Francis Charles Massingberd

The English Reformation

Francis Charles Massingberd

The English Reformation

ISBN/EAN: 9783742802088

Manufactured in Europe, USA, Canada, Australia, Japa

Cover: Foto ©Andreas Hilbeck / pixelio.de

Manufactured and distributed by brebook publishing software
(www.brebook.com)

Francis Charles Massingberd

The English Reformation

THE

ENGLISH REFORMATION.

As for my Religion, I die in the Holy Catholic and Apostolic Faith, professed by the whole Church before the disunion of East and West : more particularly, I die in the communion of the Church of England as it stands distinguished from all Papal and Puritan innovations, and as it adheres to the doctrine of the Cross. —BISHOP KEN's *Will*.

TO THE

VENERABLE EDWARD CHURTON, M.A.

ARCHDEACON OF CLEVELAND AND RECTOR OF CRAYKE,

WHOSE FRIENDSHIP

THE AUTHOR COUNTS AMONG THE PRIME

BLESSINGS OF HIS LIFE,

THESE PAGES,

UNDERTAKEN AT HIS REQUEST, AND IMPROVED BY HIS

ASSISTANCE,

ARE MOST AFFECTIONATELY INSCRIBED.

PREFACE

THE FOURTH EDITION.

THE question between the Church of England and her opponents is, in great measure, an *historical* question. That old and glorious title of *Ecclesia Anglicana* is no modern invention, nor was it assumed for the sake of contrast to the Church of Rome, or with any view to controversy whatever. All through the Middle Ages, as in previous times, national churches were recognised under their respective designations, and the Church of England was so described in all parliamentary and legal documents, and in all Councils and other transactions of the Church throughout Western Christendom. It was this Church which the Reformation found in England, and it was this which the Reformation left. And the sole ground on which any foreign bishop can pretend to justify the attempt to found a new Church of England amongst us is, either that this Church has apostatised from the faith, or that he himself has divine authority to cut off from the fold of Christ all churches and all countries that will not own his jurisdiction.

It is well that English churchmen should have this truth impressed upon their minds, because it removes at once all pretence for self-pleasing or choosing for themselves. It is no justification for quitting the Church of England, that men are pleased with the services or approve the practices of foreign churches. The question is whether the Pope has divine authority conferred on him by Christ, to rule the whole Church throughout the whole world, as His Vicegerent and in His Name; and that so absolutely that 'he whom he blesses is blessed, and he whom he curses is cursed.' Unless *that* can be shown, the attempt to sow dissension in the bosom of this Church, and to plant a new Church in this country, is the most cruel and unjustifiable act of schism that it is possible to contemplate.

It was in the hope to illustrate this view of the case that the following pages were written; not with a view to controversy as against others, but with a view to exhibit to her faithful sons the same Church of England which has claimed the allegiance of her sons for at least twelve hundred years.

As for the notion so often ignorantly assumed that Parliament has at some undefined period taken away the property of the Catholic Church in England from the 'Catholics,' and given it to the 'Protestants,' it is impossible to show a shadow of a pretext for such a supposition. No such Act of Parliament exists, nor has ever existed. It was the practice of Parliament from the very earliest times to make regulations affecting the Church. It did so under Henry VIII. in the most important particulars affecting the claim which the Bishops of Rome had for some ages made, and against which the Church and realm of England had often protested, of interfering in the internal regulations of the state, as if the Kings of England had within their dominions 'any earthly superior.' And the true notion, therefore, of the Royal Supremacy was the enunciation of the contradictory to that assumption, by which the Crown became the Protector of the liberties of the Church, against the encroachments of a foreign Court and See.

How that Court and See proceeded to cut off, by excommunication, the king and country that had ventured on what, in the Middle Ages, was thought so great presumption; how the Church and country thus excommunicated proceeded ' in despair of a general Reformation,' to reorganise their own internal affairs and to recover as best they might the primitive truth and order of the Church of Christ, is the question which History has to develope and unfold. That any set of men should have ventured on so bold a course, in that age of the world, is hardly less surprising than that they should have succeeded, surely under the Divine guidance, in steering their arduous course amidst such perils as those by which they were surrounded. That they may have been attracted sometimes too far towards those continental communities who were engaged, at the same time, though with less happy success, in a similar enterprise, is no reproach to them, but an indication rather of that yearning after Unity which never can be absent from truly Christian hearts.

And in our own day it seems as if this same principle of the independence of national churches, subject always to the review of a general council, whenever such may be had, were the one hope for any step towards the restoration of that great blessing of unity which is the subject, as it ought always to be, of so many prayers. Once at least since the Reformation, it has seemed not impossible that the Gallican Church might have entered upon some course which might have led to such results. And though this hope, as regards the Gallican Church, seems now more remote than ever, it is only so much the more incumbent on us to cling to the principle which vindicates alike the coordinate authority of bishops, and the substantial unity of Christendom grounded on that authority. That the Pope is the Patriarch of Western Christendom, and the first bishop in rank of the Christian world, we never need be afraid or ashamed to avow; what we deny and must always deny, unless we be false to all the traditions of our Church and country, is that he has any authority over our faith, while we are prepared to recognise such authority in a free General Council of the Universal Church.

But while we contend for so much as this, neither ought we to forget the danger there must always be of another sort of tyranny besides that of the Roman See. If the Royal Supremacy be the proper and constitutional guarantee of the liberties of the Church—and that it was so understood at the time when it was so welcomed as it undoubtedly was in England, is undeniable—there is an opposite danger in the tendency of the stronger to encroach upon the liberties of the weaker party. And it is surprising how often it has seemed as if statesmen thought it was their duty to stand out against what they regard as priestly encroachment, when their duty would rather be, for the sake of that very object, to be jealous of the just liberties of the Church confided to their guardianship. It was for the protection of the Church against the encroachment of a foreign power that the Royal Supremacy was established or restored, not in order that the Kings of England, still less the Parliament, should exercise the authority of the Pope. A more fatal mistake they cannot make, or one more calculated to throw back the Church towards that priestly dominion which they think they are striving to avoid.

While these sheets were passing through the press, the author became aware, by means of a learned and able article in the *Christian Remem-*

nature of the argument between the Churches. It seems that Berengarius, whose conflicts with the then dominant party are related in Chapter IV., did not finally submit to the authority by which he had, in a moment of weakness, twice been overborne, but left behind him a learned treatise on the nature of the Holy Eucharist, in reply to his great antagonist Lanfranc, which was discovered in Germany about a century ago, and has lately been republished in the German language, with many additional letters on the same subject. It is impossible to escape from the evidence which this treatise supplies to the historical fact that the doctrine first established in a Council of the Church, under the name of Transubstantiation, by Innocent III. at the fourth Lateral Council, A.D. 1214, was not generally received in the 10th and 11th centuries, and that the doctrine of Berengarius, of a real but not corporeal or material presence of the Body and Blood of our Lord, much more nearly resembled that which was held by the most learned of our own Reformers than has hitherto been supposed.

It further appears that there is ground to believe that the treatise commonly known as the Book of Bertram,* by means of which Ridley

---

* See p. 54, where for 'Scotus Erigena' read 'Johannes Erigena,' Erigena having been the name given to him as born in Ireland, the inhabitants of which island were long called Scoti.

first, and from him Cranmer, became persuaded that the then received doctrine on the Sacrament was not the original doctrine of the Church, is in fact the long lost treatise of Erigena on the same subject. This book is one of high interest to English Churchmen, the first English edition, in black letter, having been published A.D. 1560, by Augustin Bernher, the faithful friend and attendant of Latimer, in accordance with the last injunctions of Ridley, as related in the Martyrs' Letters.

One thing seems clear; that the one object most of all to be desired for the advancement of Christ's Church throughout the world is the restoration of Unity, and yet we cannot hope to bring about that blessed object by any devices of our own, or by any other ways than those of Patience and Prayer.

Such a prayer is supplied to us in the devotions of our own great and good Bishop Andrewes:—

' FOR THE CATHOLIC CHURCH,

ITS ESTABLISHMENT AND INCREASE ;

FOR THE EASTERN,

ITS DELIVERANCE AND UNION ;

FOR THE WESTERN,

ITS ADJUSTMENT AND PEACE;

FOR THE BRITISH,

THE SUPPLY OF WHAT IS WANTING IN IT,

THE STRENGTHENING OF WHAT REMAINS IN IT.

ADVERTISEMENT

THE SECOND EDITION.

THE writer takes this, the earliest opportunity afforded him, to acknowledge the obligations he was
under, in the preparation of the first edition of this
book, to his friend, now Archdeacon Churton, who not
only undertook to superintend the Press during his un-
avoidable absence from England, but generously added
several matters from the stores of his own learning.
The account of King John, in Chapter III., and that of
the persecution of the Jews, Chapter V., and some of
the earlier parts of Chapter VI., were from his pen. He
also supplied the extracts from Thomas of Eccleston, in
the History of the Friars, in Chapter VII., and some of
those from Wycliffe's writings in Chapter VIII.

The original Spanish Records of the Marian Persecution, are from a series of papers, by the same hand, in
the *British Magazine*. These researches, which Bishop
Burnet was advised, but neglected, to make, throw a
new light on those events, and can never be overlooked
by any future writer.

The author has taken the opportunity of the present
edition, to supply some historical notices of the
doctrinal innovations in the Medieval Church; and
has been able to give the events of the English Reformation somewhat more at length, as they were originally
written by him, but necessarily abridged to meet the
dimensions to which the books of the Series for which
he wrote were confined.

CONTENTS.

—◆—

CHAPTER I.

Introductory.

CHAPTER II.

Wycliffe and Pope Gregory XI.

CHAPTER III.

Rise and Progress of the Papal Power—Schism of the Popes, A.D. 1378.

CHAPTER IV.

Transubstantiation—Penance—Confession.

CHAPTER V.

Effects of Papal Supremacy in England—Jews— Good Bishops.

Chapter VI.

Monasteries and Chantries.

Chapter VII.

The Mendicant Orders; their Rise and History.

Chapter VIII.

Wycliffe's Translation of the Bible—His Denial of Transubstantiation—His Death.

xviii CONTENTS.

CHAPTER IX.

Wycliffe's Character, Opinions, and Followers—The Lollards—Their Number and Influence—Acts of Parliament against the Papacy—Archbishop Arundel.

CHAPTER X.

Usurpation of Henry IV.—Persecuting Statute—Trials of the Lollards—Lord Cobham.

CHAPTER XI.

Council of Constance—Bishop Hallam—Persecutions in England—Bishop Peacock—Wars of York and Lancaster.

CHAPTER XII.

The Church in the Fifteenth Century—Schools and Colleges founded—Decline and Vices of Monasteries.

CHAPTER XIII.

Condition of the Parochial Clergy in the Fifteenth Century—Power of the Popes, and their Character.

CHAPTER XIV.

King Henry VIII. and Cardinal Wolsey—Luther—The King's Divorce, and Submission of the Clergy.

Chapter XV.

State of Parties—Cranmer Archbishop—King excommunicated—Supremacy of Pope renounced by Parliament—Bible in English.

CHAPTER XVIII.

Edward VI.—Protector Somerset—Homilies—Suppression of Chantries.

CHAPTER XIX.

Communion Service in English—First Reformed Prayer Book.

CHAPTER XX.

Foreign Reformers—Dispute about the Habits—Popular Discontent.

CHAPTER XXI.

Fall of Somerset—Cranmer's Book—Second Reformed Prayer Book—Articles—Reformatio Legum—Death of Edward—Council of Trent.

CHAPTER XXII.

Reign of Queen Mary—Restoration of Popery—Persecutions.

CHAPTER XXIII.

The Persecutions—The Bishops at Oxford—Death of Ridley and Latimer—Troubles at Frankfort.

CHAPTER XXIV.

Fall and Death of Cranmer—Death of Queen Mary.

CHAPTER XXV.

Queen Elizabeth—Reformed Religion restored.

CHAPTER XXVI.

Conduct of Papal Party—Puritans—Conclusion.

THE ENGLISH REFORMATION.

CHAPTER I.

Speak gently of our Sister's fall :—
  Who knows but gentle love
May win her, at our patient call,
  · The surer way to prove ?—*Christian Year.*

THE history of the Church of Christ is the history of
a conflict between the powers of evil and the power
of good.   The enemy of the souls of men never sleeps in
his cruel attempt to pervert the best things, and to betray to their ruin those whom God will save.   Accordingly, since the time when Christ set up his Church as
the means in and by which he would save the world, it
might be expected that the adversary, who could not
destroy, would use all his arts to corrupt it.   And this
may supply a clue to some things in the history of
the Church which might seem inexplicable on other
grounds.

It is hardly possible to conceive anything more magnificent than the notion of the Catholic Church, as it
must have appeared to the faithful during the first ages
of its existence.   The stone cut out without hands,
which smote the image and became a great mountain
and filled the whole earth :[1] this prophetic figure seemed

---

[1] Dan. ii. 34, 35.

B

to be realised in the way in which the Christian Church without human aid, pervaded the Roman empire, and survived its dissolution. And good men might think it was thus that the kingdoms of this world should become the kingdoms of our Lord and of his Christ.[1] And yet at this very time there was growing up in the dominions of Him whose kingdom is not of this world, a temporal power which in the course of time assumed an empire unknown before, and in connexion with which the Gospel was corrupted and the truth suppressed in an almost incredible degree. That it was so is no modern fiction, but was confessed almost universally in the ages which preceded the Reformation, and even while that event was in progress. The very preachers at the Council of Trent made their pulpits ring with their laments of the profane pomp and secular delights in which faith and charity had become dead. Cardinal Pole, who presided at some of the earlier sessions of that Council, had declared that the abuses of the Court of Rome had brought the Church to the brink of ruin; and the clear-sighted Erasmus, though he did not forsake the communion of Rome, complained that 'the monks and friars would be content with nothing but the re-establishment of cruelty, ignorance, and superstition; and that popes, cardinals, and bishops, who had caused the disorder, could never apply the remedy, or extinguish the fire which their own pride and covetousness had kindled.'[2] And one of the most distinguished preachers at that Council, taking for his text the question of the apostles, 'Lord, wilt thou at this time restore again the kingdom to Israel?' describes the progress of the Gospel in the Apostolic times, 'Oh blessed ages, that beheld Israel in her beauty!' and then contrasts these ages with his own. 'But how does the Church at this day maintain this character? How have you, fathers, whom Christ left as his vicegerents, you

---

[1] Rev. xi. 15.   [2] 2 Epist. xix. 38, xxix. 69.

the bishops of his household, the watchmen and guards
of his fortress, you doctors and keepers of this city,
leaders in this warfare, preserved the purity of the holy
spouse of Christ? Suppose, oh! fathers, that Christ
should now return—He will return quickly—and require of you his spouse as He left her to your care, how
will you restore her to him? Her who goes proudly in
this profane pomp and secular apparel? Her who now
contends with princes in the magnificence of her palaces.
Her who lives at ease in the abundance of secular delights! Is this that Holy City separated from the spirit
of the world? Is this that city of God governed by
divine laws? The very same. Alas! how changed
from what she was. Is this that city of perfect beauty,
the joy of the whole world? Must we not rather call
her all hideous, all her beauty gone—" the whole head
is sick, and the whole heart faint; from the sole of the
foot to the crown of the head there is no soundness."
Where are thy ornaments with which thou wast prepared to be delivered to thy bridegroom? Where is
that faith which even raised the dead? Where thy
charity? Where that contempt of life and things present? Where that ardent desire of death and heavenly
things? Where that thirst to behold the kingdom
of God? Where that love of poverty? Alas! alas!
my fathers, who shall behold her with tearless eyes?
Oh! citizens of the New Jerusalem, that royal and
holy city, who that understands these things can remain
unmoved? Who that has a Christian's heart can hear
these things without trembling? Who can but pity his
mother? I will pray with Jeremy, " Oh that my head
were waters and mine eye a fountain of tears." [1]

But when we consider that ' an enemy hath done
this,'[2] it ought to make us humble and mistrustful as to
ourselves, as well as charitable towards others. The
very author of this beautiful oration, Carranza, Arch-

---

[1] LABBE, Concil., tom. xiv. p. 1832.   [2] St. Matt. xiii. 28.

bishop of Toledo, was himself afterwards betrayed by the false principles which he had been taught to adopt, to persecute men who sought to restore the Church to its ancient purity, and residing in England as confessor to Queen Mary, if the historians of his own country may be believed,[1] was a chief agent in the martyrdom of Cranmer. And it is thus for the most part that corruptions in religion are brought about. The net would be spread in vain if it were set in our sight;[2] but if the betrayer of men's souls can once succeed so far as to entangle them in wrong or wicked principles, he will not fail to urge them on into crimes to which those principles necessarily lead.

And the same considerations may account for the imperfect way in which whatever was done by way of reformation was accomplished. During the fifteenth century the desire of a reformation was so universal, and the acknowledgment of its necessity so general, that all men considered it inevitable, and the only question was when and how it should be done. Even so late as after the civil strifes of the sixteenth century in France, we find the widow of a French nobleman,[3] who had spent his life in promoting it, writing to her son, that 'a reformation of the Church cannot now much longer be delayed;' not contemplating a separation from the Church, but the reformation of it. And yet so it was, that the admixture of human error in all the attempts that were made, was permitted to obstruct the excellence of the design, and afforded a plea and a temptation to those whose self-love was wounded, and whose authority was questioned, to adhere more closely to their errors.

It is an inquiry too far removed from the subject of these pages, how soon the seeds might be sown from which arose that growth of corruption which claimed

---

[1] FERNANDEZ, *Hist. Eccl.*, cxxix.   [2] *Prov.* I. 17.
[3] Philip de Mornay.

the title or the sanction of the Catholic Church during the middle ages. Our business is rather to contemplate the papal system as it was at the time of the Reformation, and in the ages immediately preceding it, in order to form a judgment of what was required to be done by way of reformation, and how far and by what means it was accomplished. And if we shall find, as the result of our inquiry, that we almost alone in England, of all the people of Western Christendom, were permitted to retain the primitive form and discipline of the Church, while we regained the primitive profession of Gospel truth, it is to be hoped that we shall learn a lesson of deep thankfulness for such unspeakable mercies—of thankfulness, and yet of fear. For if such be indeed the character of our Church, we ought to expect that such a Church will be peculiarly liable to be tried by all changes of temptation, and that prosperity and adversity will each in turn be brought to undermine it.

But if the view here taken of the course by which error was brought into the Church in former ages be correct, it will be useful to bear it in mind on more accounts than one. It will teach us to mistrust ourselves, and to speak gently of others. The corruptions of popery were the growth of ages; and the course which those corruptions took was in most cases, and in the outset, the perverting or suppressing of some truth rather than the maintaining of falsehood. Only we must take care that we do not confound the boundaries of right and wrong, but remember that error is not less error because it is capable of being explained into some kindred truth.

And there is one consideration connected with this inquiry which is calculated to afford the utmost contentment to all true members of this Reformed Church, as regards their present position. It is capable of being shown that all the most important steps in the progress of our English Reformation were taken by men who found themselves providentially placed, by no seeking of their own, in circumstances in which they were obliged to act. The supremacy of the crown was already the law of England before the reign of Henry VIII., so that the convocation under Archbishop Wareham could not do otherwise than recognise what Archbishop Courtney had declared nearly two centuries before. Cranmer, whose introduction to the notice of the king might have seemed as improbable as that of any private tutor in the family of a private gentleman in the present day, found the royal supremacy already established, and the Church of England placed in what he believed to be its original state of independence, before ever he came to the primacy. And throughout his career, his object was rather to direct the current of events, and regulate as he might the tide on which he was embarked, than to carry out preconceived theories of his own. And though this course may be despised by men of the world, the Christian ever loves to wait God's time, and is content to act when circumstances, without his own seeking, show him that God's providence calls upon him to do so.

This cannot be better expressed than in the words of the great and good Lord Clarendon. ' A Church thus reformed, with such pious wariness in the observation, and after a long expectation of the just season of its reformation, and all the religious circumstances requisite thereto, chose rather for a long time to endure many errors and corruptions in the exercise and worship of the religion that had been established, than precipitately to enter upon any alteration, which might have been attended with a concussion in the state, and destroyed its peace and security; and by a Christian patience waited God's own leisure and direction; and was then so blessed as to abolish nothing that was necessary or fit to be retained, and retained nothing but what was held decent by the most venerable antiquity.'[1]

---

[1] *Essays, Divine and Moral,* p. 273.

With regard to those communities on the continent of Europe, which shared the struggle of the Reformation, but with less patience in the conflict, and with less happy results, the writer will adopt the language of another venerable authority, well worthy of attention. 'There are not many persons,' said Archbishop Sancroft,[1] 'who have a deeper or more tender resentment than I have of the sad and deplorable state of the reformed churches in some parts of the continent of Europe: and I should count it my joy and the crown of my rejoicing, if I could contribute anything besides my daily prayers (may God look to it, and require of me, as I speak!) towards restoring and advancing them to a yet better condition. . . . . But, whatever becomes of any particular scheme, I can by no means, as our brethren seem to do, give up the Protestant cause at once, as lost and desperate, and ready to breathe its last. No! God hath by the Reformation kindled and set up a light in Christendom, which, I am fully persuaded, shall never be extinguished. Heaven and earth shall pass away, but the word of the Lord endureth for ever: and this is the word which hath been preached among us. Only let them that suffer according to the will of God, commit the keeping of their souls to Him in well-doing; let them adore the unsearchable depths of His wise providence; who, when all our fine policies are baffled and defeated, will take the matter in His own hands, and perfect what concerns us in a way we think not of. For His is the kingdom and the power ; to Him be the glory for ever.'

---

* *Life*, by D'Oyley, L 108, 201.

CHAPTER II.

WYCLIFFE AND POPE GREGORY XI.

A good man ther was of religioun,
That was a poure¹ persone of a toun;
But rich he was of holy thought and werk.
He was also a lorned man, a clerk,
That Christė's gospel trewely woldė preche.
His parishens devoutly woldė he teche.—CHAUCER.

IT was towards the end of the long reign of Edward III. that the stir began in England, which
afterwards extended to almost every part of Europe,
against the papal power—that power which had for
three centuries ruled supreme in the Western Church,
and, aided at first by public opinion, afterwards strengthened by policy and arms, had often maintained a successful struggle against the kingly crown. The period
was one remarkable for great corruption of morals and
general discontent. The court was profligate; the
people were poor and oppressed. The glories of Edward's French war had faded; and the hopes of the
nation were suddenly extinguished by the death of the
Black Prince. The zeal and devotion which had animated the rude breasts of the Crusaders was now forgotten; the spirit of chivalry, which had succeeded,
and kept alive at least the soldier's virtues, was passing
fast away. The bonds of government were loosened;
armed factions and turbulent nobles harassed the state,
and gave omen of those long and grievous civil wars
which in the following century so often desolated the
face of England, and shed the best blood of her people
like water on the earth.

At this period, A. D. 1377, there had arisen at Oxford

---

¹ A poor parish priest.

a scholar in the science of theology, a plain north-countryman, who had for some time attracted great notice, and drawn many disciples after him, by teaching publicly in the schools and elsewhere the following determinations and conclusions:—

' 1. That the Church of Rome is not the head of all churches any more than any other church; and that no more power was given by Christ to St. Peter than to any other apostle.

' 2. That the Pope of Rome has no more power in binding or loosing men's sins than any other bishop or priest.

' 3. That no bishop or priest ought to excommunicate or use any ecclesiastical censure, in revenge for injuries done to himself or others, but only in the cause of God; and that no man is the worse for excommunication, unless he is first and principally excommunicated by himself.

' 4. That temporal lords and governors of state have the power of taking away the goods of fortune from a delinquent church; and that in certain cases they may lawfully and meritoriously do so.

' 5. That the Gospel is sufficient as a rule of life in this world, for any Christian; and that all the other rules invented by holy men, observed by the different religious orders, add nothing of perfection to the Gospel.

' 6. That neither the Pope nor any other prelate ought to have prisons for the punishment of offenders against church-discipline; but that such offenders ought to be left to their personal liberty.'[1]

It has seldom happened that any great impulse has been given to the public mind, unless the course of events, some common feeling of grievances, or desire of

---

[1] WALSINGHAM, ed. Camden, p. 191. A few portions of his statements are here corrected by comparing them with Wycliffe's own writings.

change has paved the way for it. Then some master-spirit, embracing with keener perception the prevailing mood, embodies the general sentiment, and seems to lead the opinions of which he is in fact the representative. The power of such a man depends as much upon the agreement of his own views with the pulse of the times, as upon his genius or skill in maintaining them. Such a man in his time was JOHN WYCLIFFE, a time of which it has been said, with too much severity, but not without a certain amount of truth, that ' the only name of Christ remained among Christians, but his true and lively doctrine was as far unknown unto the most part, as his name was common unto all men.' The minds of high and low were beginning to awake to a sense of the strange encroachments of a foreign juris-diction ; which, under pretence of asserting the liberties of the Church, had broken the sacred ties between the subject and his sovereign, had taken away the plainest duties of obedience to the laws, and not only levied taxes in other realms, but now began to put forth its hand against the liberty and even the life of private men. It was now about eleven years since Pope Urban V.—a pope of English extraction, being the son of William Grisant,[1] an English physician of the same name which he bore—had sent to give notice to King Edward III. that he intended to cite him to his court to answer for his neglect in not doing homage, as King John had done, to the see of Rome for his crown, and for not paying the tribute of seven hundred marks which John had covenanted to pay. The king asked the advice of his parliament ; and their answer was befitting the council of a free and independent nation :—' That King John had no right to dispose of his crown, or subject it to such bondage ; that the peers of England had no share in that proceeding, which was in violation of his coro-nation-oath ; and that the demand should be resisted

---

[1] Or Grimwald. Sandini.

by every means—by force and arms, if necessary.' It
must needs seem strange how it had come to such a pass
that a foreign bishop, and but lately a poor monk—for
such was Urban, should have made so preposterous a
claim, and from a monarch who was apparently his
natural sovereign.   But there were other monks in
England, who presumed on their immunity, to defend
this claim, looking probably to gain promotion to themselves, or favour to their order, from the papal court.
On this occasion Wycliffe is said first to have distinguished himself as a disputant against one of these
teachers, though he was aware of the danger he incurred.   Having therefore first professed himself a
humble and obedient son of the Roman Church, he set
forth an answer, A.D. 1367, in the form of a debate in
the House of Lords, in which he put into the mouths
of several lords the reasons why the realm of England
should not pay this tribute to the Pope, and declared
that such a claim ' could never be proved either reasonable or honest, before the day should come when all
exaction should be at an end.'

Wycliffe had been distinguished at Oxford while yet
a young man, by a book called *The Last Age of the
Church*, in which, about A.D. 1356, he had interpreted
the prevailing miseries as the signs of the approaching
termination of the world.   He was a master in all the
learning then in vogue, had committed to memory the
abstruser parts of Aristotle, and was gifted with remarkable eloquence ; but his best distinction at a time
when the study of Thomas Aquinas had almost superseded that of the Holy Scriptures in the schools, was
that he should have obtained the title of the 'Evangelical Doctor,' according to the pedantic fashion of desig-
nating celebrated scholars according to any peculiar
excellence which they were thought to possess.   About
A.D. 1361 he was chosen master of Balliol College, and
in A.D. 1372 he became a Doctor or Professor of Divinity, a rank less common then than it has since

become, and which entitled all who attained it to read lectures on divinity in the schools.

This designation of Professor of Divinity has led most of his biographers to describe him as having been then appointed to some such high office as that which is now known as a Regius Professorship. But there is no reason to suppose that it was anything more than what is now called taking a Doctor's degree, though it is obvious that such a degree was at that time reserved to distinguished merit, and conferred some such privileges as now belong to a professorship.

Wycliffe [1] was not slow to avail himself of the influence derived from his position at Oxford. He was now forty-eight years of age, and had been known as a vehement declaimer against the abuses of the Church for at least sixteen years, that is, since the publication of his *Last Age of the Church*. Yet he was so far from having lost credit by the course he had adopted, that we shall find reason to believe that almost the whole University approved his conduct. Nor was his fame confined to the schools of Oxford. Later in life, when his writings had been pronounced heretical by the authorities of the Church, but few of the great ones of the earth were found to countenance him. But now his indignant sentiments were echoed by the general feeling, and he was selected with Gilbert, bishop of Bangor, to proceed on an embassy to the Pope, to represent the complaints of the English parliament against the enormous encroachments of the papal power. That his conduct in this embassy was satisfactory to his employers, appears from the fact of his having been presented by the king, A.D. 1375, to the rectory of Lutterworth, and to a prebend in the collegiate church of Westbury, and

---

[1] The spelling of the Reformer's name has been adopted, because it is the name of the village in Teesdale where he was probably born. The last male descendant of the family, who had the same name and spelt it thus, died a few years since at Richmond, in Yorkshire

he was also chaplain to the king.   His colleague, on the other hand, seems to have given more satisfaction to the Pope, by whom he was promoted successively to the bishoprics of Hereford and St. David's, as it were in defiance of that very remonstrance against such 'Provisions' which he had been deputed to convey.

There is reason to believe that this 'Evangelical Doctor' had not yet ventured to impugn the received opinions on any point of faith.   It is, indeed, supposed from internal evidence, that a treatise of his on the Ten Commandments, designed for the instruction of the common people, and called the *Poor Caitiff*, was written, at latest, soon after he became a Professor of Divinity. But the account of his opinions about this time transmitted to the Pope, contained no allusion to the sacramental controversy.   We may therefore conclude with sufficient certainty that he had as yet confined himself to denouncing the papal power, and the general corruption of the Church.

But this was offence enough.   An outcry was raised against him, especially by the parties who seemed to be chiefly attacked, the members of the different religious orders.   Such doctrines were declared to be subversive of the Christian faith, heretical, and contrary to the determinations of the universal Church, and full of venom against the monks and their possessions.   Gregory XI. therefore issued his bulls, directed to the Chancellor and University of Oxford, and others to the Archbishop of Canterbury and Bishop of London, to urge proceedings against him.   There is something so striking in the imperious tone of these bulls, that it may be well to give some parts of the first of them at length :—

'Gregory the Bishop, servant of the servants of God, to our beloved sons the Chancellor and all the University of students at Oxford, health and the apostolical benediction.   Needs must we be grieved and surprised, that you, who are, as it were, sailing in the open sea, with

God to aid, with so many graces and privileges granted
to your Oxford school by the apostolic see, and with
such knowledge of the Scriptures—you who ought to
be strong champions of the orthodox faith, the only
health of souls, should suffer tares to grow among the
pure wheat of the field of your glorious school. This
alone is a proof of indolence and sloth, that you suffer
them to shoot and grow; it is still more pernicious, that
you suffer them to run to seed, and take no pains to
root them up, tarnishing the brightness of your good
name, periling your souls, showing your contempt for
the Roman Church, and bringing harm upon the faith.
And, what torments us worse than all, we feel the
increase of these tares at Rome, before you seem to be
sensible of it in England. But it is in England that
the remedy should be applied. It has been whispered
in our ears, by many credible persons, who were grieved
to report such things, that John Wycliffe, rector of
Lutterworth, in the diocese of Lincoln, professor of
theology—(would that we were not compelled to add
also, a master-teacher of errors!)—has burst forth into
such detestable madness as to put forth certain erroneous
and false propositions and conclusions, savouring of
heretical pravity, and plainly tending to subvert and
weaken not only the constitution of the Church, but
also the system of government of the state.

'Wherefore, considering that if such fatal pestilent
opinions be not checked in their beginnings, and plucked
out by the roots, it may be too late hereafter to prepare
medicines, when a great number are infected with the
contagion; we could not endure, as indeed we ought
not, to shut our eyes, and suffer them to pass unnoticed.
And we charge and command your whole University
strictly, by these our apostolic letters, in virtue of your
holy obedience, and under penalty of deprivation of all
the graces, indulgences, and privileges granted to you
and to your school by the said apostolic see—that
hereafter you do not suffer persons to assert or put

forth such conclusions and propositions, expressing bad
sentiments in regard to good works as well as faith,
however the proposers may attempt to defend them by
nice and difficult arguments, and abuse of words and
terms. And as to the said John Wycliffe, we enjoin
by our authority, that you apprehend him, or cause
him to be apprehended, and deliver him to be kept in
safe custody to our venerable brothers, the Archbishop
of Canterbury and Bishop of London, or either of them.
And if, which God forbid, there shall be in your University, subject to your jurisdiction, any who are corrupted with such errors, and who shall obstinately
persist in them, that you apprehend and deliver up
these gainsayers also to the same custody. This if you
shall do, and in other respects proceed with firmness
and circumspection, so as to make up for your lack of
diligence in what has passed, ye shall obtain grace and
kindness from ourselves and the apostolic see, and the
reward and favour of Divine recompense.

'Given at Rome, at Santa Maria Maggiore, in the
seventh year of our pontificate, May 22, 1377.'

Of three other rescripts, addressed to the Archbishop
of Canterbury and Bishop of London, the first directed
them to warn the old King Edward, with Joan of Kent,
the widow of the Black Prince, and the peers of England, of the danger and disgrace impending on the
devout realm of England from Wycliffe's doctrines,
which, it affirmed, were not only full of error as regarded the faith, but, if well noted, would appear
destructive of all civil government. They were therefore to charge these princes and peers very earnestly
to help them in the task of rooting out such perilous
doctrines.

The second, addressed to the same parties, enclosed
a copy of several propositions and conclusions, which
Wycliffe was accused of having taught; and directed
them, if they found this information correct, to have
him apprehended and imprisoned, to examine him upon

all the points mentioned in the enclosed paper, and having taken down his answers to send them under seal to the court of Rome. Further, to guard against a difficulty which the Pope's own entangled laws had introduced, and to prevent his own authority from being pleaded against himself, Gregory now suspended, in this case, all privileges and exemptions granted by former pontiffs to the four orders of friars, and other orders, and colleges or chapters of priests and monks, not knowing whether the accused might take the benefit of any of these to withdraw himself from the archbishop's jurisdiction. And because a law of Boniface VIII. had directed that no person should be tried by an ecclesiastical court out of his own diocese, and Wycliffe was in the diocese of Lincoln, in which Oxford, as well as Lutterworth, was then situated, the Pope, either distrusting the Bishop of Lincoln[1] or the University of Oxford, suspended this law also.

By a further document it was provided, that in case the culprit should not be found, they should cite him by public edict, to be set forth in Oxford and throughout the diocese, to appear within three months from the day of citation. But whether he should come to answer or not, they were to give notice in the edict, that the Pope would proceed upon the articles exhibited, and pronounce his condemnation on every point, 'as his demerits shall require, and the interests of the faith shall seem to render most expedient.' Such was the kind of trial to which this Italian prelate destined an English clergyman and subject of the English crown.

When these bulls arrived in England, the Oxford men were in no haste to act upon that which fell to their share. The heads of colleges and the proctors met together, and debated whether they should receive it with outward marks of respect, or refuse it not without some

---

[1] John Buckingham, a plain, unlearned man, who afterwards retired into a monastery.

appearance of contempt. The former counsel seems to
have prevailed; but after the admission of the paper into
their conclave, it was laid upon the table, and no measure
was founded upon it.

The Archbishop of Canterbury, Simon Sudbury, a
wise and moderate man, was also slow in executing
these strong mandates. It seems probable that he was
in some points agreed with Wycliffe, though he was far
from liking all his doctrines or proceedings. It was in
the year 1370, that he, who was then Bishop of London,
happened to be travelling towards Canterbury, at a time
when the Pope had ordered a jubilee in honour of Becket,
and had offered a plenary indulgence to all who should
visit his shrine on the festival kept in remembrance of
the translation of his bones. Sudbury, who, like many
good men in those times, lamented the excess of these
popular superstitions, seeing the crowds who thronged
the road, said to them, 'My friends, this plenary indulgence, which you hope to find at Canterbury, will avail
you nothing.' Such words, from a man so respected,
attracted much attention; and some of the pilgrims,
perhaps after further conversation with him, actually
turned back from their expedition. But others were
sorely offended, and followed him with curses and re-
vilings; among whom, Sir Thomas Aldon, a knight of
Kent, made himself conspicuous, by riding up to him,
and saying, 'Lord Bishop, for this division that you
have made in the people against St. Thomas, on my
soul you will die an ill death'—words which the
monks, or other superstitious persons, pretended to
consider as prophetic, when several years afterwards
this prelate, for the firm and faithful counsel which
he gave to Richard II. (which was the means of
preserving the young king's life), fell a victim to the
fury of the misguided populace in Wat Tyler's insurrection.

Sudbury, therefore, suffered some months to elapse
before he took any step in compliance with the Pope's

c

letters.[1] But Gregory seems to have known that he
should find a more efficient delegate in William Courtney, then Bishop of London, whose name he had joined
in the commission. Courtney had been at an early age
a diligent student both of the common and the canon
law, which was the best road to preferment in those
days, whether from the royal or the papal court. He
took the degree of doctor in civil law at Oxford; and,
entering holy orders, was very soon enriched with three
prebendal stalls, at York, Exeter, and Wells, and a few
livings besides. He was made Bishop of Hereford,
A.D. 1369, by a provision of Pope Urban V.; and Gregory himself had aided his translation to London, when
Sudbury was by the king's interest made primate. By
his means, it seems probable, a mandate was at length
issued by the Archbishop in their joint names, addressed to the University of Oxford, and, after reciting
the charges against Wycliffe from the Pope's letters,
requiring them to cite him to appear within thirty days
to answer to the accusation at a court to be held by the
two prelates, or their delegates, in the chapter-house of
St. Paul's. They were directed, at the same time, to
employ some scholars in theology, of good repute for
Catholic sentiments, to collect information, which they
should transmit under seal to the court, about the propositions enclosed in the Pope's letter. The mandate,
however, contained no such order as the Pope had
directed for the imprisonment of Wycliffe, and it shows
that some good had already resulted from the recent
statute of *præmunire*, which made it highly penal to
execute a papal bull without license from the crown.[2]
The date of this mandate was December 18, 1377.[3]

---

[1] It is by no means probable that these bulls should have been six
months on their way from Rome to England, as Lewis supposes. The
journey at that time was performed within two months.

[2] A few years later than this Sir W. Brian was committed to the
Tower for publishing a bull or brief of the Pope's against some persons
who had broken into his house and stolen his papers. Evidently his
offence was acknowledging a foreign jurisdiction.

[3] Walsingham says it was after the receipt of the bulls that Wycliffe

At the very period of the meeting of this court before which Wycliffe was cited, there was no want of proof that the current of opinion was in his favour.   The first parliament of Richard II., which had met at the same time, addressed the crown with a prayer, that the Pope might not be allowed to take the first-fruits of vacant benefices; that no English subject should be suffered to procure a benefice by provision from Rome; and that no Englishman should take a lease or farm of any benefice held by a foreigner, under pain of being outlawed.   They also prayed that all foreigners holding preferments in England might be compelled to relinquish them within three months, and the revenues arising from them be employed in paying the expenses of the French war, till that war was concluded.   The ground for this last demand was, that the popes, who had during this century resided for near seventy years at Avignon, in France, had shown themselves partial towards French interests; and it was supposed that the treasure exported by their nominees contributed to supply the French with resources for war.

Wycliffe made his appearance before the convocation at St. Paul's, which met, together with the parliament, in February, 1378.   The tumultuary scene which followed is characteristic alike of the age and of the parties concerned.   Wycliffe had become known to John of Gaunt while employed on his embassy to the Pope, and this prince had some personal feeling against the bishops, besides the general disgust which high-minded and chivalrous men would feel at the encroachments of the papal power.   He determined to accompany the Reformer when he went before the synod, and he came attended by Henry Lord Percy, lately advanced by his

---

was made to appear at St. Paul's (p. 191); though he relates the occurrence as before the death of Edward III., June 21, 1377, which was pretty certainly before the bulls arrived in England.   This neglect of chronology in Walsingham has led later writers into a mistake, as they speak of Wycliffe's summons as before the issuing of the bulls.

influence to the office of earl marshal, afterwards created
Earl of Northumberland, and the father of the famous
Henry Hotspur. A great crowd of people were pressing
into the court, and some angry words passed between
Bishop Courtney and the duke. For Courtney, who
besides the blood of his own ancient and royal house,
was descended, on his mother's side, from the kings of
England, was not disposed to quail before the presence
even of such noble intruders. He told the earl marshal,
as he saw him moving the crowd aside, that 'if he had
known what mastery he would have kept in the
Church, he would have stopped him out from coming
there.' This led to a fierce reply from the prince, who
heard it; and the feelings of both sides were still
further excited, when Percy afterwards in the court
called to Wycliffe to be seated, and the bishop, justly
offended at such interference with the authority of the
judges, declared he should not sit there. In the heat
which ensued, the duke said, in very threatening language, that he would bring down his pride, and the
pride of all the prelacy of England; he supposed the
bishop presumed upon the nobility of his parents;
'but,' said he, 'they shall not help thee; they shall
have enough to do to help themselves.' To which the
prelate returned a becoming answer, that his confidence
was not in his parents, nor in any man else, but in God
alone, who, he trusted, would give him courage to speak
the truth. The prince found no reply; but presently
whispered to one that sat next him, in a tone loud
enough to be heard, that sooner than endure what he
had received from him, he would drag the bishop from
the church by the hair of his head. This unmanly
insult was so resented by the London citizens, though
they were otherwise favourably disposed to Wycliffe,
that, amidst the clamour that was raised, the court
broke up in disorder. Some of the populace, with
whom John of Gaunt was never popular, went that
same evening to burn or plunder his palace at the

Savoy; but Courtney, having timely notice of it, hastened to the spot, and by his interference prevented the outrage.

The bishops, dissatisfied with the disorderly termination of their proceedings, and fearing that Wycliffe, presuming on the support of these powerful peers, would not comply with their injunction, or perhaps having been informed that he disregarded it, summoned him to another court which was shortly after held at Lambeth. The Londoners on this occasion are said to have shown so much boisterous zeal for his cause, as to have penetrated into Lambeth Chapel, and some of them to have addressed the prelates sitting there in his favour. But he had a still more powerful advocate in the widow of the Black Prince, the young king's mother, who sent Sir Lewis Clifford, afterwards a known favourer of Wycliffe's principles, with a message to the court, desiring them not to proceed further, nor pronounce any sentence on the accused. Upon which they again dismissed him with only a reprimand.

Much indignation is expressed by the historians of the time, who were most attached to the papal interest, at what they considered the poor-spirited conduct of the bishops on this occasion. But probably they may have taken a more just and constitutional view of their own responsibility than has been supposed. The Pope's bull for Wycliffe's imprisonment had not been confirmed by the king's warrant, and the statute of *præmunire* subjected them to the severest penalties, if they acknowledged a mandate from Rome without the royal license. The princess, in the childhood of her son, would have something of the authority of regent; and if the message which she sent was a refusal to grant this license, it follows that they had no power to go beyond a spiritual censure. We shall see hereafter how those churchmen, who were bent upon trying the plan of persecution, succeeded at length in obtaining this power from the Crown.

Wycliffe defended himself before these courts with much adroitness, and with something of that metaphysical subtlety for which he had been noted at Oxford. Two papers have come down to us, differing a little from each other, in which he goes through the several propositions objected to by the Pope, and offers his explanation of them. , These propositions, eighteen in number, all relate to the right by which the Church held her temporal possessions, the power of excommunication as then exercised by popes and prelates, the different orders of the ministry, and the prerogatives of the see of Rome. With respect to the first, he had said, as the original endowment of the Church was an alms-deed, or work of mercy, it might in certain cases be equally an alms-deed to withhold its revenues from a delinquent church, or, as he had expressed himself elsewhere, from churchmen who habitually abuse them. In calling church property by the name of *alms*, he only used the common name applied to it by old custom in England.[1] He now explained himself to mean that this was only to be done in cases specified both by the civil and the canon law; namely, that if a beneficed clergyman wasted and dilapidated the endowments of his living, it was the business of the patron to give information to the bishop or ecclesiastical judge; if the bishop was neglectful of his duty, then to apply to the archbishop; and lastly, if nothing was done, to complain to the king. And in such cases the law gave the king power, limited by

---

[1] One instance may suffice, recorded by Gyraldus Cambrensis. Owen Cavelloc, a Welsh prince of Powys-Land, was one day dining with Henry II. at Shrewsbury. The king, as a mark of friendship usual in those days, sent him a loaf from his own hand. Owen cut it up into fragments, and laid it out like alms-bread, or doles to be distributed to the poor, but afterwards took back the pieces and swallowed them one by one. When the king asked him his meaning, he said, alluding to Henry's appropriations of church-preferments to his own use, 'I am only calling in my *alms*, as the king does his.'

law, to sequester the living during the incumbent's
life, but after his death it was to return to his successor.

On the second point, he had said that excommunication does no harm, unless he be first and principally
excommunicated by himself.   In defence of this he
quoted the text from Isaiah lix. 2, *Your iniquities have
separated between you and your God*; from which he
argued that nothing but sin could cut a man off from
the Divine assistance.   Therefore, if cursing or excommunication should be denounced against a man who
was not an adversary of the law of Christ, it could have
no force: for *if God justifieth, who is he that shall
condemn?*   There were several propositions, all bearing
on this subject, and evidently tending to shake the prevailing doctrines of the Pope's power to bind or loose as
he pleased, forgetting that the power of Christ's vicar
could only be effectual if exercised in compliance with
the will of Christ.   'There is no Christian,' he said,
' who may not in this act of excommunication err widely
from that purity which will be found in a member of
the Church triumphant hereafter.   But if he so errs, he
does not then bind or loose, as he pretends.   And it
seems to me that he who should usurp to himself such
power, would be that *man of sin* mentioned in 2 Thess.
ii. 3, 4, *sitting in the temple of God, and shewing himself
as if he were God.*'   He also blamed those who used
such a weapon as excommunication against the with-
holders of church-dues.   This was a very common
practice in those times; but what did it prove, said
Wycliffe, but that men valued their personal convenience above the honour of God, and thought the loss of
a few temporalities more important than the interest of
the Church?   Christ would not suffer his disciples to
call down fire from heaven on those who refused him
hospitality (Luke ix. 55).   This sentence ought never
to be passed but in charity to the offender, for his spiritual correction, not for revenge.   And the vicar of

Christ ought to be moved by charity towards his neighbour more than by a love for any temporal good that this world can give.

On the third point he had affirmed, that any priest rightly ordained has power to administer all the sacraments, and therefore to give absolution for any sin to a contrite penitent. It would seem that he thought there was no difference in the power of orders between bishops and presbyters; and that, therefore, except that this was otherwise directed for convenience by the laws of the Church, priests might administer confirmation, and ordain other priests and deacons. He defended this view on the authority of Hugh de St. Victor, a famous doctor of Paris, who lived about two centuries before, and left many writings. He might also have defended it on the authority of Elfric, the great teacher of the later Anglo-Saxon Church, who held that the difference between bishops and priests is one of jurisdiction, and not of orders. But other Anglo-Saxon authorities speak of bishops as a distinct order; and this is clearly the doctrine of the primitive Church.

On the fourth point, the prerogatives and power of the see of Rome, he had said, that though all the world should agree together till the coming of Christ to give St. Peter's successors political dominion, it could not last for ever. When he was asked to explain this, he said that, though the term 'for ever' often occurred in deeds and charters of inheritance, still such perpetuity must have a limit. For at least all civil property must end before the end of the world; and he who believes the article of the creed that Christ shall come to judge the quick and the dead, must believe the truth of this proposition. There is an appearance of banter in this explanation; and it is perhaps to this and one or two similar passages that Walsingham refers, when he says, with hearty good spite, of Wycliffe, 'the double dealing hypocrite put a good meaning into his abominable propositions.'

He had said also that any churchman, even the Pope
of Rome himself, may in certain cases be corrected by
his subjects, and be brought to trial for the good of the
Church, by either clergy or laity. This proposition
was naturally very unpalatable at Rome. But it was
not very difficult for Wycliffe to defend it in point of
fact by referring to instances, in the chronicles of former
ages, of popes who had been deposed by the authority
of princes. As to the reasons for it, he said with some
grave humour: 'It is not to be doubted but that the
Pope is capable of sinning, since he is one of Adam's
race; I do not say capable of committing the sin against
the Holy Ghost, for I would not mention this under the
respect we all feel for the sanctity, humility, and reve-
rend character of so eminent a father in the Church.
But, as one of our brethren, he is liable to fall into sin,
and therefore subject to the law of brotherly reproof
(Lev. xix. 17). And therefore if at any time the college of cardinals are remiss in correcting him for the
welfare of the Church, it is plain that the rest of the
body, which *possibly may be* chiefly composed of laymen, may medicinally reprove him, and accuse him, and
reduce him to live a better life. And though we ought
not to suppose the lord Pope guilty of any great fall
from rectitude without clear evidence, yet it is not to be
presumed possible that, if he does fall, he will be further
guilty of so much obstinacy as not humbly to accept a
cure from his prince, who is his superior in the sight of
God. God forbid,' he adds, at the conclusion of his
paper, 'that this truth should be condemned by the
Church of Christ, because it sounds ill in the ears of
sinners and ignorant persons; for by this rule the whole
faith of Scripture might be liable to be condemned.'

Wycliffe professes, at the beginning of his defence,
his determination to live and die, under the grace of
God, a sound Christian, and to defend the law of Christ
with all the sufficiency he has, to his last breath. If in
ignorance or from any other cause he may have failed,

he asks pardon of God, and is ready to retract, submitting himself to the correction of the Church. But he complains that his sentiments have been conveyed to Rome ' by boys and worse than boys,' who misrepresented what they did not understand. And it is most probable that, as often happens in controversy, these propositions were taken by themselves, and made to wear a different sense from what he intended when he delivered them. However, it was not likely that the contest would end with this trial, which seems only to have excited the spirits of both parties; and both Courtney and the parson of Lutterworth were soon to appear in other scenes, one against the other.

His position in the meanwhile, though he escaped for the present, was now full of danger. For although the bishops had not as yet any coercive power, except what the Pope might pretend to give them, the king might order the execution of a convicted heretic, and it was evident that the whole power of the Pope was bent on his conviction. But in this same year in which he appeared before the convocation at Lambeth, Pope Gregory XI. died, and his death, which probably put an end to their commission, was followed by that schism in the papacy which will shortly be mentioned as marking an era in the history of the Church.

CHAPTER III.

> Rome, in happier time,
> Had turn'd the world to good; and her twin powers
> Were like two suns, whose several beams cast light
> On either path, th' imperial rule and God's.
> Now one hath quench'd the other, and the sword
> Join'd with the pastoral staff: ill fare they both,
> Their own due honour lost, their right fear dead.—DANTE.

LET any unbiassed reader peruse a narrative of the scenes recorded in the preceding chapter, and he can only come to the conclusion that the times were strangely out of joint, that both Church and State were wonderfully misgoverned, and each was acting out of its proper province. The fact of a bishop of a remote diocese in a foreign country having sent out what may be called a warrant for the apprehension of an English clergyman, having ordered him to be imprisoned, directed the form of trial, and pre-ordained the sentence which was to be pronounced against him, is so utterly opposed to all just law, spiritual or civil, that if one did not allow for the influence of opinion, one should suppose that such an experiment on English patience would be treated with contempt. On the other hand, since it is plain that, in any rightly constituted Church, the bishops ought to exercise the right of hearing charges against presbyters who give offence by their life or doctrine (1 Timothy v. 19, 20), and of imposing silence on those who teach heresies (Titus i. 10, 11); it follows that nothing could have been more irregular than the interference of the Duke of Lancaster and Lord Percy, if Sudbury and Courtney had intended only to pass a spiritual censure on Wycliffe, and if their mandate had

not been issued in obedience to a foreign jurisdiction.
Even as it was, their interference was so disorderly, as
by no means to carry the appearance of an act of the
civil power, having much more the character of a fac-
tious tumult excited by those nobles.

The inquiry which such a narrative suggests is,
' How did things arrive at this state of mutual conflict
and distrust? how were the popes thus enabled to set
up in every land, and especially in this country, a separate kingdom and laws of their own?' There is no
question that the Church in this island was originally
independent of Rome. It is not pretended that the
British Christians acknowledged any foreign jurisdiction
in the government of their churches before the Saxon
conquest. When Augustine was sent by Gregory to
convert the heathen Saxons, and planted Christianity
among a new people, the case was a little different.
Thenceforth the Church of England owed so much respect to Rome as is due from a daughter to a mother
church. The Bishop of Rome was to the Church in
England what the Archbishop of Canterbury is now to
the Church in the British colonies, a patriarch and a
founder. We can afford to be thankful to the memory
of Gregory the Great, as his virtues deserve; nor was
there any reason why the Saxon archbishops might not
continue to receive the pall, the ensign of their dignity,
from his successors. The election of the English prelates was freely conducted by the Church at home; the
unity of the Church was unbroken, and the Roman
bishop, as patriarch of Western Europe, presided among
his equals, not as a lord from whom their right to their
sees or their power to govern was derived.

It is by the good providence of God that St. Gregory
has left on record his sentiments on this point, in the
protest which he made against his contemporary, John,
patriarch of Constantinople, for assuming the title of
universal bishop. It is true, some of his successors
soon began to take this title to themselves; but in this

they were no more like him, than his namesake, who
condemned Wycliffe's doctrine about excommunication;
on which St. Gregory's doctrine was, that 'the priest
who binds and looses for his own pleasure, and not for
the moral benefit of the people, deprives himself of all
power to do either.'[1]

Again, as to independence on the civil power, this
good man speaks of his own elevation to the bishopric
as received from the Grecian emperor, to whom Rome
was then subject.[2] And if the emperor should think fit
to depose a bishop, he says, a subject has no choice but
to obey: if it is done where no law of the Church
requires it, he must bear it as he can.[3] There is no
Pope of Rome whose doctrine the Church of England is
more bound to respect than the first Gregory's; and it
does not seem that in this point either Wycliffe or the
later doctors of the Church have departed from his
teaching.

How, then, did so great a change come over the
Christian world, that such sentiments as these subjected
their proposer to prosecution? And how did the popes
find a pretence for the assumption of powers unknown in
better times?

In order to understand the progress of those innovations by which this state of things had been brought
about, it will be useful to have a definite notion of the
several steps in that progress, and the periods to which
they belong. The time between the Norman Conquest
and the separation of the English Church from the see of
Rome under Henry VIII., may be conveniently divided
into three periods. The first period, of about a century
and a half, during which the papal power was advancing
to its highest point, may be considered as extending from
the papacy of Gregory VII., or the era of the Conquest,
to the reign of King John, or the papacy of Innocent

---

[1] St. Gregory, *Homil.* xxvi.
[2] B. L. Epist. 5.
[3] B. ix. Epist. 41.

III., A.D. 1199. The second period may be reckoned
from the papacy of Innocent to the beginning of the
schism in the Western Church on the appointment of
two rival popes, A.D. 1378, a year after the accession of
Richard II., or, more conveniently, though less accu-
rately, by the termination of the dynasty of King John's
rightful heirs, on the deposition of Richard II. A.D. 1399,
thus comprising the whole of the thirteenth and fourteenth centuries. It is during this second period that
the papal power and corruptions may be considered to
be at their height. The last period, from the end of the
fourteenth century to the time of Henry VIII., is that
during which the conflict of opinions was preparing the
way for reformation, an age of persecution for the party
who desired change, but in which their views were constantly gaining ground, till the Church was eventually
reformed.

We have the authority of a most eminent Italian
writer, that until the time of Theodoric, King of Lombardy, the Pope was so far from being the lord of
Christendom, that he was hardly acknowledged to have
any superiority, even in causes ecclesiastical, above the
Church of Ravenna, a neighbouring city.[1] But it was
not long after this period, and more than two centuries
since the death of the first Gregory, when the world first
heard of the Decretal Epistles, since notorious as the
Forged Decretals. The writings purporting to express
the sentiments of the early Church are of three kinds :
the Apostolical Canons ; the Apostolical Constitutions ;
and the Decretal Epistles. The first are not indeed supposed to have been drawn up by the apostles, but they
are understood to be recognised by all the early councils,
and so far are undoubtedly genuine.[2] The Apostolical
Constitutions profess to have been set forth by the apostles

---

[1] MACCHIAVELLI. It is said that Guicciardi expressed the same in
his fourth book, but that it was erased. See Appendix A.
[2] MANSI. *Conc.* l. p. 3.

in council, Clement of Rome acting as notary. This is not supposed to be the fact, but these also are universally acknowledged as an authentic exposition of apostolical practice.[1] In neither of these documents is there any trace of the primacy of St. Peter. But the third authority, the Decretal Epistles, in which this claim is manifestly asserted, is undoubtedly a forgery, and forged for the purpose of promoting this primacy at the time when it began to be asserted. They profess to be the decrees and letters of the earlier bishops of Rome, recorded in the pontifical books of Pope Damasus, and extending from the time of St. Clement, the companion of St. Paul, A.D. 69-83, to the time of a pope named Deusdedit, in A.D. 615. The design of them is to prove, by the supposed testimonies of these earlier bishops, that all the world had then allowed the Church of Rome to be, in virtue of our Lord's promise to St. Peter, the chief of all churches; that all other bishoprics in the world were founded from Rome, and that this parent Church had the care of all the flock of Christ; that no council could give or take away these rights; that no earthly power in Church or State could judge the Roman bishop; and that whatever was done in the Church by princes, bishops, or councils, had no force without his sanction.

This forgery is said to have been brought out of Spain by an ecclesiastic named Isodorus Mercator or Peccator:[2] but it was copied into the records of the Church of Metz by a deacon named Benedict Levita, under the authority of its bishop, Riculfus, who presided over that see from A.D. 787 to 814. It was about A.D. 836 that it attracted general attention, and in the year 865 Pope Nicholas I., in a contest with the Gallican Church, appealed to these decrees as genuine, and

---

[1] Mansi, *Conc.* L p. 251.
[2] *Hincmar. Opusc.*, c. 24, quoted in Labbe, tom. L p. 78.

insisted on their authority.[1] From this time they seem to have been received without question, and thus it came to pass that all the authority they assign to the papal chair was supposed throughout the middle ages to be supported by primitive practice.

The troubled state of Italy for a long time after the death of Nicholas, gave the popes more than enough to do at home. The see became a prey to lawless princes and barons, who made and unmade bishops at will;[2] and then fell under the oppressive power of the foreign emperors of Germany. The most unfit and unworthy men were, with few exceptions, placed in St. Peter's chair, till the time of the famous Hildebrand.

Hildebrand Hildebrandini, who became pope A.D. 1073, by the name of Gregory VII., was of very humble origin; his father is said to have been a smith or carpenter at Saona, in Tuscany. In early years, having come to Rome and studied to accomplish himself for the priestly office, he found his spirit stirred within him by the sight of the prevailing corruptions. The clergy were living in great ignorance and immorality, and the episcopal office had become a matter of common traffic, a source of revenue to weak abandoned princes, who disposed of it to the best bidder, with a total dis-

---

[1] *Nichol., Ep.* 42, quoted in LABBE, *ubi supra.* The learned Labbe and Cosart, in their notice of this forgery, thus express their wonder that anyone should defend the authenticity of these epistles. 'Adeo enim perspicacibus viris deformes videntur, hoc saltem tempore, ut nullâ arte, nullâ purpurissâ fucari possint.' (tom. l. p. 78.) A modern writer, who admits indeed their falsehood, asserts that it is false that Nicholas I. *declared* them to be genuine. (PALMA, *Prælect. Hist. Eccl.*, tom. ll. pt. 2.) This is at best *suppressio veri.* The professor well knows that Nicholas 1. *appealed* to them as genuine, which served his purpose much better than declaring them to be so.

[2] Of these times, their great historian Baronius thus complains:—
'Quam fœdissima Ecclesiæ Romanæ facies, quum Romæ dominarentur potentissimæ æquè ac sordidissimæ meretrices, quarum arbitrio mutarentur sedes, darentur episcopi, et quod auditu horrendum et infaudum est, intruderentur in sedem Petri rarum amasii pseudo-pontifices qui non sunt nisi ad consignanda tantum tempora in catalogo Romanorum pontificum scripti.'—BARONIUS, An. 912, num. 14.

regard of the character of those to whom it fell. The talents of Hildebrand soon recommended him to notice; and for many years before he was himself raised to the papacy, he was employed by several popes in succession to fill high offices of trust, and administer the government. In these offices he laboured unweariedly to carry out the principles of the 'False Decretals,' and saw in them the only way of redress for the evils of the time. And seeing that the world cannot be governed while two rival authorities are at strife with each other, he was not content with asserting the independent power of the Church, but maintained its supremacy, as one to which all temporal sovereignties were subject. The Pope, according to his doctrine, derived a kind of hereditary holiness from St. Peter, and could not err in his decisions; therefore no man could be a Catholic, unless he agreed in all things with the Church of Rome. And holding, as it would seem, that a departure from Catholic truth was a forfeiture of all right to temporal sway, he followed up these principles by asserting the Pope's power to absolve subjects from their obedience, if their prince was not obedient to the laws of Holy Church; and in his contest with the rash and violent Emperor Henry IV., he showed that he was not slow to exert this power.

The character of Gregory VII. was well suited for the work he took in hand. His spirit was undaunted, his manner of life severe and self denying, and he had something of that fanatic zeal and confidence in his own inspirations, which seems necessary to qualify a man to complete a great public revolution. No text was more frequently on his lips than that which was so often heard from the remorseless puritans of Cromwell's time, *Cursed be he that doeth the work of the Lord negligently.* His successors,[1] Urban II. and Pascal II., were men of talents and character, and seemed to be cast in the

---

[1] His immediate successor, Victor III., sat only three months.

D

same mould; the first was the great promoter of the crusades; the other the successful assertor of the right of investiture, which, by the help of Anselm, he gained from King Henry I. of England,[1] and prepared the way for further encroachments on the English Church.

Although nothing can justify the assumption of such authority on false pretences, there is some reason to conclude that the papal power, thus founded, was politically a public benefit compared with the confusion and darkness which had gone before. To this period of its rise the words of Mr. Southey are meant to apply: ' The indignation, which its corruptions ought properly to excite, must not prevent us from seeing, that, raised and supported as this power was wholly by opinion, it must originally have possessed or promised some peculiar and manifest advantages. If it had not been adapted to the then condition of Europe, it could not have existed. Though in itself an enormous abuse, it was the remedy for some great evils, the palliative of others. We have but to look at the Abyssinians and the Oriental Christians, to see what Europe would have become without the papacy. With all its errors, its corruptions, and its crimes, it was, morally and intellectually, the conservative power of Christendom. Politically, too, it was the means of saving Europe; for in all human probability, the West, like the East, must have been overrun by Mahommedanism, if, in that great crisis of the world, the Roman Church had not roused the nations to an united effort, commensurate with the danger.'[2]

But it is probable that the foundation of the enormous power of the Popedom in the Middle Ages was the belief, true in itself, that the Christian Church is the kingdom of God, or the kingdom of heaven upon earth. Believing this, and untaught as yet by experience, Christians would apply to the Church such prophetic

[1] See CHEATON's *Early English Church.*
[2] *Book of the Church,* c. x.

words as that 'the kingdoms of this world are become
the kingdoms of our Lord and of His Christ.' It required only to establish a temporal head to this divine
kingdom, and those who believed in it might be excused
if they quailed before the authority which they deemed
that he possessed, forgetting the declaration of our Lord
that His kingdom is not of this world.

The moral strength of the cause was still on the side
of Rome in the violence and misrule of Stephen's reign,
and when Henry II. attempted to revive the same mis-
application and sale of Church-patronage, which Rufus
and his grandfather had begun. The contest with
Becket was maintained stoutly on either side; but the
bloody death by which that unhappy prelate fell turned
the scale against the king, by the impression that is
always produced by self-devotion and sacrifice of life
even on a mistaken principle. It now remained only
for a commanding spirit on the papal side to complete the
subjugation of the opposite power.

Such a spirit was found, when Innocent III., from
whose accession, A.D. 1199, we have dated the highest
point of the papal dominion, was forced into active hostility by the profligate and violent King John. This
prince, by seizing on the property of the Church within
his realm, provoked a power which he was unable to
contend with, wielded as it was by a man more able and
determined than had yet arisen among the successors of
Hildebrand. Innocent's notion of the supremacy was
even more exalted than Gregory's, though he only followed the same principles, when he affirmed that ' the
Church owes no reverence to any person but the Pope,
who has no superior but God.' He had, therefore, no
scruple in pronouncing sentence of deprivation on two
emperors in succession; and when John refused to allow
him to appoint bishops for the English sees, he at once
placed the kingdom under an interdict, excommunicated
him, and gave away his crown to Philip of France.

If we wonder how the peers of England, barons as

well as bishops, should have acquiesced in this humiliation of their sovereign, we must remember who that sovereign was; an usurper who had invaded the throne, and, if he is not much belied, had secured himself in it by the murder of his nephew, the rightful heir, and one whose whole reign was a series of lawless insult, treachery, and cruelty. To reduce the Church to subjection, he had seized on her estates and expelled her ministers. Those who remained in the kingdom were exempted from the protection of law; their murderers were set at liberty; and a priest who had killed a person by chance-medley having fled from the king's vindictive temper, he ordered three innocent persons to be hanged in his stead. As to the barons, if he suspected their loyalty, his way of proceeding was to deal with them as if under martial law; he required hostages from them, seized on their wives and children, and in many instances it was proved that there was but one step for them between a prison and a grave. One instance from private life, which lies out of the common records of the chronicles, will serve to mark the horrors of that time.

On the borders of Wales, in an English or Norman fortress erected in Brecknockshire, resided a baron named William de Bruce. A writer who knew him well describes his life and character, as one who set God always before him, having a constant regard to the precept of St. James, and saying in all that he designed and undertook, 'if the Lord will.' He had a large correspondence with persons of distinction in different parts of England, and charged his secretaries to begin with an acknowledgment of the Divine mercy, and to end every letter with a word about the Divine aid. In travelling, he never came to a church or cross by the way-side without turning aside to it to offer a short prayer; if engaged at the time in conversation with high or low, commoner or noble, still he would leave it for this duty, and after a brief space return. ' What was further remarkable,' says this friend, ' whenever he met children

in his way, his custom was to invite them to talk with
him with a few kind words on either side, that he might,
as it were, force the little innocents to give him their
blessing, and give them his own in return. This practice was also his wife's, Matilda de St. Valery, a good
wife and mother, and mistress of his house and property.
Would to God,' he concludes, 'that they had both met
with as much temporal happiness and comfort at the
close of their lives, as I trust they have, for their devout
lives, obtained of eternal glory!'[1]

It is not strange that he should thus draw a veil over
the dreadful sequel. King John, suspecting De Bruce's
fidelity perhaps more from his religious character than
any other cause, sent to demand his eldest son to be
given up for a hostage. The baron was absent from
home; but his lady, noble and high-spirited, indig-
nantly resenting the affront, replied to the messenger,
'Go, tell your master, his care of his nephew has not
been such, that I should consign to him any sons of
mine.' When De Bruce heard of this rash answer, he
saw that there was no safety for them, and immediately
fled with his wife and children to Ireland. There, in
the following year, the poor woman, with her eldest son
and a daughter-in-law, and other children and little
grandchildren, fell into the tyrant's hands; the old baron
himself having gone to France, where he died, and was
honourably buried by Archbishop Langton. The poor
prisoners were conveyed to Bristol, and thence to Windsor, where women, children, and infants were thrust
into a dark dungeon, and done to death by famine.[2]

> A thousand ways our mortal steps are led
> To the cold tomb, and fearful all to tread;
> But that most fearful, when with slow decay
> Pale hunger drains life's gushing fount away!

---

[1] GYRALDUS CAMBR., *Itinerary of Wales*, L 2.
[2] *Annals of Morgan Abbey*, A.D. 1210; *Annals of Waverley Abbey*.
Ibid.

After a history like this, can any Christian reader doubt on which side the scale of justice and mercy turned in this contest? Moreover, if it be true, as it is told with strong evidence of truth by Matthew Paris, this miscreant king was guilty of an act, which, even in the present state of our laws and constitution, without aid of the Pope, would have enforced the surrender of his crown. This was his secret embassy to Mohammed Ebn Yacub, caliph of the Moors in Africa and Spain, offering to turn Mussulman and pay him tribute, if the Moorish prince would assist him against his own subjects. The answer of the Miramolin was remarkable, and characteristic of the feelings of a well-educated Mussulman: ' I have lately met with a book written in the Greek language by a Greek Philosopher and Christian, named Paul; whose words and actions give me much satisfaction. There is only one thing about him which I like not, that he remained not stedfast in the law in which he was born, but, like an inconstant man and a deserter, fled from it.'

When we turn from the degraded throne of England to take a view of the Court of Rome at this period, the contrast is very striking. Instead of the insane and savage despot, who was making priest and peer his prey, we see a zealous, self-denying man, in the prime of life, unsparing of his time and care for the public state of Christendom, yet amidst all his labours anxiously stealing a few leisure hours for meditation on the book of Divine truth, and writing a commentary on the seven penitential psalms. His wealth was disposed of in charitable foundations, and gifts bestowed on the suffering Church in Palestine. Though of a noble family, he had no nephews or other relations whom he sought unduly to advance; but administered the affairs of his own little state with disinterested integrity, while with the greatest skill and determination he forced the kingdoms of Europe to obey his laws.

While, however, we give the praise which is his due

to the man, we must not look with favour or indulgence on the principles which he thus successfully
established. No sooner was the mitre exalted above the
crown, than it began to show the abuses which accompany all unlicensed sway,—with this further evil, that
the cruelties and extortions, which before affected only
the credit of the civil government, now began to be
perpetrated in the name of religion, and to bring disgrace and infamy on the office of those who sat in the
apostles' seat. Innocent III. had proclaimed a crusade
against King John. If Matthew Paris's story of the
embassy to the Moors be true, it was as lawful as that
against Saladin, at least. It is far more questionable
on what grounds he afterwards awarded the same measure to the poor sectaries called Albigenses, in Narbonne
and the south of France. But when Gregory IX. excommunicated the Emperor Frederic II., a prince who
had himself obliged the Pope by leading a successful
crusade to the Holy Land,—when he proclaimed a crusade, and excited the states of Italy to a protracted war
against him, and when for this purpose large taxes were
levied on the Church of England through the weak connivance of Henry III.,—people began to ask whether
this was a proper use to which to apply the endowments
of English churches, and whether the Pope could thus
make every prince a heretic who had given him some
personal offence.

Still this evil was tolerable[1] compared with that
which soon followed, when it was found that simony,
which Hildebrand had spent so much pains in checking
when it was transacted between churchmen and their

[1] It is well said by a late writer on this subject: 'We are far from
approving of the encroachments of pontiffs on the rights of contemporary monarchs : but considering what those princes commonly were in
education and character, and how they exercised their prerogatives, we
doubt whether it was in *this* respect that the usurpations of the
Roman see were chiefly to be deprecated.'—*Encycl. Metrop., History.*
c. lxxvii.

prince, was now transferred on a much larger scale to
the Court of Rome. It soon became notorious that the
candidate for preferment, who went best furnished with
treasure, had the best chance of prosecuting a successful suit with pope and cardinals. The issue of the
contest between Innocent and King John had taken
not only the investiture,[1] but the appointment and
patronage of bishoprics from the crown to the pope.
From bishoprics the claim was soon extended to ab-
bacies, deaneries, and other preferments; and all to be
paid for in meal or malt, a sum paid down, or an
instalment, to be followed by more. In the thirteenth
and fourteenth centuries there were sometimes as many
as five or six hundred clergymen from England occupied with business at Rome; some waiting for preferment, some to make appeals against the jurisdiction
of bishops in their dioceses, others seeking new privileges for their monasteries or their religious order. The
papal capital was filled with the noise of litigation; and
the pontiff's court was made a kind of court of chancery to every other ecclesiastical court in Europe. Even
an honest pope, amongst such innumerable temptations to be partial, must have been oppressed with the
load of business, so distracting to a mind of any reli-
ligious temper, and so foreign to the proper employment of a spiritual pastor of the Church of Christ.
What was to be expected, when from the political
situation, which he held in Italy, he was compelled
continually to use a variety of shifts to supply an exhausted exchequer, to negotiate peace on hard terms,
or hire troops to defend him in war.

All this time, the canon-law was receiving new additions from the labours of those popes, who were most
diligent in exacting these supplies. Gregory IX. and
Innocent IV. were great lawyers; and the code, which
they enlarged and made more perfect, was continually
extending its jurisdiction, so that it becomes difficult .

---

[1] See Appendix C.

to say what causes might not be brought within its circuit. For since all crimes are spiritual offences as well as transgressions of the law of the land, there would be a constant question to which of the two tribunals they should be brought. And, in fact, throughout this period the common law courts and the spiritual were continually at variance. There can be no doubt that the Church, as a religious society, has an inherent right of self-government; and even when the law of the land is founded on the revealed word of God, as it must be in every Christian country, there are cases in which the spiritual judge ought to exercise a different jurisdiction from that of the state. The loss of all penitential discipline in the Church is an evil which we deplore;[1] and it is to be feared it is one of those things which has brought the common people to think nothing a sin which the law of the land does not punish. But this discipline was not destroyed at the Reformation, when many efforts were made to restore it; but by the conduct of the ecclesiastical courts long before. The system, which came from Rome in the thirteenth and fourteenth centuries, was one which, instead of reviving discipline, overlooked the grossest offences, and multiplied positive laws, for the purpose of exacting fines when these laws were dispensed with. What other judgment can we form of those prohibitions of marriage between the most remote cousins, for violating which nothing was required but a sufficient sum paid for a dispensation to the Court of Rome? Or if this law was at first put forth by sincere, mistaken men, what sense of morality can justify those who afterwards took money for the violation of it? If the law was bad, why not rescind it? If it was just and right, it was treason to the law of God to permit it to be broken. Wills, contracts, and bonds, and all matters in which oaths were to be administered, were

---

[1] See the Commination Service, in the Prayer-book.

easily drawn within the jurisdiction of the spiritual
courts. It would have been well if this had not been
made the means of dispensing with the obligation of
oaths after they had been taken. But of all pretences
by which persons were made responsible to the laws of
the Church, none was more multiplied than that of
sacrilege. If an officer of the king took a chief out of
a sanctuary, he must be excommunicated till he had
paid his fine. If a mischievous knave docked the tail
of a bishop's palfrey, or if a stout baron played the
practical jest of waylaying the abbot's venison, and
prevented him for one day from keeping the custom of
'Bolton Abbey in the Olden Time,' it was no less
than the sin of sacrilege. Such harshness only p o-
voked the offences it was intended to check; and the
annals of monasteries are full of complains against
their country neighbours, who drained their fishponds,
broke their park-fences, and carried off their deer.

The spirit of the time is sufficiently marked by the
form of general excommunication, which, during a
good portion of this period, was pronounced four times
a year against the enemies of the Church's authority
and privileges. The foremost of the offenders enumerated as under a curse are 'those that purchasen writs
or letters of any lewd court,[1] to let[2] the process of
the law of holy Chirche of causes that longen skilfi 'ly[3]
to Christen court, the which shuld not be demed[4] by
none other law.' The next were those that should
alienate any of the Church-lands. And thirdly, those
who should withhold or diminish from the Church's
portion in tithes and offerings. No doubt these two
last were injurious and dishonest practices; but why
they should be selected alone out of all the sins against
the decalogue, it would puzzle a man to say, unless it was,
as Wycliffe said, that churchmen were more anxious

---

[1] lay court; court of common law.
[2] belong separately.
[3] hinder, or stay.
[4] doomed, judged.

to secure their own temporalities, than to maintain
the honour of God's laws. And as to the first, it only
proves the outrageous zeal they had to secure those
exemptions, which it had cost so much to obtain, and
which were so ruinous in their consequences.

These criminals, however, and these only, were on
such occasions pronounced accursed.[1] The prelate or
priest, coming into the church, mounted his pulpit,
and with bell, book, and candles burning, and the form
of the merciful Redeemer sculptured on a crucifix
lifted up before him, thundered out the words in the
plain old English of the time; for though the prayers
were in Latin, the curses were in the vulgar tongue:
'By authority of God, Fader, Son, and Holy Ghost;
and the glorious moder and maiden, our ladie St.
Marie, and the blessed apostles, Peter and Paul, and
all apostles, martyrs, confessors, virgins, and the hallows
(saints) of God; we denounce all those accursyd, that
byn so found guiltie, and all those that maintainen
them in ther sins, or given them thereto help or coun-
sell. For they be departid fro God and holy Chirche,
and they have no part of the passyon of our Lord
Ihesu Crist, ne of noe sacraments, ne noe part of the
prayers among Christen folk: but they byn accursyd
fro the sole of ther foot to the crown of ther head,
slepyng and wakyng, sittyng and standyng, and in all
ther wordes and in all ther workes, but if (except)
they have grace of God to amend them here in this
life, for to dwell in the pain of hell for ever withouten
end.' Then he shut the book with violence; the
candles were quenched, and the bells rung ; while the
congregation, receiving the sentence as if it had been
ratified above, raised a cry of terror for the fate of
the persons involved in such a doom.

[1] It is scarcely necessary to allude to the contrast presented in our
own Church-service for Ash-Wednesday, speaking the solemn sentence
of God's law in the words of God. This service is, indeed, in its original
far more ancient.

When one reads of such dreadful words, and sometimes worse than these, pronounced over trivial offences, applied in vengeance for private quarrels, and often for acts which only the canon-law had perverted into crimes,—and when one thinks of the blessings with which the Gospel was ushered in, and the brotherly love and tender pity which it is its office to shed abroad—the eye fills with tears at the record of such debasing cruelty and superstition. And yet, for raising his voice against these practices, was Wycliffe threatened with imprisonment and bonds.

The amount of influence thus exercised upon the country will be more easily judged of by considering the numbers of the clergy in proportion to the population, and the amount of their property as compared with that of the laity. But in both these respects we are left without any certain ground on which to form a calculation. The statements usually made that the Conqueror found a third of the land of England in the hands of the Church,[1] and that in the time of King John this amount had nearly reached one-half, seem in each case to exceed probability. As far as can be judged from the Doomsday survey, the amount of Church property at the Conquest would be more nearly one-tenth than one-third, and if this amount were doubled during the two following centuries, when more than five hundred monastic establishments were founded, it has been thought that this would leave a sufficiently large proportion.[2] One-fifth of the whole country, and that the best cultivated part, was a vast amount, when it is considered that the proportion which the Church property now bears to other landed property, is somewhere about a fiftieth. But in this calculation it is to be remembered that the religious houses were accustomed to lease out a great part of their lands to

[1] SIR WM. TEMPLE, *Works*, folio, II. 560. HALLAM, *Middle Ages*, II. 200.
[2] H. WARTON: HARMER's *Remarks on Burnet*, p. 4L.

laymen, for easy fines, as Bishops and Deans and Chapters still do.[1] So that they were not perhaps the direct landlords of more than one-half that amount.[2]

And precisely the same uncertainty exists as to the numbers of the clergy. In the absence of all certain information, the following may be offered as a probable conjecture. The number of chantries suppressed by 1 Edward VI., including all chaplaincies to hospitals and colleges, was 2374; of which we may suppose one priest for each, though this would exceed the actual amount. The whole number of lesser monasteries, dissolved 27 Henry VIII., was 376. If we suppose an average of six inmates for each house, this will give us 2256, a more probable number than 10,000, as stated by Stow. The greater monasteries were 186, and their average income about 600l. Calculating their numbers by the same houses, this will give the average number of inmates at

---

[1] Harmer, l. c.

[2] But it must be admitted that as far as any records extend from which a judgment might be formed, they will give a much larger proportion. It is stated by Selden (*Titles of Honour*, p. 572-3), from Ordericus Vitalis, who lived in the time of Stephen, that the Conqueror distributed the whole country into about 60,000 portions, called Knights' Fees; and the same writer, as well as Stow (*Annals*, p. 285), gives the actual number of Knights' Fees in the time of King John as 62,215, of which the proportion held by the Church was then reckoned at 28,000, or near one-half. Selden, however, elsewhere denies that a Knight's Fee was a measured quantity, as is commonly supposed, so that if the lands of the religious were taxed with a greater service than others, this may account for the statement. Besides, if this be a contemporary statement, it does not follow that those who made it were correct. They seem to have reckoned 45,000 parish churches and 52,080 townships in England,* and this can hardly be accurate. The present number of parishes is about 15,000. It should be added that in Wycliffe's answer for the Parliament against paying tribute to the Pope he gives the speech of a Lord who says, ' A third part, or more, of the land of this kingdom is held in mortmain by the Church.'—(Le Bas, p. 128.) Hence it is clear that in Edward III.'s time the proportion was reckoned at about a third; as in the time of John it has been at still more. Most probably these calculations were only made upon the cultivated lands, and a third of these at that time would be perhaps a fifth of the whole.

* Selden, ubi supra.

thirty-six, in all 6696. The number of 'religious persons,' therefore, at the time of the Reformation, from which time the data for these calculations are taken, will be 8952, besides the priests of the chantries 2374, in all 11,325. Of these a considerable proportion were not in holy orders, for there were always lay-brothers in proportion to their income, as in the case of the smaller the monasteries, besides that the nuns are included in this calculation.[1] But in forming an estimate of the actual number who under whatever designation, belonged to the order of the clergy, we must still add to this amount the whole number of parish priests, except those who served cures belonging to the monasteries, and a vast number of inferior persons employed in menial offices in the convents, all of whom had some lesser orders, as well as those who devoted themselves to the legal profession, and in some instances also to medical science.[2]

It may be affirmed that the population during these ages could not exceed 4,000,000, and if we suppose one-third of the inmates of the monasteries to have been priests, stating them at 3000, these, with the chantry priests, will make 5374, in addition to the whole number of parish priests, say altogether 15,000, which will be the same number of working clergy for a population of 4,000,000, that we have now in England when the population is 15,000,000, taking no account of the number of 'religious' who had no cure of souls. There were at least as many parishes as now, each with its own priest, besides that many Churches had one or more

---

[1] The writer is indebted for much assistance in this calculation of the number of religious persons, as for many other suggestions and contributions, to his friend, the Rev. Edward Churton, now archdeacon of Cleveland.

[2] This may account in some degree for the great discrepancy between different calculations of the numbers of these persons. A recent publication (FULLARTON'S *Parliamentary Gazetteer*), which gives the population of England in A.D. 1377 at no more than 2,300,000, reckons the total number of the religious at the same time at 47,721.

Mass Priests attached to chantries, who were often required to assist the parish priest in his duties. Then again there was hardly a neighbourhood in which there were not one or more monasteries, who were the proprietors of many of the village churches, receiving the tithes, and performing the duties by means of a vicar or substitute, answering to what we now improperly understand by a curate. There were six hundred and sixty religious houses, at least, at the time they were suppressed; but the names are preserved, in the whole, of eighteen hundred places at which some sort of religious foundation had at some time existed.[1]

The popedom was not without its reverses and disasters after it had attained its zenith. The long reigns of Henry III. in England, and Louis IX., commonly called St. Louis, in France, and the character of both these kings, had greatly favoured its advance. But when Edward I. and Philip the Fair were seated on these respective thrones, it would have required a pope of great prudence and circumspection to maintain his influence with them. Such was not Boniface VIII., a man of overweening self-confidence, and of very ques-

---

[1] An attempt has been made to calculate the revenues of the Church in the year 1317, from the fact that two cardinals who came to England that year, received 50 marks a day for their expenses, being four pennies out of every mark from every church. MACPHERSON on Commerce, vol. I. 819 (as quoted by Hallam), who cites Knighton (col. 2750), and infers that the Church revenue was therefore £200 marks a day, and 730,000 marks a year, which he observes was more than twelve times the national revenue in the reign of Henry III.—the revenue of Edward III., to whose time this record belongs, not being known. But as regards this last statement, the crown revenue in those days was merely the king's private income from his own estates; the national revenue, if it existed at all, was in occasional subsidies, and in feudal service. An old Durham MS., which appears to have been written about A.D. 1406, gives the amount of the clergy's tenth in one year at 18,870£., when the lay fifteenth was 37,952£. This would make the proportion of the Church lands rather less than one-fourth; or if we suppose the 18,870£. to include the tenth of tithes, rather less than one-fifth. And this is according to the estimate of one of the best ecclesiastical antiquaries.—See H. WARTON, on Burnet, as above.

tionable character. He is said to have gained the papacy
by a shallow trick, but one that sufficed for a weak
superstitious old man, his predecessor Celestin V. As
he was reposing himself at night in his chamber, Boniface contrived by a tube to send a voice into his ear, by
which he was warned to resign his office. He believed
it to be a celestial message, and complied; but afterwards finding how he had been deceived, he said to his
successor, on his election : ' You have stolen into the
chair like a fox; your temper will rule in it like a lion ;
but you will die like a dog.' The words were verified
in the fortunes of Boniface. He began his rule over the
Church of England by sending orders to Archbishop
Winchelsey, that the clergy should pay no taxes to the
king without his concurrence. For acting in compliance
with this order, the archbishop brought upon himself
and the Church the fierce wrath of a stern prince, who
soon made him to understand the duty of a subject.
This, and opposing Edward's ambitious designs on Scotland, destroyed this Pope's power in England. The
French king brought the contest to much closer quarters : he sent an armed force into Italy ; and proclaiming
charges of heresy, simony, and other crimes brought by
the French clergy against Boniface, and joined by two
cardinals of the powerful family of Colonna, whom he
had made his enemies, they surprised him in his country residence at Anagnia, made him prisoner, spoiled
him of enormous treasures, and left him so destitute and
heart-broken, that he died a short time after, A.D. 1304.[1]

This event broke the charm of the papal power in
its contests with kings; but over the Church it was
still undisputed. And now what the Popes could not
do by authority, they began by baser means to effect
by intrigue. Clement V., to keep up his credit with
Edward I., gave him absolution from fulfilling his coronation oath. This Pope, in A.D. 1309, removed his

---

[1] See Append.x C.

court to Avignon in France; where his successors for nearly seventy years continued to reside, and where the old palace with its dungeons still remains a monument of tyranny gone by. Here they continued their exactions, and wasted in profligate luxury the goods which a better age had lavished in piety and alms. With the English court these Popes of Avignon were deservedly unpopular; they were governed by French influence, and often thwarted, as far as they could, the designs of England against France. Hence Edward III., by some wise laws, as his grandfather had done, checked their appointment of bishops, and cut short their supplies. But while the king's consent was necessary, the Pope still 'provided,' as he called it; and it was not likely that an English clergyman would be promoted who was in bad esteem at the papal court. There were many attractions for ambitious churchmen in the patronage of the Pontiff abroad; and more than one English archbishop resigned his mitre for a cardinal's hat; while friars found lucrative employment as judges and advocates at Avignon and Rome.

There was still one step wanting to complete the disorders of the Church, and to destroy the last ties of Christian brotherhood. It had followed in other countries almost immediately after the papal triumph; but in England, though there was manifold corruption and debasing superstition in all quarters, there was as yet no avowed *persecution.* The papal lawyers had long aimed to introduce a law into all the states of Christendom, that persons convicted of heresy by the ecclesiastical judge should be capitally punished by the civil power. They had succeeded, in 1224, in Germany, where the emperor Frederick II. had enacted such a law, and another with it, that all temporal lords, who protected heretics after warning from the Church, should forfeit their estates; a law which, by a judicial retribution, the Pope afterwards turned against Frederick himself, when he declared this prince a heretic, and drove

E

him from the Kingdom of Sicily, which he gave to
Charles of Anjou. They had attempted it in France;
but St. Louis, to his great honour, was not seduced by
his pious zeal into compliance. His answer was, that
no man should suffer by his sentence, who had not been
tried by his laws. Yet it was in his time that Gregory IX., A.D. 1233, erected the courts of the Inquisition on the frontiers of his kingdom at Thoulouse; and
it would seem that this devout king had greatly aided
the fanatic warfare by which Count Raymond was
assailed. In the following reigns no country was more
disgraced by cruel executions for heresy than France.

In England the progress of this cruelty was more
slow. The fierce ignorance of the people had indeed
been shown in many dreadful persecutions of the Jews;
and in the reign of Henry II. a party of thirty foreign
sectaries are said to have perished miserably, wandering
about the country, where no man would give them food
or shelter. But as yet, down to Wycliffe's time, there
was no statute awarding the extreme penalty of the
law. And it is singular enough that the way by which
persecution was gradually introduced into England, was
by means of the privileges of the clerical order, better
known as the benefit of clergy. By this privilege, which
was contested between Henry II. and Becket, and confirmed by King John's charter, no clerical person was
liable to be tried in the king's courts, and any person,
who had been so tried, was at liberty to bring proof of
what was called 'his clergy,' on which he was delivered
to the ecclesiastical judge and a new trial took place.
He was admitted to take his oath that he was innocent,
before a jury of twelve clerks, and to produce twelve
compurgators who swore they believed he spoke the
truth: witnesses were examined on behalf of the prisoner only, and the result often was the acquittal of
those who had been condemned in the king's courts.[1]

---

[1] BLACKSTONE, iv. 367. The terms 'clerk' and 'scholar' became

It was in consequence of the powers thus exercised that the bishops, from the time of the Savoyard Boniface, archbishop of Canterbury, A.D. 1244—1270, began to have prisons in their several dioceses, which prisons, in the time of the Lollards, became places of cruel confinement.

Gregory XI. left his court, which he had brought back to Rome, in a state of miserable dissension. The Roman people assembled in large masses, and forced the cardinals, most of whom were Frenchmen, to elect an Italian to the vacant chair. They chose Urban VI.,—a man of harsh temper and manners, severe to himself, as Walsingham describes him, but more severe to others, and one who never forgave an offence. The French cardinals soon after separated themselves from him, annulled their election, and chose another pope of their own body, with the name of Clement VII. Urban immediately declared their cardinalships forfeited, and appointed a new set of cardinals. War ensued. Clement's party were defeated in a pitched battle, with the loss of five thousand men; and he escaped to Avignon, where he was supported by France, Spain, and Scotland; while Germany, England, and Italy adhered to Urban, who, suspecting even the cardinals who remained with him, soon after put six of them to the torture, and among them Adam Easton, a learned Englishman. He then ordered the rest to be thrown into the sea in sacks, but spared the life of Easton, out of regard to the English nation.

When Wycliffe heard of this double election, he felt as a persecuted man might feel, when the tyranny that had almost crushed him was, to all human appearance, tottering to its fall. He immediately put forth his spirited tract, entitled, *The Schism of the Popes.* ' Stand we firm,' he said, ' in the faith that Christ's law teacheth, —for never was there greater need,—and trust we to

synonymous, and any man who could read was admitted to claim his clergy. But it was enacted, 18 Eliz. c. 7, that no man allowed his clergy should be committed to his ordinary—that is, he should be tried in the queen's court.

E 2

the help of Christ. For he hath begun to help us
graciously, in that he hath *cloven the head of Antichrist*,
and made the one part to fight against the other. No
doubt the sin of the Popes, which has been so long continued, has brought on this division. If both these
heads last, or the one by itself, then shall the last
error be worse than the first.' He therefore called
upon emperor and king to put down the temporal
sovereignty of the Pope, and take away the territory
of the see in Italy: for this not only he, but almost
every wise and thoughtful man in Christendom at this
'time, looked upon as the source of the evil.¹ 'Maintain God's law, conquer your own heritage, and destroy
this foul sin, saving the persons. And then were peace
found for us, and simony destroyed. Let lords who
love God's law, help their princes in this cause. For
to them it belongs; and more glorious conquest did
never Christian king.'

If this reformation which he proposed was root and
branch, we cannot wonder at it, when we reflect on the
state of things which pressed upon his mind. It is
seldom that persecution leads the oppressed to regard
the oppressors with more favour than is here intimated,
in the wish to spare their persons, but to take away their
means of doing harm. But before we pass judgment on
Wycliffe, we must take a closer view of religious society
in England at the time when he appeared.

' Dante, as translated by Milton, had said long before:

'O Constantine, of how much ill was cause—
Not thy conversion—but those rich domains
Which the first wealthy Pope received of thee!'

It was believed in the middle ages that the Emperor Constantine had
given the Bishop of Rome his territory in Italy: though there was no
truth in it, and no proof that there was any lordship belonging to the
see before the age of Charlemagne. It was also a story at this time often
repeated by Wycliffe, John of Trevisa, and other English writers, from
the works of the Abbot Joachim, that when the gift was made, an angel's
voice was heard, saying, 'Alas! this day is venom poured forth into the
Church!'

CHAPTER IV.

O come to our Communion Feast;
There present in the heart,
Not in the hands, th' Eternal Priest
Will his true self impart.—*Christian Year.*

TO the same period which we have now been considering must be referred the establishment of some
points of *doctrine*, which have an equally important
bearing on the history of the Reformation. No doubt
the first advocates of transubstantiation were led by a
sincere though mistaken zeal, meaning to maintain the
consolatory and scriptural truth, that 'the body and
blood of Christ are verily and indeed taken and received by the Faithful in the Lord's Supper.' But it
is a temptation incident to human nature to bring
down everything to the level of human reason. And
so, rather than acknowledge that there are mysteries
which they could not fathom, men tried to explain the
way in which Christ is actually present, according to
his promise, by affirming that his natural body and
blood are contained in the consecrated bread and wine,
and that they cease to be bread and wine, and only
seem to be so.

Nothing is more certain than that this was not the
doctrine of the Anglo-Saxon Church. In the eighth century, the Venerable Bede wrote that, 'In the room of
the flesh and blood of the Lamb, Christ substituted
the sacrament of his Body and Blood, in the figure
of bread and wine.'[1] And in the same century, the
Emperor Charlemagne wrote thus to our countryman
Alcuin:[2] 'Christ at supper broke the bread to his

---

[1] Dp. Coers's *Hist. of Transubstantiation*, p. 82.   [2] Ibid.

disciples, and likewise gave them the cup in figure of his Body and Blood.' The modern doctrine is said by some to have been first promulgated about A.D. 820 by Paschasius Radbertus, a monk of Corbie, in the diocese of Amiens, who was forced, by the excitement which ensued, to resign the abbacy of his house. He seems to have taught that Christ is consubstantiated or rather enclosed in the bread, and corporally united to it in the sacrament. Yet even he did not go the length of transubstantiation, for he still said, 'The flesh and blood of Christ are received spiritually.' And he was answered by several learned men, some of whom, as John Erigena, our countryman, otherwise known as Scotus Erigena, the tutor of King Alfred's children, appear to have gone to an opposite extreme. But his most important antagonist was Bertram, or Rattram, whose book, written about A.D. 860, is addressed to Charles the Bald, and professes to be written by his command.[1] He asserts 'that the body and blood of Christ, which in the Church are received by the mouth of the believers, are figures, according to their outward show and visible form, but that according to an invisible substance, that is, according to the power of that divine Word, they are verily and indeed the body and blood of Christ.' And as for the change in the elements, he says, 'If they will say, that it is made in respect of the substance of the creatures, I answer that that cannot be so; for in respect of the substance of the creatures, look whatsoever they were before consecration, they are even the same afterwards. But they were bread and wine before, and, therefore, they remain the same.'[2] And further, 'This also is another prayer that is used

---

[1] This book was first printed in English A.D. 1549. It is entitled *The Boke of Bartram priest, intreating of the bodye and bloode of Chryste, written to greate Charles emperoure, and set forth viii c yeres agoo.*
[2] It is important to show this, because some modern Romanists have asserted that Bertram did not absolutely deny their doctrine of transubstantiation.

about the sacrament. Make perfect in us, good Lord, we beseech thee, the thing which the sacrament doth contain, that we may take those things in verity which now we take in figure.' And again, 'The external thing which is seen, hath a corporal form that feedeth the body ; but the interne thing which is understanded, hath a spiritual fruit that quickeneth the soul.' It was this book which first convinced our own Ridley, and after him Cranmer, by showing them that the then received doctrine was not the original faith. A little later, Ælfric, abbot of Malmsbury, A.D. 970, translated into Saxon a homily for Easter from the Latin, nearly copied from Bertram's book.[2]

The new doctrine was brought into England by Lanfranc of Pavia, made Archbishop of Canterbury by the Conqueror. His learned adversary Berenger, better known as Berengarius, who was Archdeacon of Angers, in France, wanted the moral courage necessary to a successful defence of the truth. And there was a defect in his teaching, which exposed his opinions to some just exceptions. He is thought to have been a follower of Erigena before mentioned, who is said to have denied that there is, in this sacrament, anything more than a bare sign, and no actual presence of Christ. Such an opinion was justly condemned by several councils before which he was summoned, and where he retracted it : but there is some doubt whether he had said so, for when he wrote again afterwards he taught that there is a real spiritual presence of Christ in the holy communion. He compared his own weakness to St. Peter's denial, and complained as if threats and terror had been used against him. But in his own solemn and melancholy words, in another place, ' the words of a priest must be either the words of truth, or

---

[1] External—outward.
[2] See the opinions of Ælfric in CHITRON's *Early English Church*, p. 251. See also PALMER's *Church History*, p. 127.

sacrilege.' It is a lesson for all times against a waver-
ing soul, to think what may be lost by the sinful
compliance of one trying hour.   After several recantations he was finally summoned before Pope Hildebrand
at a council at Rome, A.D. 1079, where he was made
to submit to the doctrine as propounded by the council.
Yet even the words of this formal recantation, commonly called 'the decree *Ego Berengarius*,' though
they most strongly assert the actual and substantial
change of the bread and wine into the true body and
blood of Christ, were cited by Wycliffe[1] in proof that
the Church of Rome had not even then arrived at the
point of transubstantiation.   It is confessed that the
name was then a novelty, and it shows how divided
men's minds were, on the subject, in the time of
Berenger, that he was made archdeacon by the Bishop
of Angers, and wrote, for some time, under his sanction.

It is, indeed, matter of some doubt whether this
doctrine of transubstantion was absolutely established
in the Church of Rome before the Council of Trent.
But it was generally received from the time of the
fourth Lateran Council, held under Innocent, III. A.D.
1215, a short time after his successful contest with
King John.   It was usual for the Acts of every Council
to open with a confession of faith, but, on this occasion,
the following words were introduced, under the head
of belief in the Universal Church. 'In which (Church)
Jesus Christ himself is at once both Priest and Sacrifice, whose body and blood are truly contained in the
sacrament of the altar under the appearance of bread
and wine, the bread being transubstantiated into the
body and the wine into the blood by divine power'—
a decree to be deplored by all succeeding ages for the
divisions, strifes, and sufferings which it has brought
into the Christian Church.   For, although it was still
a question whether this was sufficient to make it a

---

[1] *Dialogues*, pt. iv. ch. ii. p. 102.

matter of faith, since the Pope merely propounded
this confession on his own authority, without submitting
it to the deliberation of the council, it was soon after
adopted by diocesan and provincial synods in most
parts of Christendom, and was deemed to be the doctrine of the Church. The earliest notice of it, in any
canons of the English Church, is at a diocesan synod
at Salisbury, A.D. 1217, two years after this Lateran
Council, where it was expressed in the same words;
but we shall find that it had not been formally adopted
by the English Convocation until the time of Wycliffe.

It was a natural consequence of this belief that divine
honours should be paid to the consecrated elements,
and it was accordingly ordained, by Honorius III., the
successor of Innocent, that adoration should be made
at the elevation of the host. But it was not long before it was confirmed by a special festival, in honour,
as it is said, of this great gift of God to his Church.
This festival, called *Corpus Domini*, began to be celebrated in Flanders a little before the Lateran Council,
in consequence of some visions of a nun at Liege,[1] and
was appointed by the Bishop of Liege, about A.D. 1246,
but was not confirmed by the Church of Rome until
A.D. 1264, when Urban IV., being unwilling to sanction
it, was induced to do so by the alleged miracle of
Bolsena. The Pope was staying at Orvieto, a neighbouring city, when a priest, who had entertained doubts
about this doctrine, is said to have seen the miracle
performed as he was consecrating the sacred elements.[2]
The miraculous host was borne to Orvieto in grand
procession, and the Pope no longer hesitated to appoint
the festival for the whole Church. This is by no means

---

[1] LIGORI, *Oper. Dogmat.*, p. 324. LAMBERTINI *de Festis*, art. *Corpus
Domini*. The present Office was composed by Thomas Aquinas.

[2] Even so there seems some contradiction. The vision is said to have
been seen in *forma pietatis*, in the form of a *Pietà* or dead Christ,
whereas the present doctrine is that the elements are changed into
Christ's living body.

a single instance of the way in which those in authority
may be driven forward, beyond their own wishes or
intentions, by the intemperance of inferior persons in
carrying out opinions to which they are committed.
The *exposition* of the host upon the altar for divine
worship is first heard of about A.D. 1248, and in the
following century the *procession* of the holy sacrament
received the papal sanction.[1]

Still later, but a developement of this belief, is the
practice of 'Benediction of the Holy Sacrament,' by
which it is held that some special blessings are denied
to those who seek them by prayer *in the presence* of the
sacred elements reserved for such purposes after consecration.   This sort of 'Real Presence' is quite different from any that bears the sanction of the primitive
Church, and the difference is this.   Whereas, with the
primitive Church, we believe that we partake of the
body and blood of our Lord truly present, in and by
consecration and reception, this notion attributes the
actual presence of the Second Person of the Blessed
Trinity to the consecrated bread and wine, apart from
celebration and reception.

The practice of communion in both kinds was not
discontinued till the twelfth century, and this innovation also was gradually introduced.   It had become
usual in most parts of Western Christendom to dip the
bread in the cup, and thus administer it in a spoon.
This was forbidden by the Council of Claremont, A.D.
1095, which ordered that no one should communicate
of the altar without taking the body separately and the
blood in like manner.[2]   But instead of inducing a return to the primitive usage, this led to withholding the

---

[1] Liguori, *ubi supra.* Lambertini thinks the procession was observed from the time that Urban went in procession to conduct the
miraculous host into the town of Orvieto. The magnificent Cathedral
of Orvieto, one of the most beautiful specimens of Italian mediæval
architecture, was erected in honour of this miracle.

[2] Concil. Clare. A.D. 1095. Labbe, tom. x. p. 509, Can. xxviii.

cup altogether from the laity, and from those who did not officiate. In the thirteenth century there is evidence that it was generally discontinued, and the Council of Constance, in the fifteenth, expressly forbad it. Still a power was reserved to the Pope, of allowing it in certain cases, and the Council of Trent at one time had thoughts of restoring it.

Equally great was the departure from ancient usage which was introduced in these ages regarding the frequency of the Holy Communion. Indeed the change of the Communion into what is now understood by the Mass, is one of the most remarkable in the history of the Church. In the first three centuries there is evidence that the priest gave the Communion to all who had been present at the celebration. St. Cyprian says,[1] ' We receive the eucharist every day, as the food of our salvation, unless for some grave offence we are obliged to refrain from it.' And Justin Martyr, in his *Apology*, says the same. The Apostolical Canons, framed, as we have seen, in the third or the beginning of the fourth century, ordained that ' those who should come to church and not communicate should be excommunicated.' Here is some indication of the commencement of a departure from the primitive custom. Two centuries later, the Council of Agda ordained, A.D. 506, that every one should communicate three times in the year, at the Nativity, Easter, and Pentecost. But there is evidence from a writer who lived near that time, that in the Greek Church both clergy and laity communicated every Sunday, and those who did not were excommunicated; and he says the Roman practice was the same, but without excommunication. Meanwhile, as the priest continued to celebrate the divine mysteries every day, whether any communicated or not, the people gradually forgot the purpose for which they were instituted, and came to regard the *Sacrifice of the Mass* as a repetition of the very same sacrifice which the Scrip-

---

[1] *De Orat. Domini.*

ture teaches us was offered once for all upon the cross.
For some ages the Church continued to require attendance at the Communion, as the Church of England now
does, three times in the year at the least. But the
fourth Lateran Council made in this respect also a
a most material alteration. 'It was required that[1]
'every adult of either sex should confess, alone, to his
own priest, at least once in the year, and reverently receive the eucharist, at least at Easter.' This canon, like
the rest on such subjects, was intended to restore discipline, not relax it, but it shows that the notion of
daily or weekly communion was already abolished.
The English bishops, indeed, were slow to carry out
this provision of the Lateran Council in its full extent.
For by the canons of Walter de Cantilupe, bishop of
Worcester, A.D. 1240, it is enjoined that all shall confess
at least once a year, but they are exhorted to communicate thrice,[2] as is now enjoined by the Church of England. And the canons of Poer, bishop of Sarum, A.D.
1217, are to the same effect.[3]

Much more important, however, were the results of
this same canon, as regards the other practice to which
it refers. To enjoin the attendance at the Holy Communion was a good thing, however lax the injunction
might be. But the result of requiring communion once
a year, *preceded by confession,* was to render the confessional imperative on every one of the people, and it is
impossible to estimate too highly the consequences of
this step. These consequences have been twofold, first
to impose an intolerable yoke upon the people; and
secondly, to overthrow all discipline by the reaction it
has caused. The intention of Innocent was probably
to revive what had been neglected; for the practice of
confession had existed in the East before the end of the
fourth century, but was then discontinued on account

---

[1] LABBE, tom. xi. p. 172. This is the famous Canon, *Omnis utriusque
sexus.*
[2] Ibid. pt. 1. p. 578.   [3] Ibid. p. 254.

of some public disorders arising from it.[1] In western
Europe it had been continued without intermission, but
as a practice rather than a law, and it does not seem to
have been compulsory. One of the clergy at the cathedral churches was called a canon penitentiary, whose
office it was, in difficult cases, to advise the doubting
conscience and to direct persons in works of repentance
and acts of penance. Such confession as this, left to the
option of the parties, many good men in later times
have wished to see revived. Dean Colet told Erasmus
that he much approved of secret confession, ' professing
that he never had so much comfort in anything as in
that.' The martyr Ridley, a short time before his
death, writing from his prison, used these words concerning it : ' Confession to the minister, which is able
to instruct, correct, comfort, and confirm the weak,
wounded, and ignorant conscience, I ever thought might
do much good in Christ's congregation ; and so, I assure
you, I think at this day.' The excellent Jeremy Taylor
has left on record an equally favourable opinion of this
part of penitential discipline. And few considerate persons will judge differently of it.[2] It is surely to be regretted that it is so little practised, except on a sick
bed, between priest and people, in our time.

There is a remarkable testimony to the change
effected by this new law of Innocent III. respecting the
practice of confession, in the extant records of the Wal-
densian churches ; a testimony not affected by any
question as to the origin or antiquity of those churches
themselves. In a MS. in the Vaudois language, allowed
to be of the fourteenth century, and consequently 150
years before the Reformation, and less than that time
after the Lateran Council, under the head of the Seven
Sacraments, are these words concerning penance : ' Of
which penance we hold for faith, and sincerely at heart
confess that it is useful to man, by reason of doing

---

[1] SOCRATES, iv. c. 19. SOZOMEN, lvii. c. 17.
[2] See also Dr. DONNE. Serm. xxvi. p. 264. Ed. 1640,

away sin. To which people should be continually
admonished, and we admonish that sins be confessed
according to the form of the primitive Church, and that
men seek counsel in their needs of priests, who are wise
and who know them. The form and obligation newly
introduced by Innocent III., which the simoniac priests
commonly use, ought to be declined and avoided by the
faithful. The remedies useful to be duly counselled to
the penitent, such as are fasting, prayers, alms, and
other works of satisfaction, we confess that they are
useful and profitable. Auricular confession made only
to the priest alone, and the form and usance of absolution, and the enunciation of the penance in number, and
foot, and measure, at the will of the confessor, according to the mode which the simoniac priests adopt, and
the obligation of Innocent III., is not of the substance of
(but rather opposed to) true penance.'[1] Hence we discover two facts: first, we find that a certain kind of
confession, much resembling that now prescribed in the
Communion Service of the Church of England, existed
before this Lateran Council; and secondly, we have an
almost contemporary testimony as to the mistrust and
dislike with which the novelty of auricular confession,
with its accompanying penances, was at first received.
It matters not to brand these Vaudois as heretics. Their
testimony to the matter of fact is independent of their
opinions, and it goes to show that these innovations of
the Lateran Council were so considered at the time they
were introduced.

The advice to confess to priests *who knew them*, has
reference to a further innovation, which was introduced
by Gregory IX., when he gave authority first to the
Dominican Friars in A.D. 1227, to hear confessions,[2]
which was soon extended to other mendicant orders;
'an unheard-of privilege,' as Matthew Paris calls it.

[1] For further particulars of the very valuable MSS. of the Vaudois in
the public library at Geneva, see Appendix D.
[2] LABBE, xi. p. 333.

This was a violation of the law of the Lateran Council, which required that the people should confess to their own priests, and we shall soon have occasion to observe that it was a fruitful source of mischief, and an endless subject of complaint.

The doctrine of Purgatory was not declared an article of faith till the Council of Florence, A.D. 1438, nor has it ever been determined to be material fire. This is not the place to enter upon the lengthened discussions as to the state of separate souls, which ended in the establishment of this belief. But it is to be observed that the passages from the Fathers usually alleged in its support, relate only to prayer for the dead, except two places of St. Augustine, which disprove rather than countenance the modern notion.[1] But the belief in purgatory is so intimately connected with the doctrine of Indulgences that the one can hardly be separated from the other. It is admitted that the name of indulgences is not found in the writings of the Fathers;[2] and it is plain that they arose out of the practice of imposing penance, which the bishop, in certain cases, had the power to remit. Those who had sacrificed to idols to save their lives were excluded from full communion, by the ancient canons, for five years, being wholly separated from the faithful for three years, and then admitted only to 'communion without oblation' for two years more; that is, they were allowed to be present, but not to communicate themselves. But the Council of Ancyra, held A.D. 314, before the first Nicene Council, allowed to the bishops a power, 'either of using clemency or of adding more time.' They are, therefore, to 'consider the foregoing and subsequent life (of the penitent), and so extend their clemency.'[3] And by the Nicene Council a similar permission was expressed in

---

[1] *De Civitat. Dei*, l. xxI. c. 13. *Enchiridion*, c. 08, 09, on 1 Cor. iI. 13. 'Incredibile non est, et utrum ita sit quaeri potest.'

[2] LIGUORI, *Opera Dogmat.*, p. 501.

[3] HARDUIN, *Con.*, tom. I. p. 237. LABBE, I. 1458.

these words: 'For such (viz., the truly penitent) the
bishop shall be allowed to devise more gentle measures.'
On the occasion of the first Crusade, we find indulgences
granted by the Council of Claremont, A.D. 1096, under
Urban II., to those who should go to the Holy War;
and it is worth while to compare the style of this first
indulgence for such a purpose with that which was
granted a century later for a similar object by the
Lateran Council. 'Whosoever for devotion alone, and
not for the sake of honour or wealth, shall go to Jerusalem for the liberation of the Church of God, that
journey shall be reckoned to him in the place of all
penance.' But the words of Innocent, at the Lateran
Council, are as follows: 'We, therefore, out of that
power of binding and loosing which God has bestowed
upon us, however unworthy, indulge to all who shall go in
person, being contrite and confessed, the plenary forgiveness of all their sins; and we promise them an augmen-
tation of eternal salvation in the retribution of the just.'

Here we have the germ of that wonderful assumption
which found its completion in the following declaration
of Clement VI., A.D. 1342, in his bull *Unigenitus*; that
'in the Church there is the infinite treasure of the satisfactions of Jesus Christ, and there are also the super-
abundant satisfactions of the blessed Virgin, who, being
exempt from every actual sin, had no satisfaction to
pay for herself; and the satisfactions of the saints, who,
in the holy deeds of their lives, have paid more satisfaction than their sins deserved.' Thus did the simple
remission of penitential discipline become mixed up with
a notion that penance continues beyond this present life,
which led to the invention of this infinite store of merits
dispensed by the rulers of the Church.

The next step, in the downward progress, was the *sale*
of such indulgences; the scandalous traffic in which is almost too notorious to require description here. But we
shall have occasion to mention it when we come to speak
of the great dealers in this article, the Mendicant Friars.

CHAPTER V.

EFFECTS OF THE PAPAL SUPREMACY IN ENGLAND ON
CLERGY AND PEOPLE. TREATMENT OF THE JEWS.
GOOD BISHOPS.

> If Rome be earthly, why should any knee
> With bending adoration worship her?
> She's vicious, and your partial selves confess
> Aspires the height of all impiety.
> BEAUMONT AND FLETCHER.

TO judge of the state of religious society in England
during the time of the Papal supremacy, it will be
necessary to take a view of the different classes of which
it was composed, the bishops and clergy, the monastic
orders, the friars, and the people. All these classes had
existed before the rise of the Papal power, except the
friars, whose case will require a separate consideration.
Of the rest, the question will be whether they were
ultimately benefited or not by the system of Church
government then established. And whatever may be
thought of the influence of the Papal Court upon the
religion of these times, it is consoling to find how many
good men there were in the Church of England.

The first English bishop appointed by the authority
of the Pope was Stephen Langton, made Archbishop of
Canterbury by Innocent III., A.D. 1207; a man unques-
tionably of high character, equal to the first of his time
in sacred learning, and one who showed a high-minded
conscientiousness in his public conduct; obeying orders
from Rome, as long as they seemed bound upon him by
his religious duty, but refusing to do so when they were
injurious to the liberties of his country.[1] Nor can it be
denied that for a time afterwards some regard was shown
at Rome to the character and qualifications of the bishops

---

[1] See SOUTHEY's *Book of the Church*, cix. near the end.

F

to be invested, when, in A.D. 1234, Gregory IX. made
choice of Edmund Rich, commonly called St. Edmund,
a Berkshire clergyman of blameless life and conversation, and a diligent preacher of God's word; whom
however he forced upon the Monks of Canterbury, after
having set aside three other elections. And our respect
to both these prelates is due rather for what they did in
opposition to the popes who appointed them, than for
any act in which they complied with their commands:
to Langton, for his adherence to the barons, who stood
against an excommunication from Rome in their contest
for the Great Charter; to Edmund, for his resistance to
the rapacity of the legate, Otho, in tithing and tolling
the English Church. It is well known that this good
man, after many unavailing attempts to persuade the
king to measures more befitting the honour of his crown,
and seeing the discipline of the Church destroyed by a
shameful compact between the Pope and the government
at home, retired to the Cistercian house at Pontigny in
France, to close his days in mortification and prayer.

But the most illustrious ornament of the Church
of England in these times was Robert Grosteste, bishop
of Lincoln, in the reign of Henry III., whose works contain abundant evidence that the love of Christ, and the
study of Holy Scripture, were the foundation of his
excellence.

The following is a specimen of his sermons. It is
addressed to his clergy, and entitled, 'The persuasion of
good shepherds,' on the text (St. John x 11), 'I am
the good shepherd.' 'The good shepherd enters in at
the right door, namely, by Christ preached: he maketh
the sheep hear his voice, he calleth his own sheep by
name, for he seeks to know those who are written in the
book of life. And he not only knows them, but is
known of them, by his works, his goodness, his labours
of love; as Christ says, 'I know my sheep, and am
known of mine.' He leadeth them out of sin: link by
link as their sins connect them, so must the steps of true

repentance set them free. He goeth before them, according to the injuction of St. Paul, 'Be an example to the flock in word, in conversation, in charity, in faith, in purity.' And lastly, he lays down his life for his sheep; and why not? when the least virtue is better than the bodily life, for the body lives only through the soul, and virtue is the life of God in the soul of man. If an householder should give his servant in charge a worthless penny and a most precious sheep, and the servant should be able to save the life of the sheep by losing the worthless penny, would he not be a wretch to hesitate? Who then should refuse to lose his worthless body for the sake of saving a precious soul? when instead of the worthless penny, the corruptible body, he shall receive a golden treasure, a body incorruptible.[1]

But it is remarkable that all those who were most distinguished for their piety and learning in these times, were strong in their indignation against the Papal Court. And none more so than Grosteste, who went in person to the Council of Lyons, A.D. 1250, and there delivered a protest to the Pope and Cardinals, which contained these words, in which perhaps we may hope that there is something of the style of hyperbole, which seems to have been in fashion in the Latin orations of the day. 'Pastors who do not preach Christ, even if they have no other sin, are Antichrist, and Satan transformed into an Angel of light.' But these Pastors add all sorts of sins besides. They are all luxurious, fornicators, adulterers, incestuous, indulgent of their appetite to excess, and to be short, all defiled together with all sorts of sin and wickedness and abomination.' And then with a noble boldness, he tells the Pope and Cardinals; 'But what is the cause, the fount and origin of

---

[1] *Fasciculi Appendix*, p. 250, edition 1690.
[2] It was this sentence of Bishop Grosteste that was so much relied upon, and so often quoted by the followers of Wycliffe. 'The priest that preacheth not the word of God, though he have none other default, he is Satanas and Antichrist.'

this? I exceedingly fear to say, and yet I dare not be silent, lest I fall under that woe of the prophet who says,—Woe is me, because I was silent, for I am a man of unclean lips.[1]   The cause, the fount and origin of it is THIS COURT;[2] after which he describes the profligacy and venality of the Court of Rome.

At this same Council of Lyons, the representatives of the English nation declared that the number of foreigners to whom the Pope had given preferments in England was so great that 60,000 marks were carried out of the country yearly by foreign clergy; and this was afterwards stated at 70,000.   For the Pope now assumed the power to nominate to all preferments, and constantly bestowed the best bishoprics and livings on Italians, sometimes on boys and libertines.   Grosteste himself was afterwards suspended for refusing to induct an Italian boy to a rich living in his diocese given him by the Pope.   It is said that the exactions demanded from the diocese of Lincoln alone, in his time, were 6,000 marks in one year, equal to the value of 20,000l. of our money.   The former sum stated to have been extracted from the whole kingdom would now be not less than 200,000l.; but a better way of judging of these amounts may be to compare them with some other payment near the same time.   Thus the ransom of the King of Scots, taken prisoner by Edward III. was 100,000 marks, but the sum was so large that the Scots were allowed to pay it by instalments, 10,000 marks a year.   So the largest diocese in England, paid in one year to the Pope or his dependents, more than half as much as the kingdom of Scotland could afford for the ransom of their king.[3]

---

[1] Isaiah vi. 5.   In our version 'For I am undone,' instead of 'Because I was silent.'

[2] Foxe. App. p. 252.

[3] It is said to have been shown in Parliament, A.D. 1532, in the reign of Henry VIII., that there had been paid for the bulls of Bishops (for institution, that is, to their sees), since the 4th year of Henry VII., in fourty-four years, one million and sixty thousand pounds, besides what

Edmund Rich was succeeded at Canterbury by Boniface of Savoy, a foreigner, a rude and violent man, without any qualities befitting such an office, to which his only recommendation was, that he was uncle to the queen.   On his death the Pope sent over Robert Kilwardby, a Franciscan friar, who a few years afterwards carried off the treasures of the see to Italy, to support him in the new honour of a cardinalship, for which he resigned it.   Then came another Franciscan friar, John Peckham, a man in some respects of better stamp, a restorer of discipline, and one who strove to mitigate the harsh conduct of Edward I. towards the Welsh people; but trained by a long practice as one of the judges of the Pope's court at Rome, to deeds of severity, and blinded by cruel superstition.   After paying a sum of 4000 marks to the Pope for his presentation, equal to about 15,000*l.* of our present money, his first act was to excommunicate his brother primate, Walter Giffard, of York, for coming into his province with his silver cross borne before him.   Giffard was travelling towards London with his retinue, and the monasteries and other places of entertainment on their way shut their doors against him, so that he was soon driven by peril of famine to submission.   His next remarkable act was the issuing of an order to level to the ground all the Jewish synagogues within his province; a singular mark of the extent to which he thought it allowable to exercise the independent authority of the mitre without consulting the crown.   Here, however, his proceeding was checked by Edward I., who had his own plans to carry, by commanding forbearance.

It was in this king's reign, and during Peckham's primacy, A.D. 1296, that the Jews were finally expelled from England, where they had resided since the time

had been exacted for dispensations and indulgences.—(HOLLINGSHEAD, *Chron.* p. 928.)   The treasure left by Henry VII., the wealthiest prince of his age, was one million eight hundred thousand pounds.

of Edward the Confessor. Their history presents a
gloomy picture of the manners of the age. In the early
Norman reigns, by practising peaceful and profitable
arts, while the people neglected them, they had amassed
considerable wealth. They were physicians, goldsmiths, and jewellers, and are supposed to have directed
their industry to the working of mines in the mineral
districts; but their most gainful employment was found
in lending money, and granting letters of credit from
one part of the kingdom to another. The advantage
of this practice, at a time when travelling with a sum
of money was not quite so safe as it is now, was very
soon perceived. The kings and their ministers encouraged it, at the same time turning it to a source of
revenue, by having every money bill enrolled at some
public office, and requiring a fee upon it from the bor-
rower and lender.

They had enjoyed more than a century of peaceful
commerce, when at the accession of Richard I. they
were marked out as victims to the popular fury. The
first outbreak was in London, at the time of this king's
coronation; thence it spread to Lynn, Stamford, and
Lincoln, and Bury St. Edmund's, with less violence;
but it ended with a dreadful massacre, partly occasioned
by their own suspicious fears, in the city of York. The
leaders of the populace in this bloody deed were some
thriftless profligates, who resorted to murder to cancel
their debts, and to recover their bonds deposited in the
public office by the Jews; but it could not have been
perpetrated had not some fanatical priests and monks
encouraged it, who were seen actively engaged in the
assault. It is well known that the Jews, distrusting the
protection given them by the Norman governor, had
taken their opportunity, while he was gone out of the
castle, to overpower the guard, and close the gates
against him. This rash measure, turning their only
means of safety to their own destruction, united all
parties against them. They were closely besieged; and

in their despair the greater part, following the counsel
of an aged rabbin, fell by their own hands. The rest,
being unable to maintain the defence, offered to surrender and receive baptism, the only terms on which life
was offered them ; but they were cruelly butchered, in
breach of treaty, by a miscreant called Richard le
Maubête, or the *Ill Beast*, as soon as they had passed
the barrier.

The only life lost on the side of the besiegers (it
would be an abuse of words to call it the Christian side)
was that of a vile priest, in the garb of a hermit, who
had once been a canon in the order of the Premon-
strants. He is said to have been so persuaded that the
act in which he was about to engage was a religious
service, that he received the holy communion himself,
and administered it to a chosen party of followers, before he went to join in the fray ! There, as he was
busying himself in the foremost rank, and leading an
onset or attempt that was made to scale the wall, a large
stone hurled from the battlements scattered his brains,
and cut short his fanatic exhortations to those around.
The other instigators of the tumult discovered their real
motive in the part they took, by going immediately to
the register-office at the cathedral, and obtaining possession of the bonds deposited there, which they committed to the flames.

This atrocity was prompted in some measure by the
fierce zeal then prevalent for the crusades, which made
the ignorant people regard the destruction of the infidel,
Turk or Jew, as a religious duty. But the Church had
hitherto done something to restrain such madness. St.
Bernard, in the earlier part of the same century, indig-
nantly condemns the conduct of a monk, well named
Rodolph the Vile, who had attempted to provoke a persecution against the Jews in Germany. The famous
Carthusian saint, Hugh, bishop of Lincoln, who lived in
the time of Richard I. and John, took some commendable
pains to prevent a man from being honoured as a martyr

who had robbed a Jew, but had afterwards himself been
murdered at Northampton for the sake of his plunder.
And William of Newborough, an Austin canon residing
in the neighbourhood, and an historian of the time,
calls this tragedy at York an act of execrable butchery.

There is some difficulty in sifting the evidence with
regard to those insults which the Jews of the middle ages
are said to have committed against Christians. The
tumult at Lynn is said to have been occasioned by an
attempt which they made on the life of one of their own
nation, who had become a Christian convert, and by
their assault upon the church into which he had fled for
refuge. The stories of their cruelties to Christian children are told in the chronicles with the usual circumstances of facts; and sometimes, on a trial ensuing, the
accused are stated to have confessed their guilt. In an
age when men of different faiths were fierce in hostility
against each other, it is not improbable that the feelings
of humanity on either side should have been blunted;
that the Jews should have had their rancour against the
cross embittered by the wrongs which they endured;—
at least it is not consistent with the acknowledged principles of human nature, that all the cruelty and fa-
naticism should have been only on the Christian side.[1]

The wrongs they suffered were indeed extreme.
King John, when he made his gaol-deliveries, excepted
the Jews from the common benefit. Henry III. on one
occasion confiscated a third of all their property. Edward I. seized, imprisoned, and heavily fined the whole
body for a supposed conspiracy in clipping the coin; on
which charge great numbers suffered death. Lastly,
about nine years after he had checked the outrage purposed by Peckham, the parliament came to a bargain

---

[1] So late as A.D. 1701, a Jew of immense wealth turned his only
daughter out of doors utterly destitute for having embraced Christianity;
an act which occasioned the passing of a new statute.—BLACKSTONE,
b. i. c. 16.

with the king for their entire deportation, granting him a fifteenth of all property, on condition that the Jews should quit the realm. They were then a body of more than fifteen thousand persons, who were expelled almost in utter destitution; and they appeared no more in England till the time of Cromwell.

Only one act of a more merciful kind is recorded. In the early part of his reign King Henry III. was persuaded to found in London a religious house for the instruction and maintenance of such Jews as should be converted to the Christian faith. It stood to the east of Chancery Lane, and the church which belonged to it is now the chapel of the Rolls. It was under the government of a master and two or three chaplains, and continued for about a century and a half, or eighty years after the expulsion of the Jews. It would appear that some number of converts were received into it; and there found good Christians who sought conferences with them for removal of their prejudices. But the ill-treatment, which was more prevalent, made the time unfavourable for such efforts. The good Archbishop Bradwardine, who lived a century later, relates a conversation which passed between him and a Jew, showing the strength of his ancient prejudices. At the close of it, 'If you will not hear my reason,' said Bradwardine, ' at least promise me that you will pray for me, as I will for you, that God may remove the error from the heart of one or the other of us, and show whether of us follows that law which is most acceptable in His sight.' 'No,' said the Jew; 'for this would be to doubt concerning the truth of my own law; and I have no such doubt. I cannot therefore pray for myself as you desire, nor can I consent that you should pray thus for me.' 'Yet,' persisted Bradwardine, 'if you will not pray for yourself, nor take it kindly if I pray for you, I would still entreat you to pray for me, and in those terms in which I have offered to pray for you.' 'And this I said (the good archbishop here remarks), hoping at least to melt his hard and stubborn heart to kinder feelings by the benefit of prayer.' But this also he peremptorily refused. 'I know,' said he, 'that you will never be a good Jew; and even if you choose to doubt about the truth of your law, I will never doubt of mine.'

Such answers mark the effect of persecution on the human heart. They would not have been given had the Church during this interval produced many Bradwardines. But the prelates who, under papal influence, were employed to watch over the flock of Christ, were very few of them gifted with either talents or virtues like to his. The very pretence on which the investiture had been claimed by the disciples of Hildebrand was now virtually abandoned; and the worthless favourites of weak princes were appointed by the pope's connivance as easily as if there had been no appeal to Rome. On the death of Archbishop Winchelsey, in A.D. 1313, a man of learning and charity, though too subservient to Rome, the monks of Canterbury had chosen Thomas Cobham, canon of St. Paul's, a man whose good doctrine and innocency of life had gained him the name of *the Good Clerk*. Edward II., however, had a friend of his own to serve, Walter Raynold, a man of low origin, being the son of a baker at Windsor; but this should have been no hindrance to his promotion had he been otherwise worthy. The Avignon pope, Clement V., seems to have made little inquiry on this point, being influenced by other considerations. He gladly joined with the king to destroy the free election of bishops, and appointed Raynold on his own authority. The new archbishop made it his first object, by leaving a good retaining-fee at the papal court, and a promise of an annual payment, to secure himself against all appeals that might be made in England against his proceedings. There was some ground for this, if he could not act independently of the Pope, nor obtain the rights of his primacy otherwise; for vexatious appeals thus made

against the bishops were among the crying evils of the
system. But the next step was less equivocal. He
obtained bulls of privileges, which must be enumerated,
to show how far the papacy had restrained the due authority of bishops, while it usurped the power of licens-
ing them to do many things that were neither consistent
with good discipline or good faith. 1. A privilege to
visit his own province of Canterbury during the next
three years, during which time the suffragan bishops
were to exercise no jurisdiction. 2. A privilege to restore two hundred religious persons who had broken
their rule, to their monasteries. 3. To dispense with
the rule about ordaining none below the canonical age,
which was then twenty-five, so as to ordain one hundred
priests or deacons who had not reached that age. 4. To
give absolution to one hundred persons who had assaulted clergymen, such offenders being then bound to
seek absolution of the Pope. 5. To dispense with the
canon-law against pluralites in the case of forty beneficed clergymen. 6. A privilege to grant pardons for
every offence committed within a hundred days to all
who sought it, wherever he went on his visitation.[1]
There is scarcely one of these privileges which does not
bear upon the face of it a strong presumption that the
object was to sell his episcopal acts and functions for
money. And the long-continued term which he stipulated for has something of a mercenary appearance; for
the primate, on his visitation, expected to find free
quarters; and his attendants, a body of eighty men
mounted, man and horse, were to be entertained at the
cost of the suffragans.[2]

He was interrupted, however, in his progress by the
troubles of the state; and we must follow him to take
a view of his political character   It was only in the
spirit of the times that he interfered to prevent Adam

---

[1] GODWIN, in *Vit. Reynold.*
[2] Hist. of Rochester, in *Anglia Sacra*, 369.

Orleton, Bishop of Hereford, from answering, in the
King's Court, to a charge of treason, which his subsequent conduct proved to be too well founded. But he
had been himself tutor to the unhappy Edward II., and
owed his preferment to him; and there is something
shocking in the grey-haired perfidy of this low-minded
prelate, when we see him coming forward, in a meeting
of the rebellious Londoners, at Guildhall, at which it
was resolved to dethrone the king, and saying, 'The
voice of the people is the voice of God.'[1]   Whether influenced by fear, or deliberately joining in the revolt,
the guilt is nearly equal.

Yet in this century also, we may still trace the same
stream of good men mingling with the turbid waters,
and in each case we find them longing and praying for
better things. Of these was Richard Rolle, called the
Hermit of Hampole, from a place near Doncaster, who
lived in the reigns of Edward II. and III., and died A.D.
1349. He translated some parts of Scripture into English, and expressed his earnest desire for a translation of
the whole, by applying these words of the Psalmist, 'Oh
take not the word of thy truth utterly out of my mouth.'
He is thought to be the author of one of the earliest
English poems, called the *Pricke of Conscience*, and his
writings were very popular, and exercised an extensive
influence. What was the nature of that influence may

---

[1] It has sometimes been supposed that he brought forward these
words as a text of Scripture, and preached from them; but this seems
to be a mistake. Adam Orleton had taken as a text before the University
of Oxford, 2 Kings iv. 19: 'My head! my head!' and preached a sermon
to prove to them that the body politic would never be sound till it had
a new head. Raynold spoke indeed in a popular assembly; but it was
usual for bishops to begin their speeches in parliament with scripture
texts, and he seems to have substituted this misapplied proverb instead.
But what a departure from old English principles! 'The people must
be led according to the divine laws, not blindly followed,' says Alcuin;
'for you only trust the testimony of the good and honest. Never listen
to those who say, The voice of the people is the voice of God. There is
always something akin to madness in the sudden movements of the
multitude.'—*To Charlemagne*, Epist. cxxvii.

be judged by the following specimens from an unpublished commentary on the Book of Job.[1] 'What is man, that Thou shouldest magnify him? and that Thou shouldest set Thy heart upon him?'[2] O wondrous condescension of the Creator, oh immense benignity of the Redeemer! For what is man?—a mass of putrefaction, a vessel of abomination, food for worms :—prone to evil, slow to good, fast linked to earthly things, banished far from heavenly joys. What then is man? Man is become like unto vanity, whom God made in the image and likeness of Himself. Justly, therefore, do the days of man pass like a shadow : but if man had not sinned, he would have remained throughout unchangeable and unchanged. Wherefore, listen, O man, to thy misery, understand thy poverty, and behold thy fall. Thou hast fallen down from the delight of Paradise to want and hunger; falling among thieves, thou hast been left stripped and wounded and half dead. Arise, O man, from the nets of ruin, and breathe again toward the kingdom. There are all delights, there the odours of all sweets, there is all beauty, and the fulness of every joy.'

Tho same writer has the following beautiful contemplations on tho name of Jesus, from the Song of Solomon (c. i. 3), 'Thy name is ointment poured out, therefore do the virgins love Thee.' 'O wondrous, O delightful name; for this Thy name is most high above every name, without which no man whatever may hope for salvation. For sweet is that name and pleasant to the human heart, affording true consolation. For JESUS is in my mind a song of joy, in my ear a heavenly sound, in my mouth a honeyed taste : no wonder, then, if I love that name which affords me solace in my every strait.'[3]

Of the same age was Richard Fitzralph, Archbishop

---

[1] Lincoln Minster Library, MS. D. 5, 12.   [2] Job vii. 17.
[3] Lincoln MS. D. 5, 12. See HAMPOLE's *Seven Marks of the Spirit of God*, in Archdeacon CHURTON's *Early English Church*, p. 379.

of Armagh, and thence more commonly known as *Armachanus*, from whose *Apology against the Friars*, delivered to the Pope at Avignon, A.D. 1352, we derive the best and most authentic account of the miserable condition of the Church in the fourteenth century. He is said to have translated the Bible into Irish, at a time when there was as yet no English version of Holy Scripture, and when the policy of the Government had been to suppress and discountenance both languages. Having been invited to preach in London, he had delivered seven or eight sermons in English against the practices of the friars, and especially against the way in which they interfered with the ministerial office, by taking the confessions of the people themselves, instead of the parish priest. Churchmen did not mind abusing one another in Latin; but an appeal to the people, such as these English sermons, from the Primate of Ireland, gave great offence. The friars appealed to the Pope; and the Archbishop's apology is called the Defence of Curates, that is, of parish priests, against the friars. He laboured with all the eloquence and skill of which he was master (and he was one of the best preachers of his time), to destroy the privileges of the mendicant orders; but he pleaded at Avignon before Clement VI., one of the most prodigal and profligate of men; and the mendicants did not want money to secure their cause.

Of a mind equally sincere, and of deeper wisdom, was Thomas Bradwardine, who, at the close of a blameless life, was made Archbishop of Canterbury by the purest of all elections, the choice of the king and of the clergy of the cathedral being unanimous. This good man was a noble example of the union of religious contemplation with active benevolence. He was chaplain to Edward III., and attended his armies in France, where he was so beloved, both by the monarch and his soldiers, that he was sometimes able to mitigate the cruelty of the war by his intercessions. He was twice chosen to the archbishopric; the king refusing, on the first occasion, to part with his faithful confessor. When he went to Avignon to be confirmed in his new dignity, the profligate court received him with an act of unmannerly and heartless insult. A nephew of Clement's introduced into the hall a person habited like a peasant and seated on an ass, with a petition to the Pope that he would be pleased to appoint him to the see of Canterbury. But this was a case in which the dignity of virtue was conspicuous; the Pope and the other cardinals resented the affront, and sent him back with due honour. Unfortunately he scarcely lived to enter upon his office, dying within six weeks after.

There can be no doubt that his great work, *The Cause of God pleaded against Pelagius*, was suggested by the state of doctrine taught by the friars at the Universities in his time. All writers on the doctrines of grace are in some danger of not allowing all that is due on the other side to the consideration of God's justice. But Bradwardine wrote always with one design, to exalt the power and mercy of the Most High. Our plan does not admit of a description of the doctrinal parts of this spiritual and excellent treatise, which was the labour of his life, and gained him, not undeservedly, the title of the 'Profound Doctor.' But the following specimen of his sentiments on the subject of prayer, will show the character of the man :—'I think there cannot be any prayer more profitable or more efficacious, whether in prosperity or adversity, whether concerning what one desires or what one would avoid, than that one may always be able to say unto the Lord, with one's whole heart and soul and strength, Thy will be done. For thus it will come to pass that one shall keep back nothing to oneself, but be able to submit oneself and all one has to the divine will; wholly desiring the glory and honour of God, and never one's own, whether in great things or small, fearing nothing and caring for nothing in itself, but gladly embracing, if need be, for the sake of God, the loss of riches, honour, and fame,—

disgrace, ridicule, persecutions, and whatever miseries, except the displeasure alone of Almighty God.'

The prelates of these ages rigidly enforced the law of celibacy, as they had learned it from the practice of Gregory VII. and Innocent III.; for however this law had been attempted earlier, it is not pretended that it was generally enforced before this period. Indeed, the case of Gregory I., A.D. 590, the second founder of the English Church, is in itself a refutation of all notion of its having been a primitive practice. For he was the grandson or great-grandson of another pope, Felix III., whose father Felix was also a presbyter; and these facts are twice mentioned by Gregory himself in his works still extant.[1] And in the apostolical Canons, of the second or third century, the marriage of the clergy is expressly recognised.[2] And the clergy in England were commonly married until the time of Anselm and Henry I. The compulsion of such a law must be regarded as an unmixed evil. The immoral consequences of it, with those who were tempted to break their vow, are recorded in every page from the time of Hildebrand downwards. And it is plain that in many instances the poorer offenders against this law suffered, while the more powerful escaped. But there were other consequences, perhaps not less pernicious, to those who were enabled to keep it. 'It is not possible,' says a wise ancient,[3] 'that he can be a good member of the state, and love justice and equity, who has no children to expose to danger if his country suffers.' The law in itself had a tendency to prevent them from being good subjects, more especially when the interests of Church

---

[1] *Homil.* 38, in *Evan.,* § 15. *Dialog.,* lib. 4, cap. 16. See SANDINI, *Vit. Pont.,* pp. 130, 580. There were married priests in Spain so late as the fourteenth century. A Council at Palencia in Leon, A.D. 1388, regulates their garb and tonsure.—L'ENFANT, *Conc. Pis.,* Pref. xxvii.

[2] 'Let not a Bishop, Presbyter, or Deacon, put away his wife under pretence of religion: but if he put her away, let him be excommunicated; and if he persist, let him be deposed.'—*Apost. Canon* V.

[3] THUCYDIDES.

and State were so divided. 'Wife and children,' says Lord Bacon, 'are a kind of discipline of humanity; and single men, though they be many times more munificent and charitable, because their means are less exhausted, yet they are, on the other side, more cruel and hard-hearted, because their indulgence and tenderness is not so often called into play.' The rise of the terrible Inquisition in other countries was indeed an immediate consequence of the establishment of the papal power, and of this law rigidly enforced with it. This fearful scourge was not yet brought into England, but the spirit of it had been manifested in Peckham's mandate against the Jews; and we shall soon see it brought to its height by the primates of Wycliffe's time, Courtney and Arundel.

CHAPTER VI.

STATE OF THE MONASTERIES IN WYCLIFFE'S TIME.
CHANTRIES.   THEIR INSTITUTION, AND PURPOSES.

Vain the worshippers who strove
God with idols to divide;
Ne'er may man his spirit's love
Give to Heav'n and aught beside.

CÆDMON, § 50.

WHEN in these days we look upon the ruined abbey, standing in peaceful solitude, in scenes which
nature seems to have spread for the abode of calm
content and prayer, it is not easy nor always agreeable
to call to mind the true facts on record concerning the
usual inmates of these dwellings; how soon the piety
that reared them declined; how often their own vices,
without the aid of the arm of power, brought on their
ruin; how their numbers fell away, as their reputation
decayed; and public opinion, in the course of a few
more years, would probably have accomplished, in many
instances, what was hastened only a little sooner by the
will of an arbitrary king.

It is not to be supposed that in former days the heart
of man was inaccessible to a sense of the beauties of
creation, or that this feeling was not often called forth
in these retirements, and expressed by devout minds in
thanksgiving and adoration.   Take Gyraldus's description of one, which still remains to attest the truth of his
description—Lantony, in Monmouthshire: —'In the
deep vale of Ewias, which is about a bowshot over, and
enclosed on all sides with high mountains, stands a
church dedicated to St. John the Baptist, a structure
roofed with lead, and not unhandsomely built for the
remote situation in which it stands.   It is a spot on
which formerly stood a little humble chapel of St. David

the Archbishop, which had no other ornaments than
woodland moss and wreaths of ivy.   In truth, it is a
place fit for the abode of religion, and as well furnished
as any British monastery with the means of canonical
discipline.   Two hermits first founded it to the honour
of a solitary life, in a wild far removed from the noise
of the world, on the banks of the River Hondy, which
rolls down the deepest part of the valley. . . . . . The
rains, which mountainous districts usually produce, are
here very frequent; the winds high and strong; the
winters dark, with almost continual mists and clouds.
Yet the air of the valley is so happily tempered, as
scarcely to be the cause of any diseases; so that the
brothers from a younger foundation at Gloucester, even
when worn out with labour, and seeming past cure, if
brought for change of climate to the parent house, by a
little nursing are restored to health.   Here the monks,
sitting in their cloisters, when they choose to refresh
their eyes by looking upward from their books, may see
rising over the roofs of their dwellings on every side
the mountain-tops which seem to touch the sky; and
often the goats or wild-deer, with which this district
abounds, feeding on the summit, and appearing as if at
the verge of their horizon.   The orb of the sun is seldom visible above the hills, even in the fine summer
season, before half-past seven in the morning.   It is a spot
marked out for heavenly contemplation, a spot happily
chosen, and one that moves the kind affections; and in
its first days well provided and well governed, till it was
wronged by the intrusion of English luxury.'[1]

No doubt there were many who found refuge in such
places, in whom the flame of devotion burnt brightly,
and their sense of the mercies of redemption was a
strong solace amidst the troubles of oppressors, and
the rude manners of a half barbarous age.   We have
writings of the English monks of the twelfth century,

---

[1] *Itinerary of Wales*, b. 1. c. iiL, written about A. D. 1220.

and some of later date, which speak of divine love in
language such as might be studied with advantage now.
Nor could anything but a devoted zeal have effected
that great sacrifice of wealth, which was poured in
during the twelfth and thirteenth centuries, wherever
a monastery began to rear its head. It is a circumstance, as a well-informed and amiable man has well
remarked,[1] ' which must strike every thinking person
with some degree of wonder. No sooner had a monastic institution got a footing, but the neighbourhood
began to be touched with a secret and religious awe.
Every person round was desirous to promote so good a
work; and either by sale, by grant, or by gift in rever-
sion, was ambitious of appearing a benefactor. They
who had not lands to spare, gave roads to accommodate
the infant foundation.'   When Matthew Paris, the
historian of the time, asked Richard, earl of Cornwall,
to tell him the cost of his foundation of the Cistercian
abbey at Hayles, in Gloucestershire, ' I have laid out,'
he said, ' ten thousand marks in the erection of the
church only. And would to God that what I have
laid out upon my castle at Wallingford had been spent
as wisely and as well.' The same sentiments were felt
and expressed by the religious persons of the age.
William of Newborough, an Austin canon of Yorkshire,
speaks thus of the Abbey of Fountains, then a new
foundation : ' The place,' said he, ' is called Fountains;
where, from the time of its foundation, many souls have
drunk, as from the fountains of their Saviour, of the
waters springing up to everlasting life.' And again, of
Rievaulx and Byland, near which he lived, ' What
are such religious dwellings but the camps of God,
where the soldiers of Christ our King keep guard, and
the recruits are trained against the assaults of spiritual
wickedness ? ' Such language may be imbued with the
prejudices of the time in favour of a monastic life, and

---

[1] GILBERT WHITE, *Hist. of Selborne*, part II. lett. 7.

those prejudices may be mistaken, or such a life may be unsuitable to a different state of society; but it is the language of Christian piety, and it spoke of feelings which the writer had himself experienced.

Whatever benefit, however, these foundations con-' ferred upon their time and country, it is plain that the first fervour soon declined. The chief revival after the Norman Conquest was that effected by the Cistercians and Austin Canons; and their frugal industry, hospitality, and charity, is abundantly attested. But in the next age we find them chiefly mentioned as following Reuben's choice, 'abiding among the sheep-folds, and listening to the bleatings of the flocks.' They drove a great trade in wool, and industry degenerated into avarice. No doubt this was productive of public good; and when the military barons despised agriculture, and left the production of food to be the task of their slavish serfs and thralls, it was well if any class in society taught the people how to improve and value the wealth of the country. Their care and charity enabled them to relieve, in times of dearth, the famishing and improvident. But the public opinion of them soon followed the well-known saying of Richard I., in which he characterised three of the leading orders. A religious man in France, of high reputation for sanctity, was prompted to administer to this bold monarch a reproof: 'You have three daughters at home,' said he, 'whom you love more than the grace of God:—they are Madam Pride, Luxury, and Avarice.' The king, surprised at the suddenness of the strange address, made a little pause: 'My friend,' said he, 'they are no longer at home:—I have married my daughter Pride to the Templars, Luxury to the Black Monks, and Avarice to the Cistercians.' The pride and insolence of those military monks, the Templars, was brought to an end long before the time of Wycliffe. The most monstrous charges were advanced against them, of which it is impossible to believe that the whole body were at all guilty, of impiety and uncleanness. There is more reason to believe that they were ruined from political causes. The King of France, Philip the Fair, had the Pope at his command, and he was afraid of the wealth and power of the Templars; or, as a sincere English writer of the time reports,[1] the grand master of the Templars had lent him a large sum of money, which he took this means of cancelling. If the character of this king was like that of his daughter, the queen of Edward II., this is not improbable. But the old Temple at Paris was of such extent, and maintained so many inmates, that any King of France might well fear that these martial churchmen might prove as dangerous to him as the prætorian guards were to the Roman emperors, or the janissaries to the Great Turk.[2] It can hardly be doubted, though great cruelty and injustice was shown in the means used, that a sound policy would have advised their dispersion.

By the Black Monks, King Richard probably meant both the old Benedictines and the Cluniacs. These last were early noted for thriftless waste and selfish luxury. 'Give them,' says Gyraldus, 'a place to dwell in, furnished with handsome buildings, and endowed with large revenues and broad lands; yet within a short time you will find it impoverished and ruined.' They did not even keep the first rule of common property, by living on one common purse; but each took what he could get assigned to himself, and left the public fund destitute. The houses founded for poor monks were turned into rich bachelors' halls, where the good fellows hawked and hunted, and made a merry life of it. And charity waxed cold; they would sooner mortgage their estates, and let the poor die at

---

[1] Sir Thomas de la More.
[2] When Henry III. went on a visit to St. Louis in A.D. 1254, he was attended by a guard of honour of about 1000 mounted knights and squires. They were all easily lodged and entertained in the Temple, which had buildings large enough to take in an army.—MATT. PARIS.

their gates, says Gyraldus, than have one dish diminished from their tables. In fact, there is scarcely
one instance of a member of this order who served
either the Church of England by his piety and learning,
or the state by his counsels.

Of the old Benedictines a more respectable character
must be given. Their houses had been the nurseries of
the Church; and it was not a change for the better, when
first the bishops began to be taken from among the secular clergy or the later monastic orders. Here whatever
learning there was in England and in Western Europe,
had been preserved. And here still were to be found
those who kept faithful chronicles of their time, and re-
gistered the annals of our native land. The monks of
Westminster, St. Alban's, Croyland, Malmsbury, and
Glastonbury; and of the cathedral churches, Canterbury,
Winchester, Worcester, and Durham, and many other
Benedictine houses,—are men to whom we owe the
most instructive records of the past. It is only want of
information that has led some to speak with contempt
of monkish historians, as if they were not the best qualified of all men to give a true picture of the events and
manners of their time. 'They who indulge in such
ridicule,' says an able modern critic,[1] ' must forget that
these monkish writers were often men of princely descent; that they were entrusted with the most important
offices of state, and therefore could best explain them;
that in general they were the most accomplished and in-
telligent men whom the world could then produce; and
that, in one word, if we were to have any histories at
all of those ages, it was absolutely necessary they should
be written by the monks. Perhaps,' he adds, ' the very
best of situations for a writer of history is one not
widely differing from that of a monk; one in which he
enjoys good opportunities of gaining experimental knowledge of men and their affairs, but is at the same time

---

[1] SCHLEGEL, *Lectures on the Hist. of Literature.*

independent of the world, and has full liberty to mature in retirement his reflections upon that which he has seen.' In England especially it was the common practice for Norman kings to keep their Christmas at some of the great abbeys; and the house of parliament, in the fourteenth and fifteenth century, was most commonly the monks' refectory at Westminster.

While, however, we praise the learned diligence and candour of William of Malmsbury—the patience, good humour, and love of his country, which are the praiseworthy qualities of Matthew Paris—and something of the same praise is due to many more—there are also certain signs, by which we can judge of the defective morals, the dissipation, the quarrels and bickerings, and the worldliness, which were often found within these monasteries. The history of the monastery of Glastonbury for a long period is nothing but the record of a long-sustained quarrel with the Bishops of Bath and Wells, whose property in certain manors the monks had seized upon. The same disputes arose at Canterbury, at Lichfield and Coventry, and at Durham, and wherever there was a Benedictine priory at the Cathedral Church. As we come down nearer to Wycliffe's time, we find things growing worse. The benefits which had accrued to society were passing fast away; and irreligion and hard-heartedness succeeded. We may suppose the historian Walsingham, who was nearly contemporary with Wycliffe, to express the monastic feelings of his time. He was a man, whose mind seems to dwell with satisfaction on acts of persecution, cruel executions, and bloody laws—whose praise is given to the proud and merciless, who condemns all lenity as cowardice or connivance at crime.[1]

---

[1] It is strange that Collier should have taken the representations of this ill-tempered man, who cannot speak of Wycliffe without calling him 'an angel of darkness,'—or by his miserable pun upon his name, 'Wicked-belief,'—as a fair statement of his doctrines. Collier's account is almost all taken from Walsingham, or Walden, the Carmelite, who

There is one remarkable fact in the later history of these monasteries, which alone speaks much to prove the selfish luxury into which they had fallen. On no estates did *slavery* linger so long in England, as on those of the Benedictine Abbots and their convents. In the rebellion of Wat Tyler, the sudden extension of which through a great part of England was a sad proof of the misery of the poorer classes through the oppression of the great, the slaves on the lands of St. Alban's and other abbeys flocked to join the revolt, and to demand their freedom. The abbot temporised for his own safety, being advised by the court of the danger of the time. The mob were supplied with beer and provisions at the gate; and the monks prepared charters of freedom for the contentment of all who asked for them. It might be right that these deeds, which were so extorted, should afterwards be all cancelled: but if there had been any wisdom or mercy to advise with in the monastery, this hint would not have been lost, and they would have begun at once to turn these poor dependents into free labourers. On the contrary, these poor dependents found the monks their hardest masters; and at the dissolution of Glastonbury alone, there were on the estate of that monastery nearly three hundred bondmen, whose bodies and goods were transferred from the abbot to the king.[1]

When we recollect how much pains the early Saxon bishops and ecclesiastics had taken to promote the liberation of slaves, and the pious labours of the Benedictine bishop Wulstan at the period of the Conquest to the same purpose, it must appear that this was a strong proof of the decay of Christian charity and mercy; the more so, as at this period slavery was fast disappearing in other quarters, and free labour, with industry and

---

said of Wycliffe at Oldcastle's trial, that he was 'the mid-day devil.' This learned historian seems to have had a prejudice against Wycliffe.
[1] The number was 271: HEARNE's *Langtoft*, p. 381.

self-improvement, was advancing. They were not serfs or thralls, but the free-born yeomanry of England, whose strong arms and skill in archery gained the victories of Creci and Poictiers.

That much dissoluteness had spread into the great monasteries, as well as into those of the lesser sort and of less creditable orders, is evident from such privileges as that of Walter Raynald before mentioned as purchased at Rome, to restore two hundred religious persons who had broken their convent vows. The bishops who followed the Roman model most, often procured privileges of this kind, as Cardinal Beaufort, Archbishop Arundel, and others. The prelates who were of better character, as William of Wykeham, Wainfleet, and Grosteste, are recorded in many instances to have struggled in vain to reform the morals, the wasteful expenditure, and vagabond habits of the religious of both sexes.

But before Wycliffe's time the evil had advanced to this point, that the barons and great persons were offended by the rival pomp and state of my lord abbot, and the poor found no sympathy from the monks in their afflictions. If the Cistercian houses and Austin priories were in some degree free from the idleness and luxury of the rest, not living on rents, but by their own labour, yet they had fallen into great ignorance and neglect of humanising habits. The Cistercians and Carthusians had in their houses an equal or greater number of lay brothers with the professed monks; and these, being of an inferior class, were treated with less ceremony, expected to work harder, and sit in a lower seat. This led to divisions and difficulties. And these monasteries, which in their first age were crowded with inmates, became at last almost empty of both monks and lay brothers. Waverley Abbey, in Surrey, contained, in A.D. 1187, one hundred and twenty lay brothers and seventy professed monks. When it was dissolved by Henry VIII., there were only thirteen religious persons remaining in it. It could never have been right or wise to keep up these splendid foundations, when they were becoming destitute of inhabitants.

But when the rage for the foundation of monasteries, which was carried to so great an extent for two centuries after the Conquest, began to subside, the same opinions which, though they did not originate, had greatly tended to multiply such institutions, gave rise to a minor sort of foundation, of which some account may be given. It was the primitive belief, abundantly confirmed by Holy Scriptures, that the souls of the departed are reserved by God in some middle state of consciousness until the final judgment. And in this faith they came in very early times to commend the souls of their departed friends together with themselves to God's gracious care. It was an innocent practice in itself from which no one could have foreseen the steps by which succeeding ages would proceed to the belief of their being purified by penal fires, from which the prayers of the faithful could release them. But in proportion as this belief obtained, people became anxious to provide for themselves and their departed friends, those who should pray for their souls in purgatory, and offer what they considered the propitiatory sacrifice of the mass on their behalf. To give one instance. The beautiful Abbey of Bolton, in Yorkshire, is said to have been founded by a lady of the house of Clifford, for the soul of her only son, drowned in stepping across a narrow part of the River Wharf. And one might envy the faith which would admit such precious tributes to human sorrow, if we did not know that it is human all and earthly, whereas the Gospel is heavenly.

> There now the matin bell is rung,
> The *miserere* duly sung,
> And holy men in cowl and hood
> Are wandering up and down the wood.

It had been usual in earliest times to celebrate the Holy Communion at funerals, and our Reformers, with

their usual regard for antiquity, endeavoured to restore
the practice. Cranmer administered this holy sacrament himself at King Edward's funeral, and in the time
of Elizabeth a special service for the purpose was authorised by Act of Parliament.[1]   But the way in which
this practice had degenerated into masses for the dead is
thus told by Latimer in one of his sermons.   'The
blessed Communion, the celebration of the Lord's supper, alack, it hath been long abused, as the sacrifices
were before under the old law.   Even so it came to
pass with our blessed Communion.   In the primitive
Church, in places, when their friends were dead, they
used to come together to the Holy Communion.   What?
—to remedy them that were dead? No, not a straw, it
was not instituted for no such purpose.   But then they
would call to remembrance God's goodness and his passion that he suffered for us, wherein they comforted
much their faith.   Other came afterward and set up all
these kind of massing.'   Thus it had by degrees come
to pass that private masses, or if it were not a contradiction, the private celebration of the Holy Communion,
was deemed to be available for the souls of the departed,
and people were anxious to obtain it for themselves and
others.   The founders of monasteries were accustomed
to provide that prayers and masses should be offered for
themselves and their families or friends.   And this was
the common object specified in the foundation of chantries; not indeed the sole object—for no doubt there
were services intended by them for the living as well as
for the dead.

It is to this custom that we owe those beautiful
chapelries which still remain in the walls of many of our
cathedrals and other churches, usually over the tomb of
the person on whose behalf they were founded. Here,
a priest was retained to say daily masses on the spot,

---

[1] A.D. 1560, 2 Eliz.: see in Bp. SPARROW's *Collection*, p. 201, 'An Act
for Commemoration of Founders and Benefactors, &c.,' and a 'Form of
Administering the Holy Communion at Funerals.'

and it was believed that the intention in the mind of the priest could appropriate the benefit of the mass to the soul for whose behoof it was intended. Sometimes a chantry was a separate building with no church attached to it, in which on certain days these services were to be performed. In other instances it was connected with hospitals or similar foundations, and it would seem that in general the officiating priest was intended to perform other offices besides that of masses for the dead. Thus a deed of Simon Langham, Archbishop of Canterbury, A.D. 1368, recites the foundation of the chantry at East-. bridge Hospital by Simon Islip, his predecessor, in which the purpose of the foundation is stated to be 'the honour of God and of divine worship, and for the health of the souls of certain benefactors, of the hospital itself, and all the faithful departed.'[1] The celebration of masses in this case was far from being the only duty of the priest; on the contrary, his duties seem to have been the same as if he had been appointed chaplain to the hospital; for the deed describes them to be the administration of the sacraments and sacramentals (confession and absolution) to the poor and strangers who came there, and to the sick in the hospital. For this purpose he was to have a residence in the hospital, a chamber over the gate; and was constantly to reside, never being absent a day without leave of the warden, and then to provide another priest to take his duty. A similar deed of Archbishop Whittlesey, A.D. 1371, appointing a chantry priest to the Hospital of St. Nicholas, Herbaldowne, declares that his purpose is to supply a proper priest to perform divine service in the Church of St. Nicholas for the poor of the hospital, to hear their confessions, and duly administer the holy sacraments to them day and night. In other cases the office seems to have been little else than that of private chaplain in a nobleman's or gentleman's family. Thus a charter of the convent of St. Augustine's at Canterbury, about

---

[1] Somner's *Appendix to Hist. Canterbury*, p. 18.

A.D. 1260, gives permission to a gentleman to have a chantry in his chapel at Lukehall, in the parish of Littlebourne, to be served by his private chaplain.

But in other cases these foundations appear to have been introduced into places where the benefit of the living could hardly have been contemplated. Thus Richard de Ravenser, Archdeacon of Lincoln, obtained a licence in A.D. 1373 to alienate manors for the support of two chaplains daily to perform service in the Church of Driby, for the health of the living and the souls of the faithful dead.[1] And not long after Robert de Bernack founded another chantry in the same church; so that in a parish, of which the population at the present day does not amount to one hundred persons, and which could not be greater then, three priests were provided for the service of the church, besides the parish rector. In like manner, in A.D. 1264, a chantry was founded for two chaplains, one to officiate in a free chapel in a certain dwelling-house in the parish of St. Paul, at Canterbury, and another at the altar of St. John Baptist in St. Paul's Church,[2] and the number of these priests and their offices in cathedral churches marks the object of their institution.   There were in St. Paul's, in London, thirty-five endowed chantries, and fifty-four priests employed to serve them.[3]   The duties of these secluded ministers could scarcely have been any other than those described by one of our poets who had witnessed their suppression :—

> They whilome duly used everie day
> Their service, and their holy things to say;
> At morn and eve to sing their anthems sweet,
> Their pennie masses and their complines meet.

These chantries, however, and colleges of singing priests continued to multiply in England ; and no doubt, as Wycliffe complains, to the decay of preaching and

---

[1] *Orig. Grossi Fines*, p. 359, as referred to in OLDFIELD'S *History of Wainfleet.*
[2] SOMNER, *ubi supra.*
[3] DUGDALE, *Hist. of St. Paul's*, p. xli. Pref.

praying. In the first year of Edward VI., at which time these foundations were all suppressed and their endowments confiscated, the whole number returned was 2374.

When so much of the Church's alms, as it was still called, was thus bestowed in idle superstition, it is no wonder if the poor became dissatisfied. It was a thing which common feeling and plain good sense pointed out as injurious to them, that charity should be so lavished, and men paid for saying or singing solitary services over the dead, whose office it was to pray with the living. Long before the Reformation these poor Sir Johns, as the chantry-priests were called, were held in great aversion by the common people; and they were commonly the most ignorant and least respectable of their tribe. As the rich and powerful had been estranged by the abuse of excommunication and the other obnoxious measures of the canon-law, so the poor were offended when the old monastic charities declined, when their instruction failed them more and more, and the mendicant friars came to beg a portion of the small pittance which was left to support their daily toil.

Boniface VIII. complained, in one of his most extravagant bulls, of 'the ancient enmity' between the laity and the clergy. The same complaint often occurs in the English chronicles at this period; and the writers seem to speak of it as an incurable disease, under which the minds of the laity laboured. But where was this 'ancient enmity' before the popes had set up their divided empire? Where was it in England, when King Oswald interpreted the discourses of Aidan to his countrymen; or when the poor people crowded round a bishop as poor as themselves, and knelt to receive his blessing?[1] Where was it, when Alfred made his bishops the companions of his studies, the executors of his will, and distributors of his alms? The true state of the case is best described by an excellent candid writer of the French Church.

---

[1] See CHURTON's *Early English Church*, c. iv.

'It is true,' says the Abbé Fleury, 'that Jesus Christ said, *He came not to send peace on earth, but a sword.* But that was between his disciples and unbelievers, not among His disciples themselves. And in this war all the violence is to be on the part of the unbelievers; Christians are only to suffer without resisting. Such ought to be the conduct of churchmen; it is their part to make all advances to re-establish that unity which Christ has so recommended and given for a mark of His true disciples. It is the part of bishops to gain the respect and affection of the people by the holiness of their lives, their zeal for the salvation of their flock, their care in instructing them and procuring them all kinds of good, spiritual and temporal; by their gentleness, their patience, and all other Christian graces.

'But now they took a way altogether the opposite to this. There was nothing but sternness, high disdain, bitter complaints, piercing reproaches, threats, judicial processes, excommunications, and other censures; all means, not to extinguish the flame, but to make it burn the more. Thus the laity, provoked more and more, came often to open action and deeds of violence. They stopped on the road the persons who carried bishops' letters or mandates, took them from them, tore and destroyed them. They seized on the persons of clergymen, beat them, imprisoned them, made them ransom their lives, and sometimes even put them to death;—and for all this no remedy, but those censures which had already so often been despised. Such were the fatal effects of the division caused by the excessive extension of ecclesiastical power.'

Happy had it been for them, if even at this point they had learnt to turn and seek that better way, by which alone a spiritual empire can be won, by which the primitive Christians had overcome their pagan torturers, and converted a world which lay in darker ignorance—

Content to hold Love's banner fast,
And by submission win at last.

CHAPTER VII.

THE MENDICANT ORDERS. THEIR RISE AND HISTORY.

> He that hath seen a great oke drie and dead,
> Yet clad with relics of some trophies olde,
> Lifting to heaven her aged horie head,
> Whose foote in ground hath left but feeble holds ;
> But though she owe her fall to the first windo,
> She of the devout people is ador'd,
> And manie young plants spring from out her rinde ;—
> Who such an oke hath seene, let him record,
> That thus Rome's demon doth himself enforce
> Againe on foote to reare her mouldred corse.
> SPENSER : *Ruins of Rome.*

IT is a great error in looking back to past ages of the world or of the Church, to suppose that the human mind was less active then than it is now in striking out new notions, and attempting reforms and changes in government and society. On the contrary, where knowledge and education are less general, these revolutions are more frequent ; more is done by force, and less by argument ; fanatic ignorance acquires more followers ; and mistaken systems are more rapidly established. There cannot be a more remarkable proof of this than in the rise, progress, and extension of the orders of religious mendicants, or begging friars.[1] Their character and institutions were so different from the rules of the monks, or other regular clergy, that it is necessary to review them separately. And their influence on the Church was so great at certain intervals during the three centuries preceding the Reformation, that it is impossible to understand this great controversy without a clear view of their doctrines, discipline, and habits of living.

---

[1] That is, begging brothers—' Friar ' being the English corruption of ' Frère.'

At a time when the English nation had begun to grow a little jealous of the great increase and wealth of the monasteries, the popular mind was attracted by the arrival of some small bodies of religious persons, who professed to live supported only by their own labour, or the alms which they received from day to day, as they went from house to house to preach the Gospel. The Dominicans, or preaching friars, were the first who came, and they shortly afterwards procured a house at Oxford, by the bounty of Isabel De Vere, Countess of Oxford, A.D. 1221.   They were followed in A.D. 1224 by the Franciscans and Trinitarian friars, and about twenty years later by the Carmelites, Austin friars, Crouched, Pied, and Bethlemite friars, and other forgotten candidates for public favour, most of whom did little more than appear and disappear.   As they were distinguished from each other by little else than their dress, it will be sufficient to trace the early history of one of their orders, and that the first in point of time, as well as the most numerous and popular, and which carried out the principle of religious mendicancy to the greatest excess—the Franciscans or Minorites.   Of the Dominicans it may be allowed that they generally practised poverty more simply; they were diligent in preaching and teaching at Oxford, and other places, and maintained themselves by the wages of learning as tutors in families and domestic chaplains, or as professors and lecturers in schools.

It is scarcely possible to read the history of St. Francis of Assisi, the founder of the Franciscan order, without believing that there was in him a sincere and self-devoted, however ill-directed piety.   The injunctions to his brethren to observe perpetual poverty, without condemning those who are rich; to be clad in coarse garments without judging those who go in gay apparel; and to be cautious in receiving confessions, lest they should become too familiar with sin, are excellent.   He was himself influenced by a missionary zeal, and is said to have preached the Gospel to the Sultan of Egypt in the face of hostile armies; and some of his earliest followers imitating his example and going to preach to the Turks and Saracens, lost their lives among those infidels,[1] while some of the crusaders, struck by their example, themselves embraced the order. The peculiar regulations which he was the first to introduce, were that those who entered the order should sell all they had and give to the poor; that they should possess no money; that they should labour for their food and clothing; and receive payment for labour in clothes or food instead of money; if labour failed them they might beg the necessaries of life, a permission which his followers seemed too generally to consider as a precept enjoining them to beg, and excusing them from labour. Those who were ignorant of letters were not to care to learn them, a permission which many interpreted as making a merit of illiterate ignorance, and it seems consistent with this that he encouraged illiterate lay-brothers into his order. He called his followers *friars minors*, as being less than the least of religious sects or fraternities; and their officers not masters or prelates, as in other orders, but *ministers*, that they might remember they were to be the servants of all.

On the other hand, it is equally clear that this self-devotion was under the influence either of a very weak or very enthusiastic temperament; though it is probable that the wildest stories that are told of him were the invention of his followers, not of himself: and the mind of the age seems to have been prepared for a sort of epidemic enthusiasm. He was represented as having been honoured in many respects with a resemblance to our Lord. It was said that his mother could not be delivered till she was removed into a stable, where he was born, and that he had a precursor, who went about

---

[1] A.D. 1220. 261 years afterwards, A.D. 1481, Sixtus IV. recognised their martyrdom and allowed the Franciscans to celebrate their office. Their reliques were said to be at Coimbra.

Assisi and the neighbourhood proclaiming peace and
health to all, and vanished when he began to preach.
But the most marvellous story was that of the *stigmata*,
or five wounds of Christ, which it was said had been
impressed upon his person by way of special honour.
The history of this superstition of the stigmata is a singular instance of the growth of a popular delusion.   The
earliest allusion of the kind is the story which was
read at the second Nicene council, from a spurious
work of Athanasius,[1] which relates that some Jews
having in mockery pierced the hands and side of
an image of Jesus, blood flowed from the wounds,
and many Jews were converted by the miracle.   But
about the time of St. Francis, to show that there was
prevalent a tendency to this enthusiasm, we find that
two persons were condemned at a provincial council held
at Oxford by Cardinal Langton, in A.D. 1222, one of
whom pretended to bear the marks of the five wounds,
and to be sent on a special mission, and the other professed himself his follower; at which time, so far from
gaining any credit for their imposture, it is related that
both were punished, and one account, which we may
hope is not correct, asserts that they were crucified.[2]

These marks are said to have first appeared upon St.
Francis in A.D. 1224, and he died two years after.
There seems no reason to doubt that his body was exhibited in this state after his death, but the evidence of
their existence before his death is of the slightest possible kind.   It was pretended that he concealed them from
modesty, and only one or two of his followers professed
to have seen them by stealth before he died.   The story
was strongly objected to at the time, until Gregory IX.
undertook to confirm it, and excommunicated all who

---

[1] The learned Benedictine editors discredit the story, and say that it
is obviously not the writing of Athanasius.   It is called 'The Passion of
the Image of Jesus Christ.'

[2] LABBE, tom. x. p. 287.   MATT. WESTM., in *Flor. Hist.*

should question it. On the whole, it seems more than
probable that St. Francis, having an enthusiastic desire
to be conformed unto Christ, and placing his notions of
such conformity in abstract contemplations, might dream
or fancy that a seraphim appeared to him on a cross,
whose wounds were conveyed to himself. If he mentioned it to his followers, by whom he was idolized, and
who were enthusiasts like himself, and looking out for
miracles, prepared also as we have seen to think of such
a thing by the reports already spread in one or two
other cases, they would report that marks were visible,
and one or two afterwards might fancy they had seen
them, as Pope Alexander IV., A.D. 1254, affirmed that
he had done. It would not be difficult under such circumstances for a few of his immediate attendants to
persuade themselves when he died, that the credit of
their order, and as they might think, the interests of
religion itself, required a pious fraud to make the marks
visible which they firmly believed he had received.[1] It
was soon said to have been confirmed by miracles, and
Mount Avernia, in Tuscany, where it was alleged to
have taken place, was declared by a bull of Alexander
IV. in A.D. 1255, to be taken under the especial protection of the Holy See. A festival was appointed by the
Franciscans in honour of this event in A.D. 1337, which
was extended by Paul V. to the whole Church, in 1615,
and Sixtus IV. in 1475 forbade the representation of any
saint with these marks except St. Francis.[2]

The rapidity with which the new orders spread was
wonderful. It was in 1208 that St. Francis first began
to preach, not being yet a priest, nor in any sort of
orders. In the next year his society was sanctioned,
not without some difficulty, by Innocent III., for it
had but just been decreed by the Lateran council that

---

[1] *Storia particolare delle Stigmata.* Assisi, 1804, 4to.
[2] See further about St. Catharine of Siena and the questions between
rival communities, App. D.

no new orders should be permitted; but a cardinal who
stood by, said to him, ' Take care what you do, lest,
in rejecting this poor man, you reject the Gospel itself.'
Innocent was struck by the words, and gave his assent.
St. Dominic was then a canon of the cathedral church
of Osma, in Spain, and had engaged a few associates
on a mission to preach to the Albigenses of Languedoc,
when he heard of this new vow of poverty.   He immediately advised his companions to bind themselves by
a similar vow and rule; and thus his order arose, who,
from this first mission of ·theirs, in which their preaching was backed by the powers of the newly-founded
Inquisition, were called preaching friars.   The Carmelites appeared a few years later, when the popularity of
such fraternities was on the increase; they professed
to be newly arrived in Italy, driven out by the Saracens
from the Holy Land, where they had remained on
Mount Carmel from the time of Elisha the Prophet.
They assert that ' the sons of the Prophets' had continued on Mount Carmel as a poor brotherhood till the
time of Christ, soon after which they were miraculously
converted, and that the Virgin Mary joined their order
and gave them a precious vestment called a scapular.
But to return to St. Francis.   At the time his order
was sanctioned they numbered eleven brothers, of
whom one only was a priest.   Three years later, a
sisterhood of the same order was founded by a noble
lady of Assisi, named Clara, who absconded from her
parents for that purpose, as Francis had also done;
and A.D. 1219, ten years only after the first formation
of the order, 5000 friars were present at a general
chapter at Assisi; nobles and people thronged to bring
them provisions, and 500 novices were admitted.   On
this occasion they divided the world among them for
preaching; Syria and Egypt the founder reserved to
himself, sending 200 into Spain to preach to the
Moors; and the next year five were put to death in
Morocco in a similar attempt, as has been already re-

lated. At the same chapter Friar Angelo, otherwise called Agnelli, of Pisa, was made provincial minister of England, where some account of their proceeding must now be given.

We have a very minute and particular description of their first mission to this country, from Friar Thomas of Eccleston, one of their earliest converts, who wrote about thirty-two years after their arrival. The party, which was sent over by the charity of the monks of Fescamp, in Normandy, landed at Dover, Sept. 11, A.D. 1224. It consisted of nine persons, four in the orders of the Church, and five lay brothers. There is something to admire in the power which these rules of life had in uniting persons of different nations and tongues in the bonds of Christian brotherhood. The leader of the mission was the above-named Agnelli, and the clergymen who accompanied him were three Englishmen; one advanced in life, who had long resided in Italy, and distinguished himself as a preacher; the other two youths, eminent for zeal, obedience, and patience. The laymen were four Italians and one Frenchman, Laurence of Beauvais, to whom St. Francis, in token of his great affection for him, afterwards gave his own tunic or close vest which he wore. These were shortly afterwards joined by Friar Pedro, a Spaniard, who, following the example of St. Dominic, as he is commonly reported, wore, as a mortification of the flesh, a steel cuirass for an under-waistcoat, and exhibited, as Eccleston says, many other examples of perfection. He became warden of a friary which was founded at Northampton; while Friar Thomas, another Spaniard, was fixed as warden at Cambridge.

It is clear, from the account that Eccleston gives, that these missionaries, in the first days of their sojourn, underwent many privations, and rigidly kept their rule of poverty. Having proceeded from Dover to Canterbury, they divided their company, and four, headed by the old English priest, Richard Ingleby, proceeded to

London. Agnelli, with the other four, obtained the charitable use of a small chamber or cellar, beneath the house of a certain scholar, who seems to have come to study at one of the great monasteries in the former city. Here they sat from day to day, as if their rule had shut them into that narrow place, till, when the scholar came home in the evening, they were allowed to enter the house and sit with him. They then made their fire, and prepared their repast. It consisted of oaten short-cake, sometimes accompanied with onions and thick black beer, warmed at the fire, so thick that it often required a little mixture of water to make it potable. The same hard fare was generally adopted wherever they planted themselves afterwards. The charity of the inhabitants in many of the large towns began to flow in upon them immediately; but they showed great forbearance, sometimes sending back the parcels of cloth which were brought to them, and only taking in the pittances of food on three days during the week.

When Ingleby and his companions reached London they were entertained by the black friars or Dominicans, who had already erected some buildings, for their first convent, in the neighbourhood of Lincoln's Inn; till John Travers, one of the sheriffs, gave them a house in Cornhill. Hence they removed to the place known henceforth as the Grey Friars, the name by which the Franciscans were commonly known in England, where Christ's Hospital now stands, taking possession of a piece of ground which John Unwin, citizen and mercer, bought for them; which, as the friars then would not hold any property as their own, he made over to the Lord Mayor and Corporation of the city, for their use. This wealthy mercer afterwards himself entered the order as a lay brother. Other rich citizens poured in their bounty; one building them a chapel at his own expense, another an infirmary, another enlarging their plot of ground, another giving them a conduit. But their patrons were not confined to one order in society. At Canterbury a noble countess, Lady Baginton, 'nourished them as a mother might do her children,' and used her influence, which was very effectual, as such influence is still, in obtaining favour for them with peers and prelates. Nor were the clergy indifferent to them. Simon Langton, Archdeacon of Canterbury, and brother of the Archbishop, was a special friend to them on their arrival; two or three priests were among the first to take the friar's frock at London; and they had still further success at Oxford, when Ingleby, with one of his original companions, proceeded to try his fortunes there.

A rich mercer and the University miller were here his first patrons; the miller conveyed a site to the corporation, as had been done in London, which plan was now generally adopted in other places, for a Franciscan convent. But the great accession to their cause came from a more important quarter. A number of bachelors and students of the University, who were many of them young men of good families, came to enlist themselves as novices, and the king, Henry III., greatly patronised them, and had a lodging built for himself near their convent, being moved thereto by the miraculous death in their beds of three monks of Abingdon in the same night that they had refused them admission on their first appearance. At Cambridge their success was not so rapid. The townspeople gave them a deserted Jewish synagogue close to the town-jail; where the jailers and prisoners and the poor friars had to go in and out by the same entrance, till they procured the king's leave to make another. Here they built a chapel of lath and plaster, so small and poor that it was little more than one day's work for a carpenter to erect the wooden framework. But in spite of these difficulties they persevered; no sooner had they found footing in one place, than they began to think of sending a colony to another; and before a few years had passed they had houses and convents in Norwich, Lincoln, York, Shrewsbury, Worcester, Salisbury, Southampton, and almost every other ancient city or populous town. Within thirty-two years after their landing at Dover, there were in England ninety-nine convents or stations of these friars, and the number of enrolled members was 1242. Probably, with the other orders then spread about the country, there were not fewer than between four and five thousand.

The number of enrolled members, however, does not afford a test of the full extent of their success. We must also take into the account the congregations who came to hear their preaching, the persons of all ranks who came to confess to them, and their habit of celebrating divine service in the open air, when they went on missionary excursions to places where they had no fixed abode. We must think what must have been the strength of popular favour which could support such an army of mendicants in different quarters; for all these friars lived mainly upon the alms of the benevolent. The Dominicans, indeed, had some property in houses in London, and a few small endowments elsewhere; and this might be the case in a very few instances with the other orders; but the Franciscans, when Henry VIII. broke up their establishments, do not appear anywhere to have had rents amounting in the whole to fifty pounds a-year. It was the self-renunciation and resolute poverty of these devotees which gained them their support. The contrast it afforded to the worldly wealth of the monks and dignified clergy, was regarded as a new demonstration of the power of the Gospel; and according to the mode of argument used in those days, it was asked, if it be so praiseworthy for a man to do good works with his worldly store, how much rather to give up his worldly store with himself—to offer not the fruit only, but the stem and tree?

It was, of course, however, necessary to regulate the

system of begging alms; for if there had been no restraint, and every friar had been at liberty to wander to what houses he pleased, the alms would either soon have been exhausted by the contributors lacking means, or have been very irregularly supplied. This was effected by assigning districts to each convent, within which its members were to take their rounds, and generally each individual friar had his own limits prescribed; whence the name that was commonly given to them of *limitors*. When the system was established, the alms of bread, bacon, and cheese, logs of wood for their fire, and other ordinary gifts, were ready for the friar when he called; and he who refused to give was liable to suspicion, as if he were no good Christian. It was in the nature of things that such a system should degenerate, and deep and loud had become the complaints of all classes against these lusty beggars long before the time of Wycliffe. It was commonly said that ' no one could sit down to meat, high or low, but he must ask a friar or two, who when they came would play the host to themselves, and carry away bread and meat besides.' Fitzralph, in his *Apology at Avignon*, accused them of 'philosophising' in the chambers of the most beautiful maidens; and Eccleston says, that even so early as his time, Friar Walter of Reigate confessed that these familiarities were one of the ways by which the foul fiend vexed the order.

It appears from Chaucer, the contemporary of Wycliffe, and who was allied by marriage to his great patron, John of Gaunt, that it had become a practice of these limitors to *farm their limits*, that is, to contract with their convent to pay them a certain sum from the district assigned them, and pocket the remainder. Indeed, Chaucer's inimitable description of his friar should be studied by all who would see the manners of the age depicted to the life.

> A frere there was, a wanton and a merry,
> A limitour, a right solemne man,

> In all the orders four is none that can
> So much of dalliance and soft language.

Many a marriage had he made at his own cost, and
well was he beloved by franklins and their dames. He
had more power than the parish priest, so he said,
to hear confessions, and he made it agreeable to his
penitents.

> Full swetely heard he confession
> And plesant was his absolution.

Those who could afford to give, found him an easy
confessor, for a man shows he is well shriven who gives
money to a poor brotherhood, and since men's hearts are
hard, and they will not weep for their sins, let them give
money to the poor pious instead of tears and prayers.

It was by means of the confessional and of education
that their great influence was obtained. They had
separate places of worship, where they administered the
sacraments and heard confessions. It seems also that
they might preach when they pleased in the parish
churches, and would often come and order the bell to
be tolled to their sermons without consulting the parish
priest; and the effect of these sermons was as great as
was ever produced by Whitefield or Wesley in later
ages. There was an English friar of remarkable eloquence and talent, Haymo, of Feversham, who was afterwards promoted to be minister-general of the order.
Being at a church in Paris about Easter, and seeing a
great crowd of people hastening to receive the Holy
Communion, he felt his spirit stirred within him, and
having ascended the pulpit, he warned them of the danger of communicating in unrepented sin. The people
were so affected, that for the next three days he had full
employment in hearing their confessions.

In this instance the result seems to have been good,
but it was quite otherwise when this power, which they
had obtained from the pope, was used, as it soon was,
to draw away the parishioners from their own parochial
clergy, and in a manner to usurp the place of the latter.

Martin IV., A.D. 1281, endeavoured to compromise matters by requiring one confession in the year to be made to the parish priest; but while he left the friars their ordinary privilege, this would only lead at most to a formal appearance at the stated time before the less favoured confessor. The people liked better to confess to them, being strangers, than to their own clergy, and it thus became a common complaint that the salutary part of confession, the shame of sin, was removed, and the people separated from their appointed pastors. Archbishop Fitzralph's account of this part of their operations is given in terms which mark his own piety and good sense. He says, 'The only offices they seek are burials and confessions, because these are profitable; yet every good man but themselves shrinks from hearing confessions, for it is more than enough for each to find out his own sins, without learning those of others. And thus the people are placed under shepherds who never see their flock or know their sheep, and the shame of confession is lost.' And he describes the result of this in Ireland in a way too remarkable, as compared with the present state of things in that country, to be overlooked. 'I think I have every year in my diocese two thousand of my flock who are involved in the general sentence of excommunication against wilful murderers, public thieves, incendiaries, and the like, of whom scarce forty in a year come to me or my penitentiaries; and yet all such persons receive the sacraments like the rest, and are absolved, or said to be absolved, and doubtless they cannot be so by any one else than the friars, since no one else absolves them.'

This change in the laws of the Church was naturally followed by a change in its doctrine relative to confession. It was one of the bad systems during this period, that all literal interpretation of Scripture was abandoned, and strange notions of Church power, and abuses of its exercise, raised from distorted senses of the plainest texts. It was the interest of the friars to keep up the

confessional; and how did they do it? Scripture speaks
of confession to be made to God: *I said, I will confess
my sins unto the Lord: and so thou forgavest the wickedness of my sin* (Psalm xxxii. 6). But the friar inter-
prets it—'Unto the Lord; that is, to God's vicar, or his
priest; or otherwise, to the honour of God, as Joshua's
words are to Achan'[1] (c. vii. 19). How different from
the old doctrine of the Saxon Church! 'Every day,
once or twice, or oftener if we may, we must in our
prayers confess our sins to God, as the prophet says,
*Lord, my sin have I made known to thee, and mine un-
righteousness I hide not from thee. I said, I will confess to thee, Lord, mine unrighteousness by myself; and
thou, Lord, didst forgive the iniquity of my sin.* The
confession that we make to mass-priests of our sins doth
us this good, that receiving from them wholesome counsels and ghostly medicines for the stains of our souls,
and following their directions, we may thus do away
the habit of sin. But the confession that we make to
God alone doth us this good, that the oftener we remember them, God the rather forgets them; as the Lord
says by the prophet, *Thy sins I remember no more.*'[2]

If the influence obtained by means of education was
not so great, it was perhaps more permanent, and ought
to have been less objectionable. The first care of the
provincial Agnelli on his arrival at Oxford, was to erect
a handsome school or lecture-room at the Grey Friary,
and he was eminently successful in the lecturers whom
he engaged. The first of these was the famous Robert
Grosteste already mentioned, afterwards bishop of Lincoln, and the most distinguished man of learning of his
time. He was succeeded by Roger Wesham, a man of
the most conciliating manners, as well as a man of
learning, who was also raised to the bench of bishops,

---

[1] CARDINAL JOYCE (a Dominican, confessor to Edward I.) on the
Psalms, part ii. p. 85.
[2] *Anglo-Saxon Ecclesiastical Institutes.* THORPE, vol. ii. p. 426.

holding the see of Lichfield while Grosteste was at Lincoln; and by Thomas of Wales, so called from the land of his birth, who became Bishop of St. David's. None of these learned teachers took the order of St. Francis upon them, but their engagement with the Grey Friars shows in what esteem the new society was held in its infancy by some of the wisest and best men of the time. And the name of Friar Bacon, who was one of the first scholars of the Oxford Franciscans, must ever rescue the science and learning of the order from contempt.[1] It was not long before a similar school was set up at Cambridge; and lectureships were established at their convents in London, Canterbury, and other places.

But if they abused the office of confessors, their practices with their pupils in their schools were often not more wholesome. We may judge of the principles instilled into their scholars by a few specimens. The Italian missionaries seem to have used fables and familiar stories of the same kind as are still used in Italian sermons, where the friars rather act a comedy than preach. Friar Alberti had a fable to teach the juniors how to practice unquestioning obedience:

'A clown gained admission into paradise. He knocked at the door, and St. Peter opened to him. "You may come in and see; but you must ask no questions." He began to look about him, and the first thing he saw was a plough drawn by two oxen, one fat and one lean. The driver of the plough suffered the fat beast to go as he would, but kept goading the lean one. "Fie upon you," said the clown, " why do you so?" St.

---

[1] Roger Bacon was born at Ilchester, in Somerset, about A.D. 1215. His researches in natural philosophy were so far beyond the spirit of his age, that he was suspected of practising magic. It is said that he invented a telescope. It is certain that he had discovered the error in the calculation of time, which afterwards was rectified by some Italian philosophers at Rome, two centuries ago, and led to the difference between our old style and new style. He entered the Franciscan order at Oxford, where he resided to a good old age, and was buried in the convent church there, A.D. 1293.

Peter.was at hand, and immediately threatened to expel him; but, on his entreaty, gave him a second trial. Going a little further, he saw a man carrying a long piece of timber, and trying to enter the doorway of a house; but as he bore it transversely, he was constantly forced back. He began to direct him how to carry it straight, but was interrupted a second time by the doorkeeper of paradise, who dismissed him again after a more strict admonition. A third strange sight caught his attention; it was that of a woodman in a grove, who was felling the young growing trees and sparing the old trunks, which were of age to make good timber. The clown was unable to restrain himself, and began to chide the man who so misused his axe; when St. Peter caught him by the arm, expelled him from the sacred place, and shut the gate behind him.'

The aim of this story was plainly to inculcate that implicit faith in the commands of a superior which was afterwards taught with such pernicious effect by the Jesuits—to teach the pupil to do as he was bid, however unreasonable the command might appear. Such doctrine, under pretext of enforcing reverence to authority, destroys the exercise of the moral feelings; it checks due inquiry on one side, and tempts to abuse of power on the other. But it is a pretext which has often prevailed with young and earnest minds, bent upon self-sacrifice. 'Do you wish to go into England?' said the warden of the convent at Paris to a young English friar of his society. He had learnt his lesson: 'I do not yet know,' he said, 'what my own wish is to be.' His meaning was that he would form no wish till he knew his superior's will. The powers of persuasion exerted by the friars were certainly very remarkable, if we may trust Fitzralph's account. He declared that their practices to entice boys away from school or college to join their order were such, that parents now would rather consign their sons to the plough than send them to Oxford, where the numbers had decreased, in his memory, from

30,000 to 6,000 students. These numbers are probably stated on a loose calculation, but they are about the same proportions as are related to have quitted the University of Prague in the time of Jerome, the Bohemian Reformer; and we must remember that, as none of our public schools were then founded, all the boys who would otherwise have gone to Eton, Westminster, and the hundred other schools founded since the Reformation, went then at an early age to Oxford or Cambridge, and mixed with older students, who came from the monastic schools, and were intended for the monastic life, or to make the Church their profession.

The mendicant orders, however, continued to increase; and when the devout ceased to join them from motives of piety, the ambitious flocked to them as the best road to promotion. This was marked by the course which things took in England. Ralph de Maidstone, Bishop of Hereford, in A.D. 1240, renounced his mitre, and retired into a Franciscan convent, persuaded by a dream which he interpreted as a divine warning. He dreamt that he was presiding in state in a synod of his clergy, when a stranger came, and, sprinkling water in his face, changed him from a bishop to a beggar. The moral was, that he should go and join himself to a set of men who were in their way of life most like the poorest of the poor. Walter Mauclerc, Bishop of Carlisle, and lord-treasurer, a few years later, A.D. 1246, in like manner gave himself up to the Dominicans. But in the next generation, instead of keeping to their scapulary and cord, the friars of both these orders were vying with each other in aiming at the highest stations in the Church. 'If they maintain their state of poverty for the most perfect,' said Wycliffe, 'why forsake it for the less perfect?' Three popes, John XXI., Innocent V., and Benedict XI., were all taken from the order of Black Friars, between A.D. 1276-1303. Nicholas III., A.D. 1277, was a great patron of the Grey Brothers, for it was said that St. Francis had predicted in a vision to

him when young, his future elevation. He it was who
enabled them to hold property without violating the
letter of their vow of poverty, by giving them the
usufruct of property vested for them in the Holy See.
This order also had its popes, of whom the first, Nicholas IV., presided four years, to their great advantage,
from A.D. 1288-1292. Cardinals and bishops there were
many. And what gave them further splendour in England was, that it began to be considered, as King
Charles II. said of the system which nourished it, that it
was a comfortable religion to die in. Princes and nobles
often, as the closing scene of a life of luxury, put on the
poor mendicant's dress, and gave their hearts or their
whole corpses to be buried at their convent chapels.
' What good can the dress do,' says Erasmus, in one of his
colloquies, ' to a dead or dying man?' 'Nay,' replied the
other speaker, ' it is well if they renounce their pride
and ambition at their death-beds; for how many are
there who, even in their lifetime, please their imagination with the thought of the splendid funeral and procession that is to follow them to the grave?' ' It would
be well,' the other rejoins, ' if there were no other way
of escaping from such pomp and pride. But why not
order themselves to be rolled up in a cheap winding-
sheet, and carried out by poor pall-bearers, to be buried
in the churchyard with the poor? For this mode of
burial seems rather to change the kind of pomp, than to
avoid it altogether.' These were the sentiments of a
more enlightened age. At the time of which we write,
Eleanor, queen of Edward I., gave her heart, and that
of her son Alphonso, who died before her, to be buried
with the Black Friars. Johanna, widow of the Black
Prince, made the same present to the Minorites at
Stamford; and her son, Richard II., was buried at
another Dominican house, founded by his predecessors,
at King's Langley, Herts.

Another marvellous way, by which the rich were
brought in to share all the graces of poverty, without

practising its privations, was by *conventual letters,* or
charters of fraternisation; by which the person presented with them was entitled to all the benefit of the
prayers, masses, and meritorious deeds of the order.
A better expedient could not be devised to take in rich
patrons, and secure their alms, than this; by which, as
Wycliffe said of it, 'they made property of ghostly
goods, where no property may be, and professed to have
no property in worldly goods, where alone property is
lawful.' It was probably under the persuasion of this
benefit, that Edward II. gave up to the Carmelites
one of his own royal residences, Beaumont palace, near
Oxford, built by Henry I. for a very different purpose.

It was a singular change when the friars begun to
dwell in palaces and stately houses. When they first
came into England, their superiors rigidly enforced the
law that they should dwell within mud walls, so that
when some benefactors had built their cloisters and dor-
mitories of stone, they even went so far as to level them
with the ground, and rear them again of such materials
as the poorest labourers used for their cabins. It was
not exactly in this spirit that Richard Leatherhead, a
grey friar from London, having been made Bishop of
Ossory, in A.D. 1318, pulled down three churches to get
materials for his palace. But the conventual buildings,
especially of the Black Friars, are described by the
author of *Pierce Plowman's Creed,* a poet of Wycliffe's
time, as rivalling the old monasteries in magnificence.

There is a memorable story told by Walsingham,
which, if true, speaks plainly enough of the character
both of the friars and their great patron at the close of
their first century. The Franciscans in Italy, having
amassed immense wealth, wished to hold estates like the
monastic orders. To get permission for this they offered
Boniface VIII., in A.D. 1299, 40,000 ducats in gold,
which they lodged with a banker in Rome. The Pope
dismissed them with a dubious answer, and then,
having absolved the banker from his obligation to the

depositors, seized the money, and told them it was not good for them to depart from their rule of poverty.

It was almost a natural consequence of their precarious mode of maintenance, that they should have sought to support their credit by miraculous revelations. The wonderful story of the five wounds of our blessed Saviour impressed upon St. Francis has been already related; but this was carried still further in the following century, when a book was exhibited at the Franciscan chapter at Assisi, A.D. 1389, by Friar Bartholomew of Pisa, and approved by general consent, in which it was taught that St. Francis was made a type of Christ in his passion, that he received in a vision the same wounds, suffered the same griefs, and that the passion of Christ was renewed in him for the salvation of souls. And it declared that he was made by his merits the Son of God, and sanctified by the Holy Ghost, by reason of a scroll which Friar Leo saw descend from heaven and fall upon the head of St. Francis, wherein it was written, ' This man is the grace of God; wholly conformable unto Christ; the image of all perfection.' And again, the same book spoke of the hood of St. Francis, as conferring on all who put it on the same grace as holy baptism, full remission of sins, and deliverance both from their guilt and punishment. To such lengths can man be carried by misplaced reverence for his fellow-men.

Nor were the followers of Dominic a whit behind. ' Christ,' said they, ' raised three only that were dead; St. Dominic raised three in the city of Rome. Christ, being immortal, entered twice among his disciples, the doors being shut. Dominic, yet mortal, entered by night into the church, lest he should waken his brethren. He had the angels at his service, the elements listened to his call, the devils trembled at him, and were not able to disobey him.'[1] To which must be added what one fain would not write, ' Christ prayed once in vain, Dominic never prayed in vain.'

---

[1] LEWIS's *Life of Pecock*.

It may be asked how so many wise and learned men, as the popes often were, should have given authority to such gross inventions. It must be remembered that the papal power itself could have only been secure by keeping its hold upon public opinion; and, while the current of opinion ran strongly in favour of the mendicants, it would scarcely have been safe to oppose them. Some of them had excited seditions and civil war in Italy; and at Paris there was a sect of Minorites who set out for sale at the church of Notre Dame, a book impiously called *The Everlasting Gospel*, which raised a great commotion in that city. This book contained a prophecy that the successors of St. Peter should shortly be put down, and a new power be raised in the Church, under the patronage of St. John, which should utterly destroy the adherents of the see of Rome. This power was to stand, as might be expected, in the support of the friars, who were to be the only clergy left alive under the new system. Pope Alexander IV. ordered this book to be burned by the executioner in A.D. 1256; but the friars gave him so much trouble, that he declared 'he would rather have one of the most powerful kings in Christendom for an enemy, than a disciple of Dominic or Francis.' A decision of John XXII., A.D. 1316, revoking in some measure the permission of Nicholas III. to hold property, and condemning those who should say that Christ and his apostles had nothing of their own, gave great offence, and a section of Franciscans from this time rejected the Pope, and lurked about Italy for a century and a half, holding strange doctrines, and practising, as their enemies asserted, unheard of and unnatural rites. They were called Fraticelli, and were cruelly persecuted.[1]

It is remarkable that in the rebellion of the boors in England in the following century, shortly before the

---

[1] Some curious particulars of this persecution may be seen in a small book published in Germany, and entitled *Vier Documenten aus dem Römisches Archivva.* Leipsig, 1843.

death of Wycliffe, the same design was entertained of
leaving no clergy except the friars; and it is a very
suspicious circumstance against them, as having been
the exciters of that insurrection.   When Jack Straw
was brought to execution in London, A.D. 1381, the lord
mayor begged him to make a full confession of the designs of Wat Tyler and his accomplices, promising him
a good number of masses for his soul, if he complied.
He confessed, among other things, that after destroying
all the nobility and gentry, they meant to have killed
the king, and all the clergy who had either land or fee,
the bishops, monks, canons, and rectors of churches.
'None but the begging friars,' said he, 'should have
been left upon the face of the earth; and they would
have been enough to do all the duties of the churches.' [1]
This was not a random calculation, if, as Wycliffe says
in one of his tracts, there were then 'many thousands'
of these friars.   He calculates their collections in alms
as amounting to not less than 60,000 marks, which, as
ten marks a year was then sufficient for the maintenance
of a chantry-priest, would support at least six thousand
friars.   Among these there were, doubtless, many ignorant laymen, but the notion of consigning all ministerial
duties to the friars was natural enough at a time when
they had already, as Fitzralph and Wycliffe alike bear
witness, almost driven the rectors and curates from the
discharge of their office.

Another remarkable doctrine of the friars is the rather
to be noted in this place, as it seems to have arisen first
in England.   It was recorded at a council in London,

---

[1] WALSINGHAM, p. 265.   It is remarkable that Collier, where he relates this confession, sets down the words 'to destroy the monks, canons,
and rectors, and not to spare any of the clergy, excepting the friars
mendicant, *and some poor priests to officiate.*'   Whereas Walsingham
says nothing whatever of these 'poor priests,' but precisely what the
reader will find in the text.   Did Collier mean to hint that Wycliffe's
'poor priests' had made common cause with the friars, who were their
bitterest enemies?   Walsingham elsewhere tries to insinuate this.   But
Jack Straw's confession is alone enough to determine this question.

A.D. 1328, that St. Anselm had appointed a festival in
honour of the *Immaculate Conception* of the Virgin,
which this council accordingly ordained to be observed
in the province of Canterbury. It was asserted that the
Blessed Virgin ' was free from original sin through sanc-
tifying grace which God infused into her at the time
when the soul was united with the body.' [1] And this
assertion was for three centuries a fruitful source of
altercation in the Church, the Franciscans affirming and
the Dominicans denying the doctrine, and the popes in
vain attempting to mediate between them. Once it was
adopted by the Council at Basil, A.D. 1439; but this
council not having had at that time the papal sanction,
its decree is not received, and the question is not yet
settled, though a great living authority has written in
favour of it,[2] expressing a hope that it will yet be
affirmed by the Church.

And yet the followers of Dominic were hardly behind
the votaries of Francis in their exaltation of Mary. One
of his biographers recorded that she was present when
St. Dominic was celebrating the Lord's supper ; that she
took the sacrament at his hands, and helped him afterwards to unrobe. He calls Dominic the spouse of the
Holy Virgin, and proceeds to describe the way in which
he himself also had been in like manner favoured by her,
and presented with a ring and a chain of her hair.[3] Who
can wonder, and who can doubt, that in such times
saints and angels, images and pilgrimages, were in equal
honour with the Saviour, and other names advanced
above the holiest one? The adoration of the Virgin

---

[1] LAMBERTINI (Benedict XIV.) *de Festis*, p. 460.

[2] CARDINAL LAMBRUSCHINI on *the Immaculate Conception*. Such
was the state of the case until the decree of the reigning pope declared
this dogma to be an Article of the Faith. On which subject see the
Sermon of the Bishop of Oxford, which has been republished in French
by the 'Association for making known the Principles of the Anglican
Church.'

[3] ALANUS DE RUPE, quoted with just censure by the Bollandisti, 4th
of August, p. 361.

supplies one of the earliest instances of harmonious
cadence in English poetry :—

> Mary, mother, well thee be,
> Mary, maiden, think on me;
> Maiden and mother was never none
> Together, lady, save thee alone.

As all the services, except the sermon, were in Latin,
they had a sort of poetical description of the Old and
New Testament history, which was recited or acted on
Sundays and holydays before the people. But such was
the strange confusion of all knowledge, that one of these
rhyming stories introduces a legend of a bishop called
Antiochus, at the time of the Annunciation, before our
Saviour's birth.[1]   These histories were called Miracles,
or Miracle Plays, and were represented in churches,
sometimes by means of puppets, sometimes by the clergy
themselves dressed up in character. It was a rude device
adapted to a rude age, and perhaps we ought not to
censure any attempt, however imperfect, to represent
the sacred history to the minds of the people. But
these exhibitions were usually conducted by the mendicant orders, and considering their wandering habits, it
must have tended to give them very much of the character of roving players or minstrels. This was done
especially at Easter, when the subject was the awful
mystery of the resurrection of Christ; and these
actors were not afraid to make an idle mock-represen-
tation of the angels at the sepulchre, the soldiers, and
the women. About Christmas they kept the festival of
the Star, as it was called; and not only the wise men
from the East were represented, but a manger and oxen
were brought into the church. In like manner Balaam's
history was made a piece of profane drollery, and this
interlude was called the Festival of the Ass. This was
a custom to be matched in later times in Italy and
Spain, where it used to be a practice on St. Mark's day

---

[1] See two specimens of these plays given at length in STEPHENS'S
Supplement, L. 139. See also WARTON'S *English Poetry*, IL 92.

to bring a bull, to which they had administered a sleep-
ing potion, into their churches to hear mass. Pope
Clement VIII., about A.D. 1600, forbade it in his own
territories; but it prevailed in the last century in the
provinces of the peninsula. It is of such profanations
that a Benedictine of that country speaks, when he applies to them the text:—*Behold, I will spread dung
upon your faces, even the dung of your solemn feasts;
and one shall take you away with it* (Malachi ii. 3).
They prevailed against the wishes of Bishop Grosteste
and William of Wykeham, who laboured to suppress
them; and against the strongest condemnation expressed
by other clergymen, such as William de Wadington, a
poet of this period, who spoke his mind in Norman-
French verse:—'To make such assemblies of fools in
the streets and churchyards,—to abuse the church-
vestments, consecrated to other purposes, in these follies,
—who can believe such things to be done, as it is pretended, for the honour of God? Verily it is nothing
else but a devil's game, and an act of sacrilege, and the
spectators share the crime.'[1].

More harmless in its character was the festival of the
boy-bishop on Innocents' day, when a child from the
choir was dressed up in vestments like a bishop, and
acted his part for the day as a grave father of the
Church. Something of this kind appears to have been
kept up after the Reformation, when we find good Dean
Colet providing for the little pageant at his foundation
of St. Paul's school, and his friend Erasmus composing
a speech to be delivered by the boy-bishop. In the
next age the younger singers of the choir were taken
to play in court-masques and interludes, where, perhaps, their talents for mimicry were not better employed.[2]

[1] ' 'E jus del diable pur verité,' &c. PRICE on WARTON'S *Hist. of
Poetry*, vol ii. p. 69.
[2] Ben Jonson's pretty lines on the death of Salathiel Pavey, a child
of the Queen's chapel, speak as if he might have acted boy-bishop:—

We need not harshly condemn what such men as Dean
Colet and Erasmus thought fit to be tolerated, and what
was but a Christmas holyday game at worst.   Of a
very different character were those base representations
and corrupt scenes enacted by their elders, and which
were so bound up with the religion of the party opposed
to reformation, that they were revived again in London
in the days of Queen Mary.

Still worse was it when the festival of a saint's translation came round, and crowds of votaries came throng-
ing to the holy place.   But what the scenes were at
such places as were most celebrated, we may judge by
the only modern parallel in any English settlement, a
camp-meeting in the woods of North America.   This
again might be proved by the coarse but faithful description left us of the Canterbury pilgrimage by
Chaucer.   What was the character of these scenes at
a later date in Spain? ' The pen cannot enter upon it,'
says our Benedictine, ' without horror.   No man who
has ever been present at these meetings, will hesitate
to bear witness to the innumerable disorders which are
committed there ; vice scarcely disguises itself with
the cloak of piety ; dissoluteness triumphs in its proper
garb and form.   And no wonder ; for it is the very
end for which they go.   With very few exceptions, it
may be said that the most innocent intention with
which any appear at these meetings, is to see, and to
be seen.'   He goes on to speak of the excesses which
follow by day and night, and ends with the significant
proverb, ' No great artillery is needed to batter down
walls which are ready to fall with the slightest breath
of wind.'[1]

One other of the practices of the friars is yet to

He did act, what now we mean,
   Old men so duly,
That the three sisters thought him one,
   He played so truly, &c.

' *Feyjoo, Theatr. Crit.* vol. vi. p. 39.

be mentioned. When indulgences came to be sold, the Pope made them a part of his ordinary revenue, and according to the usual way in those, and even in much later times, of farming the revenue, he let them out usually to the Dominican friars. Here again we must refer to Chaucer for the best and most authentic description of the 'gentle pardoner.'

> His wallet lay before him in his lap,
> Brimful of pardon, come from Rome all hot.

He had reliques too, as well as pardons, our Lady's veil, and part of the sail of St. Peter's ship.

> And thus with falned flattering and gapes,[1]
> He made the parson, and the peple, his apes.

And yet he was a noble ecclesiastic, and sang an offertory better than the best.

Popular poetry, always influential, is especially so in a rude age, and these poems, and others, such as the *Vision of Piers Plowman*, and the *Plowman's Crede*, at once indicated and promoted the desire after better things. But Chaucer, with the love of virtue inseparable from a true poet, was not content to lash prevailing vices; he would also hold up ideal excellence to view; and his beautiful description of a parish priest, familiar to us all in the modern paraphrase of Dryden, has sometimes been thought, though erroneously, to be intended for Wycliffe himself; certainly it represents such a pastor as all priests may emulate, and all parishes desire to see.

> A parish priest was of the pilgrim train,
> An awful, rev'rend, and religious man.
> His eyes diffused a venerable grace,
> And charity itself was in his face.
> Rich was his soul, though his attire was poor,
> (As God had clothed his own Ambassador,)
> For such on earth his bless'd Redeemer bore.[a]

---

[1] Tricks.   [a] See the motto of Chap. II.

CHAPTER VIII.

WYCLIFFE'S TRANSLATION OF THE BIBLE. HIS DENIAL OF
TRANSUBSTANTIATION.   HIS DEATH.

> O book, infinite sweetness, let my heart
> Suck every letter, and a honey gain,
> Precious for any grief, in any pain,
> To clear the heart, and mollify all pain.
> G. HERBERT, *of Holy Scripture.*

AFTER the second citation of Wycliffe, when he
appeared before the convocation at Lambeth, A.D.
1378, an interval of three years seems to have occurred
without any further proceedings against him; but it
was a momentous period in the history of his life.   We
have seen that the papal schism, to which it is probable
that he owed the suspension of these proceedings, had
immediately become a fruitful topic of his censure.
But if his former conduct was calculated to bring him
into disrepute with the leaders of the Church, still
more were those steps on which he now adventured.
These were the translation of the Bible into English,
and the denial of the doctrine of transubstantiation.

The English people had as yet no entire version of
the Scriptures in their own language.   There were,
indeed, some parts of the sacred volume translated at
different times, which were probably in few hands; and
it is not easy to say how far the old Anglo-Saxon
translations might still have been understood.[1]   But
these were not for the people, and there was no provision that it should be read in churches.   The rulers
of the Church had neglected their duty, and any man
who should undertake to supply the want, would under-

---

[1] See the quotation from Sir Thomas More in SOUTHEY's *Book of the
Church,* cal. p. 204, 4th edit.

take an invidious task,—more especially Wycliffe, who
was already embarked in avowed hostility to them.
It happened as might have been expected; rather
than acknowledge their own neglect, the clergy found
out that the people had no right to the word of God,
and that they had done their duty in withholding it—
thus perverting and bringing into contempt another
truth; for though the Gospel is committed to the
ministry of the Church, it is that the ministers of the
Church may keep it only to teach it to the flock of
Christ, not withhold or suppress the sacred deposit.

Wycliffe's translation was made not from the original
Hebrew and Greek, but from the Latin; and he was
assisted in it, as he says in his preface, by some of his
friends, particularly Dr. Nicholas Hereford, one of the
most learned of them. Happy man and true patriot,
who amidst reproach and trouble could refresh his own
soul from the fountains of eternal life which he was
pouring forth upon his country! The Bible thus translated was first put forth in the year 1380, and the price
of it in the year 1429 is known to have been 2*l*. 16*s*. 8*d*.,
which in our money would be ten or twelve times as
much,—a vast price; for printing was not yet in use,
and the cost of transcribing was very great. But it
was soon in great request, and copies multiplied amaz-
ingly; for it seems the people were of Wycliffe's own
opinion, as expressed in his preface, 'that Christian
men and women, old and young, should study fast in
the New Testament,—should cleave to the study of it,
and that no simple man of wit, no man of small knowledge, should be afraid unmeasurably to study in the
text of holy writ.'

This translation was not immediately denounced or
put down by authority; for when an attempt to suppress it by act of parliament was made about four years
later, John of Gaunt interfered, and declared that 'all
other nations had the Bible in their own language, and
the English should not be the dregs of all men;'—a

declaration which, being made after Wycliffe's death, may perhaps mark some conscientious regret at his having abandoned the Reformer, as we shall see, shortly before his death, on account of his opinions concerning the holy sacrament of the Lord's supper. So the attempt for the present miscarried; and the translation was first condemned by Archbishop Arundel's influence in convocation, A.D. 1408.[1] The grounds on which the churchmen of those days objected to the translation were not, indeed, that it is wrong in itself for people to read the Bible, but that it is wrong for unauthorised persons to put out their versions of it. For, on another occasion, this same Archbishop Arundel, in preaching the funeral sermon of Anne of Bohemia, queen of Richard II., highly extolled her for having the four Gospels in English, and for sending them to him for his inspection and approval. If this was the only objection, however, they would have best proved it by issuing an authorised version to be read in churches. The Hermit of Hampole had made a translation of the Psalms, with an English commentary, a few years before, which is so like Wycliffe's version, that probably Wycliffe had seen it. And another version of the whole Bible appeared about the same time with Wycliffe's, by John of Trevisa, a Cornishman, chaplain to Lord Berkeley, a young baron who seems to have had a taste for better things than the usual occupations of his age. The only copy of this version known to have existed in this country was destroyed by fire; but other writings of John of Trevisa, which remain, show that he was a man of principles near akin to Wycliffe's, and opposed, on the same grounds, to the temporal power of popes and prelates.[2]

[1] Wycliffe's Bible was never condemned by act of parliament. The act 2 Henry V. c. vii., which is sometimes said to have condemned it, contains no such clause.

[2] It is singular that Foxe makes no mention of Wycliffe's version of the Bible, and Collier speaks as if he had not seen it. A specimen of HAMPOLE's *Psalter*, and WYCLIFFE's *Translation of the Book of Job*, will be found in the Appendix to this volume, E.

It is observable, however, that Wycliffe gave no countenance to the modern sectarian way of sending every private man to the Bible to make out a creed for himself. He was only careful to warn his hearers against receiving new articles of belief on the Pope's warrant; but his rule of faith was the same with that of Ridley, as learnt from Vincent of Lerins, and other fathers of the primitive Church. His words are these:

' As belief is the ground of all other virtues, it is the aim of the fiend to mar men in their troth (in what they should believe); and he begins by this, that whatever your prelate saith is the belief of holy Church; or whatever the Pope saith is true and stable, and that all men should stand by it as by their belief; or whomever he canonises, assoils, or damns, he is so treated of God ; as if God must confirm all that the Pope does, in virtue of Christ's behest to Peter.

' The cause of these errors, by which the old belief is openly suspended, and a new belief grows in its place, as antichrist would have it, is that men know not their belief, and therefore trust in falseness, and take strange truths as the belief of the whole Church. The ground against the errors is, to be established in Christ's law, and to know what His Church is, and what is the belief of His Church. What is the subject of belief? It is hidden truth; which God tells us in His law. It is declared enough in the common creed of Christian men. If thou wilt examine faith, whether it be the true faith of Christ's Church, look whether it is grounded on any article of the creed; if it be not grounded, take it not as belief.

' Shame upon this venom, that if the Pope determine thus, then it is common belief, that each man ought to trow. For thus two popes might make two creeds, and the creed of the Church should hang on the Pope; and he must needs be saved, however he may live, for he would be a God on earth. This is the friar's cry, and they blind the people with it. But ask these friars whether it is grounded on the common belief of the Church; and if they fail in this point, suspect them for fiend's children.'

To this good catholic doctrine he adds, that, in his opinion, the creeds themselves contain some things less necessary than others, and that a plain Christian may be saved without being able to dispute upon them all.

'Right belief teaches what must needs be God's truth, and that thou shouldest trust in His will. Men must trow that God is, and love Him, and their neighbour. In the general creed are contained many truths that we need not to dispute, but may leave them as unpertinent (unnecessary), as in the creed of Athanasius and of the Church; but it is an honest ordinance, and God would have us take it. Let each man trow that God is better than any other thing, and in generalty believe all truths that God will have him believe.'

'We need not muse on special questions about truths that God will hide. God will hide from thee whether thou shalt be saved or damned; but He would have thee trow, that if thou believe in Him to the death, then thou shalt be with Him in bliss of heaven without end. And thus God would have hidden from thee the hour and time when thou shalt die, and the day of the last doom, for God would have thee ever waking. God would have thee leave musing on doubts that He would hide; as of our Lady, and St. John, and other saints that fools prate of, and bring in as matters of belief, for they hope to win thereby.[1] Since God made all things in measure, we should hold us in His bounds, and trow

---

[1] This evidently alludes to such legendary tales as those of Friar Woodford, mentioned before, and the assumption of the Blessed Virgin, which he fairly owns 'is not in Scripture!' It seems that as early as the time of St. Augustine, there was an apocryphal story that St. John was not dead, but lay asleep in his grave, founded on the words in his Gospel, ch. xxi. 22, 23.

truths that He has ordained and taught Christian men
to trow.[1]

In the meantime Wycliffe continued to teach the
students who came to him, in right of his degree as
doctor of theology. There was no want of pupils to
learn his tenets; and the Oxford bachelors and scholars
were ready to enlist themselves as his disciples. It
seems to have been about this time that he adopted with
them the same plan which had been tried three centuries earlier by the unfortunate Berenger in France, who
had engaged and paid poor scholars to go about and
preach his doctrine of the Lord's supper.[2] In like
manner, Wycliffe's 'Poor Priests,' as they were called,
travelled about to different towns, preaching very
earnestly the same doctrines for which their master had
been accused, and, as is wont to happen where persecution has stirred up a spirit of resistance, often going
beyond their master.

Perhaps the very steps that were taken to suppress
his opinions might turn out to the furtherance of them.
For when his friends were banished, as we shall shortly
see, from Oxford, they travelled on foot all England
over, and preached wherever they could, thus adopting
the same system of itinerancy already practised by the
mendicant orders: so that another set of preachers thus
arose, equally opposed to the generality of the clergy.
They preached wherever they could find an audience, in
town or country; the market-crosses and stone pulpits,
which were then standing in the most populous places
of concourse, were their favourite places of harangue;
and by calling themselves poor priests, walking bare-
foot, and wearing long russet gowns, they seemed to aim
to recommend their cause to the poorer part of the people, to whose habits they so much conformed.

It is not true that Wycliffe took upon him to ordain

---

[1] *Homily on St. Matt.*, xxiii. MS.
[2] MALMSBURY, *Hist.*, b. III. § 284.

priests; but he said that the mission of a priest to preach the Gospel is the same as that of a bishop, and therefore he maintained that priests might preach everywhere without license from bishops. He, in fact, did no more, when he employed any priests who were willing to preach his doctrine without license from the bishops, than the friars already did under the authority of the Pope. They too were authorised to enter into all parishes and churches; they too preached sometimes in the open air, and were not accountable to the priest or bishop of the parish or diocese which they thus invaded. And that which these fraternities did under papal sanction, in order to preach up papal indulgences, and as he believed, to mislead the people, Wycliffe boldly resolved that any priest might do, on his own authority as the minister of Christ, in order to preach the Gospel.[1] And if it must be confessed that they did not always confine themselves to such topics as became them,—for they excited men's minds against many things which they had been taught to reverence, and thus sometimes addressed the passions of their audience,—yet on the whole they preached Christ crucified, and that name was as the sound of waters in the wilderness, or as the shadow of a great rock in a weary land.

The working of this system may be judged of by a few examples. We have an account of William Swinderby selecting two millstones for a pulpit in the Highstreet of Leicester, and declaring that he could and would preach there in spite of the bishop. They would preach in churches, however, when they could gain permission; and they made use of the chantries and free chapels, many of which were situated in lonely places, and seem to have been but little frequented. And we often find that knights and gentlemen would give notice of their preaching, and bring their armed retainers to

---

[1] M. Merle d'Aubigné, in his *History of the Reformation*, gives this as if it had been a speech of Wycliffe's, which it certainly was not.

protect them from molestation. Soon after Wycliffe's death, John Fox, mayor of Northampton, A.D. 1392, sent to hire preachers from Oxford to preach in the churchyard in the market-place during Lent, at a stone cross erected there, to which probably the penitents at that season resorted to pray or perform their penances.[1]

It is most likely that the Lollard preachers were employed in explaining the better doctrine of absolution as taught by Wycliffe, and as he had learnt it from the study of St. Jerome;[2] but the vicar of All Saints, *Sir John* Plomme, seems to have had no vote in the matter. It was worse when, on Sunday, as the same vicar, after the offertory, was going to the altar to sing his mass, the mayor followed and held him by his vestment, till he had made him promise to cease while the congregation heard a sermon from the strange preacher; and in the afternoon Richard Stormworth, a woolstapler, zealous for the other side, made an uproar which drowned the voice of reformation.

Wycliffe himself was not certainly disposed to leave too much to Church governors. He put forth a tract

---

[1] BRIDGES' *Hist. of Northants*, i. 230.

[2] 'Right as priests of the old law had power and cunning (knowledge) to tell who were leprous, and who were clean of leprosy, by signs that God taught them; so in the new law God taught His priests by what spiritual signs they should know ghostly leprosy, and by what signs they should say. This leprosy is forgiven, if the man who confesses to the priest say the truth of himself. And this is Jerome's sentence upon Christ's word to Peter.' (S. JEROME, *Comm. on St. Matthew*, b. iii. c. 16.) Again, he says, there is great danger in men's trusting in penances imposed by the priest, not perceiving how impossible it is for any priest 'to tax evenly the pain after the sin. No man in earth,' he says, 'nor angel in heaven, unless God tell him specially, can tax such a penance.'— *Schism of the Popes*. 318.

Mr. Lo[?]ias, following Dr. Vaughan, says that Wycliffe 'positively denied the necessity of confessing to a priest.' *L. of Wyclif*, p. 201. On the contrary, he in this tract says, 'this sacrament is needful to sinful men; but not so needful as confession made to God.' He says, 'it doth men good by shame and dread of their shrift, and draweth them from many sins;' and his determination is wise and just, 'that Peter's keys should not perish, but be furbished and cleansed of the rust of heresy, and the blasphemy of confessors be laid down.'

K 2

about this time, in which he plainly avowed that he
thought it contrary to God's law for bishops or clerks to
possess lands or lordships.[1]   This notion he founded
upon the texts in the New Testament in which our Lord
reproves his disciples for contending which should be
the greatest. (Matt. xx. 25, 26); and he argued that
God, in the old law, forbade priests to have any heritage
among the people (Numb. xviii. 20); therefore they
ought to live on offerings and tithes, which he calls
'God's rents;' and patrons who had endowed the
Church with lands were guilty of an offence against this
divine prohibition.

The argument was unsound, and rested on an imperfect knowledge of Scripture.   The Levites, under the
old law, had a public endowment of lands as well as
tithes; their forty-eight cities had each a suburb or
district assigned round them for gardens, and pasture
for their flocks, of the size of an ordinary parish, or
manor (Numb. xxxv. 4, 5); and it is plain that the
priests had a portion of their maintenance from these
fields of the suburbs (2 Chron. xxxi. 19).   Religious
persons were allowed and encouraged to devote a part of
their lands to the service of God, and the use of the
priests (Lev. xxvii. 16-21).   As to lordships, David,
and other religious princes, had always some of the chief
priests for their ministers of state; and it would not be
easy to find a good reason why Christian kings should
not entrust a share of the public counsels to the bishops,
whom the English constitution has ever regarded as one
of the three estates of the realm.   In this, and some
other points, Wycliffe was carried by his zeal beyond the bounds of truth and soberness.

We must, however, remember that in this time there
was enough to provoke extreme opinions, in the unsuitable occupations which many bishops and clerks pursued as a means of preferment, as well as in the unpriestly

---

[1] *Tract on Divine Dominion.* MS. WALSINGHAM, p. 208.

characters which they assumed after their elevation.
He speaks of several who gained benefices by becoming
house-stewards to noblemen, 'kitchen-clerks or penny-
clerks (accountants), or wise in building castles, or other
worldly doings, although they cannot well read their
psalter.'[1]   And when they had gained higher preferments, they used their lordships like other lords, and
often were employed on embassies abroad, or in military
enterprises within and without the realm, while they
left their episcopal duties to a suffragan.   Shortly after
Wycliffe's death, there was more than one bishop
engaged at the head of troops in the border wars, to
which Shakspeare alludes in speaking of Hotspur:—

> He doth fill fields with harness in the realm,
> Lead ancient lords *and reverend bishops* on
> To bloody battles and to bruising arms.

But a more distinguished martial prelate was one whose
exploits he lived to witness, Henry Spencer, bishop of
Norwich, Walsingham's model of perfection in all qualities befitting a father of the Church.   He had, by great
vigour and presence of mind, put down the insurgents
of Norfolk in Wat Tyler's rebellion, and executed some
number of them without the king's warrant.   Shortly
afterwards, A.D. 1383, he levied troops, and led what
was called a crusade against the French and Flemings,
to assert the cause of Urban VI. against his French
rival, Clement.   After a series of bloody actions and
sieges at Graveline, Dunkirk, and other towns in the
Low Countries, he returned with the reputation of great
personal courage, but with no permanent benefit to the

---

[1] *Why Poor Priests have no Benefices.* MS.   T. Warton thinks that
Wycliffe here alludes to William of Wykeham, the architect of Windsor
Castle.   But when all the bishops and barons dwelt in castles, there is
no need to suppose that he was the only castle-builder among the clergy.
And Wycliffe would hardly have meant to reproach the memory of
Edward III., the author of Wykeham's preferment, by whose favour he
himself had been preferred to the prebend of Westbury and rectory of
Lutterworth.

cause of the Italian pontiff. The Pope had sent an unbounded grant of indulgences to all who should follow
this mitred champion to the war; and not only knights,
squires, and yeomen archers flocked to his standard,
under this license to plunder and destroy without remorse, but also many rectors and vicars of parish
churches, monks and canons regular, and friars.
'Those priests who live by alms and tithes,' says
Friar Capgrave, in speaking of this prelate, 'are forbidden to meddle with battles; for they have nothing
in common with princes. But those who have castles,
and such kinds of royalties from princes, may with full
license be present in battles, not only against Paynims
and Saracens, but also against false Christians.'[1] If
such was the doctrine of the time, we may see that
Wycliffe had some reason to desire the abolition of
their temporal lordships. 'Take heed,' he said to his
hearers,[2] 'of the ministries of these prelates. They give
leave to priests, to monks, and friars, to travail in their
cause, although they slay men. Ah! since King David,
that was so just a man, was forbidden to make the
temple, but Solomon, that loved peace, was ordained of
God to make it, how much less should popes and priests
shed blood in their own cause! Surely it seems that
since they have forsaken patience and charity, God for-
saketh them.'

There was one class of persons, however, to whom
Wycliffe was still more opposed than 'the proud pran-
cing prelates,' as John Foxe delights to call them.
These were the mendicant friars, with whom he kept no
terms of civility, gave them no quarter, but pursued
them with all the invective which the Latin of the
schools, or the plain English of the people, could furnish.
They were 'Iscariot's children, betraying Christ and
the truth of the Gospel for money, comforting men in

---

[1] *Angl. Sacra*, ii. p.361.   [2] *Schism of the Popes*. MS.

sin and lust;' 'thieves stolen into the Church;' 'hypo-
crites, and worse heretics than the Jews;' 'adversaries
of Christ, and disciples of Satan.' He exposes without
mercy the part they had taken in Bishop Spencer's
crusade, the treasures they had raised from the king's
liege subjects for this mad expedition, more than the
king could raise for himself or his own land; the counsel that they had given to many, who, misled by a false
piety, had gone and died in the wars, who, he says, were
'Antichrist's martyrs;' and he speaks with bitter contempt of their superstitious regard for their 'rotten
habit,' their trade in letters of fraternity, the unscriptural
character of their rule of begging, and their 'stealing of
children,' as he calls it, that is, their seducing of boys
of tender age, as before mentioned, to take their order
upon them. He speaks of their many great churches
and costly houses, and complains that in many places
the old parish churches were falling by neglect, while
all this expense was lavished upon 'Cain's castles.' He
thus designated their convents, taking the first letters of
the titles given to the four orders, Carmelites, Austin
friars, Jacobins,[1] and Minorites to spell the name of the
first-born murderer. But William Woodford, a Mino-
rite, complained, fairly enough, that he had misspelt the
name, and made it *Cuim*, instead of *Cain*, to include the
disciples of Francis.

The friars, on the other hand, were not slow to retaliate. It was chiefly by their agency that some of
Wycliffe's disciples seem to have been imprisoned during
his lifetime. They disputed against his doctrines, particularly in defence of transubstantiation, which he had
now begun to oppose. And as he had argued that the
common religion taught by the Gospel, coming imme-

---

[1] The Dominicans, so called from their first house, the hospital of
St. James in Paris; which may truly be said to have been a Cain's
castle, a dwelling of murderers, when it was made the place of meeting
for Robespierre and his club in the French Revolution.

diately from Christ, was infinitely more perfect than the
private rules of Benedict, or Dominic, or Francis, they
thought it concerned their credit to maintain the contrary.   The arguments which they brought forward are
a curious specimen of the received opinions of those
days.   'The same mode of reasoning,' said Friar Woodford, 'would prove the soul of the traitor Judas to be
more perfect than the human nature of our Lord; for
the soul of the traitor was created immediately by God,
the humanity of our Lord was born from the blessed
Virgin; or that the coats of skins which the Almighty
made for our first parents were more perfect than silk
and scarlet, and cloth of gold.'   Not being quite satisfied, however, with these base comparisons, he goes on
to shift his ground, and says boldly, that God is much
more the author of these private rules than either
Benedict, or Dominic, or Francis; 'for the three principal mandates and counsels of the Gospel are poverty
without property, chaste single life, and obedience to
the counsels of a superior,' which were the foundation
of most rules of private religion.   This could hardly
satisfy; he therefore gets clear of Scripture, and takes
up his position in the stronghold of tradition, which
he evidently .thinks impregnable.   'The common
Christian religion,' he says, 'contains many traditions, which are not in holy Scripture; and yet these
traditions are good and perfect; as, for instance, the
use of the sign of the cross, and the observance of
the Lord's day.   We read in Scripture of the observance of the Jewish Sabbath, and nothing is plainly set
down of the change of the solemnity to the Lord's
day.   This is an apostolical tradition, not written in
Scripture.'   There was no harm in this; we learn the
Apostles' practice from Scripture (Acts xx. 7 ; 1 Cor.
xvi. 2 ; Rev. i. 10); and therefore believe the tradition
of the early Church, which says it was their rule.   What
next?   'Likewise, the tradition of observing the festival of the assumption of the glorious virgin is not in

Scripture; but, like many other festivals, is rightly
observed by the community of all Catholics.' As if
a tradition confirming a practice authorised by the
apostles, and a tradition of which the Church never
heard for the first eight hundred years, stood on the
same footing.[1] He next mentions the Lent-fast, and
the Ember-weeks; but the first of these is, as all Christians know, founded on imitation of our Lord in the
Gospels, the other an imitation of the Jewish Church
(Zech. viii. 19); both, therefore, in different ways,
sanctioned by Scripture. What was commonly done
by the Church at large, however, would not make out
a case for the friar. He therefore goes on: 'By the
same rule, many religious persons of private religions
observe many private traditions, *which are not found
perfectly set down to the very letter in holy Scripture.*'
Well said :—for what were they? 'St. Peter the
apostle observed the tradition of rising and weeping
every night at the crowing of the cock; which none of
the other apostles did. St. James also observed many
traditions not written in holy Scripture, and different
from those of the other apostles and other Catholics, as
you may read in his life;'—probably some legend of
Compostella. 'St. Bartholomew bent his knees a hundred times night and day—a tradition not written in
Scripture,' says the friar, 'nor observed by the other
apostles. The monks and nuns, who were instituted by
the apostles, did the like, observing many traditions of
their own, by order of the apostles.' These reasons the
learned Woodford delivered in a public disputation
against Wycliffe at Oxford, more to his own satisfaction,

---

[1] In the time of the Venerable Bede, the Scottish Abbot Adamnan of
Iona wrote a description of the Holy Land from the narrative of Arc-
wolf, a French bishop. In this book he speaks of the blessed Virgin's
sepulchre as situated in a church in the Valley of Jehoshaphat. The
Church then believed that she had died and was buried, like other
saints. This was in A.D. 701. The story of her being raised again was
of later date.

probably, than that of his hearers.[1] For it is certain
that mendicancy never recovered effectually from the
homethrusts of the patriarch of Reformation.

It would be a waste of the reader's time to offer him
any detail of the sterner stuff which Wycliffe brought
against such adversaries. It is not likely such adversaries will arise again to require arguments to put them
down. What we would rather wish to know is, by
what secret Wycliffe obtained such influence among the
people of England,—how his doctrines were so widely
extended at home, that every teacher of the reformed
party tried to imitate him in all things, and for the
next half-century they were equally popular in Germany. We have left to us a great number of his tracts,
preserved by his followers in the midst of persecution,
and when copies of them were eagerly sought to be destroyed. They seem fairly to represent to us the
character of his addresses from the pulpit, often mixed
with strong reproof of the abuses of the time, but plainly
directing the hope and faith of Christians to that central
truth which can alone sustain the soul. While every
quarter of the land was full of papal privileges, purchased indulgences, charters, bulls, and letters of the
monkish and mendicant fraternities, we may imagine
with what force such words as these must have rung in
the people's ears :—

'Look well to the CHARTER OF HEAVEN ! Every wise
man, that claims a heritage, or asks a *great pardon*,
must keep with busy pains, and often think of the charter of his challenge. Therefore, all and each of you,
keep fast the charter of heaven, and study well the wit
and meaning of that *bull* ; for the *pardon* thereof shall
endure for ever.

'Do you ask what is the charter of this heritage, and
the bull of this everlasting pardon ? It is the name of
our Lord Jesus Christ, written with all the might of the

---

[1] BROWN's *Fasciculus*, L 218, 219.

virtue of God. The parchment of this heavenly charter is neither of sheep nor of calf; but it is the holy
and blessed skin of our Lord, the Lamb that was never
spotted with wem or stain of sin. And never was there
skin of sheep or calf so sore and hard-strained upon
the tenter or harrow of any parchment-maker, as was
this blessed body and skin of our Lord, for our love,
strained and drawn upon the gibbet of the cross.[1] And
no man ever heard from the beginning of the world,
nor ever shall hear, that writer ever wrote with such
hard and hideous pens, so bitterly, so sorely, and so
deeply, as the accursed Jews wrote upon the blessed
body of our Lord, with hard nails, sharp spear, and sore
pricking thorns. They pierced his hands and feet with
hard nails. They opened his heart with a sharp spear.
They pressed upon his head a crown of pricking thorns.
These wounds upon his blessed body are the letters in
which our charter was written, by which we may claim
our heritage, if we read them aright. Thereon is
written wailing and sorrow for our sins; for the which,
that they might be healed and washed away, Christ, God
and man, must endure such hard and painful wounds.
But thereon is written joy and singing to all those that
perfectly forsake their sins.

'The *laces* that hold the seal to this charter are these
two. First, the behest or promise of God, that at what
day or hour a sinful man leaveth his sin, and heartily,
with bitter sorrow turns to him, he will receive him to
his mercy. The second is, the full trust that we have,

---

[1] The frequency of sights of executions and mortal suffering seems to
have enabled pious persons of the times of Wycliffe to realise more than
we can the bodily anguish of the cross. Thus the devout Richard of
Hampole, a little before Wycliffe, in his *Meditations on the Passion* :
'Sweet Jesu, methinketh I see thy body on the rood all bleeding and
strained, that the joints twine (part asunder) ; . . . thy skin all-to
drawn so broad, that it is marvel it is whole ; . . . thy body is *strained*
as a parchment-skin on the harrow,' &c.—See *British Magazine*, April,
1834, p. 423.

that God may not lie nor be false of his behest. And hereon hangeth surely our trust of our heritage.

'The *seal* of our charter is sealed with the blood of the Lord Christ, taken of the drops that he swate in his agony. Marry, more craftily and marvellously is it sealed than ever any bee, by craft of kind, gathereth the wax from flowers of the field. The *print* of this seal is the shape of our Lord Jesu hanging for our sin upon the cross, as the Gospel which we believe teacheth us. He hath his head bowed down, ready to kiss all those who truly turn to him. He hath his arms spread abroad, ready to embrace them. He is nailed fast, foot and hand, to the cross, to show that he will dwell with them, and never wend away.

'This charter fire cannot bren (burn), nor water drown, nor thief rob, nor any creature destroy. For this Scripture the Father of heaven hath hallowed and made steadfast, and sent into all the world. Lock not this charter in thy coffer, but set it in thine heart; and all the creatures in heaven, or in earth, or in hell, may neither rob it nor bereave it from thee.'[1]

But we must now follow Wycliffe to scenes of disquiet, in the midst of which his life of zealous labour was closed. The doctrine of transubstantiation had never been formally received by the Church of England; but from the time of Innocent III. and Stephen Langton, it had never been questioned. Wycliffe denied that it was the primitive doctrine; and asserted, on the contrary, that it had not been so held for the first thousand years after Christ. It is probable that he had already declared his own belief in his sermons, or in the work called *The Wicket*, a short English tract on this subject; but the year after the publication of his Bible, A.D. 1381, he openly delivered, in the schools at Oxford, certain *Conclusions*, in which he affirmed 'that the consecrated host which we see upon the altar is neither

---

[1] MS. in the British Museum.

Christ nor any part of him, but an effectual sign of him.'

In his more popular writings on this subject he seems to have argued against the then received opinion without propounding any theory of his own. Thus, in *The Wicket*, he says, 'They make us believe a false law that they have made upon the sacred host, for the most falsest belief is taught in it. For where fynde ye that ever Christ, or any of his disciples or apostles, taught any man to worship it?' And again. 'You cannot create the world by using the words of creation. How shall you make the Creator of the world, by using the words by which ye say he made the bread his body?' But in a more elaborate work in Latin, called his *Dialogues*, which has internal evidence of having been written late in his career, he argues very strongly that it is the body of Christ in the form of bread, and quotes the decree against Berengarius, to show that the Roman Church then thought so. He writes always as a Catholic, speaking of those who hold the other doctrines as heretics who contradict the teaching of the Church. But in proof that it still is bread, he quotes St. Augustine, who says that, 'give us this day our daily bread' in the Lord's prayer, has reference to the holy eucharist; and St. Paul, that 'the bread which we break is the communion of the body of Christ.' [1]

There seems no reason to doubt that a great proportion of the Oxford men thought with Wycliffe in their hearts. But the chancellor of Oxford that year, William Berton, or Barton,[2] was against him, and he procured a decree to be passed by twelve doctors, chiefly members of the monastic orders, or friars, affirming

---

[1] *Dialogorum*, part iv. c. iii.

[2] It seems probable that he was the same as William Burton, who had been employed, together with the Bishop of Bangor, on the first of the two embassies to the Pope in the reign of Edward III., and who, on the occasion of the second embassy, was superseded in favour of Wycliffe. The chancellor was then a resident officer of the University.

transubstantiation, and pronouncing sentence of imprisonment and suspension from office in the University, as well as excommunication, against all who should hold the contrary.

It seems that this decree, though it had the sanction certainly of the University authorities, was not obtained without some contrivance; for Wycliffe was not aware of it until it was promulgated in the schools of the Austin friars, where he was sitting in his doctor's chair, and teaching the opposite doctrine. When he had recovered from his first surprise, he declared that neither the chancellor nor those who had acted with him could refute what he had taught; and as this decree would suspend him from his functions in the University, he appealed from it to the king in parliament. This proceeding, as it was a new assertion of the supremacy of the sovereign over the authorities of the Church, was looked upon as a further proof of heresy; and probably it would have led to further conflict between the two powers. But about this time occurred that terrible outbreak of the peasantry, before alluded to, which for a time threatened destruction to the whole established order of society; and the primate Sudbury, who was informed of what had passed at Oxford, before he had time to interfere, was murdered by the mob on Tower Hill, June 13, 1381.

Courtney, whom we have seen distinguished for his activity against Wycliffe, was Sudbury's successor, elected by the Church of Canterbury, with the king's assent, in the following August; but it was not till the early part of the next year that he received the pope's confirmation. The parliament met in May, 1382, and here Wycliffe is said to have presented his petition or complaint;[1] in which, not confining himself to the matter of dispute at Oxford, he prayed the assent of the king, the Duke of Lancaster, and other great men of the

---

[1] LEWIS's *Life of Wycliffe*, p. 97. JAMES's *Two Treatises*, pp. 1-17.

realm assembled in parliament, to four articles: 1. That all members of religious orders of whatever denomination might have free liberty to leave their rule, keeping only to the rule of the Gospel. (It is mentioned that several monks and canons were favourable to his views of reformation; and this may have suggested this first article.) 2. That those who had condemned him for teaching that the king might seize the property of delinquent churchmen, might be amended of their error. He argues with great force against the immunity of churchmen from the common laws, showing how it gave them encouragement to foment treasons and conspiracies. 3. That the tithes and offerings paid to monasteries and disreputable priests should be stopped, and given to true men, or distributed to the poor. He seems to speak here of both as voluntary contributions; but he may mean to object, as he had done before, against extorting them by excommunication. 4. That Christ's doctrine of the sacrament of his body, as it is plainly taught in the New Testament by Christ and his apostles, might be taught openly in churches to Christian people. He does not explain more fully what he thought that doctrine was.[1]

There were many of the nobility and members of this parliament who were ready to listen to plans for seizing on the Church's property; but few who had any ability or knowledge to consider the proposed reforma-

[1] Walsingham speaks of a paper of different conclusions from this, as presented to parliament by Wycliffe. It relates to the preferments held by foreigners in England; their conveying of treasure out of the realm; the danger of unlimited obedience of the king to the pope; and complains of clergymen being enslaved to worldly offices; and of imprisonment as not a proper punishment for excommunicated persons. *It also recommends the seizure and sale of the Church-lands, before any act or unusual taxes were imposed.* Lewis, where he reports it, omits this remarkable article. As, however, we seem to have Wycliffe's petition extant in his own words, the substance of which is given in the text, Walsingham has perhaps reported another document, prepared by some more thorough-going reformer.

tion of the Church's doctrine. Accordingly, after his appeal had been presented, John of Gaunt came in, and forbade him to treat any more of the sacrament of the altar.[1] Yet there was a spirit evinced by the Commons which seems to have been awakened by that feeling to which he had given so great an impulse. The upper house had passed a law in the preceding session for the imprisonment of heretics, which, having the king's assent, was enrolled as a statute without being submitted to the Commons, who now insisted that it should be erased. The spiritual peers at this time made up the greater proportion of the House of Lords,[2] but this independent spirit of the Commons was a mark of the increasing influence of the middle classes in society, with whom the strength lay in the cause of Reformation.

---

[1] There is much uncertainty as to the order of events. The condemnation of Wycliffe by the University was in the summer of 1381. The register of Archbishop Sudbury states that he then appealed to the king, and that, after his appeal, John of Gaunt came in and forbade him to handle that matter any more. But his appeal was presented to parliament, and no session of parliament was held till May, 1382, at the same time with the synod at the Black Friars, which condemned his opinions and established transubstantiation. It may have been presented to that parliament, as is here assumed, according to the usual account. But if the second clause refers to the decree of the synod which had condemned 'this counsel,' and not merely to that of the University, it must have been presented afterwards. And if Foxe be correct in stating that the next parliament met at Oxford with the Convocation, it seems to reduce this intricate question to some consistency to suppose that it was then that the Duke of Lancaster, being at Oxford with the parliament, 'came in,' &c. This view is confirmed by the place which the entry in Sudbury's register occupies, for it comes after the notice of the readmission of Repington and the rest to their degrees, whereas the University decree against Wycliffe was a year before. It is probable, therefore, that the registrar inserted the account of the whole proceeding after the appeal, without noting the interval otherwise than by the words 'post appellationem.'—See WILKINS, Conc. lii. in loco.

[2] In the early part of the reign of Henry VIII., the House of Lords contained fifty bishops and abbots, and about forty lay peers. At an earlier period, the proportion of churchmen was still larger. A great difference from our times, when there are only thirty bishops to more than four hundred lay peers.

Meantime the new primate was equally prompt and resolute in his measures to suppress the doctrine of the Reformer. He convened a synod at the house of the Black Friars, in London, on the 17th of May; and a remarkable incident, which occurred at its first assembling, sufficiently denoted with what spirit he was animated. They had scarcely met, when the city of London felt a shock of earthquake. The monks and friars, who composed the great majority of the synod, were struck with superstitious fear, and would have interpreted it as a sign of the displeasure of heaven. But Courtney told them, on the contrary, it was a favourable omen; the shaking of the earth was caused by the expulsion of noxious vapours from within her bosom, and thus the removal of heretics from the communion of the Church would contribute to her health and peace. The sessions, therefore, went on; and on the 21st the synod came to a conclusion of deep importance in the subsequent history of the Church of England. Hitherto the doctrine of transubstantiation, though generally received, had rested only upon the papal authority. But this synod declared, as the Oxford Chancellor and doctors had done, that it was heresy to affirm that the material substance of bread and wine remain after consecration in the sacrament of the altar. Then followed a like condemnation of twenty-three other conclusions of Wycliffe, or attributed to him; among which last we must surely reckon that strange assertion, pretended here, and afterwards at the Council of Constance, to be collected from his writings, 'that God ought to obey the devil.' Wycliffe himself seems to have complained of it, in a tract which he put out afterwards, as invented to blacken his reputation.[1] Thus did the Church of England rivet upon herself the chains of Roman superstition, not because she had originally chosen wrong, but

---

[1] Lewis, c. vi. p. 117. See the following Chapter for a further notice of this charge.

because she hated to be reformed, and had cast God's word behind her. There is one name, however, attached to this decree, which cannot be mentioned without reverence; it is that which stands second and next to the archbishop's, the name of William of Wykeham, bishop of Winchester, the founder of Winchester College, and of New College at Oxford, a charitable and kind-spirited man, a promoter of good discipline, and as a statesman faithful and exemplary. Far be it from us to separate ourselves on this account from sympathy with such a man; rather may we learn a lesson of charity, when we see how difficult it is to root out, even from generous minds, the errors in which they have been bred, and see them led astray by that attachment to things established, which, within proper limits, is one of the first qualities requisite in a governor of Church or State.

It is uncertain whether it was before this synod, or at a convocation afterwards held in Oxford, that Wycliffe seems to have appeared in person, and to have delivered in a confession in English, and one in Latin, respecting his belief as it concerned the sacrament of the altar. In these he so far modified[1] his first statement as to admit the real presence of the Saviour in the holy eucharist, which he might before have seemed to deny, when he said only that the bread which we see is an effectual sign of Christ. He now affirmed that 'the eucharist is the body of Christ in the form of bread; and this worshipful sacrament is bread and Christ's body.' It might be supposed from these words, that he believed what has since been called consubstantiation, as attributed to Luther. But it appears from a fuller statement in another work that he had no such meaning. 'We are not to suppose,' he

---

[1] It is sometimes said that he recanted: there is no evidence of any such thing; but perhaps this modification of his opinions may have given ground to the report, though in fact he now came nearer to what we of the Church of England believe.

says, 'that the body of Christ comes down from heaven to the host consecrated in every church; no, it remains ever fast and sure in heaven. Therefore, it has a spiritual presence in the host, not such as can be measured by length or breadth. The body of Christ or his human nature, is indeed spiritually present at every point of the world; as Augustine and other doctors say, he is a king spiritually, in virtue and power, at every point of his kingdom. By the virtue of that body every part of the world is perfected. But we must believe that the body of Christ is in the consecrated host after another manner: it is, according to its constitution as a body, the host itself.' 'The body of Christ is there fairly and really. You may say, if you will, that it is there bodily and essentially, if you understand the word "bodily," as in the text of St. Paul to the Colossians, where he says that *in Christ dwelt all the fulness of the godhead bodily*.'[1]

The Latin confession is full of metaphysical argument, in which he labours to turn the tables against his opponents, and to show that the notion of an accident without a subject, by which the friars explained the dogma of transubstantiation, involved a denial of the real presence itself. But as he distinctly adhered to his denial of transubstantiation, his explanation was not satisfactory; and no less than five doctors undertook to refute his opinions, of whom the foremost was the Chancellor Barton. At the time when the House of Commons had just petitioned against the persecuting statute, it was probably thought dangerous to imprison a man so popular as Wycliffe. His opponents took what would have been a surer way, had he lived to suffer by it, that of procuring him a summons to Rome, beyond the reach of his influential supporters; and in the meantime the king was persuaded to issue

---

[1] *Trialogus*, iv. 6 and 10.

L 2

a proclamation, by which the Reformer and all who
should maintain his opinions were banished from
Oxford.

There was enough in the present aspect of things to
terrify any mind less resolute than Wycliffe's. Several
of his most distinguished disciples now recanted; his
friends in Oxford were overborne by an adverse power;
and the Duke of Lancaster declined all further interference in his favour. But there was no sign of weakness or
hesitation in his conduct. He withdrew, after the proclamation, again to Lutterworth, but continued thence
to write and encourage those whom he had instructed,
to maintain the doctrine he had taught. 'I should
indeed,' he says, 'be worse than an infidel, if I were
not ready to defend, even to the death, the law of
Christ. And I know that not all the heretics and antichrist's disciples in the world can impugn my sentiments
on the holy eucharist, proved as they are by the Gospel.
On the other hand, I put my full trust in the mercy
of the Lord, that after this short and miserable life, I
shall be abundantly rewarded by my Lord for maintaining this lawful controversy. I know, by the faith
which I have learned from the Gospel, that antichrist
and his council can only destroy the body; but that
Christ, whose part I sustain, can cast both soul and
body into hell. And I know that he cannot fail his
servants in anything that is expedient for them, since
he freely exposed himself to the pains of death, and
ordained that as many disciples as he loved should, for
their profit, be tried with sharp tribulation.' He plainly
declares that the cause of men's falling into this heresy
was their want of faith in the Gospel, and their taking
the laws of popes and apocryphal legends in its place;
which he calls of all unfaithfulness the worst, and 'the
most direct apostacy from our true father abbot, the
Lord Jesus. Be it true,' he says, 'that Innocent III.
went astray in this madness, as the friars lay it to his
charge, that cannot prove this doctrine to be founded

in the Gospel; and as I hold fast to the faith of the Gospel, I will deny this as the greatest heresy.'[1]

In such labours the last energies of the great Reformer were expended. He was seized with the palsy within a few months after the conclusion of the proceedings at Oxford; but not so as to prevent him from continuing his labours as a parish priest, in which it was confessed that his life was exemplary. To this seizure he alludes in his answer to the summons from Urban VI., which arrived in the following year, commanding him to appear at Rome, and defend himself from the heresies laid to his charge. 'If I might travel in my own person,' he says, 'I would, with God's will, go. But Christ has needed me to the contrary, and taught me to obey God rather than man.' At the same time he professes his readiness to give an account of his faith to all true men, and especially to the Pope, whom he acknowledges to be the highest vicar that Christ has here in earth. But he speaks more like one who thought himself in capacity to advise, than to be advised by, the pontiff; and counsels him to give up his wordly lordship to worldly lords, and to seek to be greatest by following most closely the example of Christ,—advice much needed by the proud, revengeful man to whom it was addressed, whose reign was secured by deeds more befitting an eastern despot than a prelate of the Church.

This was almost the last public act of Wycliffe. He was assisting at the celebration of the holy communion in his church at Lutterworth on Innocents' day, A.D. 1384; and while thus engaged, he received the final summons of his heavenly Master. He was struck by a second stroke of palsy, which was so severe that he fell with it to the ground, and continued speechless from that moment to his death, which was on the last day of the same year.

---

[1] *Trialogus*, b. iv. 6. As he speaks in this place of presenting his conclusions to the prelates, 'satrapis,' it seems plain that this was written after the decree had been passed against him.

CHAPTER IX.

WYCLIFFE'S CHARACTER, OPINIONS, AND FOLLOWERS. THE
LOLLARDS. THEIR NUMBERS AND INFLUENCE. ACTS
OF PARLIAMENT AGAINST THE PAPACY. ARCHBISHOP
ARUNDEL.

> 'Tis said that this is bitterest pain,
> To know, and prize, yet crave in vain
> The sweets that truth and freedom give:
> Thus did this suffering champion strive,
> From wealth and friends and kindred driven,
> Upholding still the weight of heaven.—PINDAR.

THERE are few men whose opinions and character have
been more variously estimated than Wycliffe's.
The Romanists abroad, whose hostility is most lively
against Luther and Calvin, have tried to prove him to
be a forerunner of both, in denying the freedom of the
will, and asserting a kind of fatal predestination. The
English Church historians have not treated him with
much more favour. Collier repeats the charges made
against him from the writings of the friars who opposed
him, but does not appear to have compared them with
his own writings. On the other side, Milner seems to
have questioned his sincerity, and scarcely allows him
the praise of a Reformer. And Dr. Vaughan, an Independent, has indeed given him praise enough, but for
opinions, which, in the view of a Church-of-England
man, if he really held them, must rather turn to his
dispraise.

We will take a few of the common charges against
him. He is accused of holding that 'dominion is
founded in grace.' The fact is, that the friars upheld
the claim of the Pope to the tribute exacted from subjects of the English crown, on the ground that 'all
things belong to the *saints*: therefore all countries

ought to acknowledge this truth by paying the demands of Christ's vicegerent.' 'But if so,' said Wycliffe, 'the claim depends upon the *sanctity* of the pope's character; it is therefore forfeited, since the popes have sinned.' And upon the strength of this argument, which was nothing else than what is known to logicians, as a *reductio ad absurdum*, has been grounded this often-repeated calumny. Again, in an instance already alluded to, in his desire to magnify the goodness and mercy of God, he represented the Almighty as calling forth from the course of his providence the utmost possible happiness for his creatures, but thwarted in various ways by the malignity of Satan. From such expressions, his opponents drew the perverse inference, that he taught 'that God must obey the devil;' and this absurd blasphemy was gravely condemned at Oxford, and at the Council of Constance, as part of his tenets.

There is no question, however, that the title often given him, of Father of the Reformation, must belong to him as the prototype of some part of the evil as well as of the good connected with that event. His opinions on Church property, though there was much in the abuses of his time to excuse such sentiments, are inconsistent with the scriptural precedents on which he founded them, and were formed on fanciful views of perfection, which hardly belong to the fallen state of man. 'In proportion,' he said, 'as a Gospel-preacher fulfils his office with greater poverty, so much the more, other qualifications being equal, does he please God.'[1] Much more enlightened is the doctrine of St. Clement of Alexandria on this point, in his treatise, entitled *What rich man can be saved?* Riches, according to him, are simply neither good nor evil; they are like beauty or strength, instruments only, which may be either well or ill employed. Worldly

---

[1] *Trialogus*, iv. 17.

goods, the abundance of which makes wealth, are necessary in order to many good works which Jesus Christ has commanded; else how could any man give alms? On the contrary, extreme poverty is a hindrance to many duties, and a source of many violent temptations, as, to fraud, to base expedients of living, and to despair. But in Wycliffe's time the writings of the Greek fathers were unknown.

He complained that priests were forbidden to say mass or to preach the Gospel in a bishop's diocese without leave of the bishop. But this is a necessary rule of Church-order; and his neglect of it can only be excused by the extreme corruptions of the time. In his invectives against lordly prelates and popes, and cardinals and archbishops, archdeacons, monks, and canons, he might seem to aim at the destruction of the different orders of the ministry; but this was not his meaning; for he affirms again and again, that ' prelates and priests, ordained of God, came in the stead of apostles and disciples;' and that it would be ' treasonable presumption' in temporal lords so to withhold their alms from the Church as to fail to 'maintain the ordinance of Christ.' [1]

While, therefore, his enmity to the temporal rank of churchmen, and some few other points, may serve to unite him in sympathy with those who dissent from the Church of the Reformation, his views of the royal supremacy, his preaching of Christ crucified, his zeal for making known the Scriptures, and his determined maintenance of the purer doctrine of the holy communion, should serve much rather to connect his name with those of the reformers of that Church. Another principle of his doctrine was to go back, as far as he had the means, to better and purer times, before, as he expressed himself, Satan was set loose, a thousand years after Christ came. He strove to form his views by the writings of St. Jerome and St. Augustine, while he gave

---

LEWIS, c. viii. *Of Prelates.* MS. *Trialogus,* iv. 17.

pre-eminence to the written Word of God. But he did not reject any light which might be afforded him by Anselm, Fitzralph, and Grostête, whom he never mentions but in terms of the greatest respect, and often fortifies his own positions by reference to his writings.[1]

It has been mentioned as a strange thing, that Wycliffe should have escaped imprisonment, and died quietly at Lutterworth. And hence some have supposed that he made submission, or recanted his opinion on the sacrament of the altar. But it has been shown that he was driven from Oxford, and his enemies were designing to have him conveyed to Rome, when a merciful Providence rescued him by a better summons. It is impossible to show any proof of this supposed weakness. Others have wondered how it was that he did not quit the communion of the Church, since he found so much of antichristian practices within it.[2] But he never professed to think it the duty of any Christian to leave the Church; he would have reformed the Church itself, not have set up a rival communion; and he did the utmost that conscience dictated in raising his voice against the corruptions which prevailed.

It had been for a long time supposed, and stated by one writer after another, that Wycliffe's enmity against popes and prelates began in his being deprived of the wardenship of Canterbury Hall, Oxford (to which he had been appointed by its founder, Archbishop Islip), by his successor, Archbishop Langham, and afterwards by Pope Urban V.[3] But it has now been proved on undeniable evidence, that there were two of his name at Oxford at the same time, and it has been inferred that the

---

[1] Mr. Hallam says of Grostête, 'It is a strange thing to reckon him among the precursors of the Reformation.' (*Middle Ages*, c. vii.) If he had examined Wycliffe's writings, he might have found reason to modify this opinion.

[2] COLLIER.

[3] Particularly by Anthony Wood, T. Warton, and other Oxford writers. Foxe says that it was 'Simon Sudburie' who deprived him.

warden of Canterbury Hall, John Wiclyve, and the
Reformer Wycliffe, were two totally different persons.[1]
The Reformer seems to have studied at Queen's College,
then newly founded by Robert Eglesfield, in A.D. 1340,
for students from the north.   In A.D. 1361 he seems to
have been made master of Balliol; and in A.D. 1375 he
was preferred to the prebend of Westbury and rectory of
Lutterworth.   If this important discovery can be fully
established, the writer who has made it justly remarks,
that the most serious charge ever brought against
Wycliffe will be entirely disproved ; and the well-head
of the Reformation shown to be untainted with any
mixture of personal resentment or disappointed pride.

It has been necessary to enter thus fully into the
public life and doctrine of this great man ; for it may
be truly said of all that was done for reformation in
England or abroad for the next half-century, that he
was the doer of it.   He was the first who dared to out-
face the wasting system of corruption and tyranny which
had overspread all Europe ; and his success had shown
how much may be done against the world by one single-
hearted man valiant for truth.   His death, however,
left the cause without a leader of ability or courage to
carry on what he had begun.   Philip Repington had
preached in Oxford in favour of Wycliffe after the decree of the doctors against him.   He had since been excommunicated and a fugitive ; and after a short interval
he came forward to retract those principles which he
had preached and maintained.   He submitted himself
to Archbishop Courtney before the Convocation, was
restored to his University-degree, and read his recantation at Paul's Cross.   Presently we find him made

---

[1] A writer, who signs his initials W. C. (Mr. Courthope), in the Gentleman's Magazine for August, 1841, pp. 146-8.   But it appears that in
the same year, 1366, in which John Wiclyve was appointed to Canterbury
Hall, another person, J. de Hungate, was chosen master of Balliol, which
leads to the inference that the warden of Canterbury Hall was the
Reformer, else why did he cease to be master of Balliol?   So that this
intricate question is reopened.

abbot of Leicester, then chancellor of Oxford, and in
A.D. 1405 the Pope gave him the bishopric of Lincoln.
Gregory XII., a pope of doubtful title, afterwards raised
him to the dignity of a cardinal. It is the unhappy fate
of apostates that they are almost forced, by the suspicion
which attaches to their character, to prove their sincerity
by fiercer zeal than common for the cause to which they
have transferred their allegiance. Repington, with these
honours upon him, became a bitter persecutor of his
former friends; so that he was called in scorn by both
parties by the nickname of *Rampington*, for his fury and
violence. Yet this unhappy man, like many others in
such sifting times, may have had at last some compunc-
tious visitings; for the end of all was, that, after having
imbrued his hands in the blood of the Lollard's,[1] he resigned his bishopric, and passed his last years in retirement.

The history of Nicholas Hereford is more uncertain.
He seems to have been one of Wycliffe's most intimate
associates, had aided him in the translation of the Bible,
and is described as the most learned and accomplished
of the Lollard preachers. He had so much simplicity
with his zeal for reformation, that he went of his own
accord to Rome to plead his cause before the Pope. He
might almost with equal safety at such a time have
ventured his head into a lion's mouth. Urban VI.
with his cardinals declared his doctrines so heretical,
that the preacher merited burning; but, through respect
to the English nation, who had honoured him for the

---

[1] Pope Boniface IX., in writing to Richard II. to root out the Lollards, says, ' They call themselves the poor of Christ; but the common
people more properly call them Lollards,—as a man should say, *withered
darnel.*' He therefore derived it from the Latin word *lolium*. But it is
more consistent with the analogy of language to suppose that the people
took the word from their vernacular tongue. Some ascribe it to their
practice of psalm-singing; from the old English verb to *loll* or *lull*, signifying to sing. Chaucer calls them ' Lollers.' But they are said to
have been opposed to psalm-singing: and others think it was the name
of a sect in Germany.

true pope, not from any feeling of generosity towards a man who had confided his life to his keeping, he changed the sentence to one of perpetual imprisonment. Some of the nobles of Italy, sensible of the disgrace brought upon them by this breach of faith, were importunate with the Pope for his release; but to no purpose.[1] Some time after, in the absence of Urban from Rome, the populace rose in tumult, broke into his palace, and set free the prisoners; among whom was Nicholas Hereford, who took the opportunity to return to England.   Here, it is said, he was again imprisoned by Courtney; before whom he had appeared and made his submission at the synod, in A.D. 1382, at Blackfriars.   He seems, however, to have been at liberty again shortly afterwards; as in A.D. 1387, he is mentioned as giving offence by recommending a dying clergyman to confess to God, and not trouble his conscience for want of priestly absolution.[2] In A.D. 1391 he was canon of the cathedral of Hereford, and sat with the bishop there at the trial of Walter Brute, a Welsh Lollard; so that he was then considered a conformist.   But the very next year he owed his safety to the king's letters of protection, obtained for him by John of Gaunt; having therefore again incurred suspicion.   It seems that at length, wearied out with the risks he had undergone, and probably with a conscience not altogether clear of the reproach of weakness, he took the habit of a Carthusian, and ended his days in a monastery at Coventry.

The same want of firmness was shown by Aston, Bedeman, Purvey, and several others, who were among Wycliffe's scholars, and after labouring to propagate his opinions, gave in their recantations.   Some doubt must rest upon the facts reported by the historians of the time respecting some of these men; since the submissions which they are said to have made do not agree with the

---

[1] KNYGHTON, col. 2657, et seq.
WALSINGHAM, p. 328.

existing records in public offices and bishops' registers.
But both the terror of punishment and hope of reward
were abundantly employed to recover them to the obedience of the Church—or, as we should rather say, of
that usurped power which then controlled the Church,
and deprived its members of their Christian liberty.
Still the new opinions continued to spread among all
classes. Knyghton, a chronicler of this period, and
canon of Leicester, in which neighbourhood Wycliffe's
influence was very great, complains that you could not
meet two persons in the street but one of them was a
Lollard. Wycliffe himself had said he believed a third
part of the clergy were with him in their hearts. And
among the laity of rank and dignity, besides John of
Gaunt, and his brother Thomas of Woodstock, duke of
Gloucester, of the royal blood, were William Montague,
earl of Salisbury, Sir John Montague his brother, Sir
Lewis Clifford, Sir Thomas Latimer, Sir William
Neville, and many others, whose names denote them
to have been of the most distinguished families in
England.

Among these distinguished persons, it is easy to see
that in many instances political motives had more than
their due influence in the part they took. The party
of the Dukes of Lancaster and Gloucester was generally
in opposition to the government of the king, and they
seem to have used the Lollards to strengthen their
influence against the bishops who held offices about the
court. Neither of these princes was of such character
that one can suppose they were much inspired with the
spirit of religious reformation. John of Gaunt had a
castle at Leicester, and a residence at Lincoln; and, as
the new doctrines had so many supporters in the
neighbourhood, it was his policy to protect them.
There is extant, among the tracts attributed to Wycliffe, but written after his death, *a Report of a Conference between a Friar and a Chaplain of Thomas
of Woodstock*. The chaplain addresses it to his patron,

in whose presence the controversy had been held,
begging him to decide the truth, and 'take the file to
rub away the rust of error in either party.' This chaplain was evidently one who had learned Wycliffe's arguments against the principles of the mendicant orders.
But there seems to be no other proof that this prince
had any sympathy with the disciples of Wycliffe. His
public character was, as Henry remarks, that of an ambitious, proud, and turbulent politician ; and he lost his
life in a bloody act of revenge taken by his nephew,
King Richard, and the rival faction.

The Montagues come in for a share of Walsingham's
abuse, for removing the images of saints from their private chapels. This was clearly a sign that they had
received a portion of the reformed doctrine, as we find
similar acts charged afterwards against Sir John
Oldcastle. Sir John Montague's will appears to have
contained no direction for masses to be offered for him
after his death.[1] And Sir Thomas Latimer's, dated
September 13, 1401, is expressed as follows :—

'In the name of God, Amen. I, Thomas Latymer, of
Braybroke, a false knight to God, thanking God of his
mercy, having such mind as he vouchsafeth, desiring
that his will be fulfilled in me and in all goods that he
hath chosen me to keep, do make my testament. First,
I acknowledge me unworthy to bequeath him anything
of my power, and therefore I pray to him meekly, of his
grace, that he will take so poor a present as my wretched
soul is into his mercy, through the beseeching of his
blessed mother and his holy saints: and I give my
wretched body to be buried where that ever I die, in
the next churchyard that God may vouchsafe me, and
not in the church, but in the uttermost corner, as he
that is unworthy to lie therein, save the mercy of God.
And that there be no manner of cost done about my
burying, neither in meat, nor in drink, nor in no other

---

[1] LEWIS, c. x.

thing, but to any such one who needeth it, after the law
of God; nor any lights, save two tapers of wax. And
anon, as I be dead, put me in the earth,'[1] &c.

Sir Lewis Clifford, whom he names as executor with
his wife, also left a will drawn up in the same strain of
penitence and humility, and directing his body to be
laid in the churchyard. These wills are remarkable
proofs of the simpler feeling and more enlightened piety
which Wycliffe's preaching had awakened. In the interval which succeeded before the Reformation, it was
considered almost a mark of heresy for a man to make
no mention in his will of masses for his soul; and the
Emperor Charles V. fell under great suspicion of Lu-
theranism, after his death, for this omission; so that his
confessor, and many distinguished Spanish clergymen
who had been his friends, were accused and imprisoned by the Inquisition. In the early part of the reign of
Henry VIII., the chancellor of Worcester took up the
body of William Tracie, Esquire, of Todyngton, in Gloucestershire, and committed it to the flames, for no other
offence than having said in his will that he believed
there was 'but one Mediator between God and men,
which is Jesus Christ. So that *he did accept none in
heaven or earth to be his mediator between him and God,*
but only Jesus Christ.'[2] As to the usual scenes acted
in these days before the death of a wealthy client of
fortune, Erasmus probably gives a picture not much
beyond the truth :—

'When Sir George had been given over by his physicians, he sent for Bernardin, the warden of the Franciscans, to take his confession. He had scarcely done
so, when a tribe of the four mendicant orders began to
crowd towards the house, like vultures after a carcass.
The parish priest was called to give him extreme unc-

---

[1] BRIDGES' *Northants*, II. p. 11.
[2] Tracie's will, having been printed by Tindal, together with WY-
CLIFFE's *Wicket* (Noromburg, A.D. 1546), will be given in Appendix P.

tion, and the holy symbol of the Lord's body; but here
arose a bitter strife between this priest and the friars;
for he said he would neither give the unction, nor anything else, to a sick man whose confession he had not
heard himself.   The quarrel was appeased by the
knight's offering to confess again, and promising to pay
handsomely all fees and dues for tolling the bells, for
funeral chaunts, monumental tablet, and burial service.
The priest did his office, and took his leave.   But then
arose another storm and tempest.   There had already
come only friars of the four orders; now came another,
one of the crossed or crouched friars.[1]   The other four
all set upon him :   "Who ever heard," said they, "of a
waggon that went on five wheels?   What impudence to
make the number of mendicant orders greater than that
of the four evangelists I   We might as well have all the
beggars here from the cross-roads and bridge-ends."
"And pray," said the crouched friar," how did the waggon
of the Church go when there were no mendicant orders
at all, or when there was but one, or when there were
three?   As to the evangelists, you might as well tell
me that a dye has four corners.   Let the Austin friars
tell me, when did St. Austin act the mendicant?   And
the Carmelites, when did Elijah do so? "   However, as
he was but one against four, he made his retreat; but he
left the Franciscan and Dominican to carry on the same
conflict against the other two orders, which they called
intrusive orders, and not genuine.   All this passed
in the ante-room, leading to the sick chamber; but so
loud that the sick man could hear.   To put an end to
the strife, he sent out a message by his wife to bid
the Carmelites and Austin friars return home; they
should be as well provided as the rest with food and
alms-gifts, but at their own convents.   He then gave
directions about his funeral, that all the orders, including

---

[1] There were a few of these friars in England ; but Bishop Grostête
had them expelled in his time, and afterwards they thrived but little.

the fifth, should be invited, nine out of each order ; the
number five in honour of the five books of Moses, the
nine in harmony with the nine orders of angels;[1] each
order to carry their own cross or crucifix before them,
and to chaunt their funeral songs. Then thirty minstrels,
according to the number of the pieces of silver for which
our Lord was sold; and twelve mourners, representing
the number of the apostles, and twelve torch-bearers
clothed in black.[2] Next, he gave directions about his
interment. The body was to be placed at the right side
of the high altar, in a marble tomb raised four feet
above the ground ; his effigy, sculptured in the finest
marble, to be laid above, armed from top to toe, with
helm and crest, and shield on his left arm; his sword,
with gilded hilt, by his side ; his belt and spurs, as be-
fitted a knight, and a leopard at his feet. The border
of the tomb was to have an inscription suitable to so
great a man. But his heart he wished to have buried
apart in the Franciscan chapel ; and his bowels he gave
as a legacy to the parish-priest, to be honourably disposed of in his lady-chapel. And, as he had been a
noble captain, who well knew how to marshal his men,
and to overrule any disputes, he provided that the Franciscans and Dominicans should draw lots for precedence
in the procession ; after them, the other three were also
to draw lots; then the parish priest and other clergy to
come last, or first, as the friars should determine.

'As the sick man now gave signs that his time was
drawing to a close, the last act of the drama was prepared. There was read a brief of the Pope's, promising

---

[1] According to a notion prevalent in the middle ages, derived from a
supposititious work of Dionysius the Areopagite, there were nine orders
of angels, differing in dignity : seraphim, cherubim, thrones, domina-
tions, princedoms, virtues, powers, archangels, and angels.

[2] This superstitious regard to sacred numbers often led to gross profaneness, being applied to the most trifling occasions ; as when a friar
would beg three fagots for his convent in honour of the Trinity ; and
such abuse led to blasphemous replies.

that all his sins should be blotted out, and setting him free from all fear of purgatory. As ill luck would have it, there was his wife's brother, a lawyer, present, who found out a flaw in the form of the instrument, and threw in a suspicion of some forgery. The knight was almost distracted; but Friar Vincent, the Dominican, manfully interfered : ' Be comforted,' he said; ' set your mind at case, Sir George. If there is any omission or correction needed in the bill, I will supply it. I have the license of the Pope to do it; and my soul for yours, if all be not right.' The dying man seemed revived at this; and the friars went on to recite some bonds, giving him partnership in all the good works to be done by their four orders, and the fifth beside ; and also an enumeration of all the masses and psalm-singings which should accompany his soul after its departure. The number was infinite. He was then stretched out upon the floor on a straw mattress sprinkled with a small quantity of fine ashes. A Franciscan frock and cowl were laid upon it, ready to be fitted to his body, and consecrated with holy water and a short prayer. Under the cowl were deposited the Pope's brief of indulgence and the bonds. When he was placed upon the mattress, he had a small crucifix put into his right hand, which he kissed, and, calling it his shield against the enemy of his soul, laid it on his left shoulder. The two friars kneeling on each side, bade him think that he had St. Dominic and St. Francis to defend him ; and as he could now no longer use his voice, he was desired to turn his head to either side in token that he heard, and was assured by what they said. Thus he breathed his last. He had before, by will, disposed of his great wealth, in different shares, to his wife and children; but on condition that his wife should become a Beguine—something between a nun and a lay woman ; his eldest son should go to Rome, and there, being made a priest, should daily offer masses and visit the holy places for the good of his father's soul; his younger son should become a friar of the Franciscan order, and carry his portion into the convent; his two daughters, one to become a poor sister of St Clare, the other of St. Catherine of Sienna.'

The scene here depicted has an appearance of exaggeration or satire, but is intended to describe the deplorable system which the writer himself had witnessed. It is placed in contrast with the will of Sir Thomas Latimer, that it may be judged against what a mass of corrupting superstition, customarily established, the old English gentlemen who embraced Wycliffe's doctrine had to contend. It was to be expected, however, that in the recoil from such debasing self-delusion and false worship, some excesses would appear in the conduct of those who had been kept in ignorance and oppression. Such appears to have been the effect of imperfect instruction on the minds of many, both high and low, among the Lollards, whose acts and words respecting the holy sacrament of the altar cannot be excused from sad impiety. Such is the account of Sir Lawrence de St. Martin, a knight of Wiltshire, as related by Walsingham, who carried home the consecrated bread to eat it in derision, as an accompaniment to his wine and oysters at supper.[1] Such is the only excuse to be given for many ribald speeches, which Foxe relates, as spoken by persons whom he mentions among the sufferers for truth. If such persons were visited with severe penances, it was no more than they might expect. As to worse punishments, if they were ever inflicted on these offenders, they were perhaps impolitic,

---

[1] Foxe tells this story of the knight of Wilts, as if 'the Earl of Salisburie' had done it; but he only says, 'he carried the sacrament home to his house.' This is not true to the record. Lewis tells it as he found it; but translates '*singulis feriis sextis*' 'every sixth holyday,' instead of 'every Friday;' on which the knight was to go to the cross at Salisbury, and do penance on his knees in his shirt. He seems, as others have done, rather to discredit the story. There appears to be no just ground for this. It is probable; and the fact of the erection of the cross must have been known. In our zeal against superstition, let us not palliate impiety.

but not wholly unjustifiable; but the misfortune was, that the governors of the Church were incapable of distinguishing bold impiety from conscientious sincerity and constancy in asserting what was believed to be the revealed will of God.

In the same year in which Wycliffe died, the parliament itself petitioned the king to put down the new sect; and this petition was followed by a royal commission to suppress their writings; on which occasion Richard II. assumed, as he did in several of his proclamations, the title of Defender of the Faith. By this commission inquisitors were first appointed to search for heretics; two of whom, Dr. Brightwell, dean of Leicester College, and Sir Richard de Barrowe, were connected with the district of Wycliffe's labours. It would seem, however, that John of Gaunt still gave the Lollards some protection. Peter Pateshall, an Austin friar, had become a preacher of their tenets; and he is called the Duke of Lancaster's chaplain. It is related of him that he was preaching in the church of St. Christopher in London, and declaiming violently against the friars, when one of them got up in the same church, and began to preach against him, in order to put him down. A riot ensued; the mob took part with the Lollard, and the friars who were present had a narrow escape of their lives. And then the mob posted upon St. Paul's doors the accusations of Pateshall against his former associates, in which he imputed to them the most atrocious practices, and the commission of many murders. Such proceedings do no credit to the cause of the reformers; for good men know that it is not the part of a Christian to become the accuser of his brethren, except in a judicial inquiry; and he who will anticipate the office of the only righteous Judge must take his account to be suspected, even though he speak the truth.

This was in the year 1387; but in the following year a priest of the name of Wimbleton delivered a sermon at St. Paul's cross of a very different temper, and which

is the more worthy of notice on account of the imputations of a disorderly spirit so often brought, and not
always undeservedly, against the preachers of these
opinions.   It was on the text, *Give an account of thy
stewardship* (St. Luke xvi. 2); on which subject he thus
speaks of the duties of all classes of the people. ‘Every
one see to what estate God hath called him, and therein
remain and labour, according to his degree.   Thou that
art a labourer or artisan, do this truly.   If thou art a
servant or a bondman, be subject and lowly, in dread of
displeasing thy lord.   If thou art a knight or a lord,
defend the poor and needy from hands that will harm
them.   If thou art a priest, rebuke, pray, reprove, in
all patience and doctrine.   Rebuke those that are negligent, pray for those that are obedient, reprove those
that are disobedient to God.’   He then enlarges upon
the duties of the several orders of priests, governors, and
people; adverting with godly indignation, indeed, but
with no ungodly abuse, to the prevalent simony and
luxury of the clergy.   And in conclusion, having dwelt
upon that exposition of the Apocalypse which all this
sect adopted, that the last times were come, he describes
the day of judgment, and ends with this apostrophe:
‘But joy, and joy, and joy to them that be saved.   Joy
in God, joy in themselves, joy in each other that are
saved.   Joy, because their labour is brought to so
gracious an end.   Joy, because they have escaped the
pains of hell.   Joy, for their bliss that they have in the
sight of God.’

It is in the same year in which this sermon was
preached, that the Lollard priests are accused of having
taken upon them to confer orders.   If this fact be correct, it is the first instance in history of presbyterian
ordination.   But it rests on the slightest possible authority,[1] and there is strong evidence the other way, as we

[1] WALSINGHAM, p. 340. He says that a Lollard confessed it to the
Bishop of Salisbury, at Sunning, Berks; but see p 211.

shall see hereafter.   Wycliffe himself did not deny that
the power of ordination is reserved to the bishops ; and
if there is any accusation of this kind made against particular persons, it is not confirmed by existing records.
It is more probable that the disciples of the first
preachers of Wycliffe's tenets might keep up the spirit
they had themselves imbibed by occasional exhortations, without any alleged authority, than that they had
as yet any definite notion of a presbyterian ministry.

During this period, while the contest between the
two parties was yet in suspense, the history of the ad-
ventures of William Swinderby may serve for a specimen of the rest.   He was a priest at Leicester, where
he preached with great earnestness against the vices of
the inhabitants, making use sometimes of the churches,
sometimes of the chapel of an adjoining hospital, and
not unfrequently addressing the people in the streets
and markets, as the friars also were accustomed to do.
He was at this time protected by John of Gaunt, who
allowed him to live in his park, where for some time he
passed his days as a recluse, and was known as William
the Hermit.   But resuming his practice of preaching,
he was cited before the Bishop at Lincoln, where several
articles were exhibited against him, as containing the
opinions which he had preached.   The friars were
earnest for his conviction, and, by way of bravado, had
prepared fuel, as if to burn him.   They could hardly
expect to do so, since, even if he were convicted of
heresy, the king's writ would be required for his execution, and no such writ had ever yet been issued.
But Swinderby denied that he had held the opinions
imputed to him, and on that ground undertook to retract them in every church where he had preached ;
and having also pledged himself to preach no more in
Lincoln diocese, he was dismissed on the intercession
of powerful friends.   He retired to the remote districts
of Herefordshire, on the borders of Wales ; and here, in
a secluded spot, called Derwoldswood, he made use of a

chantry, where mass was said a few times only in the year, in which he not only preached, but administered the holy communion to the laity in both kinds. It is singular to find those lone chapelries, which were founded for masses for the souls of the departed, converted to the use of that very class of men who were most opposed to the whole system to which they owed their origin. Here also Swinderby had powerful supporters; for the Bishop of Hereford having cited him to his court, could only succeed in bringing the preacher before him by the promise that he should be dismissed unharmed. Under this promise he appeared, and in a written answer defended with piety and constant reference to Scripture, if not always with success, the leading opinions of his sect: ' That tithes may be withheld from wicked priests; that priests have a commission to preach the gospel independent of the license of a bishop, and are bound to exercise their function; that confession to a good priest is good and salutary, but that God only, and not the priest, can remit sin; that baptism by a good priest, with the prayers of good people, is more availing than by a wicked one; that the sacrament of the altar is bread and Christ's body; that the pope is antichrist.' Swinderby being dismissed, according to the bishop's promise, would never appear again, though often cited, and was therefore pronounced excommunicate, from which sentence he appealed to the king in parliament, and in support of his appeal presented a petition, from which the following are extracts:—' Dear sirs, so as we have seen by many tokens that this world comes to an end, and all that ever have been brought forth of Adam's kind into this world shall come together at doomsday, rich and poor, each one to give account and receive after his deeds, joy or pain for evermore, therefore make we our works good the while that God of mercies abides, and be ye stable and true to God, and ye shall see his help about ye.' He goes on at great length with similar exhortations, urging

them not to be ashamed of Christ, and apparently
alluding to his own weakness in having recanted before
the Bishop of Lincoln; and he declares that his object
is ' the most worship of God, the showing of the truth,
and the amendment of holy Church.'

There is an eloquence in the very simplicity of this
appeal from a poor, and perhaps not very learned,
clergyman, zealous for what he believed the cause of
God, in the midst of contempt and danger, which claims
forgiveness for some errors in the character and in the
opinions of its author. But there must have been a
strong·feeling in favour of such opinions, when they
could be thus presented to parliament; and it appears,
from several laws enacted about this time, that the
spirit of resistance to papal encroachment was as strong
as ever. Three years before, the act of Edward III.
against papal provisions,[1] by which the Pope usurped
in fact the patronage of all dignities and preferments,
had been renewed, and sentence of banishment pronounced against all who should hereafter infringe it.
In A.D. 1391, the act of Edward I. against giving lands
in mortmain was renewed and enlarged,[2] and the
giving of tithes to monasteries was also restricted;[3] and
now in 1392 the famous act of *præmunire*[4] was repealed,
with some circumstances worthy of remark. It is said
to have been introduced by Lord Cobham, who, as
Sir John Oldcastle, may have been at this time a
member of the House of Commons, and whom we now
first meet with in that contest in which he became so
fatally conspicuous. The act recites the petition of the
Commons, in which they declare that if the present
system of papal interference be continued, ' the Crown
of England, which hath been so free at all times, that

---

[1] 25 Ed. III. st. 2, A.D. 1350.   13 R. II. st. 2, § 2, 1389.
[2] 7 Ed. I. st. 2.   15 R. II. c. 5.
[3] 15 R. II. c. 6.
[4] 27 Ed. III. st. 1, c. 1.   16 R. II. c. 5.

it hath been in no earthly subjection, but immediately
subject to God in all things touching the regalty of the
same, crown, and to none other, should be submitted
to the Pope, and the laws and statutes of the realm by
him defeated and avoided at his will, in perpetual destruction of the sovereignty of the king our Lord, his
crown and regalty, and of all his realm—which God
defend.' Here was an express assertion of that which
is now called the royal supremacy, and which is commonly thought to have been first introduced at the
Reformation. But the Commons did not rest here.
They proceeded to pray the king, 'and him require,
by way of justice, that the opinions of all the lords,
temporal and spiritual, might be taken separately on
this point.' This seems to have been aimed at the
bishops; and accordingly Courtney, the archbishop,
delivered his written answer, in which, after reciting
the above declaration of the Commons, he declared
that he adhered to it, and that he assented to the passing
of the law. It was passed accordingly; and the rest
of the bishops having given a similar answer, their
assent was solemnly recorded in the body of the statute.
A proclamation was then issued, ordering all English
beneficed clergy who were absent at Rome, to return
home, or forfeit their preferments. We shall see that
an almost similar course was pursued at the time that
Henry VIII. finally broke the power of the Roman see
in England.

It would seem as if the king had been more inclined
than the parliament to aid the bishops against the
Lollards; for in the next year, A.D. 1392, he gave them
a commission to arrest Swinderby; and two years
afterwards another commission against Walter Brute,
a Welshman of his party, who, though a layman, was
a man of considerable learning, and master of arts
at Oxford.[1] But these commissions were issued in

---

[1] One of the names in this commission is that of Thomas Oldcastle, a
gentleman of Herefordshire, and probably the father of Lord Cobham.

consequence of express and earnest representations from the Pope himself. In A.D. 1395, such was the confidence of this party in their numbers, and in the power of their supporters, that they availed themselves of the absence of the king in Ireland, to put up papers on the doors of St. Paul's, and other principal churches in London, severely reflecting on the clergy; and at the same time to present a general petition from their body to the parliament, in which, under twelve heads, they summed up their accusations against the Church, as follows :—

I. That when the Church of England began to mismanage her temporalities in conformity to the precedents of Rome, and the revenues of churches were appropriated to several places,[1] faith, hope, and charity, began to take leave of her communion.

II. That the English priesthood derived from Rome is not that priesthood which Christ settled upon his apostles.

III. That the enjoining celibacy upon the clergy is the occasion of scandalous irregularities.

IV. That the feigned miracle of the sacrament of bread induceth all men, except it be a very few, into idolatry.

V. That exorcisms and benedictions pronounced over the bread and wine, and over the cross, the altarstone, and the holy vestments, have more of necromancy than of sacred divinity.

VI. That the joining of secular offices with spiritual functions puts the kingdom out of the right way.

VII. That all religious foundations, in which special prayer is enjoined for the souls of individuals, are a breach of charity, which would have us pray for all alike; and that such prayers may be displeasing to God, since it is probable that all are damned who made such foundations.

---

[1] That is, to monasteries at a distance from the parish church; severed from it.

VIII. That pilgrimages, prayers, and offerings to images and crosses are near of kin to idolatry.

IX. That auricular confession, and the feigned power of absolution, make the priests proud, and give occasion to intrigues and unchaste conversation.

X. That it is contrary to the Gospel to take any man's life for any offence whatever.

XI. That the vow of single life undertaken by women is the occasion of horrible sins.

XII. That all unnecessary trades should be abolished, as ministering to modes of life contrary to the Gospel rule, which enjoins that having food and raiment we be therewith content.

In this document we find many things which no well-informed mind can approve. The wholesale condemnation of religious foundations is a sad foretaste of the havoc to which such principles were to lead; and the reason on which it is grounded would be just as good against praying particularly for our friends who are alive. For they did not object to prayer for the dead in itself. Again; the denunciation against war and capital punishments, though it seems to be aimed chiefly at the system of crusades, would come with strange inconsistency from a party who even now began to count up their numbers, and to boast of their fighting-men as if they would do battle for their cause. And yet we recognise in this petition the seeds of great and saving truths; and the errors with which they are intermixed, springing up together with the revival of scriptural learning, may serve to show that the Church herself must teach the truth, and not suppress it, if she would guard her people from error when the reaction comes.

It might be expected that the authorities of the Church would take alarm at such proceedings; but, it seems, they thought it dangerous to interpose. 'The bishops,' says Walsingham, 'saw and heard all these sayings and doings; but they went their ways, one to his farm, and another to his merchandise. There was not a shepherd who raised his voice to frighten the thieves, or his pastoral staff to drive them away, except the Bishop of Norwich.[1] Blessed be his name to all posterity, that he did not suffer his people to be infected with such a pestilence! For he swore, and did not repent, that if any preacher of this perverse sect should presume to preach within his diocese, he would either burn him alive, or cut his head off. And there was not one of the whole company, who, knowing this peril, was in any haste for martyrdom.' It would appear that even Courtney himself was one of those who thought it necessary to yield to the time. But now we find among the foremost against the Lollards the name of another churchman, who was soon to teach them that the little finger of an Arundel was heavier than the loins of a Courtney.

Thomas Fitz-Alan, or Arundel, who on the death of Courtney, in A.D. 1396, was promoted to the arch-bishopric of Canterbury by papal provision, was at this time archbishop of York, having been elevated to that see by the same influence from the bishopric of Ely, to which also the Pope had appointed him, though the king had nominated another candidate, and the convent had elected a third.[2] This chosen favourite of Rome was a man of small learning; for he never proceeded further than bachelor of arts; but he was the brother of the powerful Earl of Arundel, lord treasurer and lord high admiral, and he bore himself in his exalted station more as an imperious nobleman than as a father of the Church. On the presentation of the Lollards' petition, he had hastened himself to Dublin to urge the immediate return of the king, who on his arrival severely rebuked Sir Lewis Clifford and others of the Commons, who had favoured those proceedings; and shortly afterwards, in a visitation of his diocese, he compelled some Lollards

---

[1] Henry Spencer, the leader of the Flemish crusade before mentioned.
[2] GODWIN, in *Vit. Arundel.*

at Nottingham to take an oath, in which were the words,
' I swear, that from henceforth *I will worship images.*'
A most remarkable declaration, when we recollect how,
in better times, the English Church had protested with
an anathema against this very practice.[1]

But events were now at hand which were to throw
a darker shade over the history of this unhappy sect.

---

[1] See COLLIER, L 509. CREATON's *Early Eng. Church*, o. ii. p. 176.

CHAPTER X.

USURPATION OF HENRY IV.   THE PERSECUTING STATUTE.
TRIALS OF THE LOLLARDS.   LORD COBHAM.

The woe's to come: the children yet unborn
Shall feel this day as sharp to them as thorn.
    SHAKSPEARE. *Richard II.*, act iv. sc. 4.

IF, as Shakspeare has said, the angels weep over the abuses and usurpations of earthly power, there is no page of English history more worthy of their tears than all that relates to the elevation of Henry Bolingbroke to the throne.   It was a time when a weak prince, ruling in the wantonness of youth, had driven from him all faithful counsel; and a powerful faction, opposed to the court, having lost its leaders by a bloody death, was thirsting for revenge; when, exiled by an arbitrary sentence without a trial, and smarting for the unjust seizure of his patrimonial estates, the heir of Lancaster was joined in France by another exile, the primate Arundel.

He had been forced to leave England upon the death of his brother, whom the king, revoking his solemn pardon, had executed as a traitor.   The populace, counting the dead earl a martyr to the cause of public liberty, went in crowds to visit his tomb; and it was reported that his head, after it was laid with his body in the coffin, had again become united with the trunk from which it was severed.   To check this demonstration, and disprove the pretended miracle, the corpse was taken up and exposed; and the friars, at one of whose churches it lay, were ordered to remove the trophies and monument, and by levelling the tomb with the pavement, to make the place undistinguishable to beholders.   Having thus attempted to abolish the memory of the dead, to take away all hope from the surviving brother, the king declared his see vacant, and, with the sanction of the pope, appointed a rival archbishop in his room.

Thus to each of these restless spirits seemed to have arisen that 'necessity,'[1] which nothing less than the highest principle and the most enlightened judgment would have enabled them to withstand. The same necessity invited the one to seize the deserted throne, the other to defend, with the sanction of the Church, an act which restored him to his former dignity. There was no want of solemn forms fit to consecrate an usurper.[2] The sacred oil with which Henry was anointed was out of that mysterious vial which the blessed Virgin was said to have given to Becket during his exile in France, telling him that the kings who should partake of it, should be good champions of holy Church. Arundel preached at his coronation, on the text, *This man shall reign over my people* (1 Sam. ix. 19); and in his sermon contrasted the manly virtues of Bolingbroke with the childish follies of the fallen Richard. All the bishops, either openly or tacitly, concurred, with the exception of Marks, bishop of Carlisle, in a change which promised them deliverance from the questions agitated in the parliaments of the former reign; and they counted, not unreasonably, on the favour of a sovereign whom their support had done so much to secure

---

[1] See SHAKSPEARE, *Rich. II.*

[2] In calling Henry IV. an usurper, it is not intended to express an opinion against the rights of his house in their subsequent contest with the house of York. He was an usurper because he invaded the throne of the then lawful occupant. But it is highly probable that the house of Lancaster would have been preferred to the Earl of March, in case of the peaceful death of Richard II.; and as the claim of York, a younger brother to Lancaster, had not accrued until he afterwards married the heiress of March, it is difficult to see what just right he could set up against the prescription of three generations with parliamentary and national consent, though not difficult to trace the righteous judgment of heaven against the original crime of Bolingbroke.

in his new possession. When the convocation of the
clergy met at the assembling of his first parliament, instead of asking, as usual, for a subsidy more than equal
to the taxes imposed on the laity, the pious usurper declared that he would not ask for their money, but their
prayers.

This was soon followed by the statute for burning
heretics. The first instances of a persecuting spirit
which occurred in the primitive Church were checked
by the openly expressed indignation of some of the most
honourable names among the prelates of those holier
times. In A.D. 384, when Priscillian, a Spanish bishop,
of tenets undoubtedly heretical, had been put to death
by the Emperor Maximus, at Treves in France, the
Christian Church was so far from concurring in such a
sentence, that not only St. Ambrose, bishop of Milan,
but Siricius, bishop of Rome, solemnly protested against
it. The bishop by whose sentence the heretic had been
delivered to the civil power, was deposed by a council
of the Church; and St. Martin, the apostle of the
French, separated himself from his communion.[1] So
thought the Church of the Fathers. But a thousand
years had passed; the Inquisition abroad had existed
for nearly two centuries, and now it was become a common thing in other parts of Europe to put to death for
heresy. One remnant, indeed, was retained of the ancient practice: for whereas the fathers, when they delivered an offender to be corrected by the law of the land,
were accustomed to entreat that his life might be spared,
this entreaty still accompanied the sentence; but it became a mockery when those who passed the sentence
knew and intended that their victim should be committed
to the flames.

The first victim was William Sawtrey, a parish priest
of St. Oaith's in London, who the year before had recanted in St. Margaret's church, at Lynn in Norfolk, of

---

[1] *Church of the Fathers*, c. xxi. p. 408. COLLIER, I. 617.

which he had been incumbent; but being now convened before the archbishop, with the bishops and clergy in convocation,[1] and accused of preaching the same doctrines, at first denied the fact of his having recanted before, which being proved in court, he was pronounced a relapsed heretic, and having been solemnly degraded was delivered to the civil power. The parliament was then sitting which had passed the law in question. The king's writ for his execution was immediately issued; and on the 26th of February, A.D. 1401, Smithfield beheld the first of those scenes of blood and fire for which it was to be fatally notorious.

The act of parliament,[2] however, rendered it no longer necessary to await the king's writ. It was provided that whenever the bishop should see fit to proceed to a definitive sentence against a convicted or relapsed heretic, the mayor or sheriff of the place should attend; and having received the culprits at the hands of the ecclesiastical judge, should '*them in an high place do to be burned.*' Thus did Henry consent, for political purposes, to forego the noblest attribute of his new royalty — the attribute of mercy — depriving himself of the power, in matters of religion, which belongs to a sovereign in the case even of a common felon. And as he had already frustrated the loyal boast of his father, that 'he would not be the first traitor of his race,' so now was he the first to consign to a death of torture the adherents of that cause of which his father had been the patron.

Of the opinions of which Sawtrey was accused, there was scarcely one which can be called a doctrinal error. They were simply these four:—that it was not the duty of Christians to worship the cross of Christ, but Christ who suffered on the cross: that it would be fitter to worship a man predestinated to salvation than an angel of God; for our Saviour, he said, took upon him the

---

nature of man, not of angels; but the Divine law allowed neither: that a man had better distribute the expenses of his journey to the poor at home, than go on
any pilgrimage which he had vowed: and that a priest
was more bound to preach to the people than to say the
daily hours of prayer.   But on being examined, he
also denied the doctrine of Transubstantiation; and this
denial probably was with him, as with all the martyrs
in Queen Mary's days, the immediate cause of his cruel
death.

Bitter were indeed the sufferings which followed
from the enactment of this hateful law.   It is true that
many of the bishops were still, in the fifteenth century, accused of slackness in the persecution; and it
should be mentioned to their honour.   But from time
to time it broke out afresh, and none were ever safe
who held the proscribed opinions.   The prisons in the
bishops' houses, which had been simply places of confinement, were now often provided with instruments of
torture.   The Lollards' Tower at Lambeth still remains,
long since converted to better uses, but with an apartment wisely preserved as a memorial of the past, retaining its iron rings and other signs of the captives
whom it once immured.   The Bishop of Lincoln, at his
palace at Woburn, and perhaps other bishops elsewhere,
had a cell in his prison called *Little-Ease;* the name
was given because it was so small, that those confined
in it could neither stand upright nor lie at length.   The
same law which transferred to the Church the power of
life and death, left still a discretion with the ordinary of
fine and imprisonment; and frequently those convicted
of heresy were doomed to the sentence formerly inflicted
by the Church for homicide, of perpetual imprisonment
within the walls of a monastery.   It is possible that in
such abodes they may have been sometimes the blessed
instruments of imparting divine truth to the companions
of their sojourn; but if we may judge of the feelings
expressed towards them by Walsingham and other

monks of the time, we may well imagine how, with such keepers, they ate and drank the bread and water of affliction. Others were branded on the cheek with a hot iron, which if they dared to hide, they were liable to be burnt as relapsed heretics; or they were condemned to wear the device of a faggot worked upon the sleeve of their clothing, in token of their narrow escape from burning.

It is a melancholy proof how hardly a received error in practice can be amended, even when the principles which led to it have been long discarded, when we recollect how long these persecuting laws remained a part of the jurisprudence of our country. When Henry VIII. began to break with the Pope, he did indeed repeal this statute, but enacted another[1] by which heretics were still to be burnt, though not without the king's writ, while by his six articles he made all points of Romish doctrine to be as much secured by persecution as ever.[2] As the times of the Reformation approached, Erasmus began to plead for a mitigation of such horrors. 'It may be,' he said to the Duke of Saxony, 'that open enemies of the principal articles of the faith deserve burning; but it is not just that every error should be punished with fire, unless he who maintains it is a seditious person, or guilty of other crimes, for which the laws exact a capital punishment.'[3] On the accession of Edward all acts of parliament for burning heretics were repealed,[4] but the common-law still left the power to the king. Cranmer indeed seems to have designed to repeal the punishment of death in the code of ecclesiastical laws which he had just completed when King Edward died. But these laws were never ratified, and the best legal authorities in England still defended the practice. 'As in case of a disease in the body, so in case of heresy, a disease of the soul,' said Sir Edward

---

[1] 25 Hen. VIII. c. 14.
[2] Eplst. xxl. § 7, A.D. 1524.
[3] 31 Hen. VIII. c. 14.
[4] 1 Ed. VL c. 12.

Coke, 'a relapse is fatal.   And as a leper is to be removed from the society of men, lest he should infect them ; so he that has the soul's leprosy, convicted of heresy, shall be cut off, lest he should poison others, by the king's writ *de hæretico comburendo.*[1]   On such reasons the law was still retained ; and a few unhappy persons, for denying the doctrine of the Holy Trinity, or other errors, were executed in the reigns of Elizabeth and James I.   When the sectaries prevailed over the Church in Oliver Cromwell's time, the Independents put to death several Quakers.   Calvin and Beza abroad taught and acted on the same principles.   It was not till the excellent Jeremy Taylor and Chillingworth had taught the doctrine of toleration, that this practice was finally abolished in the reign of Charles II.[2]

As might have been expected, the spirit of the Lollards was not extinguished, though it was embittered, by such proceedings.   They were now almost excluded from the use of the churches, but they held their conventicles in secret ; and as the state had declared against them, they seem to have become less disposed to act the part of good subjects, and to have added more and more of political discontent to their religious opinions. The unsettled state of government, under a doubtful title, favoured this inclination to sedition.   But as yet they had hopes from their friends in parliament.   A party in the House of Commons were known as the Lollard members ; and twice in this reign they presented a petition to the king (which was almost the same as passing a bill by the lower house) for the sequestration of all Church-property.   The petition set forth that this property would suffice to maintain 15 earls, 1500 knights, 6200 esquires, 100 almshouses, and would leave the king 20,000*l.* of yearly income besides : a most exaggerated calculation doubtless, at a time when

---

[1] Coke, *Instit.,* part III, c. 5.   Collier, i. 616.
[2] 29 Car. II, c. 9.

the tenth paid by the Church did not amount in all to 19,000*l.*   But the majority of the house assented to the petition, as in after-times under Henry VIII. and Edward VI., in hope of sharing the plunder; and the statement itself breathes anything but a religious spirit, offering this kind of bribe to the king and nobles.[1]

'King Bolingbroke,' as Shakspeare calls him, was much changed in a few years from what he was at his first accession to the throne.   His faithful clergy, who had been lately requested only to aid the cause of usurpation with their prayers, were now told that the contribution of a tenth was by no means enough to ensure his protection.   They were to pay two-tenths in one year.   He is said to have sent secret instructions to the high-sheriffs of counties before the election of members, that they should take care to let the knights of the shires whom they returned be the most ignorant of law whom they could find,[2] in order that such proposals might be the more readily entertained.   Whether the king seriously contemplated the seizure of Church-property, or whether he wished only to terrify the spiritual peers into a large contribution, the danger now seemed imminent.   But Arundel showed a spirit equal to the emergency.   Turning to Sir John Cheyne, the speaker of the House of Commons, a man who was in deacon's orders, but had left the Church for the Army, and who had expressed his little value for the services of the priesthood: ' I see,' he said, ' which way the wind sets;

---

[1] One portion of this petition is remarkable, as containing the first proposal for a poor-law, which was afterwards the offspring of the Reformation.   It suggested that every township ' should keep all poor people of their own dwellers, which could not labour for their living.' And for the relief of those whom their own township could not maintain, because of their numbers, it proposed the foundation of so many endowed almshouses.   This suggestion seems to have been derived from John Purvy, a disciple of Wycliffe.

[2] WALSINGHAM.

but while Canterbury lives, it will be at your peril, if
you touch any goods or property of his.' Then, kneeling before the king, he reminded him of his coronation
oath, in which he had promised to maintain the Church
and her ministers in all their rights and privileges. He
spoke of the little profit that had accrued to the Crown
from the seizure of the alien priories and cells of Norman abbeys by Edward III., and represented, in language almost prophetic, the certain impoverishment of
a kingdom which should resort to such means of plunder
and spoliation. He had interest with the temporal
lords, some of whom he had saved from forfeiture by
pleading their cause with the king; and they joined
him in his intercession. The king appeared to be
moved, and said, 'Whatever else I do, I will leave the
Church in as good a state, or better, than I found it.'
He was as good as his word, and never listened to these
proposals afterwards.

It would have been well if this active primate had
contented himself with repressing projects of this kind,
so manifestly tending to public disorder. But having
obtained this respite from danger, he determined with
the utmost rigour to put down the growing heresy,
which he looked upon as the root of the mischief. The
memory of Wycliffe was still cherished at Oxford; and
when this prelate proposed to visit the University, he
was opposed on the plea that the Pope had exempted it
from his jurisdiction. When he afterwards, by help of
the king's authority, was received as visitor, one of those
whom he had appointed to examine the Reformer's writings, and detect the heretical opinions they contained,
refused to act with the rest. However, in A.D. 1408,
Arundel presided at a synod in Oxford, and, imitating
the practice of the popes, laid down the constitutions
to be received without debate. In these all Wycliffe's
writings were condemned; and it was made heresy to
possess any version of the Bible not authorised by the
Church; which, as no translation received such sanc-

tion, was in effect to proscribe all English versions of
the Word of God.

Two years later the University passed the same sentence, and committed the books of the Reformer to the
flames; but it did not pass without opposition, for his
popularity was not yet forgotten there.   Indeed, in A.D.
1406, some of his party had contrived to affix the common seal of the University to a testimonial highly prais-
ing him; which was afterwards published in Bohemia
as if it had been the act of the University.   This it
certainly was not; nor is it any credit to those who
resorted to such a trick: but it proves that the zeal of
his followers was not by any means extinct.[1]

Not content with these rigours against the writings of
Wycliffe, Arundel applied to the pope for permission
to burn his bones.   But for once Rome was more
merciful than Canterbury, and the permission was refused.   It was reserved for the Council of Constance
first to make this decree, A.D. 1415; and Martin V.,
elected pope by that council, sent an order into England
for its execution..   It was in A.D. 1428, nearly forty-
four years after the death of Wycliffe, that his moulder-
ing remains were taken up and committed to the flames
by Fleming, bishop of Lincoln, who, like many others
in these times of inconstancy, had in early life favoured
the doctrines of the Reformer.   The ashes were thrown

---

[1] The learned H. Wharton speaks of this testimonial as genuine.
Lewis and Dr. Wordsworth also defend it. On the contrary, Collier, in
one of his controversial pamphlets, calls it ' no better than a beggar's
pass made under a hedge.' It professes to be the unanimous decision of
the chancellor and masters, sets forth the virtues and learning of Wycliffe, and says that he had never been condemned or convicted of
heresy. This was as yet true. But that the document had not the
public or unanimous consent of the University seems plain, from internal and external evidence: the first, because it is contrary to another
authentic decision of the Oxford authorities, and has no signatures of
names to it; the second, because a public declaration of the convocation
of the province of Canterbury, A.D. 1411, states that it was a forgery
and the seal surreptitiously set to it.—WILKINS, Concil., iii. 316, iii. 302.

into the little river Swift, which flows by Lutterworth,
a tributary of the Avon; and, as a modern ballad har-
monises a thought of Fuller's on the subject—

> The Avon to the Severn ran,
> The Severn to the sea;
> So Wycliffe's dust was borne abroad
> As wide as waters be.

The principle upon which Arundel seems to have
proceeded, was one on which many persecutors have
quieted the natural feelings of remorse.   The Church
had decided against such doctrine as Wycliffe taught,
since the time of Innocent III.   From the sentence of
the Church there was no appeal; the Church itself
would be destroyed if its right to decide was called in
question.   Thus he dealt the same measure to high or
low.   John Badby, a poor artisan of Evesham, was
sent up to him by the bishop of Worcester for refusing to
abjure the Lollard opinion of the eucharist, and denying the authority of the priesthood.   He asserted, says
Walsingham, that the consecrated host was but an in-
animate substance, and so of less account than a toad
or spider, which are creatures endued with life.[1]   He
was condemned to be burnt in Smithfield.   The Prince
of Wales—afterwards Henry V.—came to the place of
execution, in hope to persuade him to recant and save
his life.   It was all in vain, nor was it likely to be otherwise; but it was a benevolent effort in the future hero
of Agincourt, and he could hardly be expected, at the
age of nineteen, to know the impotence of royal eloquence in such a case.   It is uncertain how many similar executions took place in the lifetime of Henry IV.;
but some other instances of compassion in his son,
which have lately been brought to light, have made it

---

[1] This appears to be only Walsingham's illustration of his meaning.
But Collier relates it as if the poor man had himself used such mean
comparisons. See WALS. p. 378 and p. 570.

evident that there were several more than have been recorded. For in the first year of Henry V. he granted a restoration of their forfeited property to the widows of four others, who had suffered for heresy before his own accession to the throne.[1]

We have a more full account of the trial of William Thorpe, a Lollard clergyman, who fell twice into the hands of Arundel, both before and after the primate's banishment, but seems to have been able to commit to writing his own story of his examination.[2] It is one of the most interesting of the Lollard writings, and gives a clear account of the writer's notions, shared by many of the sect, upon many points of doctrine. Thorpe acknowledged no Church-authority which he would obey, unless he could perceive those who exercised it to have and use all Christian graces and virtues. He objected to an oath on the New Testament, because swearing by any book he thought to be swearing by a creature, or a thing composed of divers creatures. He thought that all musical instruments in churches were unlawful, and interpreted David, where he speaks of them, as meaning virtues and graces, wherewith men should please God and praise His name. 'The letter killeth them that take such psalms literally,' he said. Here we have something like three several errors of the Puritan, Quaker, and Independent, stated separately. Together with these, however, he held many sounder opinions, explained his belief on most points of the Creed well, acknowledged the real presence of Christ in

---

[1] TYLER's *Life of Henry V.*, vol. ii. p. 413.

[2] Foxe says, 'it is most like to be true, that he was so straitly kept in some strait prison, that either he was secretly made away, or else died there by sickness.' But of this he brings no proof, except that Arundel was not likely to let him go, and that Thorpe was so valiant that he was not likely to have retracted. The difficulty is, to imagine how he could have written such a paper in this strait confinement, reporting many things not very complimentary to the archbishop, and how he could have sent it abroad afterwards.

the Eucharist, but denied any change of the substance
of the bread, and disputed with some success against
pilgrimages.   He offended Arundel by another extra-
vagance in declaring tithes unlawful, and saying that
priests ought ' to follow Christ and His Apostles in wilful
poverty.'   It is strange how on this point some of the
Lollards seem to have been of the same mind with their
opposites, the begging friars.   It would not be fair to
judge of the arguments of the archbishop, or his manner
of discourse, from the report of this Lollard ; it is gar-
nished with oaths, and broken by impatience ; and, as
Sir Thomas More said of it, Thorpe has attributed to
Arundel and his clerks such things as ' none but a wild
goose ' would have said.[1]

In such doctrines as these, however extravagant and
inconvenient for the Church to tolerate, there was nothing actually immoral or seditious But there is reason
to believe that the Reforming party were now becoming
more estranged from that religious simplicity which
characterised their first proceedings.   Sir Lewis Clifford, one of Wycliffe's first supporters, had become disgusted with some tenets which were now avowed, and
denounced them to the archbishop.   Among these are
said to have been the following :—that the marriage ceremony is unnecessary ; that all public worship and
receiving of the communion in churches ought to be
discontinued, those churches being synagogues of Satan ;
that infants ought not to be baptised ; and that neither
the Lord's-day nor the observance of other festivals
are binding upon Christians.[2]   It is said also that, on
the accession of Henry V., they publicly declared that
they were one hundred thousand strong, and would de-

---

[1] See WORDSWORTH's *Eccl. Biogr.*, i. 262, 3rd edition.
[2] WALSINGHAM, p. 366. Some doubt must rest on his statement, as
we find nothing so atrocious in the Lollard tracts which have come
down to us. But it is not probable that Sir Lewis Clifford, who was a
religious man, would have denounced them, if he had not met with
something to give him disgust.

fend themselves by force against those who sought to restrain them.

But that which caused the greatest offence was, that certain knights and gentlemen continued to maintain the preachers of the new sect, and to send them about the country. Of those who persisted in this practice, the most conspicuous was Sir John Oldcastle, a knight of Herefordshire, who having married the heiress of Lord Cobham, of Cowling Castle, near Rochester, had summons to parliament as Lord Cobham in right of his wife's barony. He was a man of influence and note, who had been employed in the public service both by Richard II. and Henry IV., and with whom the new king, Henry V., had contracted a personal intimacy on account of his military achievements, and whom he esteemed for his private worth and character. But he had adopted the opinions of Wycliffe; of which he declared, that 'until he knew that despised doctrine, he had never abstained from sin;' and he adhered to them with a frank and resolute spirit. And indeed the truth appears to be, that Wycliffe had revived the inquiry after that vital godliness which constitutes 'the life of God in the soul of man.' Many of his opinions might be erroneous, and those of his followers still more so. But this principle once imbibed, is calculated to make an indelible impression on the human heart. Immediately after the decrees of the Oxford synod, by which preaching without license was forbidden, the church of Cowling was put under an interdict, with several other churches in the diocese of Rochester, because a certain chaplain living with Lord Cobham had been allowed to preach there;[1] and now, in the year 1413, complaint was made in the convocation of the clergy that the same Lord Cobham maintained in his house preachers who had been convicted or suspected of heresy, and sent

[1] WILKINS, Conc., iii. 350.

them about the neighbourhood to preach.   It was related that he did this not only in Kent, but in the neighbourhood of his paternal estate in Herefordshire; and
that he was accustomed to go himself to their preaching with his attendants, to countenance and protect
them.

It was in vain that the bishops now decreed, not only
that every church or churchyard where unlawful preaching was held should be placed under an interdict, but
that wherever any such meetings were held within a parish, the church and churchyard of that parish should
incur the like penalty.[1]   Such an interdict was indeed
a terrible punishment; for by it Christian burial and
marriage, as well as all the other services of the Church,
were withheld from all the parishioners.   But it was
evident that measures of a different kind were necessary
with Cobham; for he had taken his resolution, and was
prepared to abide the consequences.   He was therefore
denounced by name as a heretic; and the clergy in convocation demanded of the archbishop that he should
proceed against him.   The bishops having thought it
best first to ask the king's permission, Henry desired
them to defer the process until he should have tried the
effect of his own persuasion with his friend.   He sent
for him to Windsor, and had several interviews with
him; at one of which his answer is reported to have
been in these words: 'You, most worthy prince, I am
always prompt and willing to obey, forasmuch as I know
you a Christian king, and the appointed minister of
God, bearing the sword to the punishment of evildoers,
and for safeguard of them that be virtuous; unto you,
next my eternal God, owe I my whole obedience, and
submit thereunto, as I have ever done, all that I have
either of fortune or nature, ready at all times to fulfil
whatsoever ye shall in the Lord command me.   But as
touching the pope and his spirituality, I owe them

---

[1] WILKINS, Conc., III. 352.

neither suit nor service, forasmuch as I know him by the Scriptures to be the great antichrist, the son of perdition, the open adversary of God, and the abomination standing in the holy place.'

Finding persuasion vain, the king permitted the archbishop to proceed according to the law. But Cobham resolved to set the ecclesiastic at defiance. He fortified his castle, and would admit no man to summon him. In vain Arundel appointed him a day to appear at Leeds Castle, then a palace of the archbishop's; in vain he caused the citation to be affixed to the doors of the cathedral of Rochester, three miles from Cowling Castle. The papers were torn down, and the authority of the bishop's court defied. In his absence, sentence of excommunication was pronounced against him; but the only result was to induce him to go again to the king, instead of the archbishop, and to deliver to him his confession of faith.

The most remarkable part of this confession is the definition it contains of holy Church, which he describes as being divided into three societies, of whom the first are in heaven; the second in purgatory, 'if such' place there be;' and the third are all good men on earth, of the several ranks of clergy, nobles, and commonalty; of whom he says, that ' day and night they contend against the crafty assaults of the devil, the flattering prosperities of this world, and the rebellious filthiness of the flesh.' Here was the same omission of any distinction between the visible and invisible Church, which has been before observed as one of the errors of the Lollards. For our Saviour describes the kingdom of heaven as a net cast into the sea *which gathered of every kind*; and the true doctrine is, that the Church on earth, in and by which the Lord will save His people, outwardly contains, until the Lord come, both bad and good. But Henry V. was no judge of controversy; he saw that his friend was resolved to oppose the laws and religion of his country, and he was determined to prevent him. He

was only the more offended when Cobham, who had
previously offered, according to the strange practice of
the times, to defend his opinions by wager of battle,
now declared that he appealed from the archbishop to
the pope.[1] He sent him, therefore, 'a prisoner to the
Tower, from whence he was brought before the archbishop, with whom sat the bishop of London and
Cardinal Beaufort, bishop of Winchester, at the chapterhouse of St. Paul's.

The archbishop having offered him absolution, if
he would conform to the doctrine of the Church, Cobham delivered his written answer, which is preserved in
the original English in the archbishop's register.[2] He
declared that ' he called Almighty God to witness that
it had been and was his intent to believe faithfully and
fully all the sacraments that ever God ordained in his
Church. That as for the most worshipful sacrament of
the altar, he believed it to be Christ's body in form of
bread. As to penance, that it is needful to all who
shall be saved to forsake sin, and to do penance for sin
committed, with true confession, contrition, and satisfaction. As to images, he thought them not *of belief*
(not a necessary part of faith), but ordained since the
Christian faith was given, to be calendars to lewd men
(that is, to ignorant or lay people), to represent and
bring to mind the passion of our Lord, and the martyrdom and lives of saints; but that whoever should pay
to them the worship due to God, or trust in them, or
honour one image more than another, would be guilty
of idolatry. And so of pilgrimage, that we all are
pilgrims towards bliss or woe; and he that knoweth not
nor will keep the holy law of God, though he go on
pilgrimage to all the world, if he die so shall be damned ;
and he that keepeth it to the end shall be saved, though

---

[1] But the author of the *History of England and France under the
House of Lancaster* (Lord Brougham) says the appeal to the pope was
impossible.

[2] WILKINS, *Conc.*, iii. 354.

he never go on pilgrimage in his life to Canterbury or
Rome.'

This answer was not sufficient; and after in vain
attempting to engage him in disputation on the points,
they adjourned the court, and sent him in writing the
substance of that faith to which they would require his
assent. It was, ' that in the sacrament of the altar the
bread and wine are so turned by the Priest's words into
Christ's body and blood, that there remaineth no longer
bread or wine; that every Christian is bound to confess to a priest; that St. Peter and his successors are
the vicars of Christ on earth; and that it is meritorious
to go on pilgrimages, and worship images and relics.'
After two days they met again at the house of the Black
Friars, near Ludgate Hill, to receive his final answer;
and it is due to his judges to say that they showed no
desire to convict him, but used all means in their power
to induce him to recant. But they had to deal with
one of those gallant spirits which rises against oppression
and despises danger. At the first trial his conduct
towards his judges had been such as not to provoke
them wantonly. But now he seems to have resolved to
denounce them openly. The archbishop began by offering him absolution as before, if he would submit and
confess to him; but he answered, ' Nay, forsooth will I
not; for I never yet trespassed against you, and therefore I will not do it.' He then kneeled down on the
pavement, and holding up his hands towards heaven,
said, ' I shrive me here unto Thee, my eternal living
God, that in my frail youth I offended Thee, O Lord,
most grievously, in pride, wrath, and gluttony, in
covetousness, and in lechery. Many men have I hurt
in mine anger, and done many horrible sins; good Lord,
I ask Thee mercy!' He arose in tears; and turning to
the people who were present, ' Lo, good people,' he
said, ' for the breaking of God's law and his commandments they never yet cursed me, but for their own laws
and traditions' most cruelly do they handle me and

others; and therefore both they and their laws, by the promise of God, shall be utterly destroyed.'[1] Being questioned on the articles of faith which had been delivered to him, he again declared his belief, that in the sacrament of the altar is bread and Christ's body, but denied that it was the true doctrine of the Church that the bread is changed; 'or if it be the Church-doctrine,' said he, 'it has become so since the Church was poisoned by endowments.' He again admitted that it is good to confess to a good priest, but denied that it is a duty to confess to the parish-priest in every case. As for images, he said he would pay no more honour even to the cross on which Christ was crucified, than to preserve it carefully; and as to the power of the keys, he declared that the Pope himself with the archbishops and prelates are the head and tail of antichrist.[2]

The court upon this proceeded to their final sentence, by which they declared Sir John Oldcastle, lord of Cobham, a convicted heretic, and delivered him as a heretic to the secular jurisdiction. All who should favour him were excommunicated and denounced; and it was ordered that these proceedings should be published in every church in England. By the law of Henry IV. the consequence of this sentence was death, though it was not the practice of the spiritual court to pronounce it. But though this new law had given authority to the secular magistrate to proceed at once to the execution of a person thus delivered over from the spiritual court, it does not appear that any such course had yet been taken without the king's writ.[3] It is not likely that Henry V. would be forward to issue such a

---

[1] Foxe, from whom this account is taken, refers to Jer. II., the prophetic description of the destruction of Babylon.

[2] This is the account in the archbishop's register. Foxe is more particular; but he does not give his authority.

[3] But there is very high authority for saying that the king's writ issued of course on conviction by a bishop.—*England and France under the House of Lancaster.*

writ in the case of such a man; and it is said that
Arundel himself interceded with the king to stay the
execution. He was sent back to the Tower, and henceforth the history of this nobleman is as full of perplexity
as it is of partial and exaggerated statements. Hitherto
we have seen him boldly and manfully standing forth
at the peril of his life in defence of principles which,
though not unmixed with error, were founded upon
precious and saving truths, too long forgotten or neglected. But now we have to thread our way through
conflicting testimony, in order to determine whether the
same Christian knight permitted himself to be goaded
by persecution, or misled by enthusiasm, into deeds
disgraceful to the Christian name.

What is certain is, that a short time after his conviction, in September 1413, he escaped from the Tower
(by what means was never known); and in January
following the king had information on which he relied,
that Cobham had conspired with twenty thousand of
his party to seize his person and overthrow the government. Henry hastened to London from Eltham Palace,
ordered the gates of the city to be closed, and proceeding with his troops to St. Giles's Fields, where the insurgents were supposed to be assembling, dispersed
some stragglers whom he found there, taking prisoners
Sir Roger Acton and Beverley, a Lollard preacher,
who with many others, thirty-six in all, were condemned and executed as traitors.

On the same day a royal proclamation was issued,
offering an immense reward, a thousand marks, for
the capture of Cobham himself, who was soon after
outlawed by sentence of the judges. It was believed
to be the intention of his party to make him regent
of the kingdom; and it was said that one Morley, a
brewer of Dunstable, who suffered for treason, was to
have been knighted by him on the field, made Duke of
Hereford, and enriched with the sequestered estates of
the abbey of St. Alban's. The parliament of the next

o

year passed a law to sequester the estates of all convicted heretics, and the public opinion seems to have turned against the Lollards.   Whenever any treason was brooding, it was now connected with rumours of Lollard insurrections; they were suspected of stirring up the Scotch invasion, which took place while Henry was in France, and of being connected with the conspiracy at Southampton, for which the Earl of Cambridge suffered; and at length, in December 1417, Cobham himself was taken in Wales, after a desperate resistance.   A standard was found, on which were depicted the emblems of the crucifixion and the consecrated elements, which was supposed to belong to him, and seemed to indicate an intention to carry on a religious war; and he was brought up, wounded and a prisoner, to London.

Henry was in France, following up his success in a second campaign after the battle of Agincourt. But the parliament was sitting, and Cobham was brought before it.   Being asked what he had to say in arrest of judgment, he replied that ' it was a small thing with him to be judged by them, or by man's judgment;' and being pressed for an explicit answer, he declared that King Richard was living in Scotland, and that he would own no tribunal the authority of which was derived from any other source.   On this he was sentenced to be hanged and burnt, as a convicted heretic and traitor; which horrible sentence was carried into effect in all its particulars.   He was drawn on a hurdle through London streets from the Tower to a low gallows erected in St. Giles's Fields, on which his body was fastened horizontally in chains, and lighted faggots being placed beneath, he was thus burned to death.

What were indeed the designs of Cobham and his party is matter of conjecture.   That they had designs against the existing government was never questioned by the king, or by any contemporary historian; and it is remarkable that the same writer who takes pains to

disprove the existence of any conspiracy, should hold
up to admiration as a Christian hero the leader of the
Bohemian insurgents, Ziska, who almost at the same
time carried on a religious war against his lawful sovereign. Perhaps the truth may be, that the persecuting
laws of the house of Lancaster led the Lollards to
concur in the wish for a change of dynasty, of which
so many symptoms had appeared in other quarters.
The insurrections of Archbishop Scroop and of the
Percys against Henry IV., as well as the conspiracy
of the Earl of Cambridge against Henry V., all had reference to some change, which was not avowed—partly,
perhaps, because the Earl of March did not declare
himself, and partly because there was a strong belief
that Richard was still alive. Whether the assembly in
St. Giles's Fields was a real insurrection, may possibly
be questioned; but that Cobham had some designs
against the government at the time he was taken, admits
of no reasonable doubt. The result, however, of these
proceedings was fatal to the Lollard cause. The party,
indeed, continued; but they had lost their credit and
influence in the state, though they remained as a despised and persecuted sect.

CHAPTER XI.

COUNCIL OF CONSTANCE.   BISHOP HALLAM.   PERSECUTIONS
IN ENGLAND.   BISHOP PEACOCK.   WARS OF YORK AND
LANCASTER.

> At last
> Of middle age one rising, eminent
> In wise deport, spake much of right and wrong,
> Of justice, of religion, truth, and peace,
> And judgment from above: him old and young
> Exploded, and had seized with violent hands.
> So violence
> Proceeded, and oppression, and sword-law.—MILTON.

THE Lollards were suppressed by degrees as a political party, but the desire for a reformation was as strong as ever, and even more general than before. Long after they had ceased to be formidable to the state, the flame of persecution breaking out from time to time showed that the spirit of religious inquiry which Wycliffe had excited was not quenched. But it was not only with those who had adopted Wycliffe's religious opinions that this desire was to be found. Kings and nobles, even the clergy themselves, on different grounds and in different degrees, all concurred in deploring and in professing to desire to remedy the degraded condition of the Church. It was no longer indeed permitted, as it had been to Petrarch and Chaucer, to lash the vices of the clergy, or to hold up their failings to ridicule. But the bitterness which had now succeeded to indifference showed an awakened sense of shame and consciousness of danger.

The most memorable event in the Church-history of the reign of Henry V. was the termination of the schism of the popes,—memorable for the restoration of a power which seemed ruined past recovery, and for the discouragement which it gave to the hopes of reformation. While the schism lasted, there was no great strength of attachment between the state of England and the pontiffs to whom the state adhered. These pontiffs were often in great distress from wars and factions at home; but they feared to levy contributions abroad, lest they should provoke their friends to transfer allegiance to their rivals. Hence they were driven to more pitiful expedients: new festivals were added to a calendar already swollen with days of idleness and superstition; new privileges were granted to monastic and collegiate churches; and the friars busily plied their private trade in papal charters for the comfort of their attendants at the confessional. The fourteenth century had witnessed the addition of many new holy-days, as All Souls after All Saints, the Conception of the Blessed Virgin, and Corpus Christi, a high day for plays and processions. Now Boniface IX., in A.D. 1392, instituted the Salutation of Mary and Elizabeth, 'cram-full of indulgences,' as Walsingham says, for those who should observe it; and Arundel obtained his sanction to raise St. Dunstan's and St. George's days to the rank of the greater festivals—an honour not allowed in all cases to the memory of the Apostles.[1] Now the monks of Bury procured some special indulgences for their shrine of St. Edmund; and those of Ely and Norwich full absolution for all who should come and confess themselves at their churches in Trinity week. And while the fires of Smithfield were burning the unhappy Lollards, the canons of St. Bartholomew, hard by, were advertising their new privileges of pardons for the devout who were guilty of any crime short of heresy.

In the meantime the protection of a pope of doubtful title had very little power in England. Henry IV., soon

---

[1] After the battle of Agincourt, the English Church ordained St. Crispin's day, October 25, to be observed as a greater festival throughout the realm.

after his elevation, had put to death eight or nine friars on a charge of treason.   He had sentenced Archbishop Scroop to the same fate, without even allowing him a trial by his peers.   The abbot of Hayles and other abbots, priests, and monks were either beheaded, or imprisoned and visited with other punishments, to strike terror into the opponents of his power.   And though a bull of excommunication came from Rome against the slayers of the archbishop, and his friends tried to make a martyr of him, these efforts had very little success. It is remarked that Archbishop Scroop was the first prelate who was tried by a lay tribunal since the time of King John. However just or unjust were these sentences—and they appear to have been often attended with circumstances of great barbarity—they are a proof that this monarch did not think the Lollards the only dangerous subjects he had. And they must have taught the Church a bitter lesson for her breach of faith, and credence to the promises of an usurper.

The schism had now continued nearly forty years, and with little mitigation of the disorders in which it had begun.   In the beginning of this century a general council had been convened at Pisa, by which a sentence of deposition had been passed against the two rival popes, and a third, Alexander V., elected in their place, who, dying shortly after, was succeeded by John XXIII. But as the other two refused to resign, the only result of this measure was that there were three prelates at once, each calling himself the pope, and claiming to be the vicegerent of Christ on earth.   In this state of things another council met at Constance in Switzerland, A.D. 1415, with the double object of promoting unity and putting down heresy.   Some Bohemians, who had come into England with the queen of Richard II., had carried back the doctrines of Wycliffe with them.   And they were joined by some English clergymen, particularly one Peter Payne, who is accused of having got up

the Oxford testimonial in favour of Wycliffe.[1] John
Huss, a teacher at the University of Prague, of high
character for learning and private worth, had imbibed
some of these opinions, and publicly maintained them in
his lectures. He had before given offence by other
tenets which touched the national prejudices of the
German students; and this new announcement was
made the signal for his prosecution. When the council
met at Constance, he was summoned to appear; and he
was persuaded to come, under the guarantee of a safe-
conduct from the Emperor Sigismund. The violation
of this safe-conduct is one of the most disgraceful acts
recorded in history.[2] He was seized and imprisoned:
the remonstrance of his friends to the council, and their
appeals to the prince, were equally vain. The emperor
is said to have declared that he would have saved him
if he could; but here, as in England, unknown and
irresponsible persons were able to prevail, and truth and
honour, not to say justice and pity, were overborne.
Huss was required to recant a set of opinions which he
declared he had never held; and though he protested he
was willing to submit to the council, and only desired
that he might not be forced to offend God and his conscience by saying he had professed those errors which it
was never in his mind to profess, he was condemned to
the stake, and burned, A.D. 1416. His friend and associate, Jerome of Prague, who had come to the council

---

[1] Bayle says that Lord Cobham caused Wycliffe's writings to be copied
out by fair writers, and conveyed them himself into Bohemia. It is
possible he might have gone to that country on some state-mission; but
the fact does not appear.

[2] Palma (*Prælect. Hist. Eccl.*, t. iv. c. iii. p. 89) thus writes: 'Est
enim cuique cognitum, salvum conductum a principe tributum, efficere
minime posse, ut ecclesiastica potestas, ab iis exercendis, quæ juris
sui sunt, impediatur.' Such is modern ultramontanism. But the Italian
author of a memoir of Pius II., prefixed to his novel of *Le Duc Amante*,
writes thus: 'Dopo l'assassinio di Giovanni Huss, fatto abbruciar vivo
contro la data fede dai Padri del Concilio di Costanza,' &c.—P. 7 of Pref.
by the Editor.

of his own accord, was also seized ; and though he at first recanted, being brought up again and withdrawing his recantation, he was made soon after to share the same fate.

Another culprit, of higher rank, was accused before the same council, and was for a time the inmate of the same prison with John Huss. This was Pope John XXIII., whose title to the see was maintained by the assembled prelates against his two rivals, Gregory XII. and Benedict XIII., but whose enormous crimes, confessed, as it would appear, by himself, rendered him not so unfit to govern as unfit to live. This miserable man, fearing sentence of deposition by the council, after many dishonest artifices resigned the popedom ; but instead of being punished, as his deeds amply merited, with death or perpetual imprisonment, he was set at liberty, and restored to the rank of cardinal, which he held as long as he lived. It was so much safer, in these unhappy times, for a man to break every precept of the decalogue than to raise his voice against the corrupt doctrines by which such transgressions grew !

It is pleasing to be able to trace any character of better temper, and with any degree of zeal for truth, in such an assembly. And this praise seems due to Robert Hallam, bishop of Salisbury, one of the English representatives both at the Council of Pisa and at Constance, equally celebrated for his eloquence, and for his earnest endeavours to terminate the schism. When Jerome of Prague was brought up for his first examination, and had given offence by one of his answers, so that several of the doctors called out, ' To the fire with him !' the accused answered, with some emotion, ' If my death is what you seek, God's will be done ! ' Hallam took up his words: ' No, Jerome,' he said, ' it is not God's will that any sinner should die, but that he should be converted and live.' It would seem by this speech that he had more mercy in his soul than the majority in that assembly. He died before the conclusion of the council,

and it seems that his death had taken place before the
execution of Huss, for he was not present at the next
session after that where this occurred.[1] He distinguished
himself by the boldness and resolution with which he
enforced upon the council the prosecution of the pope,
saying to a prelate who defended him, that he knew, if
he would speak the truth, that the man deserved a
hundred deaths. And he brought with him to Pisa
and Constance a good plan for reformation, drawn up
by his friend Richard Ullerston, an Oxford man—an
opponent of the Lollards, but very desirous to recover
the Church from its abuses in discipline. This tract
contained sixteen articles, and among the things to be
reformed were—the mode of electing popes, the simony
practised in preferments, the appropriation of churches
to monasteries, exemptions from bishops' jurisdiction,
papal dispensations, appeals to Rome, abuses of privileges, employments of clergy in worldly offices, and
generally the extortions of Church-courts, officers, sum-
moners, and other agents. 'Let the popes,' he said,
'keep within the bounds of their spiritual ministry.
Let things be brought into their natural order, and let
abuses be cut off. Let the pope employ himself, as
befits his charge, in promoting peace among Christians,
in preaching the Gospel himself, and sending everywhere
good preachers, to teach, both by their doctrine and
example, to princes and people, their different duties,
and to make a *holy war* against those passions which
are, as St. James says, the source of wars and divisions
in Church and State.' We see in these articles most of
the evils of which the Lollards complained, admitted to
exist by one who was not their friend. Hallam seems
to have laboured zealously, in concert with the Emperor
Sigismund, to effect this reformation; but his death
interfered. The other English deputies had not the same
spirit; and all the plans of reformation were defeated by

---

[1] April 23, 1415. L'ENFANT, *Conc. de Constance.*

the election of Martin V. to the papal chair, with whose election the schism of the popes was also terminated.

To return to England.   Arundel dying in A.D. 1418, was succeeded by Chicheley, a man of great abilities as a statesman, of great probity in his bishop's office, and of munificent charity; but the persecution continued.   In A.D. 1415, John Claydon and George Gurmyn were burned for heretics; [1] and several others, among whom were many clergymen, were forced to recant.   The circumstances connected with Claydon's trial, as well as with that of a clergyman named Taylor, are remarkable as illustrating the social miseries, jealousies, and distractions introduced by these unhappy laws, and also the way in which persecuting principles. once admitted, may plunge men in crimes even against their will.   It is plain that the bishops would often have spared their victims, had they dared to withstand the clamour of inferior persons.   In A.D. 1414, the University of Oxford published certain 'Articles concerning the Reformation of the Church,' [2] which had been drawn up, as they declare, by the king's express command.   For Henry V., though he adhered to all the dictates of the Church, was resolutely bent on the reformation of its abuses; and is said to have declared, that if the bishops would not reform them, he would take the matter into his own hands.   These articles are exceedingly important, as it is from such documents that we collect the most authentic and least suspicious testimony as to the real condition of the Church.   But, unfortunately, there was one of their proposals which was the most readily adopted and the most fatal to a true reformation.   This was, 'that any bishop who should be remiss in purging his diocese of heretics should be deposed; that civil officers should take an oath to aid the bishops against

---

[1] Foxe calls one of these men Richard Turming; but Mr. Tyler has found the name in the Pipe-Rolls. (Vol. IL 394.)

[2] Concil., lil. 306, ex MS. C.C.C. Oxon.

them; and that all their books and translations should be
put down by law, until proper translations should be
made.' This probably gave rise to the act of parliament
of the same year,' requiring all civil officers to take such
an oath as this, and declaring the forfeiture of all the
property of heretics. We see here the miserable alternative to which the bishops were reduced: they must
persecute to the death or be themselves denounced.
Even when they deferred the trial of Lord Cobham
until they should consult the king, the announcement
was received with murmurs. And, probably, it was this
same pressure of perhaps a few malicious spirits which
led to the cruel constitutions which bear the name of
Archbishop Chicheley, in 1416.² By these it was
ordained that the bishops should twice a year cause
inquiry to be made for heretics in every rural deanery;
and that in every parish where any were suspected,
three or four persons should be sworn to denounce all
who should be known to read suspicious books in English, or to hold private meetings; and those who were
thus denounced might be consigned to perpetual imprisonment, or brought before the convocation to choose
between recantation and the stake　Thus was a kind of
inquisition set up in every parish, and almost in every
family; and it is sad to think what a system of mutual
mistrust, and what an engine of private malice, would
thus be set in motion.

It was after the passing of the act of parliament just
mentioned, but the year before the publication of these
constitutions, that John Claydon was brought before
the bishops by the lord-mayor, who doubtless had taken
the oath which that law required. Claydon was a
tradesman in St. Martin's Lane; and it appears, from
the record of his trial, that he had for twenty years
been a known follower of Wycliffe, had been twice imprisoned—the first time for two years, and then again

---

' 2 Henry V. c. 7.　　　² Conc. iii. 378.

for three more ; after which he recanted ; and to those who had once recanted the law left no escape in case of a second conviction. Three of his apprentices were called in evidence against him, one of whom had left him, and had gone to live with the lord-mayor. The lord-mayor had by these means become acquainted with his habits, and had apprehended him and searched his dwelling; and thus were the members of his own household dragged forth to witness against him. They deposed that two of his friends, with a man who had transcribed his favourite book, *The Lantern of Light,* used to assemble with him to hear it read by another of his servants, and that he expressed his approbation and delight in it. One Sunday the transcriber and the reader were occupied with him from eight in the morning until dusk in correcting the book, and reading parts of it, when it was first transcribed. The chief articles extracted from this book, by a committee appointed to examine it, were—that the pope is antichrist, and that true and faithful priests may preach in spite of the bishops, and without their licence. There was an unfairness in these extracts; for the pope, with his 'false laws,' is there called only one of many antichrists, and the bishops are complained of as hindering all preaching, rather than their authority denied. A less partial censure would have found, what was indeed clear from the evidence, that the book contained other things : for one of the servants remembered to have heard the Ten Commandments read from it in English, and another said that it contained ' the great commandment of our Lord Jesus Christ.'[1] There was no escape—no place for pity—no room for recantation. Betrayed by those

---

[1] The *Lantern of Light* has its title from the text, Psalm cxix. 105. It has been printed, either the whole or in part, more than once, and contains much excellent matter, mixed with such bitterness as persecution creates in the minds of those who suffer by it. Claydon said he heard a good part of it in a sermon preached at Horselydown, in Southwark.

who had eat his bread—convicted of spending the
Lord's-day in reading a religious book with his family
and friends, and of returning to such practices after
having once recanted—the poor man was delivered over
to the secular arm, and committed to the flames.

But this account reveals to us the nature of those
'conventicles and schools' which this persecuted people
were accused of holding: a tradesman and his servants,
with a transcriber and a reader, for he could not read
himself, and two friends,—eight or nine persons at the
most,—listening to a religious book read to them in
his own house. Such meetings could not be held for
the purpose of preaching; and the preaching which
they frequented was that of clergymen who had adopted
their sentiments, and having done so, preached sometimes in churches or chapels, sometimes in churchyards or in the woods, but certainly not often, if at all,
without having been ordained by the bishops.[1] It was
in consequence of such preaching having been held
there, that the church and churchyard of Cowling, and
several others in Lord Cobham's neighbourhood, were
placed under an interdict, so that the daughter of
Lady Cobham by a former husband could not be
married there until it was removed.

The trial of William Taylor, a clergyman, originally
of Quorn, in Leicestershire, further illustrates the hateful system of private information which was now introduced. He was first brought before the convocation
in 1419, three years after Chicheley's inquisitorial
canon, where he abjured and promised to conform.
The next year he was again accused of holding heretical

---

[1] Walsingham says that Claydon had made his own son a priest.
Nothing of this appears in the record of his trial, which is preserved
at great length in Chicheley's Register. It seems to have been a practise
with their opponents to call the Lollard clergymen 'pretended priests,'
or 'pseudo-presbyters;' for these names are given to Sawtrey, Swinderby, and others, who were certainly ordained. In the legal record of
a trial the term would mean no more than that the accused 'professed'
himself a priest, of which the court had no certain evidence.

opinions at Bristol, and was sentenced to perpetual imprisonment; but Chicheley availed himself of an appearance of contrition to obtain a mitigation of his sentence, and he was liberated on bail. It does not appear that he preached any more, but a year had hardly passed when he was again put upon his trial; and the evidence now produced was a letter he had written to a brother-clergyman, a priest at Bristol, of the name of Smyth, in which he showed from Scripture and the Fathers, that we ought to pray to God only, and not to saints. Whether Smyth betrayed him, or by what process his letter fell into the hands of his enemies, does not appear. But it was enough: former offences were now afresh brought up against him, and his life was forfeited to a system more lenient, as we have seen by what passed at Constance, to every imaginable vice, than to the discussion of divine things, or the investigation of the truth.

There is no need to multiply instances. Enough has been already said to show that there were numbers, both among the clergy and people, who had imbibed the love of better things. And the same proofs were still afforded, after the early death of Henry V., and during the long minority of his unfortunate son, till the civil war broke out. In A.D. 1428 Garenter, a priest of London, and Monk, of Melton Mowbray, were brought to a recantation: and White, another priest, was burnt at Norwich. But the most remarkable instance—proving how the principle of persecution, once admitted, may involve its abettors in crimes they would fain avoid—is to be found in the fate of Reginald Peacock, one of the most enlightened defenders of the system which was turned to the ruin of himself. Peacock had been in early life distinguished by the patronage of Humphrey duke of Gloucester, a virtuous and learned prince, whose foul murder prepared the way to all the civil discord and savage warfare in which the house of Lancaster was overthrown. By his influence he appears to have been appointed, in A.D. 1444, bishop of St. Asaph. Being a man of genius and learning, a skilful logician, and eloquent in discourse, he was dissatisfied with the common method taken against the Reforming party; and expressed his opinion, that ' the clergy would be condemned at the last day, if they did not draw men into consent to the true faith otherwise than by fire and sword or hanging.' He therefore began to put out tracts in English, in which he aimed to convince the people that some of their complaints against the Church were unreasonable, and tried to mitigate their violence by palliating those neglects which were but too manifest. With this view he argued, in a sermon at St. Paul's Cross, A.D. 1447, that the bishops may be excused from residence and from preaching, on the ground that they have higher duties in the superintendence and government of the Church. And in pursuance of the same object he published, in A.D. 1449, a book called the *Repressor*, in which he argued against the Lollard notion, that the Bible is the only rule for human conduct in every case, by showing, very truly, that reason is in some things before Scripture, and Scripture grounded upon it. As usual in such cases, his attempt to appease the clamour against the Church, by abstract reasoning, was wholly unsuccessful ; while it raised suspicions against himself among the clergy, that he should appeal to the people's judgment on such deep questions, and argue them in their language.

In the meantime public events tended to increase these suspicions. The people, by whom Duke Humphrey was much beloved, began to rise in tumults after his death ; and two prelates who had held offices about the court fell victims to their resentment. Adam Molins, bishop of Chichester, was murdered by a party of sailors at Portsmouth ; and Ayscough, of Salisbury, the king's confessor, was dragged from his church, and put to death, with circumstances of great barbarity, by

the country-people of his diocese.   It might be with a
view of appeasing the popular indignation that Peacock,
as a friend of the duke whom they deplored, was transferred, in A.D. 1449, to the vacant see of Chichester;
where he still continued his attempts to bring over the
Lollards by argument rather than by persecution.
Among other books, he wrote *A Treatise of Faith*,
in which, not insisting on the infallibility of the Church,
he tried to persuade them that it is reasonable to take
for granted received opinions until they are disproved;
and admitted that though the priest's lips should keep
knowledge, and the people should seek instruction from
his mouth, yet neither pope nor council can add an
article to the creed, or change one that is received,
inasmuch as Holy Scripture is the only ground of faith.
This was too much for the party then ruling in the
Church; and several doctors of both universities undertook to refute him.   The bishops, however, were not
at all forward to proceed against one of themselves, who
had thus stood forth in their defence; and it is probable that no further notice would have been taken of
him, had he not, by some means not sufficiently explained, incurred the displeasure of the king and the
Lancastrian nobility.   It seems they suspected him, as
other friends of Duke Humphrey were suspected, of
favouring the Yorkists.   He was expelled the House of
Lords, and the bishops were ordered to proceed against
him.   It was in vain that he desired his books might
be examined by competent persons.   They were delivered to a committee, to extract from them what they
pleased; and the only alternative in such cases was to
recant whatever they might collect from their writings,
or to be consigned to the stake.   He was accused of
maintaining that our Lord's descent into hell, and the
belief in the Holy Spirit and in the Catholic Church,
are not necessary articles of the creed; and that the
universal Church may sometimes err in points of faith.
The last point he had admitted; but as for the three

former, he had indeed said, and truly, that the article
of the descent into hell was not in the most ancient
copies of the creed; and that, though we ought to
believe the holy Catholic Church, we ought not to say
we believe in the Church, in the same way as we believe in God. But as to the belief in the Holy Ghost,
no vestige of a doubt upon that point exists in his
writings that remain; and it has been remarked, that
the archbishop, Thomas Bourchier, himself omitted
this point in summing up the charges against him.[1]

It was no matter; he must recant these opinions
precisely in the words in which his judges chose to
clothe them, if he would save his life; and he consented
to do so. He was brought to St. Paul's Cross, A.D. 1457,
where twelve years before he had stood forth in defence
of the abuses of that system by which he was thus
requited; and there, in the presence, it is said, of 20,000
people, he acknowledged himself a miserable sinner,
who, trusting to natural reason rather than to the Old
and New Testament, and the authority of our mother,
holy Church, had held and written heresies and errors.
Wherefore he exhorted no man to give credence to
what he had before written, but to bring his books to
be burned.[2] Upon this, several of his writings were
committed to the flames in his presence; and having
afterwards attempted to obtain the interest of the Pope
for the restoration of his see, it seems probable that
the statute of *præmunire* was put in force against him,
for he was consigned to perpetual imprisonment in
Thorney Abbey.

But events were now at hand which cast for a while
into the shade all minor differences, in that terrible
civil war, which has rendered the latter part of the
fifteenth century a mournful page in English annals.
There was little leisure for religious differences, when

---

[1] Lewis's *Life of Peacock.*
[2] *Concil.* iii. 576.

P

every heart was set and every nerve was strained in the murderous conflicts between the Houses of York and Lancaster. At length, when peace was restored, on the accession of Henry VII., A.D. 1485, the religious principles of the Reforming party appear to have been more deeply rooted than ever in the minds of great numbers of the people. And this brings us to the proper place for inquiring what was the actual condition of the Church on the eve of that period, which, in the course of Divine Providence, was destined for its reformation.

CHAPTER XII.

THE CHURCH IN THE FIFTEENTH CENTURY. SCHOOLS AND COLLEGES FOUNDED. DECLINE AND VICES OF MONAS-TERIES.

> Yet still some aged ones are found, in whom
> The old time ebbies tho new; they think it long
> Ere God remove them to a better world.—DANTE.

EVER since the time of Wycliffe, there had been two parties, each of whom was sincerely desirous of a reformation in the Church. Of the opinions of the followers of Wycliffe, and their views of reformation, some account has been given, as well as of their sufferings in consequence. But there was all the while a numerous class of persons, differing entirely from them in their religious views, who were keenly alive to the abuses in the Church, and anxious to see them redressed. It is from the attempts made to redress them from time to time, that we obtain the most authentic and least suspicious testimony to the actual condition of the Church: in the investigation of which testimony we should bear in mind that these abuses were regretted by good men of all shades of religious opinion, and that, in the parties to which they severally adhered, something might still be found to commend as well as something to blame on either side. Wycliffe, indeed, was far beyond his day, and sowed the seeds of precious and saving truths. But the general spirit of discontent which at that time was brooding in the minds of the people mingled itself too much with the opinions of his followers. On the other side were some men of primitive virtue, whose love of order and obedience led them to cling to the religious system which they found, but

whose hearts were deeply imbued with a spirit of
Christianity.[1] William of Wykeham was among the
bishops engaged in suppressing Wycliffe's opinions, and
William of Wainfleet was one of the judges of Bishop
Peacock.   Yet these illustrious men were laying a sure
foundation for the revival of religious truth, in the colleges which they endowed, and were examples, in their
own persons, of ancient simplicity and charity.   The
motives which induced the former of these prelates to
devote his wealth to the foundation of a college, rather
than the erection of a monastery, are recorded by himself: ' Having long resolved to dispose of the wealth
which the Divine providence had abundantly bestowed
upon him to some charitable use for the public good,
he was embarrassed when he came to fix his mind upon
some design that was likely to prove most beneficial,
and least liable to abuse. On this occasion he examined
the various rules of the religious orders, and compared
with them the lives of their several professors; but
was obliged with grief to declare, that he could not
anywhere find that the ordinances of their founders,
according to their true design and intention, were at
present observed by any of them.   This reflection
affected him greatly, and inclined him to take the resolution of distributing his riches to the poor with his
own hands, rather than to employ them in establishing
an institution which might become a snare and an occasion of guilt to those for whose benefit it should be
designed. After much deliberation and devout invocation of the Divine assistance, considering how greatly
the number of the clergy had been of late reduced by
wars and pestilence, he determined to endeavour to
remedy, as far as he was able, this desolation of the
Church, by relieving poor scholars in their clerical
education; and to establish two colleges of students, for
the honour of God, and increase of his worship, for the

---

[1] See CHURTON's *Early English Church*, pp. 375, 376, 2nd edition.

support and exaltation of the Christian faith, and for
the improvement of liberal arts and sciences."[1] In pursuance of this design, he established, about A.D. 1379,
his two colleges at Winchester and Oxford, which
became, as it were, the commencement of a new era in
religious foundations. Among the most conspicuous of
his followers were Archbishop Chicheley, who had been
educated at his colleges, and who became the founder
first of St. Bernard's College (now St. John's), and then,
in 1438, of All Souls'; and William of Wainfleet,
bishop also of Winchester, who, following the same
example, founded Magdalen College, in 1458.[2] Nor
was the benefit of this example confined to Oxford. It
was exactly followed by Henry VI., when he fulfilled
his father's intention as to the disposal of the alien
priories, by the foundation of King's College at Cambridge, and Eton, the nursery of the youth of England,

> Where grateful science still adores
> Her Henry's holy shade.

The acts of other founders during this period fully
confirm the testimony of William of Wykeham, as to
the degeneracy of the monasteries. The earliest instance of one of these foundations being given to a
college, after the alien priories, is that of Selborne
Priory, Hants, which being entirely dilapidated by the
misconduct of its inmates, and in the end forsaken by
both prior and canons, was bestowed by Wainfleet,
with the consent of the Crown and Pope Innocent VIII.,
on his newly-founded Magdalen College.[3] Smyth,
bishop of Lincoln, a few years later, converted the

---

[1] BP. LOWTH's *Life of Wykeham*, pp. 91, 92.
[2] On the mention of the honoured name of William of Wainfleet,
the writer would beg to be permitted to adopt, pro hac vice, the words
of Foxe, who, like himself, was indebted to that good man's bounty:
'For which foundation, as there have been, and be yet, many students
bound to yield grateful thanks to God, so must I needs confess myself
to be one, except I be unkind,'—*i. e. unnatural.*
[3] In A.D. 1484. WHITE's *Selborne*, pt. ii. lett. 24.

friary and another religious house at Lichfield into a
hospital and grammar-school; and purchased a decayed
priory at Cold Norton for his foundation at Brasenose.
The colleges founded by Margaret countess of Richmond,[1] the mother of Henry VII., were partly endowed
out of several decayed monasteries, ruined by the profligate and dissolute lives of the inhabitants; so that
the worthy Bishop Fisher, a good and upright man,
though no friend to the Reformed doctrines, took an
active part in their suppression.[2] He showed that the
brethren of the Hospital of St. John, out of which St.
John's College was erected, 'had ruined themselves by
their lust and riot, sold their plate, mortgaged their
lands, and now were wandering abroad subsisting, as
they might, in total neglect of divine service and of all
their other duties.' A part of the same foundation was
the nunnery of St. Rhadegund, near Cambridge, which
was in an equally deplorable condition. It is mentioned
that the nuns had become notoriously profligate, and
their house was fallen to decay. And two other nunneries, Higham and Bromehall, were for the same
reasons afterwards devoted to the like purpose.

In the last year of his reign, Henry V. had issued
injunctions for the reformation of monasteries, with
directions evidently pointing out the decay of moral
discipline and the license prevalent in many places.
This led to the assembling of a general chapter of the
Benedictine abbeys, the most respectable as well as the
most ancient and well-endowed of these foundations;
and they made some partial reforms. And it seems to

---

[1] St. John's and Christ's Colleges at Cambridge.
[2] STEPHENS' *Appendix to Dugdale*, vol. II.   HYMERS' *Account of
Lady Margaret*, p. 13.   When Fox, bishop of Winchester, was delibe-
rating about the disposal of his wealth, at the beginning of Henry VIII.'s
reign, and thought of founding a monastery, his friend Hugh Oldham,
bishop of Exeter, said to him, 'Beware of what you do; the monks
have already more than they will be able to keep.' He took his advice
and founded Corpus Christi College, Oxford, to which Oldham contributed, A.D. 1516.

have been mercifully provided that they should have remained through the thirty years of civil war, to mitigate in some degree the horrors of that time.   For even in those cruel days the rights of the greater sanctuaries were in some degree respected; and the blood-stained Richard III., though he set guards round Westminster Abbey, to prevent all escape or access of friends to the daughters of Edward IV., who had been placed in refuge there, did not dare to invade that sacred barrier.[1]

When peace was at length restored, and the rival roses united by the marriage of Henry VII. with Elizabeth of York, we do not find that the condition of these houses was improved.   On the contrary, Innocent VIII., in a bull of A.D. 1489, addressed to Archbishop Morton, recites in particular of the Cluniacs, Cistertians, and other later orders, that their ancient rules had been abandoned, and that in many instances the inmates of these walls were living like persons given up to a reprobate sense, who had cast off the fear of God and regard for the opinion of men.   By this bull he gave power to this primate, who was a man of the most upright character, well proved in evil times, to break through all exemptions, and visit all monasteries, with liberty to punish all delinquents, and especially those who had broken their vows.   Thus furnished, the cardinal archbishop proceeded, in the first place, to the visitation of the Benedictine abbey of St. Alban's.

This abbey was one of the most ancient and of best repute, as we have already seen, in all England.   Its revenues were princely, producing at this time between 2000*l.* and 3000*l.* a-year; and the property which had once belonged to it was estimated, two centuries after the dissolution, at the annual value of 200,000*l.*[2]   The

---

[1] *Hist. of Croyland*, contin. p. 587.
[2] WEEVER, *Funeral Monuments.*

abbot had episcopal jurisdiction over all the churches
in the patronage of the abbey; he was lord paramount
of the town of St. Alban's, appointed justices of the
peace, had his own gaol-delivery, and was a lord of
parliament.   The historical and religious recollections
of the place had marked it out for distinction among
the British churches; and one cannot but concur with
Archbishop Morton in lamenting that the seat of such
sacred memorials should ever have been so disgraced.
It would seem that the records of the abbey have
omitted the name of the person under whose presi-
dency these disorders occurred; for they take no notice
of an interval between the death of Abbot Wallingford,
in A.D. 1484, and the installation of Thomas Ramridge,
in A.D. 1492; of whom it is related that he was a pious
and religious man, and that his name was celebrated
for his good works to posterity.[1]   But in this interval,
in A.D. 1489, the abbot was charged with almost every
abuse that he could be guilty of in a station where he
had this great command of wealth and power,—simony
in disposing of his preferment, dilapidation in selling
off the old oaks and profitable timber to the value of
eight thousand marks, neglect of divine service, giving
license to all the members of his society who chose to
live viciously, and persecuting with hatred those who
would have kept their rule.   It was further complained
that in consequence of his conduct his monks were given
up to all kinds of sin, the divine service almost wholly
neglected, and those who were inclined to live religiously persecuted and hated.   Besides this, such was
the old jurisdiction of these abbeys, there were in the
neighbourhood of St. Alban's two nunneries subject to
the abbot as visitor.   It was laid to the charge of this
man, that he had removed all the women of a religious
character out of these houses; that his monks were in
the habit of publicly visiting those who remained; and

---

[1] STEPHENS, *Supplement to Dugdale*, i. 284.

that he had himself appointed as prioress of the nunnery of Delapré a married woman, whose name is given, who had long been separated from her husband and was living in adultery.[1] These charges appear to have been proved before the archbishop; and they relate to the discipline of one of the chief abbeys in the kingdom. They prove indisputably the effects produced by those papal exemptions, which these religious orders had so eagerly purchased; and such proofs might be multiplied from other records of the like judicial and solemn process. They show that the corruption in morals was not, as some would make us believe, a fiction of Lollard libels or Protestant histories, but one that should convey its lesson to all surviving generations:

> To teach us that God attributes to place
> No sanctity, if none be thither brought
> By men who there frequent, or therein dwell.

At the same time, therefore, that we receive with distrust some of the particulars reported by Henry VIII.'s visitors, we may see evidence enough in memorials taken before the dissolution was thought of, and in the acts of such men as Wainfleet and Fisher, to prove that some great moral change was considered desirable by the wisest and most moderate men of the fifteenth century. The report of the antiquary Leland is equally unfavourable against the learning of these houses. It is true that, after the invention of printing, the abbeys of Glastonbury, Westminster, St. Alban's, and Tavistock established printing-presses; but the scribes that were before employed in the great abbeys in copying manuscripts, now were generally discontinued; and the manuscripts themselves were perishing by neglect. Dust and damp were obliterating the stores of past ages: and it is probable that, had the monasteries been spared, they would have left decay to do the work

---

[1] WILKINS, *Concil.* lil. 630, 632, A.D. 1489, 90, Hen. VII. 5, 6.

which was afterwards done with more heat and haste in the disorders of the Reformation.[1]

There were certainly many of these houses which were to the last assiduous in their religious services, exercising hospitality and charity on a large scale, and maintaining a good number of scholars in their schools and at the universities. The preamble of the act of Henry VIII. for dissolving the smaller monasteries bore witness that religion was well observed and kept up in the greater.[2] Even the visitors appointed under that act found several which they reported as conducted in the most exemplary manner. And if we look to facts, we find no instance in which these monks were convicted or punished for the crimes laid to their charge. Our evidence of the state of these houses, therefore, is not taken from the popular reports at the time of their suppression, but from records and historical memoirs written before they were suppressed, and by persons who harboured no intention to suppress them. There is quite enough to show that the time when they had been good schools of religious discipline was past; and as their numbers fell off, and public opinion shifted against them, they did not take warning. Gross delinquencies among them were of no uncommon occurrence; vices were indulged which naturally flow from 'pride, fulness of bread, and abundance of idleness,' and these both in the sons and daughters of the monastic system.[3]

---

[1] Leland and Gascoigne, quoted by Bale.
[2] 27 Hen. VIII., c. 28.
[3] The nunnery of Rumsey, in Hampshire, was founded by Edward the Elder, and enlarged by King Edgar in the tenth century. It was one of the richest in the kingdom, endowed with lands and tithes; and many of the inmates were of noble families; for in those days it was a common way with persons of the highest rank to provide for the younger daughters of a large family by making nuns of them. The vice of drunkenness seems to have been the besetting sin of this house. The abbess, Clementina Guilford, in A.D. 1315, appears to have been poisoned, or to have died of drink. And Joyce Rowe, another abbess, A.D. 1506, was accused before Bishop Fox of inviting the nuns every

These vices were probably still more frequent among
the friars, whose discipline was such as to subject them
to less restraint. It is on record that a Franciscan, in
A.D. 1424, had the effrontery to preach in St. Mary's
Church, in Stamford, that incontinence in a member of
a religious order is no mortal sin. He was, indeed,
cited before the convocation, and compelled to retract in
the same church; but the fact points out something of
the state of morals, which occasioned him to hazard
such a public declaration.

Nor ought we to forget that these places were, as they
were justly considered by many of the Reformers, the
nurseries of corrupt superstition. And it is superstition
which is the stronghold of intolerance and persecution.
The soul cannot live without some kind of religion;
but as the worship of false gods perverted the moral
sense of the heathen, so they who were taught to pray to
the Virgin and the saints became corrupt in their imagi-
nations, and stern and cruel to those who would have
called them to a purer worship. It has seldom been
found that the religion of a persecutor was anything
better than a devotion to a name or form. Archbishop
Arundel, after he had seen the establishment of successful rebellion in A.D. 1399, immediately obtained the
new king's consent to a decree, that a morning-bell
should toll daily in every church in England at day-
break, and that at that sound every one should offer
the same prayers to the Virgin, to whom they attributed
their success, as were already appointed for the evening
hour.[1] The controversy between the Franciscans and

<hr/>

night after compline to drink with her in her chamber; and she was
herself habitually addicted to strong potations. Marmaduke Huby,
the last abbot of Fountains, in a MS. letter to Lord Dacre. A.D. 1524.
says that the nuns of his order for the last two hundred years had
'remissly kept their vow.'

[1] If this be the origin of the morning-bell, which still sounds in many
churches, it is remarkable that it should have been meant to preserve
the memory of a revolution no less disastrous in its results than that
which the curfew calls to mind. See WILKINS, Concil. III. 1 Hen. IV.

Dominicans, on the Immaculate Conception, has been already referred to. Although the decree of the Council of Basil, A.D. 1439, in favour of this doctrine, was not recognised at Rome, it was adopted by a Gallican synod at Avignon, A.D. 1457, and the University of Paris caused all who took degrees to subscribe to it. Still the controversy continued, so that Sixtus IV., A.D. 1476, ordained that none should say it was wrong or sinful to maintain it.[1] The growth of this superstition had been gradual. We find it on the increase in the twelfth century, when St. Bernard took some pains to prevent some such festival as this from being adopted by the clergy of Lyons, though his own veneration for the Virgin was not free from superstition. The Saxon hermits and holy men, who were resorted to by the common people after the Conquest, committed her name to short hymns and prayers in verse. By degrees her altars and her images outshone those of other saints; and almost in every church the worshippers were reminded by outward signs of the value of her intercession. Frauds and fables followed next. At Walsingham, in Norfolk, she was said to work constant miracles, and consequently there was no place which attracted greater multitudes of pilgrims. The most strange titles were given to her, which the figures and types of Scripture, or an unchastened fancy, could supply:—the burning bush seen by Moses, the reconciler of the old law and the new, the window of heaven, the gate of paradise, the throne of the Trinity; or the brightest rose, the fairest lily, the light of love and beauty, and queen of courtesy. These were commonly sung in her English praises; but there was also often written on the walls of churches dedicated to her a Latin hymn to the following purpose:—

Maid and mother, raised on high,
Guard us from above the sky;
Virgin, pray for us!

---

[1] LAMBERTINI de Festis, p. 460.

She the wound of sin can close,
She, heav'n's flower, our sorrow knows;
    Mary, pray for us!

Star of ocean, help us now,
Turn on us thy gentle brow;
    Mary, pray for us!
By her gift salvation's given,
She can ope the gate of heaven;
    Virgin, pray for us!

Maid and mother, ever pure,
From temptation shield us sure;
    Mary, pray for us!
She the port in all distress,
From the world's unfaithfulness;
    Virgin, pray for us!

Gabriel's daughter, duly praised,
Listen to our voice upraised;
    Virgin, pray for us!
By thy Son, on thee we call,
Virgin Mother, help us all;
    Mary, pray for us!'

When Wycliffe preached against some of these de-
pravations, he said, with a full sense of the unpalatable
nature of his doctrine, ' I wot well that this belief
winneth not the penny.' It is marvellous what wealthy
gifts were poured in to such places as Walsingham, and
Becket's shrine at Canterbury. Of this last we have a
particular description from a distinguished eyewitness,
who saw it a short time before it was destroyed,—
Erasmus of Rotterdam. After speaking of an old altar
of the Virgin, ' where the holy man was said to have
bidden her his last farewell, and the sword by which
his skull was said to have been cut open,' he proceeds
as follows :—' Hence we went into the crypt, where is
exhibited the martyr's skull, pierced through, all covered
with silver, except the crown, which is left bare for the
devout to kiss. There also hung in darkness the hair
shirt, the girdle, and small clothes which the prelate
wore to subdue the flesh; things which it made one

' The Latin is in WEAVER, *Fun. Mon.*

shudder to look upon, and upbraiding us for the soft-
ness and delicacy of our times. Hence we returned to
the choir, and saw a wonderful quantity of bones —
skulls, jaws, teeth, hands, fingers, and arms—all to be
kissed with devout reverence; which were brought
from some closets on the north side. Then we viewed
the altar-table and its ornaments; and afterwards the
treasures stored under the altar—such a store, that if
you saw them, you would say they beggared Midas and
Crœsus. After this we were led into the vestry, where,
amidst a splendid show of silken vestments and golden
candlesticks, we saw the saint's crosier, a slender rod
overlaid with silver, of very little weight, no remarkable
workmanship, and little more than a yard long. There was
also his pall, of silk, but coarse in the thread and not orna-
mented with gold or jewels of any kind. Then there
was a napkin, or handkerchief, with marks of sweat and
blood still visible, which were the stains occasioned by
its having been worn about his neck. These things
were not shown to everybody; but I had some acquaintance with the archbishop, William Warham, who
gave me two or three words of introduction to the
monks of the cathedral. We were therefore led into
the higher parts of the church behind the high altar,
going up by steps into a kind of new chapel. There
we were shown an image of the eminent saint all gilded
over, and adorned with many gems.'

The companion' of Erasmus on this occasion, gave
offence by suggesting that some of these treasures
might with advantage be given to the poor; and he
himself, while he allows that they were perhaps as well
bestowed as if they'had been squandered by the donors
in wars or gambling, concludes with an expression of
regret, that there was now no disposition to imitate the

' Under the Latin name of 'Gratiosus Pullus,' Mr. Nichols, in his
edition of *Erasmus's Pilgrimages to Walsingham and Canterbury*,
seems to have proved that Dr. John Colet, the famous Dean of St.
Paul's, is intended.

good example of those bishops of earlier time, who had sold the holy vessels in a time of distress, and succoured the poor with the money. He goes on to describe the sight of Becket's coffin, in which, together with his bones, was packed a rich casket of jewels, the presents of kings and princes accumulated during three centuries; and a chapel of the Virgin in the crypt, secured by a double iron railing, which seems to have been the richest treasury of all. Within a few years more, shortly before Erasmus died, all these riches were scattered by Henry's prodigality: and the most splendid jewel of them all, called the Royal of France, presented by Louis VII. in A.D. 1179, was set in the monarch's seal-ring, where it seems to be represented in some of Holbein's pictures.

What drew so many gifts to Canterbury and Walsingham was, doubtless, the reputation which these places enjoyed for miracles. Those which came nearest to them in this respect were St. Alban's, St. Edmund's at Bury, and St. Ethelburga's at Barking. But there were others in the more remote districts;—the Northcountrymen had their saints, and the Welsh had theirs. Were these miracles always frauds practised on the public credulity? It seems harsh to pronounce such an opinion. The probability is, that in times when the imagination was so little under control from the reason, it had the power to effect more on the bodily system. Physicians well know, that in many cases the operation of medicine will do little without the aid of the fancy and influence of the mind upon the body. Nervous disorders, as they are called, no doubt existed in earlier ages under a different name; and these disorders are not altogether unreal, because they have so much to do with the imagination. But in cases of real disease, a strong persuasion has often been found as effectual as medicine to cause or to remove the malady. There is a remarkable story of an experiment of this kind, which was entirely successful, when loyalty, and not religion, gave it its healing power. It was at the famous siege of Breda, in A.D. 1625, when the garrison was dreadfully afflicted with the scurvy. The Prince of Orange hearing of their distress, and fearing lest they should surrender the place, wrote letters to the men promising them speedy relief, and accompanied with medicines, said to be of great value and of greater efficacy. The quantity was very small; but more was promised. In the meantime the physicians, who were in the secret, divided these medicines among them, and gave it out that three or four drops out of a small phial were enough to impart a healthful virtue to a gallon of liquor. The effects of the delusion were wonderful: the soldiers flocked in crowds to ask for the prince's remedy:—some recovered instantly; and many, who had been deprived of the use of their limbs for a month before, were seen walking about the streets, sound and straight, and perfectly whole.[1]

But that there were also many impostures practised admits of no reasonable doubt. Sir Thomas More tells the well-known story of the sham-miracle at St. Alban's as related to him by his father.[2] This story is perfectly authentic, as told with admirable effect by Shakspeare,[3] who does full historical justice to all the characters present, more especially the simple and somewhat credulous piety of Henry VI., and the shrewdness of good Duke Humphrey. The records of the time have preserved the same account, from which Shakspeare evidently derived it; of a fellow who imposed upon the king by pretending to have been born blind, and to have obtained his sight by touching St. Alban's bones. But Duke Humphrey convicted him of falsehood, by making him tell the colour of every man's dress, and thus showing that he could not have been

---

[1] Dr. LIND on the Scurvy. From Vander Mye, a Dutch physician present at the siege.
[2] Sir T. MORE's Works, ed. 1557, p. 134.
[3] King Henry VI., Part II.

blind before. There is no proof of any concert with
the monks in this case; the wretched knave seems to
have done it of his own impulse to obtain public com-
miseration. But we must judge differently of two or
three other cases on record. The blood of Hayles Abbey,
a relic deposited there in the thirteenth century as the
true blood of Our Lord, appears to have been afterwards
changed by the monks for clarified honey, with which
they deceived the people by some optical deception.
The rood of grace, as it was called, at Boxley in Kent,
was a piece of mechanism moved by wires, by which
the features of the image were made to frown or smile.[1]
The first of these impostures is like that for a long time
exhibited at Naples,—the blood of St. Januarius. A
fraud like the last seems to have been attempted in
Majorca at the time of the expulsion of the Jesuits, in
A.D. 1768, when an image of the Virgin at a church in
Palma was said to have moved the posture of her arms
in token of displeasure. There is some contradiction in
the accounts of these cheats; but the fact is not easily
disproved.

Robert Whitgift, the uncle of the able Archbishop
Whitgift, was the head of a small Austin priory at
Wellow, in Lincolnshire. Here his nephew was educated under him—for the place was a kind of school;
and he is said to have told the future primate that he
was well aware these houses must be broken up—that
their religion, as it then was, was not according to the
Gospel.[2] On the whole, the monastic system had lost
that rank in public opinion, which is often the surest
defence of established institutions. A law of Henry
VI.[3] recites the complaint of the Abbey of Fountains,
that the bailiffs of the several manors in which they had
property conspired to cite the abbot on the same day
to all their courts, in order that, not being able to attend,

[1] See WORDSWORTH's *Eccl. Biog.* ii. 279-281.
[2] *Life of Whitgift*, by SIR G. PAULE, p. 3.
[3] 33 Hen. VI. c. vi.

Q

he might be fined for default.   Such affronts would not
have been offered to the lordly abbot a century before;
and they indicate a remarkable change in the public
sentiments.

One circumstance which tended to bring the privileges of the ecclesiastical foundations into contempt,
was the abuse of the rights of sanctuary.   A bull of
Innocent VIII., A.D. 1487,[1] which restricts some of
these privileges, recites that ' there are certain ecclesiastical places in England which have such immunity,
that whatever malefactors, (whatsoever homicides, incendiaries, sacrileges, thefts, and other offences they
may have committed,) also public robbers, and traitors
resorting thither, and there remaining, cannot be dragged
from thence.   But not only so, they go out from thence
to commit other depredations, and return there, knowing that justice cannot overtake them.'   The knights of
St. John appear to have carried their claim of privilege
to an intolerable height.   Their priests took upon them
to grant absolution to whom they pleased, so that even
the excommunication of a bishop might be set at nought
by those who had the favour of these proud and turbulent ecclesiastics, who were all required to be of
noble birth, and whose grand-prior sat in parliament
next after the princes of the blood.   To such an extent
did their priests abuse their power of celebrating marriages in their churches, that complaint was made by a
bishop, in A.D. 1488, that persons thus got married contrary to divine and canon law, often while a suit was
pending respecting such marriage.[2]   In the time of
Henry VIII. their churches had obtained the name of
' lawless churches,' and were the customary resort for
clandestine marriages.

The condition of the seats of learning and of the
foundations for the poor and sick seems to have been
equally deplorable.   In the year 1421, an act of par-

---

[1] *Concil.* III. 621.   [2] Cf. *Concil.* III. 625, III. 724.

liament[1] recites that many scholars and clerks of Oxford,
armed and arrayed in manner of war, have oftentimes
put out divers persons of their lands and tenements in
Oxfordshire, Berkshire, and Buckinghamshire; and
hunted with dogs and greyhounds in divers parks,
warrens, and forests in the said counties, as well by
day as by night, and taken deer, hares, and conies, and
threatened the keepers with their lives, and rescued convicted clerks out of the hand of their ordinaries. A
short time before this, a law of the same reign recites
that many hospitals which were endowed to sustain impotent men and women, lazars, poor women with child,
and the like, are now for the most part decayed, and the
goods and profits of the same, by divers persons, as well
spiritual as temporal, withdrawn and spent otherwise,
whereby many men and women have died in great
misery for default of aid and succour.[2] And the Oxford Articles of the same reign accuse the masters and
wardens of diverting these goods to their own use. It
is too true that this imputation does not belong to their
times alone. And this information is obtained through
the vigorous attempts of a great monarch who was
nobly intent on their reformation. But our object is to
draw from authentic sources a picture of the times
before the Reformation, in order that we may not have
to seek our authority from those who may be thought
to have been interested in darkening the picture.

---

[1] 9 Henry V. c. 8.　　　　[2] 2 Henry V. c. 1.

CHAPTER XIII.

CONDITION OF THE PAROCHIAL CLERGY IN THE FIFTEENTH
CENTURY. POWER OF THE POPES AND THEIR CHARACTER.

> Alas! of fearful things
> 'Tis the most fearful when the people's eye
> Abuse hath cleared from vain imaginings,
> And taught the general voice to prophesy
> Of Justice arm'd and pride to be laid low.'
>   WORDSWORTH, *Eccl. Sketches*, II. ix.

IN pursuance of the same object as in the preceding
chapter, the condition of the parochial clergy must
now claim our attention ; and it was sufficiently deplorable, whether we consider the misconduct of the
wealthier incumbents, or the abject situation and the
ignorance of the inferior clergy.

It was among the complaints of the Oxford University, in the articles of reformation before referred to, in
the reign of Henry V., that prelates are not ashamed to
give the cure of souls to their young relations and
beardless companions, and that it tends to the subver-
sion of the Church that youths, like insolent squires, not
distinguished from laymen by dress or tonsure, occupy
prebends and chapels in the church. They proceed to
complain of those who live away from their cure, devoted only to pleasure and gain, and spend their time in
cities or in the courts of lords, intent only upon their
banquets and their cups. 'And whereas very few are
able, and they hardly, to rule a single cure, or their
own souls, as will be known at the last trump, nowa-
days 'tis wondrous how so many thoughtless persons,
panting after worldly lust rather than the safety of souls,
dare to accumulate to themselves so many benefices.'
And the luxurious habits of these semi-clerical persons

is thus again adverted to: 'Clergy in name alone, knights or soldiers in dress, in reality neither, they would fain belong to both classes, and are deserters and confounders of both.' A similar complaint was made by the convocation, in A.D. 1460, that many of the clergy dress like gallants, with scarlet collars to their doublets; and what is still more remarkable is that many of these persons are said, in a constitution of Archbishop Bourchier about the same time, to have been actually not ordained, or suspended from their orders. And a little later, the good Archbishop Warham, the predecessor of Cranmer, complains, A.D. 1529, that priests and clerks in sacred orders are not ashamed to go about publicly like laymen, with hounds in leash and hawks in hand. The higher clergy indeed were very generally given to these pursuits. Complaint was made in A.D. 1414 that bishops and archdeacons go their visitations with an excessive retinue, which those whom they visit have to maintain, and take money which is called procuration from some clergymen to be excused the expense of their visits. And it is recorded that an archdeacon of Richmond once came to Bridlington Priory, in the course of his visitation, with ninety-seven horses, twenty-one dogs, and three hawks.[1]

We have an instance of one of those youthful pluralists of high family, in the case of Fitzhugh, dean of Lincoln, about A.D. 1510. He had a papal bull to hold any benefice short of a bishopric at the age of sixteen; and held, with his deanery, the rectory of Bingham in Nottinghamshire, with the canonry of Whitington, Kirby Ravensworth, and Bedale in Yorkshire, Wintringham in Lincolnshire, a prebend in Lincoln Minster, and the mastership of Pembroke Hall in Cambridge. At a visitation of the cathedral by Bishop Smyth about this time, the dean's attendants were accused of breaking the windows and damaging the roof of the Minster

---

[1] DUGDALE, *Monasticon*, ii. 66.

with their arrows and crossbows; and it was shown
that a gentleman of his retinue had a chamber adjoining one of the chantries, to which the chaplains resorted
to play at dice and cards till past midnight.[1]   The situation of a chaplain, whether in a cathedral town or in a
nobleman's family, seems to have been sought as an exemption from residence.   For, a century before this,
complaint had been made that the clergy got themselves
made chaplains, and pretended exemption from residence, ' when in truth they would rather enjoy their
cups and their ease in towns and cities, than serve
churches with cure of souls.'[2]

It must be confessed that the inducements held out
to those who continued in the parochial cure were of
the smallest possible kind.   The stipends of curates
were limited by law, and might in no case exceed ten
marks per annum.   The tithes of many parishes were
appropriated to monasteries, and vicars maintained at
the lowest stipends : in some instances the tithes were
devoted to the supply of the bishop's table.   Lay patrons
were not slow to follow these examples, by exacting all
sorts of simoniacal contracts.   And the consequence
was that the country clergy fell into a deplorable state
of ignorance and poverty.   The University of Oxford
complained that all were so full of avarice that bishops
would put in their own relations under age into livings, that they might reserve part to themselves; that
presentations and impropriations were sold; that the
appropriation of the tithes of parishes to monasteries
and to bishops' tables caused desolation to the parishes,
deprived the poor of their alms, and caused the cure of
souls to be neglected : that in some cases the whole
tithes were appropriated, leaving only a stipendiary
priest removeable at will, and others were endowed with
so small a stipend that the vicar could not live.   Before

---

[1] ARCHDEACON RALPH CHURTON's *Life of Bishop Smyth.*
[2] *Concil.* III. 335.

this, Archbishop Courtenay, in A.D. 1391, complained of those whom he called 'chop-churches,' who by exchanges and other frauds reduced the curates to poverty, and of others who made those who were inducted take an oath to them to receive no emolument, and to resign when called upon; so that when Wycliffe assigned, as a reason why his 'poor priests' have no benefices, that they were afraid of simony, and that none could obtain livings without some simoniacal contract, there seems to have been some ground for his assertion.[1]

But that which tended most of all to the ruin of the parochial clergy was the system of provisors; by which persons who had been presented to livings by the patrons were ejected by others, who during the life of a former incumbent had obtained what was called a provision from the pope to succeed on the next vacancy. For the pope claimed to present to all the livings in Christendom, as well as to the bishoprics, by divine right; and as these provisions were openly sold, under the plea of *providing* for the Church, it entailed upon the parochial clergy a system of constant and ruinous litigation. It seems to have been the ruinous consequences of this system to which reference is made in the following words, with which the University concluded their list of the grievances of the Church: 'Simple vicars and curates are oppressed by force and violence, and maliciously indicted on false accusations by hired testimony; and while the innocent blood is shed, the simplicity of many priests does not procure legal remedy for fear of being put to death; but either they buy off these unjust vexations with the goods of

---

* See BARCLAY's *Ship of Fools*, p. 59:—

> Courtiers become priests, nought knowing but the dice,
> They priest not for God, but for a benefice,
> The clarke of the kitchen is a priest become,
> In full trust to come to promotion high,
> Nothing by virtue, cunning, or wisdom,
> But by covetise, practise, and flattery.

the Church, or are compelled for fear of their lives to
give up the care of their flocks, and fly the country.'
Many laws indeed were made both against appropriations and papal provisions. In the time of Richard II.
it was enacted that in every case of appropriation of
the tithes of any parish to a monastery, or otherwise,
the bishop should ordain a fit sum to the poor, and
a proper and sufficient endowment to the vicar;[1] and
this law was confirmed and enlarged by an act of
Henry IV.[2] which complains that the monasteries put
monks into their livings unfit for the parochial ministry.
But it was for the purpose of evading these laws that
the wholesale system of simoniacal contracts was introduced, which we have above described. More effectual
means were sometimes taken to shelter those who had
obtained papal provisions against the laws of the land.
For an act was passed by Henry IV. to pardon all who
had obtained preferments by such means, and allow them
'to put their grace in execution;'[3] that is, to avail
themselves of the pope's gift. But the vigorous hand of
his son was exerted to defend the actual possessors, and
in his reign it was enacted that all should enjoy their
livings, and no provisors be suffered to eject them.[4]

The degraded condition of the parochial clergy, consequent upon this state of things, is evinced by the
following complaint of Archbishop Bourchier, A.D. 1455.
He declares that there are priests in his diocese who are
perfect strangers, bringing with them no recommenda-
tions, nor letters of orders: and some of them so illiterate as to be not only unlearned, but hardly to know
how to read.[5] And at another time complaints were
made that foreigners, ignorant even of the English language, were promoted to the best preferments. Some

---

[1] 15 Rich. II. c. 6. See before, p. 174.
[2] 4 Henry IV. c. 12, A.D. 1402.
[3] 11 Henry IV. c. 10.
[4] 3 Henry V. c. 4.
[5] 33 Henry VI. A.D. 1455. *Concil.* III. 574.

of the more vigorous bishops, as William of Wainfleet and Smyth bishop of Lincoln, sometimes took an oath of those whom they ordained, that they would learn Latin, the very language in which all the services were which they had to perform. But it was in vain that the Church of England made regulations, when the Court of Rome would often admit those to orders who had been rejected at home as ignorant and unworthy.[1] Nay, it appears from the records of the Council of Constance, that several incumbents had dispensations from the pope, sometimes for seven years, sometimes for life, to excuse them from entering into such orders as were requisite to qualify them for their function.[2] It would not be expected that such ministers would have an elevated view of their calling, or propose an elevated standard to their people. But if we are astonished at the degraded nature of some of their teaching, let us hope that these are the worst instances, and let us remember that we should not have known them at all but for the attempts of those in authority to provide a remedy.

It does not appear that such exhibitions as the Feast of Fools, and the like, had been discontinued since the time of Wycliffe; for in a proclamation of Henry VIII., A.D. 1541, mention is made of childish observances yet to this day observed and kept in sundry parts of this realm : 'Children be strangely decked and apparelled to counterfeit priests, bishops, and women; and so led from house to house, misleading the people and gathering of money; and boys do sing mass and preach in the pulpit, with other unfitting usages, rather to the derision than to any true glory of God.' But perhaps the most extraordinary instance of this kind of abuse is the celebration of what was called 'Glutton Mass.' We learn from an order against it, made when Repington

---

[1] *Concil.* III. 361.
[2] RYMER, tom. ix. p. 337, quoted by Collier.

was bishop of Lincoln, that a custom then prevailed in
the deanery of Leicester, of celebrating early in the
morning, during the five days of the Feast of the Annunciation, a 'glutton mass;' the curates of all the
churches in the deanery going about from one to the
other in turn, and encouraging the people, instead of
attending matins or high-mass, to give themselves up
to eating and drinking in the pothouses of the town.[1]
These were acknowledged abuses, and let us hope not
of frequent occurrence. But the provision that was
made to supply the ignorant priests with subjects for
their sermons does not improve our view of the case.
A book of festivals was published[2] in the reign of
Henry VII., professedly 'for the help of clerks to excuse them for default of books,' containing sermons for
festivals, after the fashion of our homilies. In one of
these, in the office for the dedication of churches, the
following story is told to deter the people from irreverent
behaviour in the house of God : 'That St. Austin saw
two women prating together in the pope's chapel, and
the fiend sat in their necks writing a great roll of what
the women talked ; and letting it fall, Austin went and
took it up, and asking the women what they had said all
mass time, they answered, "Our Pater-noster." Then
Austin read the roll, and there was never a good word
in it.' In the same book a story is told, to deter
people from stealing, of a man dying excommunicated,
who had stolen an abbot's ox, and his spirit walked by
night and came and besought the priest to go with his
wife to the abbot, and pray him to assoil him, that so
he might rest : ' And anon the abbot assoiled him, and
he went to rest and joy for evermore.' We are not so
much surprised that such things should be believed by
the vulgar in rude times; but that which is surprising
is, that they should be taught from the pulpit, and such
teaching provided by authority.

---

[1] WILKINS, *Concil.* iii. 389.
[2] STATPS, *Eccl. Mem.* pt. i. p. 213, Oxford edit.

It is impossible here to enter upon the scandal which meets us in every page of the Church-history of these times, arising from the unhappy endeavour to enforce celibacy not only on the inmates of monasteries, but on the parochial clergy. It seems to have given rise to what are called left-handed marriages to such an extent, that the practice was not merely connived at, but in one instance declared to be expedient.[1] A similar opinion is related by a celebrated French ecclesiastic as being general in France;[2] and the Oxford divines, assuming such unions to be unlawful, complain of the scandal arising from them, and the bad example to other evil persons.[3] But it is an odious task to investigate such matters. Let us thank God that such times are past, and let us take warning how vain it is to enforce by legal sanction those high and self-devoted qualities, which, to be acceptable or praiseworthy, must be spontaneous.

And yet, amidst this obscurity of Divine Truth, and this corruption in practice, some vestige remained of purer doctrine, as well as some examples of holier practice. The bidding of beads, or the bidding of prayer, was always used in English, and preserved a remnant of the glorious intercession of the ancient liturgy of Jerusalem. A priest of Malines, in the Low Countries, known by his Latin name of Pupperius, who died A.D. 1486, published several works now proscribed by the Church of Rome, in which he maintained 'the free justification of a sinner by the Blood of Christ.' And it is related of Ernest, Archbishop of Magdebourg, that when a Franciscan friar came to him on his death-bed, and bade him not fear, 'for we communicate to you all the good works not only of ourselves but our whole order, and therefore doubt not but you receiving them shall appear before the tribunal of God righteous

---

[1] By a Council at Toledo in Spain, as quoted by DUPIN.
[2] Nicholas de Clamengo, Canon of Langres, in BROWNE's *Fasciculus*.
[3] *Concil.* lii. 864.

and blessed;' the good man replied to this hollow com-
forter, ' By no means will I rely upon my own works or
yours, but the works of Jesus Christ alone shall suffice;
upon these will I repose myself.' It may be thought a
doubtful instance of improvement in religious feeling to
mention that Henry VII. was accustomed to engage, by
an annual payment, any good men whose prayers he
valued, to pray for himself and his family. Yet certainly none can blame the pious desire to be remembered in good men's prayers. Who would not covet
them? And it may have been much the same as asking
the prayers of those who partook of his bounty. It may
be added, that the few chantries which were now
founded had schools attached to them, at which the
mass-priests were to teach grammer freely to poor
scholars. Such was the case in a chantry provided by
the Princess Margaret,[1] and in a hospital at Lichfield,
endowed by Bishop Smyth. The beautiful prayer provided by this good bishop for the use of the inmates of
his hospital, is wholly free from anything inconsistent
with the simplicity of primitive worship.

Plain it is, however, that through the whole of the
fifteenth century the one obstacle to the hopes of all
good men for a reformation in the Church, was the
power and the claims of the popes. It was in vain that
patriotic laws were made to curb the usurped interference of a foreign bishop in the disposal of the preferments of the Church, when he had no scruple in
setting those laws aside, and often was but too successful in doing so. It might be supposed that after the
stringent laws against papal provisions in the reigns of
Edward III. and Richard II., no Englishman would
dare to accept them, even though the Pope should
attempt it. But in the reign of Henry V., as soon as
the Council of Constance had terminated the schism,
Pope Martin promoted, on his own authority, no less

---

[1] Bishop Fisher's Funeral Sermon on the Lady Margaret.

than fourteen persons to various bishoprics in the province of Canterbury alone. For the kings were accustomed to connive at this irregularity, in order to evade the legitimate influence of the cathedral chapter. They found it convenient to make a compact with the pope, by means of which the electors were often obliged by him to chose their nominee. The clergy would in some instances resist it; as the dean and chapter of York, in the fourth year of Henry VI., when Martin V. having by his bull preferred Richard Fleming, bishop of Lincoln (who burnt Wycliffe's bones), to the archbishopric of York, they refused to elect him to the see, and the pope was forced to submit, and send him back to Lincoln. But again, in A.D. 1438, Pope Eugene actually gave the bishopric of Ely *in commendam* to the French archbishop of Rouen; and after some resistance, this foreigner was allowed to enjoy the revenues. A sad perversion truly of the original purpose of a commendam, which was that, when a religious house was ill-conducted, the pope would *commend* the care of it, for a while, to some pious bishop who should restore its discipline!

And it was the same source which poisoned the religion itself of the countries over which its influence extended. How much the friars had to do with the abuse of the confessional, and how entirely their power to abuse it was derived from Rome, we have already seen. But one should hardly have expected to find that the popes themselves would not only sanction but enjoin the betrayal of its secrets. Yet this was done in the reign of Henry VII., who obtained a general order from Pope Innocent VIII., that all confessors should deliver to him the confessions of as many lords as he pleased, written out, with an attestation subjoined on oath, that nothing more had been confided to them than they had delivered[1] And this is said to have

---

[1] SIR H. ELLIS, vol. I. letter 63.

been one of the ways by which that monarch contrived
to obtain such accurate information of all conspiracies
against his government. But such treachery derives,
if possible, a darker hue from the fact, that it was
directly at variance with the solemn denunciation of
the Church; for it had been determined, by the fourth
Lateran council, that whoever should reveal the secrets
of the confessional should not only be deposed from the
ministry, but consigned to perpetual imprisonment in
the dungeon of a monastery.

Meantime the attempts which had been made to
emancipate Christendom from this spiritual tyranny
were by no means confined to a single nation.   Charles
VII. of France established the *Pragmatic Sanction* in a
parliament of his kingdom at Bourges, A.D. 1438, by
which the principles assumed by the Council of Basle
were made the law of France.   For twenty-three years
after this the Church of France was free from all payments to the pope, elected her own prelates, and ordained her own clergy.   If the pope should constrain
any clergyman to pay anything to him, he might appeal
to a general council; and any who should collect his
taxes were to be fined and imprisoned.   Pius II. succeeded for a time in getting this law suspended; but
it was re-enacted by Louis XI. with additional clauses
—such as that no clergymen should go to Rome under
pain of forfeiting his preferment; that none of the
monastic orders should visit any monastery beyond the
bounds of France; and the mendicant friars were
threatened with the extirpation of their order, if they
should violate it.   This continued until A.D. 1516, when
Francis I., for political objects, entered into a covenant
with Rome.   But during this interval the Church of
France was very much in the same predicament, as
regards its relations with Rome, as the Church of England was afterwards under Henry VIII.

In Germany also, when Pope Eugene had deposed
the two archbishops of Cologne and Treves, A.D. 1445,

the whole body of the electors of the empire, being
assembled at Frankfort the following year, demanded
of the pope security for the liberties of their Church,
restoration of the deposed archbishops, and the recognition of the decrees of the Councils of Constance and
Basle concerning the authority of general councils. In
A.D. 1446 they resolved, that the relation of the Church
of Germany to the pope should be defined and secured
by the diet of the empire ; and when Pius II. had obtained the decree of the Council of Mantua (A.D. 1459),
against appeals from the pope to a council, the electors
of Germany, notwithstanding, appealed to a general
council in A.D. 1464.

In England, although the measures taken to curb the
power of the pope might not seem at the time to be
quite so decided, they were destined, perhaps on that
account, to have a more permanent influence. But
even then the Court of Rome was sufficiently aware of
the importance of the *præmunire*, and eager to have it
repealed. In the reign of Richard II., when that prince
desired to have a bull to confirm the arbitrary measures
which he had adopted towards the close of his reign,
the pope took advantage of the request to stipulate for
a relaxation of this law.[1] In the time of Henry VI. Pope
Martin V. proceeded almost to extremity against Archbishop Chicheley, to compel him to use his influence that
it might be wholly repealed. Edward IV., soon after his
accession, was glad to purchase the countenance of the
pope by granting some relaxation of it. But the law
itself, however sometimes evaded, was not by any
means inoperative. In the time of Richard II. no
individual of the mendicant order might quit the
kingdom without licence from the king; and in the
same reign, Dardain, the pope's collector, was made to
swear that he would neither execute nor permit to be
executed any of the pope's mandates to the disadvantage

---

[1] BISHOP LOWTH, *Life of Wykeham*, pp. 280, 281.

of the king, his laws, or his realm. Henry V. forbad a clergyman, named John Drennan, to go to Rome, on pain of forfeiting one hundred pounds. Nor could any intercourse be legally carried on with the papal court without the royal sanction. In 1427 Archbishop Chicheley, having received a sealed bull from Rome, a messenger came from the court to demand in the king's name that it should be given up to him, as being contrary to law; and this was followed by a writ enjoining him to keep all bulls unopened, and deliver them to the king, without whose consent he was not to execute them. And generally, in the following reigns, the leading churchmen did not often venture to act upon letters from Rome, without authority from the crown.

While the fabric of papal power thus began to be undermined, the personal character of many of the popes was calculated to aggravate the odium of their exorbitant pretensions. ' There is this special advantage,' said a politic Italian of the time, ' enjoyed by a spiritual potentate over all temporal sovereigns. The only difficulty is to gain the prince's seat; when it is once gained, whether by virtue or good fortune, it requires neither the one nor the other to maintain it. The old ordinances of religion keep the pontiffs in their state, however they may act or live. They alone have a realm without defending it; they have subjects without the trouble of governing them; and their realm, though undefended, is not taken from them, and their subjects care not for being ungoverned; they never think, nor can they manage to be rid of their masters.'[1] This was true. Nothing but a general council could depose a pope; and after the time of John XXIII., the popes took care to check all the efforts made by councils against their power. Secure in irresponsible power, they must have been more than men if they did not often grievously abuse it. But the vices of all preceding

---

[1] MACCHIAVELLI'S *Prince*, c. 11.

popes seemed to be concentrated in Roderic Borgia,
a Spaniard, who, succeeding in A.D. 1492, took the
name of Alexander VI. Of him Guicciardini, the
Florentine historian, writes, that there was in him no
sincerity, no shame, no truth, no religion. And without dwelling upon the passage said to have been originally found in this historian, but suppressed in later
editions, attributing to this monster and his family
crimes too odious to be named,[1] the following facts are
not denied. He publicly acknowledged his mistress
soon after he became pope; and of his two bastard
sons, the elder he made duke of Candia, an independent
principality, and wishing to promote the younger, Cæsar
Borgia, in the Church, he procured a person to swear that
he was his own legitimate son, without which he could
not be made a cardinal. But Cæsar Borgia, not content
to be a cardinal, caused his brother to be murdered and
thrown into the Tiber, that he might enjoy his dukedom.
It is worthy of remark, that it was in the time of Borgia,
and under his authority as pope, that the discoverers
of Spanish America put forth those unheard-of pretensions by which they claimed from the poor Indians the
possession of their lands. 'All these people,' the inhabitants, that is, of the whole world, said Alonzo de
Ojeda to the Indians of Carthagena, 'were given in
charge, by God our Lord, to one person named St.
Peter, who was thus made lord and superior of all the
people of the earth, and head of the whole human
lineage. . . . . . . This holy father was obeyed as lord,
king, and superior of the universe, by those who
lived in his time, and in like manner have been obeyed,
and honoured all those who have been chosen to succeed
him.' And then he proceeds to tell them that the
present pope has granted them and their lands to the
Catholic sovereigns of Castile, and that if they do not
submit he will invade and make war upon them, and

[1] See Appendix A.

take their wives and children, and sell them for slaves,
and do them all manner of injury, as vassals who will
not obey their sovereign.[1]   It might seem to have been
of special purpose that it was left to such a man as
Roderic Borgia to be made the subject of such pretensions.   Has it never occurred to the advocates of papal
dominion, that the purposes of God are not without
repentance, and that, even if they could *prove* the authority which they claim for the pope, such authority
might be revoked or forfeited by notorious sin? Julius
II., the successor of Alexander, was scandalous for his
wars, with which he disturbed the peace of Europe.
He was said to have thrown the keys of St. Peter into
the Tiber, declaring that from henceforth he would try
his sword.   He was succeeded, A.D. 1513, by Leo X.,
of the house of Medici, who was a friend to peace and
ease, and free from those vices which had disgraced his
predecessors.   But his magnificence led him into expense; and in order to support it, he carried to greater
excess than ever the scandalous traffic in indulgences.
In the time of this pope—when, as Erasmus speaks,
the overstretched cord of usurped power was on the
point of breaking—the luxury of the Court of Rome
was advanced to its greatest height.   The revival of
ancient arts and learning, after long ages of forgetful-
ness, had filled the capital with poets, painters, sculptors, and architects, who found in Leo a splendid
patron: but the panegyric of his flatterers addressed
him in words which modest piety cannot hear without
abhorrence.   They dared to call him, by an impious
play upon his name, 'the *Lion* of the tribe of Judah,'
'king of kings, and monarch of the world;' and added
the ascription which none but One can claim, 'All
power is given to thee in heaven and in earth.' Leo
himself appears to have had sense enough to see the
outrageous folly of these addresses, if he did not shudder

---

[1] WASHINGTON IRVING'S *Companions of Columbus*, Appendix.

nt their wickedness; but he had not the virtue to
decline them. In fact, there seems to be some ground
for the charge of irreligion which was brought against
him. His agents in foreign countries were profligate
men, who, while they preached the value of his pardons,
might be seen gambling in alehouses, and staking at
hazard the very documents which professed to contain
such awful and mysterious powers. To what could
this tend but to demoralise the many, to shock the
pious, and to shake all faith in revealed truth?

Such was the state of society and of the Church at
the time of the accession of Henry VIII. to the English
throne.

CHAPTER XIV.

KING HENRY VIII. AND CARDINAL WOLSEY—LUTHER—THE
KING'S DIVORCE AND SUBMISSION OF THE CLERGY.

> Never came reformation like a flood
> With such a heady current, scouring faults,
> As by this king.—SHAKSPEARE.

HENRY VIII. succeeded to the throne of England
April 22, 1509; and no prince, for a century or
more, had come to the crown under such favourable
circumstances. Uniting the titles of the rival houses of
York and Lancaster, each party was anxious to claim
him, and both concurred in devotion to his government.
The vast wealth amassed by Henry VII., amounting to
a million and eight hundred thousand pounds sterling
(in those days an enormous sum), enabled him to indulge
his taste for expense; and that which had made his
father unpopular served to buy him cheap applause.
His personal qualities, also, were calculated to add to
the favourable view which his subjects were inclined to
take of his character. Handsome, affable, and young,
he was calculated to win the applause of the vulgar;
while his undoubted learning and abilities obtained him
the respect of graver persons. There were not wanting
instances, indeed, which to observant minds might cast
a shade of doubt over these favourable auspices. It
was ungenerous to purchase popularity to himself by
the sacrifice of Empson and Dudley, the ministers of
his father's avarice; and it was still worse to withhold
the property of his grandmother, Margaret of Richmond, on account of some informalities in her will, and
put her executors to expense in obtaining the fulfilment
of her munificent charities. But these things were not

obvious at first; while the apparent success of his government—the deference which the greatest sovereigns
of the day found it their interest to pay to him—the
success of his French campaign, trifling as it was—and
the still more important victory over the Scots at
Flodden Field—all served to impress his subjects with
exalted notions of his greatness, which he was by no
means slow himself also to imbibe. These circumstances seem to account, in some degree, for the absolute
and arbitrary power with which he was able to govern,
and for the servile deference with which his subjects
treated him.

It is, however, manifest that a good part of the
success of Henry's earlier days was owing to the government of his great minister, the famous Cardinal
Wolsey, although the influence of this remarkable person may have had a very unfavourable effect upon his
own character. Thomas Wolsey, a person of humble
parentage at Ipswich, had received his education at
Magdalen College, Oxford; and after struggling with
many difficulties, having sought and obtained an introduction at court, had commended himself so well to
Henry VII. by his despatch in conveying a message to
the Emperor, that he was already dean of Lincoln when
Henry VIII. succeeded to the throne. In each of these
situations he gave an earnest of those qualities for
which he was afterwards conspicuous. The unrivalled
tower of Magdalen College, if not designed by him, was
completed under his auspices as bursar; and the late
deanery-house at Lincoln retained to our day the traces
of his architectural skill. Something of scandal had
attached to his character while resident for a short time
upon a country living in Hampshire; while his zealous
devotion to his employers, as well as his aspiring turn
of mind, had made him useful to those courtiers, whom
the same qualities soon enabled him to supersede in the
royal favour. Being commended to Henry by Fox,
bishop of Winchester, one of the chief counsellors of

the late king, it is said that he ingratiated himself with
his youthful sovereign, not less by his ability in all
matters of business, than by flattering his vanity, and
ministering to his pleasures and his vices.   Persons of
humble origin rise more rapidly under an arbitrary
monarch than under any other form of government.
Envy keeps them back where they contend with equals;
but a despotic sovereign is gratified to exalt the creatures of his own choice; and Henry showered greatness
on his favourite with an unsparing hand.   In A.D. 1514
he made him bishop of Tournay, his recent conquest
in France, then of Lincoln, and then archbishop of
York, all in one year.   Soon after, retaining York and
Tournay, he exchanged Lincoln for Durham; and, as
if that were not enough, on the death of Bishop Fox,
he was translated from Durham to Winchester, having
also the bishopric of Bath, and the abbey of St Albans,
the wealthiest in England, *in commendam*.   The pope
made him cardinal of St. Cecilia; and because it was
doubtful whether these honours entitled him to rank
before the archbishop of Canterbury, he procured the
office also of legate *à latere*, in virtue of which he
annulled a convocation summoned by the archbishop,
and called another in his own name.   Henry VII., to
save the expense of paying some of the papal envoys,
had given them the two bishoprics of Worcester and
Hereford; these bishoprics Wolsey took to farm, paying
a certain sum to the Italian prelates, who had no desire
to reside in England, and receiving the revenues himself.   To crown his greatness, Warham, archbishop of
Canterbury, who had been also lord-chancellor of Henry
VII., resigned the latter office, which was immediately ·
bestowed upon the favourite.

Wolsey did not bear himself in his great fortune
with such meekness as to disarm the envy excited by
his sudden elevation.   He assumed almost royal state,
had lords and gentlemen in his train, rebuilt the palace
of the archbishops of York at York Place (now White-

hall) in a princely style, and began a still more splendid
residence at Hampton Court. But the kingdom prospered under his administration; his judgments in
chancery were equitable and unbiassed, and his attention to the externals of religion was scrupulously regular. It must be feared that his religion went no further
than externals; for, without discussing the vile imputations cast upon him by his enemies after his fall, it is
sufficiently certain that he had a bastard son, whom he
permitted to assume his arms, and for whom he provided in the Church; and there was a nun at Shaftesbury at the time of the dissolution, who was also said
to be his daughter.[1] It is not from such persons that
we are to expect any great progress in purifying religious truth; yet Wolsey was too great a statesman to
be insensible to the condition of the Church, and too
confident in his own powers to be deterred from
attempting a remedy. His foundation at Oxford, of
which the noble establishment of Christ Church is but
a remnant, would have been the most splendid in
Europe. It was not indeed, like some other foundations, the result of the founder's self-denial or frugality.
But it was the measure of a bold and energetic statesman to convert a number of decayed religious houses
into a magnificent place of education. He was preparing also to redress the abuses in the Church with a
vigorous and unshrinking hand, when the fatal turn
arrived in the tide of his affairs, which was at once
ruinous to himself and to that overgrown fabric of
Church-power, of which he at once exemplified both
the splendour and the abuse. Nothing could have
seemed less probable, in the commencement of Henry's
reign, than that he should himself become the instrument of liberating his country from the dominion of
the pope. Yet even then some steps had been taken
towards restricting the privileges of the clergy, which

---

[1] Sir H. Ellis, letter cxxiii. p. 91.

are the more important as they are connected with those laws by means of which that object was afterwards more entirely accomplished. One of the greatest grievances for the last two centuries had been the exemption of all the clergy from being tried in the king's courts. This was extended not only to bishops, priests, and deacons, but even to those inferior orders which were commonly conferred on all the servants of churches and monasteries. But, in A.D. 1515, a law was made that in cases of burglary or murder, those below the rank of deacon should be tried in the king's courts. This law, which to us seems so reasonable, created the most violent sensation.

And the feeling of the clergy against it was much aggravated when the citizens of London endeavoured to prosecute in the King's Bench Dr. Horsey, the Bishop of London's chancellor, against whom a coroner's jury, influenced perhaps by momentary excitement, had brought in a verdict of murder, in consequence of a person imprisoned on a charge of heresy having been found dead in the bishop's prison. The bishops, instead of soothing the popular feelings, blindly exasperated them, by passing sentence of heresy against the dead man, and ordering his body to be burnt in Smithfield; and the convocation commenced a process against Dr. Standish, a Franciscan friar, who had argued in favour of the law, and against the exemption of the clergy. Standish having appealed to the king, the point was submitted to the judges; and they determined that the whole convocation who had proceeded against Standish had incurred the penalty of the *præmunire*. This seems to have been a great stretch of that remarkable law, which was originally passed to restrict appeals and suits in the courts of the pope; and the only ground on which this convocation could be deemed to be a papal court was, that it had been convened by Wolsey as the papal legate. But it was a severe blow to the clergy: for all the members of the convocation were forced to

go, with the cardinal at their head, and beg the king's
pardon on their knees. Henry was then content to
compromise the matter. Horsey was made to appear
in the King's Bench, but was not prosecuted; and the
proceedings against Standish were dropped. But a
great principle was thus established, and the king's
attention was called to the power of these restrictive
laws, and to his own true position; for, in answer to
the humble suit of the prostrate clergy, he used these
ominous words, 'By the permission of God we are
king of England; and the kings of England in times
past had never any superior but God only. Therefore
know you well, that we will maintain the right of our
crown.'

MARTIN LUTHER was at this time an Augustin friar,
and a professor at the University of Wittemberg, in
Saxony, to which he had been appointed by its founder,
the Elector Frederick, in consequence of his distinction
as a scholar and a preacher. He was already a man of
high character among the clergy in Germany, when he
began, in A.D. 1517, by writing first to the Archbishop
Elector of Mentz, to whom Leo had issued indulgences
to farm by way of revenue, and then to the pope himself, to complain of the shameful proceedings of their
agents. He was answered by one of them, Tetzel, a
Dominican friar, and was soon engaged in controversy
on every side. He still professed allegiance to the
pope, but being condemned by a cardinal who was sent
to treat with him, and then by the pope himself, he
publicly delivered an appeal to a general council. The
pope was not yet aware of the importance of the question. Despising the poverty of the individual, he overlooked the powerful sympathies by which he was
supported. To excommunicate Luther, and order his
books to be burnt, might have availed a century before;
but now it only widened the breach, and relieved the
Reforming party from any difficulty about separating
from the papal see, when they were thus hastily and

unjustly cut off from its communion.   Luther proceeded to further measures.   He undertook the translation of the Scriptures into German ; he demanded the restoration of the cup to the laity in the Holy Communion ; and maintained the doctrine of justification by faith alone in the strongest possible terms.   This has been called the distinctive doctrine of the Reformation, and in one sense it deserves to be so.   Placed in opposition to the vain reliance on human merits, pilgrimages, and pardons, this doctrine signifies that CHRIST alone is our salvation, and that faith is the means by which we apprehend it.   In this light it seems to have been applied by the Reformers, in opposition to the prevalent doctrine of human merit, much in the same way as St. Paul applied it to oppose the Jewish notion of salvation by the law.   But Luther certainly stated it in such a manner as to give occasion to his opponents to accuse him of disregarding holiness of life ; and the violence of his language, on this and some other points, set an example of bitterness which has been but too readily followed on either side.   However, it was the preaching of Christ crucified which was indeed the secret of his influence and of that of his fellow-labourers.   In doctrine they sometimes differed among themselves, and sometimes held nearly the same opinion with their opponents.   But they supplied a want in the teaching of the Church, without which all else is vain, and restored the doctrine of the Cross to its true pre-eminence, as the only refuge of the sinner's hopes.

The excitement which these proceedings caused in Germany was the more quickly communicated to England, in consequence of the latent spirit of religious inquiry which already so widely prevailed.   The despised followers of Wycliffe had continued to read his Bible and to cherish his opinions ; and their zeal is marked by the records of many instances of persecution.   These were sometimes attended with circumstances of great atrocity.   Henry VII. was present at Canterbury, when a poor priest, who had recanted by his persuasion, was nevertheless committed to the flames; and it was in his reign that those horrors were committed at Agmondesham, in Bucks, which charity would lead us to hope may have been exaggerated, but which Foxe relates as told to him by a spectator, when a woman was compelled to set fire to the fagots which were to burn her father. And yet, while scenes of this kind were from time to time renewed throughout the whole district between the Humber and Thames, they had no effect but to move the hearts of the people more and more towards the persecuted side. So precious were the Holy Scriptures to those in whose hearts God had placed the love of his truth, and yet so severe were the laws against what were deemed to be perverted and heretical translations, that people went out into the woods and fields to read that blessed book, which, at least in the English tongue, was banished from their churches! One man was accused to his bishop of reading the English Bible in the fields; the evidence against another was, that he had been seen in the woods looking on a book; and it was reported in evidence against a third, that he had said, he trusted to see the day ' when maids should sing the Scriptures at their wheels, and ploughmen at their plough.' This was in A.D. 1519, the year before Luther was excommunicated by the pope, and only three years after he had first set himself to oppose the sale of indulgences. It was no wonder if any man who considered the probable effect to be produced by the ART OF PRINTING, now for nearly fifty years established in the country, should have expressed this hope. The power of this discovery in multiplying the facilities of obtaining knowledge was very soon felt in England ; and it was easily foreseen that no prohibition could be effectual which was not seconded by public consent.

But it was not from the effect of the press upon the mass of the people that the Reforming party received its greatest impulse. It was much more importantly .

aided by those who now began to cultivate what was called the *new learning* at the universities. Erasmus had passed some time in England before the conclusion of the fifteenth century; and his genius and learning, spreading its influence wherever he was known, had kindled many sparks of emulation among English teachers and students. The Greek language, which had scarcely been understood by more than one or two in a century for many ages, and by them, as Grostête and his friends, very imperfectly and in authors of little value, was now earnestly studied; and with it came better principles of reasoning, a more true judgment of the laws of nature and morals, and a more just discrimination of truth and error in matters of faith. Holy Scripture began to be studied in the original tongues. Among the friends of Erasmus was the ' ever-memorable DEAN COLET,' the founder of St. Paul's School. About A.D. 1498 he had first revived at Oxford the practice of reading lectures upon Scripture, instead of Scotus and Thomas Aquinas. Being made dean of St. Paul's, his preaching there, and in Buckinghamshire also, where he had a church, was much frequented by those who had inherited the principles of the Lollards; and he did not escape suspicion of what was then called heresy. Archbishop Warham, however, was too good a man to lend a willing ear to malicious accusations, and Colet continued in his deanery. His diet was frugal, his life austere. At his meals, according to primitive practice, St. Paul's Epistles or Solomon's Proverbs were read by an attendant; and he expressed to Erasmus his dislike of the writings of Aquinas, who, he said, ' had polluted Christ's holy doctrine with man's profane teaching.'

What was done by Colet at Oxford was also done, probably with still greater effect, by George Stafford, divinity lecturer at Cambridge; from whom HUGH LATIMER, though at first strongly prejudiced against him, learned to lay aside the schoolmen, and to study

the text of Scripture instead of their glosses. Latimer's preaching was as persuasive at Cambridge as it
was afterwards popular at court. NICHOLAS RIDLEY,
then a young man, was one of Latimer's hearers, and
acknowledged his obligations to him. And it was at
Pembroke Hall, as he declares in his pathetic farewell
to his beloved college, written with his martyrdom in
view, that he committed to memory, in their original
language, all the epistles of St. Paul, and the other
epistles of the New Testament.

It is important to observe, that the principal leaders
of this new reforming party were not persons who
merely inherited or adopted the opinions which still
prevailed among the followers of Wycliffe. Doubtless
those opinions had a material influence in disposing the
public mind, as far as it was disposed, towards reformation; but the leaders of this party, and the principal
agents in the success of reformation itself, were men
who had prejudices to overcome of a directly opposite
kind; and very few of these had as yet gone so far as to
reject the novelty of transubstantiation, which they had
been taught to receive as the primitive doctrine of the
Church.

When the news of the movement in Germany was
known in this country, the bishops who opposed reformation began to be more vigilant against what was
still called Lollardy. And the king, then just entering
on his prime of manhood, undertook to refute Luther's
opinions in a book, which he dedicated to the pope.
This book was received with all possible deference by
the papal court; and the king, who had studied church-
affairs and was fond of churchmen, was gratified by the
unbounded applause with which his part in the controversy was welcomed. It was on this occasion that
the pope bestowed upon him that remarkable title of
Defender of the Faith, which has ever since been
assumed by English sovereigns. It was not, indeed,
altogether a new title; for Richard II. had frequently

adopted it in his proclamations against Wycliffe and his party; and Henry IV. had once been styled 'the Champion and Chief Defender of the Orthodox Faith,'[1] and Henry III. 'the Defender of the Church.' But it was now bestowed upon Henry VIII., in full conclave, by the pope himself. And, indeed, his book was no contemptible performance, and in some points he seems to have had the advantage of Luther. The majority of the clergy were but too ready to second the exertions of the king in what was held to be their own cause. The year after it was published, A.D. 1523, Cardinal Wolsey, the prime minister and pope's legate, was persuaded to consent that a visitation should take place at Cambridge of suspected persons, and some prosecutions took place; but the moderation of Tonstall, then Bishop of London, for a time put off the danger. Soon after, the cause of reformation derived considerable accession of strength from the publication, A.D. 1526, of an English translation of the New Testament, by William Tindal—the first English translation that was printed, and the first that was made from the original. This was printed beyond sea. A clergyman, named Garret, who was afterwards burnt, was sent with a number of copies to Oxford. And when some bishops bought up this heretical work, to destroy it, the money which they gave furnished Tindal with the means of publishing a new and more correct edition. The price of Wycliffe's New Testament, a hundred years before, we saw to be nearly three pounds sterling; but now the printed copies of Tindal's were sold for three shillings and sixpence. The effect of such a change may well be imagined. The way to judge of these prices is to compare them with wages of labour; and it appears from a law[2] of

---

[1] WILKINS, Concil. III. 354. 'Regis, tanquam pugilis, athletæ' et defensoris fidei orthodoxæ. A.D. 1411.

[2] 23 Hen. VI. c. 12.

Henry VI., that a labourer's wages in the fifteenth century were threepence a day, so that little more than two weeks' wages would buy a poor man an English Testament in the reign of Henry VIII.

Such was the state of things in England on the eve of the great public struggle, which ended in the establishment of reformation. Ten years had passed (A.D. 1527) since the first publication of Luther's Theses, and Henry had been warmly engaged in controversy with him, when the quarrel arose between himself and the pope about his domestic affairs. According to his own account, it was three years before this that he first began to entertain scruples as to his marriage with Catharine of Arragon, the daughter of Ferdinand and Isabella of Spain, and widow of his elder brother, Arthur prince of Wales. Although the pope, Julius II., had granted a dispensation for this marriage, Warham, archbishop of Canterbury, had protested against it, as contrary to the law of God; and Henry VII., who at first promoted it, had caused his son to renounce the contract, and enjoined him on his deathbed not to venture upon it. The marriage took place notwithstanding: and more than one son having died in childhood, the king found himself, eighteen years after his marriage, with an only daughter, the Princess Mary, and with no prospect of further issue by his queen. It was in some sense a national object to have a direct heir to the throne, fresh as was the recollection of the wars of the Roses in the century before. But the desire of an heir was still further enhanced, when exception was made by two of the greatest princes of Europe, the Emperor Charles V. and Francis I. of France, to an alliance with the Princess Mary, on the ground that her legitimacy was doubtful, in consequence of the affinity between her parents. But if Henry, as is probable, began with a scruple about his marriage, it is certain that he very soon had other

motives for wishing to be released from it. For, one
year after his first overtures to the pope upon the
subject, he appears to have been on most familiar
terms with Anne Boleyn, the destined successor of
Catharine in his throne. This young lady, the daughter
of Sir Thomas Boleyn, at that time a private gentleman, was nobly allied both on her father's and mother's
side, and was descended, through the family of Lord
Hoo and Hastings, from the Scottish kings. Having
spent much of her time in the French court, she was,
on her return, attached to the person of the queen,
where, if Henry were already turning his mind towards
another marriage, he had an opportunity of being
attracted by her charms. We are not concerned to
defend his conduct; all we have to do, in the judgment we pass upon it, is to abstain from exaggerated
censure. And if this be an equitable view of the
course of his feelings on the subject, there still remains a heavy account against him. If he thought
his marriage illegal, it did not follow that he was at
liberty to marry another; still less to select another
before the first tie was dissolved, even though there
might be nothing which is called criminal in the connection.

In the end of the year 1527, application was first
made to the pope, on the king's behalf, to revoke the
bull of Julius II., and declare the king's marriage void.
The pope was desired to authorise Wolsey and another
cardinal to try the cause in England, and to delegate to
them full power to proceed to a definitive sentence. It
was also requested that Cardinal Campegio, to whom
the king had given an English bishopric, and who was
supposed to be devoted to his interest, might be selected
as Wolsey's associate. Clement VII., the reigning
pope, was at this time little better than a prisoner to
the emperor, whose forces had taken Rome, and besieged
him in the castle of St. Angelo. So that, however willing to gratify the King of England, his fears withheld

him from avowing it; for Charles V. was Catharine's
nephew, and was now resolved to uphold the legality of
her marriage.   In the first place, therefore, the pope
granted the commission that was asked, but with an
express desire that it might not be acted upon until he
should be more at liberty.   He next suggested that the
forces of the French king, who was allied with Henry,
should move towards him, so as to give him an excuse
for pretending to the emperor that he acted by compulsion in yielding to Henry's wishes.   And then he
privately advised that the king should marry another
wife, and promised that he would confirm it.   But this
was thought too hazardous by the English counsellors,
lest, when it was done, the pope should change his mind.
Wolsey all the while urged the pope to proceed, with an
earnestness of entreaty, and even supplication, not consistent with his usual haughtiness.   He more than once
declared to him that he would lose England if he did not
comply.   And it is clear, as well from this as from
other circumstances, that the king had already conceived the design of renouncing the papal supremacy.
The year before, he had agreed with the French king
that each should govern his own Church, and not acknowledge any act of the Roman see, so long as the
pope should be the emperor's prisoner; and not long
after, they concerted a plan of setting up a patriarch of
their own, who should stand in the same relation to the
Churches of their kingdoms which the patriarchs of
Constantinople or Antioch hold to the countries that
acknowledge them, a most remarkable fact in regard to
our present position.

Campegio at length arrived in England (A.D. 1528),
and brought with him not only authority to himself and
Wolsey to try the cause, but a bull to dissolve the marriage.   But this was only a blind.   He was allowed to show
the bull to the king and Wolsey, and then was privately
instructed to destroy it.   Fresh delays occurred while
negotiations were carried on to obtain greater powers to

s

the legates; and Campegio in the meantime attempted
to prevail with the queen to renounce her claims and
retire to a nunnery. Similar attempts had already been
made on the part of the king, but in vain. For Henry,
like many other people of low principles, had not dis-
criminated between the complying and gentle character
of his wife, and the high sense of dignity and self-
respect inseparable from virtue. Catharine had been
brought up in implicit obedience to the doctrines of the
Church of Rome, and her dearest associations were
connected with its services. When the court was at
Greenwich, it is related of her that she used to rise at
midnight to join in the devotions of the Franciscan convent. And thus attached by interest and affection to the
papal authority, she declared that nothing short of the
same power which had allowed her marriage should avail
to dissolve it. The legates, therefore, proceeded to open
their commission, and cited the king and queen to appear
before them on the 18th of June. On that day the king
did not appear; but three days later, on the 21st of June,
1529, both king and queen obeyed the summons at the
house of the Black Friars,—the same building, and probably the same apartment, in which the convocation had
assembled which condemned the doctrines of Wycliffe.

Such a scene could not fail to excite the deepest interest. But popular feeling, as usual, was with the weaker
party; and this feeling was probably enhanced by the
course which the queen adopted. When her name was
called, she did not answer; but arising from her place,
came round to where the king was seated; and, kneeling before him, besought him to remember 'that she
was a woman in a foreign country; that even her own
counsel were his subjects; and how could she expect
justice in such a court? How had she disobliged him,
that she was thus used? She was ever obedient to his
humour; his wishes had been her will. She was his
wife those twenty years, and had borne him several
children: and he knew that her marriage with his

brother was one of contract only. If he could charge her with breach of faith, she was willing to be dismissed with infamy; but if not, she asked for justice at his hands. Their parents were wise princes, and would be well advised ere they consented to this marriage. But as she could not trust her cause in such a court, she besought him to suspend the trial till she could consult her friends.' With these words she quitted the court, and would not be induced to return, but left her cause to be defended by her counsel. On her side were Bishop Fisher of Rochester, who died for the papal supremacy; and Ridley, the uncle of the martyr of the English Reformation. On the king's side, though not actually employed as counsel, yet warmly engaged in the cause, in negotiations at Rome, and in writing to defend it, were Gardiner and Bonner. The legates, having pronounced the queen contumacious, proceeded with the cause; and on the 23rd of July it was supposed they were about to pronounce the sentence. But Campegio had other instructions. The emperor had prevailed with the pope to admit the queen's appeal to himself at Rome; and the legate, pretending that the cause could not go on during the vacation of the Roman courts, adjourned the proceedings till October. Meanwhile the citation to Rome arrived; and although the king, by virtue of his power of inhibiting bulls under the penalties of the *præmunire*, would not allow it to be executed, the authority of the legates was at an end, and Campegio prepared to return.

Henry had awaited the pope's decision now two years, and his temper was chafed by the delay. But this was not all: having an object to carry in which his passions were concerned, it appeared to him that the most effectual means to coerce the pope was by showing a disposition to reject his authority. He had got a notion from English history, and from what he found of the actual state of the laws, of the independence of his crown; and he little deemed that in making use of these laws to compass his private purposes, he was an instrument in the hands of the Divine Providence of accomplishing a mighty revolution in ecclesiastical affairs. His first indignation was directed against Wolsey, who was deprived of his office of lord-chancellor, and forced to surrender his palaces at Whitehall and Hampton Court, and all his wealth, into the hands of his master. Henry, like other spendthrifts, was fond of money, and often talked of it in his moments of relaxation; and Wolsey, who knew his character, hoped to satisfy him by a free surrender. But this was not enough. The king had called a parliament after an interval of seven years, and there an impeachment was preferred against the cardinal by some of the lords; in the first clause of which they recited the preamble of the act of *præmunire*, in which the clergy and parliament of Richard II. had affirmed that the kings of England had no earthly superior. They alleged that the cardinal was within the penalty of this statute for the exercise of his legatine functions. There were no fewer than forty-four clauses, each containing a separate charge; but they were all thrown out in the commons, through the zeal of Thomas Cromwell, a servant of Wolsey's, who, for this purpose, procured himself to be elected to parliament by the city of London, and whose affectionate adherence to his master commended him thenceforth to the notice of the king.

But the *præmunire* was not so easily disposed of: an indictment was brought upon it in the King's Bench; and to this indictment Wolsey pleaded guilty—a plea which involved the most important consequences, not to himself alone, but to the clergy and Church of England. The law required that no bull from Rome should be executed in England without the royal license, and the penalty was forfeiture of property and imprisonment during pleasure; so that if Wolsey had indeed neglected to obtain the king's license, he was within the statute. He affirmed at the time that he had not neglected to do so; and it is certain that in more than one instance he had obtained it, though possibly not to the full extent: but knowing Henry's impatience of resistance, he said he thought it the safer course to submit entirely, and throw himself on the king's mercy. And so for the time it seemed. The king granted him a most ample pardon; and once at least, during the same session, he ventured to take his seat in the House of Lords. But this gleam of favour was of short duration. He was ordered to repair to his diocese of York, which it seems he had never visited, for he had not yet been installed; and he set forth early in the spring of 1530, on his progress towards the north,—a signal instance of the instability of human greatness. It was but a year before that he had exchanged the bishopric of Durham for that of Winchester; and about the same time that, on the report of the illness of Clement VII., the popedom itself, the long-cherished object of his ambition, had seemed within his grasp.

But another person now appears upon the stage, who was destined to have the most important influence upon the affairs of the Church of England. The king was returning from a progress which he made in the autumn of 1529, between the conclusion of the trial and the meeting of the parliament, when two of his attendants, Gardiner and Fox, lodging at the house of a gentleman at Waltham Cross, fell into conversation on the subject of the divorce with Thomas Cranmer, who, having lost a fellowship at Cambridge by marriage, had, after the death of his wife, taken orders and become the tutor of this gentleman's sons, being restored at the same time to his fellowship. He expressed his opinion that the king should collect the judgments of the principal universities and divines of Europe, and that, if they were in his favour, his own clergy might then decide the question.[1] This was just what Henry was

---

[1] The author of the *Life of Bishop Fisher* says Cranmer's words

in search of. Wolsey had indeed before suggested to
consult the universities, and some steps had been taken
in it. But this was of little moment when the pope
was, after all, the last resort. But Cranmer's suggestion,
originating from those very strong views of the royal
supremacy which he maintained through life, supplied
the link which was wanting; and Henry, whose mind
was already alive to the point, seized it with eagerness.
Cranmer was immediately sent for, and received with
distinguished favour. He was employed to write in
favour of the divorce, according to the opinion he had
formed and expressed before he could possibly have
dreamed of royal favour; and was sent next year with
Ann Boleyn's father, now made Earl of Wiltshire, on
an embassy to the pope, with whom negotiations were
continued. The whole of this year was occupied in
obtaining the opinions of various universities and
divines, in which also Cranmer, with others, was engaged; and going into Germany to consult the Lutheran
clergy, he married the niece of Osiander, one of their
leading divines, though the laws of the Church at that
time still enjoined celibacy on the clergy.

The autumn of this same year witnessed the close of
Wolsey's career. Since his banishment from the court
he had spent his time in such a way as to show that he
was alive to the duties of a Christian prelate, though
he had hitherto neglected them. In his progress towards the north, at Peterborough Abbey, at Newark
Castle, at Southwell Minster, at Newstead Abbey, he

---

wore: 'If the king knew but his own power so rightly as he might he
given to understand the same, there would be no cause left him for dis-
contentment. . . . For if the king rightly understood his own office,
neither pope, nor any other potentate whatsoever, neither in causes civil
nor ecclesiastical, hath anything to do with him, or any of his actions,
within his own realm and dominions; but he himself, under God, hath
the supreme government of this land in all causes whatsoever.'—*Life
of Fisher*, p. 89, as quoted by Todd, i. 17, who however, very inaccu-
rately, describes this as if the advice of Cranmer had simply been that
the king should declare himself head of the Church within his own realms.

had won the favour of the people, and gained the
respect of the clergy. And in his retirement at Cawood
he spent his income in charity and hospitality, and his
time in preaching to the poor, and promoting good
feeling and kindness among the rich. He was about
to be installed at York with something of primitive
solemnity, when he was arrested the day before on a
charge of high-treason. Whether he had done anything
since his pardon to incur this charge is exceedingly uncertain. The king expressed great regret at his death,
'wishing rather than twenty thousand pounds that he
had lived;'[1] and perhaps it was only a feint to work
upon the pope. But it is a desperate game for princes
to play with men's lives, and think they are in sport.
The cardinal sickened in his way to London, and died
at the Abbey of Leicester, Nov. 29, 1530. On his
deathbed he was molested by an inquiry about some
money which the king had learned that he had lately
received; and it was on this occasion that he addressed
to Kingston, lieutenant of the Tower, whose prisoner
he was, those words which Shakspeare has embodied
in a speech to Cromwell:—'If I had served God as
diligently as I have done the king, he would not have
given me over in my grey hairs. But this is the just
reward that I must receive for my diligent pains and
study that I have had to do him service: not regarding
my service to God, but only to satisfy his pleasure '
The conclusion of his message to the king (none of
which, however, was delivered) was such as to show
that, whatever might have been his reluctance to persecute, he would certainly have opposed reformation with
a high hand, had he remained in power. The manifold wisdom of God is made known even to the heavenly
inhabitants, as they read the development of His providence in His dealings with His Church.[2] Much more

---

[1] Cavendish.　　　　　　[2] Eph. iii. 10.

ought we to acknowledge His Hand as we see the instruments of his purposes successively exalted and removed.

The character of Wolsey has been drawn by many pens of the highest genius, and by the faithful historic muse of Shakspeare.   Never, as Clarendon observes, was there a more remarkable instance of a man raised to distinction by his own industry and lively talent. Sprung from parents of the meanest class, he had been sent to the university, which he left for want of means, and for a time kept a poor school in the country.   He was near thirty years of age before he was noticed; yet from such beginnings he rose to as great a height of worldly glory as a subject is capable of.   He was able to converse and negotiate in the greatest courts in Christendom, and to be received into much familiarity and confidence with the greatest princes.   If these high qualities had not been accompanied by two great vices, pride in his exaltation, and abjectness in his fall, he would have preserved his claim to dignity of character. But his pride, the natural tendency of persons of mean birth when suddenly exalted, made him offend all the great nobility, who conspired for his disgrace; and his abject spirit seems to have been the occasion of his death, when his outward honours were all lost, and he had not in himself that firmness which is only learnt by fixing the hope on a kingdom that cannot be removed.

The parliament met again in January, 1531; and the opinions of the universities and divines in favour of the divorce were immediately submitted to them. Six foreign universities, besides those of Oxford and Cambridge, had decided in the king's favour; to which may be added a great number of divines in all parts of Europe, as well as the convocation of the English clergy. This body was now to take so important a part in the changes that were at hand, that it is necessary to say a word respecting it.   By the constitution of the Catholic Church, every bishop may convene his clergy to a diocesan synod, and every archbishop may summon the bishops and clergy of his province to a provincial council. These meetings are deemed to constitute the representative Church in the diocese or district to which they belong, as a national synod or council represents a national church; and a general council, assembled from the whole of Christendom, represents the Catholic or universal Church. The bishops in England have the power, like all other Catholic bishops, of calling such assemblies; but the kings by degrees adopted the practice of requiring them to convoke their clergy, not to a purely ecclesiastical synod, but to a meeting connected with the parliament, and exercising some temporal functions. This was called the Convocation, of which there was one for either province of Canterbury and York. These assemblies voted all the taxes which were paid by the clergy; and it was on this account that the kings had an interest in convening them. The archbishop still had the power to summon provincial councils; but as the convocations, being called in their name as well as the king's, were able to exercise the functions of a synod, the practice of holding any other councils had almost fallen into disuse, especially as it was discountenanced by the pope. Thus it came to pass that the convocations of the two provinces, which always sat at the same time with the parliament, were recognised as the synod of the Church in England.

We have seen that in the beginning of this reign the whole convocation of the province of Canterbury was cast in a *præmunire* for prosecuting Dr. Standish, and the members were forced to beg the king's pardon on their knees. But they were now to undergo a still more important ordeal. It was alleged that they had incurred the same penalty by admitting the legatine authority of Wolsey; and although they could not have done otherwise when he was in the plenitude of his power, it was held that as he had pleaded guilty, his guilt involved them all. An action was brought against them in the King's Bench; and Henry determined to avail himself of the predicament in which they were thus placed, not only to extort a heavy subsidy, but also to obtain a recognition of his supremacy in ecclesiastical affairs.

The royal supremacy was the turning-point of the English Reformation; for by this principle the papal power was abolished, and the Church left free, as far as Rome was concerned, for the admission of those alterations in religion which actually followed. But this principle admits of being understood in very different ways. In opposition to the claim of the pope to be supreme in all religious affairs, and even to make or annul the laws of the countries which own his supremacy, it had been long ago contended by the English parliament, and admitted by the English clergy, that their king within his dominions has no earthly superior. This was, therefore, already so clearly the law of the land, that the clergy could not deny it. And so when Henry demanded that they should acknowledge him the head of the Church, no one could refuse to admit it in the sense in which it had been already admitted. But it was evident that such an admission, in such hands as his, was capable of a very much wider interpretation. It is one thing to say that the sovereign alone is the fountain of all law within his own dominions, so that no laws shall be made without his consent;—it is quite another to affirm that he has the right to make such laws as he shall please touching religious affairs. It was in this latter sense that the clergy dreaded the royal supremacy, and were unwilling to acknowledge it. On the other hand, the king persisted that he would continue the prosecution against them, unless they would *submit* to his terms; which were, not that they should formally pass any resolution on this point, as if it were a new thing, but that, in voting the subsidy which he required, they should acknowledge him the sole protector and head of the Church. After three days it passed in the convocation of Canterbury, with the addition of the words, 'as far as is consistent with the law of Christ;' and, with this limitation, the address in which it was embodied, voting a subsidy at the same time of 100,000l., was signed by the whole convocation, including Warham the arch- bishop, and Fisher bishop of Rochester.

Some months afterwards a similar · lmission was made by the convocation of the province of York, where, however, Tonstall, now bishop of Durham, pro- tested against it. They also voted a subsidy of 18,000l.

This act of the convocation has since been known as the 'submission of the clergy.' But it may be ob- served, that the sense in which that expression has since been understood is somewhat different from that in which it was used at the time. It then was taken to imply that the clergy submitted to the prosecution under the *præmunire*; whereas it has come to be used as if they had then for the first time submitted, as to a new thing, to the acknowledgment of the royal su- premacy.

This submission was followed by an act of parliament (January 1532)[1] to abolish appeals to Rome, and to put a stop to those enormous payments to the pope, by way of annates and the like, which had, ever since the time of Wycliffe, and before, been a chief subject of remonstrance on the part of English statesmen. And this law was accompanied by clauses sufficiently signi- ficant of the temper both of the king and the nation. For it was provided, that if the pope should refuse to consecrate bishops in consequence, the king might order the archbishop, or, on his refusal, any two bishops, to do so; and that if the pope should place the kingdom under an interdict, the king should cause the sacraments and other rites of the Church to go on as usual. These

---

[1] 24 Hen. VIII. c. 12, called 'The Statute of Appeals.'

provisions were very similar to those of the Pragmatic Sanction in France ; but as the negotiations were still continued with Rome, a liberty was reserved to the king of making void or confirming any part of this statute within two years. At the same time a further concession was exacted from the clergy, and further restrictions imposed upon them. The parliament had complained, in a 'supplication,' which they presented to the king, that the clergy exercised a power of making laws, by way of canons, independent of the state ; so as to be but half-subjects. This complaint being submitted to the convocation, the clergy offered to bind themselves to make no laws *which do not affect the faith* without the king's concurrence. But this was not deemed sufficient ; and at length they were brought to consent that they would not enact or put in ure (that is, execute) any new canons whatever without the royal license. This point completed the submission of the clergy, and was in fact essential to it, and a necessary consequence of it. And by this means the clergy of the Church in England, who had hitherto, for some ages at least, claimed a right to make their own laws, without waiting for the king's assent, and by so doing had introduced the laws of the pope since he obtained the supremacy over Western Christendom, became once more subject to the crown.[1]

It is very important to distinguish between the real facts of the case, and the common opinion about the royal supremacy. The common opinion has come to

---

[1] When it is said that the Church of England had 'for some ages' only, and not from the first, made its own laws, and that by the submission of the clergy it became subject 'once more' to the crown, the theory is adopted, which has been that of common-lawyers since the Reformation. But there are not wanting those who deny its historical truth ; and, like all theories invented afterwards to suit a particular state of things, it is probably only partially correct. This, however, is clear, that before the Conquest and the subsequent separation of the two jurisdictions, the Church-laws were made under the authority of the king and the English bishops, not under the pope.

be that Henry VIII., being a king of arbitrary principles and character, made himself a sort of pope in his
own dominions, and coerced his clergy into such an
abject submission to himself, as that the state in England thenceforth may make such laws as it will in
regard to all matters affecting the Church of England.
Nothing is more certain than that this was not so understood at the time, or so intended by the clergy. That
alone to which they formally assented was that they
would not in future enact canons without the assent of
the crown—not that the crown with the parliament should
make ecclesiastical laws without their concurrence.
And in this point of view the royal supremacy might
well be regarded as the restoration of its just rights to
the crown. For it involves no more than that every
independent state is, as the statute of appeals asserts,
'an empire' within itself, or a state possessed of
imperial power, with which no foreign power may
interfere. It is in this point of view, therefore, that
'anglican liberties' and 'royal supremacy' may be
said to be convertible terms, implying that the crown
is the natural protector of the Church, within its own
jurisdiction, against the supremacy of the pope. Very
different from this is the arbitrary and unconstitutional
authority over the Church now sometimes claimed for
the parliament—an authority inconsistent with the independence, and if persisted in, fatal to the very existence
of the Church.

CHAPTER XV.

STATE OF PARTIES—CRANMER ARCHBISHOP—KING EXCOM-
MUNICATED BY THE POPE—ACTS OF PARLIAMENT RE-
NOUNCING PAPACY—ENGLISH BIBLE.

> Our mirror is a blessed book,
>   Where out from each illumined page,
> We see one glorious Image look,
>   All eyes to dazzle and engage.
> *   *   *   *   *
> O happy hours of heav'nward thought,
>   How richly crown'd, how well improved,
> In musing o'er the lore he taught,
>   In waiting for the Lord he loved!
>   *Christian Year—St. Bartholomew.*

THE feelings and opinions of individuals do not
often occupy a prominent place in the history of
events; yet they influence those events as much as
they are influenced by them.   It is, therefore, a very
interesting question, what was the state of religious
parties at the time that Henry obtained the renunciation of the papal authority from his clergy and his
parliament?

It has been before observed, that the leaders of the
new party of Reformation were not from among the
followers of Wycliffe; and it is also remarkable how
few were able, in the first instance, to endure the trials
to which they were exposed, and how bitter, in many
cases, were their regrets when they had been overborne
by fear so as to retract their opinions.   The revival of
the study of Holy Scriptures at both universities had
a material influence, long before the obstacles to an
authorised translation were overcome; and Tindal's
version, though denounced by the bishops, was read by
high and low.   On the whole, it was a time of much

excitement and religious anxiety, especially among those of the clergy who began, as was their duty, by taking the Church for their guide, but by degrees found themselves unable to reconcile many things in her teaching with the Word of God.

Of these one of the most remarkable was Thomas Bilney, Fellow of Trinity Hall, in Cambridge—a devout student of Scripture, and a man of learning, whose meek and gentle temper commended the way in which he expressed his opinions to those around him. He had been accused, a short time before the fall of Wolsey, for preaching against vows, pilgrimages, and invocation of saints; and he was suspected of approving the doctrines of Luther, which, however, he allowed to have been fairly refuted by Bishop Fisher. He expressed his wishes for reformation in some points with great moderation, not condemning all the laws which had been received on the authority of popes into this kingdom, but wishing their number lessened; not pronouncing against the use of images, if the worship was paid to Christ, whom they represented; but he earnestly desired that the people should have the Scriptures read in churches in England, and be taught the Creed and Lord's Prayer in their own language; for want of which, he said, he had found many persons ignorant even of such an article of faith as the resurrection of the dead. From the depositions taken against him, he was convicted of heresy before Tonstall, then Bishop of London; and, by the persuasion of some of his friends, he recanted, and, according to the penance enjoined in such cases, he stood during a sermon at Paul's Cross with a fagot on his shoulder, signifying the sentence he had escaped by his recantation.

What followed is as affecting as it is instructive. The remorse he suffered was such as almost to deprive him of reason; and he seemed to read in every page of Scripture his own sentence of condemnation. When at length he regained his fortitude, after spending two

years at Cambridge in preparing himself for his fate, he
went down into his native county of Norfolk; and
there preaching privately among his friends, and on
some occasions more openly, he was apprehended by
order of Bishop Nix, who had long presided over that
see, and was a cruel persecutor. He was burnt in a
place called, from the cruelties perpetrated there, the
Lollards' Pit, near Norwich, in July 1532.

The calm Christian serenity with which he suffered
had a strong effect on those who witnessed this closing
scene; among whom was Matthew Parker, afterwards,
under Queen Elizabeth, elected to be Archbishop of
Canterbury. It was evident that the Reformed doctrines
were now beginning to be preached by men of better
education and of more enlightened minds than the
poor despised Lollards. Among the things which Bilney mentioned in his dying words to the people, he
spoke of it as an offence which he repented of, that he
had preached in a church where he had no license, by
request of the curate. And he professed his belief,
'that only priests duly ordained by bishops have the
keys, by whose power they bind and loose the penitent,
if they do not err in the use of them; and that the un-
worthiness of the ministers does not diminish nor take
away the efficacy of the sacraments, as long as those
ministers are suffered in the Church.' This was very
different doctrine from that ruder zeal of some of these
poor sufferers, who had taught that the ministerial acts
of bishops and priests were not effectual without holiness of life; and so that a pious layman might be more
a priest than a vicious clergyman.

Bilney had become acquainted with Latimer at Cambridge, and found him somewhat prejudiced against
Philip Melancthon, whose name and writings now began
to be known in England. Bilney, seeing the ingenuous-
ness of Latimer's character, asked him to receive his
confession, for it was customary with the clergy to
choose their own confessor. The development of the

state of Bilney's feelings had the result whic'i he intended with his single-hearted and zealous friend; and Latimer had so far adopted these views, as to become a conspicuous preacher of them at Cambridge, though as yet he escaped prosecution. But being preferred, about A.D. 1530, to the cure of West Kingston, in Wiltshire, and continuing there the same course, he was cited before the convocation in 1532, in the same session in which that body made their submission to the crown. He appealed to the king, but his appeal was rejected; and refusing to sign all the articles required of him, he was excommunicated, and imprisoned at Lambeth. By degrees he was brought to sign some of them, and to beg pardon for having preached against the rest; and at length he acknowledged that he had erred both in doctrine and discretion, on which the mild archbishop was glad to dismiss him without further censure.

He was probably guided in this course by the cautions he had received from Bilney; and there is no circumstance more satisfactory in the lives and characters of these leaders in the cause of reformation, than the care and circumspection with which they examined the grounds of the belief which they embraced. Latimer's assent was given to two articles—one asserting the lawfulness of keeping the Lent fast, and other fasts of the Church; the other, 'that it is laudable and profitable that the venerable images of the crucifix and other saints should be had in the church as a remembrance, and to the honour and worship of Jesus Christ and his saints.' If he had preached against the fasts of the Church, we may conclude he now found himself in error; for no such doctrine appears in his sermons which have been preserved. On the subject of images, it is likely that he thought the practice had led to idolatry, but he did not think it in itself unlawful to have images or pictures in churches. His rule of acting in this case may be learnt from his own words: 'I would

T

be loath to suffer death, unless it were for necessary
articles of my belief,'—words of sound instruction,
especially to those who may be found at all times too
ready to disturb the peace of the Church, by their
adherence to some private opinion or indifferent practice, by which weak consciences are offended.   He
showed the same principle shortly after, in a conference
which he held with James Baynham, a gentleman of
Gloucestershire, then a prisoner in Newgate on a charge
of heresy, who was condemned and burnt in Smithfield,
with Dyfield, a monk of Bury St. Edmunds, during
the same year.   He desired Baynham strictly to examine
his motives and opinions, to beware of vainglory, and
to consider ' that it was not lawful for a man to consent
to his own death, unless he had a right cause to die in.'
When he heard him say, that one of the opinions which
he was charged with was, that Becket was a traitor, and
no true martyr—for he had found in an old chronicle
that this prelate had borne arms against his prince, and
provoked foreign princes to invade the realm,—' Well,'
replied Latimer, ' but this is no cause at all worthy for
a man to take his death upon; for it may be a lie, as
well as a true tale; and in such a doubtful matter it
were mere madness for a man to jeopard his life.'   He
then said that he had also spoken against purgatory and
satisfactory masses; upon which Latimer acknowledged
that he might do well to die rather than consent to doctrines opposed to the truth of Scripture.   So carefully
did this honest and humble man proceed in establishing
his own conscience and that of his fellow-sufferers !   In
the meantime his own life was in continued peril.   He
went down to Bristol, and there preached in his familiar
style as before.   His preaching was soon reported to the
convocation, where Gardiner moved that a copy of his
late recantation should be sent down into those parts,
in the hope of counteracting the effect of his sermons.
But his simple eloquence became only the more touching when he publicly bewailed his own weakness, and

confessed that he had not constantly maintained what
he believed.

Archbishop Warham died in August 1532. He was,
as Erasmus sums up his character, a man of learning
and of mild goodness, and both in morals and piety a
worthy prelate. But that for which he is chiefly
memorable is, that under his primacy the subjection of
the Church of England to the See of Rome was renounced, with his full consent and concurrence, and
without any intention of a separation from the true
Catholic Church of Christ.[1] Henry determined to give
the vacant archbishopric to Cranmer, who was then in
Germany, and sent to recal him, without informing him
of his purpose. He was at that time a private clergyman, and scarcely four years had passed since his first
introduction to the king. But it was not unusual in
those days to raise men at once to the highest stations,
and this king was fond of doing so. Cranmer, when
he had notice from his friends of the king's intention,
was in no haste to put himself in the way of such promotion.[2] He delayed his return to England for seven
weeks, hoping that Henry would change his mind; and
it was not till he had received a second message, that he
seems to have determined, not without reason, that a
higher Hand than that of an earthly king was visible
in the series of events which, without his own seeking,
and in the course of his plain and daily duties, had
brought him into the way of such promotion.[3]

---

[1] Warham was a great patron of learning, and endeavoured to prevail
with Erasmus to accept of preferment in England. On his refusal, he
gave him a pension out of a living in Kent, which he presented to
another person to hold with that condition.—COLE's MSS. Br. Museum.

[2] It has been supposed, on the authority of a letter of Erasmus
(Sir H. Ellis, Letter 117, 1st Series), that the king offered to make
Cranmer lord-chancellor also, Sir Thomas More, who succeeded
Wolsey, having resigned. But it seems rather that the offer referred to
was made to Warham, who had been chancellor before Wolsey.

[3] He has been accused of 'loitering at taverns,' when Gardiner and
Fox had that conversation with him at Waltham Cross, which being

But an obstacle occurred. The law, which took away the payment of annates to the pope, had authorised the king to cause his bishops to be consecrated without the pope's consent. But this was only in case the pontiff should proceed to extremities, by excommunication and interdict; and as he had not yet done so, the usual form of appointment was not changed. It was the custom for all bishops to take two oaths—one to the pope, and the other to the king. In the first they swore 'to be faithful and obedient to St. Peter and the holy Church of Rome, and to the pope and his canonical successors;' in the second they declared 'that they utterly renounced all such clauses, words, sentences, and grants which they had or might have of the pope, that might be prejudicial to the king's authority.' There had been an alteration made in the first oath some centuries before by Pope Hildebrand, which made the inconsistency greater than before. For whereas the original form required all bishops to swear to observe 'the rules of the holy fathers,' he had thought fit to add to those words, 'the royalties of St. Peter.' The inconsistency of these two professions, apparent in itself, was now more glaring when the Church had just renounced the papal supremacy; and Cranmer, who foresaw, and probably wished for, some further change in the relations of this country with Rome, objected to take the oath to the pope. It was suggested by the lawyers, that he should take it under a protest that he did not; hereby understand anything contrary to his duty to his king and his country. To this course he assented; the protest was three times made and recorded—first in the chapterhouse of St. Stephen's, Westminster, and twice in public

repeated by them to the king, brought him into Henry's notice. But this is a mistake, arising from inattention to the different customs of different times. Gardiner and Fox did not lodge at an inn on their journey, but at the house of a gentleman, to whose sons Cranmer was tutor; and he was come away from Cambridge with his pupils to their father's house, on account of an infectious fever.

at the high altar of that collegiate church, before his consecration, and before he was invested with the pall; and a clause was added, ' that he did not intend by that oath, or any other, to restrict himself from full liberty of saying and advising whatever might concern the reformation of religion, or the good of the state of England, or of executing such reforms as should seem to be required in the English Church.' He received the papal provision, confirming his appointment, by an instrument dated February 21, 1533, and was consecrated on the 30th of March following.

Whatever may be thought of this protest, there is evidence that his own mind was satisfied by it, and that he looked back to it as an act by which he preserved a good conscience. For long afterwards, when he was about to be brought to his trial under Queen Mary, he gave it as an objection to a bishop who was appointed for his judge—that he had taken two contrary oaths, to the queen and to the pope, on one of which he must needs be perjured : and when this bishop, Brooks bishop of Gloucester, reproached him with it on his trial, he fully justified his own conduct, as having done everything which became him, in making known his scruples to the king, and having taken the best legal advice, to prevent any appearance of deceit or collusion.[1]

One of the first acts of Cranmer after he became archbishop was an attempt to save the life of a person convicted of heresy. This was John Frith, a young man of much learning and good character, who had belonged to Wolsey's college at Oxford, and who was condemned by Stokesly, bishop of London, in con-

---

[1] It appears from his own account afterwards, that the first suggestion of the lawyers was that he should send a proxy to Rome, who should take the oaths in his name. But this he at once rejected as disingenuous ; and when Brooks and the rest reproached him for his conduct on this occasion, he asked them ' what he could do more in the case,' to which they made no answer.—*Works*, iv. 116, Letter to Queen Mary; letter ccxcix.

junction with Gardiner and Longland. As this was the last conviction under the law of Henry IV. which authorised the bishops to condemn to the flames on their own authority, so was this person the first of the new reforming party who ventured to deny the dogma of Transubstantiation. He did not attempt, as the Lutherans and Wycliffites did, to account for the doctrine of Christ's presence in the Eucharist by any reasoning of his own. He believed that Christ is really present in the Holy Communion, according to his own words—only he denied his corporeal presence, and said we ought to be content to believe him present, without pretending to explain the manner of it. And he fortified this opinion by a passage from the writings of Gelasius, an early bishop of Rome, who had said, 'That the elements of bread and wine being consecrated to be the sacraments of the body and blood of Christ, *do not cease to be bread and wine in substance, but continue in their own proper nature.*'

Cranmer at that time thought Frith in error, but he sent for him several times in the hope of convincing him, and having failed to do so, he could not prevent the law from taking its course; but two of the archbishop's officers, who had him in custody, offered to let him escape, and it can scarce be doubted that they had Cranmer's directions to do so. Frith, however, had made up his mind with the deliberation of a genuine martyr. He was a friend of Tindal, and was encouraged by him not to flinch from maintaining the truth. So long as he could remain at large unquestioned he had endeavoured to do so, but having once fallen into the power of the persecuting party, he would not avoid their sentence. He was brought to the stake in July 1533, in conjunction with a young man in humble life, who persisted that he believed as he did; and when a wretched priest exhorted the spectators not to pray for them any more than they would for a dog, Frith's only answer was by a prayer for the pardon of his persecutors. It is most remarkable that Cranmer's amiable and gentle nature should have brought him into communication with Frith at such a moment, when we consider that the doctrine he held on the Eucharist is the very doctrine adopted afterwards by Cranmer himself, and now held by the Church of England, in accordance, as we believe, with the true Church Catholic; and that Cranmer should have made use of the writings of this very person, as he himself acknowledged, in his own controversy with Gardiner on the subject.[1]

One other sentiment of the new archbishop must here be noticed. Many years afterwards he declared his opinion, that 'it pertains not to private subjects to reform things, but quietly to suffer that they cannot amend;'[2] and it was doubtless under this view of his duty that he now thought himself justified in aiding the inclinations of his sovereign to modify the relations of his country to the see of Rome. It was not the weakness of a yielding temper, but the patient spirit of a Christian watching the providential hand of God, and labouring to overrule for good the wayward temper of his master. Nor did he close his mind against the religious questions which were now so generally discussed. He left behind him many volumes of notes and extracts from the Fathers and ancient authors, whose writings he consulted for their opinion, so that he was enabled to fortify the result of his own investigation of Scripture truth by his knowledge of the tenets of the Early

---

[1] We are indebted for the interesting fact of Cranmer's interview with Frith to a letter published by Sir H. Ellis, 1st Series, Letter 114, MS. Harl. 6148. It is from Cranmer to Hawkins, ambassador to the emperor, describing the coronation of Ann Boleyn; and it establishes two other facts besides this, of almost equal importance—namely, that Ann Boleyn was not married until about January 1533, instead of November preceding, as is commonly said; and that Cranmer, so far from marrying them, was not even present, and did not know of it till a fortnight afterwards.

[2] Martyr's Letters.

Church. And that which he did himself he encouraged in others, and was well rewarded. Soon after he became archbishop, he promoted Ridley to the living of Herne, in Kent. Ridley was then, like himself, an anxious inquirer after truth, though still retaining the Romish doctrine on the subject of the sacrament. But it was here that, in the fulfilment of his pastoral duties, assiduously preaching the gospel to his flock, he became convinced by the writings of Bertram, before mentioned, that the doctrine of Innocent III. was a novelty and an error. Satisfied that the Church of our Anglo-Saxon forefathers, the contemporaries of Bertram, had not held that which the Roman Church would impose upon mankind as primitive and catholic truth, Ridley was eventually the happy instrument of bringing over the archbishop to the same conviction, as the latter publicly acknowledged on his trial at Oxford, though this change in his views did not take place until some years later. Thus it is that the obedient fulfilment of our plain duties is the way by which God will lead us into all truth.

On the 25th of January, 1533, Henry had married Ann Boleyn, thus acting on that advice which the pope had given him at first—not to wait for a divorce, but to marry another wife. Cranmer was not present at the marriage, but soon after he became archbishop, he wrote to the king, to represent the scandal that would arise if his first marriage were not formally annulled; and the convocation having decided that a marriage with a brother's widow is unlawful, he received a license to adjudge the cause, and cited both parties to Dunstable, near to which place, at Ampthill, Catharine was living. She refused to obey the summons, not accepting any other judge but the pope; and Cranmer gave sentence, pronouncing the marriage null and void from the beginning,—a sentence which may have contributed to his own death afterwards, from the resentment felt by the Spanish counsellors of Mary, for the disgrace thus done to a princess of their own. Even at the time when the sentence was given, great fears were entertained. The popular feeling was strong in favour of Catharine, and Cranmer confesses he should have been perplexed how to act, if she had actually appeared in his court.[1]

This step was highly resented at Rome, and was immediately disallowed; upon which the king and the archbishop appealed to a general council, and Bonner was sent on the part of the king to deliver his appeal to the pope. And yet, but a short time after, the pope was on the point of acceding to Henry's wishes. The French king, Francis I., sincerely promoted them, and the Archbishop of Paris had by his desire brought the pope to consent, that if Henry would recal his resolution of renouncing the supremacy of Rome, he would give him a favourable trial, and exclude the imperial party. A day was appointed for Henry's answer; but in the meantime it was reported at Rome that the English court made a sport of the papal conclave, and that the king was urging on further measures of hostility in parliament. The appointed day arrived, and no answer came; upon which the conclave, on the 24th of March 1534, hastily and in anger proceeded to a final sentence, pronouncing the marriage of Catharine valid, and the king excommunicate if he should refuse to take her back as his wife.

The parliament had met early in the year 1534, and the king, without awaiting the decision of the pope, had proceeded as if there had been no negotiation in hand with the papal court. The bishops preached in turn every Sunday, at St. Paul's Cross, in favour of the royal supremacy, and Latimer was enforcing the same topic with all his eloquence at Bristol. And now that series of laws was passed, by which the papal authority was

---

[1] Letter xii.

renounced and superseded. First, the law of Henry IV. was repealed, by which heretics might be burnt without waiting for the king's writ, and the power of the bishops in convicting heretics was restrained. The offenders were still, indeed, to suffer death by fire, but by a less arbitrary mode of proceeding, as has been above mentioned. Next, the submission of the clergy was confirmed by an act of the legislature;[1] they were impeded from making new canons for themselves without the king's sanction ; and the Crown was empowered to appoint a commission of thirty-two persons, half clergy and half laymen, to compile a new body of ecclesiastical laws, revising the old canons, and rejecting such as the altered situation of the Church made no longer applicable. This project languished during the reign of Henry ; for though the commission was issued no report was made, but it was afterwards renewed, as we shall find, in the reign of Edward VI. But this restriction of the clergy from making canons, necessary as it may have been at the time, in order to restore the due influence of the crown and the legislature in ecclesiastical affairs, has had results which could not then have been anticipated. For it has been held that they cannot deliberate on any canons without the royal license, and thus by withholding such license the crown has been thought to have the power to suppress the ecclesiastical synods altogether.

Next came the law to settle the election of bishops;[2] which is the more important, as it is by the same law that these appointments are regulated in the present day. We have seen already something of the changes which had taken place in these elections, by which the power of the cathedral chapter or convent had been reduced almost to a nullity. Edward III. claimed the right to nominate, on the ground that the kings, his ancestors, had ' founded the Church of England in

---

[1] 25 Henry VIII. c. 19.
[2] 25 Henry VIII c. 20.

the estate of prelacy;' and a similar claim had been
preferred by Edward I. What was the meaning of this
claim may be illustrated by the mode of election in the
case of an abbot or prior. First, the convent applied
to the 'founder' or patron (for the heir of the founder
had always the same title) for *leave to elect*; and
when the election had taken place, the founder's consent was asked, and if the house was not exempted by
the pope, he wrote to the bishop to confirm it. The
kings of England therefore, claiming to be the founders
of all bishoprics, assumed a right to proceed in the same
way; and when their leave was asked to elect a bishop,
it was but another step to claim a right of nomination
also. But the formal election had always been in the
hands of the cathedral chapter, whether they were
monks, as at Canterbury, or a dean and canons, as in
London and York; and while the pope's consent was
necessary, he might always overrule the choice—and in
fact for a long time had always done so, appointing by
his own provision, as it was called, even when he did
not change the name of the person recommended by
the king and elected by the clergy. It was therefore
now enacted, that on every vacancy the king should
grant a license as usual to the chapter to elect a new
bishop, still to be called a *congé-d'élire*, with a letter
bearing the name of the person to be chosen, which
was no more than had been for some time accustomed;
but it was added, that if the chapter should refuse to
elect the person so named, or the bishops to consecrate
him when elected, they should incur the penalty of the
statute of *præmunire*. It was at the same time forbidden that any bishop should be presented to the pope
for confirmation in his see.

This act, therefore, did not make an alteration in
the actual *form* of proceeding, except as regards the
confirmation by the pope. But by making it all but
imperative to adopt the nomination of the crown, it
introduced a vast change in point of fact. The object

being to prevent the pope from interfering, it may perhaps have been necessary at first to confirm the alleged right of the king to name the person who should be elected.   But this was not the ancient custom of the English Church in the election of bishops; and it is one thing to allow of a nomination by the representative of the founder, but quite another to constrain the Church into the adoption of the nominee.   It is the first article of *Magna Charta*, that the Church is to enjoy its liberty in its elections,—a liberty which Lord Coke declared to be most worthy to be retained. We must therefore consider it upon its own merits, and not defend it, as some writers have done, as a mere restitution of the customary and undoubted rights of the crown.   The Anglo-Saxon bishops in early times were appointed by the primates of the two provinces; and after the Conquest, the bishops in some cases appointed their own primate.   It then became a disputed right between the bishops and the cathedral clergy; and the kings interfered, and sometimes appointed, till the pope's usurpation fixed the course to be pursued, as has been already detailed.   As regards the practice which has resulted from this change, all that can be said is, that when the ministers of the crown are influenced by pure motives and guided by wise discretion, and pay a just regard to the wishes of the Church in these appointments, the choice is perhaps likely to be best placed in their hands.   But though a greater evil was removed, and the natural alliance of the Church with a Christian state was thus properly restored, it is plain that the act itself, like most of the other reforms of Henry's reign, only transferred the power from a priestly to a regal master; and it has proved, at some periods since, the means of making the English sees a source of patronage to unworthy statesmen, and filling them with needy courtiers and men of no public capacity, rather than learned and diligent prelates and true fathers of the Church.   Public opinion, however, may

do much to correct this evil, and prevent such an abuse
of trust.   And when the affairs of state have been
managed by such master-minds as Burleigh and Clarendon, the Church has prospered under the counsels of
its wisest and best priests—

> whom, shunning power and place,
> Their lowly minds advanced to kingly grace.'

Other acts were passed in this and the following
session, abolishing all payments to Rome for dispensations and faculties, and forbidding all persons to go out
of the kingdom, to attend any council or synod, without permission from the crown.   The king was also
declared supreme head of the Church of England ;[2] and
the *annates*, which had before been taken from the
pope, were now given to the king.

At the same time the convocation ordered the appeal
of the Church of England from the pope to a general
council to be affixed to every church ; and the whole
body of clergy, as with one consent, signed their names
to the renunciation of the pope's authority.   'The
Bishop of Rome,' it was stated in their declaration,
'hath not any more authority conferred upon him by

---

[1] The justification of a law which obliges the chapter, under the most
severe penalties, to elect the nominee of the crown, clearly was the
necessity which then existed of rescuing even the chapter itself from
the interference of the pope, who had so commonly set aside their
elections.   But now that the pope has pretended to abolish the original
Church of England by setting up a new church in its place, he has for
ever precluded himself from all pretence to interfere in the elections of
a Church which he cannot recognise.   *Cessante occasione, cessat lex.*
We need not seek to deprive the crown of the *nomination* of our bishops,
but the crown ought not any longer to *compel* the chapters to elect its
nominee.

[2] This title gave some offence at the time, and the name of 'Supreme
Governor' was substituted by Queen Elizabeth and other sovereigns.
It is fair to give Cranmer's explanation of it.   He understood it to mean,
' Head of all the people of England, as well ecclesiastical as temporal:
head and governor of his people, which are the visible Church.   In the
publication of the king's style,' he said, ' there was never other thing
meant.'   *Jenkyns' Cranmer*, iv. 117.   It is also thus stated now in the
Bidding Prayer in our L. Canon, except that the word Governor is
substituted for Head.

God in Holy Scripture, in this realm of England, than any other foreign bishop.'[1] Bishops, deans and chapters, monasteries and parish priests, all concurred in this measure; and near two hundred instruments, bearing their signatures, are now or were lately extant. All the bishops also, except Fisher, including Gardiner and Tonstall, took an oath to the king as head of the Church; and these acts of the National Church, still holding Catholic doctrines, and professing to remain in Catholic communion, with this appeal from the pope to a free general council, continue to preserve on record the justification of our division from foreign churches; the guilt of which must lie with those who refuse our communion, because we will not restore an usurped authority, rather than with those who shook it off.

Another law was made, at the close of this year, to regulate the appointment of suffragan or coadjutor bishops. This was the revival of an old custom in the Anglo-Saxon period, when the archbishop had usually a suffragan bishop at the old church of St. Martin in the suburbs, at Canterbury, who in the absence of the archbishop, or in the vacancy of the see, took his place in ordinations and all other episcopal functions. But Lanfranc, on the death of the bishop who held this office in his time, instead of appointing another, introduced an officer at Canterbury, not of episcopal rank, with the title of Archdeacon; after which, when the see of Canterbury was vacant, the monks of St. Augustine took to themselves authority to act as in the place of the archbishop. Similar officers being established in other dioceses, the use of coadjutor bishops seemed to be in some degree superseded. Yet the office was far from being discontinued, for Warham had a suffragan at Canterbury, and in the end of the preceding century Bishop Smyth had a coadjutor for the diocese of Lincoln; and the names of a great many more such bishops are

---

[1] 26 Hen. VIII. c. 14.

preserved, sometimes having the title of a see 'beyond the pale' in Ireland, sometimes *in partibus infidelium*.[1] And the episcopal character of these bishops was so completely recognised, that they were constantly employed in the consecration of the diocesans. But as it was necessary, according to the Primitive Church, that every bishop should be appointed to some particular see, it was now provided, that certain places should be the sees of 'suffragan' bishops, and that any diocesan bishop who might wish for a coadjutor, might present two persons to the king for his selection; that the person so selected should be consecrated to one of these sees, and exercise such part of the duties as his diocesan should delegate to him. By this law, which is still in force, twenty-five places are named as sees of suffragan bishops:—Thetford, Ipswich, Colchester, Dover, Guildford, Southampton, Taunton, Shaftesbury, South Molton, Marlborough, Bedford, Leicester, Gloucester, Shrewsbury, Bristol, Penrith, Bridgewater, Nottingham, Grantham, Hull, Huntingdon, Cambridge, Berwick, St. Germains, and the Isle of Wight. Two of these, Gloucester and Bristol, were soon after erected into diocesan bishoprics. Cranmer endeavoured to follow out the practice of the Anglo-Saxon Church, by nominating the Prior of St. Augustine to be his suffragan at Dover; and there were nine or ten others consecrated to some of the other sees, one of whom, the suffragan of Bedford, afterwards officiated at the consecration of Archbishop Parker. It has often been regretted, that a plan so requisite to the full-efficiency of the first order of the ministry in the Church of England, and now more than ever needed, from the great extent of sees and increase of population, has never been revived.[2]

---

[1] The learned Henry Wharton had nearly completed a collection of the names of all these bishops suffragans, which was printed from his MSS. in Lambeth Library by the Society of Antiquaries.

[2] While all the whole church is crying out for more bishops as the one

While these things were passing in parliament, A. D.
1534, the convocation agreed to a still more important
measure. On Cranmer's motion, they voted an address
to the king for an English translation of the Bible; a
step which was worthy to be the first act of a National
Church on becoming emancipated from the dominion of
the see of Rome. Gardiner and all his party opposed
it, alleging that the indiscriminate use of the Scriptures
in the vulgar tongue has a tendency to promote heresy.
But the assembly decided in favour of it, and the king
was persuaded to assent by the influence of his new
queen, who favoured the Reformed doctrine, and ventured
to possess a copy of Tyndal's interdicted translation.[1]
The work itself was not accomplished until about four
years later; but the principle, that the Church should
put the Bible into the hands of all the people, was
already carried, when the clergy had moved for it and
the king had acceded to their petition.

About the same time, Cranmer adopted a new style
in his title as archbishop. His predecessors had called
themselves Primates of All England and 'Legates of the
Apostolic See,' instead of which he described himself
as Primate of All England and ' Metropolitan '—a style
not altogether new, but which having been assumed on
such an occasion, and being still retained by his successors, may be in some degree equivalent to that of
Patriarch of the English Church.

The party which favoured reformation was now
strengthened by the promotion of Latimer to the see of
Worcester, and Shaxton to that of Salisbury, of which

---

great want of the day, and devising all kinds of schemes to attain them,
it will perhaps be thought hereafter to have been the same sort of in-
fatuation to neglect this law, that it was to oppose so long the revival
of Convocation.

[1] Her copy of Tyndal's Bible, bearing her initials as Queen, A.B., is
now in the British Museum. There is also extant a letter from her to
Cromwell, interceding for Richard Herman, a merchant at Antwerp,
who had been put out of the English house there, in the time of Wolsey,
for helping in the publication of it.

two Italian cardinals, Ghinucci and Campegio, were deprived by act of parliament. The influence of the queen was visible in these appointments. Shaxton indeed, as we shall find, disappointed the hopes of his friends. But there were others, who, not professing to favour Luther, or as yet agreed how far they would go in their plans of reform, were disposed to concur in some changes for the promotion of a better state of things. These were Goodrich bishop of Ely, Barlow of St. David's, Hilsey of Rochester, all promoted about this time; and Edward Fox bishop of Hereford, a man of zeal and learning, who would have been one of Cranmer's most valuable condjutors, had not his life been cut short in the midst of these trying scenes.

CHAPTER XVI.

DEATH OF MORE AND FISHER—MEASURES OF PAUL III. AND
CARDINAL POLE—SUPPRESSION OF THE MONASTERIES.

> Threats come, which no submission may assuage,
>   No sacrifice avert, no power dispute:
>   The taper shall be quench'd, the belfries mute,
> And 'midst their choirs, unroof'd by selfish rage,
> The warbling wren shall find a leafy cage,
>   The gadding bramble hang her purple fruit,
>   And the green lizard and the gilded newt
> Lead unmolested lives, and die of age.
>   WORDSWORTH, *Eccl. Sketches.*

GREAT changes in the social order of a country have
seldom been made without violence; and, as was
long since observed by a profound historian, a domestic
reform in the constitution is commonly as dearly bought
as a foreign conquest.[1] This was now to be exemplified
in England. The change that had been made in the
laws, and especially those which concerned things of the
highest moment, religion and the Church, gave a shock
to many of the most conscientious and sincere, who had
lived long in the world, had been content with things as
they were, and could not acquiesce in the reasons for
such great and perilous alterations.

A law had been passed by the same parliament which
abolished the papal authority, declaring the nullity of
the king's marriage with Catharine, and requiring all
persons to take an oath to maintain the succession to
his children by Ann Boleyn;[2] the refusal of which oath
was pronounced misprision of treason. This law, and
one which followed in the next session, requiring all
persons to swear to the royal supremacy on pain of

---

[1] GUICCIARDINI.   [2] 25 Hen. VIII. c 22.

treason, proved fatal to two most excellent and able men,—Fisher, bishop of Rochester, and Sir Thomas More, late lord chancellor. There had previously been some indication that the king's marriage was severely censured by those who adhered to the papal supremacy. Towards the end of tho preceding year, when it was reported as about to take place, Friar Peto, of the order of Observants, a stricter class of Franciscans, had denounced it in the pulpit in the king's presence at Greenwich. He took for his subject the death of Ahab, and compared Cranmer and the others to the lying prophets, while he himself was the Micaiah who told tho king the truth. And when on the next Sunday another preacher took the contrary side, and challenged Peto to answer him, Friar Elstow, of tho same house with Peto, standing up in the rood-loft, answered the challenge, boldly accusing the king of adultery, and those who advised him of betraying 'his soul to perdition. This was the year before, but now when tho oath of succession was tendered to all persons under the new act, Fisher and More refused to take it. They were willing indeed to swear to the succession of the issue of the second marriage, but objected to those words of the act which declared the marriage of Catharine void from the beginning, whereas the pope had now declared it valid. Cranmer earnestly advised that their proposal should be accepted,—it would be the way to procure the agreement of all parties; for, as he said, ' there was not one within the realm that would reclaim against it.' [1] But it was no part of Henry's character to admit any deviation from his will; and they were both committed to the Tower. One part of the accusation against them was, that they had listened to the oracles of one Elizabeth Barton, called by her admirers the Maid of Kent, who was executed with other ten persons, monks and priests, for having conspired to spread false prophecies threatening

---

[1] Letter cvI.

the king with the Divine vengeance if he should
marry Ann Boleyn. This poor woman had a power.
which is not very uncommon, of going into a sort of
trance, from which she could raise herself when she
pleased, and had been persuaded by some of these
accomplices, as she confessed before her execution, to
pretend she was inspired, and set up for a prophetess.
It surprises us that such a man as Bishop Fisher should
have listened to her visions, as he certainly had done;
but this only proves him to have been credulous. There
was no pretence to impute to him any participation in
the imposture; and perhaps some of the rest (his own
chaplain among them) may have been dupes rather
than culprits. But as both he and More persisted in
refusing the oath in the form prescribed, they were detained in prison.

Here they were soon joined by other sufferers. The
oath was exacted from all the king's subjects who had
completed their sixteenth year; and especially it was tendered to the members of religious orders. John Houghton, prior of the Carthusians, now the charter-house, in
London, with one of his monks, had scrupled to take the
oath of succession; but after a short imprisonment, by the
persuasion of Lee, archbishop of York, he submitted,
and persuaded his convent to submit, on the ground that
it was not a matter that concerned any article of faith.
But the next year another oath was required, acknowledging the king as the supreme head of the Church.
Understanding this to mean that he was 'supreme
primate in spirituals,' they resolved to maintain the
contrary with their lives. The prior, an aged and
learned man, called together a chapter of his convent,
and shedding tears of compassion for the younger members, who were willing to share the worst with him, he
declared he would readily yield his own life to save
them, if it might be allowed; but if otherwise, ' the will
of God be done.' They prepared for death, the prior
setting the example, and going round to each member

of the convent in succession, to ask pardon on his knees
for any offence or unkindness. This was followed by
all the rest; after which, having confessed to each other,
they celebrated the mass of the Holy Ghost, with prayers
and hymns to the blessed Spirit, to obtain the strength
and comfort of his grace for their last conflict. Two
other priors, of the same order, concurring in the refusal,
were soon after condemned and executed, together with
Houghton and another monk, and a month later three
more of the same house, Middlemore, Exmew, and
Newdigate, underwent the same fate.

Clement VII. died in the beginning of this year,
A.D. 1535, and was succeeded by Paul III., one of whose
first acts, and a most imprudent one, was to make Bishop
Fisher a cardinal. It was intended doubtless to express
his approbation of the course this prelate was pursuing
respecting the supremacy, and was so understood by the
king. Soon after both Fisher and More were tried for
treason, and convicted on evidence which would now be
considered wholly insufficient. The bishop had been
led into conversation on the point of the king's supremacy by persons who betrayed him, and his opinions,
thus obtained, were produced against him. He was
beheaded June 22, A.D. 1535, in the 77th year of his age,
venerable alike for his virtues and his years, and lamented even by those who did not concur in his
opinions. On the 6th of July, the great and good Sir
Thomas More followed his fate; and as far as Henry's
character is connected with the English Reformation,
such acts are a stain upon that event which it is better
to acknowledge and deplore than to palliate or disclaim.
On the news of Fisher's death, the pope proceeded to
those violent courses which had been too long the
custom with his court. He passed a sentence by which
the king was cited to answer for his conduct, and in
case of refusal was pronounced excommunicate, his
kingdom placed under an interdict, his subjects absolved
from their allegiance, his dominions offered to the first

invader, and all the bishops and clergy commanded to quit the country. This sentence, however, though pronounced at that time, was so far suspended for the present that the publication of it was deferred, and did not take place till after the suppression of the monasteries.

Immediately after, there appeared a publication from Reginald Pole, the king's near relative, and equally descended with himself from the House of York, which was calculated not only to exasperate but to alarm him. Pole was a man of high character and amiable mind, and had been educated by Henry, and treated with marked distinction. He was now dean of Exeter, but was chiefly resident in Italy; and there he was earnestly labouring for some salutary reforms in the Court and Church of Rome, when he heard of the destruction of his friend More. Perhaps his royal blood, as well as the associations of his foreign education, might render him the less subservient to the will of his imperious sovereign. His book was entitled a *Defence of the Unity of the Church*,[1] and was addressed to the Emperor Charles V., Henry's avowed enemy, calling upon him to invade England, and fight against the enemy of Christendom. Charles was preparing an armament against the Turks, when this English nobleman wrote to him, that though he were now in the Turkish seas, ready to join battle with those adversaries of the Christian name, he would exhort him to turn his arms against worse heretics than Turks. He reminded him that the English people had before now deposed their kings for misgovernment or wanton profuseness, and assured him that they had the same spirit still, and were only now withheld from calling their sovereign to account, by the

---

[1] That this book was written after the death of More, in A.D. 1535, is evident from the reference to that event; and that it was immediately after is equally certain, from its referring to Catharine as being still alive; for she died on the 8th January, A.D. 1536.

persuasion and the hope that the emperor must and would assist them.

There was one of Pole's assertions which seems to have been confidently made, but which was evidently incorrect. He affirmed that the king had gone against his subjects' wishes in renouncing the supremacy of the pope. If he had said that the generality of the people were not then prepared to concur in such changes in doctrine as were soon afterwards introduced, that might have been true. It is not to be expected that men should know or embrace the truth as it is in Christ when they have not been taught it; and for that very reason it is the duty of the Church to teach the truth, and of wise governors to see that it be taught. But that the rejection of the papal supremacy was, on the whole, an acceptable measure with the nation, appears not only from the long struggles against that weary yoke, but from contemporary evidence of an unexceptionable kind. The next year, one of the most upright of the English prelates, Tonstall, now bishop of Durham, who had hesitated about the king's supremacy while he concurred in renouncing that of the pope, wrote to Pole as follows: 'It is true the king hath rescued the English Church from the encroachments of the Court of Rome, and if this be a singularity he deserves praise. For the king has only reduced matters to their original state, and helped the Church of England to her ancient freedom.' And as to the assertion that the people did not wish it, 'This,' he said, 'is a mistake, to that degree, that, on the contrary, if the king should attempt the reviving the pope's power, he would find it a very difficult business to bring his subjects to this sentiment, and get a bill of that nature to pass in parliament.' And about the same time Gardiner, in his celebrated work, *Of True Obedience*, to which Bonner wrote a preface, took exactly the same ground. The opinions held at that time by those two celebrated persons are worthy of remark. Bonner declared that the chief object of

Gardiner's book was, to show that the difference between the king and the papal court did not turn upon his marriage, but upon higher grounds, and that what he had done was with the consent and approbation of the most excellent and learned bishops, and of the nobles and whole people of England.   And Gardiner thus wrote— 'The question is now in everybody's mouth, whether the consent of the universal people of England rests on divine right, by which they declare and regard their illustrious king, Henry VIII. to be the supreme head on earth of the English Church; and, by the free vote of their parliament, have invited him to use his right, and call himself Head of the English Church in name as he is in fact.   In which act,' he continues, 'no new thing was introduced; only they determined that a power which, of divine right, belongs to their prince, should be more clearly asserted, by adopting a more significant expression; and so much the rather in order to remove the cloud from the eyes of the vulgar, with which the falsely pretended power of the bishop of Rome has now for some ages overshadowed them.' [1]

Fortified by such opinions, Henry resolved to maintain the position he had assumed.   But he was not the sort of man who would be ignorant of the extent of that power with which he had to contend.   He knew that several of the emperors, and many other sovereigns, had been dispossessed of their dominions in consequence of the papal interdict; and he now found himself in that condition under which two at least of his own predecessors, Henry II. and John, had been forced to the most abject submissions.   There was no reason to doubt the willingness of Charles V. to accept the tempting invitation to invade his country, and Henry resolved to break the power of those who were likely to be his enemies at home, and to avail himself of a part of their wealth in the defence of his dominions, rather than risk

---

[1] STEPH. GARDINERI *De Verâ Obedientiâ*, Fasc. Apr. p. 166.

the ill will of his people by asking for subsidies at such a moment. There is cause to believe, from his own account, that such were his original intentions in the suppression of the monasteries. Leaving the larger and wealthier of these establishments, which were generally the best conducted, and removing into them some of the inmates of the smaller houses, he intended to suppress the latter, and to make use of their property, partly in the fortification of his seaports against foreign invasion, and partly in a measure formerly proposed by Wolsey,—the creation of new bishoprics in several places.

By virtue of his royal supremacy, he now appointed Thomas Cromwell to be his vicar-general in ecclesiastical affairs; an office evidently borrowed from that of vicar-apostolic, or legate of the Roman see; and the functions of which showed the king's design to take to himself whatever supremacy the pope had exercised before. For he gave commission to Cromwell or his officers to visit the whole body of the clergy, not excepting the bishops themselves; to correct and reform, and exercise ecclesiastical jurisdiction; to deprive or suspend archbishops and bishops, to convene synods and preside in them. Such a degree of authority is clearly inconsistent with any true liberty in the Church; and the suspension of episcopal jurisdiction was therefore very soon abandoned. But as the parliament had placed the visitation of monasteries under the crown, Cromwell appointed visitors under this commission to inquire into their present state. This visitation occupied the remainder of the year 1535; and in the course of it, some few houses were surrendered to the crown. The report of the visitors was presented to parliament the following year, and contained a long list of accusations, especially against the smaller abbeys, but admitted that some good order was observed among the more considerable houses.

It is not necessary here to repeat those accusations themselves. Enough has been said in treating of the Church before the Reformation, to show that the monastic

system had sadly degenerated, and it can do no good to
relate the imputations brought against the poor monks,
in individual cases, when their day of doom was come.
The character of the visitors is not in all cases free from
exception, and they seem to have acted as if they
thought it was their business to report all the ill they
could. Take for instance this of Layton's, one of the
most severe against the monasteries, who had applied
to Cromwell for an extension of his commission to other
places, on the ground that it would be for his own interest. He writes, ' At Bruton and Glastonbury there
is nothing notable. The brethren be so strict kept that
they cannot offend ; *but fain they would if they might,*
as they confess; and so the fault is not in *them* ;' where
the very strictness of the discipline kept up is used to
found an accusation upon.[1] In several instances, the
visitors themselves interceded for particular houses, on
the ground of their good order and regularity ; as
Catesby, Polesworth, and Woolstrop, in Northamptonshire; also the great Abbey of Ramsey in Cam-
bridgeshire. In other instances, as at the nunneries
of Chepstow and Godstow, Dr. London, one of the
commissioners, was accused of very shameful practices,
and the same man was afterwards convicted of perjury,
in an attempt to collect evidence against some persons
under the act of the six articles.[2]

---

[1] STRYPE, *Eccl. Memorials*, Henry VIII. cxxxv. This Layton was a
worthless court parasite, who had been before employed to entrap the
venerable Bishop Fisher.

[2] The course of the proceedings adopted is thus summed up by Mr.
Lodge: ' The principals of some houses were induced to surrender by
threats, others by pensions; and when both these methods failed, the
most profligate monks were sought for, and bribed to accuse their
governors or their brethren of horrible crimes. Agents were employed
to seduce nuns, and then to accuse them, and by inference their respective societies, of incontinence. Those who were engaged in this
wretched mission took money of the terrified sufferers, as a price of a
forbearance which it was not in their power to grant. Cromwell himself
accepted great sums from several monasteries, to save them from that
ruin which he alone knew to be inevitably decreed. He executed his

And yet it would be idle to doubt that great abuses existed. The visitors may have been interested parties, though there is no ground to question the respectability of the greater part of them : but the evidence of many other disinterested persons is to the same effect. Such is the testimony of one who had seen the state of the monasteries, and whose character is unimpeachable : ' Truly the monstrous lives of monks, friars, and nuns, have destroyed their monasteries and churches, and not we.'[1] The evidence of Bernard Gilpin, a still more unexceptionable witness, is to the same effect.[2] And further testimony may be found by those who would know more of these things than we care to produce in this place.[3]

It was determined to suppress by law all those monasteries whose revenues were not sufficient to maintain the numbers required to constitute 'a convent,' or chapter, and the preamble of the act of parliament, by which this was done, places the justification of that course on their own corrupt condition. It recites, that ' manifest sin, vicious, carnal, and abominable living, is commonly committed in the small abbeys and priories, whereby the governors and servants spoil and waste the churches, farms, and lands ; and although continual visitations have been held, by the space of two hundred years and more, for reformation of such unthrifty, carnal, and abominable living, yet none amendment is hitherto had, but their vicious living shamefully increaseth and augmenteth.' And then it grants to the king all such religious houses and their property as are not above the yearly value of 200l., but with a provision that the grantees, or purchasers of them, shall be bound to keep hospitality as formerly.

---

mission, however, to Henry's entire satisfaction, and received the most splendid rewards.' LODGE's *Portraits, Life of Cromwell.* Perhaps this account is *overcharged.*
[1] NOWELL's *Reproof of Dorman.*
[2] STRYPE, *Eccl. Mem.* i. 397.   [3] *Ibid.* p. 336.

It is remarkable that this act was passed in a parliament where twenty-six mitred abbots sat as barons, and that the whole number of spiritual lords was at that time greater than the whole number of lay peers who had seats in the upper house. The number of these smaller houses thus dissolved, was three hundred and seventy-six, and their annual revenue amounted to 32,000*l.*, besides about 100,000*l.* in plate and money.

It is said that Ann Boleyn interested herself to save some of the monasteries. But the catastrophe of her own fate occurred in the same year in which this act was passed, and before any steps could be taken in consequence of it. The history of her fall must be sought elsewhere. We can do no more than relate that her death took place in May 1536, and that the king married Jane Seymour, the next day after the execution of her who had so lately been the chosen object of his affection.[1]

Henry proceeded with the suppression of the lesser monasteries, as the act had enabled him; and a commission was appointed to value and dispose of the lands, and receive their revenues, which was called, from its purpose being to increase the royal revenue, the Court of Augmentations. But the attempt had well nigh cost him his crown. It does not appear that many houses were actually suppressed when the rebellion broke out; but the popular feeling, which had been against the monastic orders when they were in the enjoyment of envied wealth, now took part with them in their adversity. Some were already turned adrift with a very small pittance, some were drafted into the larger abbeys, where they would excite compassion, and perhaps not

---

[1] The question of the innocence of the unfortunate Ann Boleyn does not enter into the plan of this work. It can, however, scarcely admit of doubt with any candid reader. The slanders against her early life were not heard of till nearly forty years after her death, when they were put forth by Sanders, an English Jesuit, who died in an Irish rebellion. The Spaniards at the time took up the calumnies in their zeal for Catharine of Arragon; but one of their best later writers defends Ann's entire innocence.—FEYJOO, *Cartas Eruditas*, iv. § 5.

be welcome inmates, while the suspension of their usual charities would touch the people themselves. It happened also that this law, though it appeared to attack the weakest, included those who were the most likely to engage the public sympathies. These were the inmates of the nunneries, places which had long been an asylum for the unmarried daughters of the gentry, and where, in many cases, persons of gentle lives and kind deeds, had drawn to them the warm attachment of the poor. The people saw their benefactresses turned adrift with the allowance of a small pittance, or sent back to seek a maintenance in an unfriendly world; and the suspension of their usual charities was an evil which they immediately felt. To appease the growing discontent, the king first signified his pleasure to give back some thirty of these houses, the greater half of the number being nunneries. At the same time, perhaps with a view to give a religious colour to the proceeding, and to recal men's minds to one of the chief abuses in these foundations, some injunctions were set forth by authority, condemning the worship of saints and images. But the storm kept gathering. Towards the end of harvest it broke out in Lincolnshire, where Mackrell, abbot of Barlings, and suffragan Bishop under Bishop Longland[1] of Lincoln, disguised as a mechanic, and calling himself Captain Cobbler, headed twenty thousand men. This tumult was soon appeased; but it was followed by a much more formidable rising. By the month of October almost the whole of the northern counties were in arms. In this portion of England there had been very little persecution; and high and low were generally averse to the new changes. Forty thousand men assembled in Yorkshire, under the command of a private gentleman named Aske. They marched with a crucifix before them; their banners

---

[1] H. Wharton's account of Suffragan Bishops in England, printed from his MSS. in Lambeth Library by the Society of Antiquaries.

and dress were marked with a cross, and they called
their expedition *The Pilgrimage of Grace.* They.
avowed their object to be 'the removal of low-born
counsellors (alluding to Cromwell, who was a fuller's
son at Putney), the suppression of heresy, and the
restitution of the Church.' They restored the ejected
monks, as they went, to their houses; and having taken
Pontefract, where were Lee archbishop of York, and
the Lord Darcy, they obliged both, perhaps not altogether unwillingly, to join them. The king's forces
were at Doncaster, not six thousand strong, when they
were threatened with an attack from insurgents more
than five times their number. But the Duke of Norfolk
and the Earl of Shrewsbury, who commanded them,
contrived to temporise. Promises were made, and
pardon offered, and the rebel troops melted away without a battle. Aske was for a time taken into favour,
and probably by his means the king discovered who
were at the bottom of the plot. But fresh risings taking
place the next year, in which he was implicated, he
was beheaded for treason; and Lord Darcy underwent
the same fate on Tower Hill; while Lord Hussey, for
having been concerned in the Lincolnshire rebellion,
was executed at Lincoln.

Nothing so strengthens a government as an unsuccessful resistance. Henry knew this, and resolved to
press his advantage. In the year 1537, it was made high
treason by act of parliament to deny the royal supremacy;[1] and by means of this law, and the knowledge
he had of the participation of some abbots and priors
in the Pilgrimage of Grace, he was able to work upon
the fears of some, while bribes and promises were held
out to others. This year twenty-one houses surrendered, and of these some were of the class of larger

---

[1] Latimer preached this year before the Convocation, and told them
'this man ye would have baked in the coals, because he would not
subscribe certain articles that took away the supremacy of the king.'—
Sermons, p. 13, ed. 1635.

abbeys.   In the following year, A.D. 1538, one hundred
and fifty-nine resignations were obtained,—among them
the abbeys of Woburn and Burlington, whose abbots,
with three others, had been executed for having joined
the rebels.   But the impediments he had found caused
the king to resort to a fatal expedient in the disposal
of the immense domains which he thus obtained.   It
was suggested that the only way to content the nobility
and leading gentry, was to bribe them with grants of
the sequestered lands; and this course was adopted
with a lavish hand, sometimes by selling them at a rate
infinitely below their value, and sometimes by granting
them in free gift.   It was hoped the new proprietors
would thus become, as it were, parties to the suppression, and so would concur in maintaining what was done.
The success of this scheme was soon manifest.

In this year Henry seized upon the treasures at
Becket's shrine at Canterbury, ordered the bones of
the saint to be burnt and scattered to the winds, and
his name to be erased from the calendar.   In order to
justify it, a solemn trial was held, in which the dead
archbishop was pronounced a traitor, perhaps in imitation of the process acted a century earlier over Wycliffe.[1]
Such vengeance over dead men's dust can only disgrace the man who is guilty of it.   But it served to
exasperate the papal court, and now it was resolved
that the bull of excommunication and deposition should
be published, which, though passed three years before,
had been as yet suspended.   Directions were therefore
given for its publication, by affixing it to a church in
each of the three kingdoms of France, Scotland, and

---

[1] Professor Jenkyns has shown some reasons for doubting the fact
of this trial (*Cranmer's Works*), i. 202.   There seems to be some error
about the date, which might easily happen in a period of public dis-
turbance, when, as Fuller says, people ' cannot well hear what the
clock of time doth strike.'   But the account is circumstantial; and it
was the practice of Henry, and one great secret of his power, to do
nothing without the *forms* of law.   The state paper which the Professor quotes speaks in that place not of Becket, but of St. Swithin.

Ireland; and the pope at the same time wrote to the kings of Scotland and France, exhorting them to invade the country, of which he was willing to confer the sovereignty on them. But the king only proceeded with the greater earnestness and severity. The Countess of Salisbury, the mother of Cardinal Pole, a lady of great age and of royal birth, being the daughter of the Duke of Clarence, had been in prison some time for having been concerned in an insurrection in the west for which her eldest son was taken and beheaded. A standard had been found in her possession bearing the royal arms, and there was some reason to suspect a design of setting up her family as next heirs to the throne, of the house of York. When the Pilgrimage of Grace broke out, Reginald Pole was sent by the pope as his Legate into the Netherlands, to distribute a manifesto in approbation of the rebellion, and to incite the continental sovereigns to assist in it. Henry was resolved to retaliate upon Pole, and he ordered his aged mother to be brought to the scaffold, in bloody retaliation.

The next year, A.D. 1539, he obtained an act of parliament, not, indeed, to suppress the larger monasteries, but to grant and confirm to him all such monasteries as had been or should be surrendered. In order to obtain this law, he had already made very large grants to his nobility and others, which would not be valid without it, and he promised to make up the number of the House of Lords, which would be diminished by the removal of so many abbots, by creating as many new peers. There were twenty abbots still left in the House of Lords when this act was passed, but it sealed their doom. Without it, the lands of any houses suppressed would by law have reverted to the heirs of the founders, and as the king only represented the royal foundations, he would have had no title to the rest. Cranmer attempted, on this distinction, to found a claim for preserving some of them. He proposed that all such houses as were not of royal foundation should be turned into schools and colleges for education, or hospitals for the sick and poor. And Latimer the year before had written to Cromwell, to intercede for the priory of Great Malvern in his diocese, a house ruled by a worthy old man, who was his friend, and who would gladly have seen his society reformed on a plan which he proposed, to combine a system of education with extended charity, adding, 'Alas! my good lord, shall we not see two or three in every shire changed to such a remedy?' If such plans had been adopted, and if the king had devoted the royal foundations in part to the establishment of the full number of bishoprics which he had originally designed, and the rest to purposes of charity and education, and the maintenance of colleges of clergy to supply the want of ministerial functions in populous places, much good could not have failed to result. But Henry's power was too great for any one man to be trusted with. The parliament which made such laws ought to have been at liberty to provide for the fulfilment of his professions, whereas, being obliged to trust to his promises, they left all to his mercy ;—and he had squandered so much beforehand that he had not the means of acting up to his intentions, and, as usual in such cases, made that his excuse which was his greater blame. This year, however, a law was passed to empower him to erect new bishoprics, under which six were eventually founded—namely, at Westminster, Chester, Gloucester, Peterborough, Osney near Oxford, afterwards removed to Christ Church, and at Bristol. But this was a poor fulfilment of his own design, which appears by a document in his handwriting, to have embraced these nine other places besides: St. Alban's, Waltham, Dunstable, Leicester, Fountains, Bury St. Edmund's, Shrewsbury, Welbeck, and Launceston.

Every effort was now made to obtain the surrender of the remaining houses. It certainly appears that a considerable number of their inmates concurred in desiring a reformation. But, on the other hand, there can be no doubt that the greater part were unwilling to resign, and some few could not be induced to do so. Of these, the abbots of Glastonbury, Reading, and Colchester paid the forfeit of their refusal with their lives. Richard Whiting, last abbot of Glastonbury, was a very aged man, of unblemished character. He had one hundred monks in his monastery, and three hundred monks or lay brothers in the cells dependent on it. He maintained many young men at college, distributed abundant alms, and exercised princely hospitality. But it was one of those periods in this uncertain life, when the best and noblest spirits are called to suffer for the sins of those who belong to their class without partaking of their virtues. He was summoned to London, in the hope that, away from home, the old man's heart would fail. But when this was found to be in vain, he was sent home again; and passing through Wells on his way, he found the whole county assembled, and himself summoned into court on a charge of burglary and treason. The trial was public, the jury respectable, and the fact appears to have been proved, of his having applied some of the jewels of the abbey to some purpose not explained, but which probably was the support of the northern insurrection the year before. He was found guilty, but no sentence appears to have followed; and he was sent home to Glastonbury. But the next day, as he approached the abbey, a priest came to his litter, and bade him prepare for death. He begged only that he might take leave of his brethren, but this was denied him. He was dragged on a hurdle to the Tor Hill, overlooking the splendid church and buildings of his monastery, and there, with two of his monks, was hanged and quartered.

The fate of this church and its surrounding buildings is one among too many instances of the bad spirit in which these things were done. It was one of the finest churches in England, and superior to most cathedrals.

The length of the church itself was four hundred and twenty feet; that of St. Joseph's Chapel, beyond it, one hundred and ten feet;—in all five hundred and thirty, being the same length as Canterbury Cathedral, and longer by six feet than York or Lincoln Minster.[1] But all the buildings were unroofed by order of the king, including the library, and the whole house was desecrated. Similar proceedings took place elsewhere. The visitors who took the surrender of the abbey of Tewkesbury, for instance, reported that they had left to stand the abbot's lodging, pantry, cellar, stable, and barn; while the beautiful church, with its chapels, cloisters, chapterhouse, and the rest, are placed in a schedule with this title, *Deemed to be superfluous,* and then follows a valuation of the lead and bells. This church was saved by the parishioners, who bought it of the king. The abbey of St. Alban's was granted with its immense possessions to Sir Richard Leu, and its church was also condemned; but the townspeople bought it for 400*l.* In other instances, as at Croyland, a part only of the church has been preserved; while the inhabitants of the place are left to bury their dead in the roofless nave of that once splendid and celebrated structure. Others were less fortunate. Burlington Priory was held to be forfeited for treason; and Bellasis, the visitor employed, wrote that he had taken down all the lead, and deferred pulling down the house till the next summer, to *save the expense of working in short days.*[2] The abbey of Abingdon is another example. Its church was a stately cathedral, standing in a close, with two western towers lately completed, and with cloisters, chapterhouse, and a magnificent library. It was the burialplace of the Harcourts and other noble

---

[1] See a valuable table of the dimensions of the chief churches in Europe, in the Appendix to *Ancient Models,* by SIR CHARLES ANDERSON, BART., second edition, p. 205.

[2] STEPHENS, vol. II. p. 129.

families, and was the mother-church of the surrounding district. Yet it shared the same fate.

The immediate consequences of these proceedings were lamentable enough. It is not indeed correct to attribute to the dissolution of the monasteries the abject state of the country clergy, or the still more deplorable condition of the poor which existed for some time after. For there is certain evidence that these were of earlier date. A supplication presented to the king before this time,[1] complains that 'noble and worshipful men, as well of the clergy as of the laity, abuse their presentations to parsonages and vicarages, giving them to surveyors of their lands, receivers of their rents, stewards of their household, falconers, and gardeners.' A similar complaint was made in another book,[2] towards the end of this reign, that surveyors of buildings, goldsmiths, and others are rewarded with benefice upon benefice. And as for the state of the poor, we may judge from the description of Sir Richard Gresham, then lord mayor, a friend of Cranmer, and father of the famous Sir Thomas Gresham, who set a noble example to the courtiers who were scrambling for the plunder of the abbeys for their own advancement, by applying to the king, not on behalf of himself or his family, but of those whom he justly called 'Christ's very images, created to His own similitude.' 'There be,' he said, 'near and within London, three hospitals endowed with great possessions only for the relief of the poor and impotent, and not to the maintenance of canons, priests, and monks to live in pleasure, nothing regarding *the miserable people lying in every street*, offending every person passing by the way.' He then proceeds to entreat the king to make over these hospitals to the lord mayor and aldermen, for the use

---

[1] *Harl. Misc.* x. 450.

[2] *The Supplication of the Poor Commons*, A.D. 1546. The other book was called *The Supplication of Beggars*, and was printed in A.D. 1524. STRYPE, *Eccl. Mem.* I. 608.

of the poor; 'and then your grace shall perceive that
where now a small number of canons and monks be
found for their own profit only, a great number of poor
and sickly persons shall be refreshed and maintained,
and also healed and cured.'[1] By his intercession, St.
Bartholomew's and St. Thomas's Hospitals were preserved, and the trusteeship consigned, as he requested,
to the lord mayor and aldermen for the time being.
And his good example was followed by Sir Richard
Dobbs and Sir George Barnes, the friends of Ridley,
and Sir Thomas White, the founder of St. John's College, Oxford, and of the Merchant Taylors' School.

But though the dissolution of the monasteries did
not originate these evils, it certainly augmented them.
The sort of hospitality exercised by the monasteries
was not indeed calculated to elevate the character of
those who depended upon it. But its loss was severely
felt when the new proprietors ceased to spend their
revenue on the spot, and, generally looking only to
profit, raised the rents, and turned the lands into
pasture, by which means the tenants were oppressed,
and the labourers deprived of employment. But the
cause of religion suffered still more. Many monks
were put into small livings, to save the expense of
paying the pensions granted them on the dissolution
of their houses, and thus the country clergy became
more imbued than before with hostility to the Reformation. Nor was this the worst. Poor as were the
stipends of the vicars who depended on the monasteries, the bishop of the diocese had the power, by
several statutes, to augment them; and the new lay
impropriators received the impropriate tithes on the
same condition. But by degrees it was broken through;
where the monastery had supplied its own chaplain, the
new proprietor hired a curate on the lowest possible
terms, and where a vicar was endowed, in no single

---

[1] STRYPE, *Eccl. Mem*, I. 410.

instance was his endowment augmented.   Nor was this
a transitory evil; it has been felt ever since, especially
in large towns, the churches of which, from their position, were usually in the hands of the monasteries, and
where the stipend of the vicar is, in general, wholly in-
adequate to provide for the parochial duty.

But few of Henry's court were found to follow the
example of Sir Richard Gresham.   In general it was a
struggle who should get the most, and very dishonest
means were adopted in obtaining it.   A paper presented
afterwards to Queen Elizabeth, concerning these grants
in her father's time, declares that the value of gold and
silver from the shrines, plate, bells, and furniture was
not less than a million in gold; yet of this only a very
small proportion came to the king, the rest being pilfered.   And the same document relates the various
cheats practised upon the king, by withholding the
title-deeds, making false returns of value, that those
who made them might buy the cheaper; omitting to
make return of woodlands, and then, when they had cut
down all the wood, exchanging with the king for other
lands where wood was standing.[1]   It is no wonder that
these things should bring no real wealth either to the
king or his courtiers.   The whole number of religious
houses suppressed amounted to six hundred and sixty,
and their revenues, as returned, to 140,785*l.* per
annum, which at the present value might be a yearly
revenue of two millions.   But what with large pensions paid to the abbots and monks, and profuse grants
and cheap sales to all sorts of persons, little was left for
the endowment of the few bishoprics that were founded,
except impropriate tithes; and after fortifying some few
places on the coast, the king found his exchequer so low
that the very next year he was forced to come to parliament for a subsidy, and twice again afterwards before
his death; though he had professed, and perhaps in-

---

[1] Information of Abuses, &c. WEEVER, *Fun. Mon.* p. 124. *Harl.
Misc.* x. 276.

tended, to maintain his state and provide for the defence
of his kingdom out of those revenues alone.

Nor did this sudden wealth prosper any better in the
hands of his subjects. Some few families,[1] indeed, have
preserved even to the present time the lands they thus
acquired; and let us hope that the way they have preserved them, has been by not forgetting the conditions
of charity and hospitality on which they first were
granted. But it was observed that, in far the larger
number of cases, one or two generations sufficed to dis-
sipate the whole. It is not for us to anticipate God's
judgment, and pronounce upon such results : sudden
wealth is proverbially inconstant, especially if it come
in an indirect way. But such things are certainly a
subject of grave and serious reflection; and there is
one part of these grants, the impropriate tithes, on
which it may not be wrong to express a stronger
opinion. If the monasteries themselves received them
on condition of making an adequate provision for the
service of the churches to which they belonged, and if
they were granted to laymen on the same condition, no
human law can release any future purchasers from the
moral obligation of making the like provision. If they
bought them ignorantly or thoughtlessly, the duty is
the same when they become aware of it. More than
this,—we had no right, as a nation, to seize these tithes
at all. Whatever may be thought about the lands of
the monasteries, the tithes did not belong to them, but
to the service of God, and to that service they ought to
have been restored. And when we shall have grace
and faith, as a nation, to act upon the exhortation of the
Word of God, ' Bring ye all the tithes into the store-
house, and prove me now herewith, saith the Lord of

---

[1] Burnet thus enumerates the great families raised under Henry
VIII. and still flourishing in his time :—Seymour, Paulet, Russell,
Wriothesley, Herbert. Rich, Cromwell, Brown, Petre, Paget, North.
Montague. (Appendix against Saunders, vol. L p. 279.) But some of
these were previously important families.

Hosts, if I will not open unto you the windows of heaven, and pour you out a blessing, that there shall not be room enough to receive it;' then may we hope that the promise will be fulfilled, 'All nations shall call you blessed : for ye shall be a delightsome land, saith the Lord of Hosts.' [1]

It would be unjust to the memory of Cranmer and his friends to suppose that they shared in the appetite for destruction, or in the unworthy motives of the agents by whom it was effected. Nothing is more remarkable than the decline in the influence of the Reformers at court from the time of the downfall of the abbeys ; and this is attributed, by more than one writer of the time, to the opposition made by their party to the spoliation that was going on.[2] Latimer gave great offence by saying, in one of his sermons, ' that it was not decent the abbeys, which were ordained for the comfort of the poor, should be used for keeping the king's horses.' He was told that such preaching was seditious, and against the king's honour ; and he was obliged, on this or another occasion, to plead his own cause to Henry on his knees : ' If your grace allow me for a preacher,' said this sincere man, ' I would desire to be suffered to discharge my conscience.' He escaped for the present ; but the storm was gathering, and deeper politicians were at work to remove so honest a monitor from the king's court and chapel.

There was all this while a numerous party of temporising opponents of the reformed doctrine, who had

---

[1] Malachi iii. 10, 12.—There were two acts of parliament, 12 Rich. II. cap. 6, and 4 Hen. IV. cap. 12, by which the bishop is empowered to see that the vicar of each impropriate rectory be well and sufficiently endowed. As these laws have not been repealed, it has been thought that the bishops might still exercise the power of augmenting vicarages. But this seems to be a mistake : for the words of each of these laws seem to be confined to the power which the bishop might exercise *at the time of the endowment.*

[2] Treatise on Unwritten Verities. JENKYNS' *Cranmer*, vol. iv. p. 168. FOXE, p. 1816.

yet joined in asserting the king's supremacy, and prosecuting those who denied it, and had many of them
been concerned in the commission against the monasteries, and had obtained large grants of abbey lands.
Among these were the Duke of Norfolk and Sir
William Petre; and, of the churchmen, Bonner, and
Gardiner, of whom Cranmer said, that 'he lacked
neither learning in the law, nor witty invention, nor
craft, to set forth his matters to the best.' When these
men joined with the courtiers, whose religion consisted
chiefly in kindness to themselves, they were often too
strong for Cranmer and the friends of reformation; and
they appear to have urged on the extreme measures
with no other view that can be supposed, but to gratify the king's humour, and to gain power or advantage
to themselves.[1]

The colleges and chantries yet remained, and the
houses of the knights of St. John. These high-born
and wealthy knights would not surrender, and so they
were dissolved by act of parliament the following year,
A.D. 1540. Their illustrious grand master, De l'Isle
Adam, had paid a visit to England some time before
this,[2] on his expulsion from Rhodes after its memorable
siege, to intercede for his order with the king, who is
said to have granted some slight favors to the hoary and
venerable suppliant. It may have been owing to the
recollection of his visit, that their church in London
was spared for the present; it had a bell-tower lately
finished, which is described by an eyewitness as one
of the finest he had ever seen. And it perhaps was on
the same account that such large pensions were granted
to the grand prior of England, Sir William Weston, and
to the grand prior of Ireland, whose house was at Kilmainham, near Dublin—1000l. a year to the former,

<hr />

[1] TANNER, *Notitia Monastica*, Pref. p. xxv. COLLIER, *Eccl. History*,
II. 117.

[2] Between the surrender of Rhodes, A.D. 1523, and the settlement at
Malta, A.D. 1530.

and 500*l.* to the latter.   But Weston died of grief the day his house was dissolved.

On the whole, the country has, doubtless, been a gainer by the dissolution of the monasteries.   So much land in the hands of such corporations was calculated, as we have seen, to cripple the energies and suppress the enterprise of the people.   Nor did it seem likely that these societies could be so reformed as to efface the memory of the superstitions they had cherished, and to promote the interests of true religion.   This was certainly Cranmer's opinion, as it may be read in the *Homily of Good Works*, which was composed by him.   We may be humbled when we think how many bad passions were at work in their suppression; and regret the injustice that was done to many erring but conscientious men, whose worst crime was a stubborn adherence to the principles under which they had been brought up.   But let us not be ungrateful for all the good which Providence has raised out of the dust of these ruined piles.

> From those deserted domes new glories rise,
>   More useful institutes, adorning man;
> Manners enlarged, and new civilities,
>   On fresh foundations build the social plan.
>
> Science, on ampler plume, a bolder flight
>   Essays, escaped from superstition's shrine;
> While freed religion, like primeval light
>   Bursting from chaos, spreads her warmth divine.
>
> Yet here may Pity meditate alone,
>   Nor scorn, within the deep fane's inmost cell,
> To pluck the grey moss from the mantled stone,
>   Some holy founder's mouldering name to spell;
>
> And when, amid the wavering ivy-wreaths,
>   Or clustered column hung with matted brier,
> The whispering wind its pensive music breathes,
>   Recall the measured hymn and chanting quire.

CHAPTER XVII.

Ye blessed angels! If of you
There be, who love the ways to view
Of kings and kingdoms here;
(And sure 'tis worth an angel's gaze,
To see throughout that dreary maze,
God teaching love and fear),
O say, in all the bleak expanse,
Is there a spot to win your glance
So bright, so dark as this?

Christian Year. 1 Lent.

HAD Cranmer aimed to gain himself a name, instead of pursuing his great object of recovering
forgotten truth, he would not have been able to adapt
his measures so circumspectly to the uneven current
of the time. The praise of firmness and decision is
easily given to more daring men, who brave the tor-
rent's force, and stake their life and reputation on a
point; the world is not so just to that more rare but
not less resolute fortitude, which waits for the floods to
subside, and can endure to suffer and be silent, till
calmer times give room for more salutary counsels.
Cranmer justly judged that both the corruptions which
had overspread the Church, and the disjointed condition of society, were mainly owing to the establishment of the pope's laws and power; and that truth and
good government could not be restored till the king's
authority was acknowledged over all persons and in all
causes, and the people had shaken from their neck 'the

yoke and halters which they had made for themselves.'[1]
Judging also that *a king's heart is in the hand of the
Lord, to turn it whithersoever He will,* it was a part of his
religion, as it has been of all the most excellent teachers,
both of the Primitive and of our Reformed Church,
to be *subject to the higher powers for conscience' sake*;
not to resist evil, which was done with the forms and
authority of law, but to try to mitigate it; to plead for
the sufferers who were unworthily condemned, and to
gain over by persuasion those who, from a mistaken
principle, held sincerely those errors which he strove
to overthrow. And no patient chemist ever replaced
his broken retorts, or watched his experiments in the
laboratory, with more earnest pains than the meek archbishop submitted his course of proceedings to the furnace
of the king's wrath, which was so often seen to go forth
as the roaring of a lion, and as messengers of death.

And an impartial judgment will confess, that there
were qualities in the king whom he served which might
well persuade a Christian bishop, at least before the
systematic cruelty of Henry's later years, that he was
an instrument of Providence, raised up for some great
purposes. He had certainly that great princely talent
of discerning merit, and selecting for his ministers men
who were equal to the burden of those difficult times.
These were again removed when their services were
no longer needed—not, as in former reigns, with harm
and loss to the public safety, but to their own absolute
ruin and eclipse, showing that all their greatness had
stood in the sunshine of their sovereign's favour. Hence
a people, habitually turbulent and nominally free, bowed
down before his will; and it is nothing strange if he
learned to believe and turn to account the flatteries
with which he was beset. His parliament told him, to
his face, that he was the most learned and most illustrious of kings; and he thought it modesty to answer,

---

' CRANMER's *Answer to the Devonshire Rebels.*

that he gave the glory to God. It was not difficult for such a man to persuade himself that the least resistance to his will was the blackest treason. The remorseless system of the civil war, during the preceding century, had made it a principle of self-preservation with the prevailing party to show no mercy; and while none dared remonstrate, and all were familiar with scenes of blood, his own heart unhappily suggested no compunction. And yet, amidst his tyranny, there was the same vigorous intellect conspicuous to the last, and the same resolute pursuit of a grand design. He had conceived the idea of a National Church, holding Catholic truth, independent of the Roman pontiff, and of a patriot king presiding over such a Church. But understanding, as he did, by Catholic truth every doctrine then held in the Church of Rome, he had no mind or feeling to relax the established way of maintaining it undisputed. He therefore persecuted either party in turn, as each seemed to be opposed to these his favourite notions.

In May 1539, the same parliament which confirmed the surrender of the larger abbeys, decreed that proclamations issued by the king, on his own authority, should have the force of law; and passed an act to establish, under the severest penalties, *six articles of faith*, on the following points:—

1. That in the sacrament of the altar, after consecration, there remaineth no substance of bread and wine; but the natural body and blood of Christ are present under these forms.

2. That communion in both kinds is not necessary to salvation to all persons by the law of God. (This was to establish a custom, which had now prevailed for more than a hundred years, of denying the cup to lay people.)

3. That priests might not marry.

4. That vows of chastity, taken either by men or women, ought to be observed. (So that monks and nuns, though they had lost their monasteries, were to

live as if they were still enclosed, except they had
taken the vows before they were of age.)

5. That solitary masses were agreeable to God's law,
and ought to be continued; for men received great
benefit by them.

6. That auricular confession was necessary, and ought
to be retained in the Church.

It was enacted that all who should deny the first
article should be burnt as heretics; to impugn the rest
was made felony without benefit of clergy. This law
was introduced by the Duke of Norfolk, having been
previously submitted to the clergy in convocation, where
it was opposed by Cranmer and other bishops; but the
inferior clergy had assented. When it was before parliament, Cranmer again argued against it for three days
successively in the House of Lords; and, though the
king came in person to require him to withdraw before
it came to the vote, he refused to do so, and recorded
his vote against it. The immediate consequence was,
that Latimer, now bishop of Worcester, and Shaxton.
of Salisbury, were thrown into prison, and resigned
their bishoprics; and in a short time more than five
hundred persons were imprisoned. Many of the clergy
who were now married were forced to separate from
their wives, of whom Cranmer himself was one. But
the more dismal results of this disgraceful statute did
not appear till after the fall of Cromwell.

In the next year after the convocation had passed
their vote for an English translation of the Bible,
the hopes of the nation had been gratified by the
birth of a Prince of Wales, who was baptised by
the name of Edward, and had Cranmer for his god-
father. The death of his mother, Jane Seymour, ten
days after the prince's birth, had left the king again a
widower; but the loss was sensibly felt by him in this
instance, and he did not immediately seek to supply it,
till Cromwell, towards the close of the year 1539, promoted his marriage with a German princess, Anne of

Cleves.   The event of this marriage is well known ; the
king conceived a dislike to her as soon as he saw her;
he married her as a point of honour—such is the name
the world assigns to the most selfish and ungenerous
cowardice—with the intention to divorce her ; the divorce was obtained from the compliant opinions of the
clergy without difficulty ; but the minister who had
brought him into this predicament was not to be forgiven.   The Duke of Norfolk and Gardiner hated
Cromwell as an upstart, and as one whose policy had
been opposed to theirs, and favourable to the Reformers.
And there is reason to believe that the king, finding his
late measures unpopular, was willing to shift the blame
upon his agent, who now appeared to be no longer
serviceable.   It was natural that Cranmer, who had
been in long correspondence with him on matters of
Church policy, should have interposed, as he did, in his
favour.   But the disgrace of this minister, as of others
in these dangerous days, was but a prelude to his death.
He was condemned by a bill of attainder, the first victim
of a law which he had himself procured, by which an accused person might be condemned without a trial ; and
in spite of his own abject supplications, and the intercession of Cranmer, suffered as a traitor, July 28, A.D. 1540.

It is a singular mark of the nature of the struggle of
opinions which was going on, that the very ballad-
singers in the streets were divided into opposite parties
on this occasion ; and rival ditties carried on the controversy, whether Cromwell was more of a traitor or a
victim to the cause of The Reformation.   Cromwell seems
to have contrived his dying speech in answer to one of
these ballads, which accused him of irreligion, when
he desired the bystanders ' to bear him record, that he
died in the Catholic faith, not doubting in any article,
nor denying any sacrament of the Church.'[1]   By these

---

[1] Both sacramentes and sacramentalles
Thou woldyst not suffer within thy walles, &c.
                                    PERCY's Reliques, vol. II. 00.

words, as Collier justly remarks, it is plain that he died in the religion professed by the king at this period, and in the communion of the Church which had sanctioned the Six Articles.   But it is to be feared he had been all his life an irreligious politician, and had little serious thought upon these subjects.   He was a man of little learning but great natural talents; he was a faithful friend, but had no other public principle than to execute his master's purposes with profit to himself.   Hence he had nothing to restrain him from becoming the resolute agent of the most sweeping measures of destruction.[1]

His death, however, was followed by the execution of many better men.   A few days afterwards, one of those dreadful spectacles was exhibited in Smithfield, by which Henry thought to prove his impartiality in the system he had resolved to uphold.   Barnes, a divine of some note, who had once been employed on the king's service abroad, and two other clergymen, Garret and Jerome, were burnt for heresy; and Featherstone, Abel, and Powell were tied to the same stake, for adhering to the pope and denying the royal supremacy. When the sword of persecution was thus provided with two edges, it is not wonderful if, as Lord Clarendon asserts, Henry caused more men to be put to death for their religion than afterwards suffered in the reign of his daughter Queen Mary.[2]

---

[1] Foxe tells a story of his meeting with a friar in St. Paul's Churchyard, wearing his frock and cowl after the suppression of his house. Cromwell threatened him with hanging at a few hours' notice, if he did not change his apparel. This was much akin to the kind of law which he directed the Wardens of the Marches to deal to the poor gipsies, who were all to leave the realm by a certain day, or to be hanged without judge or jury. See SIR H. ELLIS's *Letters*, No. 137.

[2] LORD CLARENDON's *Essays*, p. 205. This is more probable than Bishop Burnet's statement, which affirms the contrary.   But Burnet perhaps means only to reckon the sufferers on one side.   Cranmer himself says (*Answer to Devonshire Rebels*) that 'the statute of Six Articles continued in force little above the space of one year.'   But he seems to mean that Henry moderated the execution of it in some cases, which perhaps he knew of, but they are not recorded.

It is not necessary, and it would be only painful, to enumerate these cases one after another. Henry himself sometimes took part in the public examinations of the accused, as he did at the trial of Lambert, a clergyman of Cambridge, who, in 1538, was condemned for denying transubstantiation, and burnt with circumstances of peculiar cruelty. And now a remarkable agent in such atrocities, the notorious Edmund Bonner, had been appointed bishop of Hereford, in the room of Cranmer's friend, Edward Fox, and within two years was translated to the more important see of London. It is said that he had disguised his principles so much before he was elevated, that Cromwell was deceived by him, and recommended him to the king. The possession of power discovered his true nature; and after Cromwell's fall there was no longer any occasion to dissemble. Soon after the execution of Barnes and his fellow-sufferers, he caused a boy of fifteen, Richard Mekin, to be tried for heresy. The act of the Six Articles, cruel as it was, was so far better than the statute of Henry IV., that it required the evidence to be submitted to a jury; and in this instance the grand jury refused to find a bill. But Bonner acted as Cromwell had done at the trial of the Carthusians; he told the jury they were perjured, threatened them with personal danger, and made them put the boy on his trial. He was found guilty; and though he recanted at the stake, he was burnt—an ominous prelude of the horrors in which this prelate was to steep his soul

The king had married Catherine Howard, a niece of the Duke of Norfolk, shortly after his divorce from Anne of Cleves; but it was not long that she enjoyed his favour. She was confessedly a woman of unchaste life ; and she was condemned and executed for treason, with the accomplices of her guilt. Had such a calamity befallen another king, he would have obtained some share of public sympathy; but Henry's domestic misfortunes were regarded as a divine retribution.

His marriage with Catharine Parr, his sixth and
last wife, which took place in July 1543, was calculated to give some advantage to the cause of the Reformation.　This lady, who had been before twice married,
had profited by the practice, which arose with the
revival of letters, of instructing women in the higher
departments of learning.　A good man who lived at
that time, speaks of it, in writing to Catharine herself,
that it was now 'no strange thing to hear gentlewomen,
instead of most vain communication about the moon
shining in the water, to use grave and substantial talk in
Latin and Greek, with their husbands, of godly matters;
and for young damsels in noble houses and in the
courts of princes, instead of cards and other instruments
of vain trifling, to have continually in their hands
either psalms, homilies, and other devout meditations,
or else St. Paul's Epistles, or other book of Holy Scripture; and as familiarly to read or reason thereof, in
Greek, Latin, French, or Italian, as in English.'　It
was a part of the wisdom of Henry VIII., that he himself set an example to his nobility, in giving a learned
education to his daughters as well as to his son; and
nothing helped more than such social improvement to
spread the knowledge of religion. As to Queen Catharine
Parr, she was of eminent service in this way; she was
herself the author of a religious treatise,[1] and it was by
her desire and at her expense that the commentary of
Erasmus on the New Testament was translated into
English; and she persuaded the king to have it set up
in churches, together with the Bible.

Thus were the two parties balanced; the translated
Bible giving an increased advantage to the Reformers,
while the persecuting statutes presented a strong barrier
of defence to some of the most corrupt doctrines and
practices of the papal times. The king, in these last
years of his reign, seems in turn to have favoured both,

---

[1] *The Lamentation of a Sinner*, printed in 1548.

but with evident fear and distrust of the spirit of
liberty which the change of his own making had raised
up. He would not retract his permission that the
Bible should be read, but he sanctioned a law of
Gardiner's to limit the rank and condition of those who
should be allowed to read it ; so that none of the lower
classes of society, no artificers, apprentices, husbandmen, or labourers, might possess copies for themselves.
Gardiner had attempted a further restriction, by pro-
posing that in the next edition several words of great
doctrinal importance should be given only in Latin.
But the king saw the absurdity, and probably alluded
to it when he complained, in one of his last speeches,
that ' some of the prelates were as stiff in retaining
their old *mumpsimus*, as others were over-forward in
asserting their new *sumpsimus*.' There was some
ground for both these complaints. People used to
collect round the place at which the Bible was set
up in churches; and one would read aloud and expound what he read, even during divine service. An
injunction was therefore issued, that none should read
Scripture aloud in any assembly, or expound it, without license from the king or the bishop of the diocese.

The old abuse of acting plays and interludes in
churches, which the monks and friars had so long
sanctioned, was now turned against themselves. Plays
were brought in to ridicule the exploded religious
orders ; but, as the progress is easy from things indifferent to things sacred, and there was little reverence
in the inventors of such drolleries, they did not refrain from turning into burlesque the highest mysteries
of religion. This evil was very properly restrained by
some injunctions which Bonner issued in A.D. 1542,
probably acting under direction of the king.

In these abuses there was, doubtless, something to
justify those who looked upon the progress of things
with suspicion, but much more to convince a deliberate judgment of the necessity of persevering and

labouring more earnestly for the advancement of religious knowledge. Henry had discernment enough to appreciate the integrity of Cranmer, and this alone was a powerful motive to keep him from yielding too far to the designs of his enemies. And though he retained doctrines and practices, which could not stand the test of Scripture, he still saw that his own cause had need of the support of the awakened thirst for knowledge. Yet his selfish nature led him to act as if he were pleased to be the spectator of a tragedy in which his subjects played for life or death, interfering only when the danger threatened his personal convenience. There is a gleam of greater generosity in his treatment of Cranmer on one occasion. It was near the close of his reign, in A. D. 1545. He revealed to him the machinations of his enemies, and bade him investigate the authors of a plot against his life. Thornden, his suffragan bishop of Dover, formerly a monk of Christchurch, Canterbury, and Dr. Barber, a civilian, whom he retained in his own family as his legal adviser, had been corrupted by Gardiner, and employed in collecting evidence against their patron and benefactor; and several other members of his cathedral, to which Gardiner himself had once belonged, were engaged in the conspiracy. It is a remarkable proof of the confiding simplicity of the archbishop, that he had always entertained the highest opinion of Thornden's character, as 'a right honest man, of good learning, good judgment, without superstition, and ready to set forward his prince's cause,' and on these grounds had petitioned Cromwell for his preferment.[1] When he was informed of their treachery and ingratitude, he led aside Thornden and Barber into his garden, told them that some whom he had trusted had disclosed his secrets and accused him of heresy, and asked how they thought such persons ought to be

---

[1] Letter ccxlii. JENKYNS' Cranmer. Thornden lived to be an active agent in the persecution of the Reformed clergy under Queen Mary.

treated.   They were loud in expressing their indignation, and declared that such traitors deserved to die.
' Know ye these letters, my masters?' said the primate,
and showed them the proof of their own falsehood.
The two offenders fell upon their knees to implore forgiveness, for it was evident that their lives were in
his power; but all the revenge he took was to bid
them ask forgiveness of God.   His charity and forbearance on this and other similar occasions must be acknowledged as very remarkable, when we remember
amidst what personal dangers they were manifested;
and it is not wonderful if it became a kind of proverb
among those who knew him,—' Do my lord of Canterbury an ill turn, and he is your friend for ever.'

The protection, however, which Henry afforded to
Cranmer was not extended to inferior men, and it
allowed but little relaxation to those who were suspected.   Latimer lay for some years a prisoner in the
Tower, till, near the end of the reign, he seems to have
been dismissed; for we find him preaching again where
he could in Warwickshire and Derbyshire.   Shaxton
was prosecuted under the statute for some words spoken
in prison against transubstantiation.   He was condemned
to be burnt, but was permitted to save his life by sign-
ing a recantation; and then forced to do what to a
feeling mind must have been worse than death—to
preach the condemned sermon, as it may be called,
at the dying scene of another, one of the most innocent and gentle sufferers for the doctrine which he had
not courage to maintain.

Anne Ayscough, or Askew, was the second daughter
of Sir William Ayscough, of Kelsey in Lincolnshire.
She had been reluctantly persuaded by her father to
marry a gentleman of the same county, of the name of
Kyme, on the death of her elder sister, who had been
engaged to him.   She had borne him two children; but
having embraced the Reformed doctrine, she was driven
from his house by unkindness, his prejudices being

strong against it. She was questioned by some of the clergy at Lincoln, who found her in the Minster, reading the Bible on her knees, according to the good custom which then prevailed, of admitting private devotions in church. She soon afterwards came to London, and there resumed her maiden name, intending to sue for a divorce; and was taken into the household of Catharine Parr, where she was admired for her beauty, esteemed for her learning and piety, and pitied for her misfortunes. Gardiner and his party were at this time labouring to effect the queen's ruin; and it appears, from the examination of Anne Askew, that one of their objects with her was to extract evidence against Catharine. She was first taken before what was called 'the Quest,' that is, persons appointed to hold inquisition for heresy, under the act of the Six Articles; and then, being sent to the lord mayor, was by him committed to prison. But her friends were influential, and made interest to have her bailed; to which the lord mayor, and afterwards the lord chancellor, assented, if they could have the consent of the Bishop of London. Upon this she was brought before Bonner, and each of these persons seems to have shrunk from extreme courses, and to have been willing to release her if they could but obtain from her some sort of acquiescence in their creed. The main point was transubstantiation; at this time she fully admitted the real presence in the holy eucharist, but that, unhappily, was not enough. People were required to acknowledge that Christ's own body is so present in every morsel of consecrated bread, and so remains, as that it cannot cease to be His corporeal body, whatever may become of it; and it was customary to invent imaginary cases by way of testing this belief. Accordingly she was asked, if a mouse should eat the consecrated wafer, whether he received God or no. Anything more irreverent, or more calculated to drive people away from the truth into opposite extremes, it is hardly possible to conceive. But that such questions were commonly asked is so absolutely certain, that there is no reason to doubt the artless narrative as related by herself. She smiled at this question, and made no answer; but her woman's delicacy was offended at what she called the 'unsavoury similitude' by which Bonner tried to persuade her to speak her mind to him, 'because if a man had a wound, no wise surgeon would minister help to it before he had seen it uncovered.' She was accused to Bonner of having called the mass idolatry. But she replied, 'No; I said not so. Howbeit the Quest did ask me, whether private masses relieved souls departed or no? Unto whom then I answered, What idolatry is this, that we should rather believe in private masses, than in the healthsome death of the dear Son of God!' So that, in common with the most learned of the Reformers, she drew a distinction between private masses and the service of the Church in the administration of the Holy Communion, then called the mass. For she expressed her readiness to communicate at the approaching Easter, and her joy that the time was near. As she admitted the real presence, Bonner resolved to release her if possible, being urged, as he said, by her influential friends, and let us hope also by some compassion in himself. So he drew up a confession, in which the point of transubstantiation was not very prominently stated, and invited her to sign it. She desired him to add, that she admitted so much as the Holy Scripture doth agree unto; but at last she put her name with this explanation only, 'I do believe all manner of things contained in the faith of the Catholic Church.' The confession, however, was enrolled without the explanation, and was published afterwards as a recantation, which she earnestly protested it was never in her mind to make.

This was in A.D. 1545; but the next year, when the council were carrying on their plots against the queen, she was examined before them by the king's command;

and Gardiner especially pressed her to acknowledge the
corporeal presence. But she had made up her mind,
and now would not say more than, that 'so oft as we do
receive the bread, in a Christian congregation, in remembrance of Christ's death, and with thanksgiving,
we receive therewith the fruits also of his most glorious
passion.' She was committed to custody, and being
seized with violent illness, desired to see Latimer, who,
it seems, was then a prisoner. But this was refused,
and, ill as she was, she was removed to Newgate, where,
continuing her journal, she wrote that she 'neither
wished for death nor feared his might, but was as merry
as one bound towards heaven:' adding this text,
'Labour not for the meat that perisheth, but for that
which endureth unto life everlasting.' Now again she
was taken before Bonner, and the wretched Shaxton
also was brought to try to persuade her by his example; but when all was vain, and her spirit was
goaded into answers still more strong against what
they would have had her say, she was sent to the
Tower, to endure a more horrible trial. She was questioned about the faith of the ladies of the queen's court,
and was especially asked who maintained her in prison,
in the hope of eliciting something which might be produced as evidence against the queen herself. What
follows must be told in her own words: 'Then they
put me on the rack, because I confessed no ladies or
gentlewomen to be of my opinion, and thereon they
kept me a long time. And because I lay still, and did
not cry, my lord chancellor and another [1] took pains to
rack me with their own hands till I was nigh dead.'

'The might of woman appeareth in weakness.' These
words of the martyr Philpot were exemplified in all the
conduct of this Christian lady. She swooned when
taken from the rack; and when recovered, she sat for

---

[1] The lord chancellor and another. Wriothesley was chancellor.
She gives the name of the other, but as Foxe names a different person,
it is better to mention neither

two hours on the bare floor, while Wriothesley, having failed to coerce her, now tried as vainly to persuade her by words of kindness. At length she was brought to the stake, in company with Lascelles, a gentleman of the king's household, and two others. The scene was in Smithfield, near St. Bartholomew's Church, under which the lord chancellor and others of the council were provided with seats. Unable to stand, she was brought in a chair and chained up to the stake, while Shaxton preached; after which the chancellor sent to each of them to offer them their lives if they would recant. But her answer was that she came not there to deny her Lord and Master. And the rest having in like manner refused, the lord mayor commanded the fire to be kindled. It was nearly dark, and the spectators, intent upon this appalling scene, rendered more awful by the surrounding gloom, perceived at the moment a few big drops of rain and a single clap of thunder. At a time of strong excitement men's minds are peculiarly apt to entertain thoughts of communion with the unseen world. It was much noted at the time, and one who was present declared in relating it, ' there fell a few pleasant drops upon us that stood by, and a pleasing noise from heaven; God knows whether I may truly call it thunder, as the people did in the gospel, but methought it seemed that the angels in heaven rejoiced to receive their souls into bliss.' But this tragedy was long remembered, and being the last of these horrors in Henry's reign, people were the more prepared to acquiesce in the changes that afterwards took place.

The queen had wellnigh been sacrificed, and Gardiner and his party supposed that they had carried their point; but having had notice of the plot, she contrived to allay the king's suspicion; and the result was, that he removed Gardiner's name from among the counsellors appointed to act during the minority of his son. Cranmer also escaped a still more imminent danger;

and Henry's anger turned against the opposite party. The Earl of Surrey, a man of high accomplishments and noble character, was brought to the scaffold; though the only ground of accusation was his having expressed indignation at being superseded in his military command in France, and having quartered the arms of Edward the Confessor without a difference, like one of the royal family. The truth was, probably, that Henry dreaded the power of the house of Norfolk during the minority of his son, and so for reasons of policy resolved to remove them. The Duke of Norfolk himself was attainted, Cranmer absenting himself from the house, that he might take no part against a political opponent. He was condemned, and would have suffered, like his noble son, on the very next day, when the king was summoned to his last account. He had been ill some time, but none dared to speak to him of his danger, for he had made it treason to speak of the king's death. When one ventured at last to ask whether he would have spiritual consolation, he put it off till it was too late, and then sent for Cranmer. He was speechless when the archbishop came, but he pressed his hand, and expired. In imitation perhaps of former kings, he founded on his deathbed Trinity College in Cambridge, and designed the foundation of Christ's Hospital: and in accordance with the faith in which he died, the heralds proclaimed at his funeral, ' Pray for the soul of the high and mighty Prince Henry VIII. of England.' He died on the 27th of January 1547, in the 56th year of his age, and the 38th of his reign.

The great event of this reign, as regards the Reformation, was the setting forth of an English Bible. This was the right foundation to lay for further measures. Not that the people in this country had been always denied the Scriptures in their own language; we have seen that it was otherwise: the prohibition came in with the era of persecution. There were old

English translations, as there were old translations in
Spain, till persecution put them down. And a king of
France had ordered a French translation to be made at
the very period that Wycliffe's Bible was condemned in
England. But the Church for a century or more had
betrayed this important trust; and the recovery cannot
well be too highly estimated. It is remarkable, that
the Bible now published was the same translation
which had so lately been condemned by the bishops,
as 'corrupted by William Tyndal.' Tyndal had translated the New Testament and the five books of Moses,
and the rest was done by Miles Coverdale, afterwards
bishop of Exeter, with some assistance from Bilney and
others. Tyndal did not live to witness this fruit of his
labours, for he was betrayed by an acquaintance, and
put to death as a heretic, in the Low Countries. But
he died with the prayer upon his lips, ' Lord, open the
eyes of the King of England.' The first edition of this
translation was published in 1537, and was called
Matthew's Bible, by a name which appears to have
been fictitious. It was printed partly at Paris, under
the supervision of John Rogers, afterwards the first
sufferer in Mary's reign, and under the patronage of
Bonner, who was then the king's ambassador to the
Court of France. Another and better edition came
out in the year 1541, which is generally known as
Cranmer's, because it had a preface written by him.
It was required that each parish should be provided
with a copy, which should be placed upon a desk in
the body of the church, where all might come to read.
It is said that some aged persons learned to read on
purpose, and it may well be imagined with what thankfulness such a boon would be received by those who
but a short time before were forced to hide the precious
portions of God's Word which they might possess, and
go into the woods and fields to read it unobserved.
When the first edition came out, Cranmer wrote to
Cromwell that he 'rejoiced to see this day of reforma-

tion, which he concluded was now risen in England, since THE LIGHT OF GOD'S WORD DID SHINE OVER IT WITHOUT A CLOUD.'

Besides the Commentaries of Erasmus, already mentioned as having been placed with the Bible in churches towards the end of this reign, other books were set forth by authority at different times. The chief of these were—an explanation of the Church Services, containing some valuable matter mixed up with Romish doctrine; several editions of a collection of prayers called the King's Primer, and two books of devotional instruction. The first, entitled the *Institution of a Christian Man*, and called also the Bishops' Book, was drawn up with the consent of the convocation, and printed A.D. 1537, a year after some 'Articles of Faith' had been agreed to, upon which it was grounded; but the second, which was intended to supersede it, was put forth after the act of the Six Articles, and was the result of deliberations among some of the bishops and other learned men, which were not concluded for three years: it was published with a preface from the king himself, by the title of the *Necessary Erudition of a Christian Man*, but it was also called the King's Book. It maintained and defined transubstantiation, whereas the Institution had been silent on the subject. Except in this point, the Erudition was an improvement upon the Institution. The Institution had commanded devotion to images, honouring of saints, and masses for the dead; whereas the Erudition omitted the mention of them, and advised the people to abstain from discussing the doctrine of purgatory, under colour of which it declared that great abuses had been advanced, to make men believe that masses said at prescribed places did in those places more profit the souls than in another: thus gradually did they begin to impugn the practice of private masses.

The latest edition of the Primer was published in the

year 1546, the last of Henry's reign; but this was by
no means the best edition, for several things were now
omitted, when the king was become jealous of the progress
of the Reformed doctrine, which had been inserted, by
way of caution against some prevailing errors, in the second
edition, published under Cranmer's auspices, in A.D. 1535.
These books, called Primers, had existed in the English
language for two centuries before this time, and probably from an earlier period.[1] They were doubtless
originally intended, as the name imports, to be among
the first things which young persons should learn; but
they were not designed for them alone, but for all classes
of the people, being a collection of admirable prayers
and devotions suited for all ages, many of which were
taken from the old services of the Church translated
into English. In Cranmer's edition,[2] the second commandment was distinguished from the first, and recited
at length; whereas the Roman way of uniting them,
and omitting the greater part of the second, was restored
in the later copy. In this also there was a general
confession of sins, an instruction how to pray, an explanation of the Lord's Prayer, and an especial caution as
to the *Ave Maria*, or Hail Mary,—that it is not a
prayer to the Virgin, but that the grace and favour
given her of God giveth us an occasion to praise God
and give thanks. There were devotions for the seven
hours of primitive worship, including a translation of
the Matins and Evensong as then used in Latin; next
came the Litany in English; a 'Dirige' or Dirge for
funerals and for the anniversary of the death of friends;
the seven penitential psalms; the history of our Saviour's passion from the gospel of St. John; and, in
conclusion, a great number of admirable prayers, of
which those especially for the concord and for the peace
of Christ's Church are replete with piety.

[1] See MASKELL's *Monumenta Ritualia*, vol. II.
[2] The editor was Dr. Marshall, archdeacon of Nottingham, but he
probably was employed and directed by Cranmer.

The Primer was not intended to be used by the minister in public worship, but to form the devotional manual of the people either in the closet or in church. For it was then the custom to resort to the churches for private as well as public prayer; and when the devout worshipper had such a book in his hand, and the Bible in his native language open for his perusal, much progress must have been made towards a better state of things, though the services themselves continued to be in Latin.   We have cause to regret that we have lost this practice of resorting to our churches at all times, and going down upon our knees to say our prayers or read our Bibles.   We have seen that Anne Ayscough spoke of having been daily in the Minster, when at Lincoln, reading in the Bible.   Who does not wish to see these noble churches again visited by such worshippers, and means afforded for private prayer or Scripture reading, instead of their being made, as they are now, the resort of idle curiosity?

In the last year of his reign this king advanced yet another step, by ordering lessons from the Bible in English to be read after the Latin hymns, and the Litany to be said or sung in English instead of Latin.   This litany differs only in the following particulars from that now in use: after calling upon the Holy Trinity, as at present, there followed three invocations to the Virgin, the Angels, and all Patriarchs, Prophets, Apostles, Martyrs, to pray for us; and where we now pray to be delivered from sedition, privy conspiracy, and rebellion, these words were inserted, 'From the tyranny of the Bishop of Rome, and all his abominable enormities.' It appears from a letter of Cranmer's to the king, that this litany was translated by him, with a few alterations, from one already in use.   Henry, however, was preparing to go further than this.   He had agreed with Francis, the French king, that they would each put forth a revised communion-service, instead of the old Latin service of the mass, in the language of their respective countries. Cranmer had received orders to prepare that for England; and the two kings had resolved to invite the emperor to concur with them in the total abolition of the supremacy of the pope throughout their respective dominions.

It was about a year before Henry's death, on the 15th of December 1545, that the first session was opened of the famous Council of Trent. It had become evident that both Germany and France would follow the example of England, unless something was done for reformation by the Court of Rome; and Paul III. determined to hold a council, which he accordingly summoned to Mantua in 1536. But both France and England resolved not to acknowledge any council which should be held in Italy, under the immediate influence of the pope; and both these powers sent ambassadors to the Lutherans assembled at Smalcald, to dissuade them from agreeing to it. The pope next attempted to hold it at Vicenza, but against this Henry protested, and neither the emperor nor the French king would permit their bishops to attend. At length Trent was decided upon in 1542, but in the meantime the bull of excommunication had been published against Henry; so that, besides that the council was called in the name of the pope, instead of being in the name of Christian princes, Henry had now no option unless he chose to prejudge his own cause, and come as a suppliant to the very authority which he had disavowed. Martin Luther died in the year 1546, soon after the council had begun to sit, but his death made little difference in its proceedings. The subjects of discussion were of two kinds, discipline and doctrine, and some very important improvements in discipline were adopted, and very salutary regulations made. They would have been, indeed, much more so, had not the pope overruled them. The Spanish bishops were earnest to go to the root of the evil of non-residence, by declaring that a bishop's residence was of divine obligation and indispensable; and many of the Gallican Church were desirous to have had the Pragmatic Sanction re-established. But in point of doctrine they were not so fortunate. They did not as yet meddle with transubstantiation and similar points; but in their anxiety to counteract what they deemed Lutheran errors, they reckoned some things as Lutheran tenets which no Protestant holds; and they proceeded to establish as doctrines of the Church some points which can scarcely be thought to be probable opinions, much less ought they to be positively required as part of Christian faith: such as, that traditions are part of divine revelation—that all the books of Scripture, including those called apocryphal, are of equal authority—and that the old Latin translation of the Bible, called the Vulgate, should be received as of equal authority with the original Greek and Hebrew. These decisions were not calculated to promote the peace of Christendom, and that relating to tradition especially has done almost irreparable mischief; for when people saw it placed on a level with Scripture, they went to the other extreme of denying that any respect at all is due to the collective voice of antiquity. How much it tended at the time to widen the breach between the two parties, may be judged by the mention which Bernard Gilpin makes of its effect upon his own mind. He was then a young man, anxiously seeking the truth, and hesitating between the fear of schism and the duty of following the Word of God. And his prepossessions in favour of Rome were first shaken by this decision.

Such were the first acts of this famous synod, for which the Church of Rome claims the allegiance of the whole of Christendom, as a general council of the Universal Church. But it wants no fewer than three requisites to entitle it to that character. First, it was not called by the consent of the Christian princes of the countries over which it claims authority, but by the sole authority of the Bishop of Rome, without consulting them. Secondly, so far from representing the whole Christian world, it did not even represent more than one half of Europe. No bishops were present from Poland, none from Sweden or Denmark, England or Ireland, very few from any part of Germany, and none at all from several of its independent states; to say nothing of the whole of the Greek Church, embracing Russia and its provinces, the Christians in Greece, and those in European and Asiatic Turkey. Thirdly, in not one of these countries, except Poland, has it ever been acknowledged; whereas it was always deemed essential to the ratification of a council that it should be universally received. These points may to some appear of little importance; but when the Roman Church places its claim to our allegiance on the decrees of this council, and denounces us as heretics, separate from Christian communion, because we will not adopt them, we cannot tell how important it may become to show that this council is not entitled to that character, which, by a singular coincidence, was omitted in describing it. For it was proposed when the synod was opened that the words 'representing the Universal Church of Christ' should be added to its title; but the proposal was overruled by the pope's legates, of whom Cardinal Pole was one, not because they did not claim that character for the synod, but lest it should be inferred that the pope himself is subject to the council.

CHAPTER XVIII.

EDWARD VI.   PROTECTOR SOMERSET.   HOMILIES.
SUPPRESSION OF CHANTRIES.

This pretty lad will prove our country's bliss,
His looks are full of peaceful majesty ;
His head by nature framed to wear a crown,
His hand to wield a sceptre ; and himself
Likely, in time, to bless a regal throne.
Make much of him, my Lords.

SHAKSPEARE.—*Hen. VI.*

THE reign of Edward VI., if regarded only in reference to the temporal prosperity of his subjects,
would not be calculated to excite any feelings of satisfaction.   We see the people poor and discontented, and
the nobles actuated often by selfish motives, even in
their adherence to religious improvements.   But this is
not the only way in which history may be read.   It is
possible to divest even the sacred records of their religious lesson, if we will regard the events which they
relate apart from that commentary which the Spirit of
God reveals ; and on the other hand, it is also possible
to trace, amidst the selfishness of man, the overruling
Providence of God, directing that very selfishness to
the accomplishment of his own mysterious but bene-
ficent designs.   And the character of the princely boy
himself who presided over the changes that now took
place, was worthy of one appointed to such a destiny.

Edward, the sixth since the Conquest,[1] was born on

---

[1] The Norman Edwards, and other sovereigns for three or four centuries after the Conquest, did not designate themselves absolutely as
t he first or second king of England of their name, but as the first or
second (or as the case might be) *since the Conquest.* This style was
adopted even by those sovereigns whose christian name had never been

the 12th of October, 1537, and had not, therefore, completed his tenth year when he succeeded to the throne, on the death of his father, in January, 1547. The wisdom of his father was in nothing more conspicuous than in the choice of preceptors for his son; for he did not suffer his own religious prejudices to prevent him from selecting good and learned men, though they might be disposed to carry the Reformation much further than he was himself. The first of these was Sir Anthony Cook, to whose care the young Edward was entrusted when only six years of age. But those to whom belong especially the praise of having formed his character, were Dr. Richard Cox, afterwards Dean of Christ Church, and lastly Bishop of Ely, and Sir John Cheek, professor of Greek at Cambridge. The natural talents of their royal pupil, and his progress in all human learning, were such as to move the admiration of elder scholars; his amiable temper, which shone forth in his conversation, made it appear as though his soul was the abode of all the virtues, and his gravity and piety gained him the name of the Youthful Saint.[1] There are now remaining in the British Museum letters of his in French and Latin, written before he was nine years old, and at thirteen he was reading Aristotle in the Greek. His virtues were regarded by good men at the time as a singular blessing to his country, and many expressed their belief that it was an answer to their prayers. But this early promise rather encouraged hopes for the future than aided counsels for the present. The unsettled state of things was left to the direction of statesmen little agreed among themselves, and none of sufficient capacity and influence, nor, indeed, of sufficient character and prin-

borne by a Saxon king, as Richard II.; *Ricardus, post conquistum secundus.* It is to be regretted that we have lost this vestige of a recognition of our Anglo-Saxon Monarchs; two of whom by the name of Edward have a place in our calendar.

[1] ROGER ASCHAM, *Epist* I. 2, and II. 29.

ciples, to preside firmly at the helm of state. Cranmer, therefore, judged with some reason that his difficulties were rather increased than diminished by the death of a king, of whom his daughter, the Princess Mary, truly said, that 'he was a prince not only of power, but of knowledge how to order his power.'

The chief of these ministers was the young king's maternal uncle, Edward Seymour, Earl of Hertford, who was now created Duke of Somerset, and made protector of the realm and governor of the king's person. He was a man who had been employed in military services under Henry VIII., in which he had shown fidelity and courage; his manners were mild and conciliating, and his popularity was secured by the desire which he professed for an object he kept steadily in view—the improvement of the condition of the poorer classes. His religious sentiments, as far as they were declared, were in favour of the reformed doctrine; and it appears from a beautiful prayer found afterwards among his papers, that he did not enter upon his office without a solemn devotion of himself to God, and a committal of his cause to the guidance of His providence. 'Thou, Lord, by thine order, has committed an anointed king to my governance, direct me with thy hand that I err not from thy good pleasure. . . . . . I ask victory, but to show thy power upon the wicked. I ask prosperity, but for to rule in peace thy congregation. I ask wisdom, but by my counsel to set forth thy cause.' But if Somerset desired to serve God, he was willing also to serve the world. Even his very office of Protector he obtained, not indeed without the consent of the other counsellors named by the late king, but by no direct appointment from him, and not without some contrivance of his own. And this very prayer betrays the deception he was practising upon himself, in attributing that power to the will of God which he had in some measure obtained by his own management. It is not surprising that such beginnings should have ended

as they did.   Open, generous, and undesigning, he made
no secret of his intentions, and thought himself secure
in the affection of the people whose cause he honestly
espoused against the oppression of the nobility.   But
proud and vainglorious, he assumed royal state, and
thinking himself religious because he opposed popery,
he made it consist with his religion to enrich himself
with' the plunder of the Church.   The signal victory
which he obtained over the Scots at the battle of
Pinkey, in the first year of his government, confirmed
his power for the time, though it probably tended to
augment that vainglory which in the end contributed
to his ruin.

It had been the policy of the two kings of the house
of Tudor to take every means to depress the power of
the old nobility of England.   They had procured laws
to restrain the number of their retainers, and they had
carefully excluded them from the highest offices of
government.   There was a good reason for this.   The
public peace had been continually disturbed by them
and their factions, from the time of Richard II. till the
wars of York and Lancaster; and Henry VII. had still
battles to fight and rebellions to put down, after he had
gained his throne.   He judged, therefore, that he might
more certainly rely on the fidelity of those who owed
their exaltation to himself, and whose greatness was not
placed on an eminence obtained by ancestral honours.
This system worked well, while the throne was filled
by monarchs of vigorous age, with talents for command.
It did much to bring forward the gentry of the middle
ranks, and the mercantile interest, and to give stability
to the order of society.   But it had this inconvenience.
The men who were now employed in public business
were commonly of low origin and needy; for after the
downfall of Church-power, it was no longer possible to
employ clergymen, like Archbishop Morton and Wolsey,
who might be paid, without expense to the king, by
being advanced to great preferments.   The plan now

pursued, begun by Henry VIII., and carried on without
much check during this reign, was to give these ministers grants of abbey lands or other church endowments ;
and some of them, who were intended to receive a
peerage, declined the honour, because they were not to
receive with it what their circumstances made them
consider the most substantial part of the benefit.

Of such men was the council of state under Somerset
composed. Every one, except the bishops who belonged to it, was on the watch for spoils ; and as the
monks and all that they had were by this time nearly
disposed of, they began to turn their attention to the
bishops' lands, and the property of the chantries and
colleges. Somerset had received grants of three religious houses from Henry VIII.; he now procured
himself five or six more, among which were the rich
nunnery of Sion near Brentford, and Glastonbury, which
he turned into a worsted manufactory for some French
Protestant refugees.

There was still something of public spirit in the uses
to which he turned his acquisition ; it was the dignity
of his office, not his private wealth, which he sought to
advance. Others were influenced by baser motives,
and peculation in sales, falsifying their accounts, and
retaining good part of the price, was confessed by
several who were accused of it. But the ostentation of
Somerset, and the small thefts of other officers of state,
were all far outdone by the grasping avarice and cold
ambition of John Dudley, Viscount Lisle, afterwards
Earl of Warwick and Duke of Northumberland, who
was preparing to play a prominent part in the proceedings of this reign.[1]

The causes of this irreligious profligacy, it is easy to
trace. The impostures and superstitions of the exploded
system had disgusted and revolted the minds of the

---

[1] He was the son of Dudley, the minister of Henry VII., who was executed by Henry VIII., together with Empson, in the beginning of his reign.

nobles and gentry, which had now begun to be cultivated by learning; and they were in a state bordering
on unbelief. Besides, there was now a common practice
for young men of family to go abroad on travel, or reside, as attached to embassies, in foreign courts. There
was a great admiration of foreign manners, particularly
of Italian, that country having now the repute of being
the most polite in Europe, and having taken the lead in
the revival of learning. But the vices of Italy were
more easily imitated than its works of genius and
wonders of art; and the English residents became so
conspicuous for this kind of imitation, that even the
Italians had a proverb against them.[1] There were
many men in the court of the young Edward who had
studied the political writings of Machiavelli, and learnt
to separate religion from rules of state, and to treat the
common sort of men as the prey of the more ingenious
and longheaded. Others, of a more military turn, had
fallen in with some of the companies of adventurers in
the emperor's service, and thought the Church might
be turned to good account in raising the like at home;
as Sir Philip Hobbey, master of the ordnance, who
proposed to suppress all the cathedral clergy, and turn
their stalls into a fund for an artillery corps. But what
tended still more to the corruption of morals was that
idle romances were now imported from Italy and Spain,
translated into English, and read with too much effect,
as they ever will be, by the young and susceptible.
These works are often mentioned by writers of the age
of Elizabeth. Their names are now forgotten; and we

---

[1] 'Inglese Italianato è diavolo incarnato.' 'An Englishman turned
Italian is a devil incarnate.' A proverb mentioned by Ascham and other
writers of the time. It was doubtless much more to his own times than
to those of Richard II. that Shakspeare referred when he wrote

Report of fashions in proud Italy ;
Whose manners still our tardy apish nation
Limps after in base awkward imitation.
Richard II. act II. scene I.

have had others to succeed them of native growth. They were often the production of Italian monks and priests,[1] and were a proof of the state of discipline in that country, and that it was safer to be of no religion than to deny transubstantiation. It was in the memory of some of the English clergy, that Cardinal Campegio, the pope's nuncio, who, as we have seen, held an English bishopric a few years before, had publicly maintained that it was much more befitting a priest to live as St. Augustine did before his conversion, than to wed a wife. In short, the spirit of covetousness was encouraged by irreligion and immorality; and the sanctity of life, which should have been the barrier against sacrilege, was not found among those who ministered at the Church's altars.

Such were the times and men, when Cranmer, having witnessed the destructive part of the Reformation carried out with all its crimes, was called upon to use redoubled efforts to construct a system of faith and worship to revive the dying Church. It was well that some sense of religion was yet alive in the breast of Somerset, and that the young king had a heart tender to impressions of piety; for while one set of his courtiers were instilling into his mind maxims of Italian policy, others were contriving to remove the Bible from his chamber, and to substitute an effeminate romance in its place.[2]

The state of affairs, as regards religion, was not immediately affected by the death of Henry. Several indeed who were imprisoned under the Six Articles were set at liberty, among them Coverdale and Hooper, afterwards bishops, and Philpot and Rogers, both of whom as well as Hooper were put to death under Mary. Nor was there the same facility of prosecution for religious

---

[1] Pope Pius II. (Æneas Silvius Piccolomini), was himself the author of a romance, which is still extant, and is disgracefully profligate.
[2] STRYPE, *Eccl. Mem.*, Ed. VI., b. 1, ch. xiii. ASCHAM's Works, p. 254, ed. 1771.

opinions. For Dr. John Harley, of Magdalen College, at Oxford, afterwards also a bishop, and a confessor, having been sent up a prisoner to London, for preaching against popery, was liberated without a trial. The people also began in some places to show their expectation and desire of a change, by taking down images from the churches, and setting up the king's arms where the Holy Rood had been placed. The Holy Rood was a crucifix placed over the entrance to the chancel, representing the body of our Saviour on the cross; and whatever may be thought of the impropriety of having such images of our Redeemer, it must have seemed irreverent to substitute the king's arms in their place; but it does not appear that this was ever commanded,[1] and if so, the universal adoption of the practice seems to imply that the royal supremacy was popular. But in the royal injunctions issued immediately after this time, it was ordered that all such images as had been abused to superstition should be removed, and this was enlarged the next year by an order in council, extending to all images whatsoever. The consequences, however, of these directions are not to be confounded with that mutilation of our churches which was accomplished by the Puritans in the time of Charles I., when the beautiful statues which adorned the exterior of most cathedrals were broken and disfigured.

The party who were adverse to any further change, endeavoured to found their opposition on the fact that the king was a minor, and that as he was head of the Church, nothing ought to be done in the matter of religion until he was able to judge and act for himself. Gardiner especially, who was at the head of that party, and was an able, and in some respects a learned man, wrote to the Protector to remonstrate: 'Some,' said he, 'are for one new thing, some for another, till they have nothing old left them but their folly;' and this sentence

---

[1] See Burnet's Answer to Saunders, vol. ii., Append. p. 353.

is characteristic enough of the disposition and temper of the man. More of a statesman than of a divine, with a strong intellect exercised in the ways of the world, he was content with the religion that he found, and attributed religious zeal to a defective understanding. But Cranmer had now the power to carry on the Reformation, and was resolved to avail himself of it. Holgate, Archbishop of York, was willing to concur, and four other bishops were decidedly in his favour, one of whom was Ridley, who had been nominated to the see of Rochester before the late king's death.[1]

But it was no part of Cranmer's character to innovate thoughtlessly or hastily. He weighed every step he took, and never acted without having investigated for himself. First, therefore, he endeavoured to give effect to everything that had been ordered in the late reign, and then to proceed upon the steps that had been agreed upon for a further progress. The Convocation had resolved, in 1542, that a book of Homilies should be prepared, and although Gardiner now objected that this decision had been superseded by the publication of the *Erudition of a Christian Man*, it was determined to act upon it. Twelve homilies were drawn up under Cranmer's directions, three of which were written by himself on Salvation, Faith, and Works. That on Salvation was also called at the time the homily of Justification, and is so referred to in the Articles. It maintained the doctrine so strongly advocated by Luther and the continental reformers, of justification by faith alone, and was immediately objected to on that account by Gardiner and his party. Cranmer defended it on the ground that the object was 'only to set out the freedom of God's mercy,' which is precisely the same ground on which the same doctrine was afterwards explained by Bishop Jewel.

---

[1] The others were Holbeach of Lincoln, Gooderick of Ely, and Barlow of St. David's.

The bishops under Henry VIII., and Bonner among
the rest, had received the patent of their offices under a
clause, that they were to retain them during the king's
pleasure, like the judges or other officers of state. And
they were now obliged, as it would seem with the advice
of Cranmer, to take out new commissions to the same
purpose, under a new sovereign. The design was to
leave no question as to the acknowledgment of the royal
supremacy; but the archbishop has been much blamed
for it, as if he had thus meant to acknowledge, that a
king can make a bishop, without regard to the succession
of this order from the apostles. Such an accusation
seems entirely unfounded. A king's authority to a
bishop to exercise his function is quite distinct from a
claim to the power of consecration. The power of consecration Cranmer doubtless believed to reside in the
order of bishops, and to be derived to them, not from
the king, but from God; but he thought that they
should consecrate other bishops as the king should
command them, and hold their office and exercise their
functions only in obedience to the laws of the land.
The case of a government which should attempt to
abolish the order of episcopacy had never yet occurred,
nor is it probable that the thought of it had entered
Cranmer's mind. 'The ministration of God's Word,'
he said, 'which our Lord Jesus Christ did first institute,
was derived from the apostles unto others after them by
imposition of hands and giving of the Holy Ghost, from
the apostles' time to our days. This was the consecration, orders, and unction of the apostles, whereby they
at the beginning made bishops and priests, and this
shall continue in the Church even to the world's end.'[1]
Again, in complaining of Gardiner, who had objected to
his title of Metropolitan, he said he feared that Diotrephes,
who *loved to have the preeminence in the Church*, had
found more successors than all the apostles. 'But I

---

[1] Sermon on the Keys, in the translation of Justus Jonas's Catechism.

would that I, and all my brethren the bishops, would
leave our glorious styles and titles, and write the style
of our offices, calling ourselves *apostles of Jesus Christ*;
so that we took not upon us the name vainly, but were
even so in deed; so that we might order our dioceses in
such sort, that neither paper, parchment, lead, nor wax,
might be the letters and seals of our offices, but the very
Christian conversation of the people, as the Corinthians
wore unto Paul, to whom he said, *our epistle and seal
of our apostleship are ye.*'[1] These are not the words of
a man who looked upon his commission as dependent
on the patent of any earthly power.

Next followed a general visitation of the kingdom by
commissioners appointed by the crown, under the authority imparted to the council by King Henry's will.[2]
And as the bishops had just renewed their commissions
to exercise their functions during the king's pleasure,
their authority was suspended for a time while this
visitation was carried on. Such interference with the
episcopal functions, however, has never since been attempted, and this condition was not exacted from the
new bishops appointed in this reign. The injunctions
delivered by the commissioners in this royal visitation
to the clergy of each Rural Deanery, are a valuable
record of the state of religion as left by Henry VIII.,
both as regards the vestiges of a former state of things,
and the indications of an approaching change. They
began by requiring all ecclesiastical persons, four times
in the year at least, to preach against the usurped authority of the bishop of Rome. The clergy were next
commanded to abstain from extolling images and relics,
and not to allow any lights before images, but only two
lights upon the high altar, 'for the signification that

---

[1] Letter cxlvii.
[2] Which authority Henry had the power to impart under an Act of
Parliament, 28 Hen. VIII. c. 7, and 33 Hen. VIII. c. 1.—See CARDWELL's
Documentary Annals, L 5, where these injunctions are given at length,
which is not done by Collier or Burnet.

Christ is the very light of the world.'¹ They were to
provide a large Bible and the Commentaries of Erasmus
for every church, and discourage no man from reading
the Bible: they were to examine all who came to them
for confession, as to their knowledge of the Creed, the
Lord's Prayer, and the Ten Commandments, and admit
none to the 'blessed Sacrament of the altar' who did
not know them. They were to keep a book for registering
baptisms, burials, and weddings; and to provide a strong
chest, with a hole in the upper part of it, into which
the parishioners should put their oblations and alms for
the poor. All non-resident clergy of a certain income
were publicly to give away a tenth part of their income
to the poor of the place whence it was derived; chantry
priests were to exercise themselves in teaching youth to
read and write; and whoever had a hundred a year in
church preferment (equal perhaps to more than a thousand
now), was to maintain a poor scholar either at Oxford
or Cambridge. In divine service the Epistle and Gospel
read at high mass were to be in English, a chapter of
the New Testament in English was to be read at matins,
and a chapter of the Old Testament at evensong; and
immediately before high mass, the Litany which used
to be chanted in procession, whence that service was
also called a Procession, was to be said or sung in English
by the priests and choir, kneeling in the middle of the
church. This injunction as to the place at which the
Litany shall be said, was renewed under Queen Elizabeth,
and has not since been rescinded. It is self-evident,
how much it would tend to give life and reality to our

---

¹ It seems doubtful whether this injunction for having the lights upon
the altar is now in force. They were to be placed *before the sacrament*.
Transubstantiation was still the doctrine of the English Church: and
as the Host was always kept upon the altar, the lights were probably in
honour of the supposed corporeal presence of the Redeemer; whereas
in the Injunctions put forth A.D. 1549, after the passing of the Act of
Uniformity, the clergy were ordered to omit the reading of all such
(previous) injunctions 'as make mention of the popish mass, of chantries,
of *candles upon the altar*, or any such like thing.'

devotions, if the priest were now to kneel during this
service in the midst of the people; to say nothing of the
scriptural allusion, ' that the priests, the ministers of the
Lord, should weep between the porch and the altar, and
say, Spare thy people, O Lord, spare them.'

The first parliament of King Edward assembled in
November, 1547, and with it, as usual, the convocation
of the clergy. The proceedings of both were of the
greatest importance. The convocation passed a vote for
communion in both kinds, and for the marriage of the
clergy. The first of these resolutions was unanimous;
that for the marriage of the clergy was carried in the
Lower House by thirty-five against fourteen. They
also petitioned that the reformation of the Ecclesiastical
Laws, begun in the late reign, might be continued; and
that the divines and others, appointed to revise the
Church Services, might proceed with their labours.[1]
The Parliament began by repealing all the statutes
against heretics, including the odious act of the Six
Articles. The law of Henry IV. had been already repealed, and it might have been hoped that the intention
was now to abolish the punishment of death for religious
belief; but, unhappily, we shall find proof, in this very
reign, that the common law was still sufficient for the
purpose. It was next enacted, that the mass should be
changed into a communion, and that the Sacrament
should be administered to all persons under both kinds;
and thus this long-desired boon was restored to the
people by the full consent both of the clergy and the
Parliament. But the permission for the marriage of the
clergy, though carried in their convocation, could not
pass as yet, and was deferred till the following session.
A very important alteration was also made in the law
for the appointment of bishops. We have seen that

---

[1] The remarkable petition of this convocation for the restoration of
the proctors of the clergy to their seats in the Lower House of Parliament, belongs rather to civil than to ecclesiastical history.

Henry VIII. had not actually altered the mode of their appointment which he found, but had obliged the chapters then entitled to elect, to choose his nominee; but it was now enacted, that no election should take place at all, but that the crown should nominate the bishop by letters patent.[1] This law having been repealed with the rest by Queen Mary, was not re-enacted by Elizabeth, so that the mode of election established by Henry resumed its force, and is now the law in England, but the Irish bishops are still nominated directly by the crown. Another law passed by this parliament was for the dissolution of chantries and colleges. These had been granted to the late king just before his death, but as he had not got possession another law was required for the purpose, and it met with great opposition in both Houses. It was foreseen that the nobles wanted these revenues for themselves, while Cranmer, who had in vain interposed to rescue the lands of the monasteries for religious purposes, was the more anxious that these should be devoted to such objects, as the loss of the impropriate tithes had almost deprived a great many churches of any ministry at all. He argued, therefore, that the dissolution should be deferred till the king should come of age. But those who assisted him in overruling this argument when Gardiner would have used it to stop the reformation, now overruled him in his turn, and all colleges, chantries, and free chapels, with the exception of the public schools and universities, were given to the king. Their number was two thousand three hundred and seventy-four, and among them the chapel of St. Stephen's, at Westminster, afterwards so long used as

---

[1] This seems a remarkable instance of the tendency of human affairs to be altered for the worse by temporary expedients. If it be a sort of contradiction to allow certain presbyters to elect their bishop, and yet compel them to choose a particular person, the obvious way would be to release them from that compulsion, not to deprive them of the vestige of their rights. Such compulsion may, however, have been, at the time, a necessary protection to the Chapters themselves against the overbearing and arbitrary interference of the See of Rome.

the Commons' House of Parliament, became vested in the crown. The act professed that their estates should be converted to godly uses, in erecting grammar-schools, in further augmenting the universities, and making better provision for the poor. It was out of these lands that those called King Edward's Grammar Schools were endowed in so many parts of England, but a large proportion of the property was shared amongst the courtiers.

CHAPTER XIX.

When we had heard God himself speaking to us in his words, and had seen and considered the illustrious examples of the ancient and primitive Church, and that the expectation of a General Council was uncertain, and the event that would follow it much more uncertain, and especially when we had the utmost certainty what was the will of God; and therefore thought it a sin to be too solicitous or anxious what the opinion of men might be; after all this, I say, we conferred not with flesh and blood, but proceeded and have accordingly done that which both may lawfully be done, and which already had been often done by many pious men and catholic bishops, that is, to take care of our own Church in a provincial synod.—JEWEL's *Apology.*

IT remained to give effect to those important matters which had been resolved upon by the convocation and the parliament; and the bishops proceeded to examine the service for the mass, with a view to putting it forth in English. Several attempts had been made, in the time of Henry VIII., to agree upon a general confession of faith for all the reformed Churches. But they proved ineffectual, because he would not give up the practice of private masses. In the year 1538, the ambassadors of the German princes wrote to him that 'Whereas the mass is and ought to be nothing else than a communion, as Paul calls it, and was used no otherwise in the primitive church, as may be shown from the holy fathers, something quite different has now been made of it, and wholly repugnant to the communion, and to the true use of the mass.'[1] And they added, 'That it is plain that private masses are recent, introduced by the Roman Pontiff, and not even in the present day admitted in the

---

[1] BURNET, Appendix I. 304, 306.

A A

Greek Church.' A year later it appears that Luther
and Melancthon and the German States had been willing
to retain the service of the mass, if only they might
have abolished private masses; and this seems to have
been proposed as a general plan of pacification with the
Church of Rome.[1]   But the state of affairs as regards
the foreign Protestants was materially altered : it was
now about ten years since the Elector Frederick, the
devoted adherent of the reformation in Germany, had
been deposed and imprisoned by the Emperor Charles V.;
and about the same time that Herman, elector and
archbishop of Cologne, who had attempted a reform of
religion in his dominions on catholic principles, had
been excommunicated and deposed.   In this state of
things it was the more necessary for the English Church
to look to itself alone; and the parliament and convocation having both sanctioned the measure, a committee
of sixteen bishops and six other divines was appointed,
including Bonner, but not Gardiner, to carry their intentions into effect.

Their consultations were carried on in writing, and
they supply us with authentic information as to the
state of opinions at that time.   In the first place they
were nearly agreed that private masses for souls departed
should be abolished.   They agreed also that it was to
be wished that the people would always communicate
with the priest; but they were not all of a mind as to
the discontinuance of the private celebration of mass by
the priest when the people will not partake; and still
less so as to the meaning and nature of the oblation in
the eucharist.   Private masses were of two kinds : first,
the mass itself, as celebrated at that time in England
and still continued in the Church of Rome, was for the
most part a private commemoration by the priest, and
not a communion.   This practice was stated by Tonstal
to have arisen from the slackness of the people in coming

---

[1] See COLLIER, 5, 44 (New Edit.)

to the daily communions of the early Church, in consequence of which the priest was obliged to receive alone; and this was not denied by Cranmer, though he thought the practice did not prevail for the first six hundred years. But there was much diversity in the answers to the question now proposed among the bishops, ' What is the oblation and sacrifice of Christ in the mass? ' Cranmer said, ' The oblation and sacrifice of Christ in the mass is not so called because Christ is indeed there offered and sacrificed by the priest and the people, for that was done but once by himself upon the cross; but it is so called because it is a memory and representation of that very true sacrifice and immolation which was before made upon the cross.' But on the other hand, Bonner and five other bishops maintained, ' That it is the presentation of the very body and blood of Christ, being really present in the sacrament; ' while the Bishop of Carlisle ventured to assert, that ' The oblation and sacrifice of Christ in the mass, *is even the same which was offered by Christ on the cross.*' It was however agreed by Bonner and his party that the ' Sacrifice of thanks,' that is, the eucharist, is to be received not of one man for another, but of every man for himself, and thus a foundation was laid for what was then called ' changing the mass into a communion.'

But as for masses satisfactory, or as they were then usually called private masses, the case was somewhat different. It was held by the early Church that the representation of the memorials of the precious death of Christ is acceptable to God for the sake of that atoning death, and so draws down His favour upon the whole Church as well as upon those who partake in the celebration. But this notion of drawing down God's favour upon the whole Church came by degrees to include the spirits of departed friends, as being still a part of the communion of saints, for whose peace and final acceptance it was not forbidden to pray even before the notion of purgatory came to be adopted. And as the primitive Christians were accustomed to celebrate the holy communion at funerals, it came to be thought that masses satisfactory might be offered which should be available to the especial benefit of those souls for whom they were intended. But when purgatory had become a popular substitute in people's minds for hell itself, nothing was more natural than that they should desire to procure such masses for the sake of liberating their friends from that imaginary abode. Nor was this all: when such masses were deemed available to the especial benefit of particular persons, it was held that they might be offered as sacrifices were under the law, for the obtaining of any particular blessings. If a prince went to battle, masses were said for his success; if a nobleman was ill, masses were said for his recovery; and similar offerings were sometimes made for more questionable purposes, and for objects for which good men would deem it presumptuous to pray. The priests were accustomed to take money for the performance of these masses, as well as for those which were offered for the dead, which were usually performed in what was called Trentals, that is, thirty by the year, celebrated by three at a time on particular festivals. We have seen that the chantry priests had often other duties besides these celebrations; but it was always a condition of the endowment that they should say mass for the health of the living and for the souls of the faithful dead, especially of the founder, his family and friends; and as they had private altars in the chantries where they officiated, the notion of a communion could hardly enter at all into the services which were there performed.

The immediate result of these consultations, and of the decisions of the parliament and convocation, was that a service was drawn up for the administration of the holy communion to the people under both kinds, which was appointed to come into use on Easter-day, 1548. This book left the Latin service of that part of the mass in which the consecration takes place, and

only added some prayers and an exhortation in English.
This exhortation was to be said on the preceding
Sunday or holy-day, and was nearly the same as that
which is now in use, and at the time of celebration,
when the priest had gone through the usual service of
the mass, making no difference except in consecrating
wine for the congregation, and had received himself, he
was to say the address which we now use, 'Dearly
beloved in the Lord,' and then, after a caution to such
as might not yet be fit to come, having paused to see if
any man would withdraw, he proceeded to the invitation, 'You that do truly and earnestly repent you of
your sins.' The general confession which followed,
'Almighty God, Father of our Lord Jesus Christ, Maker
of all things, Judge of all men,'—might be said either
by the priest or deacon, or by one of the communicants
in the name of the rest. Then came the absolution,
beginning thus, instead of the words now used, 'Our
blessed Lord, who hath left power to his Church to
absolve penitent sinners from their sins, and to restore
to the grace of the heavenly Father such as truly believe
in Christ,—have mercy upon you.' The prayer, 'We
do not presume to come to this thy table,' was the same
as now, immediately after which the consecrated
elements were delivered with these words only: 'The
body of our Lord Jesus Christ, which was given for
thee, preserve thy body unto everlasting life.' 'The
blood of our Lord Jesus Christ, which was shed for
thee, preserve thy soul unto everlasting life.' When
all had partaken, the congregation was dismissed with
the blessing without any further prayer or hymn. No
change was here made in the doctrine as to the presence of Christ in the sacrament; but there was a
material alteration respecting confession, which had
hitherto been absolutely required of all persons since
the thirteenth century, but which was now, by the
words of the exhortation, left to the option of the penitent.
But this service was not intended to be any other than

a temporary measure, for it was accompanied by a
proclamation, in which a promise was given of 'other
such godly orders as might be most to God's glory, the
edifying of the people, and for the advancement of true
religion.' In the meantime, other proclamations had
been issued forbidding people to discuss the nature of
the sacrament of the altar, and interdicting any of the
clergy from preaching, except in their own churches,
unless specially licensed for the purpose; the object
being to prevent variety of doctrine, until the new order
for divine service should be completed.

In the summer of this year, A.D. 1548, was published
what is commonly called Cranmer's Catechism. It is
not the same as that which is now printed in the Prayer
Book as the Church Catechism, but was an explanation
of the Ten Commandments, the Creed, and the Lord's
Prayer, drawn up in short sermons for the instruction of
the young. This work was originally written in German,
and translated into Latin by Justus Jonas, a Lutheran
divine, who was at this time residing with the archbishop. It was translated into English, if not by
Cranmer himself, under his immediate superintendence,
and some alterations and additions were made by him.
The Lutheran tenet of the Corporeal Presence was explained spiritually, and an entire discourse was added
on the second commandment. The Lutheran Church
did not depart from the Romish division of the ten
commandments, omitting the second, and dividing the
tenth into two. This division was retained in this
catechism, but after the explanation of the first, the
archbishop added that the more gross idolatry of wor-
shipping images is also forbidden in this commandment, quoting the words of the second commandment to
that effect, and adding, that 'These words by most
interpreters of late time are made to belong to the first
commandment, although, after the interpretation of
many ancient authors, they are the second commandment.' He then enlarges upon the practice which he

calls 'the abuse of our time,' of having images in churches, and especially condemns those pictures of the Trinity in which God the Father was represented, quoting St. Augustine's opinion, that 'it is a detestable thing for Christian men to have any such image of God in the church.' This catechism is further remarkable as containing a very strong recommendation of the practice of confession, and an equally decided opinion in favour of what is called the power of the Keys, and the divine authority of the Christian ministry.

The commissioners appointed to draw up a BOOK OF COMMON PRAYER had assembled at Windsor on May 9, A.D. 1548, and it was fitting that such a work should be carried on at the royal abode of the first monarch who had placed himself at the head of the reformed party, and professed the reformed faith. Their labours were continued through the summer, A.D. 1548, and as it was found that not only the clergy in general, but some even of the licensed preachers did not refrain from expressing their wishes or opinions respecting the various important matters to be comprised in the new Prayer Book, it was thought fit to interdict all preaching whatsoever for a short time until the book should be completed. The object of this was declared to be, 'that the clergy might apply themselves to prayer for a blessing on what the king was about to do; not doubting but the people would be employed likewise in prayer and hearing the homilies read in their churches, and be ready to receive that uniform order that was to be set forth.' The parliament met in November, and the first business submitted to them relating to the affairs of the Church, was the marriage of the clergy, which the convocation had agreed to the year before, but which did not then pass through parliament. It was now agreed to, though not without difficulty, and with this restriction: 'That it were better for the ministers of the Church to live chaste and without marriage, whereby they might better attend to the ministry of the gospel

and be less distracted with secular cares; but since
great evils had followed on the laws that prohibited
marriage, it was better they should be suffered to marry
than so restrained.' It is to be observed that the vows
of celibacy taken by the clergy in some countries, had
not of late years been imposed upon the English clergy
in general, but only on those belonging to the monastic
orders; but as this act seemed to convey some stigma,
notwithstanding, on those who chose to marry, another
law was passed three years afterwards, in which those
words were omitted.

While the parliament was thus employed, the new
liturgy was submitted to the convocation, which met
also in November, and having been agreed to by that
body, it was brought into parliament, where a law was
passed on January 21, 1549, since known as the Act of
Uniformity,[1] which declared that the bishops and other
learned men had now, ' by the aid of the Holy Ghost,'
concluded upon one uniform order of divine worship,
having respect to the pure religion of Christ taught in
Scripture, and to the practice of the primitive Church;
and it was therefore enacted that from the feast of
Whit Sunday next all divine offices should be performed
according to it. Another law that was now made enjoined the observance of fasting on Fridays and
Saturdays, on the Ember days, and during Lent, which
practice seems to have been already in danger of being
discontinued, through the reaction that was taking
place.[2]

---

[1] 2 and 3 Edw. VI. c. 1.

[2] As the sentiments of Bishop Burnet will not be suspected of leaning
too much to what are called ' High Church opinions,' it may perhaps be
useful to subjoin what he says on this occasion. ' It was much lamented
then, and there is as much cause for it still, that carnal men have taken
advantages from the abuses that were formerly practised, to throw off
good and profitable institutions; since the frequent use of fasting with
prayer and true devotion joined to it, is perhaps one of the greatest
helps that can be devised, to advance one to a spiritual temper of mind,
and to promote a holy course of life. And the mockery that is discern-
able in the way of some men's fasting is a very slight excuse for any

The new liturgy was used at Easter in some places where the clergy were favourable to it, though the law did not require it to be adopted before Whit Sunday, on which day, being June 10, in the year 1549, it was solemnly performed at St. Paul's Cathedral and in most other churches in the kingdom. The day of Pentecost was fitly chosen as that on which a National Church should first return, after so many centuries, to the celebration of divine service in the native tongue, and it is a day to be much observed in this Church of England among all our generations for ever. The actual change introduced by this service was not so great as might at first be supposed. The litany had been already used in English, since the end of the late reign, as well as a lesson from the Old and New Testament, after one of the Latin hymns at matins and evensong. By an injunction in the present reign, the epistle and gospel at the mass were also in English, besides the communion service lately put forth. A considerable part of the old Latin service for matins and evensong had been already translated in the King's Primer, and what was now done, as regards that part of divine worship, was chiefly to leave out all rubrics and prayers which had references to indulgences, or which contained prayers to the Virgin or other saints, and to order the old hymns and collects which had remained from primitive times to be said or sung in English. Accordingly, the morning service, which was still called the Matins, began, not as now with the exhortation, confession, and absolution, but with the Lord's Prayer and the sentences following, after which, between Easter and Trinity Sunday, alleluiah was to be added. The 95th Psalm preceded the psalms for the day, as at present, and after the first lesson Te

to lay aside the use of that which the Scriptures have so much recommended.'—*Hist. Ref.*, vol. ii. p. 91. Thomas Becon, a learned Reformer, who was rector of St. Stephen's, Walbrook, in this reign, in his *Potation for Lent*, quotes the words of St. Basil, 'Thou shalt find that fasting hath made all the saints friends and neighbours unto God.'

Deum was to be sung in English, except in Lent, and
then the Song of the Three Children instead.   The
Benedictus followed the second lesson, without any
option of having the 100th Psalm instead, which was
added when the book was revised.   The Apostles'
Creed also was not introduced in the first Prayer Book,
but as soon as the hymn after the second lesson was
finished, the Lord's Prayer was repeated with what is
called the Smaller Litany, as we now have it, and then
the service closed with the collect for the day, and the
two other collects, for peace and for grace.   No alteration was made in the time at which this office was to
be used, which was then about six in the morning.
The evensong corresponded in all particulars.   The
only hymns to be used after the lessons were the *Mag-
nificat* and the *Nunc dimittis*.   The second and third
collects were the same as those now in use at evening
prayer.   Although the Apostles' Creed was not yet
introduced, the Athanasian Creed was to be said on a
few great festivals, in the same part of the service where
we now have it.

The service was to be performed in the choir, but in
reading the lessons, the minister was to stand and turn
so as to be best heard by the people.   By a rubric in
the communion service the Litany was to be said on
Wednesdays and Fridays, according to the form appointed by the king's injunctions, which directed, as we
have seen, that the priest should say it in the body of
the church kneeling at the head of the congregation,
immediately before he began the communion service.
It was the same as that already printed in the Primer,
except that the invocation of the Virgin, and of the
saints and angels, was now omitted.

In the communion service several important changes
took place from that which had been set out the year
before, as the whole of the office was now to be in
English.   It was entitled ' The Supper of the Lord, and
the Holy Communion, commonly called the Mass.'

The rubrics preceding the service requiring the communicants to give in their names to the curate, and the curate to forbid notorious sinners, were almost the same as ours; to which was added a direction to the officiating priest to use the customary dress. The clerks were to begin by singing a psalm especially appointed for each Sunday and holiday, and printed before the collect for the day. This was called the Introit, because it was sung while the priest entered within the rails to begin the service: it was a very ancient custom, which was omitted in the second Liturgy, but has tacitly found its way back into our practice by the almost universal introduction before the communion of a congregational psalm or hymn. The priest began with the Lord's Prayer and collect, after which the commandments were not recited, but the *Gloria in excelsis*, which is now sung or said at the conclusion, was here inserted at the beginning, as in the primitive liturgies. The prayer for the King, and the collect, epistle, and gospel for the day, were the same as now, except where a few of the collects, epistles, and gospels have been varied, and at the end of the gospel the people were to say, *Glory be to Thee, O Lord*. This was omitted in the second Liturgy, but it was inserted in that prepared for the Church of Scotland in the seventeenth century, and has since found its way back into our practice. After the Nicene Creed, the sermon or homily was to follow, as now; immediately after which, unless the people had been exhorted in the sermon itself to the worthy partaking of the sacrament, the exhortation was to be read, which we now have later in the service, 'Dearly beloved in the Lord, ye that mind to come,' in the end of which, instead of saying merely that Christ hath left us holy mysteries as pledges of his love, and for a continual remembrance of his death, it was expressed that 'He hath left us in those holy mysteries, as a pledge of his love, and a continual remembrance of the same, his own blessed body and precious blood, for us to feed upon spiritually to our endless comfort and consolation.' Then came the Offertory, with the sentences to be sung or said while the people were offering their alms, after which those who were partakers of the holy communion were directed to remain in the choir, the men on the one side, and the women on the other, and all the rest to depart out of the choir. The minister was to prepare the bread and wine, mixing a little water with the wine, which was a most ancient practice, supposed to be in memory of the blood and water from our Saviour's side; after which came the angel's hymn, 'Therefore, with angels and archangels,' and the prayer 'for the whole state of Christ's Church.'

It will be observed that this prayer comes at an earlier part of our present service; but this is not the only alteration that was made respecting it in the second Prayer Book of King Edward. It is now entitled a prayer for the Church militant only, and not for the whole Church absolutely; and for this reason, that in the Liturgy as first compiled, it contained a commemoration of departed saints, and a prayer for their everlasting peace. After blessing God for the wonderful grace and virtue declared in his saints, and chiefly in the glorious and most blessed Virgin Mary, Mother of our Lord Jesus Christ, these words were added, 'We commend unto thy mercy, oh Lord, all other thy servants, which are departed hence from us with the sign of faith, and now do rest in the sleep of peace; grant unto them, we beseech thee, thy mercy and everlasting peace; and that at the day of the general resurrection we, and all they which be of the mystical body of thy Son, may altogether be set on his right hand, and hear that his most joyful voice, Come unto me, oh ye that be blessed of my Father.' The prayer of consecration followed, in which were these words, omitted in the second Liturgy, 'With thy Holy Spirit vouchsafe to bless and sanctify these thy gifts and creatures of bread and wine, that they may be unto us the body and blood of thy most

dearly beloved Son Jesus Christ;' which sentence, taken
from the primitive liturgies, has lately been partially
restored to the communion service of the Church in the
United States of America.[1]   After the consecration, the
prayer of self-dedication followed, which was afterwards
put in the post communion, 'We offer and present unto
thee ourselves, our souls and bodies.'   The confession
was next to be said, as before appointed, either by the
priest, or by one of the congregation, and then the
absolution by the priest, the recitation of the 'comfortable words of Christ, Come unto me,' and the prayer,
'We do not presume to come to this thy table, trusting
in our own worthiness.'   During the delivery of the
sacrament, the clerks were to sing, 'Oh, Lamb of God,
that takest away the sins of the world; have mercy
upon us:' and in repeating it, 'Grant us thy peace.'
Sentences of Scripture were added, one of which was to
be sung every day 'after the holy communion, called
the post communion;' and the service closed with a
blessing, preceded by a prayer of thanksgiving for having
been fed with the spiritual food of the most precious
body and blood of our Saviour Christ.[2]

It will be observed, that in this service, prayer for
the dead was retained, though in such language as
wholly to exclude the notion of purgatory.   On the
other hand, the presence of Christ in the eucharist was
declared to be a spiritual presence, a statement which

---

[1] The words of the American office are—'And of thy Almighty goodness
vouchsafe to bless and sanctify with thy Word and Holy Spirit, these
thy gifts and creatures of bread and wine, that we, receiving them according to thy Son our Saviour Jesus Christ's holy institution, in remembrance of his death and passion, may be partakers of his most
blessed Body and Blood.'

[2] It was intended that there should be two communions on Easter
Sunday and Christmas Day, for which occasions two collects, epistles, and
gospels were provided, and soon after, when it was found that some
private masses were still celebrated at St. Paul's, permission was given
to have an early service for the communion, at any time when the people
wished to attend it, instead of these private celebrations.

could not be reconciled with the Romish doctrine of transubstantiation. Another practice that was modified but not abandoned, is yet more important—confession to the minister, which in this, as in the service of the preceding year, was no longer enjoined as necessary, but yet was still permitted. For those whose consciences might be troubled, were invited to come to the priest of the parish, or to any other, and open their grief secretly, that they might receive comfort and absolution; but with a caution to those who were satisfied with a general confession, not to condemn such as choose to confess privately, and to these in like manner not to judge the other. This caution was omitted in the second Prayer Book, and absolution was mentioned in a more general way: but the invitation to confess to the priest was retained, and a special form of private absolution is also still to be found in the Visitation of the Sick, 'for those who earnestly desire it,' which form, in the first Prayer Book, was also directed to be used in all private confessions. It is further to be observed, that permission is given in both Liturgies, to those who wish for this privilege, of choosing their own confessor; for the invitation says, 'Let him come to me *or to some other minister.*'

The greater part of this first reformed Liturgy[1] was compiled from the ancient services of the Church of England. The matins and evensong were little else than the ancient hymns and collects of the primitive Church, with the insertion of Scripture lessons and portions of the Psalms. The Litany was a translation of one previously in use, and the communion service was taken from the various liturgies then used in England, known respectively as Salisbury use, Lincoln use, and the like, as these were from still older forms which had come down from the first ages of the Church. But the com-

---

[1] The word 'Liturgy,' however, *properly* applies only to the communion service.

missioners were not unwilling to make use of other
assistance; and though but few of the foreign divines,
whose influence was so great in the second edition of
the Prayer Book, had yet arrived in England, they are
known to have consulted the book drawn up with the
advice of Melancthon and Bucer, at the instance of
Herman, archbishop of Cologne, before mentioned, from
the older Liturgy of Nuremberg, and published in his
name with the title of *A Christian Reformation founded
on God's Word.* Cranmer had corresponded with this
prelate, and several of the occasional services were indebted to his book.[1]

In the office for public baptism a form of exorcism
was retained, as well as the putting on of the chrism or
white robe in token of baptismal purity, and the child
was to be dipped thrice in the font, unless too weak to
bear it. The exorcism and the chrism were omitted in
the second Liturgy, but the primitive doctrine of baptismal regeneration was carefully retained; and it is
evident that this was not done without consideration,
from the fact that the same doctrine was held by Cranmer
in his book upon the Eucharist; not so as to imply that
no future renewal is required, but that the seeds of
grace are sown when the infant is transferred into the
family of God.[2] The catechism which we now call the
Church Catechism was placed at the end of the service
for Confirmation, to be learned before the person was
confirmed; but the questions and answers relating to
the sacraments were added by Bishop Overal, in the
reign of James I. The marriage service was nearly the
same as now, but in both prayer books it was enjoined
that the married persons 'the same day of their marriage should receive the holy communion.' The form
of absolution in the Visitation of the Sick has been al-
already mentioned. In addition to which the priest
was permitted in the first book to administer extreme

---

[1] CARDWELL, *Two Liturgies,* Pref. p. xvi.   [2] See Appendix G.

unction, if the sick person earnestly desired it; but this was omitted in the second.[1] For the communion of the sick, the consecrated elements were to be carried to the sick man's house from the church, if it was on a day of public communion, but otherwise it might be consecrated at his house. But this also was omitted when the book was revised. Prayer for the dead was retained in the first burial service, and an office for the communion at funerals. Both were omitted in the second; the communion office for funerals was again separately sanctioned in the time of Queen Elizabeth, but not replaced in the Prayer Book. At the churching of women, the woman was to kneel, not as is now often the case in some private pew, but near the choir-door, or near the place where the holy table stood, and was to receive the holy communion if it was administered. The service for Ash Wednesday has come down to us as then first compiled, attesting at once the solemn piety of the ancient Church, and the faithful diligence of our reformers. But it was intended by the introductory words to prepare the people's minds for the restoration of ancient discipline, which they hoped to effect by the reformation of the ecclesiastical laws.

This brief account of the first reformed Prayer Book, and of the changes in the second, may serve to show with what care and caution our English divines proceeded in their solemn task. We may say of this, as Edmund Burke says of our civil constitution, 'All the reformations we have hitherto made have proceeded upon the principle of reference to antiquity; and let us hope and be persuaded, that all which may possibly be made hereafter will be carefully formed on precedent, authority, and example.'[2]

---

[1] The beautiful exhortation of the minister to the sick is repeated almost word for word by Ridley in his 'Farewell' before his martyrdom. Possibly it may have been written by him.

[2] *On the French Revolution.*

CHAPTER XX.

Pray'rs too are daughters of great Jove; but slow,
Wrinkled with care, and sad of mien they go,
Healing the gifts of mortals, where forlorn
They pine from swift Revenge, his eldest born.
                                        HOMER. *Iliad*, ix.

IT had been a suggestion of the wise and moderate
Melancthon, many years before, that a general confession of faith should be agreed upon by all the
reformed. It was one of those healing measures by
which this amiable man merited the character given
him by Erasmus, that he followed Luther as the prayers
personified in Homer follow after the goddess of Re
venge. The design was eagerly embraced, and long
cherished by Cranmer. In the year 1538 a conference
had been held in London upon the subject, at which
several foreign divines were present; but it was broken
up on the refusal of Henry to consent to other points,
and particularly to the abolition of private masses; for
he was a firm believer in purgatory, and had given
Latimer a severe lecture for disputing the existence of
such a place. The English divines and the foreigners
had, however, agreed upon a statement of doctrine
founded upon the Lutheran Confession of Augsburg;
but in consequence of this rupture it was not published.
On the accession of Edward, Cranmer renewed the
attempt, and especially invited Melancthon himself to
come over for this purpose. The request was more
than once renewed; Latimer spoke of it in his Court

D B

sermons; and it appears that Edward wrote in his own name to invite him only two months before his own early death, in May, 1553.[1] But he came not; and thus the meeting of the two men, who were perhaps the best qualified to unite the counsels of the reformers, was never realized. Instead of Melancthon, Cranmer secured the help of Martin Bucer, a German divine, born at Sclectstat, near Strasburg, and of Peter Martyr Vermiglio, a native of Florence.

Both these learned men had been originally members of monastic orders. Bucer having been left an orphan at a very early age, his grandfather induced him, when no more than fifteen, to become a Dominican friar; a common mode by which guardians of that period got rid of an inconvenient responsibility for their wards. The Dominicans sent Bucer to study at Heidelberg, where he was soon distinguished by his progress in philosophy and in the ancient languages. The labours of Erasmus in the revival of learning soon attracted his notice; and he began to study the writers of the Greek Church in the first ages. He was then invited to the court of the Elector Frederick; and in 1521, he first met with Luther at the Diet of Worms, where that bold man, in the presence of the Emperor and States of Germany, made his public defence of his writings. It was that famous occasion on which his friends had done their utmost to dissuade him from going, and Luther had replied, 'If I were sure to be assailed by so many devils as there are tiles on the house-tops of the town, I would still venture my life among them.' Bucer had many conferences with Luther, and either then or before he became an associate of the reformers; but he never approved of the Lutheran doctrine of consubstantiation. After teaching with great repute in different places in Germany, he came, in 1548, into England, and was made Regius Professor of divinity

---

[1] MELANCTHON, Epist. iv. 813.

at Cambridge. Here he was extremely acceptable to the English doctors and students, and greatly influenced the studies of the place. But he had scarcely completed the third year of his sojourn, when he died there. He was publicly buried at St. Mary's, with every mark of honour; the gownsmen and citizens, to the number of three thousand persons, followed him to his grave, and the most eminent scholars employed their pens in orations, sermons, and poems to his memory.

Bucer had a strong sense of the desolate condition of the German reformed churches, and with his prayer that God would have mercy on his poor country, he used to join a petition that England might be preserved from the same errors. He saw that the three orders in the ministry were appointed in the beginning by the Holy Ghost; and he called it a device of Satan to destroy the order of bishops, that the churches might be given up to spoil. His error appears to have been, that he was too much inclined to alter everything that had been once abused, though he knew that it was not wrong in itself. Hence he persuaded Cranmer to remove from the communion service in the second Prayer Book, the primitive petition for the consecration of the bread and wine. Though his own belief about baptism was agreeable to that which has always been held in the Church, he wished to do away with those instructive forms and usages which the Church had long practised, and which he confessed to be more ancient than the errors which had been engrafted upon them. In some of these objections Cranmer listened to him, perhaps too far; but when he advised that godfathers should undertake only to see the child religiously brought up, without answering in his name, the archbishop did not comply.[1]

---

[1] It may be well here to give Bucer's opinions on a practice which is now happily reviving,—baptism in the presence of the congregation. 'It is very meet and right that those who are members of each other in Christ should be assembled, when any one born from among them, a child of wrath, is to be born again in the Church to everlasting life, and

On the contrary, he distinctly refused to sanction anything which should contradict the belief 'that grace is
conveyed by the sacraments,' alleging that to do so would
be plainly contrary to the teaching of St. Augustine.[1]

Peter Martyr, an Italian by birth, was in his youth
an Austin canon, and had been made prior of a convent near Lucca; but meeting with some writings of
Zwingle the Swiss Reformer, he gave up his valuable
preferment, and went into Switzerland. His doctrine
became more like that of Calvin and the Geneva school,
than that of the English reformers. When he was settled
at Oxford, he was nearly as successful there as Bucer had
been at Cambridge; and the celebrated Bishop Jewel,
Nowell, Parkhurst, and many others, became his scholars
and admirers. It cannot be said that his influence was
altogether beneficial. He was a man of vehement spirit,
without the subdued reverential temper of Bucer; he
had not the same view of the dignity of the sacraments,
nor a like regard to ecclesiastical order. As his friends
were zealous for him and his opinions, so he also contrived to offend the opposite party by the warmth of his
disputations, and they broke his windows, and assailed
him with abuse. And he found too many imitators, of
a class not yet quite out of date, who seem to think they
are betraying truth, if they use any civility to those
whom they believe to be in error. But with all this,
the Florentine reformer was a man of learning and eloquence, and a diligent expositor of scripture. The
beautiful address, in our present communion service, to
be used when the people are negligent to come, was
composed by him.

With Bucer there came to Cambridge Paul Fagius,

---

received among the children of God; that they may at once pray for that
benefit, and the Church of Christ by its minister confer it; that as the
child is made a member of each of them by this sacrament, so each may
bind himself before God by a promise to show him all the offices of
Christian fellowship, both ghostly and bodily.'

[1] Zurich Letters.

or Buchlein, a Hebrew scholar, who, dying soon after his arrival, was succeeded by Emmanuel Tremellius as professor of that language. These men are not otherwise known than as promoters of the new learning, as the study of the most ancient tongues was at that time included under that title.

Another foreigner, of less learning, but of more activity, and turbulent zeal, was John Laski, commonly called A'Lasco, a man of a noble Polish family, but an exile from his country, who was received by Cranmer, and permitted to superintend a Dutch or German congregation in London. Melancthon draws his character, in a letter to a friend, as daring and self-opinionated; and he was one of those who made him despair of concord among the reformed party. Laski's opinions were what have since been called Calvinistic; but the reformation in Poland was early infected with Socinianism, and a spirit of self-will is too often the parent of heresy.

The effect of this influx of foreigners was nothing correspondent to the designs of Cranmer. Instead of promoting union with the churches abroad, it brought division into the counsels of the English reformers. John Hooper, an eminent preacher of the reformed doctrine, who with many others had passed some years abroad, during the persecution raised by the Six Articles, was appointed bishop of Gloucester. The dress of a bishop was not as now, of black satin mixed with lawn, but of scarlet silk, and this dress Hooper refused to wear, whereas the rubrics of the first Liturgy required that the bishops and clergy should retain precisely the same vestments that were in use before. It soon became not merely a question as to the propriety of such dresses, but as to the much more important point of the right of particular churches to make regulations in matters indifferent, which should be binding on all their members.[1] In this point of view it was now

---

[1] CARDWELL, *Two Liturgies*, Pref. xix.

regarded by Cranmer, who refused to consecrate Hooper
unless he would comply with the order in the Prayer Book.
He persisted in his refusal, in which he was supported
by the Earl of Warwick, and even by the young king
himself.   Cranmer referred the matter to Bucer and
Peter Martyr.   They both, as concerned their private
opinions, wished the dresses discontinued, and it seems
that Peter Martyr would not wear them himself at
Oxford, but both agreed that under such circumstances
they ought to be complied with.   Bucer, especially,
admitted that such garments had been used by the
primitive fathers before popery, and thought that 'the
retaining them might be expedient to show that the
Church did not of any lightness change old customs.'
And Peter Martyr expressed his dissatisfaction at
Hooper's perseverance.   Ridley also attempted in vain
to persuade him, and the attempt led to an estrangement of these two earnest and honest spirits; but
their hearts were drawn together again when they were
both afterwards involved in the same persecution.   It
was not till the next year that Hooper, finding himself
blamed by those even who agreed with him in the
main, consented to a compromise by which he undertook to wear the rochet on all public occasions, and
was consecrated to his bishopric.

But a more congenial associate in Cranmer's labours
was now promoted to a prominent situation.   The see of
London had been kept vacant for half a year, after Bonner
had been deprived for disobeying the orders of the council, and Ridley was then translated to it from Rochester,
A.D. 1550.   It is refreshing to dwell for a moment upon
the conduct of this Christian bishop, amidst the conflict
of selfish passions by which this period is darkened.   A
short time before, he had been sent down to Cambridge
as a commissioner to execute some of the acts of spoliation which Somerset was too forward to promote; and
not knowing the purport of his mission until his arrival,
he then refused to coerce the master and fellows of

Clare Hall into a surrender of their college. It was a
serious matter in those days to resist those who exercised the authority of the king; but Ridley persevered,
in spite of remonstrance, and that society, which exists
at this day, owes its preservation to his honest resolution.

There is no reason to distrust the testimony of Fox,
that after he became a bishop 'he so occupied himself
in teaching and preaching, that a good child never was
more loved by his dear parents than he was by his
flock and diocese. Every Sunday and holy-day he
preached in some place or other, unless hindered by
weighty business. The people resorted to his sermons
swarming about him like bees, and coveting the sweet
flowers and wholesome juice of the fruitful doctrine,
which he not only preached, but showed the same by
his life as a shining light, in such pure order, that even
his very adversaries could not reprove him.' With all
his studies and public cares, he was still diligent in the
religious instruction of his household, reading a lecture
to them every day at their family prayer, and enticing
them by gifts to learn parts of the New Testament by
heart. Nor did he forget to cherish those who had
suffered by his promotion; for it was his custom, when
at Fulham, to send for Bonner's mother and sister
every day at dinner, and place them beside him at his
own table.

It is remarkable that Ridley, one of the most learned
and most moderate among the reformers, should have
set the example of directing the old stone altars to be
taken down in churches, and 'the Lord's Board, after
the form of an honest table decently covered, to be set up
in such place of the quire or chancel as shall be thought
most meet by the discretion of the curates and the
churchwardens.' It appears that this had already been
done in some places, and Ridley's injunctions were soon
afterwards confirmed by a royal proclamation extending
to all the churches in the kingdom. This was one of

the greatest changes that had yet been made, especially
as there is evidence that the Lord's Supper had been
called a Sacrifice, though not in the Romish sense, from
very early times.   But it was a favourite notion that
Christian kings ought to imitate Josiah and Hezekiah
in the abolition of unscriptural practices, and as Hezekiah broke in pieces the brazen serpent because it had
been abused to idolatry, venerable as it was in itself as
a record of a signal deliverance and a type of greater
things to come, the Reformers argued that they might
abolish the form of an altar when it had been abused to
signify the daily repetition of the material sacrifice of
Christ.   As usual, violent men were not satisfied on either
side.   Not content with the abolition of altars, many refused to kneel to receive the holy communion, and this
became afterwards a fruitful source of contention, while
others would desecrate the table to common purposes
for fear of what they called superstition.   But these
evils have been gradually remedied.   An injunction of
Queen Elizabeth required that the tables should be set
as we now have them, and decently covered, and a sense
of propriety has confirmed the practice.   So that it
would surely be unthankful and undutiful now to
attempt to alter it, without authority, and without
general concurrence.   But the chief opposition which
this measure encountered at the time was from the
opposite party, and two of the bishops, Heath of Worcester, and Day of Chichester, were soon after deprived
of their sees.   Heath objected chiefly to the new ordination service; but the ground of the deprivation of
Bishop Day was that he would not concur in the
order for the removal of altars.   He was brought
before the council, where Cranmer acknowledged that
ancient writers sometimes call the table an altar, and
he was told that he might so call it still.[1]   But not
being content with this, and refusing to comply, he was

---

[1] H. WHARTON, *Harmer.* No. 32, p. 114. and No. 39, p. 116.

deprived. These were the only two bishops removed during this reign on merely ecclesiastical grounds. Both Bonner and Gardiner seem to have been willing to retain their bishoprics, and outwardly to comply with everything, perhaps as being the most effectual means of retaining the power to thwart the government in the changes that were going on. And although it had the appearance of injustice to remove those who gave an outward compliance, their conduct was calculated if not intended to drive the government to extreme courses. Bonner insulted the council when he was summoned before them, and his behaviour towards Cranmer may be illustrated from a trick he played him in order to bring him into contempt. On some occasion the archbishop was to hold a court in St. Paul's Cathedral, for which it was necessary that a temporary seat should be erected, as is still done on some great occasions. Bonner had it so contrived that the archbishop should sit, without knowing it, over one of the private altars, of which there were several in the church; and this circumstance he afterwards converted into an accusation against Cranmer, that he had seated himself above the altar of God, as if he had done it wilfully and in contempt. We shall see that Tonstal, who was also deprived towards the end of this reign, was merely the victim of political intrigue; and it is remarkable with what kindness and consideration the two bishops were treated who were now removed. The Bishop of Chichester was sent to reside with the Lord Chancellor, and Heath became the guest of Ridley at Fulham, where he remained till the accession of Queen Mary; and he acknowledged that he had been treated with the utmost kindness.[1]

The state of religious excitement which had prevailed so long in Germany, had now communicated

---

[1] His words are reported to have been, that he was dealt with 'more like a son than a subject.'

itself to this country, and the sect of Anabaptists were
spreading opinions subversive of all religion. They
did not merely hold what is now held by those who
bear that name, that children ought not to be baptised,
but many of them denied the Divinity of Christ, and
others indulged in wild speculations tending to the same
point. The dread of these opinions, and the desire of
showing that the Church of the Reformation did not
sanction that which is truly called heresy, led to the
deplorable execution of two persons, in this and the
following year. Joan Bocher[1] had been condemned
the year before by Cranmer, assisted by Latimer and
others, for saying that Christ took no flesh of the substance of the Virgin his mother, an opinion which, if it
have any sense in it, is equivalent to denying that our
Redeemer partook of our human nature. As all the
statutes against heresy had been repealed, those who
might now be convicted could not be executed except
by the king's writ, according to the common law of the
land. It is not certainly known by what means the
king's signature was obtained, or whether the council
may have ventured to act for him in his minority. The
story told by Foxe on this subject is wholly unsup-
ported, and not consistent with other evidence.[2] What
is certain is, that the execution was suspended for
several months, and when at length it took place, in
May, 1550, Cranmer himself was not present when it
was determined upon by the council. The next year,
Van Parre, a Dutchman, being also convicted of affirming that Christ is not very God, was in like manner
committed to the flames. These events have always been
considered as a blot upon the character of the English
Reformers. Certainly it is a subject of regret that the
men of those times did not distinguish between the

---

[1] Her name is by some written Bourchier, and by others Butcher.

[2] Strype remarks that, contrary to his usual custom, Foxe gives this
story of his being persuaded by Cranmer, without quoting his authority;
and that it is not noticed by Saunders, nor in King Edward's diary.

sinfulness of such doctrines and the right to inflict such
a penalty.

It might seem to a superficial observer, that the cause
of the reformers was all this while in favour with the
powers of the world. And yet it would in fact be a
judgment much more near to the truth, that they had
now as great difficulties as in the days of Henry;[1] or
even greater, as the law had less power to protect them,
and they had to reconstruct the Church when everything was tending to ruin. The irreligion, which was
now unchecked, was the bitter fruit of former neglect
and oppression. There was not a friend of the reformation who did not raise his voice against it. They
preached of sacrilege and simony in the king's court;
but the seats of the great offenders were left empty.
The Philistines, said Bernard Gilpin, had stopped up the
wells of faithful Abraham. The patrons of livings which
had been under monasteries gave them to be farmed
by their stewards and huntsmen; and hired for vicars
those who would serve them cheapest. Others, who
had pensions to pay to the dissolved monks, placed the
monks in the parish churches, to quit themselves of the
burthen. There was a famous Welsh idol which Henry
had burnt in Smithfield, called Darvol Gatheren, who
had the power, as the people thought, of doing wonderful things for his worshippers. ' I believe,' said Gilpin,
' that if Darvol Gatheren could come back and sign an
agreement with a patron, to give him the best part of
the profits, he might have a benefice.' Bucer sympathised with Hooper against ' the dress of antichrist;'
' but,' said he, ' the sinews of antichrist are the church-
robbers, that hold and spoil parish churches.'

The poor were also great sufferers, while they were
thrown out of the help of the old charities, and not yet
provided for in their need by a poor-law. A great
part of their misery, indeed, was owing to the change

---

[1] PROFESSOR JENKYNS, Preface to Cranmer.

that was taking place in the state of society. A century before, the poor were serfs, bondmen of the soil, and maintained by their respective owners. The transition from such a state to one of independence would in any case have been attended with difficulty and hazard. And when it was so soon followed by the dissolution of those houses, which in every neighbourhood were sure to supply some aid towards their support, their suffering was doubtless much increased. This explains the meaning of an act of the preceding year, by which all sturdy beggars who should be convicted before a magistrate, should become the slaves of the person who should prosecute them to conviction : that is, they should return to the condition of serfs, which was still familiar to people's minds, and not yet wholly abolished. At the same time, an alteration took place in the mode of cultivating the soil which was highly disadvantageous to them. The great landowners used to let their land at easy rents to tenants who paid them partly in kind, partly in feudal service. These tenants lived in comfort from tillage, and were a contented and thriving race. But now the landlords were tempted by the high price of wool to turn arable land into pasture ; and the enclosure of commons deprived cottagers of an old right, which even now is not everywhere extinct, derived from Saxon times. In a sermon of Latimer's, preached before the king in the year 1549, he told his Majesty that his own father was a farmer at Thurcaston in Leicestershire, where he paid a rent of 3*l.* by the year, and was able to bring up his children in comfort, and could always find a man and horse for the king's service : but that the man who now held the same land was paying 16*l.* instead of 3*l.* or 4*l.*, and was a beggar.

And this system was carried to the greatest extremes by the new proprietors of the abbey lands. Spending no money on the spot, and anxious only for profit, they had in general little regard for the tenants, and their avarice contrasted ill with the easy yoke of the monas-

tic proprietors.[1] Many of the monks being put into
the parish churches, would of course foment the popular
discontent, and many more wandering and begging
about the country would be objects of compassion when
they were no longer objects of envy.   The Protector
was willing enough to take the part of the commons
against the oppressions of the nobility ; and there are
instances of his writing in a way that does him credit to
those whom he knew to be guilty of oppression.[2]   But
his own hands were not clean from acts of spoliation,
though he may not have been guilty of similar oppression.   Fifty manors were alienated to him and his
family by the dean and chapter of Westminster, in the
hope to save themselves from a threat of dissolution,
and he was beginning to build a palace for himself in
the Strand, called Somerset House, on a scale of royal
magnificence.   Three bishops' houses and a church
were pulled down to make room for it, and when the
materials did not suffice, he attempted to demolish the
church of St. Margaret's at Westminster, giving the
abbey church to the parish instead.   But the parishioners resisted, and drove away the workpeople by
force.   So he took down a cloister and two chapels at
St. Paul's Cathedral, and when that was not enough, he
ordered the finest church in London except St. Paul's,
that of the Knights of St. John, which King Henry had
spared, to be blown up with gunpowder, and converted
to his use.

The oppressions referred to led to several risings and
rebellions ; one in Devonshire and Cornwall, and a more
alarming one in Norfolk and the eastern counties.   The
Devonshire rebels were taught by some priests to demand restitution of the abbey and chantry lands to
pious uses, the revival of solitary masses, and that the

---

[1] CARDWELL, Two Liturgies, Pref. xix.
[2] See a letter published by Mr. Tytler, from the Protector to Lord
Cobham, on behalf of a poor woman whom that nobleman had oppressed.

communion should be administered to the people only
at Easter, as it had been before; images to be restored,
old customs to be brought back, and the Bible and
English service to be put down.   It is to be observed
that the Cornish men at this period spoke a language
near akin to the Welsh, and few understood English.
But Cranmer, who put out an answer to this manifesto,
rightly judged that it was the work of a few cunning
heads, by whom the peasantry were misguided. These
troubles were not put down without lamentable slaughter;
and Lord Russell, who commanded, is said to have
hung several priests in retaliation.   Kett, a tanner,
who led the Norfolk men, professed no attachment to
anything of older time, but was a reformer of Wat
Tyler's kind, meaning to destroy the gentry, who had
given the poor too much reason to regard them as enemies.   It is said that the disorders were quelled chiefly
by the aid of foreign troops, who were employed because
the nobles could not trust the disposition of the people.
The rising in Devonshire led to an order in council to
take down all the bells save one out of every steeple,
because they had been used to summon the people
together for rebellious purposes; and contractors were
readily found to turn bells and clappers into a means
of profit.   Altogether, it was too evident that, in the
English Reformation also, the fiery speed of revenge for
the sins of former generations had far outstripped the
healing progress of the Prayers.[1]

---

[1] See the motto of this chapter.

CHAPTER XXI.

FALL OF SOMERSET. CRANMER'S OPINIONS ON THE EUCHA-
RIST. SECOND REFORMED LITURGY. ARTICLES. REFOR-
MATIO LEGUM. DEATH OF EDWARD VI. COUNCIL OF
TRENT.

> What custom wills, in all things should we do,
> That dust on antique time would lie unswept,
> And mountainous error be too highly heaped
> For truth to over-peer.—SHAKSPEARE.

INDEED the state of England during the reign of
Edward was languishing and distracted. The prince's
minority had left the sovereign power as a prize for competition amongst the nobles; and the people, as we have
seen, were distressed and easily disposed to rebel. The
Protector Somerset found his first enemy to be his own
brother, Thomas Seymour, the lord admiral; and a bill
of attainder was brought against him. He was accused
of having hired German troops to aid him in a design to
seize the person of the king, to displace his brother, and
gain the power into his own hands. It is certain that
he was a vicious man, dangerous, and turbulent; and
his proceedings may have been treasonable: but it was
a miserable spectacle, when the country saw a brother
condemned to the traitor's axe by the influence of a
brother. In setting his hand to the death-warrant,
Cranmer was guilty of a strange departure from the
practice of an English bishop, whom the laws of the
Church and of the country alike forbade to meddle with
causes of blood. His justification was, that he acted as
one of the council of regency, exercising the royal
authority. Latimer, in a sermon, justified the extremity
that was used towards the admiral, because he had
in his last moments prepared two secret letters, to be

delivered to the two princesses, Mary and Elizabeth, to caution them against the designs of the Protector. If he died in malice against his brother, the more unfit he was to die. It is only lamentable that Cranmer should have consented to the act, and that honest Latimer should have used such reasons to defend it.

The root of a power watered with kindred blood is seldom found to flourish long. There was one of the most ready agents in the attainder of the admiral, who within six months had compassed the overthrow of Somerset himself. The rise of Dudley, Earl of Warwick, and the ruin of the Protector, are matters of history. There is no faith in courts, when ambition governs, and avarice suggests to every man the path of personal advancement. Paget, the confidential friend of Somerset, was the instrument of his betrayal, and sent a message from Windsor to tell the associated nobles how he might best be apprehended.[1] He prolonged his life by submission; but it was impossible to avoid suspicion; and it seems that he could not brook the loss of his authority.

With regard to the government of Dudley, or Northumberland, the title which he procured himself after the fall of Somerset, it was altogether guided by a selfish desire of aggrandisement. With what crimes he gained his dangerous elevation, with what dark and dangerous counsels he tried to bring the crown into the line of his own family, is all recorded in the public annals of this period. It was natural enough that he should have been suspected of hastening the young king's death, when he had so laid his designs for his own more absolute power. Our plan only requires us to notice those circumstances which concern the state of religion among the people.

It was now that the young king's religious education was of essential service in the maintenance of the reformed religion. Northumberland was a man merely

---

[1] Sir H. Ellis, vol. ii. p. 173.

devoted, as we have said, to his own ambition, but his inclination was towards what was called the old religion. He seems to have brought over Wriothesley, Earl of Southampton, to his party, by promising to impede the reformation, and Gardiner, who had been imprisoned with Bonner for disobedience to the council, wrote to him from the Tower, congratulating the change of ministers, and hoping for release. There was a general expectation among those who wished to restore the Latin service and the private mass, that their wishes would be gratified, and they began to desist from attending the new service. Bonner also, who had been sentenced the year before to be deprived of his bishopric of London, prayed that the sentence might be reversed, and an appeal entertained which he had entered against it. But Edward showed himself so entirely resolved to proceed in the same course, that Northumberland made no attempt to alter his resolution, but professed to go along with all his wishes. A proclamation was issued for calling in all missals, and other books of the old devotion, which were to be delivered to visitors appointed for the purpose, and this was confirmed by the parliament, which met in January, 1550, by which also a new form for an ordination service, which had been drawn up by the commissioners, was ordered to be used. This service gave more offence to the Romish party than the English Liturgy, and their hostility was much increased by the orders which soon followed for taking down the stone altars in churches, as has been already related.

It was in the year 1550 that Cranmer published his *Defence of the True and Catholic Doctrine of the Sacrament of the Body and Blood of our Saviour Christ*; and no book had so great an influence as this upon the belief of the English Church. There had been considerable difference of opinion among the reformers respecting the manner of our Saviour's Presence in the holy Eucharist. They agreed in rejecting the Romish doctrine; but Luther and his followers maintained what was called a

c c

Corporeal Presence, asserting that, although the bread and wine did not cease to be bread and wine, yet the Real Body of Christ is in some ineffable way associated into their substance ; and this is what came to be called Consubstantiation. But the Swiss divines, of whom Zwingle was the leader, rejecting the corporeal presence altogether, were themselves divided into two parties, the one holding that there is a spiritual presence, with a participation of the benefits of Christ's death, while the rest went the length of denying that this holy sacrament is anything else than a bare commemoration. Attempts had been made to arrive at an agreement between them, and there is a remarkable paper sent from Luther to Bucer some time before, discussing the possibility of a reconciliation by a mutual concession, by which the Lutherans should acknowledge that it is only bread, and the Zwinglians should concede that Christ is really present ; and it had been agreed by Frith and Tyndal that they should abstain as much as possible from agitating the question. But the foreign divines who were invited over in the beginning of this reign were generally opposed to the Lutheran notions, and the year before the publication of Cranmer's book there had been disputations held with the Romish party, both at Oxford and at Cambridge. Peter Martyr undertook to maintain that there is no Transubstantiation ; that the Body and Blood of Christ is not carnally or corporeally present in the sacrament (which was Luther's doctrine), and that they are united to the bread and wine sacramentally. And it is a circumstance well worthy of remark, so short a time before the doctrine of Transubstantiation was finally established by the Council of Trent, that several of their own divines were then prepared to abandon it. One of those who took part in the debate against Peter Martyr was Bernard Gilpin, who being then a young man, had not yet made up his mind to abandon what he found received as the doctrine of the Church. He is said to have publicly owned, that he could not maintain

the cause he had undertaken, and being dissatisfied upon
the subject, he went to Bishop Tonstal, who was his
near relation, and to others of that party, for their
opinion. The answers he obtained were afterwards related by himself. Tonstal told him, that ' Innocent III.
was much overseen, to make transubstantiation an article
of faith,' which opinion this learned and moderate bishop
soon afterwards publicly maintained in a book he wrote
upon the sacrament. Another told him the Communion
Book, as then put out, was very godly, and agreeable to
the Gospel ; and he was told, that Dr. Chedsey, one of
the leading opponents of Peter Martyr in this disputation,
had said among his friends, ' the Protestants must yield
to us in granting the presence of Christ in the sacrament,
and we must yield to them in the opinion of transubstantiation,' the very thing which the Church of England
has done.

It was generally supposed that Cranmer held the
Lutheran opinion of the sacrament for some time previous to his final adoption of those sentiments which he
now put forth in his book.[1] He had made copious
selections from the fathers, and had gone through the
whole subject, with his usual accuracy, before the time
of the trial of Frith, at which time his opinion, at all
events of the Corporeal Presence, remained unshaken.
But when Ridley had been convinced by the writings
of Bertram that such had not been the doctrine of the
earlier Church, the archbishop was induced by his
opinion to go over the whole subject again, the result of
which was the conviction that such notions are a
novelty, equally inconsistent with Holy Scripture and
with the teaching of the early Church. Thus deliberately and gradually did he arrive at that conclusion
which he finally embraced. His mode of stating the
doctrine appears to have agreed with the more moderate

---

[1] See the reasons for adhering to this opinion fully stated by Mr.
Jenkyns, in his Preface to his Edition of Cranmer's works, p. 74.

of the Swiss divines, that it is a Spiritual Presence,
which he expressed in these words, 'that the cup is a
communion of Christ's blood that was shed for us, and
the bread is a communion of his flesh that was
crucified for us; so that although in the truth of his
human nature, Christ be in heaven, and sitteth at
the right hand of God the Father, yet whosoever
eateth of that bread in the Supper of the Lord, according to Christ's institution and ordinance, is assured
of Christ's own promise and testament, that he is a
member of His Body, and receiveth the benefits of His
passion which he suffered for us on the cross.'   And he
declared that he was equally anxious to guard against
the error of those who went to the extreme of 'despising this blessed sacrament as a thing of small or of none
effect,' as he was to do away with 'the abuse of it to
other purposes than Christ did first ordain.'   It may be
doubted whether he did not define too far, and whether
it be not preferable to confine ourselves to our Lord's
words, with the explanation that we take them spiritually.   But we are not bound by the opinions even
of Cranmer, and happily this moderate course, though
not immediately followed, has since been adopted by
our Church.   In the forty-two Articles drawn up by
him, and published in the end of this reign, 'the Real
Presence' was expressly denied, though in such a way
as to limit the meaning to a Corporeal Presence, and in
the Liturgy, as then revised, the words before directed
to be used at the delivery of the sacrament, 'The Body
and Blood of Christ, preserve thy body and soul,' were
altogether omitted; instead of which these words only
were to be said, 'Take and eat this in remembrance
that Christ died for thee,' as if it were only a memorial.
But the clause in the article denying the real presence
was omitted on the accession of Queen Elizabeth, and
the words originally used in delivering the sacrament
were united with those subsequently introduced.   In
the addition to the Catechism also, made under James I.,

it was expressly declared that 'the Body and Blood of Christ are verily and indeed taken and received by the faithful in the Lord's Supper.' So that, provided we acknowledge that it is after a spiritual manner, we are at liberty to affirm, and many of the best learned men of our Church have constantly affirmed, that there is a Real Presence of Christ in the Holy Eucharist.[1]

---

[1] This term 'Real Presence' is claimed by Romanists as expressing their doctrine, and it was so used by many of the Reformers, and by Cranmer himself. It seems clear, however, that Frith and Bucer were willing to retain that expression, as many have since been who have been as far as possible from holding Transubstantiation, or any other notion of a Carnal or Corporal Presence. A learned modern writer indeed has said that the Reformers ought to have learned, 'by exposing the absurdities of transubstantiation, not to contend for equal nonsense of their own;' and the same author having described the Zwinglian notion, that there is nothing in the sacrament but a sign or symbol, to which he justly says, the three opinions of the Romanists, the Lutherans, and of those who hold a real presence without any change of substance, were equally opposed, calls this last opinion 'a jargon of bad metaphysical theology,' and says that, 'as the Romish tenet of transubstantiation is the best, so this of the Calvinists is the worst imagined of the three that have been opposed to the simplicity of the Helvetic explanation.' It is very useful for Churchmen to be aware of the way in which men of the world regard those questions which seem to them of the greatest importance; so that we may take Mr. Hallam's strictures in good part. But does he mean to say, that the doctrine of transubstantiation is one of little importance? And when men saw with their own eyes the consequences of that doctrine, and became convinced that the theory was groundless on which it depended, and were persecuted to the death if they denied the doctrine; what else could they do than endeavour to state what was the true doctrine? That they persecuted one another for their opinions on this point is not true: that they would differ might naturally be expected, and that many would rush to an opposite extreme, and not be content to state without defining it. But when we are told that this doctrine of a Real without a Corporeal Presence is a jargon of bad metaphysics, perhaps such statements may arise from not having considered that those who say so *do not profess to explain the matter, but to adopt the language of scripture without explanation.* It is not *impossible* that Christ should, *after some spiritual manner,* 'give us his flesh to eat,' and we believe it because of his word, only we determine that it is not a corporeal or bodily presence of his flesh, and we define no further. On this subject let us hear the words of Hooker (*Eccl. Polity,* b. v. lxvii. 12), 'Let it be sufficient for me, presenting myself at the Lord's Table, to know what I there receive from Him, without searching or inquiring of the manner how Christ performeth his promise. What those elements are in them-

The general feeling of the reforming party was now pressing for further alterations. The new liturgy, excellent and beautiful as it was, had failed to satisfy almost any class of opinions. The advocates of the old learning were opposed to any sort of change, and many of the Reformers were unwilling to retain anything that the Church of Rome had held. Calvin had written to

---

selves, it skilleth not; it is enough that to me which take them they are the Body and Blood of Christ.' So Dean Brevint (*Christian Sacrament and Sacrifice*, p. 44), 'How these mysteries become, in my behalf, the supernatural instruments of such blessings, it is enough for me to admire. One thing I know, as said the blind man after he had received his sight, *He laid clay upon my eyes, and behold I see.*' And Bishop Patrick (*Christian Sacrifice*, p. 24), having cited St. Chrysostom and Eusebius to the like effect, quotes thus from Fulgentius (*De Fide*), 'In the time of the New Testament, the Holy Catholic Church throughout the world offers the sacrifice of Bread and Wine in faith and charity. For in those sacrifices (of the law) the flesh of Christ was *figured*, which he was to offer; but in this sacrifice there is a *commemoration* of the flesh of Christ, which he hath offered.' And then he adds, ' This is sufficient to show what the sacrifice is which we make when we do *do this*, and that our Church doth now the same that the ancient Church did. By feasting upon this sacrifice, we not only commemorate that oblation of Himself with the sacrifice of praise and thanksgiving, but likewise offer ourselves to Him to be entirely His.' To this may be added the well-known language of Bishop Ken. 'Oh God Incarnate! how thou canst give us thy flesh to eat, and thy blood to drink; how thy flesh is meat indeed! how thou who art in heaven art present on our altar, I can by no means explain; but I firmly believe it all, because thou hast said it; and I firmly rely on thy love, and on thy omnipotence to make good thy word, though the manner of doing it I cannot comprehend.' But if any think this mode of expression too strong, the Church, though it admits, does not impose it, provided we keep clear of the two extremes of denying, on the one hand, that in this sacrament the faithful are partakers of Christ, on the other of affirming that it is a gross and carnal partaking of Him. It is thus expressed by a modern divine: 'When we recollect what there is in the Lord's Supper beyond the mere meeting of Christ and his disciples; what it is which the bread and the wine commemorate; of what we partake when, as true Christians, we eat of that bread and drink of that cup; then we shall understand that God indeed is brought very near to us, inasmuch as he who is a Christian, and partakes sincerely of Christian communion, is a partaker also of Christ; and as belonging to his body, his living spiritual body, the universal Church, receives his share of all those blessings, all that infinite love which the Father shows continually to the head of that body, his own well-beloved Son.' (ARNOLD's *Christian Life*, Serm. xxii. p. 242.)

Somerset when it first came out, approving it as far as
it went, but hoping for further change, and all the
foreigners who were in England concurred in the same
wish, and were backed by a strong party at home. The
change' in Cranmer's views on the. eucharist would incline him to some alteration; and the long cherished
hope of uniting all the reformed churches at home and
abroad in one confession of faith, when it was proposed
that those on the continent should receive episcopal
government from England, the loss of which both
Luther and Calvin had lamented, made it seem desirable to approximate towards their views. The king
also was bent upon 'a further Reformation,' in which
he was confirmed by a paper upon the subject presented
to him about this time by Bucer; and not long after the
commissioners had completed· the new ordination services, they were directed to proceed to a revision of the
Prayer Book, some questions connected with which
subject had already been moved in convocation. However willing the foreign divines may have been to give
their assistance, it does not appear that their suggestions were implicitly followed, and there is reason to
believe, on the contrary, that what was done was, for
the. most part, the work of the commissioners themselves.[1] The alterations made by them in the communion service have been already noticed, except that the
practice of reading the Ten Commandments at the beginning of that service was now first introduced. The
earlier liturgies had begun with more of joy than of
humiliation and sorrow, but it has been remarked as
appropriate to the condition of a repentant and returning Church that we should for awhile stand afar off
and bethink us of our sins and our duties, before we
draw nigh to the most sacred and glorious mysteries.[2]
And the same observation applies to the beautiful introduction to the morning prayer, which also was now

[1] CARDWELL, *Pref.* p. xxv.
[2] This remark is taken from one of the Oxford Tracts, attributed to
the late revered Isaac Williams.

first added, consisting of the sentences of Scripture, the
Exhortation, Confession, and Absolution.[1]   These are
not to be found in this place in the primitive liturgies,
and the idea seems to have been taken from the Liturgy
of Calvin, and from one then used in England by John
Laski in his German congregation.   But Calvin had no
absolution in his service, having been overruled in his
own wish to introduce it; nor did they copy that of
Laski, but seem rather to have availed themselves of
the numerous forms for that purpose with which they
were already familiar, in the ancient services of their
own Church.   It was now required that prayers should
be said every day by all clergymen in their churches,
and that all persons should receive the holy communion
three times a year at least, instead of once only as in the
first book, this being a suggestion which had been made
by Bucer.   But it was only returning to the practice of
the Church of England before the Lateran Council.   An
important alteration was also made in the rubric respecting clerical vestments, by which, instead of continuing the use of such dresses as were in the Roman
Catholic churches, a simple surplice, with the hood,
was all that was required.   The omission of Prayer for
the Dead, both in the communion and burial services,
has been already mentioned, a practice which has been
silently discontinued by the English Church.   These
alterations were drawn up in the year 1551, but as the
parliament did not meet till the next year, the law for
the use of the Prayer Book thus revised was not made
until April, 1552, and the observance of it was to begin
from the feast of All Saints following.   It may be mentioned here that the prayers for the Parliament, and
for all Conditions of Men, and the General Thanksgiving, were not added until the restoration of Charles II.,
after the great Rebellion.   A slight alteration was now

---

[1] This part was not added to the service for *evening* prayer, until the
Restoration.

made as to the holidays to be observed in this church, by omitting the festivals of St. Mary Magdalen, and St. Clement of Rome; and the observance of the rest was soon afterwards enjoined by act of parliament.[1]

Cranmer was soon engaged in controversy in consequence of his book on the eucharist. It was answered by Gardiner, who thought fit to exhibit his answer before the council when he was called up for judgment in the causes alleged against him, as if he had been questioned for his doctrine on that point. On this occasion he called his judges 'heretics and sacramentaries,' and was at length deprived of his bishopric, in February, 1551. Cranmer produced a reply to Gardiner's answer in the September following, in which he gave the whole of his adversary's arguments at length, and answered them in order. He had greatly the advantage of Gardiner, both in his knowledge of the fathers, and in solid reasoning, and these books of his have hardly been surpassed for the ability and research with which they state the question.

But the archbishop had other work upon his hands at this time, in the preparation of the Articles of the English Church. It was not until the year 1552 that it became apparent that the design of a general confession of faith for all the reformed churches was hopeless, and then the archbishop proceeded, with other divines, under a royal commission, to draw up forty-two Articles of Faith, founded upon those which had been agreed upon with the German divines in 1538, as these were in great measure upon the Confession of Augsburg.[2] They were published by royal authority in 1553, as having been agreed upon in a London synod in the year 1552, but whether this meant the convocation itself, or the assembly of bishops and divines by whom they were drawn up, has not been certainly

---

[1] 5 and 6 Edw. VI. c. 3.
[2] JENKYNS, *Pref.* pp. xxil. and cvl.

determined. They do not differ essentially from the
thirty-nine Articles of Elizabeth, which to this day
form the Confession of Faith of the English Church;
except that the 'real or corporeal presence' in the
eucharist was denied, on the ground of its being impossible that the body of Christ should be in many
places at once. There was no article on the Holy
Ghost, but there were four more at the end, which
were omitted at the revision under Elizabeth, on the
following points: That the resurrection of the dead is
not passed already. That the souls of men departed do
not perish with their bodies, or sleep till the day of
judgment. That the notion of the millennium is a fable
derived from Jewish traditions, and against the sense of
scripture. That it is a grievous error to teach that all
men, however they may live, shall be saved at last. The
first of these four had reference to some doctrine denying the future resurrection of the body, and confining
the power of Christ to a spiritual reviving of the soul.
The others were pointed against some opinions which
have found supporters in these times; and it may be
well to remember what such men as Cranmer and Ridley
thought of them.

One thing was wanting to complete the design of a
reformation, by putting forth a new code of ecclesiastical
law. The clergy having agreed in their submission to
Henry VIII., that they would cease to claim an ex-
clusive right of legislation, the laws respecting ecclesiastical matters were left as they existed before the
Reformation; but it had been intended from the first
that they should be revised, and the Act of Submission
had authorised the king during his life to appoint commissioners for that purpose, and what he should so put
forth was to have the force of law. A commission was
appointed by him for this purpose, but no canons were
drawn up, and as the power was limited to his life, a
similar power was granted to his son, according to the
petition presented by Convocation in the beginning of

his reign.[1] Thirty-two commissioners were named under this act, in 1551, consisting of eight bishops, eight divines, eight civilians, and eight common lawyers, but it was chiefly carried on by Cranmer, assisted by Taylor, soon afterwards bishop of Lincoln, Peter Martyr, and Walter Haddon, a civilian, President of Magdalen College, Oxford. Their work was finished and ready for the king's signature, which was prevented by his death, and the want of such a code has since been considered by many to be the great misfortune of this Church.[2] Having enumerated the chief heads of Christian belief, and the principal heresies, they proceeded to the punishment of heresy. The offender was first to be excommunicated, and if he continued obstinate was to be delivered to the secular power; upon which, as the common law of the land then stood, he might have been consigned to the flames. But in the last draft of these canons the following limitation was added; having been delivered to the secular power, he was to be either condemned to perpetual banishment or imprisonment, or punished in such other way as should seem most conducive to his conversion: so that it would seem that at least their desire was to abolish the penalty of death for heresy. As regards clerical duties, preachers were to be appointed in each district, under the bishop's authority, who should go round to the several parishes to preach in turn; pluralities were to be wholly abolished; prebendaries in residence were to expound the scriptures thrice a week in the cathedral; rural deans were to be annually appointed to superintend the clergy and laity of each deanery, and report to the bishop every six months, the archdeacon being as it were the head over the rural deans; diocesan synods were to be held every year in Lent, at which, after the

---

[1] By act 3 and 4 Edw. VI. c. 2. But Collier says, ii. 297, that Cranmer protested against the Bill.

[2] This code is usually known as the 'Reformatio Legum Ecclesiasticarum.'

litany, followed by a sermon and the holy communion, the clergy were to retire with the bishop and report the state of the diocese to him, upon which he was to give his orders, which were to be obeyed at once.   Bishops in their old age or infirm were to have a coadjutor bishop, subject only to appeal to the archbishop; visitations were to be held besides the diocesan synods; each bishop was to bring up young men in his family for the ministry, and his wife and children were to avoid all levity and vain dress; each archbishop was to visit his whole province once, and on great occasions, with the king's licence, was to hold provincial synods.   As regards correction of morals, seducers were to be excommunicated if they would not marry those whom they had seduced, or if this should be impossible, they were to give them a third part of their whole property. An adulterer, if a clergyman, was to forfeit all his property, be deprived of his benefice, and banished or imprisoned for life; if a layman, he was to restore his wife's portion, give her half his goods, and suffer the like banishment or imprisonment; and the punishment of women was similar.   Divorce might be had on sufficient grounds, but there was no 'separation' without divorce.   In cases of notorious scandal, persons might be called upon to clear themselves upon oath before the bishop, with four compurgators who should swear they believed the accused spoke the truth.   The form of excommunication, and of that for receiving penitents back to the Church, were exceedingly beautiful, and these were retained in some canons which were drawn up under Queen Elizabeth.

One other thing provided for in these laws was of such importance as to deserve separate notice.   It was required that on every holiday, the curate or minister of each parish should catechise the children for an hour in the afternoon.   And this was in accordance with several injunctions in this reign, as well as with the frequent publication of forms of catechetical instruction.

The rubric at the end of the catechism annexed to the confirmation service in both the prayer books of King Edward, required that the curate, that is the clergyman of the parish, should *once in six weeks at least* instruct and examine the children for half an hour before evensong. It was not said that the people should be taught to read, which was a privilege as yet possessed by few; but it was required that the clergy themselves should instruct the youth of their parish in the elements of Christian doctrine, and should admit none to the holy communion who were not so instructed. Similar orders and still more express were given under Queen Elizabeth; for it was then, as it is still, required to be done every Sunday, after the second lesson; by which means the elder people might witness the instruction of their children and servants, and profit by it themselves. Nor can it be expected that any Church should possess the affections of the people, or succeed in training them in Christian courses, where this shall be neglected.[1]

Amidst these important changes, the turbulent ambition of the courtiers was bringing disastrous results upon themselves and their country. Somerset had prolonged his life by submission; but it was impossible to avoid suspicion, and his imprudence gave advantage to his enemies. It has been supposed that the king had been prejudiced against him by his brother;[2] and he is known to have once expressed himself as if he had thought the removal of his uncle would be an advantage. But the truth seems to be that from his youth and state of pupilage he had no choice in the matter.

---

[1] The canons of James I., which are now in force, say that the catechetical instruction shall be given before the service in the afternoon. But as they are not sanctioned by parliament, the rubric which directs that it shall be after the second lesson, must be held to supersede them, though probably it may be considered optional.

[2] By Mr. Tytler. *England under the Reigns of Edward VI. and Mary.*

The death of Somerset is recorded in his journal without a word of affection or regret; and if this marks anything, it is the ascendancy which Dudley had now gained over him.   It is indeed evident, from the king's journal and other records, that he was at the time engaged in a round of amusements, court masques, and tilting-matches, and it is probable that it was so contrived by Dudley, to keep him from reflection.   The execution of the late Protector took place on Tower Hill in January, 1552, and his speech and conduct on the scaffold tended to confirm the impression that, however vain-glorious and unguarded, he was not without a sincere desire to act on Christian principles.   It was much noted at the time that he had obtained a grant of the demesne of Glastonbury Abbey, and had converted the remains of its noble buildings into a manufactory of woollen.[1]   And as one of the popes had formerly entailed an especial curse upon any one who should desecrate that venerable foundation, his miscarriages were thought to be a signal instance of the divine displeasure upon sacrilege.   But the country was no gainer in this respect by the government of his rival.

Warwick had got himself made Duke of Northumberland, and, that he might have a principality to support his dukedom, not content with the domains of the Percies, he now endeavoured to deprive Tonstal, bishop of Durham, that he might get the palatinate to himself. Some letters were found which were construed to implicate the bishop in Somerset's affair, and he was attainted of misprision of treason.   But Cranmer vehemently opposed the bill, and with Lord Stourton, protested against it, and the commons threw it out. Notwithstanding which Tonstal was deprived a year afterwards, and an act passed to divide the bishopric, erecting another for the county of Northumberland, and

---

[1] See p. 342. But yet there was something good even in this scheme, for it was made an asylum for French refugees, who had their chaplain there.

leaving the palatine jurisdiction to the king, who bestowed it upon this duke, who obtained no less than
twelve grants of lands from the crown during this short
reign, the first being the castle of Warwick, and the
last the palatinate of Durham. But this treatment of
Bishop Tonstal was equally unjust towards him and
unfavourable to the cause of the reformation. He had
not refused to comply with any of the changes that had
taken place, and was the personal friend of Cranmer
and Somerset. Cranmer declared afterwards that
Northumberland had for some time laboured to accomplish his own ruin also, and the deprivation of Tonstal
was merely a political act; but it placed him in the
position of one of the deprived bishops, and probably
precluded his acquiescence in the restoration of the reformed religion under Queen Elizabeth. Ridley had
been actually promoted to the see of Durham,[1] when
all these matters were stopped by the king's death. It
was also during the latter years of this reign that the
greater part of that scandalous impoverishment of the
bishops' sees was carried on. Cranmer was forced to
surrender Knowle Parke in Kent ; Beaudesert had been
already taken from the bishopric of Litchfield. The
new bishopric of Westminster was suppressed, and
most of the land seized. When Gardiner was deprived,
which was not till after Somerset had been deposed
from the Protectorate, two thousand marks a year was
all that was allowed to his successor, Bishop Poynet ;
and when Miles Coverdale, the associate of Tyndal in
translating parts of the Bible, was promoted to the see
of Exeter, almost the whole of the lands had been

---

[1] There is no doubt that H. Wharton is right in saying that Ridley had
been translated to Durham, though possibly he might not yet have taken
possession, as he signed himself bishop of London, as Strype has shown,
on the last day of King Edward's life. But not only does the register of
the Council in Queen Mary's reign declare him to have been deprived of
the see of Durham, and not of London ; but he himself mentions the fact
in his letters to his family, printed by Coverdale among the Martyr's
letters, immediately before his death.

conveyed away. It was usual to give impropriate tithes
to the bishops instead of their lands, thus placing them in
a false position, as if they were withholding the tithes
which ought to have been restored to the parishes when
the monasteries were suppressed. This had been done
when Holbech was made bishop of Lincoln;[1] but
Veysey, the bishop of Exeter, did not get even so much
as this, and had nothing to leave to his successor but
the record of promises which were never fulfilled. Latimer had been pressed to return to his bishopric of
Worcester, and the house of commons had done him the
well-deserved honour of petitioning that he might have
it.   But he distinctly refused ; and it is most probable
that one reason which weighed with him was that he
would not be a party to that alienation of the lands of
his see which was exacted of almost every new bishop
in these times.   Latimer frequently and boldly protested against this prevailing covetousness in his sermons
at Court, and did not scruple to call upon the possessors of ill-gotten wealth to make restitution, and that
so persuasively, that he was once or twice successful.
At another time he mentioned a case of injustice which
had come to his knowledge, adding that the man who
had done it was present, though he might have thought
he had done it secretly.   Such a preacher was not the
sort of person who was likely to be accessory, even
though a passive agent, to the spoliation he condemned.
But it had become a convenient doctrine that it was
good for religion that the clergy should be poor.

The condition of the parochial clergy, at the same
time, was as bad or worse.   Many of them exercised
common trades for their own support, or kept houses of
public entertainment ; not that such practices were new,
for similar instances may be found in the preceding
reigns.   But it shows that very little improvement had

---

[1] It is said that the spire of the great tower of Lincoln Minster fell
down the day after the manors of the see had been surrendered, and it
is certain that it took place within the same year.

yet taken place, though many attempts were made to
remedy the deficiency. If now preaching was rare, a
little while before there were many churches in which
there was not even a pulpit. And wherever a zealous
man could be found favourable to the reformation, he
was licensed to preach, not only in his own church, but
in a certain district, and the king's chaplains especially
were so employed, among whom were Grindal, afterwards archbishop of Canterbury, whom Ridley had the
merit of first bringing into notice, and John Knox, the
too impetuous reformer of Scotland. Indeed, it would
appear from the intended reformation of ecclesiastical
laws, that a modified system of itinerancy, in the place
of that which had been introduced by the friars, and
carried on in spite of them by the poor priests of Wycliffe, was designed by the Church of the Reformation.
It is to be remembered also, that great as were the
evils which the above causes had tended to cherish, the
fault was not with those who were concerned in carrying on the Reformation itself. Many were the instances
of a self-denying and apostolical spirit by which the reforming clergy commended their doctrine to the hearts
of the people in every part of the country. Hooper, at
his bishopric of Gloucester, went about the towns and
villages of his diocese, teaching and preaching to the
people, so that 'no father in his household, no husband-
man in his vineyard, was more employed than he.'
Every day he entertained the poor at dinner in his
hall, and himself and his chaplains instructed them
in religion, and dined after them upon the same fare.
Dr. Rowland Taylor, at Hadley in Suffolk, by his assiduous labours, brought over a manufacturing population, not to his own opinions only, but to that sincere
religion which is proved by an altered life and conversation. And Bernard Gilpin, having been presented
by the Crown to the vicarage of Norton, in Durham,
in 1552, had already entered upon those labours which
afterwards gained him the appellation of the *Apostle of*

the North. A general license to preach was granted him in consequence of the sermon above referred to; for it was an excellent practice that was then observed, that every man who had a crown living given him should preach once before the king.

Indeed, nothing is more remarkable in the history of these times than the number of true-hearted and devoted men whom the primate was enabled to rally round him. Of all those who were preferred by his advice, or who shared his labours, there was scarcely one who in the day of trial was found wanting. Let a few more instances be taken of the most eminent.

Nicholas Ridley must always be named as the first of his associates—as the one to whom we especially owe the revival of the true doctrine of the Lord's Supper, and from whom Cranmer himself gratefully acknowledged that he had received it.[1] The part which he took we have already seen, from the time of his early studies at Cambridge. He was of an old family in Northumberland; and, educated under the care of an uncle of eminent learning in the canon-law, his early prejudices were by no means favourable to the cause of the Reformation. But the study of the Scriptures in the original tongue, and the acquaintance he made with the works of the Fathers, set him upon inquiries which the canonists could not satisfy; and though his uncle sent him to Paris and Louvain, he returned to Cambridge more confirmed in his desires after the truth as it was taught in more primitive times. He was then for some time employed in teaching at the university, where he gained the affection of his pupils, as one of them testifies,[2] by piety without hypocrisy or austerity, and an obliging familiarity, often condescending to join in their amusements

---

[1] It is probable that Ridley acquiesced with Bucer in wishing to omit the petition for consecrating the elements, because he thought St. Dionysius and St. Basil directed that part to be spoken in silence.'—Answers on the Mass, Q. 9.

[2] Turner, Dean of Wells, in Strype.

at tennis or archery, while he took care to imbue them
with hard Greek.

Latimer has been already frequently before the reader.
He does not appear to have been one who had any hand
in the consultations at Windsor or elsewhere. His ready
popular talent at preaching was his chief service. His
sermons, though we have them only as they were taken
down by his bearers, and therefore necessarily conveying
an imperfect notion of what he was, will always be
among the most pleasing memorials of the time : they
breathe the spirit of a plain Christian sincerity, delivering its message to all ranks and parties without fear or
favour, and with a strong vein of native humour and
good sense, which wins its way, as it did at first, to every
English heart.   His mind and memory seem to have
been somewhat impaired before his last conflict ; but the
old man's courage and faithfulness were firm and unbroken to the last.

Another martyred bishop who had a share in the consultations about the Prayer Book, was Ferrar, bishop of
St. David's.   He is said to have been guilty of some
harshness in his diocese, and offended some of his clergy,
who accused him, as it would seem, of an offence against
the statute of *præmunire*, and procured him to be imprisoned.   This severity, however, did not shake his
attachment to the Reformation ; for we shall find, that
after remaining two years in prison under Edward,
he freely gave himself to be burned under Queen
Mary.

Next to these five martyrs among the prelates (including Hooper), we may mention Poynet, bishop of
Rochester, and afterwards of Winchester, to which see
he was removed on Gardiner's deprivation.   He was the
author of the second catechism, commonly called Edward
VI.'s Catechism, published at the end of this king's
reign, and wrote a Treatise of Reconciliation, as he
called it, on the Eucharist ; by which he showed the
primitive doctrine with much clearness, and also, how

far he was willing to grant the terms which the Romanists insisted on, of the 'truth, nature, and substance' of
Christ's body in the Communion, provided he were not
required to believe that the matter was changed.[1]   He
was a most ingenious man, well read in ancient languages,
able to converse in modern ones, and a skilful mathe-
matician and mechanist, being the constructor of an improved clock, which he presented to Henry VIII.   He
fled abroad in the reign of Mary, and died at Strasburg,
at the age of thirty-nine.[2]

Harley, bishop of Hereford, was a fellow of Magdalen
College, Oxford, and we shall meet with his name again
as a confessor in Queen Mary's reign.

Holbech, bishop of Lincoln, died two years before the
death of Edward.   He had been a Benedictine monk,
and prior of the cathedral at Worcester.   He was consulted on the communion service, and his answers show
how well he had studied the subject, though they prove
that he had not unlearnt all the old learning; for he
quotes the false decretals as genuine.   He was succeeded by John Taylor, another confessor in the reign
of Mary,

---

[1] Poynet also was the author of 'a notable sermon concerning the right
use of the Lord's Supper,' preached before the Kyng at Westminster,
A.D. 1550, in which he makes two ways of feeding on the Body and Blood of
Christ: 1st, by Faith; 2nd, Sacramentally, in which last he says—' And
yet is it true that Christ's very Body is present at the ministration of
the Lord's Supper, yea, even Flesh and Blood and Bone, as he was born
of the Virgin,'—and then explains that he is so present to the eye of
Faith, though being in heaven.

[2] Stow reports in his Chronicle that Poynet was engaged in Wyatt's
rebellion; but Collier, as well as Burnet, rejects the report, as such a man
could hardly have been known to be engaged, and not attainted for
treason afterwards. A Treatise on Political Power was published with
the initials D. I. P. B. R. W. in the year of Poynet's death, advocating
something like rebellion as well as puritanism; and the design of the
letters was to make it believed that the author was Doctor John Poynet,
bishop of Rochester and Winchester. But as he appears to have avoided
the society of Knox and the other puritans abroad, and remained with
those exiles who kept the English Prayer Book at Strasburg, it seems
improbable that he should have written thus, and it ought not, as Collier
says, to be ascribed to him without better evidence.

Miles Coverdale, bishop of Exeter, has been already mentioned as aiding Tyndal in his translation of the Bible. The version of the Psalms in our prayer-books, suited well for the chanted prayer, is said to be his work. He was, like Hooper, too much in love with the Genevan model, and this disposition was unfortunately confirmed by a second residence abroad during the Marian persecution. But he was a devout man, a friend of peace, and an assiduous parish-priest.

Bradford the martyr was a chaplain and friend of Ridley, by whom he was ordained. He was some time before in some office under government, in which he had, like many more exalted persons at that time, appropriated to himself a portion of the public money. A sermon of Latimer's, in which he inveighed against this common dishonesty, had such an effect upon him, that he came voluntarily to the old bishop to confess and make restitution. When Latimer paid back the money into the treasury, he was pressed, as he tells us in one of his sermons, to discover the culprit; 'but no,' said he, 'they should sooner have had this wensand of mine.' Bradford was a man of deep piety, but so zealous a predestinarian, that he carried on a warm dispute in Newgate against some 'froward freewillers,' who were confined with him on the same charge of heresy.

The only personal friend of Cranmer who escaped in the persecution was Matthew Parker, afterwards very properly selected by Elizabeth, on the re-establishment of the Reformed faith, to be Archbishop of Canterbury. He was a wise and moderate man, to whose prudence we shall have occasion to observe that the Church was much indebted for its quiet settlement.

A commission was appointed, in the last year of this reign, to take possession of what was called the 'superfluous' plate and other ornaments belonging to divine service in all churches, leaving only sufficient for the decent administration of the holy offices. The commissioners were also empowered to examine who had seized

any plate or altar-cloths, and to proceed against them;
for such had been the waste of these things, that the
cups for the holy communion were used as drinking-
vessels, and the costly altar-cloths converted into car-
pets and cushions.   Nor did the schools of learning escape
from the general pillage.   Commissioners were employed,
according to the proclamation before-mentioned as having been issued immediately after the first disgrace of
Somerset, to erase the vestiges of superstition from the
missals and books of devotion throughout the kingdom.
Many of these books were illuminated with pictures,
some of them indicating much superstition and ignorance.   For instance, there were missals in which the
Trinity was painted—God the Father and God the Son
as an old and a young man, with the Holy Ghost above
them in the form of a dove, and the Virgin sitting between them, according to the blasphemous legend of
some of the friars of her assumption into the Trinity,
which, though condemned by the Church, seems to have
found a place in the popular devotion.   But such was
the ignorance of the commissioners, or their dishonesty,
that they destroyed many books merely for having the
cross richly gilt upon them; and at Oxford especially,
invaluable manuscripts are said to have been ruined, in
the library, since restored by Bodley, but originally
founded by 'the good Duke Humphrey,' a munificent
patron of learning, and one who read Wycliffe's Bible[1]
in the reign of his nephew Henry VI.   At the same
time, the buildings called 'the Schools,' also founded by
him, went to decay—some are said to have been used
by glovers and laundresses; and the divinity school, a
beautifully-ornamented building, was left with its roof
unrepaired, the lead pilfered, and the stained-glass windows broken.[2]   But it would be unjust to conclude, from
this circumstance, that sound learning was altogether

---

[1] His own illuminated copy of Wycliffe's Bible is now in the British
Museum.

[2] INGRAM'S Memorials of Oxford.

neglected. It is more probable that the public buildings of the university were ruined for want of funds,
and that the lectures were carried on elsewhere : For it
was at this very time that Peter Martyr's instructions,
as Professor of Divinity, were frequented by the whole
university, and the lectures of Jewel at Corpus-Christi
College were hardly less celebrated. Many private individuals of the laity expended large sums of money in
maintaining young men at college who were religiously
disposed, and Jewel himself had a pension from Chambers, a gentleman of fortune, who was foremost in such
good works, and who employed him also sometimes to
preach to the poor people to whom he distributed his
bounty.[1]

King Edward died July 6, 1553, of a pulmonary
consumption, at the age of fifteen years and nine months.
Among his last instructions for his will, was a charge to
his successors to engage in no war, except the realm
should be in danger of invasion; to preserve the Reformed Religion, and complete it by the body of ecclesiastical laws; to reduce the wasteful expenses of the court
and household; to increase the endowment of St. John's
College, Cambridge, the college of his learned tutor, Sir
John Cheke; and to found another college, which he
wished to be still larger, within the next seven years.
He confirmed the grant of the rich Savoy Hospital,
which he had given a few days before to the City of London as an endowment for Bridewell—an institution
founded by him at the request of the citizens, and one
much needed for the correction of the idle and disorderly. He also fulfilled his father's design for the foundation of Christ's Hospital, on the site of the Grey
Friars, and desired that his father's tomb should be
made up (for it seems that this funeral honour to the
great destroyer was yet unpaid); that all his debts should

---

[1] STRYPE, Mem. iii. Pt. 1, p. 117.

be discharged, and that all who had reason to complain of injuries done them should be recompensed.

With regard to the lands which he had granted or sold, being chiefly church-lands, he directed that the grants should remain undisturbed, and any bargains for which money had been paid should he completed. It is certainly remarkable that this young king, with all his religious feeling, should have shown so little perception of the sacrilege and oppression that was going on around him. He does indeed speak in one of his papers of the 'impropriation of benefices' as one of the public evils which he wished to have remedied ; but otherwise it seems as if he had been taught to look upon all charitable institutions, with their endowments, as subject to be changed, diminished, and even broken up, at the will and pleasure of the Crown. Nor would the practice of even those whom he most regarded go far to discountenance such opinions. For Cranmer himself, though none could justly accuse him of self-interest or extortion, who when the king died had barely more than would pay his debts, had not scrupled to purchase from the crown, in the reign of Henry VIII., the rectory of Aslacton (his native place and the seat of his family), in Nottinghamshire, and the site of the abbey of Kirkstall near Leeds.[1]

The same circumstance of his education and inexperience led the young king to take part with those who now began to triumph in their separation from Rome, as if the division of Christendom was a thing to be gloried in, and as if a reformation of the Universal Church ought not rather to have been the object of both their prayers

---

[1] Possibly, it may have been on this occasion that Cecil wrote to Cranmer, in friendship, telling him he was accused of avarice, and of laying by money for his children ; to whom the archbishop replied, that as to falling under the temptation of 'them that will be rich,' he feared it not half so much as he did stark beggary. As this incident in Cranmer's history has sometimes been made the ground of violent censure, the proof of his having *purchased* and not taken a grant of these lands is subjoined in Appendix H.

and endeavours. But his sincerity and his piety are as undoubted as the rest of the gentle qualities which endeared him to his people. And his last prayer was for his country: 'O my Lord God, bless my people, and save Thine inheritance. O Lord God, defend this realm from papistry, and maintain Thy true religion, that I and my people may praise Thy holy Name, for Jesus Christ's sake.' The archbishop, heart-stricken at such a loss, performed the funeral rites, and administered the Holy Communion according to the primitive form, which he had himself restored for such occasions, little thinking over whose bier it would so soon be used. It is said that Ridley and he had for some time foreboded the ruin of their hopes, from the grievous profligacy and avarice by which the courtiers had disgraced the Reformation they pretended to promote; and at the end of the reign their efforts had left them equally objects of dislike to those by whom they were opposed, and those who professed to support them.

It is important to observe, that the Church thus reformed was, beyond the possibility of doubt, at the time of King Edward's death, the original Catholic Church in England. It inherited its authority alike from the ancient British and from the Anglo-Saxon Church; nor could it be pretended, at this period, whatever might be said against a National Church which had resolved to reform itself in despair of a general reformation, that it had ceased by that course to be still the Church of England. Even while these things were going on, the Gallican Church had once more been on the point of pursuing a similar course. The Reformation was gaining ground in France, and when on the death of Paul III., his successor, Julius III., had resolved to reopen the Council of Trent, the French King, Henry II., protested against a council held in the emperor's dominions, and summoned in the name of the pope, and not in the name of Christian princes. It met notwithstanding, and in October, 1551, this synod proceeded to its most important business, in the absence of any representatives not only of the Protestant states but also of the Catholic Church in France. The only point relating to the Eucharist which they condescended to adjourn in deference to the wishes of the Protestants, until their ambassadors should arrive, was the question of the cup. Although it was admitted that 'one can hardly express the manner of the Real Presence of Jesus Christ in the Eucharist,' yet they determined that it is 'fitly and properly called Transubstantiation.' Thus was a fatal obstacle opposed to the reunion of Christendom, and a definition finally imposed upon the Roman Catholic Church which many of their own writers wished to avoid, and which the decrees of Innocent III. need not have obliged them to adopt. This decree was passed the year after the publication of Cranmer's sentiments on the subject, and the year before the completion of the Articles of the Church of England.

CHAPTER XXII.

Suffering for Truth's sake
Is fortitude to highest victory,
And, to the faithful, death the gate of life.
MILTON.

THE Church, says Bishop Hall, is represented by the emblem of the burning bush. How oft has it been flaming, yet never consumed! The same Power that enlightens it preserves it; and to none but His enemies is He a consuming fire. An earnest was given in the first victim.

Who does not know, and who has read without pity and admiration, the story of the young and innocent Lady Jane Gray? She had the wisdom to see the vanity of the ambition that offered her a crown, and the defect of her own title. 'I am not so young,' she said, 'nor so little read in the guiles of Fortune, to suffer myself to be taken by them. If she enrich any, it is but to make them the subject of her spoil; if she raise others, it is but to pleasure herself with their ruin; what she adored but yesterday, is to-day her pastime; and if I now permit her to adorn and crown me, I must to-morrow suffer her to crush me to pieces.' Her father and Dudley told her that the throne was hers by law and right; and she then 'turned herself to God,' as she spoke of it afterwards, imploring His grace and spirit, that if she was to govern, she might do it to His honour and service, and the good of the realm. They carried her to the Tower, and proclaimed her queen; but one brief fortnight saw her friends discomfited, and herself and her husband detained as prisoners in the same fortress.

It appears that a few years earlier the hopes of the English Reformers had looked forward to a union for her with the young Edward. A Swiss Reformer, in a letter to Bullinger, in A.D. 1551, mentions the report as a thing then talked of. 'But this matter,' he adds, 'must be ordered by God most high, who alone foresees and disposes all things,'—a pious and prophetic sentence, when we remember how different an alliance and far different a fate, crossed the fortunes of this gentle girl. Her own letter, which accompanied this, quoted the Hebrew and Greek Scriptures in the original tongue, and is written in excellent Latin, but without betraying any consciousness that such attainments were rare.[1] Her last moments were marked by the serene piety of the pure in heart, whose lives have been unspotted from the world, and for whom death has no terrors.

Queen Mary, on hearing of the proclamation of Jane as queen, had escaped in her retreat on a double horse behind the servant of one of her friends ; but she had right on her side, and the people of the eastern counties flocked to her standard. Dudley, who went down with a force against her, marched to Cambridge, and sent for Sandys, the vice-chancellor, to preach for his cause, as he had before unfortunately persuaded Ridley to do in London. Sandys took for his text Joshua i. 16, 'All that thou commandest us will we do,' and managed it so cautiously as to show that he had done no more than he was commanded. The troops of Dudley deserted him, and he himself went with the mayor to proclaim Queen Mary. He threw up his cap as if in joy ; but the beholders rather believed the grief confessed by his streaming eyes. 'What is more poor and prostrate,' says Fuller, 'than pride when reduced to extremity !' This proud man, who just before seemed

---

[1] Published lately at Zurich, 1840. 'Johannes ab Ulmis,' the writer of the above letter, is well known among the foreign Reformers. He was erroneously confounded with Aylmer in the first edition.

to have a sceptre within his grasp, fell at the feet of
Lord Arundel, who came to arrest him, to crave his
mercy. He suffered on the scaffold in the following
month, declaring that he had been all the while a
Romanist at heart; that his adherence to the other side
had been only to advance his own purposes; and told
the people they would never enjoy peace till they returned to the faith of their forefathers. It was remarked
that this unhappy man, whose only principle was the
aggrandisement of his own family, left behind him six
married sons; but they all died without issue.[1]

The events which followed are well known, as filling
some of the saddest and darkest pages of English history.
There is every proof that Edward before his death, in
his zeal for the Reformed religion, had been persuaded
by Dudley to direct the succession so as to exclude his
sisters: and the arbitrary way in which his father had
repeatedly changed the laws, at one time declaring the
two princesses illegitimate, and again restoring them,
had left a precedent for other sovereigns to treat the
crown as a thing placed at their disposal. But Henry
had a power conferred on him by act of parliament to
make such changes, which was wanting to Edward.
Cranmer had of late shared little in the public councils;
and it is certain that he had no confidential communication with Dudley, who was indeed his enemy, and,
as he himself declared, had been long seeking his destruction. It was Edward who had persuaded him by
his dying request, after he had publicly opposed it in
the council; and the archbishop, satisfied of the deliberate intentions of one who was as dear to him as a son,
being also informed that all the judges had complied,
and being denied a private interview with the king,
whom it was his duty to advise on such a subject, unhappily yielded against his better judgment, and lost

---

[1] FULLER's *History of Cambridge.*

one of the noblest occasions he had ever had of a truly magnanimous conduct.[1]

Mary was, both by interest and affection, devoted to the Church of Rome. One pope had authorised her mother's marriage, another had refused to dissolve it, and her own claim to be the legitimate daughter of Henry VIII. depended on these acts. On the other hand, the misfortunes of her mother were connected with the changes that had taken place, and her own severe and mortified character sympathised with the creed which her affections and her sorrows had alike endeared to her. Although she had promised the people of Suffolk that she would not interfere with their religion, a messenger was sent, who travelled in nine days to Rome, to announce her accession, and her adherence to the religion of the pope; and the only doubt seems to have been how matters should be carried towards the accomplishment of this object.

The deprived bishops were immediately set at liberty, and Gardiner, being restored to his diocese, was made lord-chancellor, and principal minister of the crown. His advice was to proceed by degrees, and especially to avoid alarming the prejudices of the people by immediately restoring the supremacy of the pope, but rather to profess at first to bring things back to the condition in which they were at Henry's death. The queen in consequence assumed the title of Head of the Church, and it was as such that she acted for two years in bringing back the dominion of the pope. She at first declared in the council, as she had done to the people of Suffolk, that she would compel no man's conscience in religion;

---

[1] Cranmer says in his letter to the Council of Queen Mary: 'Some of you know by what means I was brought and trained unto the will of our late sovereign lord, King Edward VI., and what I spake against the same; wherein I refer me to the reports of your honours and worships.'— JENKYNS, vol. i. p. 366. After reading this simple appeal to those living witnesses, it is impossible to admit the doubt of Lingard, the Romanist historian, whether the account of the interview with Edward is, or is not, to be believed.

but this was soon modified by the limitation that was
added, 'until public order should be taken therein by
common consent.' On the day that Bonner publicly
resumed his station at St. Paul's, as bishop of London,
a tumult occurred, and a dagger was thrown at a
preacher who advocated 'the old religion.' It was
appeased through the influence of Rogers, one of the
prebendaries, who had been appointed by Ridley; but
a proclamation was issued by which all preachers were
silenced, except those who should be licensed by Gardiner; and Rogers himself, and Bradford, another prebendary, also of Ridley's appointment, were soon after
committed to prison, probably on the ground that they
were intruded into their prebends by a bishop not
canonically appointed. Miles Coverdale bishop of
Exeter, and Hooper bishop of Gloucester, were summoned before the council, and refusing to promise to
refrain from preaching according to the order in council,
they were also imprisoned. This was in August 1553,
a month after the queen's accession, and while the laws
of the late reign remained in force. But the system of
making orders in council and proceeding against those
who would not comply with them, by which Gardiner
and Bonner had been formerly deprived, was now
carried to a much greater extent. Judge Hales, having
ventured to say, in charging a grand jury, that the laws
of King Edward relating to religion ought still to be
observed, was immediately committed to prison, though
he had been the only man among the judges who had
ventured to withstand the illegal will of that prince for
excluding his sister from the throne. The mass was
restored in many churches in London, contrary to law;
the celebration of it was enforced at Cambridge, where
Gardiner was chancellor; and although the marriage of
priests had been allowed by act of parliament, the
Master of Clare Hall was ejected for having a wife.
The same prelate extended his authority to Oxford,
where he was visitor of Magdalen College, as the

successor of its founder in the bishopric of Winchester.
This college was distinguished for its attachment to the
Reformation. Harley, now bishop of Hereford, and
John Foxe, the martyrologist, had been among its
fellows, as well as Parkhurst, afterwards bishop of
Norwich under Queen Elizabeth, who there imbibed
the principles of the Reformation, which after his removal to Merton College he infused into the mind of
Jewel, the most distinguished of his pupils. At the
time of Gardiner's visitation, the president and fourteen
others were turned out, though as yet there was no
law to compel them to comply with the Romanising
practices.

Peter Martyr upon this quitted Oxford, and came to
his friend the archbishop, at Lambeth. Some of the Reformers had already fled beyond the sea, and many
more were preparing to follow them. Cranmer was advised to adopt the same course, and with his usual
moderation he recommended it to others to save themselves, quoting the example of Our Saviour, who went
into Samaria when his hour was not yet come, and of
St. Paul, let down by a basket[1] to escape out of Jerusalem. But, as concerning himself, he is said to have
spoken to this effect : ' If I were accused of parricide, or
any such crime, I might perhaps be induced to fly,
though innocent. But now that it is a question of my
faith not towards man but God, and of the truth of Holy
Scripture against papal errors, I am resolved to act with
the constancy that becomes a Christian prelate, and to
quit my life rather than the country.'[2] He directed his
steward to pay all his debts, and expressing his satisfaction that none could now be a loser by his fall, quietly
awaited the result. It was thought that Gardiner had a
design to succeed to the archbishopric, and wished Cranmer not to be deprived till he should have laid his own

---

[1] See his letter to Mrs. Wilkinson, in the Martyr's letters, p. 23.
[2] GODWIN, De Præsul, art. 'Cranmer.'

plans to keep out Cardinal Pole. But, however this may be, when people saw some of the bishops already imprisoned, while the archbishop was still at large, they began to suspect that he was coming over, and this suspicion was confirmed when it was known that the mass had been set up again at Canterbury Cathedral. The person by whom this was done was Thornden, Cranmer's suffragan at Dover, of whose base treachery to his benefactor in the reign of Henry VIII., and of the archbishop's generous forgiveness, an account has been already given. The only two occasions on which any record has been preserved of Cranmer's having been carried beyond the bounds of moderation, are in connection with the conduct of this man. When he found that the very same man whom he had once forgiven for plotting with Gardiner against his life, was now so regardless of his good fame as to set the example in his own cathedral of undoing all that he had done, he drew up a paper on the subject, in which he declared that 'although he had been well exercised these twenty years to suffer and bear evil reports and lies, and had not been much grieved thereat, but had borne all things quietly; yet untrue reports, to the hindrance of God's truth, are in nowise to be tolerated and suffered. Wherefore,' he continued, ' these be to signify to the world, that it was not I that did set up the mass at Canterbury, but it was a false, flattering, lying, and dissembling monk which caused mass to be set up there, without mine advice or counsel;' and he offered, if the queen would consent, that he, with Peter Martyr, and four or five more, would ' by God's grace take upon them to defend, that not only the common prayers of the Church, the ministration of the sacraments, and other rites and ceremonies, but also that all the doctrine and religion set out by our late sovereign lord King Edward VI., is more pure and according to God's Word than any other doctrine that hath been used in England these thousand years . . . . . And we shall prove that the order of the Church set

E E

out at this present in this realm by act of parliament, is
the same that was used in the Church fifteen hundred
years past. And so shall they never be able to prove
theirs.' Whether he would have published this declaration precisely in these terms cannot now be known, for
having given a copy of it to Scory, bishop of Chichester,
for his opinion, that bishop permitted other copies to be
taken, and so it was published everywhere, till London
rang with it.¹ Upon this the archbishop was sent for to
the council, who expressed their hope that he would be
sorry for having put forth such a paper. 'Sorry am I,
indeed,' he replied, 'that it should have so gone forth,
for I intended to have enlarged it, and to have had it fixed
to the doors of St. Paul's, and of all the other churches
in London, with my hand and seal to it.' Upon this he
was committed to the Tower, on the 8th of September,
'as well for his late treason against the queen, as for
spreading about seditious bills.' Latimer was already
a prisoner, and Ridley was soon after also committed.

The foreign protestant clergy, of whom a great number were in England, both from France and Germany,
being no longer allowed the exercise of their religion,
were, however, permitted to depart, and Peter Martyr
went among them. Many English at the same time
took the opportunity to escape disguised as their attendants, but when this was discovered, strict orders
were given to prevent it; notwithstanding which, great
numbers contrived to get away. Most of the bishops
who had been appointed in the late reign had now been
imprisoned, including the two archbishops, and five
others;² so that when the parliament met on the 5th of
October, three months only after the king's death, there

---

¹ Valerian Pollen, minister of the French Protestants at Glastonbury,
who afterwards removed with them to Frankfort, mentions the fact of
its having been publicly read on Change. See ARCH. TODD's *Cranmer*,
vol. II. 377.

² Cranmer, Holgate archbishop of York, Hooper, Latimer, Ridley,
Coverdale, and Ferrar.

remained but two bishops attached to the religious changes which he had introduced—Taylor of Lincoln, and Harley of Hereford.

Taylor had resolved to speak in favour of the Reformation, and he went down to the House of Lords for that purpose. But Gardiner was what the world would call too good a politician not to have a resource to prevent it. A mass of the Holy Ghost was solemnly performed in the queen's presence before the opening of the parliament, which all the members of both houses were required to attend before they took their seats; and these two bishops refusing to do so, they were excluded from the house. It is said also that false returns were made, and other extreme measures taken with the members of the House of Commons; and a clergyman who had been chosen, and who was of the party of the Reformation, was now for the first time excluded.[1] The first thing the parliament did was to release the clergy from the penalty of the præmunire for any of those acts to which the laws of Henry VIII. had made that penalty extend. This was in order that convocation might proceed to business, in their own right, without the royal licence, which they immediately did with great solemnity. The lower house chose Weston, dean of Westminster, for their prolocutor, an office answering to that of Speaker to the House of Commons; and he immediately proposed that they should condemn the Book of Common Prayer, and define the doctrine of Transubstantiation. Six members ventured to oppose it, two of whom were Aylmer archdeacon of Stow, who had been the Lady Jane's tutor, and Philpot archdeacon of Winchester, afterwards burnt to death. By their desire a public argument was appointed, at which a great number of the nobility and others were present; but their request to be assisted by some of the leaders of their party, especially by Ridley and Rogers,

---

[1] Nowel, prebendary of Westminster, afterwards dean of St. Paul's.

was not complied with. The discussion lasted three days; and it was remarkable as the first and last scene of this kind, in which something like equal liberty seems to have been allowed to either side. The end however was, as on other occasions, that the Reformers were overpowered by numbers and clamour, and they left the house of assembly. After their departure, four articles of faith were agreed upon, which in substance were made the test of heresy to all the sufferers in this reign:—

I. That in the sacrament of the altar there is a true and real presence of Christ's body and blood in either kind; and therefore that the laudable custom of communicating in one kind is to be retained.

II. That the fathers of the Lateran Council aptly expressed the mode of Christ's presence in the sacrament by the new term of Transubstantiation, as the Nicene fathers had expressed that the Son is of one substance with the Father by the new term of Consubstantial.

III. That, since we confess that the true body and blood of Christ is present in the sacrament, how can we but worship Him?

IV. That this holy and life-giving and unbloody sacrifice we offer up for the healing of our infirmities, considering that there is on the holy table the Lamb of God who taketh away the sin of the world, there sacrificed by the priests, though without bloodshedding.

There is a tone of reverence and piety in these articles, which makes them to be as good a statement of the Roman doctrine as can easily be found. They were often put forward in a more harsh and thorny style, requiring the person to whom they were offered to say the substance of bread and wine no longer remained after consecration, but only the natural body and blood conceived by the Blessed Virgin. And this must form the lasting condemnation of the agents in the bitter persecution that followed, that they were not content with the most solemn declarations from the prisoners, that they truly believed that the body and blood of Christ were verily and indeed taken and received by the faithful in the Lord's Supper; but they forced this contradictory article upon all who came before them, put it home and pressed it with the most ensnaring terms, and would admit no such answer as with a moderate lenity of construction would have been sufficient to save a man's life. What more can be required of a Christian's faith, in this point, than is expressed in one of Cranmer's answers, ' Christ's body is truly present to them that truly receive Him ?'—what more than Latimer's assertion of a real presence, ' Because to the faithful believer there is given the real or spiritual body of Christ ?' ' Let no scorner or sycophant suppose,' said the old man, ' that I make nothing of the sacrament but a bare and naked sign.' And what language more suitable to describe the virtue of this heavenly mystery than Ridley's, where he says, ' By grace the same body of Christ is present with us; even as the same sun, which in substance never removes from its place in the heavens, is yet present here by his beam, light, and natural influence, where it shines upon the heart ?'

The early part of the year 1554 was occupied in preparing the way for the queen's marriage, and in bringing back the clergy to the obedience of the religious system now restored. A vast number were excluded from their livings, chiefly for being married. This number has been stated at twelve thousand, the whole number of parochial clergy being put at sixteen thousand. But it has been shown that in the diocese of Canterbury, out of three hundred and eighty beneficed persons, not more than seventy-three were expelled, and there is no probability that the whole number throughout the kingdom would exceed this average; but it was a sufficiently sweeping measure which dispossessed one-fifth of the whole clergy at a stroke. A much larger proportion of the bishops was ejected. Five of course were removed to make way for the restoration of those who had been

deprived under Edward. But in the month of March,
1554, seven more were turned out—among them Holgate
archbishop of York, who had before been imprisoned.
These changes, with the death of one bishop and the
resignation of another, placed fourteen sees at the disposal
of the government within less than a year of the queen's
accession; besides that of Canterbury, which was legally
void from the time that Cranmer was convicted of treason, though he was still treated as archbishop, until deprived by the pope.

The crowd of prisoners in the Tower after Wyatt's
rebellion was a providential means of bringing some of
the chief Reformers together, to their mutual edification
and comfort. They had before been kept separate, but
now for want of room Cranmer was placed in the same
apartment with Latimer and Ridley, to whom was added
Bradford, then a prebendary of St. Paul's. So they remained till near Easter,[1] confirming one another in the
truth of doctrine and in mutual edification and prayer.
Then the three bishops were sent, without previous
notice, to Oxford, where they were separately imprisoned,
the means of writing being denied them, and their servants removed. A deputation had been appointed from
the convocation, to dispute with them on the points of
doctrine already mentioned as having been agreed upon
at the last meeting of that body. Accordingly, these
three propositions were put to them, as the judgment of
the Church to which their assent was required:—'i. In
the sacrament of the altar, by virtue of the Lord delivered by the priest, there is really present, under the
appearance of bread and wine, the natural body of
Christ, conceived of the Virgin Mary, and his natural
blood.—ii. After consecration the substance of bread
and wine does not remain, nor any other substance, but
the substance of Christ, God and man.—iii. In the mass
is the life-giving sacrifice of the Church, propitiatory as

[1] Ridley to Grindal: *Martyrs' Letters*, pp. 12-3.

well for the sins of the living as of the dead.'   On the
14th of April, Cranmer was brought alone before the
commissioners, who sat, thirty-three in number, before
the high altar in St. Mary's Church.   Not a single bishop
was there, the chief person being Weston, the prolocutor
of the lower house of convocation, who a short time before was a private London clergyman.   But the archbishop
made no objection on that account, but bowing to them,
declined a seat, with such gentle dignity that some of
the audience were affected to tears.   With regard to the
first proposition, he would not answer until he had
made them explain what they meant by a real presence ;
but when they said it is the same body that was born of
the Virgin, he replied that he denied it utterly, and
the same of the two remaining questions.   On the day
appointed for the disputation, Cranmer's answer to this
first point was that ' Christ's true body is truly present,
to them that truly receive him, but spiritually.'   He at
the same time delivered in a paper, in which his opinions
were contained at length ; and a few days after, having an
opportunity to renew the dispute in the schools, he so
confounded the doctors that they gave all sorts of contradictory answers as to the manner in which the Lord's
body is in the sacrament ; and one of them at last said,
that Christ being there after such form as it pleased him,
we are not to inquire as to the manner of his tarrying
or descending into the body—which was precisely the
point at which the archbishop wished to arrive.   The
second proposition, of course, he absolutely denied : and
for the third, he said it was ' intricate and wrapped in
doubtful words, differing much from the true speech of
Scripture; but as the words seem to imply' (namely,
that Christ is again sacrificed by the priest in the mass),
' it is most contumelious against our only Lord and
Saviour Christ Jesus, and a violation of His precious
blood, which upon the altar of the cross is the only
sacrifice and oblation for the sins of all mankind.'

The disputation with Cranmer, though carried on with

some confusion, was managed on the whole not without
a show of respect for the man, and an acknowledgment
of the dignified modesty of his own demeanour.   But
that which was held the next day with Ridley was disgraced by every sort of unfairness; so that he said 'he
could never have thought that it had been possible to
have found any within the realm, being of any knowledge, learning, and ancient degree of school, so brazen-
faced and so shameless, as to behave themselves so vainly
and so like stage-players, as they did in that disputation.'   His voice was drowned by hissings, taunts, clap-
ping of hands, and cries of ' blasphemy !' and when they
answered him, he said he ' was forced to hear such great
reproaches and slanders uttered against him, as no grave
man without blushing could abide the hearing of the
same spoken of a most vile knave against a most
wretched ruffian.'   He therefore drew up an account of
his answers in writing, which he desired might be delivered to the bishops in the upper house of convocation.
And he afterwards employed himself in prison in writing
a treatise on the subject, in which he said that all the
questions relating to this sacrament, such as whether the
priest offers up Christ therein, and whether the Host
was therefore to be worshipped as God, depend upon the
one point, whether there be therein the corporeal substance of the natural body of Christ.   And he added
that they who deny this corporeal presence do not therefore take away, simply and absolutely, the presence of
Christ's body and blood from the sacrament; ' they deny
indeed the presence of His Body in the natural substance
of His human and assumed nature, but they grant the
presence of the same by grace.'   Latimer was next
brought before them, and he also gave in his answers in
writing.   Concerning the first conclusion, he said that
' to a right celebration there is no other presence of
Christ required than a spiritual presence, and this is
sufficient for a Christian man ; as a presence by which
we both abide in Christ, and Christ in us, to the obtain-

ing of eternal life, if we persevere in his true gospel.'
'And this same presence,' he added, 'may be called a
real presence, because to the faithful believer there is the
real or spiritual body of Christ: which I here rehearse,
lest some sycophant or scorner should suppose me to
make nothing else of the sacrament but a bare or naked
sign.'

The disputations with these illustrious prisoners were
each concluded in a day, after which, on the Friday in
the same week, April, 1554, they were brought all three
together to St. Mary's Church, where the delegates were
assembled. They were told they were overcome in disputation, and were asked whether they would subscribe
or no. Each having answered that he would not, sentence of excommunication was read over them, and they,
with all who should maintain their doctrine, were condemned as heretics. Upon this Cranmer said : 'From
this your judgment I appeal to the just judgment of
God Almighty, trusting to be present with Him in
Heaven, for whose presence in the altar I am thus condemned.' Ridley expressed his hope that his sentence
'would send them sooner than the course of nature to
another place, where he hoped their names were written,
though cast out from that society;' and Latimer 'thanked
God most heartily that he had prolonged his life, to the
end that he might glorify God by his death.' They
were then committed to custody—Ridley and Latimer
to the charge of private persons, but Cranmer to the
common prison of the town, at a place called Bocardo.
It was a gateway tower over one of the entrances to
the city, crossing the lower part of what is now called
the Corn Market, in a line with the old town-wall.

Hitherto no step had been publicly taken towards a
reconciliation with Rome; and these proceedings were
carried on in the name of the convocation or synod of
the English Church. It was afterwards declared that
they were illegal on that account, and so they were in
the eyes of the papal court; since the Church of England

was still held to be in schism, but it does not appear
that they were illegal as the laws then stood. And
indeed the condition of parties at this period deserves
some consideration. At the time of King Henry's
death, the members of the Church of England, agreeing
in all points of doctrine with that of Rome, but denying
the supremacy of the pope, might most properly perhaps
have been described as Latin Catholics, members of the
Catholic Church in Western Christendom, which had
originally been called the Latin Church, to distinguish it
from the Greek or Eastern part of Christendom, yet
not connected with or subject to the Roman pontiff.
To this state of things Gardiner had still adhered; while
Cranmer, without altering the internal relations of the
Church, had been the means of bringing its doctrine to
some degree of conformity with the Reformed Churches
abroad, and, as we also believe, to a nearer resemblance
of the primitive model. And all parties in England had
been so far sincere in the adoption of this intermediate
position, that Tonstal bishop of Durham, though deprived and imprisoned by King Edward's Government,
had been far from recognising the acts of the Council of
Trent: on the contrary, he had published a book, as before mentioned, in which he blamed Innocent III. for making transubstantiation an article of faith, about the same
time that the council had decreed directly the reverse.

But a great change was now about to be introduced. The queen was married to Philip of Spain
in July, A.D. 1554. In September, Bonner issued injunctions to his diocese indicating a more decided return
to former practices, requiring among other things that
all the scripture texts that had been painted on the walls
of churches should be absolutely effaced. And in
October, the first indication appeared of an intention to
proceed to extremities with those they called heretics,
in the following directions to the council from the queen
herself:—‘Touching punishment of heretics, we think it
ought to be done without rashness, not leaving (that is,

not omitting) in the meanwhile to do justice to such as by learning would seem to deceive the people: and especially within London, I would wish none to be burnt without some of the council's presence, and both there and everywhere good sermons at the same.' In November, Cardinal Pole's attainder having been reversed by act of parliament, he came to London in quality of legate from the pope, and delivered a long oration to both houses of parliament in the presence of the king and queen, to induce them to return to their obedience to the papal see. Gardiner had informed the emperor a year before that he could not hope to carry the point of the papal supremacy and the marriage both together ; and Pole had been purposely detained upon his journey in consequence. The emperor made no secret of borrowing 400,000*l.* towards accomplishing his son's designs in England, and on his arrival, and afterwards, twenty-seven chests of bullion were carried in cartloads to the Tower. In what manner this wealth was employed is matter of conjecture only. There were still found in the House of Commons those who objected to submit to the pope : but the majority carried it, and both houses brought up a humble address to the king and queen, that they would intercede with the cardinal for their absolution, and that they might be received as penitent children into the communion of the Church. The cardinal accordingly pronounced a solemn absolution. Te Deum was sung in the chapel-royal in the presence of all the members, and St. Andrew's Day, on which this was done, was appointed to be ever after observed as the Feast of Reconciliation. It only remained that these acts should be ratified at Rome, for which purpose three ambassadors were sent, who arrived there on the day that a new pope entered upon his office, with the title of Paul IV. It is needless to say that they were welcome, but the pope took care to keep up his claim of granting kingdoms ; and as Henry VIII. had assumed the title of King of Ireland, instead of

Lord, a bull was sent conferring that title as a gift from the pope upon Philip and Mary. He also complained that the church-lands were not restored; but this was more than could be accomplished, and the convocation had been induced to make a formal surrender of all claim to them on the part of the Church, before the act of reconciliation was passed; which surrender and the ratification of the cardinal were confirmed by law. We have seen that the laws for the punishment of heretics had been wholly repealed, though this, unfortunately, had not prevented the common-law from being enforced: but now it was thought fit to revive them all, so that the ex-officio statute of Henry IV., which had been too odious to be maintained even by Henry VIII., was once more placed upon the statute-book—an ominous presage of the intentions of those by whom these affairs were directed. The parliament was dissolved in January 1555, and was concluded by a solemn procession to St. Paul's Cathedral, to return thanks for the reconciliation of the nation; and a form of absolution was appointed, by which the clergy first, and then the laity throughout the country, were to be readmitted to what was considered Catholic communion.

The scenes which were acted through the last three years of this short reign are such as pity would veil from the sight of day, if truth could admit of their being blotted from remembrance. What can be more horrible to thought, than that the sacrament of Christ's passion, the solemn remembrance and communion of the most transcendent mercy that came to bless mankind, should have been turned to a symbol of destruction, a snare to the conscience of the weak-hearted, and an instrument of condemnation to the resolute, who would not deny with their lips what they inwardly believed! It is the most unhappy sign in the English Romanists of the present day, that they do not unreservedly give up the defence of these deeds of their forefathers.

But it is well. The finger of God was in it; and it

taught the English nation how to estimate the men who
had been engaged in the Reformation, and to try their
work. A cause for which three hundred persons gave
their bodies to be burned, and no fewer than thirty thousand endured exile and the spoiling of their goods,[1]
showed in the eyes of Europe and Christendom a moral
strength, foretelling that, as these shores had witnessed
and borne the brunt of persecution, they should be in
years to come the vantage-ground of a purer faith, the
asylum and refuge of other sufferers.

It has been a subject of much uncertainty who was
the chief originator of these terrible proceedings. The
general opinion at and near the time seems to have
attributed them to the queen herself; and the assertion
of Gardiner, when the protomartyr Rogers accused him
of having counselled that course, that 'The queen went
before them in those counsels, which proceeded of her
own proper motion,' confirmed as it was by other
bishops who were present, and by Rochester, the comp-
troller of Mary's household, a very confidential servant
of hers, would strengthen that impression. But afterwards, when it was considered that Gardiner was her
prime-minister, that he had been employed in all that
had been done as yet towards bringing back the papal
authority, and on the other hand that Cardinal Pole,
the other chief person apparently concerned, was a man
whose amiable character in private seemed to render his
participation in such courses improbable, an impression
gained ground that Gardiner and Bonner, who were
certainly her ostensible agents, were also her guilty
advisers. It is to be feared that Pole, amiable as he was
in private life, is not altogether free from blame. The
writers of the Church of Rome extol him as the greatest
champion of their afflicted cause in the unhappy time
at which he lived. They point to his amiable corres-

---

[1] This number is stated in the Life of Carranza, the Spanish confessor
of Mary, and by other Spanish writers of that period.

pondence, the good men with whom he was intimate in
youth—such as Sir Thomas More in England, and Sadolet
and Contarini, friends of learning and moderate reformation abroad. His natural temper was certainly mild
and gentle; and when he presided at the Council of
Trent, he was always an advocate for gentle measures,
wishing the decrees against the Lutherans, as he says,
to be drawn up in the language of affection, such as
parents use to erring children. But with all this he
was one of the many whose better nature has been en-
thralled by a fanatic devotion to a false principle. When
his aged mother and his brothers wrote to him from
England, that he was endangering their lives by his
open excitement of rebellion against Henry, he continued the same course, and left them exposed to the
monarch's vengeance, which was only satisfied with
their blood. Though he and his Italian friends were
aware of the abuses which had so long been heaped
together in the Church and Court of Rome, and confessed
that the whole Church was brought 'to the brink of
ruin,' and into 'a state of mortal disease,' under them,[1]
he had not energy of mind to seek redress by renouncing
the usurped power which was the source of all these
abuses, but fondly contended still, that the maintenance
of one Head was the only safeguard for the Christian
faith, the only defence for all that was to be preserved,
the only oracle of law for what was to be reformed.
And as a plain consequence of this false principle, he
did not disguise his opinion, that a person of pernicious
opinions, and industrious in corrupting others, was
worthy of capital punishment, and ought to be cut off
as a rotten member from the body of the Church.[2]
Hence, when he had heard that Ridley and Latimer had
refused to listen to the solicitations of the Spanish
ecclesiastic whom he desired to try to reclaim them, he

---

[1] RIDLEY's *Review of Philips*, p. 79.
[2] POLE's *Epistles*, by Quirini, Pt. iv. p. 156.

expressed his approbation of their sentence, coolly observing that 'no man can save those whom God has
abandoned.'[1] He gave his consent to the burning of
Cranmer, after his recantation, as is affirmed by good
authority;[2] though he had before written to him,
to say that 'if he could by any means rescue him
from that dreadful sentence, not only of body but of
soul, which was hanging over him, he would gladly
prefer it, God knows, to all the riches and honours
which this life could afford.'[3] And as in his own
diocese of Kent he did little to check the cruelties of
Thornden and Harpsfield, who burnt nearly sixty
persons at Canterbury, Maidstone, and other towns; so
it is remarkable that in the diocese of Lincoln the only
sufferer during this reign was a poor man at Leicester,
who was committed to the flames under a sentence, not
of his own bishop, but of the delegates of Pole during
his archiepiscopal visitation.   There is no getting rid of
the evidence of these facts; and they prove that high
moral worth and a highly-cultivated mind were not
enough to save a man from abetting persecution, who
had persuaded himself that to disown the pope for head
of Christendom was the same thing as renouncing
Christianity.

With regard to Stephen Gardiner, he was a political
enemy to Cranmer, and thus he has gained the credit of
being as much the adviser of these atrocities as Bonner
was their executioner.[4] But first it must be observed,
that he had presided in the queen's council as lord-

---

[1] Pole's *Epistles*, by Quirini, Pt. v. p. 47.
[2] By Abp. Parker, *Antiq. Britann.* p. 533.
[3] Philips' *Life of Pole,* ii. 203.
[4] The long arguments for and against persecution, which the historian
Hume puts into the mouth of Gardiner and Pole, are nothing more
than what Catharine Parr's correspondent would call 'most grave discourse about the moon shining in the water.' Burnet and Collier had
set down something of the kind before; but Philips, the Roman Catholic
biographer of Pole, justly remarks, that there is no trace of it in any
of the records.

chancellor more than a year before the persecuting laws
were revived; and he died within ten months after the
first blood, that of Rogers the protomartyr, had been
shed.   And it is well known that the burnings were
rather increased than mitigated after Gardiner's death.
The character of this prelate has been undeservedly
loaded with the weight of this charge, however he may
have given support to it by a few instances of harshness.
His aim was to hold political power and distinction, and
to secure this his means were not such as become a prelate; but he had no delight in the task that was laid
upon him in coercing heretics, which he soon gave up to
other hands.   It is only just to acknowledge that as a
statesman he did his duty to his country, in excluding
all Spaniards from offices of government under Philip
and Mary, and taking care that no innovation should be
made in the laws of succession and other customs of
the realm.

There remains only a third party to be considered;
and the chief of this party was certainly one whose
subsequent conduct renders it no injustice to suspect
him of having used his influence to drive matters to
extremity.   This is Philip of Spain, the son of Charles
V., who was induced, by the ambitious hope of uniting
England to the Spanish crown, to ally himself to the
reigning queen.   The re-establishment of the papal
cause in England was one of the first objects with both
these affianced princes: Mary was bent upon it, as
necessary to the good of her soul, as well as the security
of her reign; and Philip was the son of a father whose
chief regret in his retirement was, that he had suffered
Luther to escape alive, after he had given him letters of
safe-conduct.

It is so long since we have known in England the
name of any persecuting sovereign, and the principles
of the powerful opponents of the Reformation are now
so near forgotten, that there will be something instructive
in a glance behind the scene at this remarkable despot,

whose arms and policy so long held the fate of Europe
in suspense, and in turns annoyed the German Protestants and shook the papal throne. It is well known
with what solemnity Charles V. at length forsook the
toils of state, and retired to end his days in a monastery.
From this retreat, however, he still sent his advice and
directions to the ministers of state and the governors of
provinces, and two days before his death, he wrote his
advice about religion to his son:

' I have written,' he said one day to the monks of the
convent where he closed his life,—' I have written to
Juan de Vega, the president of the council of Castile,
and to the inquisitors, to employ all their care in seeing
heretics burnt. Let them indeed try to make them
Christians before their punishment; but not fail to burn
them, for I am persuaded that none of them will become
in future true Catholics, because of their love for reasoning and disputing; and if the magistrates let them off,
they will commit as great a fault as I did in suffering
Luther to live. I ought to have remembered that this
heretic had offended a greater master than me—namely,
God himself. I might and I ought to have forgotten
my promise, and to have avenged the wrong which he
did to God.'

' It is very dangerous,' he said again, ' to dispute
with heretics : their reasons are so convincing, and they
offer them with such skill, that they can easily impose
upon a man ; and for this reason I have never chosen to
listen to them when they wished to state their opinions.
When I went to attack the Landgrave, the Duke of
Saxony, and the other Protestant princes, there were
four of them who came to seek an interview with me.
" Sire," said they, " we do not come before your majes·y
as enemies ; we do not purpose to make war with you,
nor to refuse the obedience we owe, but only to declare
to you our sentiments, for which we are reputed heretics,
though we are not so. Suffer us to come into your
majesty's presence, attended by some divines, and give

F F

them leave to defend our faith before you. If your majesty will only hear us, we engage to submit to whatever you shall judge it expedient to direct." I told them that I had not knowledge sufficient for such a discussion, and that they must communicate with my divines, who would make a report to me. In fact, I have had very little instruction in learning; I had scarcely studied my grammar when I had to begin attending to public business, and from that moment it has been impossible for me to continue my studies. If they had succeeded in making me relish some of their propositions, how could I ever have driven them out of my mind, and have become disabused? This was my motive for refusing to hear them, though they had promised, if I would have granted their prayer, to march with all their forces to aid me against the King of France, who had then crossed the Rhine.'

To the same purpose were his last instructions to Philip: 'I desire above all things,' he said, ' to inspire my son, of whose Catholic sentiments I am well aware, with a wish to imitate my conduct. I pray and recommend him as earnestly as I can, and feeling it my duty to do so, and more, I command him as a father, by the obedience which he owes me, to labour with care, as for an essential object in which I take a special interest, to see that the heretics in his dominions be pursued and chastised with all the public exposure and the severity which their crime merits, without allowing any guilty person to escape, and without regard to any prayers, or to the rank and quality of any one. I bind him above all to protect the holy office of the Inquisition, in respect to the great number of crimes which it prevents, as well as those which it punishes, remembering what I have charged him to do in my last will, that he may fulfil his duty as a prince, and make himself worthy of the protection of the Most High.'[1]

[1] LLORENTE, from Sandoval, *Hist. of the Inquisition*, ii. 155.

When we read these private thoughts of one of the
great contemporaries of Henry VIII., we may well be
content with the lot of our own country, which was
visited at least with a tyrant who would listen to the
arguments on both sides, and had knowledge enough to
burst the bonds which Charles and his son riveted with
such dark zeal upon the neck of Spain.

Under such a father was Philip trained, and with
such a religion he came to England.   In this country
his own part was kept secret; but a few years later, in
his own kingdom, he showed his gratitude to the Providence which had saved him from a danger of shipwreck, by condemning thirteen persons at once to the
stake, and shortly after by being present at a scene of the
same kind at Valladolid, when twenty-eight more, many
of the first nobility in Spain, were sacrificed; and to
prevent the importunities of relations and friends of
the accused, he vowed that ' he would himself carry the
faggots to make up the pile for his only son Don Carlos,
if that young prince should ever become a Lutheran.'

There is no need to look further for the instigator of
the persecution.   Philip and those whom he brought
with him directed the queen's conscience, and inspired
her natural bigotry with a zeal only to be appeased with
blood.   Before his own arrival, he had sent over Bartholomew Carranza, who was afterwards promoted by him to
the archbishopric of Toledo, attended by a number of
other ecclesiastics, who were to be employed in reconvert-
ing England to the religion of the Inquisition.[1]   Of these
the most celebrated were Pedro de Soto, a Dominican friar,
confessor to Charles V., who was made Regius Professor
of Theology at Oxford, the office lately occupied by
Peter Martyr; and Juan de Villagarcia, of the same
order, who from the name given him by Foxe seems to

---

[1] The account here given of the Spanish part in the Marian persecution is chiefly derived from three papers in the *British Magazine* (1839
and 1840, Nos. 96, 98, and 102) by the Archdeacon of Cleveland, who has examined many of the Spanish authorities with equal diligence and success.

have been known at Oxford as Friar John, and who read divinity lectures at Lincoln and Magdalen Colleges. The historian eulogises the success of these divines in bringing back that famous university to Catholic doctrine, and says of Carranza, that 'on his counsel and disposal depended the major part of the spiritual government of the kingdom,' which may be the rather believed, as he was soon appointed to the office of confessor to the queen. 'By his contrivance,' says the same writer, 'many were consigned to the flames, and among them was burnt alive Thomas Cranmer, usurping archbishop of Canterbury, *who gave sentence against Catharine.*'[1] Here then we have an additional motive avowed for these proceedings. It was a national quarrel, and the life of Cranmer was due to Spanish honour, which had been wounded by the divorce of Catharine. It were a pity to deprive them of that share in the credit of these proceedings which they were so anxious to claim; and it is no longer difficult to understand how the unhappy queen, accustomed to place her conscience at the disposal of her confessor, and that confessor acting under the direction of a husband whom she longed in vain to conciliate, should have been brought to sanction measures from which her woman's heart must surely have revolted.[2]

Further evidence to the same effect is supplied from the conduct of another of these Spaniards in the following year, when the indignation of the people appeared to be directed against Philip after the persecutions had begun. It was seen that the attempt to put down the Reformation by force had failed. After the first executions, other prisoners remained equally resolved to stand

---

[1] FERNANDEZ, *Historia Ecclesiastica del Nuestros Tempos.* Toledo, A.D. 1611.
[2] But it is necessary to the truth of history to mention that on one occasion, at least, Mary exhibited the pitiless spirit of a persecutor in the most undisguised form. See, in the Appendix, an extract from the report of Noailles, the French ambassador, of his interview with her on this subject.

to their doctrine to the death, and the nation was exasperated against the authors of the persecution. Gardiner had been willing to make a trial of severities, but he now became reluctant to interfere any further; and the odium was laid upon the king. It was at this period that a sermon was preached at court by Alphonso de Castro, the confessor of Philip, in which he condemned these proceedings in the most pointed manner, as contrary both to the text and the spirit of the Gospel. He said it was 'not by severity but by mildness that men were to be brought into the fold of Christ, and that it was not the duty of bishops to seek the death but to instruct the ignorance of their misguided brethren.' Such sentiments excited much notice from such a quarter. The persecution had a short respite; and when it was resumed, the guilt was naturally laid upon the bishops, who seemed to be indulging their own resentments contrary to the wishes of the court. But an investigation of this preacher's character and writings places his conduct in a very different light.[1] Eight years before, he had published a book entitled *On the Just Punishment of Heretics*, which he dedicated to Charles V., and in which he said they ought to be dealt with, 'not with words, but with clubs and whips and swords.' And lest it should seem that subsequent reflection had mitigated his feelings on the subject, he put forth in the year 1556, the very next year after this sermon was preached, a second edition of the same book, which he dedicated to Philip himself, stating that he had enlarged it while resident in England, serving his master *in public sermons* and matters of faith. He tells Philip that he had well deserved his title of Defender of the Faith, by reconciling a kingdom in four months, after twenty years' apostacy; and he devotes one of his chapters to an account of this reconciliation, and another

---

[1] ALPHONSUS A CASTRO, *De Justa Hæreticorum Punitione*. Ed. sec. Leyden, A.D. 1566.

to the description of the different modes of putting
heretics to death in different countries, which he seems
to have collected as a matter of curiosity, and some of
which he had witnessed.[1]   And this was the man who,
while employed upon such a book, stood forth as the
advocate of moderation, to turn the popular indignation
away from his master against the English bishops !

---

[1] See *British Magazine*, ut supra.

CHAPTER XXIII.

Yet I tell you
You tender not your person's honour, nor
Your high profession spiritual; that therefore
I do refuse you for my judge.—SHAKSPEARE.

WE are now to see what was the course of that process, by which modern Romanists would tell us
it was intended to ' terrify the party of the Reformers by
some instances of justice, which, as it usually happens,
degenerated into something like cruelty.'[1] A commission was issued by the cardinal legate to Gardiner,
Bonner, Tonstal, and other bishops, to proceed against
the heretics. On the 29th of January, 1555, Rogers
and Bradford, the two prebendaries of St. Paul's before
mentioned, Hooper bishop of Gloucester, and Rowland
Taylor, the learned and assiduous parish-priest of
Hadleigh, were brought before this commission, and
refusing to conform were delivered to the secular
power. Of these John Rogers was the first victim. He
was a man of great learning, had been a friend of Tyndal, and with regard to the chief point of the sacrament, was so far from holding extreme opinions, that
he said on his trial, he was suspected by some to be
of a contrary opinion to many of his brethren. But he
would not allow the corporeal presence. All these four
were married men, yet so far was this circumstance
from daunting their courage, that it was rather an ad-

---

[1] Dod's *Church History,* a work lately republished in a cheap form
for Roman Catholic readers. Dr. Lingard also says that Cranmer and
his associates were dealt with 'on their own principles.' What! did
they burn those who believed transubstantiation?

ditional motive with them to suffer, for the sake of the character of their wives and children ; for the system to which they were opposed stigmatised their wives as concubines, and their children as illegitimate.   Rogers was brought to the stake in Smithfield on the 4th of February, A.D. 1555.   His wife was a foreigner; and when he found he was to leave her a widow, with ten orphan children, he asked that she might come to visit him till his death, that he might advise her what to do ; but Gardiner refused it, telling him she was not his wife.   Very different, however, was the effect of this first spectacle of blood from what had been expected by the contrivers of it.   His children met him on his way to execution, and stood by to encourage him during the fiery trial.   He washed his hands in the flame, and endured it with triumphant resolution, while the spectators greeted his devoted spirit with loud acclamation. And such an indication of the temper of the people was thought so important, that the French ambassador reported it to his court, and said that the man went to be burnt as if he had been going to a marriage.[1]   But the work went on, and it was thought expedient that some should suffer in those places where their labours had been most conspicuous.   Saunders had been well known at Coventry, at which place therefore he was brought to the stake on the 8th of February.   On the day following, Hooper suffered in front of his cathedral at Gloucester; and Taylor was burnt at his own parish of Hadleigh, amidst the blessings and prayers of his parishioners. His wife being refused admittance to his prison, but having learned the day when he was to be sent down into Suffolk, watched for him all night with his children in the porch of St. Botolph's Church, in Aldgate, and there he knelt with them in prayer, and gave them his parting blessing; nor can we fail here to record how richly that parting prayer was answered, if it be true

---

[1] See NOAILLES, *Ambassades en Angleterre.*

that one of those children became the father, or grandfather, of one of the most eloquent and illustrious men
whom the English Church can boast, Bishop Jeremy
Taylor.

It was now that some delay took place, when it is supposed that the English bishops were unwilling to proceed; but on the 16th of March an artisan was burnt in
Smithfield, and not long after two gentlemen suffered
near their own houses in Essex, and a priest and some
others in Suffolk. Another bishop was executed in his
own diocese in the end of the same month, being condemned to the flames by the person who had succeeded
to his bishopric. This was Farrer bishop of St. David's,
whose fate was peculiarly hard; for he had been imprisoned almost ever since he came to his bishopric, during
the reign of Edward VI., on a false accusation. He
suffered with great fortitude at Carmarthen. Coverdale,
late bishop of Exeter, had a narrow escape: the King of
Denmark, who had known him abroad, begged his life,
which was reluctantly and ungraciously granted, and he
was permitted to retire to the Continent. Instructions
were sent down to several counties, that the justices of
the peace should divide their county into districts, and
have one or two in every parish secretly employed to
discover heretics; and Bonner having abstained for some
weeks from condemning any to death, the king and queen
wrote to him in May, to have more regard to the office
of a good pastor and bishop. Bradford, the companion
of the three bishops in the Tower, though condemned
together with Hooper and Rogers, had been respited for
awhile; but in the month of July, after many endeavours
had been made to induce him to recant, his doom also
was fixed. Attempts were now made to have these
executions less public, and Bradford was conveyed at
midnight to Newgate, to be ready for his fate in Smithfield the next morning; but even at that hour multitudes watched for him, and Smithfield was crowded by
four o'clock on the morning of his death, which he

underwent in company with a youth of nineteen, an apprentice, who was condemned for the same opinions. It will be no surprise to find the notorious Thornden, Cranmer's suffragan, so often mentioned, forward in persecution, and he had a worthy associate in Harpsfield, archdeacon of Canterbury. These men condemned two priests and two laymen to the stake at Canterbury, and a woman and four men in other parts of that diocese. And in the three succeeding months, from thirty to forty more were burnt in different places in the kingdom.

The three bishops at Oxford had remained in custody since their condemnation the year before, and it was determined that fresh proceedings should be taken against them under the authority of the pope. Cranmer had occupied himself in preparing a reply to Gardiner's answer to his book upon the Sacrament, and Ridley wrote a small treatise on the subject. Latimer did little else than read his Testament, and pray for strength to endure his trial, and for a restoration once again of gospel truth to England—often repeating the words, 'Once again, Lord, once again!' A most interesting record of the feelings and sufferings of these confessors, and of their brethren in London, is preserved in the letters which passed amongst them, which were afterwards collected by Coverdale, and published in the reign of Elizabeth, in a book still well known as the *Martyrs' Letters*. A more interesting document, or one which, with a few exceptions, breathes a more holy and heavenly spirit, it would be difficult to find; and it is, at the same time, the most authentic record of their opinions on many points of importance. But in none are they more conspicuous than in the well-assured confidence in the justice of their cause, and joyful anticipation of reward. Ridley writes to the brethren in captivity in London—' Trust to the truth of our cause, which, as it may by the malice of Satan be darkened, so can it never be clean put out. For we have (high praise be given to God therefor!), most plainly, evidently, and clearly on our side, all the prophets, all the apostles, and undoubtedly all the ecclesiastical writers which have written until of late years past.' And in another letter, after his condemnation, he said, 'Know ye, that I doubt no more but that the causes for which I suffer are God's causes, and the causes of the truth, than I doubt that the gospel which John wrote is the gospel of Christ, or that Paul's epistles are the very word of God.' The consent of the ancient Church in their opinions was a point on which they were peculiarly strong. Cranmer's challenge to prove the agreement of the Reformed Liturgy with that of the Primitive Fathers has been mentioned; and Taylor, in his examination before Gardiner, declared his belief, that this Liturgy had been 'by that one reformation (meaning the revision of the first Prayer Book) so fully perfected, that no Christian conscience could be offended with anything therein contained.' And when Gardiner upon this called him an ignorant beetlebrow, he answered that he 'had read over and over again the Holy Scriptures, and St. Augustine's works through, and St. Cyprian, Eusebius, Origen, Gregory Nazianzen, with divers other books, throughout.' But the temper with which they took their trials is still more remarkable. 'Lament not our state,' said Ridley, in answer to a letter from his friend Grindal, who was among the exiles at Frankfort; 'but I beseech you and them all, to give unto our heavenly Father, for His endless mercies and unspeakable benefits even in the midst of our troubles, most hearty thanks.' And in a letter to his own relations and family, he invites 'all that be his true lovers and friends, to rejoice and rejoice with him again, and render with him hearty thanks to God our heavenly Father, that for His Son's sake, our Saviour and Redeemer Christ, He had vouchsafed to call him, being else, without His gracious goodness, in himself but a sinful and a vile wretch—to call him unto this high dignity of his

true prophets, of his faithful apostles, and of his holy
elect and faithful martyrs, that is, to die and spend this
temporal life in the defence of His eternal and everlasting truth.' And Taylor, so far from condoling with the
Oxford prisoners, told them that he praised God again
and again for their excellent promotion : ' I cannot
utter with pen how I rejoice in my heart for you three
such captains in the forward under Christ's cross or
standard. This is another manner of nobility than to
be in the forefront in worldly warfare. For God's sake
pray for us, for we fail not daily to pray for you. We
are stronger and stronger in the Lord (his name be
praised !), and we doubt not but ye be so in Christ's own
sweet school. Heaven is all and wholly on our side.
Rejoice in the Lord alway, and again rejoice.' And such
also were Hooper's sentiments : ' Blessed shall we be if
ever God make us worthy of that honour to shed our
blood for His sake : and blessed then shall we think
the parents which brought us into this world, that we
shall from this mortality be carried into immortality !'

Many affecting incidents might be collected from
these letters of mutual kindness among the martyrs and
their friends. The three bishops at Oxford had everything in common, and presents were sent them from
time to time—sometimes of clothes, sometimes of money,
for all had been taken from them. Several ladies of
quality, in some instances personally unknown to them,
were forward in thus ministering to their wants, and
they repaid it with their gratitude and their prayers.[1]
Another touching record of these times is the reconciliation of Hooper with Ridley. It will be remembered
that Ridley had attempted in vain to convince Hooper
of the impropriety of his conduct in refusing to wear the

---

[1] It was now that a lady sent to them in prison to know whether she
might have her child baptized by a ' Romish Priest:' and they replied
that she might, 'for the Church of Rome had departed less in regard to
baptism from Scripture and primitive truth than in any other matter.'
.—*MS.* inscribed in a copy of the New Testament, penes *E. Duncombe
Shafto, Esq., M.P.*

episcopal dress, and that their intercourse was suspended in consequence. But now that each was preparing to render his life for the common cause, Hooper wrote twice to Ridley, whose confinement was at that time so strict that he had difficulty in answering it; but as soon as he was able he replied, in a Latin letter, in these affecting terms: 'Howsoever at one time we have each of us, I confess, your wisdom and my simplicity, had our own opinion in smaller matters and the appendages of religion, yet now let my friend be assured that I love you, my brother, from my heart in the bowels of Christ, for the sake of the truth which abideth in us, and I am persuaded, by the grace of God, shall abide for ever;' and he concluded thus—'Farewell, and yet once more and for ever in Christ, dearest brother, a kind farewell!' The more moderate sentiments of Ridley, and his friends Bradford and Rogers, were displayed in other matters besides that of the clerical dress, which had caused the temporary estrangement from Hooper, thus so happily concluded. He confessed that he had not liked some things that were done, and admitted, as has been before noticed, that he wished to have retained auricular confession; not probably in the way it was then used in the Church of Rome, but in the manner provided for in the first Reformed Liturgy. It also appears that while he rejected the invocation of saints, he was not afraid to bespeak the prayers of those who were going before him to the abodes of bliss; for when he knew that Bradford's doom was fixed, he wrote to him—'Brother, so long as I shall understand that thou art in thy journey, by God's grace I shall call upon our heavenly Father, for Christ's sake, to set thee safely home; and then, good brother, speak you and pray for the remnant that are to suffer for Christ's sake, according to that thou then shalt know more clearly.'

On the 12th of September, a year and a half almost after his first condemnation by the delegates of the English Convocation, Cranmer was brought into St. Mary's

Church, to a solemn hearing before the commissioners of
the pope and the queen.   The pope's commissioner was
Brooks, master of Balliol College, who had lately been
made bishop of Gloucester.   He was seated on high in
front of the altar, the two commissioners of the king and
queen being placed on lower seats at either side.   The
prisoner was cited by the name of Thomas archbishop
of Canterbury, and he stood forward accordingly, and
made low obeisance to the royal commissioners, but
without noticing the papal delegate ; assigning for his
reason that he meant no personal disrespect, but that he
had sworn never to admit the pope to have henceforth
any authority in England.   The accusations against
him were divided under three heads—blasphemy, incontinence, and heresy ; but the arguments chiefly turned
upon the papal authority, and upon his own part in
taking an oath to the pope under a protest, when he was
made archbishop.   The imputation of incontinence was
founded upon his having been married, which he
acknowledged and justified ; but the other accusations
he of course repelled.   He was not now degraded, but
was sent back to prison, and was soon after cited to
appear at Rome before the pope himself.   This citation
upon a prisoner, who had not liberty to appear, was a
mere form ; but it afforded him an opportunity of writing a letter to the queen, to express his readiness to go
if he might be permitted to do so, in which letter he
gave a summary of his answers before the commissioners,
which is the best account of his defence which has been
preserved.   He expresses his grief at having been
accused before a foreign power by the king and queen
in their own dominions, and tells her he had sworn to
her father never to consent to such authority.   He
shows that the laws of England are in many respects
contrary to those of the pope, and supposes that these
things were not sufficiently opened in the parliament
house when the pope's authority was received again
within the realm : as to which matters he says, ' Ig-

norance may excuse others, but he who knoweth that I do know cannot be excused.' He also sums up very forcibly the answers he had given respecting the Eucharist : ' As touching the sacrament, I said, —— I would be judged by the old Church, and which doctrine could be proved the elder that I would stand unto. And forasmuch as I have alleged in my book, many old authors, both Greeks and Latins, which about a thousand years after Christ continually taught as I do, if they could bring forth but one old author that saith in these two points as they say, I offered six or seven years ago, and do offer yet still that I will give place to them.—— Yea, the old Church of Rome about a thousand years together neither believed nor used the sacrament as the Church of Rome hath done of late years. For in the beginning, the Church of Rome taught a pure and a sound doctrine of the sacrament, but after that the Church of Rome fell into a new doctrine of transubstantiation, and with the doctrine they changed the use of the sacrament, contrary to that Christ commanded and the old Church of Rome used above a thousand years. —— The body of Christ in the sacrament, by their doctrine, —— goeth into the mouth with the form of bread, and entereth no farther than the form of bread goeth, and tarrieth no longer than the form of bread is by natural heat in digesting, so that when the form of bread is digested that body of Christ is gone.'——It seemeth to me a more sound and comfortable doctrine, that Christ hath but one body, and that hath form and fashion of a man's true body, which body spiritually entereth into the whole man, body and soul; and though the sacrament be consumed, yet whole Christ remaineth, and feedeth the receiver unto everlasting life, if he continue

---

' That this is literally the teaching of the Church of Rome in the present day appears from their books of catechetical instruction. In one of these, after an injunction not to spit after communion, the question occurs ' How long does the Body of Christ remain after you have communicated?' Answer : ' About a quarter of an hour.'

in godliness, and never depart until the receiver forsake him.'

A week after Cranmer's trial, Ridley and Latimer were brought to the same place, before three bishops holding commission from the cardinal in the name of the pope. Brooks bishop of Gloucester was again on the commission, and his colleagues were White of Lincoln and Holyman of Bristol. They in like manner declined to show any token of respect to the pope's authority, and both refusing to recant, were condemned as heretics. A fortnight was still allowed them, during which every endeavour was made to shake their fortitude. But they had long ago armed themselves by mutual conference and prayer, and their endurance was a reward of the humility and fearfulness with which they had prepared themselves. We have seen that Cranmer acted boldly and spoke manfully; it is worthy perhaps of remark, in reference to the final conduct of both, that Ridley, when first imprisoned, feared for his own constancy, and sought to confirm his steadfastness by frequent conferences with Latimer, whose characteristic answer on one occasion was, ' I only learn to die in reading of the New Testament, and am ever now and then praying unto my God, that he will be a helper unto me in time of need.' On the 15th of October they were brought again before the commissioners, to be degraded, who, however, would not admit their character of bishops, but degraded them only as priests; and the next morning was fixed for their execution. The place selected was the ditch outside the city-wall, in that part immediately facing the lodgings of the master of Balliol College, who, as already mentioned, was at that time Brooks bishop of Gloucester, one of the commissioners who condemned them. In their way they had to pass under the gateway tower, called Bocardo, where Cranmer was imprisoned; and Ridley, who came first, looked up, hoping to receive his friend's farewell; but the archbishop was engaged in controversy with one of the Spanish

friars, and was not aware till they had both passed.
Latimer was not far behind, and when he was come to
the spot, Ridley embraced him and said, ' Be of good
heart, brother, for God will either assuage the fury of
the flame, or strengthen us to abide it.'   They kneeled
down and prayed together, and after a short sermon
against their doctrine, to which they were not permitted
to reply, they prepared for the stake.   When Latimer's
clothes were taken off, it was found that he had on a
shroud for his under-garment; and now the bystanders
observed that he whom they had seen a poor old man,
bowed down with years and infirmity, stood upright,
with an air of venerable dignity that bespoke the high
resolve of his soul. ' Be of good comfort, Master Ridley,'
he exclaimed, when a lighted faggot was laid at Ridley's
feet ; ' we shall this day light such a candle, by God's
grace, in England, as I trust shall never be put out.'
When the pile was lighted for himself, he bent towards
the flames, as if he would embrace them, exclaiming.
' Oh, Father of heaven, receive my soul ! ' and soon
expired. Ridley's sufferings were much more protracted.
Most of the spectators were adherents of the opposite
party, for the Reformers were fled or silenced.   The
magistrate who presided was Lord Williams of Thame,
who had been rewarded with a peerage for having been
the first in Oxfordshire to proclaim the queen ; and
Dr. Smith, the preacher, who was one of those unhappy
persons who had abjured the Reformed doctrine, and
who, like Shaxton formerly, was requited with such an
employment.   But a few friends had still adhered to
them, among whom were Shipshed, a clergyman, who
had married Ridley's sister, and Augustine Bernher.
the faithful attendant of Latimer, who had been employed
to convey most of the letters and messages that passed
between the prisoners in Oxford and those in London,
and who afterwards himself became a preacher of the
Reformed doctrine.   Nor was this spectacle without its
effects upon some of those who came to witness it with

different feelings.   Julius Palmer, a fellow of Magdalen
College, was induced to embrace their doctrine, and
afterwards suffered for it at the stake; and even one of
the Spanish friars, Constantine Ponce, a man of great
learning, a canon of Seville, and preacher to Charles V.,
imbibed the opinions which he was brought to England
to refute, and died a prisoner of the Inquisition at
Seville.

It was a question of painful interest, in these times,
how far it was allowable to comply with the restored
religion. There is no doubt of its being a Christian duty
to submit to the ordinances of man, when we can do so
consistently with our higher duty towards God.   And
probably this consideration may have had weight with
such men as Sir William Cecil, who, though he had
been of King Edward's council, and was attached on
principle to the same sentiments, attended mass once
at least during this reign in the parish church of
Wimbledon, where he lived.   It was a very different
case with those who were publicly called upon to
answer for their opinions; and we have seen that in
Henry's reign, Frith and some others were willing to
keep their sentiments to themselves, at the same time
that they were resolved not to deny them if challenged.
And this was the genuine spirit of martyrdom, and
those who did so deserve to be called martyrs; not
wantonly throwing away their lives, yet refusing to
compromise or suppress what they believed to be God's
truth.   But amidst these fiery trials it is no wonder that
some should have been found unequal to the task of
maintaining their faith with their lives.   One of the
first of those who renounced his former profession, and
that apparently under no coercion, was Harding, who
had been a chaplain in the Duke of Suffolk's family,
and to whom Lady Jane Gray wrote, before her death,
a letter of indignant reproof for his apostacy.   He
appears to have changed his religion within one week
after King Edward's death, having been before among

the most violent and abusive opponents of the opinions
which he so suddenly adopted; and this circumstance
may account for the very strong language which the
Lady Jane adopted towards him. He became afterwards a bitter controversionalist on the side which
she had espoused, and was the great opponent of Jewel
in the time of Queen Elizabeth. It does not appear
that more than one of the reforming bishops recanted.
This one was Scory, Bishop of Chichester, who, having
been removed from his see, afterwards renounced his
marriage, and received absolution from Bonner. It
seems, however, that he soon repented, and fled abroad,
for he is mentioned a year after in a letter from Grindal
to Ridley as having an English church, with some other
exiles, at Frisland, and we find mention of him soon
after at Emden. Another person, of whom better
things seem to have been expected was West, chaplain
and steward[1] to Ridley when bishop of London. This
man having recanted, wrote to Ridley when in prison
urging him to save his life by doing the same, remind-
ing him that he had always disliked extreme courses.
The bishop's answer and the fate of the man are equally
remarkable. ' I say unto you, in the word of the Lord,
that if you do not confess and maintain to your power
and knowledge, that which is grounded upon God's
Word, but will either for fear or gain of the world,
shrink and play the apostate, *indeed you shall die the
death.* You know what I mean; and I beseech you
remember what I say, for this may be the last time per-
adventure that ever I shall write unto you.' Ridley of
course alluded to his own approaching fate, and little
could either of them at that time foresee how differently
these words should be fulfilled from the way in which
they were meant. But we find it thus adverted to not

---

[1] Coverdale, or the editor of the *Martyrs' Letters*, calls him chaplain.
Ridley makes mention of him as 'sometime mine officer,' and others
call him steward. As such offices were probably still performed by
clergymen, it seems likely that he was both.

long after in a letter of Ridley's to Grindal—'West, your old companion and sometime mine officer, alas, hath relented, as I have heard; *but the Lord hath shortened his days, for anon he died and is gone.*'

A still more distressing case was that of Sir John Cheke, one of King Edward's tutors, and brother-in-law of Sir William Cecil.   Having been imprisoned for joining the party of Lady Jane Gray, he was pardoned and went abroad.   But having joined the church of the exiles at Strasbourg, he was entrapped into visiting his wife at Brussels, where he was seized by order of King Philip and brought to England.   Here he was told to choose between recantation and the stake, and after some conferences with Pole he sacrificed his conscience for his life.   They carried him about to the public disputations with the reformed, and paraded him as their convert; but it was not for long, for he sickened soon, and died of a broken heart.   Equally lamentable was the fall, but more happy the recovery of Jewel, a man already celebrated at Oxford, and who ventured to remain there for some time, and was employed to take notes of the first examinations of the bishops.   But through the agency of Marshall, Dean of Christ Church, who had himself professed the same opinions during the former reign, though now among the bitterest persecutors, Jewel was brought into St. Mary's Church and required to subscribe to the Romish doctrine in the fullest and most ample sense.   Veiling under an air of levity the bitterness of his soul, he asked if they wished to see how he could write, and affixed his name.   But he fled soon after, and being pursued, escaped with difficulty through the kindness of Latimer's faithful servant, Augustine Bernher.   He went to Frankfort, and there made public confession of his apostacy, with abundant tears, in the pulpit of the English Church.   Upon this he was hailed by them as a brother, and he lived to prove that their forgiveness was well bestowed.   There was another clergyman, Thomas Whittel, who recanted, but afterwards returned to his former confession, and expiated his offence at the stake. But these instances are enough to show what a time of trial it was.

A little before the time that Jewel arrived at Frankfort, those occurrences among the English exiles were brought to a conclusion, which have obtained a painful celebrity as the 'Troubles at Frankfort.' A large number of refugees had settled at that place the year before, and had obtained permission of the magistrates to make use of a church which had been assigned to the French Protestants, alternately with the French congregation. The magistrates stipulated, in order to prevent disputes, that they should conform to the confession of faith of the French, and in general to their usages also, to which the English agreed at first, apparently without considering what important principles were involved in such a step. For, in fact, if each separate congregation of a national Church was to be at liberty to remodel its doctrine and discipline according to its own pleasure, there would be an end of the principle on which the English Reformation had been conducted, as the act of a national Church under the authority of its civil and ecclesiastical rulers. But the Frankfort exiles, not considering this, and looking upon all that was opposed to popery with equal indulgence, agreed not only to abandon the use of the surplice, but to give up making the responses aloud, and to omit the whole of the litany, which was objected to, for no other reason, than that which ought to be its chief recommendation, that this precious portion of the service had been received from primitive times, with but little variation, even in the Church of Rome. They then sent to invite their brethren at Strasbourg, Zurich, and elsewhere, who perhaps had not obtained the privilege of a church for public worship, to join them at Frankfort and partake of the advantages they enjoyed. The Strasbourg exiles, who were men of more learning, proposed that Bishop Scory, who was then at Emden, and was the only bishop of their party, for Coverdale probably had not yet been liberated, should undertake the charge of this Church; but before his answer arrived, John Knox had come from Geneva with some others of like sentiments, and had been elected by those at Frankfort as their minister. Those at Zurich were disposed to join them, but only on condition that the whole of the English service was retained, and they sent Mr Chambers, the benevolent layman already mentioned as promoting good deeds in King Edward's time, to arrange matters on their behalf. Grindal also was sent from Strasbourg for the same purpose, with a letter signed by many influential names, setting forth the importance of adhering to the liturgy of the national Church. If this principle could be admitted, they were willing to acquiesce in some changes in minor points, but after many discussions and fruitless consultations, the congregation at Frankfort resolved that the English liturgy should be translated into Latin and sent to Calvin for his opinion. Not content with this, they sent at the same time a letter pointing out their own objections, in which they complained of the Angels' Hymn in the communion service, ' Glory to God in the highest,' as *popish*, though, in fact, it is found in all the primitive liturgies, besides being taken from the Word of God; and then they added that they concealed some other blemishes *out of shame and pity*. Calvin's answer was such as they probably anticipated, that the English liturgy contained ' *tolerable weaknesses*,' [1] which ought to be endured no longer than the necessity of the case required. Knox and his party, one of whom was John Foxe, ' the martyrologist,' now proposed to adopt the Geneva service, but this not being relished. a compromise was made and a form was adopted partly from Calvin, partly from the English Prayer Book, which both parties pledged themselves to observe. So matters rested until the arrival at Frankfort of Dr.

---

[1] *Tolerabiles ineptias.* The word 'fooleries,' by which this is sometimes translated, seems somewhat more severe than the original.

Cox, King Edward's tutor, with some others of similar
opinions with himself, who came there in March, 1555,
for the express purpose of bringing about a better state
of things.   Cox was a man of great learning, who would
at once perceive the importance of the principle involved
in these concessions, and the dangerous consequences
of them to the national Church if ever the Reformation
should be restored in England.   He may be supposed
to have had a personal attachment to that system which
had been established under his royal pupil, and it
would be so much the dearer to him when many of its promoters were called to shed their life's blood in the cause.
And as he was not bound to any agreement to which he
was no party, so he thought himself entitled to assume
that in every English congregation the English Liturgy
would be used.   When, therefore, he and his friends
went to church, the whole party said the responses aloud
according to the rubric, and one of them the Sunday
after read the litany from the pulpit.   Upon this, Knox
preached a sermon the same afternoon, in which he
declaimed violently against the whole Liturgy, and
declared that one cause of the present afflictions of the
English Church were the half measures taken in its Reformation.   The whole question was thus re-opened,
and some proposed that Cox and his friends should not
be allowed to vote upon the question, as not being
members of the congregation.   It is to the credit of
Knox that this proposal was overruled by him.   But
the result was, that the arguments of the new comers
were so successful, and they had the reason of the
matter so much on their side, that in a short time they
obtained a majority, who dismissed Knox from his
office as their minister.   The minority appealed to the
senate of the city, and after some fruitless attempts at
reconciliation, the whole congregation had orders to
conform to the discipline and services of the French
Protestants, under pain of their church being closed.
Cox, upon this, advised them to submit, but as the

minority under Knox had frustrated the decision of the majority by unfairly appealing to the magistrates, the other party were tempted to forget the maxim which would enjoin them to overcome evil with good. They thought themselves justified in informing the magistrates as to the former conduct of the person who had been mainly instrumental in disturbing the harmony of their church ; with which view they showed a book which Knox had published, containing, among other things, a sermon preached by him in Buckinghamshire against the queen's marriage, in which he had said that the emperor, the father of her intended husband, ' was no less enemy to Christ than was Nero.' The author of such sentiments could not be tolerated in a city subject to the emperor ; and Knox received an intimation to quit the place, upon which he retired to Geneva, and was joined there by Foxe and others of his party. The heart-burnings engendered in these disputes had afterwards a most fatal effect, as we shall see, upon the Church at home. Yet it is worthy of remark, as showing the opinion of one who had the best means of judging at the time, that Grindal wrote to Ridley soon afterwards from Frankfort, entirely approving of what Cox had done. His words are, ' Here is a Church now well settled (God be thanked), by the prudency of Master Cox and other which met here for that purpose, who most earnestly and unceasingly do cry unto God for the delivery of his Church.'[1] This letter was written on the 6th of May, and it was on the 26th of March preceding (1555) that Knox had been obliged to leave the place. So that Grindal, whose own opinions were so moderate, that he was afterwards accused of favouring the opposite party, must have known the whole transaction and decidedly approved of it.

It is not to be denied that some zealots at home gave the government cause for complaint, and afforded some

---

[1] *Martyrs' Letters*, p. 51. Black letter edition.

sort of excuse for severity. The insurrection of Wyatt, who himself seems to have professed the reformed faith,[1] and such sermons as that of Knox just mentioned, were represented as such things usually are at the time, as if they were the general sentiments of the party. So was the wild and wicked advice of a person named Thomas, who had formerly written a violent book under the title of *Pelerine Inglese*,[2] and who now proposed to assassinate the queen, and being taken up stabbed himself in prison. Afterwards, when the bitterness of the persecution had goaded the minds of the people, a priest was wounded at the altar, and two Observant friars, the very same men who preached against Henry's marriage with Anne Boleyn, Elstow and Peyto, were pelted as they went to Greenwich, where the queen had re-established their house, which had sometimes been the scene of her mother's devotions. Such things require to be mentioned, the rather because they were assiduously collected afterwards by the opposite party, as if in justification of the severities that were exercised, whereas, in fact, many of them did not take place till the worst of these severities had been perpetrated, and certainly were not sanctioned by the leaders of the party; who were so far from justifying Wyatt's rebellion, that when he set open the prison doors of the Marshalsea, none of those committed on the charge of heresy would avail themselves of it to escape. Another charge which has been brought against them is altogether unfounded. While these horrors were going on, during the first year after the queen's marriage, there was a very general belief, in which she herself participated, that she was about to have an heir to the throne. It went so far, that public prayers were ordered for her safe delivery, and in more than one instance, at Norwich, and at one church in London, on a false report that a

---

[1] Lady Wyatt, probably his widow, was among those who contributed to the relief of the martyrs in prison.

[2] This treatise has lately been printed in English by Mr. Froude.

prince was born, Te Deum was solemnly sung on the
occasion. Foxe, who wrote soon after, in the reign of
Elizabeth, at a time when people's minds were maddened
by the cruelties that had been exercised against their
friends, indulged in some sallies of unmanly exultation
and ridicule on this affair, which cannot be sufficiently
blamed, and which have afforded an opportunity to the
other side of pointing to such things as if they were
the usual sentiments and common language of his party.
Yet, so far was this from being the case, that when
Ridley had reason to believe that his own death was
deferred till after the queen's confinements, he wrote to
Grindal, that after that event, 'which we daily expect,
and have now some time expected (*and may God vouchsafe for the glory of his name to give her a prosperous
time!*), we look for nothing else than to receive the
crown of our confession in the Lord.'

A short time after the execution of Latimer and
Ridley, Bishop Gardiner died. There is no reason to
believe a story that has been told of his having waited
dinner till he heard of their death, and having been
seized with mortal illness while at table. This story is
inconsistent with other facts. And what we know of
his death, would rather incline us to hope that he began to repent of what he had been doing. It is said
that Bonner also was reluctant to proceed: but if this
was so, his wishes were soon overruled, and the little-
ness of his character rendered his cruelty the more re-
volting. Philpot, Archdeacon of Winchester, was long
detained by him in prison at his palace near St. Paul's,
and he often argued with him, and almost always lost
his temper and descended to low personalities. At
length he condemned him to the stake, and his execution, which took place in Smithfield on the 18th of December, concluded the horrors of this year, during which
sixty-seven persons had been burnt, of whom were
four bishops and thirteen priests.

CHAPTER XXIV.

> To God the fruits of sorrow
> His broken heart had giv'n,
> And he rose upon that morrow,
> Strong in the strength of heaven.
> CHURTON'S *Lays of Faith* and *Loyalty*.

CRANMER had remained in prison from the time of his examination in September, but in February, 1556, a commission arrived from the pope to proceed to a final sentence against him. In the meantime many endeavours had been made to bring him back to the Church of Rome, and the history of the steps by which this was at last, for a time, accomplished, will always remain in some degree of mystery. It appears that some hope was conceived of his fortitude having given way on the execution of Ridley and Latimer, and that he soon after expressed a wish to have an interview with Pole. There is also reason to believe that many of the most powerful of the Protestant nobility were urgent for his pardon, and it is said that Pole himself had begged his life of the queen if he would recant. It seems probable that the knowledge of such powerful intercession may have induced him to set his hand to some declarations, in which he did not retract his former religious opinions, but which contained a submission to the will of the king and queen, and an acknowledgment of the pope as supreme head of the Church of England, in deference to their will. This was to some extent in accordance with his well-known sentiments, as to the duty of submission to the ruling powers, and he was willing probably to try how far such submission, coupled with a declaration that he would be ruled, as to his book upon the sacrament, by the judgment of the Catholic Church, and of the

next general council, might avail to save his life. Three
papers to this effect were certainly signed by him before
the 14th of February; but they were not deemed sufficient, and as he would not go any further in his submission, nor retract his opinion and submit to the doctrine of the then Church of Rome, it seems to have
been determined that the law should take its course.
He was therefore on that day brought before Thirlby,
Bishop of Ely, and Bonner, who sat as the papal delegates in the choir of the cathedral of Christchurch, and
sentence of degradation pronounced upon him.   The
conduct of Bonner on this occasion is such an exhibi-
tion of unmanly insult and mean tyranny as must have
shamed those whose misfortune it was to employ such
a person in their service.   To say nothing of better
motives, a sense of his own dignity should have withheld
him from insulting a fallen man at such a moment.
Thirlby, on the contrary, was deeply affected, and declared with tears, that if it had not been for the king
and queen's command, no worldly advantage would have
induced him to undertake such an office.   To him Cranmer delivered an appeal from the sentence of the pope
to the next general council, in which he declared that
his intention was 'to speak nothing against one Holy,
Catholic, and Apostolic Church, or the authority thereof;'
but having set forth that 'a holy general council, lawfully gathered together in the Holy Ghost, is above the
pope, especially in matters concerning faith,' he proceeded to show the injustice of the proceedings against
himself, the evils that had arisen in England from the
pope's usurped authority, with the reasons why he would
not acknowledge that authority, contrasting the later
corruptions of the see of Rome with its ancient purity
and holiness, and concluded by appealing from his decision to 'a free general council held in a sure place.'
Here was, however, a departure from some part of those
submissions which he had made, in which he agreed to
acknowledge the pope, and perhaps it may have been

on this account that his adversaries accused him of insincerity, and alleged it as a ground for proceeding to extremities against him.   Be this as it may, it is probable that from the time of his degradation his doom was fixed; for whatever hesitation there may have been as to his death before that event, a recantation after definitive sentence was not held sufficient, according to papal laws, to entitle the penitent to a pardon.   And if they were incensed against him for renouncing the pope in his appeal after having consented to acknowledge him, this may have been the reason why Pole no longer interceded for him, but is even said to have advised his execution.

But now we arrive at a still more intricate part of this affair.   Only two days after he had delivered this appeal at his degradation, namely, on the 16th of February, he exhibited to Bonner a fourth paper, written and signed by himself, in which, without saying anything about the pope, he asserted his steadfast belief in ' all the articles of the Christian religion and Catholic faith, as the Catholic Church doth believe, and hath believed from the beginning.'   Nothing could be more natural than that Bonner should visit him after his degradation, and remonstrate with him for having receded from his late subscription to the pope's authority, upon which it was equally natural that Cranmer should protest, as he had indeed always protested, that he did not intend to separate from, or renounce the Catholic Church, and being required to give that sentiment in writing, he of course would do so.   But he had permitted himself, as he afterwards acknowledged and lamented, to be seduced with the hopes of life.   Certainly it seems that he had some good reason to expect it from the intervention of his friends.   And now that these attempts had failed, and he found himself condemned notwithstanding, he was the more open to the temptation to make a more desperate effort.   But near a month intervened, during which time he would be plied with all those

arguments which might best suit his case, and to a man
of his moderate sentiments, who had always maintained
the authority of the Catholic Church, and who perhaps
placed his rejection of the papal supremacy chiefly on
the question between the regale and pontificate, it was the
more easy to suggest that he ought not to put his
individual opinion in competition with that which
professed to be the collective voice of Christendom.
During this interval also he was treated with a
degree of kindness which had not before been shown
him. He was removed from prison to the lodgings of
the Dean of Christchurch, and such treatment was peculiarly apt to operate upon his gentle character. But
whatever the arguments may have been by which it was
brought about, thus much is certain, that before the 12th
of March[1] he had signed a paper, in the presence of
Villagarcia and another person, which amounted to a most
full and absolute recantation. He anathematised the
heresy of Luther and Zwingle, acknowledging one only
church, of which the pope is head, the Vicar of Christ,
to whom all the faithful must submit themselves, admitted
transubstantiation, seven sacraments, purgatory and
prayers to saints, and acknowledged that he agreed in all
things with the belief of the 'Catholic and Roman
Church.'

It is certain, from his own assertion, that he made
this confession with the hope that it might yet avail to
save his life; and there is reason to believe that his
friends at court once more interceded for him, and were
severely rebuked for doing so; but it seems to have
been resolved to turn his recantation to account, by
extorting from him a still more absolute act of self-con-
demnation. On the 18th of March, a tract was printed
by Bonner's authority, but immediately suppressed,
professing to give an account of all the submissions and

---

[1] The paper is without date; but Mr. Churton has shown from the
despatch of Noailles to his court, announcing the fact, that it must have
been before that date.

recantations of Thomas, late Archbishop of Canterbury. This tract contained not only the five papers already mentioned, including the last recantation, but two more; the one purporting to be a still more ample recantation, in which he especially lamented his sin in the divorce of Catharine, and the other a dying speech. As this tract was printed three days before his death, and contained words which he did not deliver, it is clear that his enemies must have arranged the whole matter beforehand, and that this represents what they wished and intended he should say. The sixth paper is in Latin, as the recantation also was, and it is therefore probable that it was drawn up by one of the Spanish ecclesiastics, who would naturally insert the national offence in the matter of the divorce. But it seems to have been intended as the groundwork of a dying speech, such as the seventh paper actually was; and it can therefore hardly be doubted, that Cranmer being now informed that his doom was fixed, was required to prepare a confession to be publicly made before he died, grounded perhaps upon this paper, and that he drew out himself that pathetic and eloquent lamentation, only with a different conclusion, which being transmitted to London, was sent to the press by Bonner, without waiting for the news of his death.[1]

Matters being thus arranged, the Lord Williams came to Oxford on Saturday, the 21st of March, with some other noblemen and magistrates, and Cranmer was brought from prison to St. Mary's Church, no longer dressed as a bishop, but clothed in mean attire as a poor civilian. There was a vast concourse, for those of the Romish side were expecting the triumph of their opinions, while those of opposite sentiments would not believe that he whom they had thought the champion of their cause, would desert that cause now at his last extremity. After a sermon from Dr. Cole, not unmixed with some

[1] For the grounds on which this view of the recantation is founded and for the authorities for the same, see again ARCHDEACON CHURTON's *Papers on the Marian Persecution,* as before referred to.

dash of kindness, as far as there could be kindness in
such courses, the archbishop was called upon ' to express
the true and undoubted profession of his faith, that all
might see he was a Catholic indeed.' He had been
placed upon a platform opposite the pulpit, slightly raised
above the people, and during the sermon he wept so
bitterly that all hearts were moved to see an old man's
tears, and such a man's, flowing from him as from a
child. ' Good people,' he said, ' I had intended to desire
you to pray for me, which because Mr. Doctor hath
desired and you have done already, I thank you most
heartily for it, and now will I pray for myself, as I
could best devise for my own comfort.' He then read
a prayer as he stood, and afterwards kneeled down and
said the Lord's prayer, the whole assembly with one
impulse kneeling and joining in it aloud. And then he
proceeded to read his dying speech. He exhorted all
to set their minds above this world, upon God, and the
world to come; to obey the king and the queen; to
study brotherly love, and the rich to remember the
account they shall give of their riches. He next recited
the Apostles' Creed, emphatically declaring that he
believed the whole faith of the Catholic Church, and
then he said he came to that great thing that so much
troubled his conscience above everything he did or said
in his life past. It was here intended that he should
express his sorrow for having written against the faith
of the Church of Rome; and such was the tenor of the
speech printed by Bonner, and which he was now
expected to deliver. But so far from doing so, he proceeded thus. ' And that is the setting abroad of writings
contrary to the truth which I thought in my heart, and
written for fear of death, and to save my life if it might
be, and that is all such bills and papers which I have
written or signed with my hand since my degradation,
wherein I have written many things untrue. And forasmuch as my hand offended, writing contrary to my
heart, my hand shall first be punished therefore, for

may I come to the fire it shall first be burned. And as for the pope, I refuse him as Christ's enemy and Antichrist, with all his false doctrine. And as for the Sacrament, I believe as I have taught in my book against the Bishop of Winchester, the which my book teacheth so true a doctrine of the Sacrament, that it shall stand at the last day before the judgment of God, when the papistical doctrine, contrary thereto, shall be ashamed to show his face.' He could scarce finish reading for the interruptions with which he was assailed, and they began to accuse him of falsehood and dissembling. But he answered, 'Ah, my masters, do not take it so. Always since I lived, I have been a hater of falsehood and a lover of simplicity, and never before this time have I dissembled;' then he wept again bitterly. He attempted further speech, but his voice was drowned with hootings, and they hurried him away to the spot where his happier associates had witnessed their good confession. On this spot he knelt for a short time in prayer, and then undressed for the stake; how much happier now again than if he had been permitted to live with the brand of apostacy on his name, and the stings of conscience in his heart. The conflict was over. The martyrdom which his cowardice had shrunk from was given him, under the good Providence of God, by the cruel mercy of his enemies, and he was restored in death to the God whom he had served, and to the Church which he had reformed. We are told that his shirt was made long, down to his feet, which were bare, and when his cap was off, his head was seen without a single hair, while his beard, which he had suffered to grow ever since the death of Henry VIII., 'covered his face with marvellous gravity.' When the fire was lighted, he extended his arm, and thrust his right hand into the flame, which he held there without flinching, except that he raised it once to wipe the death-drops from his brow, exclaiming often, *This unworthy right hand.* His last words were, 'Lord Jesus, receive my spirit.'

H H

Cardinal Pole was consecrated as archbishop of Canterbury the day after Cranmer's death.   But he does not seem to have exercised so much influence in affairs connected with religion as might have been expected. That he was personally amiable has never been denied, and there is preserved a letter of his, written from Canterbury, which indicates an affectionate interest in his episcopal functions.   He thanks his friend for enquiring after his health, and says that it would especially grieve him to be sick now that he was amongst his flock.   Once he interfered to save three out of sixteen persons whom Bonner had condemned together to the stake, yet on other occasions he permitted the fury of persecution to rage unrestrained.   A man and four women were burnt at Canterbury, by order of Harpsfield and Thornden, a short time before he became archbishop.   This perhaps he could not help; but the same can hardly be said when six men were burnt in one fire in the same place in the January following, and fourteen persons in two days in June of the same year, A.D. 1557.   Perhaps his Italian notions might lead him to think it necessary to permit these cruelties. But his situation, both as regards the pope and the queen, was one of great difficulty. The pope was his personal enemy, and endeavoured to supersede him as legate, by creating Peyto, the friar of Greenwich, a cardinal, and sending him legatine powers with his nomination to the bishopric of Salisbury.   The queen refused to admit his legatine authority, and Pole being thus beholden to her, was the less able to oppose the influence of Carranza, the secret agent in these scenes of blood.

The queen now proceeded to establish, as far as she could, all those parts of the ancient religion which had been broken down.   The houses of the Franciscan and Dominican friars were restored at Greenwich and in Smithfield, and the nunneries of Sheen and Sion.   The new bishopric of Westminster having been suppressed, the monks were reinstated, and the deanery converted

into a foundation for the abbot. Not long after, the house
of St. John of Jerusalem was also restored, and Sir
Thomas Tresham was made Grand Prior of England.[1]
Nor was this confined to England, for the Grand Prior of
Ireland was also reinstated at Kilmainham.[2] For these
and similar purposes, the queen deprived herself of all
the church property remaining in the crown, and that
at a time when her necessities were urgent. Encouragement was also given to those who should choose to give
lands for such purposes, and a few chantries were founded
for masses for the dead. Attempts were made to restore
the discipline of the Church. These attempts were
praiseworthy, so long as they were confined to the correction of notorious offenders, however doubtful it may
be whether any religious discipline can be truly correc-
tive of vice which shall not be voluntary. But some
parts of this discipline were calculated to bring the censures of the Church into contempt.

It is an odious task to trace the course of persecution
throughout these awful times; and some of the occurrences that took place are almost too horrible to mention.[3]
In the year before the queen died, seventy-nine persons
were burnt, and the same spirit continued to the last; so
that Harpsfield is said to have hastened the death of
three men and two women at Canterbury, who suffered
on the 10th of November, 1558 only a week before her
death, lest that event should stop the persecution. A
kind of inquisition was established, to carry on the investigation into the opinions of all persons who did not
come to church; and the Sheriff of Hampshire having
ventured to stop the execution of a victim who recanted

---

[1] But in Horsfield's *Hist. of Sussex*, vol. I. p. 376, we are told that Sir
Richard Shelley was English Grand Prior of the Order of St. John of
Jerusalem, in the reigns of Mary and Elizabeth.
[2] Sir James Ware, *Annales Hibernia*. It would seem from what
Sir James Ware says as if Pole had gone over to Ireland for the purpose.
But there does not appear to be any ground for thinking so.
[3] Such as the horrors perpetrated at the island of Guernsey, of which
an authentic record was preserved in the reign of Queen Elizabeth.

at the stake, was severely reprimanded, and was ordered
first to bring the culprit to the fire, and then to come up
to London to answer for his own presumption.   The
total number of sufferers recorded by Foxe is two hundred and eighty-four, besides about sixty who died in
prison; of these there were five bishops, twenty-one
clergymen, eight gentlemen, eighty-four artificers, one
hundred husbandmen, servants and labourers, twenty-
six married women, twenty widows, nine unmarried
women, two boys, and two infants.   But another account,
said to be given on the authority of Archbishop Grindal,
stated the number at eight hundred.   Yet it is gratify-
ing to know that the principal part of these horrors was
confined to a few dioceses.   The northern parts of England were almost wholly exempt from them, and in the
diocese of Durham especially, Tonstal did not permit a
single prosecution to take place.   In that of Worcester
also, Bishop Pates, who had been restored after having
quitted the country in the time of Henry VIII., is said
to have expressed the following noble sentiments to a
physician whom he sent for, and whom he knew to be a
Protestant.   Seeing him betray some alarm on being
sent for to him, he said: 'I am not ignorant what your
religious sentiments are.   But never fear: for I am resolved not to injure or punish any one on account of
the faith, which does not propagate itself by force and
terror, but by the influence and persuasions of reason.'[1]

   In the midst of the trials to which they were exposed,
there were not wanting those who continued to exercise
in secret the services of the Reformed religion.   A
clergyman named John Rough had a congregation at
Islington, to whom he administered the rites of the
Church of England according to the Liturgy of King
Edward; but he was taken and condemned to the
flames.   Two other clergymen, who were afterwards respectively bishops of Peterborough and Lichfield under

---

[1] GODWIN, *De Præsul.* Bishop Godwin tells this story on the authority of his own father, who was the physician referred to.

Queen Elizabeth, Scambler and Bentham, continued
their ministrations undiscovered, and Harley bishop of
Hereford, one of those two of King Edward's bishops
who attempted to take their seats in the House of
Lords in the beginning of this reign, 'instructed his
flocks in woods and secret places, as a faithful and holy
shepherd, preaching to them and administering the
sacraments, and for this purpose lurking up and down in
England, at last died like an exile in his own country.'[1]
But these terrors were to have an end. The queen's
health had been failing for some time, and her distress
of mind, arising from the coldness and frequent absence
of her husband, was augmented by her mortification on
the loss of Calais, which had been the possession of
England for above two hundred years, and was taken
by the French in January, 1558, because through the
mismanagement of her government and their jealousy
of Philip, they had left Lord Wentworth, the governor,
with no more than five hundred soldiers for its defence
in a time of war. Towards the latter end of the same
year reports were frequent that her life could not be
much longer continued, and the hopes of the nation
were directed to the Princess Elizabeth, whose inclinations as well as her interest were on the side of reformation. There was a gentleman of Shropshire, Edward
Burton, of Longnor, who was strongly attached to the
reformed doctrine. He had been compelled to hide
himself frequently for fear of being called to account for
his religion, the exercise of which he had privately
continued at his own house throughout these dangerous
times. He was an aged man, but his feelings were
alive to the miseries of his country, and to the afflictions
of the Church. The reports of the queen's illness had
reached his residence near Shrewsbury, when one
morning the church-bells of St. Chad's were heard to
ring merrily, and he thought it possible these sounds

[1] WARTON, Harmer, p. 141.

might announce the accession of Elizabeth to the throne.
His son undertook to go to Shrewsbury to learn the
news; and as the road by which he would return passed
in front of the house on the opposite side of the Severn,
to reach the bridge below, it was agreed that if the sur-
mise should prove correct, he should wave a handkerchief as he passed to signify it to his father.   The old
man watched for his return, and saw the signal; it told
of returning peace and liberty, not to himself only, but
to his country and his religion; and he went into his
house, breathed his nunc dimittis, and laid him down
and died.   They buried him in his garden, because it
was not yet lawful to bury a 'heretic' in a churchyard;
and his epitaph, preserved by his descendants, who
have continued at the same place,[1] relates the incident,
and why he was like his Saviour in his place of sepul-
ture.

Tho queen's death took place on the 17th of November, 1558, and Cardinal Pole, who had been ill some
time, died a few hours after.   It is instructive to follow
out the history of another agent in these miserable
persecutions, her confessor Carranza, already mentioned.
He was a man of great distinction in his own country,
and one of the divines sent from Spain to the Council of
Trent.   He was firmly attached to the Church of Rome,
as Pole was, with whom, during his residence in England, he formed a great intimacy.   He had preached at
many executions of heretics in Spain, and he was not
slack in the same kind of occupation while he resided in
England.   But he was not quite bad enough for the
spirits of his own party.   He was learned, and had been
captivated in his youth with the writings of Erasmus.
He thought that terror was a good instrument to maintain unity, but instruction a better.   He was employed
in England, in preparing a catechism in the Spanish

---

[1] It is believed that the late Dr. Edward Burton, the lamented Regius
Professor of Divinity at Oxford, was a descendant of this gentleman.

language, to give a little knowledge to the people ; and
he thought that all ought to be allowed to read the
Scriptures. This was enough to raise a host of enemies
against him.   He was, however, promoted by Philip,
in A.D. 1559, to the dignity of archbishop of Toledo
and primate of Spain ; and he came into his province, and was shortly after summoned to the deathbed of Charles V.   When he came he found the emperor near his end : holding in his hand a crucifix,
and falling on his knees by his bed side, he said : ' Let
your Majesty be of good comfort; sin has no more
power—the death of Jesus Christ has blotted out all
that was against you—all is pardoned.'   A monk of the
order of St. Jerome, who was in the apartment, noted
down his words, and cited others who were present
as witnesses.   It was considered that he had by these
words intended to express his contempt for the sacrament of confession, since he had given the emperor absolution before he had confessed him.   He was accused
to the Inquisition, seized and imprisoned, and passed the
remainder of his life, sixteen long years, a prisoner, first
at Valladolid, and afterwards at Rome.[1]   At length he
was made to abjure Lutheran tenets, as if they were his
own, though he had never held them; and after the most
abject submission and protracted sufferings, he died a
short time before he was to have been liberated, the
victim of that ruthless system of which he had been the
too willing agent.   Who would not rather have died like
Cranmer? Carranza declared upon his deathbed, that he
had done everything that he did in England by order of
the king his master.[2]

---

[1] LLORENTE, Hist. of the Inquisition.
[2] British Magazine, loco citato.

CHAPTER XXV.

QUEEN ELIZABETH.   RESTORATION OF THE REFORMED
RELIGION.

> The city, which thou seest, no other deem
> Than great and glorious Rome, queen of the earth,
> With gilded battlements conspicuous far,
> Turrets, and terraces, and glittering spires,
> All nations now to Rome obedience pay,
> To Rome's great emp'ror—these two thrones except.
>
> *Paradise Regained.*

THE Princess Elizabeth was twenty-five years of age
when she succeeded her sister, A.D. 1558. The
hopes of the people had long been turned towards her;
and public sympathy was excited, when they knew that
she had been in danger from accusers, and when it was
perceived that the jealousy of Mary had kept her often
in restraint, and as far as possible out of public view.[1]
It is said that on entering the Tower as queen, where
she had before been a prisoner, she expressed her thankfulness to God for the preservation of her life during
her sister's reign; and on her way to her coronation,
she confirmed the favourable impression of her character, by receiving, with an appearance of satisfaction, an
English Bible which was lowered from a triumphal arch
as she passed, and pressing it to her bosom. The
Marian bishops were unwilling to recognise her title;
and although she consented to be crowned according to
the rites of the Church of Rome, which was then the
religion of the country, there was but one of them,
Oglethorpe bishop of Carlisle, who could be induced
to perform the ceremony. And her position as regards
the Roman see was rendered still more precarious when
the pope, Paul IV., refused to recognise her as Queen
of England, declaring that the British Crown was a fief

---

[1] NOAILLES, v. 85.

of the popedom, and that it was high presumption in her to assume it without his consent.

Elizabeth proceeded with that sagacity in the choice of her ministers, and that resolution in the accomplishment of her purposes, which have rendered her reign remarkable. She gave her chief confidence to Sir William Cecil and Sir Nicholas Bacon, the first of whom became her Secretary of State, and the other Lord Keeper, in the room of Heath archbishop of York, who resigned the post of Lord Chancellor. She took the advice of Cecil, as to the best mode of proceeding in the restoration of the Reformed religion, and his answers show that his sagacious mind was able to foresee every one of those obstacles with which she had afterwards to contend: the sentence of excommunication and deposition by the pope, the hostility of foreign sovereigns, the opposition of the Marian bishops, the inclinations of a party at home, and the violence of another party, who would desire to carry the Reformation to unreasonable lengths. But Cecil hoped that these obstacles would be overcome, and measures were taken accordingly.

The parliament was called in January, 1559; and a proclamation had been previously issued, similar to those which had been put forth both by Edward and Mary, to put a stop to all preaching for a time, but allowing the litany and the epistle and gospel in English, as they had been in the time of their father. This was a significant indication of the intentions of the queen. But as the clergy were not yet brought again under those restrictions upon their deliberations in convocation which Henry VIII. had imposed, they were no sooner assembled with the parliament than they resolved to anticipate the measures of the court by a solemn declaration of their adherence to the Roman doctrine. They therefore passed resolutions, in which they declared their belief in transubstantiation, and maintained that the clergy alone have authority to

determine points of faith. Harpsfield was prolocutor of
the lower house of convocation, and he delivered these
articles to Bonner, to be presented by him to the Lord
Keeper. But the only result was, that a disputation
was appointed to take place in Westminster Abbey,
between the bishops and others of their party, and certain of the most eminent divines holding the Reformed
opinions. The points to be discussed were three:
'Whether it is against the Word of God and the custom of the ancient Church, to officiate and administer
the sacraments in a language unknown to the people?
Whether every Church has authority to appoint, change,
and set aside ceremonies and ecclesiastical rites, provided it be done to edification? And whether it can
be proved, by the Word of God, that there is offered
in the mass a propitiatory sacrifice for the quick and
dead!' The disputation was to begin on the last day
of March, four bishops and four other divines, of
whom Harpsfield was one, being appointed on the
Roman Catholic side; and on that of the Reformation,
Scory late bishop of Chichester, with seven others,
among whom were Cox, Horne, Aylmer, and Grindal,
names already distinguished, and Jewel, who soon became more eminent than any of them. The Romish
bishops could hardly have refused, in any case, to defend their doctrine, when thus challenged; but their
present position made it impossible to do so. They
owed the situation which they occupied to the violent
and arbitrary proceedings of the late reign, by which
the Reformed Church of England had been subverted,
its prelates removed by banishment or by a violent
death, and the doctrines and supremacy of Rome restored by foreign influence, even though by the forms
of law. Whatever, therefore, had been done in the
late reign by the parliament and the government for
restoring the papal supremacy and the creed of modern
Rome, the same means might now be taken for revert-
ing to the system which had previously been established.

But they were not willing to submit their doctrine to public disputation, and therefore, though they accepted the challenge, they would not adhere to the terms on which they had at first agreed that it should be conducted. Being rebuked for this non-compliance by the Lord Keeper, who presided, the Bishops of Winchester and Lincoln threatened to excommunicate the queen, for which they were committed to the Tower, and the conference ended greatly to the disadvantage of the Romish party.

Before this conference took place, though not before the convocation had passed the resolutions out of which it arose, the parliament had passed an act for restoring the royal supremacy, and the other laws of Henry VIII. and Edward VI. which depended upon it. The measures of the late reign had been so unpopular, and the cruelties by which they were enforced had so alienated people's minds from the government of Queen Mary, that no less than sixty-five members of the House of Commons had absented themselves during her two last parliaments. It was not therefore surprising that the parliament of Elizabeth should willingly revert to the previous state of things. By this law the Queen was declared to be Supreme Governor of the Church, very properly declining the appellation of its Head, as a term belonging only to Our Saviour. But it would have been well if she had shown equal moderation in the kind of government she intended to exercise over the Church. It is most true that the kings of England are supreme in their own dominions over all persons and causes, ecclesiastical as well as civil; so that the pretence of the pope with his clergy, to make laws relating to religion without consulting the laws of the land, is a most unjustifiable usurpation. But Elizabeth attempted to affix a further meaning to this supremacy. It was enacted that she should have power to appoint commissioners, for an indefinite period and with indefinite powers, to execute all manner of jurisdiction in

Church affairs; and we shall have occasion to observe
the ill-effects resulting from the manner in which this
power was executed. The Archbishop of York and
the Bishop of Chester spoke against passing the bill;
and though they were clearly in the wrong in maintaining the papal supremacy, it must be confessed that
the strongest part of their argument was derived from
the fact, that such a measure seemed to make the kings
of England a sort of spiritual governors, to which both
the Puritans and the Romanists equally objected, and
which the Church of England has never acknowledged.

Another law which encountered much opposition from
the Romish bishops, and not without reason, was that
which gave back to the crown the impropriate rectories
which Mary had restored to the Church, and authorised
the queen to give them in exchange to the bishops and
take their lands to her own use, on every vacancy of a
see. But that to which they were chiefly opposed was
the Act of Uniformity, for restoring the Liturgy of King
Edward and enforcing its observance. It has been constantly objected to the Reformed Church of England,
that it is a religion by act of parliament, because its
liturgy was sanctioned by law. But no imputation can
be more unjust, in the sense in which it is intended. If
the parliament had now assumed the functions of a
synod, and had put forth a liturgy of its own, the accusation would have been just. But the Liturgy of Edward
VI. had been adopted equally by the convocation and
parliament, forming together the great national council
of a national Church. This Church had awaited in vain a
general reformation, which all Christendom had for two
centuries desired; and when at length, in despair of universal concurrence, the whole realm of England had resolved to take measures for the reformation of their own
Church, the reformation thus accomplished had been
overthrown by violence. There are occasions, and this was
one, which are a rule by themselves; and if ever a people
and a government were justified in a national act, they

were justified in resolving at once to restore a form of worship and a system of church-government, now doubly dear to them for the sake of those who had given their life's blood in its cause. Commissioners had been appointed, soon after the queen's accession, to consider whether any alterations should be made; and it was appointed that the words used in the delivery of the holy eucharist should be such as we now have them, embodying the two forms together which were in the two Liturgies of Edward VI. This was done in order to restore the words which declare the consecrated elements to be the Body and Blood of Christ; and a corresponding alteration was made when the Articles came to be reviewed, so as to admit the doctrine of a real presence. None of the bishops who remained could be induced to acquiesce in these measures, and the Abbot of Westminster as well as the Bishop of Chester spoke strongly against them. But the law was passed in the end of April, and the Liturgy was ordered to come into use on St. John Baptist's day, June 24, 1559; but it was used in most places on Whit-Sunday, nor have its sweet and holy services been ever since discontinued, except during one short and memorable period.

The first act of the royal supremacy was to issue injunctions relative to religion similar to those of King Edward. But they differed in some particulars, where they were wisely modified to consult the feelings of the Romish party. Where stone altars had not yet been removed, it was stated to be ' a matter of no great moment, saving for an uniformity, so that the sacrament be duly and reverently ministered.' And while it was implied that they were better removed, it was ordered that it should not be done but by the oversight of the curate and churchwardens. Again, in the ' Form of bidding the prayers the queen's supremacy was thus moderately expressed by the words, ' Supreme Governour of this realm, as well in causes ecclesiastical as civil.' A general visitation was next appointed by royal authority, during the vacancy of the see of Canterbury, and the visitors were empowered to eject all those of the clergy who would not conform to the religion now restored. A more permanent commission was soon afterwards appointed, by virtue of a clause for that purpose in the Act of Supremacy, and this became the famous High Commission Court. It has been objected to this commission that the powers which it granted to the commissioners were similar to those of the Inquisition which Philip II. attempted to establish in the Low Countries. It is too true that these powers were of an objectionable kind, but they were copied from a commission of Queen Mary, by whom the model attempted in the Low Countries by her husband was introduced into England.

The first business of these commissioners was to administer the oath of supremacy to the clergy, and require the observance of the Reformed Liturgy. As soon as the parliament was dissolved, the queen sent for the bishops, and urged them to comply with the laws. The archbishopric of Canterbury was vacant since the death of Cardinal Pole, and several other bishops having died about the same time, there remained at this time no more than fourteen bishops in possession of their sees. All of these had complied with Queen Mary's proceedings, though many of them had supported Henry VIII. in his opposition to the see of Rome—especially Heath archbishop of York, Tonstal of Durham, and Thirlby of Ely. But Heath had been ejected for nonconformity under Edward, and Tonstal, who coincided with Cranmer in many of his views, had been unhappily forced into the opposite side to gratify the ambition of Northumberland, who coveted his lands. There were three bishops remaining alive who had been ejected under Mary — Coverdale of Exeter, Barlow of St. Asaph, and Scory of Chichester; and a bill had been brought into parliament to restore them to their sees, but it was dropped, probably because the government then hoped to conciliate the Marian bishops. In this expectation they were disappointed. The Archbishop of York answered for himself and his brethren, entreating the queen to observe the engagements which her sister had contracted with the see of Rome. Elizabeth replied that she and her subjects were resolved to be governed by the resolution of Joshua, that himself and his house would serve the Lord; that she had called her parliament together, in imitation of Josiah, to make a covenant with God, and not with the Bishop of Rome; that it was not in her sister's power to bind her successors to an usurped authority; that her crown being wholly independent, she would own no sovereign except Jesus the King of kings; that the pope's usurpation over princes was intolerable; and that she should look upon all her subjects, both clergy and laity, as enemies to God and the crown, who should from henceforth abet his pretensions.

The result was that all the bishops except one refused to comply, and were successively ejected from their sees; though much hope was entertained both of Heath and Tonstal, whose bishoprics were kept vacant for nearly two years. They were all treated with respect, and with a degree of moderation which contrasted favourably with the violence of the late reign. Bonner alone was imprisoned; of the rest a few retired abroad, but the greater part remained in England, residing either at their own houses, or in the families of the newly appointed bishops. Tonstal lived and died at Lambeth, the honoured guest of Archbishop Parker, and Heath was sometimes visited by the queen at his own house at Cobham, in Surrey. They appear to have conformed to the Liturgy, and it is due to them to say, that they repaid the generosity with which they were treated, by never making any attempt to continue their episcopate, or to set up a rival succession in the English Church. Of the rest of the clergy, a considerable number of dignitaries were ejected: one abbot, four priors, and one abbess—twelve deans, fourteen archdeacons, and sixty prebendaries. But almost the whole body of the parochial clergy conformed to the Reformation, for out of nine thousand four hundred livings then computed in England, not more than one hundred parish-priests refused to comply. Those who were turned out had pensions assigned them, proportioned to the value of their preferments. An offer was even made to Fecknam, abbot of Westminster, that his abbey should remain if he and his monks would conform, but on their refusal it was converted into a collegiate church. The houses of the Knights of St. John were now also finally dissolved, both in London and at Kilmainham in Ireland, where the last Grand Prior, Sir Oswald Massingberd, was attainted by Act of Parliament[1] for refusing to surrender, and thus the monastic life was banished from the kingdom.

Everything that had yet been done had been done in a spirit of conciliation. The offensive petition, to be delivered 'from the Bishop of Rome and all his detestable enormities,' had been omitted from the Litany, and every conciliation had been attempted that was consistent with the resolution to maintain the independence of the Church of England. And the general concurrence of the parochial clergy appears to indicate that they were satisfied on the whole. But the refusal of the bishops gave rise to a serious difficulty. No instance had occurred in the Church Catholic, until the period of the Reformation, in which ordination had been conferred by any who were not bishops. And although the Lutheran and Genevan Churches had ventured to adopt the Presbyterian system, they had done it reluctantly, and as a matter of necessity, acknowledging their wish to retain episcopal government. But if all the bishops of the English Church had refused to concur in the Reformation, that Church might possibly have resorted to the same alternative. The opinions

[1] Irish Statutes, 2 Eliz. c. 7 & 8. Sir James Ware, An. Hiber.

prevalent at that time among some of the Reformers, render it not improbable that such a course would have been pursued. This is what seems to have been done in Denmark; and the convention at Leith, by which bishops were allowed in the Reformed Church of Scotland, appears to have acted upon these principles. But it is the happiness of the Church of England, and it seems to have been by the especial Providence of God, that she alone of all the Reformed Churches was not tempted to this course; and while we have gained that pure faith which it is our blessing to inherit, we have not been deprived of the succession of our bishops, and of their apostolical commission from the original Church in England. It has been mentioned, that there were still alive three bishops of the Reformed opinions who had been formerly in possession of sees—Coverdale, Scory, and Barlow. There were also two suffragan bishops, of Thetford and Bedford, besides Kitchen of Llandaff, who alone of those now in possession of their sees had complied with the law, but whose character rendered his compliance suspicious. All the Irish bishops conformed except three, but their sentiments were not favourable to the Reformation, except in the case of Bale, Bishop of Ossory, who had been in exile. The queen had made choice of Matthew Parker for the see of Canterbury, who had been chaplain to her mother, Anne Boleyn, a man of great learning and equal piety, of tried devotion to the cause of reformation, and of such modesty that he was only with the greatest reluctance, and after long delay, persuaded to accept the office by the express command of the queen. At length, on the 9th of December 1559, he was consecrated at the chapel at Lambeth by Barlow, Scory, and Coverdale, assisted by Hotchkin, the suffragan bishop of Bedford; and he soon after filled up the other sees, to which some of the most distinguished Reformers were appointed—Grindal to London, Cox to Ely, Sandys to Worcester, and Jewel to Salisbury, while Barlow was translated from

I I

St. Asaph to Chichester, and Scory from Chichester to
Hereford.   There was a foolish story invented some
forty years afterwards, as if Archbishop Parker had not
been duly consecrated.   It was attributed to a chaplain
of Bonner's, who said the new bishops dined together at
the Nag's Head, in Fleet Street, and that he looked
through the key hole and saw Scory lay a Bible upon
the head of each, saying, ' Take thou authority to preach
the Word of God;' upon which they were deemed to be
bishops.   This story was never heard of at the time, not
even by Saunders, who wrote most violently against the
Reformation; and its falsehood was established by the
testimony of a nobleman who had been present at the
consecration of Parker, and who was yet alive when the
story was told, as well as by the original records of
that event which are still preserved, and in which the
whole proceedings are minutely described.[1]

It might have been hoped that bright days were now
at hand, and that the Church which had passed through
such trials, and which seemed to be restored by the
especial Providence of God, would be permitted to enjoy
in peace that pure form of worship which had been
bought by so many sacrifices.   And for a little while it
seemed so; and amidst the conflict of opinions which
so soon broke out again, we ought not to forget how
many there have been ever since, unknown indeed and
unrecorded, yet not less blessed, to whom the holy
services of this Church have afforded peace in life and
hope in death.   It is a remarkable instance of the
enthusiasm which prevailed in many places in favour of
the Reformation, which Bishop Jewel mentioned in a
letter to Bullinger, that he had seen five thousand people
singing a psalm together at Paul's Cross.   The practice
of parochial psalmody does not seem to have made much
progress in England during the earlier time of the Re-

---

[1] For further particulars, see *The Validity of the Holy Orders of the
Church of England*, by the Rev. JOSEPH OLDKNOW, D.D.

formation. The Lollards were so much opposed to the
abuse of church-music which they witnessed, that they
would have banished it altogether. But the Psalms
were translated into English metre by Sternhold and
Hopkins in the time of Edward, and the exiles who had
adopted the practice from the example of the Reformed
Churches abroad, now promoted it in every way. A
complaint was made about this time to the queen's
council, against the Dean and Chapter of Exeter, that
they had hindered the people from assembling to sing
psalms in their cathedral before divine service. The
morning prayer was then at six o'clock, and it appears
that before that hour the church was thronged by the
inhabitants, who came to join with some persons from
London, who met there to sing psalms.[1] The council
insisted that they should not be prevented, and it would
have been well if the royal supremacy had never been
exerted in any more offensive way. On the other hand,
those whose inclination or principles would have leaned
towards the ancient services, had no notion as yet of
forming separate congregations. They might disap-
prove of some things that were done, but they continued to come to church, and nothing is more certain
than that the whole nation complied with the national
religion for the first ten or twelve years after the accession of this queen. It remains to see by what means
the separation which followed was brought about, which
may be traced to three principal causes—the conduct of
the papal court, the violence of the puritan party, and
the mistaken notions of church-government adopted by
Queen Elizabeth.

[1] See the account of this in the *Concilia* of Wilkins.

CHAPTER XXVI.

CONDUCT OF THE PAPAL PARTY. CONDUCT OF THE PURITANS.
HOOKER. CONCLUSION.

> But, dearest Mother, (what those miss)
> The mean, thy praise and glory is,
> And long may be!
> Blessed be God, whose love it was
> To double-moat thee with his grace,
> And none but thee.
>
> G. HERBERT's *British Church.*

PAUL IV. was succeeded in the papal chair, in August 1559, by Pius IV., a prelate of energy and character, and of more moderation than his predecessor. In the following May he sent a letter to the queen by the hands of a legate, couched in terms of respect and affection, entreating her to return to the allegiance of the papal see. There is reason to believe that the nuncio was empowered to propose to the queen, that if she would abandon the supremacy and acknowledge the pope, he would sanction the English liturgy, permit the sacrament to the English nation in both kinds, and confirm her mother's marriage. But Elizabeth had taken her part, and she resolved to abide by it. The nuncio, therefore, was sent back without having been permitted to land in England, doubtless under the authority of the statute of *præmunire*, which had often been enforced in this way before. And, indeed, there were many other points which must have been surrendered, even if she had been able to obtain these terms. On the 26th of November, 1559, a sermon had been preached at Paul's Cross by Jewel, then bishop-elect of Salisbury, in which he openly challenged the papal party to defend twenty-seven tenets, which he enumerated as then held by them; and he repeated the challenge before the court the following year. He declared that 'if they' would bring any one sufficient sentence out of any old Catholic doctor, or father, or general council, or holy Scripture, or any one example in the primitive Church, whereby it may clearly and plainly be proved, during the first six hundred years,' that any one of these tenets was held, 'he should be content to yield and subscribe.' The chief of them were as follows :—' That there was at any time any private mass in the world : or any communion ministered under one kind: or that the people had their common prayer in a strange tongue : or that the Bishop of Rome was then called an universal bishop, or the head of the universal Church : or that the people were then taught to believe that Christ's body is really, substantially, corporeally, carnally, or naturally in the sacrament : or that the lay-people were then forbidden to read the Word of God in their own tongue : or that images were then set up in churches, to the intent the people might worship them.' This challenge was answered, among others, by Harding, who has been mentioned as having been severely rebuked by Lady Jane Gray for deserting the Reformation, of which he had been a violent advocate, within a week after Queen Mary's accession. He was now a divine of Louvain, and his answer caused Jewel to write his famous *Apology for the Church of England*, which was followed soon after by a longer treatise, entitled the *Defence of the Apology*. It may be regretted that the tone of this famous work was not of a more conciliatory character; but the language of the other party called for some severity. Harding asserted that the Bishop of Rome is always infallible in his determinations; that he is under the constant direction of the Holy Spirit; that we are to learn God's pleasure from him; that he is the centre of unity, and the main support of the Church; that whoever separates from his communion is a heretic; and that there is no hope of salvation without submission to the apostolic see. The *Apology* was translated

into Latin in A. D. 1562, and was put forth with the
approbation of the queen and the bishops.

But in the meantime another attempt had been made
by the papal party.   The pope had resolved to convene
another session of the Council of Trent, and he again
sent a conciliatory message to the queen, inviting her to
send either bishops or ambassadors to the council.   But
this also was declined, partly on account of some rebellions in Ireland which the pope's nuncio at that same
moment fomented, but mainly on the ground that England was resolved to acknowledge no council that was
called by the authority of the pope.   This was in A.D.
1561, and it was the last attempt at conciliatory measures
made by the papal court.   The French had induced the
young Queen of Scots, who was married to their king,
to lay claim to the throne of England, on the ground of
Elizabeth being illegitimate : and they had urged the
pope to pass sentence against her of deposition and
excommunication.   To provide against such courses, a
law was made in the parliament of 1562, called an 'Act
of Assurance of the Queen's Power,' by which all
persons in holy orders, lawyers, and civil officers were
required to take the oath of supremacy; the first refusal
of which should incur the *præmunire*, and the second
should be high-treason.   But it was not to be offered
the second time to any who had not been ecclesiastical
persons either in the reign of Mary, or her two predecessors, unless they should refuse to observe the rites of
the Church of England; and this law was not enforced
except in extreme cases.   For Archbishop Parker wrote
to the suffragans of his province not to force the consciences of inoffensive persons by offering the oath without necessity, and when it was refused the first time, in
no case to tender it the second, which involved the
penalty of treason, without consulting him.   Nor was
it offered to any of the deprived bishops, excepting
Bonner, who refused it.   But the favourers of the pope
continued to come to church, and the government was

chiefly occupied for some years in the contests with the
Puritans, which had now arisen to an alarming height.
At length, about the year 1567, it was found that Harding and Saunders were going about England, with authority from the pope to absolve all those who should
return to his communion; and a year later a discovery
was made, calculated to excite feelings of just indignation. Thomas Heath, a brother of the deprived archbishop of York, had obtained permission from the
Bishop of Rochester to preach in his cathedral; and
affecting puritan opinions, took occasion to impugn the
English Liturgy, as not being such prayers as are to be
found in Scripture. But he dropped a letter in the pulpit, by which it was discovered that he was a Jesuit in
disguise, and was in correspondence with the leaders of
that order in Spain, by whom he was employed to spread
puritan opinions, in order to sow dissension in the
Church of England. His lodgings were searched, and
a licence was found from the Jesuits, and a bull from
the pope, Pius V., authorising him to preach such doctrines as his superiors should enjoin; and several books
were found in his possession against Infant Baptism, for
the purpose of disseminating the tenets of the Anabaptists. Such were the first operations in England of
that famous society which had lately been founded by
Ignatius Loyola, and such the crooked courses to which
the Church of Rome was willing to resort, in order to
recover the grand idea of an Universal Church. The
punishment inflicted upon Heath was barbarous. But
it ought to have been a warning to the Puritans, who
were now rending the Church of England by their
factions, to suspect their own principles when they were
propagated by those whom they themselves rightly
regarded as their bitterest enemies. And there is good
reason to believe that this system was long carried on
by the Jesuits. Near eighty years afterwards the British
ambassador at the Hague gave intelligence to Archbishop Laud that the pope had given indulgences to the

several fraternities of the Roman Catholic communion, to educate young Englishmen in all manner of tenets contrary to those of the Church of England. He sent him the names of two who had lately come over, and he added that 'above sixty Romish clergymen were gone within two years out of the monasteries of the French king's dominions, to preach up the Scottish Covenant, and to spread the same about the northern parts of England.'[1]

It was in great measure owing to the contrivances of the same party that a formidable rebellion broke out in the summer of 1569, headed by the earls of Northumberland and Westmoreland. The insurgents professed a design to restore the Roman Catholic religion, and one Morton, who took a leading part, was believed to be an emissary of the pope, and to have instructions to declare the queen a heretic and her dominions forfeited. They marched to Durham, where they burnt the Bibles in the churches and set up the mass. But, however the people of those parts might stand affected, they did not join them in such numbers as was expected ; so that the Roman Catholic party began to fear that in another generation their adherents would forget their attachment to the see of Rome. To prevent this, colleges were founded, first at Douay, and then at Rome and elsewhere, for the education of English priests to preach up popery in England. Dr. William Allen was principal of the college at Douay, and Parsons the Jesuit of that at Rome, from which two places three hundred priests had been sent into England before the end of the reign of Queen Elizabeth. The zeal and self-devotion with which this object was prosecuted was worthy of a better cause.

But all these measures were incomplete, and would

---

[1] Letter to Abp. Laud from Sir. Wm. Boswell, ambassador at the Hague, 12th June 1640. Abp. Usher's *Letters and Life*, by Parr, App. p. 27.

have been insufficient, had not the pope confirmed them by his bull of excommunication and deposition against the queen and her adherents. This document bears date at Rome in the year 1570, and begins by declaring that He who reigns above hath consigned his one Holy Catholic Church, out of which there is no salvation, to the sole government of St. Peter and his successor the Bishop of Rome. By virtue of this authority, Pius V. proceeds to denounce Elizabeth, ' the pretended queen of England,' as a vassal of iniquity ; and after enumerating her offences, he declares her a heretic and an encourager of heretics ; that all who adhere to her are under anathema, and cut off from the unity of the body of Christ ; also, that she is deprived of all pretended right to the kingdom, that all her subjects who have sworn to her are for ever absolved from their oaths, and that all who shall henceforth obey her are involved in the like sentence of excommunication. This sentence was fatal to the unity of the English Church : for though the adherents of the pope for the most part still came to church for a few years longer, it is obvious that those who believed in the power thus claimed by him, must have done so with an uneasy conscience ; and it led to acts of retaliation on the part of the government, which they justified on the score of self-defence. In the year 1571 it was made high-treason to publish that the queen is a heretic, or an usurper ; and the like penalty was enacted against those who should publish any bull of reconciliation or absolution from Rome. A person was hanged as a traitor for posting up the bull of excommunication on the gates of the Bishop of London's palace ; and when the conduct of Roman Catholics, both at home and abroad, gave reason to believe that a design was entertained to assassinate the queen, still severer measures were passed. The massacre of St. Bartholomew at Paris, in A.D. 1572, approved as it was by the pope and hailed with universal joy at Rome as a sacred act of piety, could not fail to alarm the English Government. On that awfully memorable day, two thousand Protestants, collected at Paris under pretence of a royal marriage, and under the solemn protection of a royal promise, were massacred in cold blood; and this atrocious act, followed as it was by similar wickedness in the principal cities in the rest of France, was avowed by the king and his court, and solemnly approved by the Roman conclave. It is to be hoped that they believed the assertion falsely propagated by the French king, that the Protestants had engaged in a conspiracy against him; but this could not justify them in going in procession to return thanks before the altar, as for a victory, for an event which has stamped an indelible stigma upon their cause.

It was such things as these, and the dread of similar atrocities, which led to the severities that were exercised against the Roman Catholics in a later period of this reign. In the year 1580 it was made high treason to draw off any person from the Church of England to that of Rome, and all that should absent themselves from church were to incur the penalty of 20*l.*, while those who should willingly hear mass, were to pay one hundred marks, and be subject to a year's imprisonment. The Jesuits, Campion and Parsons, were active in spreading the Roman Catholic doctrine at the hazard of their lives, and at length, in 1581, Campion and three others were executed for treason, and several more suffered the like penalty soon after. Their party called them martyrs, while the government denounced them as traitors. It is certain that they did not suffer on account of their faith, but because it had seemed necessary, in self-defence, to affix the penalties of treason to the propagation of a creed which was now embarked in deadly hostility to the established religion and government. Such measures are defended on the ground of political necessity; but if nations would learn to forgive on Christian principles, it is probable they would find that to do right was their best defence.

But another evil, which sapped the vitals of this Church, arose from the dissensions among the Reformers themselves. Next to the proceedings of the Church of Rome, and in strange connection with them, the separation of the Puritans from the English Church tended to impair and weaken it. The principle on which the English Reformation was conducted was essentially different from that of the foreign Churches. In England, the avowed object had been to reform the Catholic Church, to recover its independence, and restore it to a primitive state, without destroying those ancient usages which had descended from primitive times. The foreign Reformers had gone further. They had sought to form for themselves a system of faith and worship according to their own views of Scripture alone. It was inevitable that such opposite principles should lead to differences between their respective advocates. We have seen something of those differences already, in the refusal of Hooper to wear the episcopal dress, and in the troubles at Frankfort. But now that the English Reformation was restored, there was a large party who had imbibed the opinions of the Reformed Churches abroad during their exile, who were bent upon carrying out those principles at home. This party, not adverting to the notion of reforming the Catholic Church, considered every vestige of Catholic usages as a badge of Popery; and having learned to regard the foreign Protestants as in some sort their spiritual fathers, were dissatisfied with the intermediate position adopted by the English Church. It is probable that many of them would be averse to the royal supremacy, since Calvin had expressed himself against it, and John Knox was also opposed to it. But they did not stop here. The following are some of their objections, as given, not by an enemy, but by one of their own writers.[1] They disapproved of the use of the

---

[1] Brown's *History of the British Churches.*

surplice and other garments worn by the priests or
bishops; they did not allow the office of bishops to be
superior to that of priests or presbyters; they disliked
the titles and offices of archdeacons, deans, and chapters;
they complained of the restriction of ministers to *set
forms of prayer*, and of what they called the vain repe-
titions prescribed in the Book of Common Prayer;
they disapproved of instrumental music, of singing of
prayers and other papal forms, as they termed them, in
cathedral churches, of kneeling at the communion,
turning to the east, bowing at the name of Jesus, and
the use of the ring in marriage.

It is obvious that the concession of all these points
would have involved a total surrender of those principles on which this Church had been reformed. And it
should be remembered that large concessions had been already made, when the first Liturgy of King Edward had
been modified as it was, in accordance with the advice of
foreigners. But when it had been resolved to concede
no further, another question naturally arose,—how far it
was incumbent upon those who might differ in some
respects from what was done, to yield to the decision of
the National Church and Government. Jewel and many
others, who had wished the use of the surplice abolished,
wisely considered it their duty to adopt it; and Coverdale, who was entirely of that party, officiated in a surplice at the consecration of Archbishop Parker. It
appears that the bishops were reluctant to force the
observance of ceremonies, however becoming in themselves, especially upon men some of whom had been
their own friends and fellow-exiles, and perhaps they
hoped that time would wear out their scruples. But in
the year 1564 the queen insisted that the archbishop
should take measures for enforcing uniformity, and
certain Articles were drawn up for that purpose. In
these it was, among other things, provided, that none
should preach without a license from the bishop; that
the principal minister officiating at the Holy Commu-

nion in cathedrals should use a cope, and all other clergymen a surplice; and that all communicants should receive kneeling.   These Advertisements, and the proceedings which followed upon them, occasioned the first open separation of the Nonconformists from the Church of England; and that so much the more, because they appeared to emanate from the bishops and not from the queen.   For although it was done by her express command, she chose to throw the responsibility upon them; and the odium was increased by some of her ministers, Leicester and Walsingham especially, taking the part of the Puritans.   The most eminent of those who refused to comply were Cartwright, Regius Professor of Divinity at Cambridge, and Sampson and Humphries, the Dean of Christchurch and President of Magdalen College at Oxford.   The last wrote to consult Bullinger and Gualter, whose authority was highly respected in England, and their advice was that they should comply. And Grindal, now bishop of London, who had decidedly inclined to the same opinions, wrote also to Bullinger as follows: ' When they who had been exiles in Germany could not persuade the queen and parliament to remove these habits out of the Church, though they had long endeavoured it, by common consent they thought it best not to leave the Church for some rites which were not many in themselves, nor wicked, especially since the purity of the Gospel remained safe and free to them; nor had they at this present time repented themselves of this counsel.' [1]

Unhappily, there were many who were not content to adopt this course; and in the beginning of the year 1566, the archbishop, still acting by the queen's express command, convened the whole of the London clergy, and required them to promise conformity.   All who would not promise were suspended, with sentence of deprivation if they did not conform in three months;

---

[1] See CARDWELL's *Documentary Annals*, i. 299, note.

and the number of those who refused, and thus became
the first nonconformists, amounted to thirty-seven.
Their first congregation was formed in the following
year, A.D. 1567, the very same year in which the emis-
saries of Rome began to absolve those who would return
to their communion, and in which also the first discovery was made of the attempts of the Jesuits to foment
the discontent of the Puritans.   Thenceforth the history
of nonconformity is one of mutual recrimination between the two parties into which the English Reformation was thus unhappily divided.   It can hardly be
doubted now, that the decision of the Church of England
on the main points at issue was right; still less can it
be denied, that the wise and moderate course was that
of those who chose to submit to the ordinances of that
Church, even in spite of their own particular wishes.
Nor could it fail to excite something of indignation in
those who saw the work of reformation tarnished by
such mistaken pertinacity; but, on the other hand, it
must be for ever regretted, that the strong arm of the
civil government should have interfered in such a case.
It is impossible to say whether any concessions would
have reconciled the party holding such opinions to
remain in the communion of the Church.   But the
course that was adopted had the effect of precipitating
a separation which was perhaps inevitable, at the same
time that it seemed to afford a justification to those who
wore the immediate sufferers.

A third cause which operated to mar the success of
the English Reformation, was stated to be the mistaken
notions of Church government adopted by Queen Elizabeth.   The proper notion of a National Church is that
in which the clergy and the people so concur in the laws
relating to religion, that no such laws can be made by
the clergy without the consent of the people, nor by
these without the consent of the clergy.   In opposition
to this principle, the clergy in the Church of Rome had
for some ages usurped the whole legislative power of

the Church; and the royal supremacy was originally nothing more than the resumption of a right inherent in the crown, on behalf of the authorities of the state, to be assenting to all such laws as should be made. But Henry VIII. was so absolute a monarch, that he in fact engrossed the whole legislative power; and his daughter, though she wisely rejected the offensive expression of the Head of the Church, was resolved to govern it notwithstanding. According to her notions, the legislative authority of the Church would have resided in herself and the convocation of the clergy, in the same way as that of the state resided in herself and the parliament; and having made use of the parliament to restore the religion of the Reformation, her object was to prevent that body from meddling any more. But this would have been in fact to bring back, under another form, the very evil that had been before complained of; and so it was thought by the House of Commons, one of whose members, Wentworth, said once to the bishops, 'Make you popes who list, for we will make you none.' It was upon this principle that the queen twice prevented the parliament from making laws relating to the discipline of the Church. Not that she was averse to discipline, but that she wished that the clergy alone should make such laws, by way of canons, to be promulgated in her own name. When the Articles were agreed upon by the convocation, the parliament wished to adopt them; but she forbade them, alleging that 'she was minded to put them forth on her own authority alone,' nor was it till some years later that this point was carried. But the strongest instance of her resolution to be the sole governor of the Church was her treatment of Archbishop Grindal. She had promoted him from the see of London to the archbishopric of York, and from thence, on Parker's death, to that of Canterbury. Not long after, she ordered him to put down certain religious exercises among the clergy called Prophesyings, of which she disapproved. These were meetings held by the clergy among themselves at their different churches, where passages of Scripture were discussed, and other matters debated. It seems that some of the Nonconformists came sometimes, and that some things were said against the Liturgy. The archbishop, however, was of opinion that they might be useful if duly regulated, and he wrote to the queen a letter of respectful but firm remonstrance against her interference in the government of the Church in spiritual matters. Elizabeth was so offended that she suspended him from his functions; and though the rest of the bishops, and afterwards the convocation, petitioned on his behalf, he never afterwards fully regained her favour. It is by such acts as these that the royal supremacy has become a name of doubtful import, and that the Church of England has been thought to be subject to a new tyranny in the place of that of Rome. But it is not necessarily so; what we require is, that it should be understood that no laws relating to spiritual matters should pass without the clergy, but that the clergy should make no such laws except with the consent of parliament. This point secured, the pastoral office may be exercised, without gainsaying, by those to whom it belongs by the divine appointment.

The Thirty-nine Articles were agreed upon by the convocation of the clergy in the year 1562. It has been already mentioned, that the doctrine of the Church relating to the Eucharist was now modified so as to admit a Real Presence. Another alteration that was made related to the authority of the Church. It was declared that the Church has power to decree rights and ceremonies, and authority in controversies of faith, subject, however, to the written Word of God. The whole of this sentence was omitted in some printed copies, which gave rise to a suspicion of its having been clandestinely inserted, but it has been positively shown that such was not the case. It is probable that those by whom this article was drawn, intended to signify that such au-.

thority resides in the synod of the clergy, but it appears that such a principle was not recognised by parliament. At the same convocation an attempt was made in the lower house to modify some of the usages, with a view to meet the wishes of the Puritans. It was proposed that the use of the cross in baptism should be optional, that the practice of kneeling at the sacrament should be left to the discretion of the ordinary, and that the minister in time of prayer should turn his face to the people. These proposals were negatived by a majority of one, and have never since been revived; and although the practice of turning to the people has pretty generally prevailed, it is contrary to the recorded decision of the Church. Like the rest of the practices on which the Puritans insisted, it involves the adoption or rejection of an important principle. To turn to the people in preaching and reading the Bible, and in offering prayer to God to turn away from them towards the more sacred part of the Church, where the holy mysteries are celebrated, has nothing in it superstitious in itself, but implies a recognition of the immediate presence of Him to whom our prayers are offered. But, to use the words of Archbishop Laud, ' Scarce anything hath hurt religion more in these broken times, than an opinion of too many men, that because Rome hath thrust some unnecessary and many superstitious ceremonies upon the Church, therefore the Reformation must have none at all ; not considering the while, that ceremonies are the hedge that fence the substance of religion from all the indignities which profaneness and sacrilege too commonly put upon it. And a great weakness it is, not to see the strength which ceremonies (things weak enough in themselves, God knows) add even to religion itself.' [1]

It was not until A.D. 1571, that the parliament succeeded, after more than one attempt, in obtaining the queen's consent to an act for the ratification of the Thirty-

---

[1] LAUD'S *Conference with Fisher*, Dedi. p. 1039.

nine Articles,[1] in which Act, without pretending to alter what the National Synod had decreed as articles of faith, they excepted those which relate to the authority of the Church, so as not to require subscription to them. Unhappily, the queen proceeded on her own authority in the way already mentioned, and in the canons which were passed in the same year, no such exception was allowed, nor would she allow the canons to be ratified by Parliament.

It remains to mention some other alterations that took place in this reign, relating to the services and doctrine of the Church. The Prayer-Book of Edward had contained no proper lessons for Sundays, but only for holidays; but when revised before the Act of Uniformity of Elizabeth's reign, certain lessons were appointed for Sundays also. And in the year 1560 a more complete arrangement of the lessons was made by Archbishop Parker, under the royal authority, which was very similar to that now in use. Some discretion, however, was left with the minister to vary the chapters occasionally, which remained till after the last Act of Uniformity at the Restoration. In the year 1561 it was ordered, that in addition to the Catechism in the Prayer-Book, which was intended for young persons before confirmation, and which did not as yet contain that part relating to the sacraments, a larger catechism should be provided for the further instruction of communicants, and a third in Latin for more learned persons. This work was confided to Dean Nowel, and the Catechism which bears his name was drawn up by him in 1562, and publicly authorised by the canons of 1571. There is nothing in the present condition of the Church more to be regretted than the discontinuance of the practice of public catechism in church; nothing which would tend so much, under God's blessing, to restore a healthy tone to the religion of the people as the revival of such a practice,

---

[1] 13 Eliz. c. 12.

and nothing for which the Reformers themselves more
assiduously laboured.

In the year 1568 a new translation of the Bible was
published by Archbishop Parker, which is generally
known as the ' Bishops' Bible.' It was a sort of revision of former translations, and was thought the more
necessary in consequence of the extensive sale of a Puritan edition, generally called the ' Geneva Bible,' which
contained marginal notes and comments, in which, together with much that was valuable, there was also
much that partook of a more questionable character.
For example, in one of these notes, bishops and archbishops were called ' apocalyptic locusts.' It is to be
feared that such language was only too true a sample of
much that was current among a certain class of Reformers. The *Book of Martyrs* of John Foxe, the most
popular book next after the Bible, was written in this
style. Foxe was a man of true piety, and of great
simplicity of character, nor can the honesty of his intentions be justly impeached ; but being also a man
whose judgment was less strong than his feelings, he
was easily led to adopt the opinions of the more violent
of his party. Having joined himself therefore with
John Knox at Geneva and Frankfort, he wrote his
laborious book after his return from exile, in the spirit
of one who believed that the whole Catholic Church was
apostate, and that all who had ever belonged to it were
servants of Antichrist. It is too true that the Catholic
Church had become awfully corrupt. It may be that
the papal power is or was a development of Antichrist ;
certainly it was thought to be so not by Puritans only,
but by such men as Cranmer and Ridley, and by many
before their time ; but such writings as those of Foxe,
valuable as they are by way of historical records, were
calculated to widen the breach between the two Churches,
and to engender a spirit of bitterness that is much to
be regretted.

And yet amidst this conflict of violent opinions on

either side, we still may trace an unbroken succession of good and holy men, who sought their happiness and found their reward in moderate opinions and laborious piety. Misunderstood perhaps at the time, because they would not belong to a party, they were suspected by both; yet theirs was the middle course between extreme opinions, and it is that course by which the Church of England has remained a witness to the world of Catholic principles on the one hand, and of primitive piety on the other. Archbishop Parker himself, however traduced by the party to whom he was opposed, was one of these: a man of most simple manners, without ambition and without ostentation, yet who knew the value of the Catholic Church, and by whose aid, under the divine blessing, Catholic principles were preserved to us. And such, in a different sphere, was Bernard Gilpin: a man who did not think it wrong to accept a living from his uncle Bishop Tonstal during the reign of Queen Mary, yet so far from being a papist, that he was on his way to London as a prisoner on a charge of heresy, under a warrant from Bonner, when he was delayed by a fall from his horse till after Queen Mary's death. As he made no scruple afterwards of maintaining Catholic principles, the Roman party made overtures to bring him to their side; but they found him among their most strenuous opponents. Firm in his conviction of the original right of independence in a national Church, he was instant in season and out of season in preaching the reformed doctrine, and his name is still revered among the inhabitants of the north of England. A little later was RICHARD HOOKER. It is not the smallest part of the praise of Bishop Jewel that he should have been the early patron at Oxford of such a man as Hooker. His five books of Ecclesiastical Polity, written in the retirement of a country parsonage, were called forth, as such works usually are, by the writings of Cartwright, under whose auspices the Puritan opinions seem to have sapped the foundations of the English Church. But Hooker undertook the defence of a reformation on Catholic principles, and he did it with a master's hand.

Three centuries have since elapsed, and the Church of England, through various fortune, has still continued a witness to the truths for which Hooker wrote and Ridley died. In the meantime some alterations of importance have taken place, which are the more deserving of notice, because they have been silently introduced. Of these the earliest, if not the most remarkable, has been the alteration effected in the use of the Liturgy by putting all the services together. So early as the reign of Edward VI., there had been an injunction that the communion service on holidays should follow the morning prayer. But in the year 1571, when Grindal was Archbishop of York, he issued injunctions to his province, in which he 'directed the minister not to pause between the morning prayer, litany and communion; but to continue and say the morning prayer, litany and communion, or the service appointed to be said when there was no communion, together, without intermission; to the intent the people might continue together in prayer, and hearing the Word of God ; and not depart out of the church during all the time of the whole divine service.' It is obvious that this injunction to the province of York could not be binding upon the National Church, but it is evidence of the state of things at the time, and the probability is that this practice had been already adopted elsewhere, and perhaps had been admitted by the exiles during the preceding reign. The original usage was for a length of time preserved in cathedral churches, and has been continued even to the present day in those of Winchester and Worcester, where the morning prayer is at an early hour, and the liturgy properly so called, that is, the communion service, is introduced by the litany at ten o'clock.[1]

---

[1] Since this was written, the practice has been discontinued at Worcester.

How far this change may have helped to give a different character to our services from that which was originally intended, need not be here discussed. But it is probable that it led to another equally remarkable alteration. One of the great complaints before the Reformation had been the infrequency of the holy communion, and it was intended to remedy this evil by appointing that it should be administered every Sunday and holiday at the least, and that some should always communicate with the priest. But this soon ceased to be the case, and it was appointed that some part of the service should still be used when there was no communion. At length, when it was complained that the service was too long, this part was also omitted, and the divine service, which ought to close with the holy communion, was concluded by the sermon. It is worthy of consideration how far this practice may have tended to give to the office of preaching a sacramental character. The proper food of our souls is the mystical body and blood of Christ; and if they are not fed with that, the more they love God, they will seek to satisfy their cravings after Him by other means; whence there may be a danger of expecting other things from the office of preaching than those which it is designed to convey. Another primitive usage which has silently been discontinued is, that of the bidding of prayer. The preacher before the sermon used to bid the people to pray for all sorts of persons, a practice which admitted of some variety and was very simple and natural, especially if he paused afterwards a little to allow them to pray in private. A specimen of such a prayer has been given above, as used a little before the Reformation, and it was continued afterwards in the royal injunctions of Elizabeth, and in the canons of James I. Instead of this, the Puritans indulged in long extempore prayers before their sermons, and when these were discontinued, the parochial clergy for the most part adopted one of the collects appointed to be said at the end of the communion

service, and when the rest of the post-communion also
was omitted, another of these collects was usually selected
after the sermon.[1]

It is not correct to suppose that the office of parish
clerk, or the practice of his answering alone for the
congregation, has been introduced since the Reformation.
In Bishop Ridley's book upon the Sacrament, where he
objects to the use of a Latin ritual, he says, ' The
people, or he which supplies the place of the people, is
compelled to say Amen, when he has not heard what the
priest has spoken.' And in one of King Edward's injunctions, ' parish clerks ' are mentioned as an office
already in existence. Another office was instituted
in the earlier part of the reign of Queen Elizabeth,
the loss of which has been regretted. It was agreed
by Archbishop Parker and the rest of the Bishops to
license persons as 'Readers,' who were to be in a
manner subsidiary to the priest or curate of the parish,
assisting him in the performance of divine service, and
intended to form a link between the minister and his
flock.[2] They were also employed to read the service
in those churches which by reason of the poverty of
their endowments had no incumbent, and might perform
all ecclesiastical functions except the celebration of the
Holy Communion. They might also read the Homilies,
but were not licensed to preach.[3] But this was afterwards
discountenanced, because the Puritans objected that the
readers were not preachers, and thus it seems to have
been found necessary to admit pluralities. The office
of deacon also has practically been merged in that of
priest, and the practice of consecrating coadjutor or

---

[1] The expression ' Bidding Prayer' seems to be another example of the
explanation of an obsolete word being added to the modern word, like
' let and hindered' in one of the collects. ' Bidding' is the same as 'Praying' in Anglo-Saxon and early English.

[2] BURN, Eccl. Law, iii. 283. STRYPE, Annals, v. i, p. 806.

[3] See also the Parker MSS. in C.C.C. Library, Cambridge.

suffragan bishops, which was continued in the reign
of Elizabeth, has unhappily also fallen into disuse.

An important change has arisen in the internal
arrangement of our churches, which deserves to be
considered. It is not indeed the case that there were
no pews before the Reformation. The name itself is
sometimes found, and although these were often open
seats, it is evident that distinguished persons had an
enclosed seat for themselves and their families. In the
record of a scandalous fray which took place in the reign
of Henry VI., in the church of St. Dunstan in the East
on Easter Sunday, between two noblemen and their
partisans, it is mentioned that one of them, Lord
L'Estrange, came out of a place called 'the closet,' in
which he had been hearing divine service, and the other,
Sir John Trussel, fell down when assaulted, between a
seat and a desk. And in the 'Supplication of poor
Commons' to Henry VIII. after the Act of the Six
Articles, complaint was made that the priest and others
put the Bible (which was ordered to be set up in
churches) 'either into the quire, or into *some pew where
poor men durst not presume to come.*' [1] But in general
the body of the church was fitted up with open seats,
such as still remain in many country places, the choir
being wholly reserved to the clergy, except that a seat
there was sometimes permitted to the patron, as is
mentioned in the diocesan canons of Bishop Grosthead.
It was not uncommon to fence off the upper end of
the side aisles with a beautiful screen of open wood-
work, which usually enclosed a small chantry reserved
for the burial of private families and for masses for
their souls. When these places ceased to be used for
the latter purpose, it is probable that the families to
whom they belonged would use them for attending
divine service, and thus the notion would be introduced
of having a distinguished 'pew' for the chief families

---

[1] STRYPE, *Eccl. Mem.* I. 612.

in a parish. By degrees, others would think themselves
entitled to the same, until the whole church was divided
into separate enclosures. But much has been done and
is now doing towards a return to a greater simplicity in
this respect.[1]

Another most important alteration has been effected
by the gradual substitution of a compulsory poor-rate
in the place of the weekly collection for the poor appointed to be made in church by the rubrics in the
Prayer Book. There is no doubt that the Act, commonly
known as the Poor Law Act, of the 43rd of Elizabeth,
was nothing else than an enlargement of several previous
statutes, by which it had been provided that the weekly
collection should be compulsory. It is probable that it
was not intended to discontinue the practice of collecting
also at church, but merely to enforce the contribution
upon those who are less willing; and it is a noble
provision of a Christian country. But at a time when
it has been found necessary to restrict the liberality with
which this fund had been administered, it is peculiarly
worthy of consideration how far we might provide
against the suffering incidental to the recent change, by
resuming the practice of Church collections.

In conclusion, it is probable that the just light in
which to contemplate the Reformed Church of England
is that of a providential dispensation, appointed to accomplish certain purposes, and be a witness to certain
truths, in the history of the Church of Christ. It would
not be difficult to trace many particular incidents which
appear to have been especially overruled towards the
accomplishment of this purpose. But as we need not
doubt that a National Church was justified in attempting
a reformation by itself, in despair of a general reformation, so have we much ground for thankfulness, amidst
some causes of regret, as to the mode in which it was

---

[1] It may be proper to mention that the above was written before the
publication of the Cambridge Camden Society's 'Tract upon Pews.'

accomplished.[1] That this Church was so justified in that course may be safely left to the simple unbiassed judgment of unprejudiced minds, and it will be on such grounds that the majority of persons will ever decide such questions. And there is this further observation to be made respecting the British Churches. Either the original Church in England and Ireland has ceased to exist, or it exists in those Reformed Churches which are now recognised by law. Those who now assume the name of 'Catholics' in either country, derive their orders and the origin of their religion from Rome, since the Reformation, and have no pretence to inherit the authority or the succession of those Churches which were planted by Patrick or by Augustine, or of that which existed in England before Augustine. The succession of those Churches has been continued with our bishops and presbyters, *and with them alone*; the bishops ejected by Elizabeth never attempted to continue the succession, and those who now exercise the functions of bishops or presbyters amongst us by authority from Rome, must allege that they come as missionaries to an apostate or heretical country, to found a new Church, without a pretence that they have any authority by descent from that Church which originally existed amongst us.

We hear that great exertions are now making, and great expectations raised, of the reunion of this nation with what is called 'the Catholic Church.' We are

---

[1] When we speak, then, of the good and of the evil side in human life, —in any society whether smaller or larger,—this is what we mean, or should mean. The evil side contains much that is, up to a certain point, good: the good side,—for does it not consist of human beings?—contains, unhappily, much in it that is evil. Not all in the one is to be avoided,—far from it, nor is all in the other by any means to be followed. But still, those are called evil, in God's judgment, who live according to their own impulses, or according to the law of the society around them; and those are to be called good, who, in their principles, whatever may be the imperfections of their practice, endeavour in all things to live according to the will of Christ.—ARNOLD's *Christian Life*, Serm. ix.

told also that associations are formed in Roman Catholic
countries for offering up constant prayers for such a
result.   Very different indeed are such weapons from
those which were formerly in use against us.   May the
result be different !   May those prayers be heard, though
it be otherwise than is intended.   May He whose alone it is
to turn the hearts of the parents to their children, enlighten
the minds of those who thus pray for us, that they may
see and acknowledge their own imperfections, and the
sins of their forefathers.   Then they will perceive that
it was themselves who made the schism, by separating
us from their communion because we would not continue
in their errors.   In the meanwhile, so long as Rome
continues what she is, we may not, dare not, unite ourselves with her again.   To do so would be to forego the
best inheritance of our country, if not also to forsake
still higher and holier destinies.   We know not what
purposes the gracious providence of God may yet accomplish towards us.   But this we know, that our Church,
imperfect as it is (and we need not fear to acknowledge
our imperfections), is yet a beacon to the nations of
apostolical authority on the one hand, and of scripture
truth on the other.   It has been attempted, in the
course of events which have been here related, to point
out the influence which the PRAYERS of those who were
attached to the reformed doctrine may have had upon
those events.   Individuals may have judged amiss, but
God has given us a Church according to their prayers;
be it ours to PRAY for its increase in all Christian graces.

APPENDIX.

A. Page 30.

GUICCIARDINI'S HISTORY.

The following is said to be the passage omitted in the common editions—'By these steps, the Popes being raised to their worldly grandure, and by degrees becoming unmindful of the salvation of souls and the divine commands, applied their minds wholly to mundane greatness; and abusing the divine authority, by making it instrumental only to acquire secular power, affected to seem princes of nations rather than dispensers of divine things. Sanctity of life, the advancement of religion, love towards God and Man, were no longer their concern; but armies and wars among Christians took up their thoughts, and they performed divine offices with hands besmeared with blood. They were intent on amassing money, making new laws, and finding new tricks to get wealth and riches from every quarter. For this end they most audaciously made use of their heavenly artillery, and most shamefully exposed to sale both profane and holy things. Hence their wealth and the grandure of their court vastly increased; and hence spring Pride, Luxury, Dissoluteness of Manners, Lust, and Wicked Pleasures. No regard was had to the good of posterity, nor concern for the dignity of the Papal Chair: but instead thereof an anxious pernicious desire of advancing their bastards and nephews, friends and dependents, not only to excessive wealth, but also to kingdoms and empires; bestowing honours and profits not only on the good and deserving, but very often by setting them to sale, they granted them to men abandoned to ambition, covetousness, and most abominable licentiousness.'—Translated from the Latin at the end of HEIDEGGER's *History of the Papacy.* 4to. Amsterdam, 1684, and printed in 'Papal Usurpation and Persecution, &c. in Two Parts.' London: Downing, 1712. Pt. ii. is PERRIN's *History of the Waldenses.*

C. Page 48.

From Bossuet's *Defensio Cleri Gallicani*, ii. 57.

'Anno 1301, passim circumferebantur brevissimæ Bonifacii ad Philippum, et Philippi ad Bonifacium litteræ omnibus notæ. Bonifacii epistolæ tale est initium:' 'Scire te volumus, quòd in spiritualibus et temporalibus nobis subes.' Quæ ne in prejudicium traheretur, die Dominicâ post octavam Purificationis B. M. 1301, rex Franciæ fecit comburere bullam Papæ, in medio omnium nobilium et aliarum personarum, quæ erant eâdem die Parisiis, et cum trumpis fecit combustionem hujus bullæ per totam villam Parisiis præconisari : item a die Veneris ante diem Dominicam erant elapsi quindecim dies, quòd idem rex condemnavit filios suos in præsentiâ totius curiæ suæ, et procerum omnium qui erant præsentes, si advocarent ab aliquo vivente, nisi a Deo, regnum Franciæ.

'Quòd ergo regia potestas; alteri quàm Deo in temporalibus subjici diceretur, id non modò regi, sed et universæ genti adeò intolerabile visum, ut nullâ unquam in re fuerit omnium ordinum tanta consensio. Eâ de re consultus Petrus de Bosco regius advocatus, ita respondebat :' 'Quod Papa sic scribens et intendens, sit et debeat hæreticus reputari.' Neque tantum ministri regis hæc Pontificia cogitata adversabantur, sed etiam gravissimi hujus ætatis theologi scriptis editis confutabant; ac ne jam privatos appellemus, Franci principes, duces, comites, barones, nobiles, in iis actis quæ ad cardinalium collegium ediderunt, illos horruerunt, quod exprobabant à Bonifacio dictum, Regem in temporalibus subjectum ipsi esse propter regnum Franciæ, cum reges Francique omnes semper dixerint, omnibusque sit notorium, id regnum in temporalibus soli Deo subdi.'

Bossuet afterwards states, that Philip did not rest until he had compelled the successors of Boniface, Benedict XI. and Clement V., to rescind all the acts of Boniface in this matter; and that Clement declared that all was restored to the condition it was in before.—*Ibid.* p. 57.

How Boniface himself was driven into exile, and at length to death, by Philip, is matter of history.

D. Page 62.

VAUDOIS MSS.

In the public Library at Geneva there are three separate Books of MSS. belonging to the Vaudois' Churches, of which

the first (No. 207 in the catalogue) contains *La Nobla Leiçon*
and several other pieces, and is said by the compiler of the
catalogue to be in the language of the Troubadours, and of the
12th century. The second, No. 208, he says is in *Patois Vaudois*,
and he assigns it to the 14th century. It is from this MS. that
the translations are given in the text. The third MS., No. 209,
called *Les Conseils des Barbets*, is also said to be in *Patois
Vaudois*, but of the 15th century. A few extracts from the
second of these volumes are here subjoined in the original. ' De
li articles d' la fe. Lo prumier article d' la nra fe ca qy nos
creyen en un dio payre tot poissant creator del cel e de la terra.
lo qual dio es un e trinita. Coma ca scrpt enlaley (q. d. est
script' en la loi), Q'Israel au (audiat Israel) lo tco Segnor dio es
un. Eph. e (q. d. Eph. v.) un signor, una fe, un baptisme, un
dio paire d' tuit. E. Joh. ept. a 4 [6?]. Trey son qui donã
testimoi al cel, lo paire, lo fills, e lo sant sp't, agsti (e questi)
trey son un. E. enlevangli d' Joh 17, es d'mostra lo paire e lo
fills e lo sant spit css un, &c.' Then follows an attribution of
the several articles of the creed successively to the several
apostles. ' Sãt Peyre apostol pause lo pmer article dizent, Io
creo en dio lo payre tot poissant, creator del cel e d'la tra [with
confirmations from ss.] Sant Joh pause lo 2 article dissent Io
creo e ȳ x° uniant fills di dio nre Segnor, &c.'

After the creed there follows in the same vol., ' de li sept
sacrament,' where under the head of ' Penance ' is given the passage translated in the text. ' De la qual fima nos tenefñ p fe e
confessen puramèt di cor qu ella es besogmuol a lome cagi p
sfaczar lo pecca. A laqual se deo continuåt amonestar e amo-
nestem qu li pecca se confesson segond la forma de la p'mtiva
gleisa, e requerir consells e las besognas spl prudent e savi desi.
la forma e obligatio introduct novellaful d'ynocent terz laqual
solon husar cofunnamèt li puer symoniach se deo squinar e fugir
d'lifidel, &c.'

On the subject of ' the fourth sacrament,' that of orders, there
is a remarkable agreement between some of their opinions and
those of Wycliffe, who wrote about the same time. For instance,
they say, ' Alla gleisa conven haver dos mãieras domes generat.
egoes. (It belongs to the Church to have two ways of generating
men) egoes (Italicè *cios*) spl'ial' e corporalmèt—(namely, spiritually
and bodily). Empyo só dui sacrament hacrear paires daquesta
muneira. Lo prima es lorde loqual es a crear paires spũals, di
qual si parla al p's'nt. Lautre ca lomatmoi loqual es a dir di
sot.' (Wherefore, there are two sacraments to create fathers, in
this manner. The first is orders, which is to create spiritual
Fathers, of which we speak at present. The other is matrimony,
which is to be spoken of below.) Compare this with the follow-

ing extract from Wycliffe's Dialogues, Pt. 4, c. 1, p. 3. 'Sed quia ecclesiam oportet habere duas maneries hominum generantium, scilicet spiritualiter et corporaliter, ideo duo sunt sacramenta ad patres hujusmodi procreandum. Primum est ordo, qui est sacramentum ad clericos, et specialiter ad presbiteros procreandum—secundum vero est matrimonium, &c.'

D. Page 101.

STIGMATA OF ST. CATHARINE.

The *Stigmata* of St. Francis of Assisi, gave rise to a similar claim on behalf of other Saints, and especially of St. Catharine of Siena. And these claims led to controversy, and even to contradictory decrees on the part of the Popes themselves, the Dominicans asserting and the Franciscans denying that St. Catharine had been thus honoured. Pius II., being himself a Sienese, canonised her, and declared that she had the Stigmata. But Sixtus IV., a Franciscan, who became Pope, A.D. 1471, on the death of Paul II., who was the successor in 1464 of Pius II., decreed on the contrary A.D. 1483, according to Melchior Canus, *that it was not true that she had them*. Melchior Canus was a Spanish Dominican, much reputed at the Council of Trent, who died A.D. 1560. He was censured for having said so, as if he had accused the Popes of disagreeing among themselves; but his editor (p. cxiii.) who defends him, asserts that Sixtus merely forbad St. Catharine to be *represented* with the Stigmata. Such were the questions which agitated the Church during these ages, and such the quibbles by which they were eluded.

E. Page 126.

SPECIMENS OF OLD ENGLISH VERSIONS OF SCRIPTURE.

I. Richard of Hampole's Psalter. About A.D. 1340. With a comment.

PSALM XCI.

1. He that wonnes in help of the Heghest,[1] in hillyng[2] of God of heven he shal dwell.

2. He shal sey til Lord, Myn uptaker ert thou, and my fleyng; my God, I shal hope in him.

---

[1] Highest (Yorkshire dialect).

[2] Covering, or protection. So Wycliffe, 1 Cor. xi. 6, 'Therefore the woman shal have an *hilyng* on her heed.'

3. For he delyverd me of the snare huntand and of sharpe word.

4. With his shuldurs he shal um-shadow[1] til the, and undur his feithurs thou shal hope.[2]

5. With shilde shall um-gif (encompass) the his sothfastnes; and thou shal not drede of the drede of nyght;

6. Of arow fleand in day, of nedis gangand in merknes,[3] of inras,[4] and mydday devyl.[5]

7. Fal shal fro thi syde a thousande, and fro thi rigt syde ten thousande; bot til the he shal not nyghe.

8. Trought for thi,[6] with thin een thou shal behold, and the yeldyng[7] of synful thou shal see.

9. For thou art, Lorde, my hope: heghest thou selt thy fleying.[8]

10. Ill shal not cum til the, and swyngyng[9] shal not nyghe til thi tabernakul.

11. For til his aungels he bad of the, that thei kepe the in all thi wayes.

12. In thair handis thei shal bere the lest when[10] thou hurt til stone thi fote.

13. On the snake and the basiliske thou shal go, and thou shal defoule the lion and the dragon.[11]

---

[1] Shadow thee about. The old Saxon preposition *umb* or *ymb*, around or about.

[2] Hampole's note is, 'Thou shal hope to be *hild* fro the hete (heat) of synne. He spekis at the lyknyng of the hen, that *hilles* her briddes (birds) under her wynges fro the glede (the kite).'

[3] Of needs, or business going in darkness. Hampole's note: 'That is when a man is in doute (doubt) what he shal do or what he shal fle.'

[4] In-raids, *i.e.* inroads (north-country dialect, from the Saxon *onræf*) Hampole's note: 'The rysing of ill men ageyns the.'

[5] Hampole's note: 'When the fiend transforms him in aungel of ligth, and makes him to seem brigt as mydday for to deceyf men.'

[6] For thy truth.

[7] Yielding.

[8] Hampole's note: 'Ful pryne (prone, willingly, and readily), thou gaf me grace to fle til the in al my nede.'

[9] Swingeing, stripes or blows.

[10] Lest at any time.

[11] Hampole's note: 'The snake is ill eggyng (evil tempting), that with delite and assentyng til synne bringis forth the basiliske, that is, grete synne in dede. The basiliske is cald (called) king of serpentes, and his sigt sleeth (slayeth) al lifand (living) thing. So grete synne in dede with ill ensample slees alle the virtues of the soule. The lyon is cruelte to his neybur. The dragon is gyle (guile) and pryve malice. But the rightwis

14. For he hopid in me, I shal delyver him : I shal hilt (*i. e.* cover) him for he knew my name.

15. He cried til me, and I shal here him : with him I am in tribulacyou ; I shal out-take him, and I shal glorifie him.

16. In lengthe of dayes I shal fille him, and I shal shew til him my hele.[1]

II. Wycliffe's Bible. A.D. 1380.

From Job xxxix. xl. xli.

Wher thou schalt gyve strengthe to an horse: ether (either) schalt gyve neiyng aboute his necke?

Wher thou schalt reise him as locustis ? the glorie of his nosethirles is drede.

He diggith erthe with the foote : he fulli joieth booldli : he goith agenst armed men : he dispisith ferdfulnesse, and he gyveth not alide to swerd.

An arrow-caas schal sowne on him : a spere and scheelde schal florische.

He is hoot and gnashith and swolewith the erthe: and he arettith not (recketh not) that the cry of the trumpe sowneth ; whenne he herith a clarioun, he seith joie, he smelliih batel afer, the exeityng of duykis (dukes), and the gelling (yelling) of the oost.

WYCLIFFE'S NOTE.

Bi the name of an olifaunt and of a whal God descryveth the power and malice of the fend, and of his membris, how they be knyt to gider in malice, and hardid in synne, that no man may overcome the dovel and also membris by man's virtu, but onely by Goddis virtu and help.

Lo, behemot, whom Y made with thee, shal as an oxe ete hey.

His strengthe is in hise leendis (loins), and his vertu is in the nawle of his wombe.

He stryneth his tail as a tedre (tether): the senewis of his buttokis ben folded to gidere.

His boonys ben as pipis of bras: the gristil of him is as platis of iron.

---

man, like the weasll, goes on it with his fote of gode-wille, and over comes it.'

[1] Hampole's note: 'That is, I shall fille him with endlesse life, that suffices til fillyng of mannes appetite. And I shal shew him, that he secco til ea (eye to eye), and speke mouth til mouth, my hele (health), that is, Crist ; in whose magrete the sigt is filled, all is mede (reward) and joy that none maytelle.'

He is the begynnyng of the waies of God: he that made him schal sette his sweerd to him. (That is, power to annoye, which he may not use, no but by Goddis suffring.—Wycliffe's note.)

Hilles beren erbis to this behemot; all the beestis of the feeld playen there.

He slepith undur schadewe in the pryvyte of rehed (reed): in moist places schadewis hilen his schadewe.

The salewis of the ryver campaasen him: he schal soup up the flood, and he schal not wondre.   He hath trist that Jordan schal flowe into his mouth.

He schal take hem by the igen of hym as bi an hook, and bi scharpe schaftis he schal perische hise nesethirles.

Wher thou schalt mow drawe out levyathan with an hook, and schalt binde with a roop (rope) his tonge?

Wher thou schalt putte a ryng in his nesethirles, ether schalt peerse his cheke with an hook?

Wher he schal multiplie praieris (prayers) to thee? ether schal speke softe thingis to thee?

Wher he schal make a covenaunt with thee, and thou schalt take him a servaunt everlastynge?

Wher thou schalt scorne him as a brid, etherschalt bynde him to thin handmaidis?

Schulen frendis kerve him, schulen marchauntis depart him?

Wher thou schalt fille nettis with his skyn, and a leep'·of fischis with his heed?

Schalt thou put thyn hand on hym? have thou mynde of the batel, and adde no more to speke. (Wycliffe's note:—to speke ony thing, that sowneth to decreessing of Goddis rightfulnesse and wisdom.)

Lo, his hope schal disseyve him; and in the sigt of alle men he schal be cast doun.

F. Page 159.

TRACIE'S WILL.

'The Testament of Master Wylliam Tracie Esquier, expounded by William Tindall: wherin thou shalt perceive with what charitie the chauncellor of Worcester burned when he toke up the dead man's carkas and made ashes of hit after it was buried. —M D.XXXV.'

The Testament hitself. In the name of God, Amen. I

' A leep—a weel, or twigren snare to catch fish: in Lancashire now called a kup.—BOSWORTH's Dictionary.

Wylliam Tracie of Todyngton in the Countie of Gloceter Esquier, make my Testament and last wyl, as here after folowith.

First, and before all other thinge, I com̄yt me unto God, and to his mercye, trustyng without any dowte or mystrust, that by his grace and the merytes of Jesus Christe, and by the vertue of his passion, and of his resurrection, I have and shall have remission of my synnes and resurrection of my bodye and soule, accordyng as hit is written, Job xix., I believe that my redeamer lyveth and that in the last day I shal ryse out of the erth, and in my flesh shal se my Saviour, this my hope is laid up in my bosome.

And towchyn the wealth of my soule the fayth that I have taken and rehersed, is suffycient (as I suppose) without any other man's worke or workis. My grounde and my beliefe is, that ther is but one god and one mediatour betwene god and man, whych is Jesus Chryste. So that I do not except none in heaven or erthe to be my mediatour between me and god, but onely Jesus Chryst, al other be but petitioners in recevinge of grace, but one able to give influence of grace. And therefore wyll I bestowe no part of my goodes for that intent that any man shoulde saye, or do, to healpe my soule, for therein I trust onely to the promyse of God, he that beleveth and is baptized shal be saved, and he that beleveth not shal be damned. Marke, the last chapter.

And touchyng the burying of my body, it amyleth me not what be done therto, where in Sainct Austin *de cura agenda pro mortuis* saith that they are rather the solace of them that live than wealthe or comfort of them that are departed, and therefore I remit it onely to the dyscretion of myne executors.

And touching the distribution of my temporal goodes, my purpose is by the grace of God to bestow them to be accepted as frutes of faith. So that I do not suppose that my merite be, by good bestowinge of them, but my merite is the faithe of Jesus Chryst only, by whych faith such workes are good accordiug to the wordes of our Lord, Matt. xxv., I was hongrye and thou gavest me to eate, and it folowith, that ye have done to the least of my brethren ye have done to me &c. And even we should consyder the trew sentence that a good worke maketh not a good man, but a good man maketh a good worke, for faith maketh the man both good and ryghtwyse, for a ryghtwyse man lyveth by faith, Rom. i. and whatsoever springeth not of faith is sin. Rom. xiiii.

And all my temporal goodes &c. Witness this myne owne hande, the x daye of October, in the xxii yere of the rayne of King Henry the viii.

Printed 'at Noremburch 1546.'

G. Page 367.

BAPTISMAL REGENERATION.

A conclusive proof that the doctrine of Regeneration in Baptism was deliberately retained by our Reformers is afforded by a letter from Peter Martyr to Bullinger, written while the Review of the Prayer Book was in progress, and printed by the Rev. Wm. Goode out of the Zurich collection. The act of Parliament for the observance of King Edward's second Prayer Book was passed in April, 1552; and the book was ordered to come into use on the 1st of November. In the interval, viz., on June 14th, 1552, Peter Martyr thus wrote concerning what had been done:—'The book of Ecclesiastical Rites is reformed, for all things are removed from it which could nourish superstition,'—and then proceeds to say, that 'the chief reason why other things which were purposed could not be effected, was, that . . . . many have hesitated whether grace be conferred by the sacraments, and some absolutely affirmed it, and would have wished it to be so decreed.' He then states his own opinion, that 'in the case of children, when they are baptized, since, on account of their age, they cannot have that assent which is faith, the sacrament effects this,—that pardon of original sin, reconciliation with God, and the grace of the Holy Spirit, bestowed on them by Christ, is sealed to them; and those *belonging already* to the Church are also visibly implanted in it.' But this view, he adds, 'was opposed, and many contend, and these otherwise not unlearned nor evil, that *grace is conferred*, as they say, through the sacraments. . . . Nevertheless, no little displeasure is excited against us on this account—namely, that we altogether dissent from Augustine. And if our doctrine were approved by public authority, then say they, Augustine would most manifestly be condemned.'

As there can be no doubt that this letter is genuine, it affords positive proof of the fact that the writer had endeavoured to persuade the Archbishop and the English Reformers to give up the doctrine of regeneration in baptism when the second Prayer Book was put together, and *had failed.* For further proof that the same decision had then been come to in regard to the Articles, and that the doctrine of the Church as it was to be expressed in the Articles was then already settled when this letter was written, see my 'Letter to Mr. Goode' (J. W. Parker, 1850), pp. 30, 31, 32; where also extracts may be found from the writings of Cranmer, Ridley, and Bucer, showing them to have held this doctrine; and Cranmer especially, in that last work of his against Gardiner, which he ratified, as it were, immediately before his death. To which may be added these words of Coverdale, 'Look, then, that ye declare this joyful method unto all men, and *plant them in with baptism* into the Father, Son, and Holy Ghost.' —Works by Parker Society, p. 370.

II. Page 408.

CHARACTER OF CRANMER.

An imputation has been cast upon Cranmer's memory, because it appears that he had bought from the crown, temp. Ed. VI., some abbey lands at Kirkstall, and elsewhere.

As this story, which rests on the authority of 'Thoresby's History of Leeds,' seems to be the main foundation of much that is said of Cranmer as a 'weak' and 'rather self-indulgent' person, it is important to place it in the true light. And it appears, on other and equally good authority, 1st. That this grant was obtained from Henry VIII., so that the deed of Edw. VI. was merely a confirmation of the act of his father; and consequently that the accusation of having obtained it 'during the royal minority' falls to the ground. 2ndly. That the lands thus obtained *were not granted in free gift to the archbishop, but purchased by him from the crown*; and that some of them were not abbey lands.

The passage from Thoresby is as follows. 'Cookridge is a village four miles distant from Leedes .... The first notice I find of this town is in the Monasticon Anglicanum, as part of the possessions belonging to Kirkstall Abbey, to which it was given during the time of the very first Abbot, Alexander, and continued to the last, being part of their demesnes where the dairy was kept. Upon the Dissolution of the house it was granted by K. H. VIII., together with the site of the monastery, &c., by indenture dated 10 June, 1540, to Robt. Pakeman Gent., of the king's household, under the yearly rent of 51*l.* 14*s.* King Edw. VI., by letters patent dated 1 June, in the first year of his reign, gave it to Archbishop Cranmer, the famous martyr, whose son, Thomas Cranmer, Esq., sold it with several other places therein mentioned to Sir Thos. Cecil—and Willm. Carnock, Yeoman, for the sum of 2800*l.*, which deed bears date 23 Feb., 25 Eliz.'

The authority given by Thoresby for his statement is *Lit. Pat. penes Thos. Kirke Armr.*, apparently the original Letters Patent of King Edward. But Dr. Whitaker, in his edition of Thoresby, subjoins the following note:—'King Edw. VI., did not give Kirkstall to the archbishop, but sold it with Cookridge, Arthington Nunnery, and the rectories of Aslacton Com. Notts, Whalley and Rochdale Com. Lanc. for 429*l.* 13*s.* 2*d.*, which made them (?) 569*l.* 3*s.* pr. ann. A good Pennyworth though no gift.'

In his own work, however, Dr. Whitaker says (art. Kirkstall, p. 120), 'The site and demesnes were granted by Ed. VI. to Thos. Cranmer, archbishop of Canterbury, and by him settled upon his younger son.'

Thus far the statements of Thoresby and Whitaker. But additional information is supplied in the following more detailed account of the same transaction, in Dr. Thoroton's 'History of Nottinghamshire,' a book of high authority, vol. i. p. 262, article 'Aslacton,' and in Bishop Tanner's *Notitia Monastica*, 'Yorkshire, 68'—compared with Dugdale, new edn. v. 529.

Dr. Thoroton's statement is as follows:—' King Edward the Sixth, by his indenture, bearing date the 20th of March, in the first year of his reign, for the sum of 429*l.* 13*s.* 2*d.*, granted to Thomas Cranmer, Archbishop of Canterbury, the scite of the Priory of Arthington, and divers lands thereunto belonging, and the scite of the Monastery of Kirkstall, and the demesne lands thereof, and other lands belonging to it, both in Yorkshire, and the Rectories of Whatton and Aslacton, with the advowson of the churches, both which then lately belonged to the Monastery of Welbeck; and the Manor of Woodhall (in Ratcliffe), in this county (Notts), late part of the possessions of Thomas Grey, Esq., and the advowson of the church of Kingesworth, in Kent, to him and his heirs for ever.

'His nephew, Thomas Cranmer, son of his brother John, by his said first wife, died, seized of the Rectory of Whatton and Aslacton, 8 December 5 Ed. VI., to which belonged one hundred acres of land, twenty of meadow, thirty of pasture, in Whatton and Aslacton, and also the Manor of Aslacton, six mess. &c., and two mess. in Whatton, and left his son, Thomas Cranmer, his heir, then above twenty-two years of age.'

[In the 'Additions to Thoroton,' follow some absurd stories about the archbishop having 'thrown up a hill, on the summit of which he used to sit and listen to the tunable bells of Whatton.' He never can have lived there since his youth. It was not his property. He merely bought the great tithes and sold or gave them to his nephew, the head of his family. It is necessary to mention this, lest these *tolerabiles ineptiæ* should discredit the authority of Thoroton, by whom nothing of the kind is said.]

Bishop Tanner further says, art. 'Kirkstall,' 'The site was granted in exchange, to Archbishop Cranmer, and his heirs, 34 *Hen. VIII.* and 1 Edw. VI.,' which is repeated by the editors of Dugdale, l. c.

If it be said that the purchase money was less than the actual value, this is admitted; but it is not clear that it was so much less as Dr. Whitaker supposes. Tanner says that Kirkstall ' was endowed with 329*l.* 2*s.* 11*d.* per ann. according to Dugdale,

513*l*. 13*s*. 4*d*. according to Speed.' If a part of these vast domains, those, viz. called the Demesne of the Abbey, with two rectories and two manors elsewhere, may be supposed to have been worth 200*l*. per ann. at the time of the dissolution, the instance of Latimer's farm being raised from 3*l*. to 16*l*. per ann., shews that rents might be quintupled in those times, and thus what was bought for 429*l*. of King Henry VIII., in the midst of the insecurity inseparable from such changes, might well be worth 2800*l*., near forty years later, in the prosperous reign of his daughter. It is not very clear what Dr. Whitaker's meaning is—'which made them 669*l*. per ann.' But if he means that the lands acquired by Cranmer were worth so much, we still require to know at what period this was.

But granted that Cranmer contracted with Henry VIII. for a purchase, partly of abbey lands, partly of a forfeited estate. We differ from him as to the propriety of buying or acquiring abbey lands at all. And we regret that he, of all men, should have had any concern in it whatever. But does it follow from this obscure transaction, of which absolutely nothing is known beyond the record in the title-deeds of a private gentleman, that he was basely intent upon sordid aggrandisement, when we know that he had barely enough at last to pay his debts? Aslacton was his native place, and he obtained the rectory for his nephew, the head of his family and owner of the place. As regards Kirkstall, it would be no wonder if subsequent events, and his own poverty, which he pleaded to Cecil, as related in the text, had obliged him to leave this property as the only provision for his family.

The character of Cranmer is of public interest. We never can flatter ourselves that it does not signify what were the motives of the chief agents in our Reformation. If truth compels us to censure them severely, by all means let us speak it. But let us not admit as truth, in such a case, any statements or inferences which are fairly capable of a different sense. When so many families were enriched by free grants from the crown, it is no great matter if Cranmer should have purchased from his master some part of a forfeited estate and some abbey lands, which the king wanted to sell. They were in the market, and he bought them; and in the vast depreciation of property consequent upon such events, he bought them on favourable terms, as land might now be bought in Tipperary or Jamaica; or, as Falstaff says, on the insurrection of the Percies,—'You may buy land now as cheap as stinking mackerel.'¹ But selfish or sordid Cranmer certainly was not.

---

¹ *Henry IV.*, first part, act. II. scene II.

This story, however, does not end here. For it appears that this very property, or some part of it, caused the ruin of the great Archbishop's family. His son or grandson spent his life in suits at law respecting it, and died a ruined man—a memorable epilogue to the tragedy of Cranmer's fate.

I. Page 436.

CHARACTER OF MARY.

If we would know what Mary was in these days of bitterness, we may learn it from a sketch by the hand of a contemporary, not John Foxe, nor any English or Protestant writer, but a bishop in the orders of the Church of Rome, Francis de Noailles, then residing as ambassador in the English Court: his letter is dated May 7, 1556, and addressed to the King of France:—

'After receiving your majesty's command, and having learned that Lord Clinton was returned from France the day before, I sought an audience with the queen, and expressed to her in many words your majesty's satisfaction with the friendly demonstration and good purposes which you had received from her by Lord Clinton. With this language, and everything that I said to this purpose, she put on an appearance of pleasure, and said, first of all, that she would never be less disposed than she had been in time past to procure a good peace between you, sire, the Emperor, and the king her husband, as one of the things which of all others she desired most. She said she had received great pleasure and satisfaction from the gracious reception which your majesty had given to Lord Clinton, and the good and laudable purposes which you had professed, as my lord had reported them; especially she felt herself much obliged to your majesty that you had been pleased to promise to send her as prisoners some of her subjects who were in France, "abominable wretches, heretics, and traitors! Well might she call them so," she said, "in regard to their crimes, which were so vile and execrable. She had no doubt that as a good and virtuous prince, attentive to the duties of a common amity, you would make your deeds answerable to your words, and that you would not keep them in your kingdom. For her part, she would not fail of her promise one jot, to gain three such kingdoms as England, France, and Spain; much less in so detestable a matter, as that of her said subjects." And here she appealed, and repeated the question two or three times with a loud voice, to Lord Clinton, "Was it not true that your majesty had promised to send them?" Clinton replied, "Yes, provided your majesty could discover them." When I then made answer, speaking of these persons as "banished men," or "transfugees," she prayed me not to call them so, but "abominable heretics," and "traitors," and "even worse, if possible;" although she was very sorry to have occasion to call her own subjects by such bad names. I willingly complied with her pleasure, telling her that, as to this point, the good and friendly understanding between your two majesties was the reason why gentlemen and other subjects of hers had been usually well received in the realms and countries owing obedience to your majesty, but if those "abominable wretches and traitors" had come there, and were now in your dominions, I was assured, since they were now known as such, your majesty would satisfy her wishes, provided they could be apprehended.

'These demands of the queen were made with such vehemence, and so often repeated, that it was evident, though she forced herself to give me a good and gracious reception, the very little I had said to contradict her (and it was very little), had thrown her into an extreme passion; and I took care to be on my guard, that she and her ministers should not suppose that the intention was to excuse our not delivering up these banished men sooner than was necessary. I must needs tell you, sire, that this princess lives constantly in two great extremes of anger and suspicion, for which we must excuse her, because she is in a continued madness of disappointment, not being able to enjoy either the presence of her husband, or the love of her people; and she is also in great fear of losing her life by the treachery of some of her domestics, it having been lately found out that one of her chaplains had attempted to kill her, though they do not like to say much about it.'[1]

---

[1] NOAILLES, vol. v. pp. 352, 3, 4. This seems to allude to one Thomas mentioned in the text as ' Pelerine Inglese.'

INDEX.

[JULY 1865.]

GENERAL LIST OF WORKS

PUBLISHED BY

MESSRS. LONGMANS, GREEN, AND CO.

PATERNOSTER ROW, LONDON.

Historical Works.

The **HISTORY of ENGLAND** from the Fall of Wolsey to the Death of Elizabeth. By JAMES ANTHONY FROUDE, M.A. late Fellow of Exeter College, Oxford.

> VOLS. I. to IV. the Reign of Henry VIII. Third Edition, 54s.

> VOLS. V. and VI. the Reigns of Edward VI. and Mary. Second Edition, 28s.

> VOLS. VII. and VIII. the Reign of Elizabeth, VOLS. I. and II. Third Edition, 28s.

The **HISTORY of ENGLAND** from the Accession of James II. By Lord MACAULAY. Three Editions as follows.

> LIBRARY EDITION, 5 vols. 8vo. £4.

> CABINET EDITION, 8 vols. post 8vo. 48s.

> PEOPLE'S EDITION, 4 vols. crown 8vo. 16s.

REVOLUTIONS in ENGLISH HISTORY. By ROBERT VAUGHAN D.D. 3 vols. 8vo. 45s.

> VOL. I. Revolutions of Race, 15s.

> VOL. II. Revolutions in Religion, 15s.

> VOL. III. Revolutions in Government, 15s.

An **ESSAY on the HISTORY of the ENGLISH GOVERNMENT** and Constitution, from the Reign of Henry VII. to the Present Time. By JOHN EARL RUSSELL. Third Edition, revised, with New Introduction. Crown 8vo. 6s.

The **HISTORY of ENGLAND** during the Reign of George the Third. By WILLIAM MASSEY, M.P. 4 vols. 8vo. 48s.

The **CONSTITUTIONAL HISTORY of ENGLAND**, since the Accession of George III. 1760—1860. By THOMAS ERSKINE MAY, C.B. Second Edition. 2 vols. 8vo. 33s.

A

HISTORICAL STUDIES. I. On Some of the Precursors of the French Revolution; II. Studies from the History of the Seventeenth Century; III. Leisure Hours of a Tourist. By HERMAN MERIVALE, M.A. 8vo. 12s. 6d.

LECTURES on the HISTORY of ENGLAND. By WILLIAM LONGMAN. Vol. I. from the earliest times to the Death of King Edward II. with 6 Maps, a coloured Plate, and 53 Woodcuts. 8vo. 15s.

A CHRONICLE of ENGLAND, from B.C. 55 to A.D. 1485; written and illustrated by J. E. DOYLE. With 81 Designs engraved on Wood and printed in Colours by E. Evans. 4to. 42s.

HISTORY of CIVILISATION. By HENRY THOMAS BUCKLE. 2 vols. 8vo. £1 17s.
> Vol. I. *England and France,* Fourth Edition, 21s.
> Vol. II. *Spain and Scotland,* Second Edition, 16s.

DEMOCRACY in AMERICA. By ALEXIS DE TOCQUEVILLE. Translated by HENRY REEVE, with an Introductory Notice by the Translator. 2 vols. 8vo. 21s.

The SPANISH CONQUEST in AMERICA, and its Relation to the History of Slavery and to the Government of Colonies. By ARTHUR HELPS. 4 vols. 8vo. £3. Vols. I. and II. 28s. Vols. III. and IV. 16s. each.

HISTORY of the REFORMATION in EUROPE in the Time of Calvin. By J. H. MERLE D'AUBIGNÉ, D.D. Vols. I. and II. 8vo. 28s. and Vol. III. 12s.

LIBRARY HISTORY of FRANCE, in 5 vols. 8vo. By EYRE EVANS CROWE. Vol. I. 14s. Vol. II. 15s. Vol. III. 18s. Vol. IV. nearly ready.

LECTURES on the HISTORY of FRANCE. By the late Sir JAMES STEPHEN, LL.D. 2 vols. 8vo. 24s.

The HISTORY of GREECE. By C. THIRLWALL, D.D., Lord Bishop of St. David's. 8 vols. 8vo. £3; or in 8 vols. fcp. 28s.

The TALE of the GREAT PERSIAN WAR, from the Histories of Herodotus. By GEORGE W. COX, M.A. late Scholar of Trin. Coll. Oxon. Fcp. 7s. 6d.

ANCIENT HISTORY of EGYPT, ASSYRIA, and BABYLONIA. By the Author of 'Amy Herbert.' Fcp. 6s.

CRITICAL HISTORY of the LANGUAGE and LITERATURE of Ancient Greece. By WILLIAM MURE, of Caldwell. 5 vols. 8vo. £3 9s.

HISTORY of the LITERATURE of ANCIENT GREECE. By Professor K. O. MÜLLER. Translated by the Right Hon. Sir GEORGE CORNEWALL LEWIS, Bart. and by J. W. DONALDSON, D.D. 3 vols. 8vo. 36s.

HISTORY of the ROMANS under the EMPIRE. By CHARLES MERIVALE, B.D. Chaplain to the Speaker.
> CABINET EDITION, 6 vols. post 8vo. 48s.
> LIBRARY EDITION, 7 vols. 8vo. £5 11s.

The FALL of the ROMAN REPUBLIC: a Short History of the Last Century of the Commonwealth. By the same Author. 12mo. 7s. 6d.

The CONVERSION of the ROMAN EMPIRE: the Boyle Lectures for the year 1864, delivered at the Chapel Royal, Whitehall. By CHARLES MERIVALE, B.D. Chaplain to the Speaker. Second Edition, 8vo. 8s. 6d.

CRITICAL and HISTORICAL ESSAYS contributed to the *Edinburgh Review*. By the Right Hon. LORD MACAULAY.
  LIBRARY EDITION, 3 vols. 8vo. 36s.
  TRAVELLER'S EDITION, in 1 vol. 21s.
  In POCKET VOLUMES, 3 vols. fcp. 21s.
  PEOPLE'S EDITION, 2 vols. crown 8vo. 8s.

HISTORICAL and PHILOSOPHICAL ESSAYS. By NASSAU W. SENIOR. 2 vols. post 8vo. 16s.

HISTORY of the RISE and INFLUENCE of the SPIRIT of RATIONALISM in EUROPE. By W.E.H. LECKY, M.A. Second Edition, revised. 2 vols. 8vo. 25s.

The BIOGRAPHICAL HISTORY of PHILOSOPHY, from its Origin in Greece to the Present Day. By GEORGE HENRY LEWES. Revised and enlarged Edition. 8vo. 16s.

HISTORY of the INDUCTIVE SCIENCES. By WILLIAM WHEWELL, D.D. F.R.S. Master of Trin. Coll. Cantab. Third Edition. 3 vols. crown 8vo. 24s.

EGYPT'S PLACE in UNIVERSAL HISTORY; an Historical Investigation. By C.C.J. BUNSEN, D.D. Translated by C.H. COTTRELL, M.A. With many Illustrations. 4 vols. 8vo. £5 8s. VOL. V. is nearly ready, completing the work.

MAUNDER'S HISTORICAL TREASURY; comprising a General Introductory Outline of Universal History, and a series of Separate Histories. Fcp. 10s.

HISTORICAL and CHRONOLOGICAL ENCYCLOPÆDIA, presenting in a brief and convenient form Chronological Notices of all the Great Events of Universal History. By B.B. WOODWARD, F.S.A. Librarian to the Queen.
  [*In the press.*

HISTORY of the CHRISTIAN CHURCH, from the Ascension of Christ to the Conversion of Constantine. By E. BURTON, D.D. late Regius Prof. of Divinity in the University of Oxford. Eighth Edition. Fcp. 3s. 6d.

SKETCH of the HISTORY of the CHURCH of ENGLAND to the Revolution of 1688. By the Right Rev. T.V. SHORT, D.D. Lord Bishop of St. Asaph. Sixth Edition. Crown 8vo. 10s. 6d.

HISTORY of the EARLY CHURCH, from the First Preaching of the Gospel to the Council of Nicæa, A.D. 325. By the Author of 'Amy Herbert.' Fcp. 4s. 6d.

The ENGLISH REFORMATION. By F.C. MASSINGBERD, M.A. Chancellor of Lincoln and Rector of South Ormsby. Third Edition, revised and enlarged. Fcp. 6s.

HISTORY of WESLEYAN METHODISM. By GEORGE SMITH, F.A.S. Fourth Edition, with numerous Portraits. 3 vols. cr. 8vo. 7s. each.

VILLARI'S HISTORY of SAVONAROLA and of HIS TIMES, translated from the Italian by LEONARD HORNER, F.R.S. with the co-operation of the Author. 2 vols. post 8vo. with Medallion, 18s.

LECTURES on the HISTORY of MODERN MUSIC, delivered at the Royal Institution. By JOHN HULLAH, Professor of Vocal Music in King's College and in Queen's College, London. FIRST COURSE, with Chronological Tables, post 8vo. 6s. 6d. SECOND COURSE, on the Transition Period, with 40 Specimens, 8vo. 16s.

Biography and Memoirs.

LETTERS and LIFE of FRANCIS BACON, including all his Occasional Works. Collected and edited, with a Commentary, by J. SPEDDING, Trin. Coll. Cantab. VOLS. I. and II. 8vo. 24s.

PASSAGES from the LIFE of a PHILOSOPHER. By CHARLES BABBAGE, Esq. M.A. F.R.S. &c. 8vo. 12s.

LIFE of ROBERT STEPHENSON, F.R.S. By J. C. JEAFFRESON, Barrister-at-Law; and WILLIAM POLE, F.R.S. Memb. Inst. Civ. Eng. With 2 Portraits and 17 Illustrations. 2 vols. 8vo. 32s.

LIFE of the DUKE of WELLINGTON. By the Rev. G. R. GLEIG, M.A. Popular Edition, carefully revised; with copious Additions. Crown 8vo. with Portrait, 5s.

Brialmont and Gleig's Life of the Duke of Wellington. 4 vols. 8vo. with Illustrations, £2 14s.

Life of the Duke of Wellington, partly from the French of M. BRIALMONT, partly from Original Documents. By the Rev. G. R. GLEIG, M.A. 8vo. with Portrait, 15s.

HISTORY of MY RELIGIOUS OPINIONS. By J. H. NEWMAN, D.D. Being the Substance of Apologia pro Vitâ Suâ. Post 8vo. 6s.

FATHER MATHEW: a Biography. By JOHN FRANCIS MAGUIRE, M.P. Popular Edition, with Portrait. Crown 8vo. 3s. 6d.

Rome; its Rulers and its Institutions. By the same Author. New Edition in preparation.

MEMOIRS, MISCELLANIES, and LETTERS of the late LUCY Aikin; including those addressed to Dr. Channing from 1826 to 1842. Edited by P. H. LE BRETON. Post 8vo. 8s. 6d.

LIFE of AMELIA WILHELMINA SIEVEKING, from the German. Edited, with the Author's sanction, by CATHERINE WINKWORTH. Post 8vo. with Portrait, 12s.

LOUIS SPOHR'S AUTOBIOGRAPHY. Translated from the German. 8vo. 14s.

DIARIES of a LADY of QUALITY, from 1797 to 1844. Edited, with Notes, by A. HAYWARD, Q.C. Second Edition. Post 8vo. 10s. 6d.

FELIX MENDELSSOHN'S LETTERS from *Italy and Switzerland,* and *Letters from 1833 to 1847,* translated by Lady WALLACE. New Edition, with Portrait. 2 vols. crown 8vo. 5s. each.

RECOLLECTIONS of the late WILLIAM WILBERFORCE, M.P. for the County of York during nearly 30 Years. By J. S. HARFORD, F.R.S. Second Edition. Post 8vo. 7s.

MEMOIRS of SIR HENRY HAVELOCK, K.C.B. By JOHN CLARK MARSHMAN. Second Edition. 8vo. with Portrait, 12s. 6d.

THOMAS MOORE'S MEMOIRS, JOURNAL, and CORRESPOND-ENCE. Edited and abridged from the First Edition by Earl RUSSELL. Square crown 8vo. with 8 Portraits, 12s. 6d.

MEMOIR of the Rev. SYDNEY SMITH. By his Daughter, Lady HOLLAND. With a Selection from his Letters, edited by Mrs. AUSTIN. 2 vols. 8vo. 28s.

VICISSITUDES of FAMILIES. By Sir BERNARD BURKE, Ulster King of Arms. FIRST, SECOND, and THIRD SERIES. 3 vols. crown 8vo. 12s. 6d, each.

ESSAYS in ECCLESIASTICAL BIOGRAPHY. By the Right Hon. Sir J. STEPHEN, LL.D. Fourth Edition. 8vo. 14s.

BIOGRAPHICAL SKETCHES. By NASSAU W. SENIOR. Post 8vo. price 10s. 6d.

BIOGRAPHIES of DISTINGUISHED SCIENTIFIC MEN. By FRANCOIS ARAGO. Translated by Admiral W. H. SMYTH, F.R.S. the Rev. B. POWELL, M.A. and R. GRANT, M.A. 8vo. 18s.

MAUNDER'S BIOGRAPHICAL TREASURY: Memoirs, Sketches, and Brief Notices of above 12,000 Eminent Persons of All Ages and Nations. Fcp. 10s.

Criticism, Philosophy, Polity, &c.

PAPINIAN: a Dialogue on State Affairs between a Constitutional Lawyer and a Country Gentleman about to enter Public Life. By GEORGE ATKINSON, B.A. Oxon. Serjeant-at-Law. Post 8vo. 5s.

ELEMENTS of LOGIC. By R. WHATELY, D.D. late Archbishop of Dublin. Ninth Edition. 8vo. 10s. 6d. crown 8vo. 4s. 6d.

Elements of Rhetoric. By the same Author. Seventh Edition. 8vo. 10s. 6d. crown 8vo. 4s. 6d.

English Synonymes. Edited by Archbishop WHATELY. 5th Edition. Fcp. 3s.

BACON'S ESSAYS with ANNOTATIONS. By R. WHATELY, D.D. late Archbishop of Dublin. Sixth Edition. 8vo. 10s. 6d.

B

LORD BACON'S WORKS, collected and edited by R. L. ELLIS, M.A. J. SPEDDING, M.A. and D. D. HEATH. Vols. I. to V. *Philosophical Works*, 5 vols. 8vo. £4 6s. VOLS. VI. and VII. *Literary and Professional Works*, 2 vols. £1 16s.

On REPRESENTATIVE GOVERNMENT. By JOHN STUART MILL. Third Edition, 8vo. 9s. crown 8vo. 2s.

On Liberty. By the same Author. Third Edition. Post 8vo. 7s. 6d. crown 8vo. 1s. 4d.

Principles of Political Economy. By the same. Sixth Edition. 2 vols. 8vo. 30s. or in 1 vol. crown 8vo. 5s.

A System of Logic, Ratiocinative and Inductive. By the same. Fifth Edition. Two vols. 8vo. 25s.

Utilitarianism. By the same. Second Edition. 8vo. 5s.

Dissertations and Discussions. By the same Author. 2 vols. 8vo. price 24s.

Examination of Sir W. Hamilton's Philosophy, and of the Principal Philosophical Question discussed in his Writings. By the same Author. Second Edition. 8vo. 14s.

MISCELLANEOUS REMAINS from the Common-place Book of RICHARD WHATELY, D.D. late Archbishop of Dublin. Edited by Miss E. J. WHATELY. Crown 8vo. 7s. 6d.

ESSAYS on the ADMINISTRATIONS of GREAT BRITAIN from 1783 to 1830. By the Right Hon. Sir G. C. LEWIS, Bart. Edited by the Right Hon. Sir E. HEAD, Bart. 8vo. with Portrait, 15s.

By the same Author.

A Dialogue on the Best Form of Government, 4s. 6d.

Essay on the Origin and Formation of the Romance Languages, price 7s. 6d.

Historical Survey of the Astronomy of the Ancients, 15s.

Inquiry into the Credibility of the Early Roman History, 2 vols. price 30s.

On the Methods of Observation and Reasoning in Politics, 2 vols. price 28s.

Irish Disturbances and Irish Church Question, 12s.

Remarks on the Use and Abuse of some Political Terms, 9s.

On Foreign Jurisdiction and Extradition of Criminals, 2s. 6d.

The Fables of Babrius, Greek Text with Latin Notes, PART I. 5s. 6d. PART II. 3s. 6d.

Suggestions for the Application of the Egyptological Method to Modern History, 1s.

An OUTLINE of the NECESSARY LAWS of THOUGHT: a Treatise on Pure and Applied Logic. By the Most Rev. W. THOMSON, D.D. Archbishop of York. Crown 8vo. 5s. 6d.

The ELEMENTS of LOGIC. By THOMAS SHEDDEN, M.A. of St. Peter's Coll. Cantab. 12mo. 4s. 6d.

ANALYSIS of Mr. MILL'S SYSTEM of LOGIC. By W. STEBBING, M.A. Fellow of Worcester College, Oxford. 12mo. 3s. 6d.

The ELECTION of REPRESENTATIVES, Parliamentary and Municipal; a Treatise. By THOMAS HARE, Barrister-at-Law. Third Edition, with Additions. Crown 8vo. 6s.

SPEECHES of the RIGHT HON. LORD MACAULAY, corrected by Himself. 8vo. 12s.

LORD MACAULAY'S SPEECHES on PARLIAMENTARY REFORM lu 1831 and 1832. 16mo. 1s.

A DICTIONARY of the ENGLISH LANGUAGE. By R. G. LATHAM, M.A. M.D. F.R.S. Founded on the Dictionary of Dr. S. JOHNSON, as edited by the Rev. H. J. TODD, with numerous Emendations and Additions. Publishing in 36 Parts, price 3s. 6d. each, to form 2 vols. 4to.

THESAURUS of ENGLISH WORDS and PHRASES, classified and arranged so as to facilitate the Expression of Ideas, and assist in Literary Composition. By P. M. ROGET, M.D. 14th Edition. Crown 8vo. 10s. 6d.

LECTURES on the SCIENCE of LANGUAGE, delivered at the Royal Institution. By MAX MÜLLER, M.A. Taylorian Professor in the University of Oxford. FIRST SERIES, Fourth Edition, 12s. SECOND SERIES, 18s.

The DEBATER; a Series of Complete Debates, Outlines of Debates, and Questions for Discussion. By F. ROWTON. Fcp. 6s.

A COURSE of ENGLISH READING, adapted to every taste and capacity; or, How and What to Read. By the Rev. J. PYCROFT, B.A. Fourth Edition. Fcp. 5s.

MANUAL of ENGLISH LITERATURE, Historical and Critical; with a Chapter on English Metres. By THOMAS ARNOLD, B.A. Post 8vo. 10s. 6d.

SOUTHEY'S DOCTOR, complete in One Volume. Edited by the Rev. J. W. WARTER, B.D. Square crown 8vo. 12s. 6d.

HISTORICAL and CRITICAL COMMENTARY on the OLD TESTAMENT; with a New Translation. By M. M. KALISCH, Ph.D. VOL. I. Genesis, 8vo. 18s. or adapted for the General Reader, 12s. VOL. II. Exodus, 15s. or adapted for the General Reader, 12s.

A Hebrew Grammar, with Exercises. By the same. PART I. Outlines with Exercises, 8vo. 12s. 6d. KEY, 5s. PART II. Exceptional Forms and Constructions, 12s. 6d.

A **LATIN-ENGLISH DICTIONARY.** By J. T. WHITE, M.A. of Corpus Christi College, and J. E. RIDDLE, M.A. of St. Edmund Hall, Oxford. Imperial 8vo. pp. 2,128, price 42s. cloth.

A **New Latin-English Dictionary**, abridged from the larger work of *White* and *Riddle* (as above), by J. T. WHITE, M.A. Joint-Author. Medium 8vo. pp. 1,048, price 18s. cloth.

A **Diamond Latin-English Dictionary**, or Guide to the Meaning, Quality, and Accentuation of Latin Classical Words. By Rev. J. E. RIDDLE, M.A. 32mo. 2s. 6d.

An **ENGLISH-GREEK LEXICON**, containing all the Greek Words used by Writers of good authority. By C. D. YONGE, B.A. Fifth Edition. 4to. 21s.

Mr. **YONGE'S NEW LEXICON**, English and Greek, abridged from his larger work (as above). Square 12mo. 8s. 6d.

A **GREEK-ENGLISH LEXICON.** Compiled by H. G. LIDDELL, D.D. Dean of Christ Church, and R. SCOTT, D.D. Master of Balliol. Fifth Edition. Crown 4to. 31s. 6d.

A **Lexicon, Greek and English**, abridged from LIDDELL and SCOTT's *Greek-English Lexicon*. Eleventh Edition. Square 12mo. 7s. 6d.

A **PRACTICAL DICTIONARY of the FRENCH and ENGLISH LANGUAGES.** By L. CONTANSEAU. Ninth Edition. Post 8vo. 10s. 6d.

Contanseau's Pocket Dictionary, French and English, abridged from the above by the Author. Third Edition, 18mo. 5s.

NEW PRACTICAL DICTIONARY of the GERMAN LANGUAGE; German-English and English-German. By the Rev. W. L. BLACKLEY, M.A. and Dr. CARL MARTIN FRIEDLANDER. Post 8vo. [*In the press.*]

Miscellaneous Works and Popular Metaphysics.

RECREATIONS of a COUNTRY PARSON: being a Selection of the Contributions of A. K. H. D. to *Fraser's Magazine*. SECOND SERIES. Crown 8vo. 3s. 6d.

The Common-place Philosopher in Town and Country. By the same Author. Crown 8vo. 3s. 6d.

Leisure Hours in Town; Essays Consolatory, Æsthetical, Moral, Social, and Domestic. By the same Author. Crown 8vo. 3s. 6d.

The Autumn Holidays of a Country Parson; Essays contributed to *Fraser's Magazine* and to *Good Words*. By the same. Crown 8vo. 3s. 6d.

The Graver Thoughts of a Country Parson. SECOND SERIES. By the same Author. Crown 8vo. 3s. 6d.

Critical Essays of a Country Parson. Selected from Essays contributed to *Fraser's Magazine*. By the same Author. Post 8vo. 9s.

A CAMPAIGNER AT HOME. By SHIRLEY, Author of 'Thalatta' and 'Nugæ Criticæ.' Post 8vo. with Vignette, 7s. 6d.

FRIENDS in COUNCIL: a Series of Readings and Discourses thereon. 2 vols. fcp. 9s.

Friends in Council. SECOND SERIES. 2 vols. post 8vo. 14s.

Essays written in the Intervals of Business. Fcp. 2s. 6d.

LORD MACAULAY'S MISCELLANEOUS WRITINGS:
LIBRARY EDITION. 2 vols. 8vo. Portrait, 21s.
PEOPLE'S EDITION. 1 vol. crown 8vo. 4s. 6d.

The REV. SYDNEY SMITH'S MISCELLANEOUS WORKS; including his Contributions to the *Edinburgh Review*.
LIBRARY EDITION, 3 vols. 8vo. 36s.
TRAVELLER'S EDITION, in 1 vol. 21s.
In POCKET VOLUMES, 3 vols. fcp. 21s.
PEOPLE'S EDITION, 2 vols. crown 8vo. 8s.

Elementary Sketches of Moral Philosophy, delivered at the Royal Institution. By the same Author. Fcp. 7s.

The Wit and Wisdom of the Rev. Sydney Smith: a Selection of the most memorable Passages in his Writings and Conversation. 16mo. 7s. 6d.

The HISTORY of the SUPERNATURAL in All Ages and Nations, and in all Churches, Christian and Pagan; demonstrating a Universal Faith. By WILLIAM HOWITT. 2 vols. post 8vo. 18s.

The SUPERSTITIONS of WITCHCRAFT. By HOWARD WILLIAMS, M.A. St. John's Coll. Camb. Post 8vo. 7s. 6d.

CHAPTERS on MENTAL PHYSIOLOGY. By Sir HENRY HOLLAND, Bart. M.D. F.R.S. Second Edition. Post 8vo. 8s. 6d.

ESSAYS selected from CONTRIBUTIONS to the *Edinburgh Review*. By HENRY ROGERS. Second Edition. 3 vols. fcp. 21s.

The Eclipse of Faith; or, a Visit to a Religious Sceptic. By the same Author. Tenth Edition. Fcp. 5s.

Defence of the Eclipse of Faith, by its Author; a rejoinder to Dr. Newman's *Reply*. Third Edition. Fcp. 8vo. 3s. 6d.

Selections from the Correspondence of R. E. H. Greyson. By the same Author. Third Edition. Crown 8vo. 7s. 6d.

Fulleriana, or the Wisdom and Wit of THOMAS FULLER, with Essay on his Life and Genius. By the same Author. 16mo. 2s. 6d.

An INTRODUCTION to MENTAL PHILOSOPHY, on the Inductive Method. By J. D. MORELL, M.A. LL.D. 8vo. 12s.

Elements of Psychology, containing the Analysis of the Intellectual Powers. By the same Author. Post 8vo. 7s. 6d.

C

The **SECRET** of **HEGEL**: being the Hegelian System in Origin, Principle, Form, and Matter. By JAMES HUTCHISON STIRLING. 2 vols. 8vo. 28s.

SIGHT and **TOUCH**: an Attempt to Disprove the Received (or Berkeleian) Theory of Vision. By THOMAS K. ABBOTT, M.A. Fellow and Tutor of Trin. Coll. Dublin. 8vo. with 21 Woodcuts, 5s. 6d.

The **SENSES** and the **INTELLECT**. By ALEXANDER BAIN, M.A. Professor of Logic in the University of Aberdeen. Second Edition. 8vo. price 15s.

The **Emotions** and the **Will**, by the same Author; completing a Systematic Exposition of the Human Mind. 8vo. 15s.

On the **Study of Character**, including an Estimate of Phrenology. By the same Author. 8vo. 9s.

TIME and **SPACE**: a Metaphysical Essay. By SHADWORTH H. HODGSON. 8vo. pp. 588, price 16s.

HOURS WITH THE MYSTICS: a Contribution to the History of Religious Opinion. By ROBERT ALFRED VAUGHAN, B.A. Second Edition. 2 vols. crown 8vo. 12s.

PSYCHOLOGICAL INQUIRIES. By the late Sir BENJ. C. BRODIE, Bart. 2 vols. or SERIES, fcp. 5s. each.

The **PHILOSOPHY** of **NECESSITY**; or Natural Law as applicable to Mental, Moral, and Social Science. By CHARLES BRAY. Second Edition. 8vo. 9s.

The **Education of the Feelings and Affections**. By the same Author. Third Edition. 8vo. 3s. 6d.

CHRISTIANITY and **COMMON SENSE**. By Sir WILLOUGHBY JONES, Bart. M.A. Trin. Coll. Cantab. 8vo. 6s.

Astronomy, Meteorology, Popular Geography, &c.

OUTLINES of **ASTRONOMY**. By Sir J. F. W. HERSCHEL, Bart. M.A. Seventh Edition, revised; with Plates and Woodcuts. 8vo. 18s.

ARAGO'S POPULAR ASTRONOMY. Translated by Admiral W. H. SMYTH, F.R.S. and R. GRANT, M.A. With 25 Plates and 358 Woodcuts. 2 vols. 8vo. £2 5s.

Arago's Meteorological Essays, with Introduction by Baron HUMBOLDT. Translated under the superintendence of Major-General E. SABINE, R.A. 8vo. 18s.

SATURN and its **SYSTEM**. By RICHARD A. PROCTOR, B.A. late Scholar of St John's Coll. Camb. and King's Coll. London. 8vo. with 14 Plates, 1s.

The **WEATHER-BOOK**; a Manual of Practical Meteorology. By Rear-Admiral ROBERT FITZ ROY, R.N. F.R.S. Third Edition, with 16 Diagrams. 8vo. 15s.

SAXBY'S WEATHER SYSTEM, or Lunar Influence on Weather. By S. M. SAXBY, R.N. Instructor of Naval Engineers. Second Edition. Post 8vo. 4s.

DOVE'S LAW of STORMS considered in connexion with the ordinary Movements of the Atmosphere. Translated by R. H. SCOTT, M.A. T.C.D. 8vo. 10s. 6d.

CELESTIAL OBJECTS for **COMMON TELESCOPES**. By the Rev. T. W. WEBB, M.A. F.R.A.S. With Map of the Moon, and Woodcuts. 16mo. 7s.

PHYSICAL GEOGRAPHY for **SCHOOLS** and **GENERAL READERS**. By M. F. MAURY, LL.D. Fcp. with 2 Charts, 2s. 6d.

A **DICTIONARY**, Geographical, Statistical, and Historical, of the various Countries, Places, and Principal Natural Objects in the World. By J. R. M'CULLOCH. With 6 Maps. 2 vols. 8vo. 63s.

A **GENERAL DICTIONARY** of **GEOGRAPHY**, Descriptive, Physical, Statistical, and Historical: forming a complete Gazetteer of the World. By A. KEITH JOHNSTON, F.R.S.E. 8vo. 31s. 6d.

A **MANUAL** of **GEOGRAPHY**, Physical, Industrial, and Political. By W. HUGHES, F.R.G.S. Professor of Geography in King's College, and in Queen's College, London. With 6 Maps. Fcp. 7s. 6d.

The **Geography of British History**; a Geographical Description of the British Islands at Successive Periods. By the same. With 6 Maps. Fcp. 8s. 6d.

Abridged Text-Book of British Geography. By the same. Fcp. 1s. 6d.

The **BRITISH EMPIRE**; a Sketch of the Geography, Growth, Natural and Political Features of the United Kingdom, its Colonies and Dependencies. By CAROLINE BRAY. With 5 Maps. Fcp. 7s. 6d.

COLONISATION and **COLONIES**: a Series of Lectures delivered before the University of Oxford. By HERMAN MERIVALE, M.A. Professor of Political Economy. 8vo. 18s.

MAUNDER'S TREASURY of **GEOGRAPHY**, Physical, Historical, Descriptive, and Political. Edited by W. HUGHES, F.R.G.S. With 7 Maps and 16 Plates. Fcp. 10s.

Natural History and Popular Science.

The **ELEMENTS** of **PHYSICS** or **NATURAL PHILOSOPHY**. By NEIL ARNOTT, M.D. F.R.S. Physician Extraordinary to the Queen. Sixth Edition. PART I. 8vo. 10s. 6d.

HEAT CONSIDERED as a **MODE** of **MOTION**. By Professor JOHN TYNDALL, LL.D. F.R.S. Second Edition. Crown 8vo. with Woodcuts, 12s. 6d.

VOLCANOS, the Character of their Phenomena, their Share in the Structure and Composition of the Surface of the Globe, &c. By G. POULETT SCROPE, M.P. F.R.S. Second Edition. 8vo. with Illustrations, 15s.

A TREATISE on ELECTRICITY, in Theory and Practice. By A. DE LA RIVE, Prof. in the Academy of Geneva. Translated by C. V. WALKER, F.R.S. 3 vols. 8vo. with Woodcuts, £3 13s.

The CORRELATION of PHYSICAL FORCES. By W. R. GROVE, Q.C. V.P.R.S. Fourth Edition. 8vo. 7s. 6d.

The GEOLOGICAL MAGAZINE; or, Monthly Journal of Geology. Edited by HENRY WOODWARD, F.G.S. F.Z.S. British Museum; assisted by Professor J. MORRIS, F.G.S. and R. ETHERIDGE, F.R.S.E. F.G.S. 8vo. price 1s. monthly.

A GUIDE to GEOLOGY. By J. PHILLIPS, M.A. Professor of Geology in the University of Oxford. Fifth Edition; with Plates and Diagrams. Fcp. 4s.

A GLOSSARY of MINERALOGY. By H. W. BRISTOW, F.G.S. of the Geological Survey of Great Britain. With 486 Figures. Crown 8vo. 12s.

PHILLIPS'S ELEMENTARY INTRODUCTION to MINERALOGY, with extensive Alterations and Additions, by H. J. BROOKE, F.R.S. and W. H. MILLER, F.G.S. Post 8vo. with Woodcuts, 18s.

VAN DER HOEVEN'S HANDBOOK of ZOOLOGY. Translated from the Second Dutch Edition by the Rev. W. CLARK, M.D. F.R.S. 2 vols. 8vo. with 24 Plates of Figures, 60s.

The COMPARATIVE ANATOMY and PHYSIOLOGY of the VERTE-brate Animals. By RICHARD OWEN, F.R.S. D.C.L. 2 vols. 8vo. with upwards of 1,200 Woodcuts.   [*In the press.*

HOMES WITHOUT HANDS: an Account of the Habitations constructed by various Animals, classed according to their Principles of Construction. By Rev. J. G. WOOD, M.A. F.L.S. Illustrations on Wood by G. Pearson, from Drawings by F. W. Keyl and E. A. Smith. In 20 Parts, 1s. each.

MANUAL of CORALS and SEA JELLIES. By J. R. GREENE, B.A. Edited by the Rev. J. A. GALBRAITH, M.A. and the Rev. S. HAUGHTON, M.D. Fcp. with 39 Woodcuts, 5s.

Manual of Sponges and Animalculæ; with a General Introduction on the Principles of Zoology. By the same Author and Editors. Fcp. with 16 Woodcuts, 2s.

Manual of the Metalloids. By J. APJOHN, M.D. F.R.S. and the same Editors. Fcp. with 38 Woodcuts, 7s. 6d.

The SEA and its LIVING WONDERS. By Dr. G. HARTWIG. Second (English) Edition. 8vo. with many Illustrations. 18s.

The TROPICAL WORLD. By the same Author. With 8 Chromoxylographs and 172 Woodcuts. 8vo. 21s.

SKETCHES of the NATURAL HISTORY of CEYLON. By Sir J. EMERSON TENNENT, K.C.S. LL.D. With 82 Wood Engravings. Post 8vo. price 12s. 6d.

Ceylon. By the same Author. Fifth Edition; with Maps, &c. and 90 Wood Engravings. 2 vols. 8vo. £2 10s.

A FAMILIAR HISTORY of BIRDS By E. STANLEY, D.D. F.R.S.
late Lord Bishop of Norwich. Seventh Edition, with Woodcuts. Fcp. 3s. 6d.

MARVELS and MYSTERIES of INSTINCT; or, Curiosities of Animal
Life. By G. GARRATT. Third Edition. Fcp. 7s.

HOME WALKS and HOLIDAY RAMBLES. By the Rev. C. A.
JOHNS, B.A. F.L.S. Fcp. 8vo. with 10 Illustrations, 6s.

KIRBY and SPENCE'S INTRODUCTION to ENTOMOLOGY, or
Elements of the Natural History of Insects. Seventh Edition. Crown 8vo.
price 5s.

MAUNDER'S TREASURY of NATURAL HISTORY, or Popular
Dictionary of Zoology. Revised and corrected by T. S. COBBOLD, M.D.
Fcp. with 900 Woodcuts, 10s.

The TREASURY of BOTANY, on the Plan of Maunder's Treasury.
By J. LINDLEY, M.D. and T. MOORE, F.L.S. assisted by other Practical
Botanists. With 16 Plates, and many Woodcuts from designs by W. H.
Fitch. Fcp.   [In the press.

The ROSE AMATEUR'S GUIDE. By THOMAS RIVERS. 8th Edition.
Fcp. 4s.

The BRITISH FLORA; comprising the Phænogamous or Flowering
Plants and the Ferns. By Sir W. J. HOOKER, K.H. and G. A. WALKER-
ARNOTT, LL.D. 12mo. with 12 Plates, 14s. or coloured, 21s.

BRYOLOGIA BRITANNICA; containing the Mosses of Great Britain
and Ireland, arranged and described. By W. WILSON. 8vo. with 61 Plates
42s. or coloured, £4 4s.

The INDOOR GARDENER. By Miss MALING. Fcp. with Frontispiece, printed in Colours, 5s.

LOUDON'S ENCYCLOPÆDIA of PLANTS; comprising the Specific
Character, Description, Culture, History, &c. of all the Plants found in
Great Britain. With upwards of 12,000 Woodcuts. 8vo. £3 13s. 6d.

London's Encyclopædia of Trees and Shrubs; containing the Hardy
Trees and Shrubs of Great Britain scientifically and popularly described.
With 2,000 Woodcuts. 8vo. 50s.

MAUNDER'S SCIENTIFIC and LITERARY TREASURY ; a Popular
Encyclopædia of Science, Literature, and Art. Fcp. 10s.

A DICTIONARY of SCIENCE, LITERATURE, and ART. Fourth
Edition. Edited by W. T. BRANDE, D.C.L. and GEORGE W. COX, M.A.
assisted by gentlemen of eminent Scientific and Literary Acquirements.
In 12 Parts, each containing 240 pages, price 5s. forming 3 vols. medium 8vo.
price 21s. each.

ESSAYS on SCIENTIFIC and other SUBJECTS, contributed to
Reviews. By Sir H. HOLLAND, Bart. M.D. Second Edition. 8vo. 14s.

ESSAYS from the EDINBURGH and QUARTERLY REVIEWS;
with Addresses and other Pieces. By Sir J. F. W. HERSCHEL, Bart. M.A.
8vo. 18s.

D

Chemistry, Medicine, Surgery, and the Allied Sciences.

A **DICTIONARY** of **CHEMISTRY** and the Allied Branches of other Sciences: founded on that of the late Dr. Ure. By HENRY WATTS, F.C.S. assisted by eminent Contributors. 5 vols. medium 8vo. in course of publication in Parts. VOL. I. 31s. 6d. VOL. II. 26s. VOL. III. 31s. 6d. are now ready.

HANDBOOK of **CHEMICAL ANALYSIS.** Adapted to the Unitary System of Notation. By F. T. CONINGTON, M.A. F.C.S. Post 8vo. 7s. 6d.—TABLES of QUALITATIVE ANALYSIS adapted to the same, 2s. 6d.

A **HANDBOOK** of **VOLUMETRICAL ANALYSIS.** By ROBERT H. SCOTT, M.A. T.C.D. Post 8vo. 4s. 6d.

ELEMENTS of **CHEMISTRY**, Theoretical and Practical. By WILLIAM A. MILLER, M.D. LL.D. F.R.S. F.G.S. Professor of Chemistry, King's College, London. 3 vols. 8vo. £2 13s. PART I. CHEMICAL PHYSICS. Third Edition, 12s. PART II. INORGANIC CHEMISTRY, 21s. PART III. ORGANIC CHEMISTRY, Second Edition, 20s.

A **MANUAL** of **CHEMISTRY**, Descriptive and Theoretical. By WILLIAM ODLING, M.B. F.R.S. Lecturer on Chemistry at St. Bartholomew's Hospital. PART I. 8vo. 9s.

A **Course** of **Practical Chemistry**, for the use of Medical Students. By the same Author. Second Edition, with 70 new Woodcuts. Crown 8vo. price 7s. 6d.

The **DIAGNOSIS** and **TREATMENT** of the **DISEASES** of **WOMEN**; including the Diagnosis of Pregnancy. By GRAILY HEWITT, M.D. Physician to the British Lying-in Hospital. 8vo. 16s.

LECTURES on the **DISEASES** of **INFANCY** and **CHILDHOOD.** By CHARLES WEST, M.D. &c. Fifth Edition, revised and enlarged. 8vo. 16s.

EXPOSITION of the **SIGNS** and **SYMPTOMS** of **PREGNANCY**: with other Papers on subjects connected with Midwifery. By W. F. MONTGOMERY, M.A. M.D. M.R.I.A. 8vo. with Illustrations, 25s.

A **SYSTEM** of **SURGERY**, Theoretical and Practical. In Treatises by Various Authors. Edited by T. HOLMES, M.A. Cantab. Assistant-Surgeon to St. George's Hospital. 4 vols. 8vo. £4 13s.

Vol. I. **General Pathology. 21s.**

Vol. II. **Local Injuries:** Gunshot Wounds, Injuries of the Head, Back, Face, Neck, Chest, Abdomen, Pelvis, of the Upper and Lower Extremities, and Diseases of the Eye. 21s.

Vol. III. **Operative Surgery. Diseases** of the Organs of Circulation, Locomotion, &c. 21s.

Vol. IV. **Diseases** of the Organs of Digestion, of the Genito-Urinary System, and of the Breast, Thyroid Gland, and Skin; with APPENDIX and GENERAL INDEX. 36s.

LECTURES on the **PRINCIPLES** and **PRACTICE** of **PHYSIC.** By THOMAS WATSON, M.D. Physician-Extraordinary to the Queen. Fourth Edition. 2 vols. 8vo. 34s.

LECTURES on SURGICAL PATHOLOGY. By J. PAGET, F.R.S. Surgeon-Extraordinary to the Queen. Edited by W. TURNER, M.D. 8vo. with 117 Woodcuts, 21s.

A TREATISE on the CONTINUED FEVERS of GREAT BRITAIN. By C. MURCHISON, M.D. Senior Physician to the London Fever Hospital. 8vo. with coloured Plates, 18s.

ANATOMY, DESCRIPTIVE and SURGICAL. By HENRY GRAY, F.R.S. With 410 Wood Engravings from Dissections. Third Edition, by T. HOLMES, M.A. Cantab. Royal 8vo. 28s.

The CYCLOPÆDIA of ANATOMY and PHYSIOLOGY. Edited by the late R. B. TODD, M.D. F.R.S. Assisted by nearly all the most eminent cultivators of Physiological Science of the present age. 5 vols. 8vo. with 2,853 Woodcuts, £6 6s.

PHYSIOLOGICAL ANATOMY and PHYSIOLOGY of MAN. By the late R. B. TODD, M.D. F.R.S. and W. BOWMAN, F.R.S. of King's College. With numerous Illustrations. VOL. II. 8vo. 25s.

A DICTIONARY of PRACTICAL MEDICINE. By J. COPLAND, M.D. F.R.S. Abridged from the larger work by the Author, assisted by J. C. COPLAND, M.R.C.S. 1 vol. 8vo, [In the press.

Dr. Copland's Dictionary of Practical Medicine (the larger work). 3 vols. 8vo. £5 11s.

The WORKS of SIR B. C. BRODIE, Bart. collected and arranged by CHARLES HAWKINS, F.R.C.S.E. 3 vols. 8vo. with Medallion and Fac-simile, 48s.

Autobiography of Sir B. C. Brodie, Bart. Printed from the Author's materials left in MS. Fcp. 4s. 6d.

MEDICAL NOTES and REFLECTIONS. By Sir H. HOLLAND, Bart. M.D. Third Edition. 8vo. 18s.

A MANUAL of MATERIA MEDICA and THERAPEUTICS, abridged from Dr. PEREIRA'S Elements by F. J. FARRE, M.D. Cantab. assisted by R. BENTLEY, M.R.C.S. and by R. WARINGTON, F.C.S. 1 vol. 8vo. [In October.

Dr. Pereira's Elements of Materia Medica and Therapeutics. Third Edition. By A. S. TAYLOR, M.D. and G. O. REES, M.D. 3 vols. 8vo. with Woodcuts, £3 15s.

THOMSON'S CONSPECTUS of the BRITISH PHARMACOPŒIA. Twenty-fourth Edition, corrected and made conformable throughout to the New Pharmacopœia of the General Council of Medical Education. By E. LLOYD BIRKETT, M.D. 18mo. 5s. 6d.

MANUAL of the DOMESTIC PRACTICE of MEDICINE. By W. B. KESTEVEN, F.R.C.S.E. Second Edition, thoroughly revised, with Additions. Fcp. 5s.

The Fine Arts, and Illustrated Editions.

The NEW TESTAMENT, illustrated with Wood Engravings after the Early Masters, chiefly of the Italian School. Crown 4to. 63s. cloth, gilt top; or £5 5s. elegantly bound in morocco.

LYRA GERMANICA; Hymns for the Sundays and Chief Festivals of the Christian Year. Translated by CATHERINE WINKWORTH; 125 Illustrations on Wood drawn by J. LEIGHTON, F.S.A. Fcp. 4to. 21s.

CATS' and FARLIE'S MORAL EMBLEMS; with Aphorisms, Adages, and Proverbs of all Nations: comprising 121 Illustrations on Wood by J. LEIGHTON, F.S.A. with an appropriate Text by R. PIGOT. Imperial 8vo. 31s. 6d.

BUNYAN'S PILGRIM'S PROGRESS: with 126 Illustrations on Steel and Wood by C. BENNETT; and a Preface by the Rev. C. KINGSLEY. Fcp. 4to. 21s.

SHAKSPEARE'S SENTIMENTS and SIMILES, printed in Black and Gold, and Illuminated in the Missal Style by HENRY NOEL HUMPHREYS. In massive covers, containing the Medallion and Cypher of Shakspeare. Square post 8vo. 21s.

The HISTORY of OUR LORD, as exemplified in Works of Art: with that of His Types in the Old and New Testament. By Mrs. JAMESON and Lady EASTLAKE. Being the concluding SERIES of 'Sacred and Legendary Art;' with 13 Etchings and 281 Woodcuts. 2 vols. square crown 8vo. 42s.

In the same Series, by Mrs. JAMESON.

Legends of the Saints and Martyrs. Fourth Edition, with 19 Etchings and 187 Woodcuts. 2 vols. 31s. 6d.

Legends of the Monastic Orders. Third Edition, with 11 Etchings and 88 Woodcuts. 1 vol. 21s.

Legends of the Madonna. Third Edition, with 27 Etchings and 165 Woodcuts. 1 vol. 21s.

Arts, Manufactures, &c.

ENCYCLOPÆDIA of ARCHITECTURE, Historical, Theoretical, and Practical. By JOSEPH GWILT. With more than 1,000 Woodcuts. 8vo. 42s.

TUSCAN SCULPTORS, their Lives, Works, and Times. With 45 Etchings and 28 Woodcuts from Original Drawings and Photographs. By CHARLES C. PERKINS. 2 vols. imperial 8vo. 63s.

The ENGINEER'S HANDBOOK; explaining the Principles which should guide the young Engineer in the Construction of Machinery. By C. S. LOWNDES. Post 8vo. 5s.

The ELEMENTS of MECHANISM. By T. M. GOODEVE, M.A. Professor of Mechanics at the R. M. Acad. Woolwich. Second Edition, with 217 Woodcuts. Post 8vo. 6s. 6d.

URE'S DICTIONARY of ARTS, MANUFACTURES, and MINES. Re-written and enlarged by ROBERT HUNT, F.R.S. assisted by numerous gentlemen eminent in Science and the Arts. With 2,000 Woodcuts. 3 vols. 8vo. £4.

ENCYCLOPÆDIA of CIVIL ENGINEERING, Historical, Theoretical, and Practical. By E. CRESY, C.E. With above 3,000 Woodcuts. 8vo. 42s.

TREATISE on MILLS and MILLWORK. By W. FAIRBAIRN, C.E. F.R.S. With 18 Plates and 322 Woodcuts. 2 vols. 8vo. 32s.

Useful Information for Engineers. By the same Author. FIRST and SECOND SERIES, with many Plates and Woodcuts. 2 vols. crown 8vo. 10s. 6d. each.

The Application of Cast and Wrought Iron to Building Purposes. By the same Author. Third Edition, with 6 Plates and 118 Woodcuts. 8vo. 16s.

The PRACTICAL MECHANIC'S JOURNAL: an Illustrated Record of Mechanical and Engineering Science, and Epitome of Patent Inventions 4to. price 1s. monthly.

The PRACTICAL DRAUGHTSMAN'S BOOK of INDUSTRIAL DESIGN. By W. JOHNSON, Assoc. Inst. C.E. With many hundred Illustrations 4to. 28s. 6d.

The PATENTEE'S MANUAL: a Treatise on the Law and Practice of Letters Patent for the use of Patentees and Inventors. By J. and J. H. JOHNSON. Post 8vo. 7s. 6d.

The ARTISAN CLUB'S TREATISE on the STEAM ENGINE, in its various Applications to Mines, Mills, Steam Navigation, Railways and Agriculture. By J. BOURNE, C.E. Sixth Edition: with 37 Plates and 546 Woodcuts. 4to. 42s.

Catechism of the Steam Engine, in its various Applications to Mines, Mills, Steam Navigation, Railways, and Agriculture. By the same Author. With 100 Woodcuts. Fcp. 8s. The INTRODUCTION of 'Recent Improvements' may be had separately, with 110 Woodcuts, price 3s. 6d.

Handbook of the Steam Engine. By the same Author, forming a KEY to the Catechism of the Steam Engine, with 67 Woodcuts. Fcp. 9s.

The THEORY of WAR Illustrated by numerous Examples from History. By Lieut.-Col. P. L. MACDOUGALL. Third Edition, with 10 Plans. Post 8vo. 10s. 6d.

COLLIERIES and COLLIERS; A Handbook of the Law and leading Cases relating thereto. By J. C. FOWLER, Barrister-at-Law, Stipendiary Magistrate. Fcp. 6s.

The ART of PERFUMERY; the History and Theory of Odours, and the Methods of Extracting the Aromas of Plants. By Dr. PIESSE, F.C.S. Third Edition, with 53 Woodcuts. Crown 8vo. 10s. 6d.

Chemical, Natural, and Physical Magic, for Juveniles during the Holidays. By the same Author. Third Edition, enlarged, with 38 Woodcuts. Fcp. 6s.

The Laboratory of Chemical Wonders: a Scientific Mélange for Young People. By the same. Crown 8vo. 5s. 6d.

TALPA; or the Chronicles of a Clay Farm. By C. W. HOSKYNS, Esq. With 24 Woodcuts from Designs by G. CRUIKSHANK. 16mo. 5s. 6d.

H.R.H the PRINCE CONSORT'S FARMS: an Agricultural Memoir. By JOHN CHALMERS MORTON. Dedicated by permission to Her Majesty the QUEEN. With 40 Wood Engravings. 4to. 52s. 6d.

LOUDON'S ENCYCLOPÆDIA of AGRICULTURE: comprising the Laying-out, Improvement, and Management of Landed Property, and the Cultivation and Economy of the Productions of Agriculture. With 1,100 Woodcuts. 8vo. 31s. 6d.

Loudon's Encylopædia of Gardening: comprising the Theory and Practice of Horticulture, Floriculture, Arboriculture, and Landscape Gardening. With 1,000 Woodcuts. 8vo. 31s. 6d.

Loudon's Encyclopædia of Cottage, Farm, and Villa Architecture and Furniture. With more than 2,000 Woodcuts. 8vo. 42s.

HISTORY of WINDSOR GREAT PARK and WINDSOR FOREST. By WILLIAM MENZIES, Resident Deputy Surveyor. With 2 Maps and 20 Photographs. Imp. folio, £3 3s.

The Sanitary Management and Utilisation of Sewage: comprising Details of a System applicable to Cottages, Dwelling-Houses, Public Buildings, and Towns; Suggestions relating to the Arterial Drainage of the Country, and the Water Supply of Rivers. By the same Author. Imp. 8vo. with 9 Illustrations, 12s. 6d.

BAYLDON'S ART of VALUING RENTS and TILLAGES, and Claims of Tenants upon Quitting Farms, both at Michaelmas and Lady-Day. Eighth Edition, revised by J. C. MORTON. 8vo. 10s. 6d.

Religious and Moral Works.

An **EXPOSITION of the 39 ARTICLES,** Historical and Doctrinal. By E. HAROLD BROWNE, D.D. Lord Bishop of Ely. Sixth Edition, 8vo. 16s.

The Pentateuch and the Elohistic Psalms, in Reply to Bishop Colenso. By the same. Second Edition. 8vo. 2s.

Examination Questions on Bishop Browne's Exposition of the Articles. By the Rev. J. GORLE, M.A. Fcp. 3s. 6d.

FIVE LECTURES on the CHARACTER of ST. PAUL; being the Hulsean Lectures for 1862. By the Rev. J. S. HOWSON, D.D. Second Edition. 8vo. 9s.

The LIFE and EPISTLES of ST. PAUL. By W. J. CONYBEARE, M.A. late Fellow of Trin. Coll. Cantab. and J. S. HOWSON, D.D. Principal of Liverpool Coll.

LIBRARY EDITION, with all the Original Illustrations, Maps, Landscapes on Steel, Woodcuts, &c. 2 vols. 4to. 48s.

INTERMEDIATE EDITION, with a Selection of Maps, Plates, and Woodcuts. 2 vols. square crown 8vo. 31s. 6d.

PEOPLE'S EDITION, revised and condensed, with 46 Illustrations and Maps. 2 vols. crown 8vo. 12s.

The VOYAGE and SHIPWRECK of ST. PAUL; with Dissertations on the Ships and Navigation of the Ancients. By JAMES SMITH, F.R.S. Crown 8vo. Charts, 8s. 6d.

A CRITICAL and GRAMMATICAL COMMENTARY on ST. PAUL'S Epistles. By C. J. ELLICOTT, D.D. Lord Bishop of Gloucester and Bristol. 8vo

Galatians, Third Edition, 8s. 6d.

Ephesians, Third Edition, 8s. 6d.

Pastoral Epistles, Third Edition, 10s. 6d.

Philippians, Colossians, and Philemon, Third Edition, 10s. 6d.

Thessalonians, Second Edition, 7s. 6d.

Historical Lectures on the Life of our Lord Jesus Christ: being the Hulsean Lectures for 1859. By the same Author. Fourth Edition. 8vo. price 10s. 6d.

The Destiny of the Creature; and other Sermons preached before the University of Cambridge. By the same. Post 8vo. 5s.

The Broad and the Narrow Way; Two Sermons preached before the University of Cambridge. By the same. Crown 8vo. 2s.

Rev. T. H. HORNE'S INTRODUCTION to the CRITICAL STUDY and Knowledge of the Holy Scriptures. Eleventh Edition, corrected and extended under careful Editorial revision. With 4 Maps and 22 Woodcuts and Facsimiles. 4 vols. 8vo. £3 13s. 6d.

Rev. T. H. Horne's Compendious Introduction to the Study of the Bible, being an Analysis of the larger work by the same Author. Re-edited by the Rev. JOHN AYRE, M.A. With Maps, &c. Post 8vo. 9s.

The TREASURY of BIBLE KNOWLEDGE, on the Plan of Maunder's Treasuries. By the Rev. JOHN AYRE, M.A. Fcp. 8vo. with Maps and Illustrations. [In the press.

The GREEK TESTAMENT; with Notes, Grammatical and Exegetical. By the Rev. W. WEBSTER, M.A. and the Rev. W. F. WILKINSON, M.A. 2 vols. 8vo. £2 4s.

VOL. I. the Gospels and Acts, 20s.

VOL. II. the Epistles and Apocalypse, 24s.

The FOUR EXPERIMENTS in Church and State; and the Conflicts of Churches. By Lord ROBERT MONTAGU, M.P. 8vo. 12s.

EVERY-DAY SCRIPTURE DIFFICULTIES explained and illustrated; Gospels of St. Matthew and St. Mark. By J. E. PRESCOTT, M.A. 8vo. 9s.

The PENTATEUCH and BOOK of JOSHUA CRITICALLY EXAMINED. By the Right Rev. J. W. COLENSO, D.D. Lord Bishop of Natal. People's Edition, in 1 vol. crown 8vo. 6s. or in 5 Parts, 1s. each.

The PENTATEUCH and BOOK of JOSHUA CRITICALLY EXAMINED. By Prof. A. KUENEN, of Leyden. Translated from the Dutch, and edited with Notes, by the Right Rev. J. W. COLENSO, D.D. Bishop of Natal. 8vo. 8s. 6d.

The FORMATION of CHRISTENDOM. PART I. By T. W. ALLIES. 8vo. 12s.

CHRISTENDOM'S DIVISIONS: a Philosophical Sketch of the Divisions of the Christian Family in East and West. By EDMUND S. FFOULKES, formerly Fellow and Tutor of Jesus Coll. Oxford. Post 8vo. 7s. 6d.

The **LIFE of CHRIST**: an Eclectic Gospel, from the Old and New Testaments, arranged on a New Principle, with Analytical Tables, &c. By CHARLES DE LA PRYME, M.A. Trin. Coll. Camb. Revised Edition, 8vo. 5s.

The **HIDDEN WISDOM of CHRIST and the KEY of KNOWLEDGE**: or, History of the Apocrypha. By ERNEST DE BUNSEN. 2 vols. 8vo. 28s.

HIPPOLYTUS and his AGE; or, the Beginnings and Prospects of Christianity. By Baron BUNSEN, D.D. 2 vols. 8vo. 30s.

Outlines of the Philosophy of Universal History, applied to Language and Religion: Containing an Account of the Alphabetical Conferences. By the same Author. 2 vols. 8vo. 33s.

Analecta Ante-Nicæna. By the same Author. 3 vols. 8vo. 42s.

ESSAYS on RELIGION and LITERATURE. By various Writers. Edited by H. E. MANNING, D.D. 8vo. 10s. 6d.

ESSAYS and REVIEWS. By the Rev. W. TEMPLE, D.D. the Rev. R. WILLIAMS, B.D. the Rev. B. POWELL, M.A. the Rev. H. B. WILSON, B.D. C. W. GOODWIN, M.A. the Rev. M. PATTISON, B.D. and the Rev. B. JOWETT, M.A. Twelfth Edition. Fcp. 8vo. 5s.

MOSHEIM'S ECCLESIASTICAL HISTORY. MURDOCK and SOAMES's Translation and Notes, re-edited by the Rev. W. STUBBS, M.A. 3 vols. 8vo. 45s.

BISHOP JEREMY TAYLOR'S ENTIRE WORKS: With Life by BISHOP HEBER. Revised and corrected by the Rev. C. P. EDEN, 10 vols. price £5 5s.

PASSING THOUGHTS on RELIGION. By the Author of 'Amy Herbert.' Eighth Edition. Fcp. 8vo. 5s.

Thoughts for the Holy Week, for Young Persons. By the same Author. Third Edition. Fcp. 8vo. 2s.

Night Lessons from Scripture. By the same Author. Second Edition. 32mo. 3s.

Self-Examination before Confirmation. By the same Author. 32mo. price 1s. 6d.

Readings for a Month Preparatory to Confirmation, from Writers of the Early and English Church. By the same. Fcp. 4s.

Readings for Every Day in Lent, compiled from the Writings of Bishop JEREMY TAYLOR. By the same. Fcp. 5s.

Preparation for the Holy Communion; the Devotions chiefly from the works of JEREMY TAYLOR. By the same. 32mo. 3s.

MORNING CLOUDS. Second Edition. Fcp. 3s.

Spring and Autumn. By the same Author. Post 8vo. 6s.

The **WIFE'S MANUAL**; or, Prayers, Thoughts, and Songs on Several Occasions of a Matron's Life. By the Rev. W. CALVERT, M.A. Crown 8vo. price 10s. 6d.

SPIRITUAL SONGS for the **SUNDAYS** and **HOLIDAYS** throughout the Year. By J. S. B. MONSELL, LL.D. Vicar of Egham. Fourth Edition. Fcp. 4s. 6d.

The **Beatitudes**: Abasement before God; Sorrow for Sin; Meekness of Spirit; Desire for Holiness; Gentleness; Purity of Heart; the Peacemakers; Sufferings for Christ. By the same. Second Edition, fcp. 3s. 6d.

HYMNOLOGIA CHRISTIANA; or, Psalms and Hymns selected and arranged in the order of the Christian Seasons. By B. H. KENNEDY, D.D. Prebendary of Lichfield. Crown 8vo. 7s. 6d.

LYRA DOMESTICA; Christian Songs for Domestic Edification. Translated from the *Psaltery and Harp* of C. J. P. SPITTA, and from other sources, by RICHARD MASSIE. FIRST and SECOND SERIES, fcp. 4s. 6d. each.

LYRA SACRA; Hymns, Ancient and Modern, Odes and Fragments of Sacred Poetry. Edited by the Rev. B. W. SAVILE, M.A. Fcp. 5s.

LYRA GERMANICA, translated from the German by Miss C. WINKWORTH. FIRST SERIES, Hymns for the Sundays and Chief Festivals; SECOND SERIES, the Christian Life. Fcp. 3s. each SERIES.

Hymns from Lyra Germanica, 18mo. 1s.

HISTORICAL NOTES to the '**LYRA GERMANICA**:' containing brief Memoirs of the Authors of the Hymns, and Notices of Remarkable Occasions on which some of them have been used; with Notices of other German Hymn Writers. By THEODORE KÜBLER. Fcp. 7s. 6d.

LYRA EUCHARISTICA; Hymns and Verses on the Holy Communion, Ancient and Modern; with other Poems. Edited by the Rev. ORBY SHIRLEY, M.A. Second Edition. Fcp. 7s. 6d.

Lyra **Messianica**; Hymns and Verses on the Life of Christ, Ancient and Modern; with other Poems. By the same Editor. Fcp. 7s. 6d.

Lyra **Mystica**; Hymns and Verses on Sacred Subjects, Ancient and Modern. By the same Editor. Fcp. 7s. 6d.

The **CHORALE BOOK** for **ENGLAND**; a complete Hymn-Book in accordance with the Services and Festivals of the Church of England: the Hymns translated by Miss C. WINKWORTH; the tunes arranged by Prof. W. S. BENNETT and OTTO GOLDSCHMIDT. Fcp. 4to. 12s. 6d.

Congregational Edition. Fcp. 2s.

The **CATHOLIC DOCTRINE** of the **ATONEMENT**: an Historical Inquiry into its Development in the Church; with an Introduction on the Principle of Theological Developments. By H. N. OXENHAM, M.A. formerly Scholar of Balliol College, Oxford. 8vo. 8s. 6d.

FROM SUNDAY TO SUNDAY: an attempt to consider familiarly the Weekday Life and Labours of a Country Clergyman. By R. GEE, M.A. Vicar of Abbott's Langley and Rural Dean. Fcp. 5s.

FIRST SUNDAYS at **CHURCH**; or, Familiar Conversations on the Morning and Evening Services of the Church of England. By J. E. RIDDLE, M.A. Fcp. 2s. 6d.

The JUDGMENT of CONSCIENCE, and other Sermons. By RICHARD WHATELY, D.D. late Archbishop of Dublin. Crown 8vo. 4s. 6d.

PALEY'S MORAL PHILOSOPHY, with Annotations. By RICHARD WHATELY, D.D. late Archbishop of Dublin. 8vo. 7s.

Travels, Voyages, &c.

OUTLINE SKETCHES of the HIGH ALPS of DAUPHINÉ. By T. G. BONNEY, M.A. F.G.S. M.A.C. Fellow of St. John's Coll. Camb. With 13 Plates and a Coloured Map. Post 4to. 16s.

ICE-CAVES of FRANCE and SWITZERLAND; a Narrative of Subterranean Exploration. By the Rev. G. F. BROWNE, M.A. Fellow and Assistant-Tutor of St. Catherine's Coll. Cambridge, M.A.C. With 11 Illustrations on Wood. Square crown 8vo. 12s. 6d.

VILLAGE LIFE in SWITZERLAND. By SOPHIA D. DELMARD. Post 8vo. 9s. 6d.

HOW WE SPENT the SUMMER; or, a Voyage en Zigzag in Switzerland and Tyrol with some Members of the ALPINE CLUB. From the Sketch-Book of one of the Party. In oblong 4to. with about 300 Illustrations, 16s. 6d.

MAP of the CHAIN of MONT BLANC, from an actual Survey in 1863—1864. By A. ADAMS-REILLY, F.R.G.S. M.A.C. Published under the Authority of the Alpine Club. In Chromolithography on extra stout drawing-paper 25in. x 17in. price 10s. or mounted on canvas in a folding case, 12s. 6d.

The HUNTING-GROUNDS of the OLD WORLD. FIRST SERIES, Asia. By H. A. L. the Old Shekarry. Third Edition, with 7 Illustrations, 8vo. 18s.

CAMP and CANTONMENT; a Journal of Life in India in 1857—1859, with some Account of the Way thither. By Mrs. LEOPOLD PAGET. To which is added a Short Narrative of the Pursuit of the Rebels in Central India by Major PAGET, R.H.A. Post 8vo. 10s. 6d.

EXPLORATIONS in SOUTH-WEST AFRICA, from Walvisch Bay to Lake Ngami and the Victoria Falls. By THOMAS BAINES, F.R.G.S. 8vo. with Map and Illustrations, 21s.

SOUTH AMERICAN SKETCHES; or, a Visit to Rio Janeiro, the Organ Mountains, La Plata, and the Paraná. By THOMAS W. HINCHLIFF, M.A. F.R.G.S. Post 8vo. with Illustrations, 12s. 6d.

VANCOUVER ISLAND and BRITISH COLUMBIA; their History, Resources, and Prospects. By MATTHEW MACFIE, F.R.G.S. With Maps and Illustrations. 8vo. 18s.

HISTORY of DISCOVERY in our AUSTRALASIAN COLONIES, Australia, Tasmania, and New Zealand, from the Earliest Date to the Present Day. By WILLIAM HOWITT. With 3 Maps of the Recent Explorations from Official Sources. 2 vols. 8vo. 20s.

The **CAPITAL** of the **TYCOON**; a Narrative of a Three Years' Residence in Japan. By Sir RUTHERFORD ALCOCK, K.C.B. 2 vols. 8vo. with numerous Illustrations, 42s.

LAST WINTER in **ROME**. By C. R. WELD. With Portrait and Engravings on Wood. Post 8vo. 14s.

AUTUMN RAMBLES in **NORTH AFRICA**. By JOHN ORMSBY, of the Middle Temple. With 16 Illustrations. Post 8vo. 8s. 6d.

The **DOLOMITE MOUNTAINS**. Excursions through Tyrol, Carinthia, Carniola, and Friuli in 1861, 1862, and 1863. By J. GILBERT and G. C. CHURCHILL, F.R.G.S. With numerous Illustrations. Square crown 8vo. 21s.

A **SUMMER TOUR** in the **GRISONS** and **ITALIAN VALLEYS** of the Bernina. By Mrs. HENRY FRESHFIELD. With 2 Coloured Maps and 4 Views. Post 8vo. 10s. 6d.

Alpine **Byeways**; or, Light Leaves gathered in 1859 and 1860. By the same Authoress. Post 8vo. with Illustrations, 10s. 6d.

A **LADY'S TOUR ROUND MONTE ROSA**; including Visits to the Italian Valleys. With Map and Illustrations. Post 8vo. 14s.

GUIDE to the **PYRENEES**, for the use of Mountaineers. By CHARLES PACKE. With Maps, &c. and Appendix. Fcp. 6s.

The **ALPINE GUIDE**. By JOHN BALL. M.R.I.A. late President of the Alpine Club. Post 8vo. with Maps and other Illustrations.

Guide to the **Western Alps**, including Mont Blanc, Monte Rosa, Zermatt, &c. 7s. 6d.

Guide to the **Oberland** and all **Switzerland**, excepting the Neighbourhood of Monte Rosa and the Great St. Bernard; with Lombardy and the adjoining portion of Tyrol. 7s. 6d.

CHRISTOPHER COLUMBUS; his Life, Voyages, and Discoveries. Revised Edition, with 4 Woodcuts. 18mo. 2s. 6d.

CAPTAIN JAMES COOK; his Life, Voyages, and Discoveries. Revised Edition, with numerous Woodcuts. 18mo. 2s. 6d.

NARRATIVES of **SHIPWRECKS** of the **ROYAL NAVY** between 1793 and 1857, compiled from Official Documents in the Admiralty by W. O. S. GILLY; with a Preface by W. S. GILLY, D.D. Third Edition, fcp. 5s.

A **WEEK** at the **LAND'S END**. By J. T. BLIGHT; assisted by E. H. RODD, R. Q. COUCH, and J. RALFS. With Map and 96 Woodcuts. Fcp. price 6s. 6d.

VISITS to **REMARKABLE PLACES**: Old Halls, Battle-Fields, and Scenes Illustrative of Striking Passages in English History and Poetry. By WILLIAM HOWITT. 2 vols. square crown 8vo. with Wood Engravings, price 25s.

The **RURAL LIFE** of **ENGLAND**. By the same Author. With Woodcuts by Bewick and Williams. Medium 8vo. 12s. 6d.

Works of Fiction.

LATE LAURELS : a Tale. By the Author of ' Wheat and Tares.' 2 vols. post 8vo. 15s.

A FIRST FRIENDSHIP. [Reprinted from *Fraser's Magazine.*] Crown 8vo. 7s. 8d.

ATHERSTONE PRIORY. By L. N. Comyn. 2 vols. post 8vo. 21s.

Ellice : a Tale. By the same. Post 8vo. 9s. 6d.

STORIES and TALES by the Author of ' Amy Herbert,' uniform Edition, each Tale *or* Story complete in a single Volume.

Amy Herbert, 2s. 6d.	Ivors, 3s. 6d.
Gertrude. 2s. 6d.	Katharine Ashton, 3s. 6d.
Earl's Daughter, 2s. 6d.	Margaret Percival, 5s.
Experience of Life, 2s. 6d.	Laneton Parsonage, 4s. 6d.
Cleve Hall, 3s. 6d.	Ursula, 4s. 6d.

A Glimpse of the World. By the Author of 'Amy Herbert.' Fcp. 7s. 6d.

ESSAYS on FICTION ; reprinted chiefly from Reviews, with Additions. By Nassau W. Senior. Post 8vo. 10s. 6d.

ELIHU JAN'S STORY ; or, the Private Life of an Eastern Queen. By William Knighton, LL.D. Assistant-Commissioner in Oudh. Post 8vo. 7s. 6d.

THE SIX SISTERS of the VALLEYS : an Historical Romance. By W. Bramley-Moore, M.A. Incumbent of Gerrard's Cross, Bucks. Third Edition, with 14 Illustrations. Crown 8vo. 5s.

The **GLADIATORS :** A Tale of Rome and Judæa. By G. J. Whyte Melville. Crown 8vo. 5s.

Digby Grand, an Autobiography. By the same Author. 1 vol. 5s.

Kate Coventry, an Autobiography. By the same. 1 vol. 5s.

General Bounce, or the Lady and the Locusts. By the same. 1 vol. 5s.

Holmby House, a Tale of Old Northamptonshire. 1 vol. 5s.

Good for Nothing, or All Down Hill. By the same. 1 vol. 6s.

The Queen's Maries, a Romance of Holyrood. 1 vol. 6s.

The Interpreter, a Tale of the War. By the same. 1 vol. 5s.

TALES from GREEK MYTHOLOGY. By George W. Cox, M.A. late Scholar of Trin. Coll. Oxon. Second Edition. Square 16mo. 3s. 6d.

Tales of the Gods and Heroes. By the same Author. Second Edition. Fcp. 5s.

Tales of Thebes and Argos. By the same Author. Fcp. 4s. 6d.

The WARDEN: a Novel. By ANTHONY TROLLOPE. Crown 8vo. 3s. 6d.

Barchester Towers: a Sequel to 'The Warden.' By the same Author. Crown 8vo. 5s.

Poetry and the Drama.

SELECT WORKS of the BRITISH POETS; with Biographical and Critical Prefaces by Dr. AIKIN; with Supplement of more recent Selections by LUCY AIKIN. Medium 8vo. 18s.

GOETHE'S SECOND FAUST. Translated by JOHN ANSTER, LL.D. M.R.I.A. Regius Professor of Civil Law in the University of Dublin. Post 8vo. 15s.

TASSO'S JERUSALEM DELIVERED. Translated into English Verse by Sir J. KINGSTON JAMES, Kt. M.A. 2 vols. fcp. with Facsimile, 14s.

POETICAL WORKS of JOHN EDMUND READE; with final Revision and Additions. 3 vols. fcp. 18s. or each vol. separately, 6s.

MOORE'S POETICAL WORKS, Cheapest Editions complete in 1 vol. including the Autobiographical Prefaces and Author's last Notes, which are still copyright. Crown 8vo. ruby type, with Portrait, 7s. 6d. or People's Edition, in larger type, 12s. 6d.

Moore's Poetical Works, as above, Library Edition, medium 8vo. with Portrait and Vignette, 14s. or in 10 vols. fcp. 3s. 6d. each.

TENNIEL'S EDITION of MOORE'S LALLA ROOKH, with 68 Wood Engravings from original Drawings and other Illustrations. Fcp. 4to. 21s.

Moore's Lalla Rookh. 32mo. Plate, 1s. 16mo. Vignette, 2s. 6d.

MACLISE'S EDITION of MOORE'S IRISH MELODIES, with 161 Steel Plates from Original Drawings. Super-royal 8vo. 31s. 6d.

Moore's Irish Melodies, 32mo. Portrait, 1s. 16mo. Vignette, 2s. 6d.

SOUTHEY'S POETICAL WORKS, with the Author's last Corrections and copyright Additions. Library Edition, in 1 vol. medium 8vo. with Portrait and Vignette, 14s. or in 10 vols. fcp. 3s. 6d. each.

LAYS of ANCIENT ROME; with Ivry and the Armada. By the Right Hon. LORD MACAULAY. 16mo. 4s. 6d.

Lord Macaulay's Lays of Ancient Rome. With 90 Illustrations on Wood, Original and from the Antique, from Drawings by G. SCHARF. Fcp. 4to. 21s.

POEMS. By JEAN INGELOW. Ninth Edition. Fcp. 8vo. 5s.

POETICAL WORKS of LETITIA ELIZABETH LANDON (L.E.L.) 2 vols. 16mo. 10s.

PLAYTIME with the POETS: a Selection of the best English Poetry for the use of Children. By a LADY. Crown 8vo. 5s.

BOWDLER'S FAMILY SHAKSPEARE, cheaper Genuine Edition, complete in 1 vol. large type, with 36 Woodcut Illustrations, price 14s. or with the same ILLUSTRATIONS, in 6 pocket vols. 3s. 6d. each.

ARUNDINES CAMI, sive Musarum Cantabrigiensium Lusus canori. Collegit atque edidit H. DRURY, M.A. Editio Sexta, curavit H. J. HODGSON, M.A. Crown 8vo. 7s. 6d.

Rural Sports, &c.

ENCYCLOPÆDIA of RURAL SPORTS; a complete Account, Historical, Practical, and Descriptive, of Hunting, Shooting, Fishing, Racing &c. By D. P. BLAINE. With above 600 Woodcuts (20 from Designs by JOHN LEECH). 8vo. 42s.

NOTES on RIFLE SHOOTING. By Captain HEATON, Adjutant of the Third Manchester Rifle Volunteer Corps. Fcp. 2s. 6d.

COL. HAWKER'S INSTRUCTIONS to YOUNG SPORTSMEN in all that relates to Guns and Shooting. Revised by the Author's Son. Square crown 8vo. with Illustrations, 18s.

The **DEAD SHOT**, or Sportsman's Complete Guide; a Treatise on the Use of the Gun, Dog-breaking, Pigeon-shooting, &c. By MARKSMAN. Fcp. 8vo. with Plates, 5s.

The **FLY-FISHER'S ENTOMOLOGY.** By ALFRED RONALDS. With coloured Representations of the Natural and Artificial Insect. Sixth Edition; with 20 coloured Plates. 8vo. 14s.

HANDBOOK of ANGLING: Teaching Fly-fishing, Trolling, Bottom-fishing, Salmon-fishing; with the Natural History of River Fish, and the best modes of Catching them. By EPHEMERA. Fcp. Woodcuts, 5s.

The **CRICKET FIELD**; or, the History and the Science of the Game of Cricket. By JAMES PYCROFT, B.A. Trin. Coll. Oxon. Fourth Edition. Fcp. 5s.

The **Cricket Tutor**; a Treatise exclusively Practical. By the same. 18mo. 1s.

Cricketana. By the same Author. With 7 Portraits of Cricketers. Fcp. 5s.

The **HORSE'S FOOT, and HOW to KEEP IT SOUND.** By W. MILES, Esq. Ninth Edition, with Illustrations. Imp. 8vo. 12s. 6d.

A **Plain Treatise on Horse-Shoeing.** By the same Author. Post 8vo. with Illustrations, 2s. 6d.

Stables and Stable-Fittings. By the same. Imp. 8vo. with 13 Plates, 15s.

Remarks on Horses' Teeth, addressed to Purchasers. By the same. Post 8vo. 1s. 6d.

On DRILL and MANŒUVRES of CAVALRY, combined with Horse Artillery. By Major-Gen. MICHAEL W. SMITH, C.B. Commanding the Poonah Division of the Bombay Army. 8vo. 12s. 6d.

The HORSE; with a Treatise on Draught. By WILLIAM YOUATT. New Edition, revised and enlarged. 8vo. with numerous Woodcuts, 10s. 6d.

The Dog. By the same Author. 8vo. with numerous Woodcuts, 6s.

The DOG in HEALTH and DISEASE. By STONEHENGE. With 70 Wood Engravings. Square crown 8vo. 15s.

The Greyhound in 1864. By the same Author. With 24 Portraits of Greyhounds. Square crown 8vo. 21s.

The OX; his Diseases and their Treatment: with an Essay on Parturition in the Cow. By J. R. DOBSON, M.R.C.V.S. Crown 8vo. with Illustrations price 7s. 6d.

Commerce, Navigation, and Mercantile Affairs.

The LAW of NATIONS Considered as Independent Political Communities. By TRAVERS TWISS, D.C.L. Regius Professor of Civil Law in the University of Oxford. 2 vols. 8vo. 30s. or separately, PART I. Peace, 12s. PART II. War, 18s.

A NAUTICAL DICTIONARY, defining the Technical Language relative to the Building and Equipment of Sailing Vessels and Steamers, &c. By ARTHUR YOUNG. Second Edition; with Plates and 150 Woodcuts. 8vo. 18s.

A DICTIONARY, Practical, Theoretical, and Historical, of Commerce and Commercial Navigation. By J. R. M'CULLOCH, Esq. 8vo. with Maps and Plans, 50s.

The STUDY of STEAM and the MARINE ENGINE, for Young Sea Officers. By S. M. SAXBY, R.N. Post 8vo. with 87 Diagrams, 5s. 6d.

A MANUAL for NAVAL CADETS. By J. M'NEIL BOYD, late Captain R.N. Third Edition; with 240 Woodcuts and 11 coloured Plates. Post 8vo. 12s. 6d.

Works of Utility and General Information.

MODERN COOKERY for PRIVATE FAMILIES, reduced to a System of Easy Practice in a Series of carefully-tested Receipts. By ELIZA ACTON. Newly revised and enlarged; with 8 Plates, Figures, and 150 Woodcuts. Fcp. 7s. 6d.

The HANDBOOK of DINING; or, Corpulency and Leanness scientifically considered. By BRILLAT-SAVARIN. Author of 'Physiologie du Goût.' Translated by L. F. SIMPSON. Revised Edition, with Additions. Fcp. 3s. 6d.

On FOOD and its DIGESTION; an Introduction to Dietetics. By
W. HINTON, M.D. Physician to St. Thomas's Hospital, &c. With 48 Woodcuts. Post 8vo. 12s.

WINE, the VINE, and the CELLAR. By THOMAS G. SHAW. Se-
cond Edition, revised and enlarged, with Frontispiece and 31 Illustrations
on Wood. 8vo. 16s.

A PRACTICAL TREATISE on BREWING; with Formulæ for Public
Brewers, and Instructions for Private Families. By W. BLACK. 8vo. 10s. 6d.

SHORT WHIST. By MAJOR A. Sixteenth Edition, revised, with an
Essay on the Theory of the Modern Scientific Game by PROF. P. Fcp. 3s. 6d.

WHIST, WHAT TO LEAD. By CAM. Second Edition. 32mo. 1s.

HINTS on ETIQUETTE and the USAGES of SOCIETY.; with a
Glance at Bad Habits. Revised, with Additions, by a LADY of RANK. Fcp.
price 2s. 6d.

The CABINET LAWYER; a Popular Digest of the Laws of England,
Civil and Criminal. Twentieth Edition, extended by the Author; including
the Acts of the Sessions 1863 and 1864. Fcp. 10s. 6d.

The PHILOSOPHY of HEALTH; or, an Exposition of the Physiological and Sanitary Conditions conducive to Human Longevity and
Happiness. By SOUTHWOOD SMITH. M.D. Eleventh Edition, revised and
enlarged: with 113 Woodcuts, 8vo. 15s.

HINTS to MOTHERS on the MANAGEMENT of their HEALTH
during the Period of Pregnancy and in the Lying-in Room. By T. BULL,
M.D. Fcp. 5s.

The Maternal Management of Children in Health and Disease. By
the same Author. Fcp. 5s.

NOTES on HOSPITALS. By FLORENCE NIGHTINGALE. Third Edition, enlarged; with 13 Plans. Post 4to. 18s.

C. M. WILLICH'S POPULAR TABLES for ascertaining the Value
of Lifehold, Leasehold, and Church Property, Renewal Fines, &c.; the
Public Funds; Annual Average Price and Interest on Consols from 1731 to
1861; Chemical, Geographical, Astronomical, Trigonometrical Tables, &c.
Post 8vo. 10s.

THOMSON'S TABLES of INTEREST, at Three, Four, Four and a
Half, and Five per Cent. from One Pound to Ten Thousand and from 1 to
365 Days. 12mo. 3s. 6d.

MAUNDER'S TREASURY of KNOWLEDGE and LIBRARY of
Reference: comprising an English Dictionary and Grammar, Universal
Gazetteer, Classical Dictionary, Chronology, Law Dictionary, a Synopsis
of the Peerage, useful Tables, &c. Fcp. 10s.

INDEX.